NEAREST THING TO CRAZY

NEAREST THING TO CRAZY

Elizabeth Forbes

Cutting
Edge
Press

The world of reality has its limits;
the world of imagination is boundless.

Jean-Jacques Rousseau

To darling Jamie
For being in my life, always

Prologue

'It's like waking from a dream; the brief moment which divides fantasy from reality; the tenuous bridge of perception between the two. That's when I think I glimpse something; and if I can only just hold on to the moment for long enough I'll be able to understand everything that happened.'

'And what can you remember, what do you see, in that moment?'

'Mixed, incorporeal images that I can't quite make out, save for their colours. I see colours. I see red; and blindingly bright white, and green . . . Yes, green. A green curtain, I think. A green curtain which separated me from my baby. I couldn't see her, you know. I was awake. Flat on my back with a green curtain above my stomach I was listening for a cry. They handed her straight to Dan while they stitched me up. And he just kept hold of her. I asked him to give her to me, but he wouldn't. You know he shouldn't have done that, should he? He should have given her to me. If he'd only given her to me, right then, then everything would have been all right. All this . . . everything would have been all right.'

CHAPTER

1

Memory can play strange tricks on you, but there are some things I recall so clearly it's like a movie replaying in my mind, like the first time I saw her. I was sitting at the table on Sally and Patrick Priestley's terrace chatting with my friend Amelia; a Sunday lunch party on a perfect summer's day. I'd seen the car coming up the drive: a green convertible driven by a lone woman. I think they call it British racing green. It had a personalized number plate, ELI 40. Amelia had her back to the drive but I was watching the car, over her shoulder. The engine was so smooth that the sound of it was drowned out by the crunch of crushed gravel beneath the fat tyres. As the car door opened I saw the shoes. They were red; scarlet, shiny, blood-red and high-heeled. I remember thinking: how unusual. Sunday lunch in the country was usually fairly informal. And *she* was wearing bright red high-heeled shoes. Amelia was still chatting to me, but I was only half-listening. I was watching *her*. And then I noticed a lull in everyone else's conversation as their eyes drifted, like mine. Even Amelia turned around, drawn by everyone else's glances. She unfolded herself from the car in one fluid movement as if she'd practised to make it perfect. And as she stood up she smoothed her dress before ducking back in to collect her handbag and a small be-ribboned gift box. The box was shiny and the ribbon showy; not at all like the usual family-sized offering of Maltesers we were used to in these parts. Her dress was white, splattered with roses, sort of fifties style, with a belted waist and big skirt; tight over her bust.

'Blimey . . .' I heard Amelia murmur.

Sally, our hostess, was standing on the edge of the terrace at the top of the steps, and she called out, 'Ellie, hi! You found us!'

We were all watching; all thinking, I imagine, the same thing: who *is* she? She walked up the steps and Sally kissed her on each cheek. She tossed her hair back like the girl in the L'Oréal ad. It was a rich, coppery-red colour. Not ginger or orangey red, more saffron I guess you'd call it. And red shoes. Brave, I thought. Sally brought her over to the table to perform the introductions.

When it was my turn I gave her a big smile and mouthed 'hello', but she barely made eye contact. Sally put her hand under her elbow and led her over to meet our men. I carried on watching her. I watched my Dan pause mid-conversation with Amelia's William. I saw both Dan and William put on their best smiles, while Patrick placed a glass of champagne in her hand. Amelia muttered to me, 'Who is she?' and I shrugged.

'Don't know. No idea. Glamorous, though.'

'Isn't she? I wonder if there's a husband.'

I laughed because that just about summed up what we were both thinking.

As Amelia and I continued to chat, I kept stealing glances towards her. She was smoking a cigarette, showing off her red lipstick and neat, matching fingernails. Patrick hates smoking but I noticed an ashtray had been found for her. And I noticed that Dan was smoking too, in spite of the fact he'd given up nearly five years ago.

Lunch was really fun, but for some reason I felt quiet on the way home. I'd been sitting at one end of the table, next to Patrick, in pride of place, I suppose. I wondered why Sally hadn't put Ellie next to him, considering she was new blood. Sally was at the other end of the table, with Dan beside her, and then Ellie beside him. Sally was jumping up and down all the time, doing her hostess duties, leaving Ellie to chat to Dan. They seemed to be hitting it off pretty well; so well that after the pudding Ellie went outside to have another cigarette and Dan joined her, to keep her company. That was Dan for you: affable, easily led.

'You're very quiet,' Dan said.

'Me? No, just feeling relaxed after all that wine.'

'Did you have fun?'

'Yes. It was lovely. Sally's such a good cook.'

'Yes. Lucky Patrick!'

'Very lucky Patrick. I only hope he realizes just how lucky he is.'

'All that business sorted now?'

'I think so. Sally hasn't mentioned it for ages.'

'Poor bugger.'

'Stupid bugger, more like. I hope you'd never be that stupid.'

'God no – and have to buy you a new kitchen, like Patrick had to do? And besides, I think I'd go for a younger model, not some old dog I was at school with.'

'Dan!'

'Joke! Ouch . . . there's no need to pinch me. Your nails are really sharp.'

'Good. Anyway, what was she like?'

'Who?'

'You know who, silly.'

'Oh *her*.'

'Who is she?'

Dan shrugged. 'A writer, on a retreat, she said. To work on her novel.'

'Wonder why she'd come here? You'd think a retreat would be in the middle of nowhere . . . and we're hardly that. Still, it depends what you're used to.'

We'd stopped at the T-junction and Dan was checking the road. He didn't respond. 'So,' I wondered aloud, 'does that mean she's here for a while?'

'No idea.' We were driving past the Gales' barn conversion. 'That's where she's going to be living.'

'Really? Jules hasn't wasted any time. It's barely finished.' I'd seen the carpet company's van only a few days before.

'The Gales never hang around where money's concerned.'

'No. But they work damned hard. I'd have made more effort to talk to her if I'd known she was going to be our nearest neighbour.'

'I shouldn't worry. You'll have plenty of opportunity.'

'Hmm. Husband?'

'Yes, wife?'

'No, silly. Does *she* have a husband?'

He looked at me sideways. 'Now why would you ask that?'

'Just curious . . .'

He lifted his eyebrows in a silent 'wouldn't you like to know . . .'

'Well?' I persisted.

'As far as I know she's separated, or divorced. Didn't really take much notice, to tell you the truth.'

And that was that.

It was a hot day. I should have taken the roof down but I didn't want to get my hair all blown about and arrive looking like I'd swallowed a cattle prod. Vain of me, perhaps, but first impressions do count, don't they? Obviously I wanted to make a good one.

I was aware of them all watching me as I got out of the car. I'd bought Sally a really nice present because I was touched that she'd asked me. Probably trying too hard, but you know how it is. Anyway, everyone was really polite, introducing me and all the usual stuff.

I remember meeting Dan. I was glad I was placed next to him at lunch. It was good. I enjoyed it. I remember laughing. He was funny.

◇ ◇ ◇

Amelia called on Monday: 'Come to lunch on Friday. I want you to see the new border – and show it off to everyone.'

'That's really kind, I'd love to . . . but honestly, please . . . I'd be embarrassed. I'm just relieved that you like it.'

'I love it! And I want people to see it. You're far too modest, and word of mouth is the way to get you more work. It's really filled out this month.'

'It's June. It's bound to look good now.'

'Stop doing yourself down, it's beautiful. And I've invited Ellie, to give her a chance to get to know the girls, to introduce her properly.'

'Good. I barely talked to her the other day. Dan says she's on some kind of retreat, writing a book.'

'I didn't know that. She didn't mention it. But I think she sounded pleased to be asked. I suppose as she doesn't know anyone she might be feeling a bit lonely.'

'Does she really not know anyone at all? I thought she was an old friend of Sally's.'

'No. She was just being neighbourly, you know what a one Sally is for taking up new projects.'

'Well I'll look forward to getting to meet her properly.'

'Lovely. See you Friday. Any chance you could bring a salad, something from that amazing veggie patch of yours?'

'Of course,' I laughed. Amelia was perfectly capable of putting together an amazing salad from her own walled garden, but she knew how much I enjoyed fiddling about with my edible flowers.

The Gales' barn was on my way to Amelia's and so I decided I'd stop and see if Ellie would like a lift. We didn't often get fresh blood in the village, but when we did we all leapt upon it like crows on roadkill. You could never call us unfriendly. We were all far too nosy and desperate for news from the outside world to let a new neighbour slip into the community unbothered. I could almost feel sorry for her if she was looking for peace. For the next few weeks she'd be inundated with lunch and supper invitations as we all jostled and elbowed each other in the fight to make her our new best friend. It was quite undignified, really, but that's one of the handicaps of country living.

I nosed into the drive and parked next to ELI 40, thinking that Jules Gale would be unimpressed by the deep furrows gorged by those fat black tyres into the smart new white gravel. I knocked on the door and a dog started to bark. It sounded small and yappy and terrier-like. I heard Ellie's voice. 'Coco, shut up!' The barking continued and she opened the door. From the blank way she looked at me, I realized that she didn't have a clue who I was.

'We met at Sally's. Lunch last week. Dan's wife,' I added, guessing she might remember my husband.

'Of course, I remember.' Her eyes swept over my cotton dress, down to my ancient suede kitten heels and then back to my face. And then she smiled a big warm smile. 'I'm so sorry, I was just going –'

'. . . to lunch at Amelia's? You're on my way so I thought I could give you a lift. It's only a van, I'm afraid, but it'll save you driving.'

It was a beautiful smile that made me think of Beach Boys' songs – 'California Girls', 'Good Vibrations', all perfect teeth and freckles.

'How incredibly kind. Come on in.'

I stepped into the sitting room. It smelled of paint and new carpets, all fresh and clean. 'Gosh, it's lovely, isn't it? Jules is so clever. It's hard to believe it was a ramshackle old barn a matter of months ago.'

'Isn't it? I knew as soon as I saw it that it was perfect. Exactly what I wanted. I've just got to get my bag. I'll be two minutes. Don't mind Coco. She's just excited to see a new face.'

Ellie left the room, and while the wiry little Jack Russell started to sniff around my shoes, I, too, had a chance to nose. There was an enormous sofa to the side of the wood-burner covered in a kilim throw and assorted tapestry cushions. An open paperback book straddled the arm. *Rebecca* . . . I remembered Rebecca, the raven-haired temptress; and beside that a drier looking tome entitled *The Daphne du Maurier Companion*. There was another ancient brown leather sofa with a brown and white goatskin on it. By the window was a desk with a computer monitor flashing photographs from her screensaver: pictures of her on a beach; round a restaurant table with friends; bikini-clad on someone's yacht; wearing a fur-edged hat on a ski slope. Juan-les-Pins? Saint Moritz? Sacha Distel? Another song.

The desk was neat, with papers stacked in tidy piles. And on one end was a vase full of old English roses. I could detect the faint apple scent wafting towards me. Then I heard light footsteps skipping back down the stairs.

'Okay. Let me just shut Coco in the kitchen, otherwise she'll chew something in protest.'

We got into my ancient van, me being careful not to scratch ELI 40's paintwork with the driver's door. 'I'm sorry it's a bit of a mess,' I said, moving an old trug off the passenger seat. Along with a pair of secateurs, some gardening gloves and a weeding claw, there were discarded supermarket receipts, scraps of old shopping lists and Tesco carrier bags littering the interior of my van. There was also an unwholesome layer of dust which covered pretty much everything. I was so embarrassed that I almost wished I hadn't stopped to collect her. Ellie just seemed so neat and clean and organized in her perfect little house with her beautifully ordered desk.

I brushed her seat with my hand before she sat down. 'I think it's okay,' I grinned, sheepishly. She was wearing jeans and a pair of

Converse trainers with pink stars and pink bows on them. If I hadn't seen them on her I would have thought they were designed for ten year olds, but on Ellie they looked just right.

'You have a business?' she asked.

'Fledgling, really. I do gardens. Anything from weeding to designing. Hence the van. I've always yearned for a smart sports car like yours, but I wouldn't be able to cart my kit around – you know, wheelbarrow and Strimmer, stuff like that – very easily.'

'No. Mine's hopelessly impractical, but I do love it.'

Amelia's was only another five minutes away, but Ellie was full of questions. Whereabouts do you live? How long have you been there?

I'm always surprised when I say it was fifteen years ago that we finally found the house of our dreams. We'd been living in Bath in a rambling old town house until Dan was invited to head up the new Birmingham office. He'd wanted a glitzy city apartment two minutes from Harvey Nicks which would have been hopelessly impractical; so instead we bought a three-hundred-year-old cottage an hour and a half away. If money had been no obstacle he'd probably have bought an apartment too, maybe stayed there two or three nights a week, who knows? Fifteen years. It seemed a lifetime ago.

'So you're renting?'

'That's right. Just for six months. At least to start with. See how I get on.'

'Well it's lovely round here, I'm sure you'll enjoy it.'

And then we were at Amelia's, turning into the mile long drive with the vicious speed humps, the smart estate fencing edging the neatly mown verges and the outgrown warning signs 'BEWARE OF WILD CHILDREN'. The house was hidden by a screen of ancient trees to make the final reveal all the more impressive. It was beautiful. Georgian. One of my favourite styles. I liked the symmetry of the crisp, white-painted windows set against the mellowed brickwork. It was ordered and classical; the total reverse of our house, with its ramshackle extensions and air of neglect. Iceberg roses smothered the facade, their delicate white clusters perfectly complementing the mood of gracious restraint. In the distance I could see a gardener on all fours in front of the new border, a wheelbarrow placed picturesquely beside him. The front door was thrown open, tempting us inside, into the delicious coolness. Satin floors marinated in centuries of beeswax and designer dust shed from the skin of hundreds of aristocratic ancestors; vases stuffed with roses and lavender, making a seductive, scented cocktail. Log baskets brimming, even though it was the middle of summer; worn sofas that didn't match, but somehow blended together harmoniously, like their owners, providing overly elegant beds for generations of terriers, spaniels and Labradors. I was conscious of Ellie at my side, barely glancing around, not making the usual 'oh what an amazing house . . .' noises, suggesting to me that she was obviously born to all this sort of thing.

We crossed the hallway, Ellie's rubber soles squeaking and my heels click-clicking over the polished floorboards, following the sound of voices towards the kitchen. Amelia's housekeeper was busy with lunch, quietly efficient. She was wearing a starched, professional chef's apron and marshalling plates of pulses, peppers and aubergines, all glistening with extra-virgin olive oil and scattered with freshly picked herbs. I placed my salad bowl on the counter. I'd spent ages on the salad, picking the most tender leaves, carefully washing them and drying them, then arranging them in my favourite wooden bowl with nasturtium and chive flowers over the top. I'd placed four violas in the centre, and I must admit I was quite pleased with the result, even though they were just beginning to wilt.

'Ah, here you are.' Amelia rushed over. 'Wow! That looks amazing. Thank you, my darling. You are so clever, almost looks too perfect to eat. Hello, Ellie, and well done for coming together. Don't you think she's creative? And just wait until you see what she's done in the border.'

'Oh shush. Anyone could have done it, it's just having the time.'

'I couldn't have done it. Not as beautifully as you, anyway.'

'Nonsense.'

Amelia was pouring wine into glasses which she then handed to Ellie and me.

'Thank you. Just what I need after a hard morning at the keyboard.'

'Your novel?' I said.

'Yes. That's right.' I was just about to ask her what it was about, but Amelia grabbed Ellie's arm.

'Come on, Ellie, come and meet everyone . . .' I stepped aside so that she could be propelled towards the crème of village society. It also gave me chance to take a few moments to see how the border appeared from the French windows. I was pleased to see that the gardener and the wheelbarrow had disappeared. From my vantage point even I had to confess that it looked pretty. The roses were at their most perfect; the lavender was just beginning to flower; and the cosmos was beginning to fill the gaps left by the spent peonies and bearded irises. The sweet peas on my home-made willow supports had also bloomed, and provided height and structure, or what I imagined grander people might call punctuation marks.

I was tempted to go and inspect my work more closely, but then Sally tapped my arm.

'You're going to be furious with me.'

'Why?'

'I can't come next week, on the garden tour. I'm sorry. It's all Patrick's fault. He forgot to tell me that he's got a client coming for lunch. I'm livid with him and asked him to change it, but he says he can't. I was so looking forward to it. I'll pay for my ticket if you can't get rid of it.'

'Can't you leave them a sandwich – or, God forbid, couldn't Patrick do lunch?'

'Don't be ridiculous. Patrick? He's far too hopeless even to open a fridge, or turn on an oven. A corkscrew's about his limit.'

'You spoil him. It would do him good to fend for himself.'

'I'm sure you're right, darling, but it suits me to have him in a state of dependency.'

'Like a toddler, you mean.'

'Something like that.'

'Well maybe you should be more . . .' I hesitated. It wasn't really any of my business, other than the fact I was genuinely disappointed.

But the words were out, and I sensed a chill in Sally, perhaps a cool shell of defensiveness.

'I should be more what?'

'Oh nothing.'

'No, go on.'

'Who am I to say?' I wanted to back-pedal, but it was too late. 'Perhaps, maybe, a bit more assertive. Let him appreciate you, not take you for granted . . .' I'd lowered my voice, not wanting anyone to overhear us.

Sally chewed on her bottom lip. 'I suppose . . . but I don't know. It's difficult to explain. I know this sounds stupid . . . I just feel grateful to have him there.'

'Sally! He's the one that needs to feel grateful.' I wanted to add that it would have done Patrick a hell of a lot of good not to have her at his beck and call, but instead I said, 'Don't worry. I understand, really I do.' But I didn't understand, not really. It irritated me that she was being such a doormat.

'You're sweet. And I know I'm being silly. Honestly, if anyone had told me before it happened that I'd react like this I'd have told them they were bonkers.'

'But surely he knows how lucky he is? Surely he realizes how stupid he was and what he nearly lost?'

'I guess. He has said as much, many times. But I just couldn't bear it to happen again. I think everyone thought I was so strong and capable, but I'm not – not really, not without Patrick. Maybe if I'd had a career, or even a job, like you, I'd feel more confident, more of a person in my own right. But the house, the domestic bit – it's the mundane routine of wifehood that defines me. Without that I simply don't know who I am. How sad is that? And it's not as if he was ever a bad husband. I mean he didn't come home drunk and knock me about every night, did he? So I've got some things to be grateful for.'

'I'm sorry, Sally. I'm so insensitive, really I am. I just don't want you to be taken for granted. If Dan –'

'But that's the difference, isn't it?' she interrupted. 'You don't know what you'd do, how you'd feel, until it happens to you. And it won't. You and Dan are welded together at the hip, anyone can see that.'

'We have our ups and downs.'

'Oh shush. Everyone knows you two are fine. More than fine.'

'I suppose. But it's not always a bed of roses. You know how it is.' Dan and I were okay. In our own way. We just sort of got on with it. Wasn't that normal marriage? Dan said you could hardly expect bells and whistles after thirty-two years together. We muddled along all right. But I knew what Sally meant about the house and Patrick being the axis of her world. When Laura went off to university Dan and I had a kind of readjustment crisis. I think we both felt a bit redundant, but I believe it was harder for me than it was for Dan. He had his career, his other life where he could feel useful and needed, whereas I, like Sally, felt pointless. We were in a sort of post-parent hinterland, with all the years of love, sweat and tears screwed up in the back of Laura's wardrobe along with the cast-off teddies. No doubt each might come in handy for the grandchildren one day. I didn't know whether Dan had wondered, like me, whether our relationship would be enough to make up for her absence. Were we enough for each other, just the two of us? Could we be all the things to each other that were necessary for a happy marriage? And what were those things? Friendship, love, mutual support, trust, great sex, financial security . . . Not much to ask, was it? Not much! And did everybody else's marriages measure up to that, or were we all just muddling through, making the best of things? Just the easy questions in life . . . But we *were* muddling through pretty well, considering. We'd even managed a holiday together, just the two of us. And it had been lovely. And life had been so much better since I'd followed Dan's suggestion and turned my hobby into a little business.

Sally sounded like she was making an effort to be cheerful. 'Perhaps we can do something another time. Why don't you ask Amelia?'

'I already did. But she couldn't.'

Sally chuckled over her glass. 'I bet you bloody asked her first, before me, didn't you? Go on, admit it, I was second best.'

'Honestly,' I laughed back. 'Relax. *Obviously* I would have got three tickets if she'd wanted to come.'

'Maybe you should ask *her*.' Sally said, *sotto voce* and nodding in Ellie's direction.

'Ellie?'

'Why not? Be neighbourly, wouldn't it?'

'Yes, I suppose it would.'

> ◇ ◇

I found myself sitting diagonally opposite Ellie at lunch, and reflecting that spending a day with her could be really good fun. She laughed easily, an infectious belly laugh that was somehow unexpected, slightly incongruous but attractive nevertheless.

Everyone was asking her lots of questions: 'What brought you to this part of the world . . . and how brave, when you don't know anyone . . .' But she was good at turning the questions around, almost methodically working her way around the table in order to find out about all of us; the usual stuff such as who we were married to, where we lived, what children we had, whether we were locals or not. In fact I did think she was rather adept at deflecting our curiosity. She used the fact that she was cultured and well-read as a way of diverting the more direct, personal questions. She chatted about exhibitions she had seen, books she had enjoyed and countries she had visited. I admired the way she seemed so relaxed and unselfconscious in the company of relative strangers.

I also wondered what she would be making of us, how she would be viewing us, through her writer's eye. Amelia's housekeeper was busy, bustling away in the background, making sure everything appeared at the right time, making sure that the kitchen remained immaculate, making sure that our hostess only had to worry about keeping up a constant patter of lively conversation. It was a theatre of sorts, and the uninitiated audience would presume that Amelia was playing the spoilt one: the rich-man's over-indulged wife, the latest in an uninterrupted line of rich men's wives captured in oil paint and pinned to the wall, required to be decorative not only in life, but after death too. On the face of it, I don't suppose the casual observer would feel too sorry for Amelia, but I did. For instance, I knew that she never really felt the house was hers, or a home exactly. William's mother was there, undead, but with her spirit already haunting everything Amelia did, along with the spectres of all the other Mrs Armitages. Newly widowed, she had been packed off to the dower house, from where she attempted to rule the latest incumbents of the big house. She managed to convey her censure in subtle little ways that we all pretended not to notice, such as asking you if you'd like *another* drink or hunting down *the* ashtray for a hapless smoker. She made us feel like naughty teenagers, which only served to make us *want* to behave badly.

William's parents had lingered far too long in the big house, while Amelia and William and their fast-growing brood, escaping from London at weekends, had occupied the old servants' quarters over what was now the pool house. It had been ridiculous, really, the way they'd crammed themselves into what was effectively an attic while the ageing parents rattled around the vast rooms. I suppose one could admire the way Mrs Armitage senior had perfected her demeanour of haughty disapproval, but she was quite scary. When I'd taken the saw to some horrid old shrubs in the border she'd crept up behind me, and then yelled in my ear, 'I planted those twenty-five years ago and I thought they were looking rather fine,' I nearly chopped my finger off.

'I'm sure they'll look even better once they've got space to stretch out a bit. And they were starving everything around them.'

'Well I suppose you know what you're doing. Of course I used to do all the gardening myself . . .'

When I told Amelia about it later, she just laughed. 'My diplomatic skills have been both tested and honed, darling. The trouble is, she still thinks of this as her house. And who can blame the old trout, she was here for thirty-five years. She's just a bit lost, really. All those years running everything, making all the decisions, feeling important and necessary, and now there's nothing for her to do. I do feel sorry for her and sometimes I find myself thinking I'll probably be just like her. I just wish she didn't make me feel like an incompetent child – a houseguest who's outstayed her welcome.'

It seemed to me, sometimes, that the house owned William and Amelia, rather than the other way around, and while it was indeed a beautiful place to live, it came at a high price.

At coffee the conversation turned to schools, as it invariably did, and Amelia said that they were hoping Lucy, their youngest, would get a place at Wycombe Abbey.

'My old school,' Ellie said.

'Really? Mine too,' said Amelia. 'Though I don't suppose we would have been there at the same time.'

'No, probably not,' she said.

In reality it was hard to tell how old Ellie was, but I imagined she was probably at least ten years younger than me, so early forties maybe. And there was that number plate of hers. Of course she might be younger and have worn rather badly, or older and have worn rather well.

When it was time to leave, everyone around the table had taken her telephone number, promising future invitations: lunches, suppers, even shopping trips, if she fancied it, 'sometime'. And I felt really pleased for her that she was slipping so effortlessly into our little group.

On the way back she seemed to be making a particular effort to be warm towards me and I must admit I rather liked this feeling of having my friendship overtures reciprocated so enthusiastically.

'I want to know all about you,' she said, smiling at me from the passenger seat. 'Tell me again exactly where you live? Oh my God you're in that gorgeous cottage down the road from here? The one with the beautiful garden? Every time I drive past it I slow down to look at it – to envy it. You're *so* clever. I wouldn't have a clue what to do. I haven't had much time for gardening, but I always thought it would be something I'd enjoy in the future.'

'I feel lucky, really, that finally I'm getting paid to do something I love. Amelia's been very kind, getting me a few commissions here and there. You know what it's like, word of mouth, things lead on . . .'

'It must be so satisfying, nurturing things, knowing that you're leaving something behind for future generations, a bit like children.'

'Maybe. But frustrating too. Unlike children, you don't always get to see them fully grown.'

'No. I s'pose not. Did I hear you say you had a daughter?'

'Yes, Laura. She's at university in Birmingham.'

'That's very grown up.'

'Twenty-one in January. I can barely believe it. And you?'

'No, sadly not. Never happened for me, which is probably just as well. I don't seem very good at doing settled domesticity.'

We'd reached her house and I pulled into the drive. I was just about to mention the garden day when she said, 'Listen, I don't feel like going back to work this afternoon, why don't you come in for a cup of coffee and I can show you the garden? Maybe you can tell me what you think I should do with it.'

I glanced at the dashboard clock. Ten past three. Actually I could spare a bit of time. Dan wouldn't be back until 7.30 and I'd only got a few non-vital jobs to attend to before that.

'Why not.'

'Great.'

I was so busy looking out of the French windows onto the flat expanse of uninterrupted new lawn that I didn't notice that instead of putting the kettle on, Ellie was unscrewing the top from a chilled bottle of white wine. I must have seemed a bit surprised.

'What the hell!' Ellie laughed. 'We're celebrating new friends. I'm really happy to be here and especially to have met you – a kindred spirit!'

'Me too. It's going to be great having you here livening us all up.' I smiled and took the proffered glass, and then we stepped outside. The dog, freshly released from imprisonment in the kitchen, raced around the perimeter fence, sniffing and yapping with excitement. The sun's warmth washed over Ellie's terrace and so we drifted towards the slatted wooden table and chairs.

Ellie hooked one of her long, lean legs onto the chair beside her and offered me a cigarette, which I declined, before lighting one for herself. She closed her eyes as she exhaled. 'Hmm, isn't this just heaven?'

At last the dog, satisfied that the boundary was successfully patrolled, had shut up and was now sitting quietly by its mistress's chair and eyeing me suspiciously.

'So peaceful. I just can't hear anything, oh, except for that tractor throbbing away somewhere and the sparrows – I think they're sparrows – chattering to each other. At first I found the quiet really eerie. At night, in the dark, when all the lights are off, and there's no moon, it's like being swaddled in black felt.'

'I know what you mean. It takes a bit of getting used to, after the city. I should imagine it will be good for you . . . for your work . . . to have the peace and quiet.'

'I hope so.' She continued to talk while gazing at the view across the woods and to the hills beyond. Above us I could count four jet trails, little white scars criss-crossing the perfect blue ceiling. I sipped my wine and sank down in the chair, closing my eyes as I listened.

'Before I came down here so much in my life was going wrong. I got awful depression and then I couldn't write so I knew I had to do something to try and sort myself out.'

I opened my eyes and glanced over at her, but she was still staring dreamily into the distance. I didn't quite know what to say; I mean, I hardly knew her, and she'd been so good over lunch at deflecting any personal questions. I felt both surprised and vaguely awkward that she was being so open about herself. 'God . . . I'm sorry to hear that. But the move, coming here, do you think it's helped?'

'Yes, I really do. Especially knowing there's people like you around. Lovely warm people who are prepared to welcome this stranger into their midst. I feel so lucky. I'm sorry, I probably shouldn't be talking to you like this. I can't imagine your life being anything other than perfect, living here in this beautiful place, surrounded by good friends.'

'Yes, I suppose I am lucky. But depression, it's an awful thing. Especially when people expect you to just snap out of it and pull yourself together. And of course you'd love to, but you can't, can you?'

She looked across at me. 'No you can't. You sound as though you know what it's like.'

I took a deep breath. 'After Laura was born I had it. It wasn't diagnosed for ages and I just thought what a really terrible mother I was, just hopeless at not being able to cope. Actually, it was all so dreadful that I try not to think about it. I just want to forget it ever happened. But you do get through it.'

Ellie picked up the bottle and refilled my glass.

'God, how awful. But you seem so capable now. I can't imagine you ever not being a good mother.'

'That's kind of you to say so, but I wasn't. I think something in the bonding process eluded me. It wasn't at all how I thought it was going to be, it was just a fog of exhaustion, a screaming baby and no clue as to what I was supposed to do. I wasn't what you'd call a natural.'

'And what about your husband – was he supportive?'

'As much as he could be. It was hard for him. I mean he just didn't know what to do. He was scared of what was going on – we both were – scared I might do something to myself . . . or worse . . .'

'Worse?'

I shuddered, suddenly feeling cold, despite the balmy afternoon. 'It was all a long time ago.'

'But you know . . . you understand what it's like to feel really low, desperate, even . . . I can't tell you how good it feels to talk to someone who knows, who's not going to judge me for being pathetic.' Her hand drifted over towards me and she rested it lightly on my arm as she stared directly into my eyes. 'I don't know if I should really ask you this, and tell me to piss off and mind my own business if you wish, but did you ever feel like ending it all?'

Her hand suddenly felt very hot, burning into my skin uncomfortably, but I felt too embarrassed to push it off, as it would have appeared like a rejection, a literal brush off. I didn't want to talk about it. Even now, after all these years, it was still a place I chose not to revisit, but I didn't know how to back-pedal without appearing rude. And if she was really feeling vulnerable it might even be dangerous to upset her.

'Perhaps I thought about it, at times.'

'And was there anyone you could talk to?'

'My doctor, my psychiatrist . . .' I laughed drily. 'There's an army of help available when it's almost too late. I was lucky – we were all lucky – that it wasn't too late.'

I swear that Ellie's eyes had filled with tears as she continued to stare at me. I squeezed her hand and lifted it gently from my arm. 'But I'm okay now. Thank God.'

'Yes, thank God. And amazing to have an understanding husband who stood by you.'

'Amazing,' I echoed. 'I think Dan used to worry that I'd have some kind of relapse. That's the worst of it, people wondering if you can ever really be better. But I know I am and I know that he knows I am. But it took a long time to shrug off the suspicion that you're somehow a bit flaky.'

'Well you don't seem remotely flaky to me. You seem like the least flaky person around.'

'Thanks. But I could say the same about you. I mean, you just appear so sorted, with your career and everything. You seem really successful and together.'

'Well doesn't that go to show?'

'Show?'

'What you see on the outside. My front, everybody's fronts, are only what we choose to show. Underneath, well, who knows?'

'I've always thought of myself as being rather open. Dan says I wear my heart on my sleeve. Always have done. Pretty much what you see is what you get, I'm afraid. Straightforward old me.'

'But you're not exactly straightforward, are you? As you've just told me.'

She was staring at me again, but this time she made me feel uncomfortable, as though there was some hidden meaning behind her words, and it bothered me somehow. It just felt, I don't know, maybe not quite right. 'All of that is so far back in the past I tend to forget it ever happened. And I never talk about it, not with anyone. I can't believe I've been boring you with it. I suppose I thought it might help for you to know that you weren't alone, that I could understand the concept . . .'

'Concept?'

'Of depression.'

'Oh yes, my depression. Of course it does. I knew there was something about you that I could connect with. You're a very warm and caring person, aren't you?'

'Golly. I don't know. I suppose I'd like to think so. Wouldn't we all?'

She made a sound like a derisory snort. 'Some more than others, believe me.' And then she gave me a rather enigmatic smile, and I sensed the shadow of some deep hurt, a feeling that she was emotionally damaged in some way. I didn't really know what to make of her. On the one hand she displayed an almost disarming honesty and openness and yet, on the other, I still felt I knew hardly anything about her at all. Maybe it was the wine clouding my judgement, but she seemed lost. I placed my hand over hers. 'Listen, Ellie. I do know what it's like. More than you think. Any time you want to talk . . . Please, you must feel able to . . . I'm only down the road after all.'

'Oh God . . .' now her tears really did start to flow. 'Sorry . . .' she choked. 'I don't know about you, but I find sympathy really hard to deal with.' She pulled a tissue from her sleeve and dabbed at her eyes. 'I'm much better when people are being foul.'

I smiled. 'I know what you mean. But would you like to talk

about it?'

She nodded. 'You don't mind?'

'Of course I don't mind. I'd be flattered that you felt able to confide in me.'

'Perhaps it helps that I hardly know you.'

'Perhaps . . .'

'I've run away.'

I felt my eyebrows shoot skywards, but I didn't say anything.

'From London, from a man . . . obviously. That's why I came here, to this lovely village, where I don't know anyone. I found the barn on a property website and I just thought it looked perfect and I could move in straight away and I'd be safe. So I did a runner.'

'Golly. How dramatic.'

'My boyfriend, live in lover, whatever you'd like to call him . . . bastard . . . was violent. I thought he was going to kill me.' She pulled her hair up from her shoulders and I could see faint blueish-purple marks around her neck. 'See these – three weeks ago and you can still see where his bloody hands were.'

'Oh Ellie, poor you. But why?'

'Drink. And drugs. I refused to give him money and so he thought he'd show me what he thought of me. Luckily I managed to fight him off and call the police. But the worst of it is that they didn't catch him. I'm just praying that he'll fall down drunk somewhere and they'll realize who he is . . . That, or – God I can't believe I'm saying this – he'll find another victim.'

I must have looked horrified because she quickly shook her head and said, 'No, no, I promise I didn't mean that. But I just want it all to be over, to get my life back. I can't tell my friends where I am – my family, anyone – just in case they let it slip. It's a complete nightmare . . . like . . . well like something you'd read in a bloody novel, not in real life. I just can't believe it's happening to someone like me.'

'Neither can I. Sorry, but I'm finding it hard to believe.'

'I know. It's just ghastly. But you must promise me, please, not to breathe a word of any of this to anyone – even your husband. Will you promise me?'

'Well, of course I will. I won't tell a soul.'

'Then you must say it.'

'Say it?'

'Say "I swear, Ellie, not to tell a soul".'

It felt vaguely childish but as she seemed so intense I repeated, 'I swear that I won't tell a soul.'

'Good. Thanks. He's very clever, you see – when he's sober. He'll trick people into telling them the smallest thing they know. He can be very charming, obviously, which is why I fell for him in the first place. He'll no doubt say he's really worried about me, that he loves me, he wants to look after me . . . God only knows what he'll come up with but I'm sure it'll be something good. So I do feel pretty scared, to be honest. And I am so glad I've got you up the road.'

'Anything I can do, anything at all . . . Just call me, pop in, whatever.' I grasped her hand and gave it a giant squeeze. 'Poor you. It all just sounds terrible.'

'Thanks. You are very sweet.' Ellie slipped her hand away from mine and stood up. 'I'm sorry. I'd love to talk some more, but I'd better take that stupid dog for a walk seeing as she's been shut up for so long.' I drained my glass and realized that we hadn't talked about her garden or next week's tour. It all seemed rather trivial compared to what she'd just told me. But I reasoned a little trip might cheer her up a bit.

'I almost forgot. I was thinking, if you were interested, I've got a spare ticket for a garden tour next week. Sally was coming, but now she can't. We see three gardens, have a good lunch, these things are usually quite jolly in a gentle way, and if you were thinking about picking up some ideas, you might get inspired . . . next Tuesday?'

'Tuesday?'

'I could collect you, around nine.'

'I'd love to. How kind of you.' We passed through her sitting room on the way to the front door. She picked up the paperback copy of *Rebecca* and held the book towards me. 'Here, scribble your number down for me on the inside cover. I'll need to double check my diary, but if you don't hear from me, then assume "yes please".'

I handed the book back to her after I'd written both my numbers down. 'I loved it . . . I remember the brooding Maxim and the evil Mrs Danvers.'

'Danny . . .' she corrected me.

'Yes. Danny. Hmm, it's a while since I've read it. I always felt so sorry for the poor nameless wife, terrified she's losing her sanity, treated like a child by her husband, haunted by the ghastly Rebecca –'

'I *adored* Rebecca, not giving a damn what anyone thought of her, attacking life, taking what she wanted, all that sexual power . . .'

I was taken aback. 'Maybe that explains its enduring qualities, the way we can either relate to one or the other. I must admit I'd always thought Rebecca was evil incarnate.'

'Really?' She smiled a rather knowing little smile and I couldn't shake off a really uncanny feeling. Perhaps I'd had too much wine. 'I think I might leave the van here, and walk back, if you don't mind. I'm probably way over the limit. Maybe Dan'll pop up later to get it for me.'

'No problem.'

As I walked back down the lane I resolved to do whatever I could to help my new friend. I couldn't begin to imagine how scared she must be feeling, and she was putting on such a brave front.

◇ ＞ ◇

She picked me up. That was nice of her. I have to say when I opened the door I didn't have a clue who she was. She seemed familiar but I suppose as I hadn't talked to her much at Sally's lunch then I had no cause to put a name to her face. I only really remembered the husband, Dan. Anyway, it was kind of her to stop for me. I suppose if you were to ask me to describe my first impressions, I'd call her typical of her type, if you know what I mean. Country housewife, a bit worn around the edges, cosy and comfortable. Not going to set the world alight, but nice. Nice with a capital N. My mother always used to say that you should never use the word nice. It's a sort of shorthand, isn't it, when you say, 'They're terribly nice.'? Like, God, they're really dull and straight. But she was. Just Nice. Nondescript, but pleasant. Ordinary, without wishing to sound rude. Just goes to show, doesn't it? One would never have guessed . . .

But then, thinking about it, she did hint that she'd had problems. Depression, possibly even suicidal thoughts. I was a bit uncomfortable the way she disclosed all that. Seemed a bit early in our friendship, but then I wasn't going to tell her to shut up or anything because you don't know what people might do, do you? So I decided I'd just be sympathetic. I got the impression she needed a good ear and I felt I could easily provide it. I really did have the best of intentions towards her, I honestly did. Her husband, Dan, came up later to collect her van. He apologized for disturbing me, but I said I didn't mind, was glad of the company. He had a quick glass of wine and said, 'Don't tell, or I'll be in trouble.' We gossiped about the locals, from memory. I found out who their closest friends were, useful stuff like that. I thought I might talk to her friends, to see if she was okay, just in case she really did need help.

2

'I'm sorry. I hope you don't mind about the coach. I don't think it's too far, though. You don't get sick, do you? I know some people can't stand them.'

We were both giggling as we climbed up the narrow steps. It was a lovely day, with just the hint of a breeze. Ellie could have been dressed for a garden party in a lime-green linen dress, with an enormous straw hat perched on her head, the front brim held up from her face with a fresh Gertrude Jekyll rose. Once again she made me feel dowdy and ordinary but hopeful that her glamour might be contagious.

'I'm loving it. What a laugh. I haven't been on one in years. Oh my God, that's not a loo, is it? You'd have to be pretty desperate – imagine if they did an emergency stop!'

We found a couple of seats.

'This is so nice of you to invite me. I'm beginning to feel human again.'

'I'm pleased to hear it.' I lowered my voice. 'So everything okay? I mean, you're all right . . .?'

'Fine. All quiet, thanks. I've had perfect peace. Chance to get some writing done, healthy walks with Coco, and I'm beginning to feel really at home. I've been sleeping better than in months. So today I'm going to try not to think about any of that stuff.'

'Good plan. I hope you won't be bored. They're a sweet bunch of people. Some of them have been quite famous in the garden world in their day.'

Ellie scanned the heads of our fellow travellers. 'I love all the different characters. All the weathered faces and gnarly old hands. Do they have secateurs stuffed in their pockets ready to steal bits of other people's gardens?'

'I'm afraid they do. All part of the perks of the trip. They're quite adept at surreptitious snipping. Watch for the carrier bags stuffed into their pockets.'

'I was thinking how nice it would be if you helped me with my garden. We didn't get a chance to talk about it the other day. I don't want to spend much, or plant stuff that will take years to appreciate. Instant gratification – is that possible?'

'Sure. I can give you lots of things from my garden. But I think pots would be best. Then if you move you can take them with you, and Jules won't object to you digging up her carefully laid lawn.'

'Did you train?'

'No. I'm just an enthusiastic amateur, learning from books, magazines, other people's gardens. It's just since we've lived in the cottage that it's become a passion of mine.'

'My mother was very keen. Too keen. I used to think she cared more about those bloody plants than she did about me.'

'Is she still alive?'

'No. She died last year. Electrocuted in her bath.'

'Oh my God! How absolutely dreadful!'

'Yes. She dropped her radio. Wireless, as she always called it. Shame it wasn't wireless, as it happened. She struggled with getting batteries in and out because her fingers were so arthritic – thanks to the bloody gardening, no doubt. Bet you never realized how lethal *The Archers* could be. She might have got away with it had she not had a pacemaker fitted.'

'Ellie, I'm so sorry. What a shock that must have been for you. Oh . . . God . . . I can't believe I've just said that.'

'Don't worry. You're not the first. They tell me she wouldn't have known much about it.'

I didn't know what else to say. It just seemed such a horrible thing to have happened. I was beginning to realize that Ellie, this woman who seemed to have everything going for her, was marked by tragedy. As she had said only the other day, it just goes to show that you never really do know about people, do you?

'I'm just so sorry . . . really.' I squeezed her hand.

'Well the way I see it you've got to die of something, haven't you? And she didn't have some awful lingering illness . . .'

'I suppose not,' I said. 'My own mother's in a care home. It's . . . well, it's difficult a lot of the time.' But I didn't want to talk about my mother today, and I couldn't imagine that Ellie wanted to talk about hers. We were supposed to be enjoying ourselves. 'Anyway, let's change the subject, shall we? Talk about something more cheerful.'

'Absolutely,' she said. 'What about Laura, your daughter. What's she studying?'

'She's doing a degree in media studies. She's just finished her second year but she's staying in her student flat in Birmingham so that she can use the library for a project. It's a worrying time, jobs being so scarce.'

'Perhaps I'd be able to give her some contacts.'

'Really?'

'Possibly. I've been out of journalism for a while, but I still know a few people.'

'That would be fantastic. Laura would be thrilled.'

'Well I can't promise, but I'll help if I can. You must miss her.'

'It's not so bad now. Not like at first . . .'

'No. I can imagine that must have been difficult, especially as she's your only child. And your husband, where does he work?'

'He's in Birmingham too. In advertising.'

'Yes, I remember now. He did tell me. He's a sweetheart, you're lucky. Well both of you are very lucky. How long have you been married?'

'Twenty-eight years. How can we be *that* old already?'

'Well you don't look it. So many marriages break up these days. It's a bit of an achievement, isn't it, to have been together so long? I envy you.'

'It's not all been plain sailing,' I said. It was the fact that she'd said she envied me, the fact that she seemed to have suffered so much tragedy herself that made me feel I should underplay my own happiness. I felt guilty for being okay and so as a result I was far more open than I would otherwise have been – even, perhaps, overplaying my insecurities. 'We went through quite a rough patch after Laura left home. I think I'd been so focussed on her that I'd neglected our marriage.'

'Really?' Her face was a picture of sympathy, so I went on, foolishly.

'It worries me sometimes with Dan, you know, involved in such a glamorous world of creative people, copywriters, shoots, models, photographers . . . and then there's plain old me.' I laughed. 'He tells me off for putting myself down.'

'He's right. It's a shallow world. I'm sure you and the home you provide are far more important to him. How did you meet?'

'We were both in London. He did uni, but I didn't. I just did suitable jobs for a young girl – the usual, secretarial stuff. We met through a friend's brother. I had assumed he fancied my friend, and do you know, to this day, I honestly think he did. But she knew how much I liked him and she wasn't that fussed, so she left the way clear. I suppose I always felt amazed that Dan should have chosen to marry me. That's the thing about Dan. He's got this craving for the sophisticated creative stuff, the nice cars and the designer labels, but then there's his working-class background and his lovely down-to-earth mum . . . So he's a bit of a social chameleon, the original champagne socialist. Balsamic vinegar on his fish and chips.'

She laughed. 'So both Dan and Laura are in Birmingham. That must be lovely for them. He must get to see lots of her – more than you do, I imagine.'

'Dan always seems to be flat out with work, meetings and things, but sometimes I'll go up and meet them for a concert, or something. We're lucky, really, that she's so close.'

'Oh my God, what is that woman wearing?'

'Which woman?'

'The one with the orange hat and peacock feather . . . what *does* she look like?'

I giggled. 'A little jaunty, isn't it?'

'Definitely. Do you think she spent hours getting ready? What can have gone through her mind? They all look so wonderfully eccentric, don't they, like they've stepped out of the wrong end of the 1950s? I can almost smell the camphor. I do wonder if I'm actually allergic to old people –'

'Ellie!' I laughed. 'Shush, they'll hear.'

'Don't be silly, of course they can't hear us, they're probably all deaf.'

'We'll get thrown off the bus for bad behaviour.'

'Sorry. I promise to take it all much more seriously and to behave myself from now on.'

'No, no, it's fine. Honestly. I just wouldn't want to hurt their feelings. They're a sweet bunch.'

'You must excuse me. I'm afraid all this,' she said, with a wave of her hand, 'is rather alien to me. You'll have to make allowances for my lack of country sensibility.'

I was surprised at how defensive she sounded. It wasn't that big a deal. 'Don't be silly, it's fine,' I said. 'Forget it. I'm sure they didn't hear. Just me being over-sensitive.'

We fell into an uncomfortable silence but thankfully we soon arrived at our first destination, and I could mask my discomfort as we filed off the coach. We were swept along by the tour organizer towards coffee and home-made shortbread on the terrace, followed by an hour-long guided tour of the garden. I'd turned off my mobile, but Ellie's rang about four times – she even answered it while our host was in mid-flow about how she'd dealt with her box blight. I wanted the earth to open up and swallow me when she said, without any attempt to lower her voice: 'Darling, you'll never guess . . . I'm going round a garden . . . Yes, a bloody *garden* for God's sake. Can you believe it?'

Everyone heard, and everyone seemed very shocked.

I couldn't help feeling that it was almost as though she was going out of her way to embarrass me. It was all so *weird*. And I'm pretty sure I heard her tell a member of the group that she wasn't remotely into gardening because she found it boring and, this is where I question my hearing, because I couldn't believe she really *would* have said it, that she 'always thought it was for people who didn't have a life'.

During lunch she appeared to be avoiding me by pointedly taking up the last seat on one of the dining tables so that I was left to find alternative company. I acted as if I didn't mind a bit and just waved at her as I took my place at the other table and tried my best to enjoy the company of my fellow horticulturalists. It was fine, really it was, and I didn't want to spoil the afternoon, and I really didn't want to create an atmosphere between us. So during the next tour I carried on as if nothing had happened, chattering away inanely about planting schemes and the usefulness of specimen trees, but something had changed in her. On the way home I tried to engage her on the subject of her garden, asking her whether she'd seen anything to inspire her; what she'd particularly liked, or disliked, the usual sort of conversations you'd have on a garden tour.

Even though she was pretty unresponsive, I carried on, regardless: 'I thought the roses were heavenly. I fell in love with that beautiful orangey-red one, Vespers I think it was called. And I wish we'd got the space for some catalpas, the Indian bean trees. There's a place where I could probably get you a really good deal on pots. I could take you there, if you like.' I knew I was wittering on to cover up my embarrassment.

'Would you? Thanks. That would be great.' She sort of smiled, vaguely, but I could sense her eyes glaze over as if I was speaking Urdu, and then she looked at her watch and yawned.

The garden tour. That was the first time I glimpsed some cracks in her marriage.

I do feel bad about it, but I honestly went with the best of intentions. I was a bit silly on the coach, I suppose, making comments about the other people, but there's something about people like that that just brings out the worst in me . . . Did I mention my mother? Gardening. God, I don't know but there's something about it that really gets to me. I can't really explain why. I think it makes me a bit claustrophobic, which is odd, as you'd think with the fresh air and all that greenery and colour and open skies claustrophobia would be the last thing you'd feel. But I did find it claustrophobic in the sense that it was so totally her world; it enveloped her completely. There was always something that demanded her attention, her loving care, her patience and time. If I'm honest, I did feel that she loved those plants, that garden, more than she loved me. She looked truly happy when she was on her knees, her ancient tattered straw hat on her head, scrabbling about in the earth. Sometimes when I watched her closely from the window I could see her lips move as if she was having all the conversations out there with her plants that she never seemed to have with me. I'm not sure she was an especially demonstrative person, my mother. But she was very practical. You should have seen her larder shelves. Stuffed full of everything: pickles, jams, preserves, potted fruits. You could stand in front of those shelves and imagine you were viewing a little piece of my mother's soul. She lined the jars up so that all the labels faced neatly in one way. The handwriting, so carefully penned, sloped to the right and was perfectly centred. She made sure that she put the date of bottling in the bottom right-hand corner. I could tick off the years of my life with that bottom right-hand corner. Then to show how much she cared, she would place a little circle of fabric over the top of the jar and tie it up with a piece of coloured twine in a pretty little bow, like they were bonnets on her little girls. But I'm getting off the subject, aren't I? I suppose I'm describing it so carefully because she was always so meticulous about it. And, yes, if I'm honest I was jealous. What was I saying? Oh yes, the garden tour. I suppose that's why I didn't really want to spend time with those people. They reminded me so much of my mother. It was unreasonable of me to take it out on her, and I'm sorry for that. But to be honest she did spend quite a lot of time talking about herself, and her daughter . . . and gardening . . . I realized that she was a tiny bit dull, I'm afraid. And provincial. And yes, a bit touchy, too.

I didn't hear anything from Ellie after our trip. It was weird. Really weird. I kept going over what I'd said, trying to work out if I'd offended her in some way. I kept wondering if I had imagined the change in her; perhaps I had been over-sensitive, or just plain unsophisticated and unable to enter into her idea of fun. Maybe I was losing my sense of humour. I told myself that I needed to chill out about it, that I was becoming too set in my country ways, that I couldn't appreciate her metropolitan edginess. I was genuinely happy at the prospect of having a glamorous new friend. I was confused, because we *had* bonded, hadn't we, otherwise why would she have chosen to confide in me? And I'd been pretty open with her on the bus about Dan and me. The more I thought about it, the more I thought perhaps I had sounded prissy and priggish and why would she want to spend a day with a bunch of geriatrics? No, I should never have asked her. It had been a stupid thing to do. She'd be more a champagne and oysters in Selfridges kind of girl. She'd been a proverbial fish out of water, an exotic hothouse orchid placed in the centre of a staid old herbaceous border. And then I finally remembered what she'd said about her mother preferring plants to her. Maybe that was it. I cursed myself for being so stupid and insensitive. Of course she would have hated the whole garden tour thing, and the oldies. It must have brought it all painfully back to her.

With all of that on top of the boyfriend problem I felt really worried about her, and so I called her mobile and left a message saying I was sorry about dragging her on the trip, and that I hoped she was all right. But I didn't hear anything back. So the next day I called her landline and left another message saying, 'Pop in for coffee if you feel bored . . .' but again I got no response. A couple of days after that I picked her a bunch of sweet peas and took them round to her house, and although her car was there and the dog barked, she didn't come to the door. Perhaps she was working and didn't want to be disturbed. I scribbled a note on a scrap of paper saying:

Hope you're okay. Call and see me when you feel like it. C.x

I didn't want to become a pest, and I reasoned she'd come and see me when she was ready, and besides I had things to do, such as getting my stuff ready for the farmers' market in the local village hall.

I was always up at six on the Saturday market mornings, and I loved the mixture of peace and promise of the unwritten day. I loved the taint of ozone as the veil of mist dissolved, exposing the new morning; the dew-soaked grass washing my rose-printed rubber over-shoes as I paced around the garden clutching my mug of tea. The hens were always waiting for me, clucking their annoyance, impatient to be released. This was my world.

Dan, however, liked to lie in at the weekends. Monday to Friday, he was showered, dressed and out of the door by 6.45, ready to catch the 7.30 train to his office in Birmingham, and so at weekends it seemed only fair that he should rebel. He liked to slob around, not shave, drink his coffee at his leisure and catch up with the newspapers.

This morning, by the time he appeared in the kitchen I'd loaded up the car with most of the produce I intended to sell and was just putting the finishing touches of gingham hats on my raspberry jam.

'Hi,' I said.

He grunted, which I knew meant, 'Good morning, darling.' He was wearing a pair of worn jeans and an ancient, white linen collarless shirt which made his head seem small, like a tortoise poking out of its shell. I got chilling mode and scruff-order while the office got the cool Dan. This Dan was the Dan I liked best, my cosy Dan. He shuffled over to the kitchen table and pulled out the chair which scraped painfully across the uneven flagstones, and then dropped heavily into it. It was the large Windsor chair with arms, and if it had a label it would say 'most important person in house chair'.

'I can't find the newspaper.'

'It's in the sitting room.'

'Well I couldn't see it.'

'On the coffee table?'

'It's not . . .'

'Do you want me to go and look?'

'No . . . no . . . but . . . well . . . if you know where it is . . .'

I was back in the kitchen a few seconds later holding the newspaper. 'It was underneath the table, on the floor.' I laughed. Dan could never find anything unless it was exactly where he expected it to be.

'Thanks. No wonder I couldn't see it.'

'It wasn't difficult. Coffee?' I plonked the cafetière down in front of him, together with the giant breakfast cup he preferred. He spread the *Guardian* out in front of him and rested his chin in his left palm while he rubbed, distractedly, at the back of his neck with his right hand, and fiddled with his hair. It was thick and black, with the merest threads of silver, and he liked to wear it long so that it curled over his collar. He looked young for fifty-three. People were usually surprised to learn he'd passed the five-O point. I'm two years younger, but people generally never voiced surprise that I'd passed mine. Maybe I'd look younger if I had a wife like me.

'Toast?' I put a couple of slices in the toaster without waiting for a reply. Then I took out a jar of my home-made marmalade from the cupboard, picked up the butter dish and set them down beside him. With his unbrushed hair and stubbly chin, he looked rather worn and comfortable and eminently loveable. I planted a kiss on the top of his head and ruffled his curls affectionately, and then the microwave pinged, so I fetched the small jug of hot milk and placed it on the table.

'Thanks, sweetheart,' he said.

'Sleep well?' I asked, as I picked up the toast and passed it to him. But I could guess the answer. He hadn't slept properly in weeks. The last few months had been really tough on Dan, with the agency haemorrhaging accounts, staff redundancies, and executives having to take salary cutbacks; there'd even been talk lately of closing the office completely and shifting what business remained to London. If that happened Dan wasn't even sure he'd be invited to go too. The strain he was under was enormous. Sometimes I felt like we were walking on eggshells around each other, like I had to tiptoe, being careful not to say the wrong thing, not put my foot in it and make things more stressful for him. I was trying to cut back on the household budget, and I hoped that the tiny income from my gardening business was a help. It was definitely better than nothing.

'Not bad. You?'

'Fine. I hope I didn't wake you when I got up.'

'No.'

I poured myself a mug of coffee and leaned against the Aga rail.

'I'm off to the market.'

'Hmm . . .'

'I've got loads of veg to sell and a couple of dozen eggs.' I calculated I might make thirty quid at most, if I was lucky.

'Hmm . . .' he repeated. His attention was fixed on the newspaper.

'I could get some local lamb, if you'd like, for lunch tomorrow.'

He lowered the paper slightly and frowned at me over the top of his glasses. 'We haven't got anyone coming, have we?'

'No, no, it's just us.'

'I'd be happy with a pack of sausages, if it's just for me.'

'It's not just for you, so let's have a nice lunch, and a decent bottle of wine . . . I'll make you a rhubarb crumble.' He always said it was his favourite, the way his mum made it, as long as it had hot yellow custard made from Bird's Custard powder. I loved the way, for all his metropolitan sophistication, he still appreciated the ordinariness of such homely things. You could take the boy out of Manchester, but you couldn't take Manchester out of the boy. I'm not sure that Dan fully appreciated why I needed to keep performing my homely role. When Laura was back I had a reason for providing a proper Sunday lunch, a reason for feeding and nurturing my family, one of the things I felt good at. But since she'd settled into university life, got a flat of her own and collected a myriad friends around her, she came home less and less. Sometimes I could hear the disappointment in my voice when I'd ask 'And this weekend, darling . . .?' and she'd say, 'No way, Mum . . . too much going on,' and I'd say 'Oh, well, never mind, then . . .'

'The plums are going to be spectacular this year.' I brought myself back to the present, and to my major solace.

But Dan was distracted once more, focused on the front page of yesterday's newspaper. 'Hmm? Whatever, darling. Whatever you'd like, sounds great . . .'

As I returned to the sink to rinse out the coffee grounds from the cafetière, I could see, from the window, the sweet peas that were splashing their vivid purple and red frills along the fence like burlesque showgirls. I loved the view from this window, which was lucky as I seemed to spend a fair bit of time here. I could see the tumbledown picket fence that separated the so-called lawn area from the orchard. Most of the wooden posts were rotted and crumbling, another job on our ever-lengthening 'to do' list. But they had a rustic charm, embossed as they were with a silvery tapestry of fungal spores and gossamer, and pitted with crazy labyrinths that provided homes for the ants and the woodlice. The steel wire which once held the posts in place was loose and twisted, but the unruly couch grass filled the gaps and provided a verdant secondary barrier. Part of me longed for it all to be neat and tidy and classically ordered, like Amelia's, but then there was also a part of me that loved the romantic chaos. I had made mood rooms in the garden to pander to my horticultural schizophrenia. I suppose my need to nurture manifested itself in an obsessive relationship with the garden.

I sometimes wondered if Dan found my passion mildly dull, no doubt bourgeois and middle-aged. Perhaps it wasn't an ideal image to sit comfortably with that of an uber-cool advertising guru. I was in the cottagey-home-making phase of my life, while he was still going through minimalist monochrome which, luckily for me, he restricted to his professional life. He wouldn't be seen dead in a Cath Kidston shop, for instance. And I still remember the scene he made when I buried the teapot under a rose-print tea cosy. I used to tease him, tell him that he loved it really; that in another life he'd have been down on his allotment chewing the cud with his digging mates, just like his father would have done. 'You're a country bumpkin now, and you can't get away from it. A three-hundred-year-old cottage, a couple of acres and a compost heap, you can't pretend you don't secretly yearn to get some good old dirt under those pristine fingernails . . .' But I'm not sure that Dan really liked being reminded of his dad's allotment. I suspected he viewed it as a mark of his success that he could pay someone else to get his dirt under their fingers. Only now that we couldn't afford to pay anyone to help maybe it was a mark of failure. But I loved the fact that it was all down to me. It gave me a role and a way of feeling useful. Growing things made me feel more anchored; weighted down by the clods of mud caked on my wellington boots, weaving my own roots into the fertile earth. It somehow kept me grounded and safe.

'Are you okay?' His voice made me jump.

'Yes. Why?'

'You were slurping your coffee, you know, making that slurp and aah sound that you do when you're thinking. I don't think you know you're doing it.'

'Sorry.' I emptied the dregs of my coffee down the sink, placed my mug – the one that's got 'There's nothing like a cup of tea in the garden' written on it – in the dishwasher, and picked up my purse and the car keys.

'Market,' I said and grinned, trying to seem cheerful.

He nodded and smiled, lifting his cup as if he was toasting me, and then returned to the paper. He was caught up in distant, more interesting worlds.

I climbed into the car, shut the door, and stuffed the key into the ignition. And then I sighed, loudly and deeply, and said out loud to the car and to myself, for no reason at all, 'Fuck!'

It was a short drive, relatively; just over two miles to the neighbouring village. The valley spread out before me, bordered in the distance by the looming ridges of the Malvern Hills. The landscape had a majestic, biblical beauty, and I told myself we were so lucky. We *almost* had everything, didn't we? If only Dan wasn't so worried about his job all the time, and the lack of money. The holiday had been really good for us, giving us space to recover ourselves, to remind each of us of who we were. Time apart from life, together. I think Dan had enjoyed it as much as I had. I *hoped* he had enjoyed it as much as I had. He'd slept better, laughed more, talked more. By the third day we'd even taken a walk holding hands. Of course it would have been good if it could have been for longer. Five days on Dartmoor wasn't ideal, but then he had needed to be back in the office, fire-fighting as usual. Short and sweet, as Dan said.

When the market first opened it buzzed with enthusiastic punters, but now the novelty had worn off the custom was drifting away a bit. Signs sprouted along the hedgerows and at crossroads once a month to advertise the event. It was a real labour of love, the dispatching of signs. They sprang up, magically, like mushrooms a few days before the event, and then vanished as though foraged in the night. We had a mishmash of produce and craft-type stuff. Wooden bowls and breadboards, exotically flavoured home-made fudge, a couple of good meat stalls, a designer baker and, of course, lots of fruit, veg and eggs. And if all of that was just too exhausting, you could recover over a decent cup of proper coffee and a home-baked cupcake with corrugated frosting.

As I fiddled around laying out my gingham cover on my assigned trestle table and arranging my produce, despite all the little problems, and even the bigger ones that I managed not to think about, I felt a warm core of contentment deep inside of me. It was good to see all the locals and to catch up with what was going on in their lives. There was Beth, whose mum ran the village shop, who'd just had her new baby and had brought it along so that we could all bill and coo over it; Alex, the old boy whose wife had died a few months back and who limped down from his cottage with a bag full of giant cucumbers and juicy ripe tomatoes from his greenhouse; Jennifer, who used to clean for me but was now chief baker for the cake stall. I loved chatting to everyone, getting all the news and gossip and feeling a real part of our little community.

'Boo!' I felt a finger poke my back and a female giggle which I recognized. I turned around to find Amelia grinning at me. She was struggling under a stash of sourdough loaves.

'Thank God you're here. I need some eggs. How many have you got? Two dozen? I'll take the lot. I've got a cake to make, pudding, breakfast for two days . . . How much? One-twenty a half dozen?'

'You know I hate charging you. You can have them for seventy-five . . .'

'Absolutely not. This is business. Ooh look, you've got some of last year's plum chutney. William will be *thrilled*. You know how he says only yours cuts the mustard . . . Oh ha, listen to me . . . cuts the mustard.'

'You're in a good mood!' I laughed. 'And thanks again for lunch the other day.'

'Not at all. It was lovely to see you. But I'm in a bit of a muck sweat. I've got William's ancient godfather and carer staying for the weekend, together with some distant cousins who I barely know. I can't be too churlish about it as I don't suppose they've got too many more years left. I only hope they don't die over the weekend, especially if I'm going to make a cake. Perhaps I'll cheat and buy one from Jennifer, be much better than mine. God, I nearly forgot to ask, are you feeling better?'

'Better?'

'Yes. Ellie said you were feeling a bit low when you went on the garden tour, and that you didn't feel like joining us on Thursday.'

'Why? What happened on Thursday?'

'The cinema. It was a real shame you couldn't come, it would have done you good . . .'

'Couldn't come . . .?' I said, vaguely.

'We all went – well, all the girls, that is. It was really jolly. We missed you. Makes such a change going to the new theatre rather than that crappy old fleapit. We had decent drinks beforehand, and nibbles, and it was all rather fun. We're going to do it again, and next time you really must try and come.'

'Well, yes, I would love to . . .' I didn't really know what else to say. And what did she mean, I was feeling low? Amelia must have misunderstood Ellie. Unless Ellie had completely misinterpreted what I was saying about Dan and me. I couldn't actually remember precisely what I'd said, but I don't think I'd led her to believe I was low, not now. But I was a little surprised that she hadn't asked me, especially after I'd taken her on the garden tour, *and* I'd left all those concerned messages, and the flowers. *All* the girls had gone? Which girls? Amelia continued, oblivious of my confusion.

'Next time. And Ellie's such good news, a really sweet girl. She said she loved the garden tour, but she was terribly concerned about you. I've been meaning to call you, but what with this weekend and everything I just haven't had a minute. Are you sure you're okay now?'

'I'm fine. Absolutely fine. No need for her to be concerned. I always *was* fine,' I said, firmly.

'That's great. I'm so glad. Anyway, darling. I've got to run. God . . . I've just had an awful thought . . . I hope they don't drink sherry. Oh bloody hell, I'd better stop off at the Spar and see if they've got any of that ghastly Hardy's stuff. Speak soon . . .'

'Bye,' I called after her. But I was left feeling deeply confused. What did she mean, I was feeling 'low'? I tried to concentrate on pushing my lettuces and runner beans at the trickle of customers, but when I counted up my takings I'd only got a grand total of ten pounds and seventy pence. And I used all of that to purchase the lamb I'd promised myself. I'd been too distracted to focus on my sales patter.

When I got home the kitchen was deserted and so was the study. I felt I needed to talk to Dan, to sound him out, to see what he thought about this Ellie business. When he wasn't preoccupied with his work he could be a sympathetic listener. Lots of my friends envied me the fact that Dan could be so 'girlie' when he chose to. I suppose it helped that he'd grown up with an elder sister, and that he had a daughter. And perhaps the fact that he worked in an industry that had needed to adapt itself to an increasingly significant female target market. Getting inside women's heads was a part of his job description.

'Dan?' I called out. But the house seemed empty. It had that familiar slumbering quality that I often felt when I returned alone, as though it was shrugging off the inconvenience of our presence, settling back into itself and making almost imperceptible little sighs and creaks of contentment, stretching and relaxing like a host body free at last of its irritating little parasitical fleas and bugs. I went upstairs to the bathroom, keeping my footsteps light in deference to the mood of the house, past the open door of our bedroom and the bomb site of a bed that Dan had been the last to vacate. I made a mental note to tidy it up once I'd been to the loo. After I'd flushed, and rinsed my hands, I heard a dog barking. I looked out of the window and saw Dan by the woodshed, an axe dangling from his hand. Ellie was walking towards him, striding out with her long hair flowing in the wind. She had come from the direction of the footpath which ran along the fields between us and the Gales' barn. Her cheeks were glowing and she was smiling. I took a step back instinctively, so that they couldn't see me watching them. She kissed Dan on the cheek, and then placed her arm on his, and left it there for a moment. Dan ran his fingers through his hair as she talked. He said something and she laughed and then he gestured to the woodpile and shrugged. He leaned the axe next to the pile of logs and looked at his watch, and then put his hands into the front pocket of his jeans and rocked on his toes, as if he was thinking, and then he spoke again, his arms spreading in wide gestures which took in both her and the house, as though he were sweeping her towards it. She looked at her watch and she nodded. I could see her smile getting wider, and they both started walking back towards the house.

I flew into the bedroom and flung off my baggy jersey, exchanging it for one of my best cashmere V-necks, and dragged a brush through my hair. I could hear Ellie's voice filtering up the stairs. And I could hear Dan's dark-chocolate-coated baritone filling in the gaps. He sounded animated and engaged. The smell of coffee combined with cigarette smoke hit my nose as I pushed the kitchen door open.

'Hi!' I said. 'What a lovely surprise!'

Ellie was leaning with her back to the Aga, in my favoured position, clutching the rail with one hand and holding a mug of coffee in the other. Dan was sitting at the head of the table, also drinking coffee, and stubbing out a cigarette. I noticed that Ellie's terrier was sitting on his lap, its head resting comfortably on the table. We had never had a dog because Dan thinks they're unhygienic, even though Laura had been desperate for one.

'It's so lovely to see you . . .' She moved towards me, and as my lips almost met her cheeks I sensed her recoil slightly so that I was left kissing the air. 'I was walking Coco along the footpath and didn't realize it cut through the bottom of your garden.'

'I'm just really glad you're all right,' I said. 'I was really worried about you when you didn't return my calls. I popped round but you were obviously busy. I feel awful now about taking you on the garden tour . . . that it might have been difficult for you . . .'

'Difficult? Why would it have been difficult? I loved it. All those characters . . . It was huge fun, and great research material for me. I'm just one big sponge, soaking it all in. I knew I'd get loads of inspiration in a place like this.'

'So you're okay then, and the writing's going well?' I said.

'Yes, really well thanks.'

'I've just seen Amelia at the village market and she said you all had a lovely time at the cinema.'

'On Thursday night. I'm really sorry you didn't join us.'

'I would have loved to, but I didn't know about it.'

'Oh no! You obviously didn't get my messages. I just assumed you were busy.'

'Messages?'

'Yes. I left a couple on your mobile, saying give me a call if you wanted to come . . .'

'I didn't get any messages.' Now I was even more confused. 'Then you must have thought me very rude.'

'Not at all. Just assumed you were busy. How stupid. I must have written your number down wrong – you'd better give it to me again. What a shame. It would have been great if you'd been there, and everyone missed you and wondered where you were.'

Written my number down wrong? But I'd written it down myself in her book, the inside cover of *Rebecca*. And what about the messages I'd left on *her* phone?

'What's this?' Dan didn't have a clue what we were talking about, nor could he have guessed at the subtext going on.

'Ellie organized for a group of girls to go to the cinema on Thursday night –'

'. . . and it was such a pity you didn't get the messages,' she interrupted.

'Perhaps you forgot to charge your phone again, sweetheart.' He turned to Ellie, 'She does that, often. It can be really difficult to get hold of her.'

I turned my face away from Dan to hide my frown. Having a go at me about my phone-charging habits was not helpful right now. And there was still the fact that she'd told the girls she was worried about me, that I was feeling 'low'. I suppose it was possible that Amelia had misheard her.

I started to unpack the box of produce I'd brought back from the farmers' market: a wilting pile of red and green oak-leaved lettuces and some fat broad beans.

'God, did you grow those yourself? You're so clever . . .'

'I sell them at the village market. You should go – it's the third Saturday in the month.'

'What a pity I missed it,' she said. 'I'd love to have bought some home-grown veg like this.'

'I'll get you a bag,' I said. 'You can take some home.' A couple of earwigs escaped onto the table and the dog pricked up its ears, obviously hoping they might provide free-range elevenses. I scooped them into my hand and chucked them out of the open window. I think I caught Ellie shuddering, but she chatted on, gamely.

'I was going stir crazy locked up in the house with just Coco and the computer for company. I felt I had to escape . . . and Dan sweetly asked me in, for coffee. I so love your house. I loved it from the outside, of course, but it's got so much character inside. Dan's been telling me all about how you found it.' I glanced at Dan, and saw that his eyes were glued on Ellie, no doubt appreciating the aesthetics; the shampoo-ad hair, the short, peppermint green cotton dress, the little-girl sugar pink cardigan draped over her skinny shoulders and, of course, those long brown legs ending in the cool All Stars. She would have looked perfect on the cover of *Country Living*.

'It was a complete wreck.' I swept my eyes around the crumbling beams, the flaking plaster, the uneven flagstones. 'Still is.'

'I think it's utterly charming,' Ellie said.

Coco jumped down from Dan's lap and came over to me to sniff my shoes. Both Ellie and Dan watched as my feet became the centre of attention.

There was an awkward silence which I felt I needed to fill. 'Dan, they've put the new wood-burner in the village hall, ready for the whist drive next weekend. It's all very smart. They've even got a club fender, and they've found one of those old wheeled laundry baskets for the logs. It's all terribly chic.'

Dan snorted unkindly. 'Village hall and chic . . . Hmm, bit of an oxymoron, I'm afraid –'

'That sounds really sweet' Ellie interrupted 'What *is* a whist drive? It's the kind of thing I remember maiden aunts used to talk about.'

'Yes . . . what an enticing picture that conjures up,' Dan sneered.

'Well, to be honest, I don't really know what it is either. But I just feel we're lucky to have the hall, and we should support it.'

'I'm all for supporting it if they put on something worth going to. So far we've had a Bridge and Scrabble night and a Promise Auction in aid of the local donkey sanctuary. Hardly a big pull for a Saturday night out. We'd ask you to come, Ellie, but it's not quite Chelsea Arts Club, is it?'

'If it means I have to dye my hair silver and don a printed frock and crocheted cardigan, then I'm game.'

'Trust me, it's really not your thing.'

'I think you're being unkind, Dan. At least they're trying to get everyone involved to encourage a sense of community.' It was almost as though he was showing off in front of Ellie, trying to be Mr Uber Cool.

'Quite right. I intend to practise my pickling skills so that I get well and truly accepted in the village,' Ellie said.

'God preserve us,' Dan sighed.

'And our prize preserves . . .' she quipped.

Dan laughed almost cruelly, as if it was the funniest little pun he had heard all week. I didn't think it was that funny. Dan knew I entered my pickles into the local competitions. Sometimes they even won, thanks in no small way to Dan's mother's own recipes.

'I ought to get going, leave you two in peace,' she said. 'I left my car at the Gales' last night. We had quite a boozy supper – it was really good fun. I couldn't believe how late it was when the party finally broke up. Thank God someone gave me a lift home. I think if I keep walking they're not too much further, are they?'

'About another fifteen minutes or so.'

"I was hoping I'd make it there before the heavens opened. Looks pretty threatening, doesn't it?' Ellie said, staring out of the window at a smattering of clouds which showed the tiniest tinge of grey.

'Dan, why don't you run Ellie up there?' I said. 'You wanted to talk to Nick about the quiz, didn't you?'

'God, no. No, really, there's absolutely no need. Coco and I will enjoy the walk . . .'

'Nonsense. Dan really does need to talk to Nick, so it's no trouble. Dan?'

'No trouble at all.' He picked up his car keys.

'Well, if you really are sure, that's terribly kind.'

Ellie patted her leg, summoning the dog to follow her. 'I feel really lucky to have you both so close to me. I know I'm going to love living here.'

'Me too.' I smiled. I don't know why I'd suggested Dan give her a lift. Perhaps I was still imagining that we were friends, kindred spirits, but after they'd gone I was left with only the silence of the house for company once more, the ticking of the clock the only disturbance in the room. Tick-tick-tick it went on, relentlessly . . . and for once I didn't find its steady march soothing; I wanted to stop it, to make time stand still. I couldn't tell why, I only knew that I did.

Dan didn't come back for almost an hour, and in the meantime I'd pulled out the straggling remains of the spent broad beans and made a start on digging over the bed, enjoying the repetitive movement of the spade slipping into the soil aided by my boot. The few clouds that Ellie had found so threatening had magically disappeared, and the warmth of the sun on my back and the soporific sound of the insects buzzing around me was soothing. I assumed he'd probably stopped for drinks with the Gales. I rarely saw Jules, Nick's wife, these days as she was always so busy with the lettings business, but I imagined she would be forming part of Ellie's new gang, especially as she was her new tenant. I wondered who else would have been at supper last night. Amelia perhaps, and Sally?

When I heard Dan's car I didn't look up, but carried on with my labours. I didn't want him to think I'd been fretting over how long he'd been.

'Here you are. I couldn't find you. Might have guessed . . . Jules and Nick send their love, and I've invited Ellie for lunch tomorrow.'

'Really? That's good.' I shoved the spade back in the soil. I turned over the earth and pulled the spade out once more before slicing it back in. I was so caught up in my thoughts that I don't think I realized I hadn't answered him.

'You okay?'

'Yes, fine . . . it's just . . . oh I don't know . . .'

'What?'

'Nothing. No . . . nothing.'

'No, what?'

'I just think there's something a bit troubled about Ellie.'

'What do you mean, troubled?'

'I probably shouldn't say anything. Probably better just left.'

'Well you've started now, so you might as well tell me.'

This was what I meant about his 'female' side. There was nothing Dan liked better than a good girlie gossip.

'I didn't tell you, but when we went on that garden outing the other day, she was really quite off . . . embarrassingly so, to be honest. I called her after that and left messages – actually because I felt a bit worried about her – and I even popped round with some flowers. I think she was in, but she didn't come to the door. I thought it was a bit odd that she never called to say thank you. And then – I was going to tell you, but I didn't have a chance – I saw Amelia at the market, and she told me all the girls had gone out to the cinema. And I know she said she'd left messages, but I don't believe she did. I wrote my number down for her, inside a book, so she couldn't have got it wrong. And, anyway, she would have got my messages, so my number would have come up on her phone, wouldn't it? I feel as though I must have done something to offend her and I don't know what it is.'

'I'm sure you haven't, babe. I think you're just reading too much into it. Anyway, like I said, you probably didn't charge your phone. Maybe there's a message on there, you just haven't heard it.'

'There isn't, Dan. And my phone was charged. Otherwise I couldn't have texted her, could I?'

'I think you're being over-sensitive. I'm sure there's some perfectly simple explanation. So stop fretting.'

'You're right. I probably am just being silly. And maybe she didn't find the gardening tour the most exciting event in her life. You know what it's like when something's a passion, you expect others to share it . . . like you with the weeding and digging,' I said, and laughed.

'And like you with Man U.'

'So lunch tomorrow is a good thing. Give us chance to get it sorted out.'

'That's my girl.' He stepped around the edge of the vegetable bed to avoid getting soil on his shoes. 'Come here,' he said, pulling me towards him. I relaxed against him, enjoying the sense of security Dan's arms seemed to offer.

'Love you,' I said.

'And I love you too, silly sausage.'

Of course I knew she was mad about the cinema trip. I mean, she would have to have been a fool to believe that I had asked her. I can see from her point of view it would have seemed unkind of me. But I honestly was doing it in her best interests. I wanted to have a chance to ask the others about her, her state of mind, just in case. Amelia was quite guarded, but Sally was sweet, really willing to chat because she felt that if I was concerned, then she should be concerned, too. It was easy to get her on to the subject. I just had to drop in a few hints about her feeling suicidal, her depression, worries about Dan, the usual stuff, and Sally was all ears. We went outside for a cigarette. Amazing how many non-smokers are more than happy to blag a sneaky one from me. It's a great ice breaker. I learn so much from my pavement ciggie chats. Anyway, Sally confirmed that she'd had this bad post-natal depression. It was all a long time before they'd moved to the village, but people knew about it. 'Oh God,' Sally said, all concerned. 'I thought that was all in the past. Poor thing. I thought she sounded a bit preoccupied at Amelia's lunch the other day. And I don't think that Laura's been the easiest child. She's very much a daddy's girl, if I'm honest.'

'Well I'm just a bit worried,' was all I had to say, and in Sally's eyes

I was already best friend and confidante.

'I love Dan but . . . sometimes he's so involved in his work I don't think he realizes what's going on at home. And because he hasn't been around he does the usual over-indulgent parent bit to make up for it. Laura's got him round her little finger, and he can be a bit . . . insensitive. I don't think he means to be. I mean I'm not saying they're not happy or anything. But, oh, you know . . .'

'Yes,' I said. 'I do know.'

I did the right thing not asking her to come out with us because it really did give me chance to bond with the others.

The following morning I woke up feeling cold, even though we were barely past mid-summer. The curtains sighed under a draught from the open window, and I could hear a duck quacking frantically on the pond. The wind carried the sound of the drumming of wings against the water's surface. And closer to the house I could hear the swallows chirruping away manically to each other. These were the sounds that I loved to wake up to, the morning percussion that reminded me that I lived a perfect life, with everything I had ever wished for.

Dan was sleeping soundly. He was facing me in the bed and his breath waxed and waned rhythmically. I wanted to slide into his warmth but at the same time I didn't want to disturb him as he looked so peaceful. I lay on my back, blinking at the ceiling for several moments, tracing the cracks in the plaster and thinking about the day to come. I was secretly annoyed with Dan for inviting Ellie but it wasn't fair to have a go at him for just being his usual kind self. I had really wanted it to be just the two of us because I was enjoying the rediscovered closeness we had brought back with us like a memento from our holiday. I suppose I knew I was being stupid over Ellie. But here, lying in bed, we had our own little world, of sorts, and everything that I ever wanted was in Dan's circle of warmth.

I couldn't resist him or the possibility of a reassuring cuddle, and so I turned around and shuffled against him, easing myself into the folds of his body, slipping my buttocks into the bend of his lap, so that my knees buckled against his. He shifted slightly and then placed his arm around my waist. His hand dropped onto my stomach and he pulled my body closer, nuzzling his nose against my hair. I sighed, savouring the delicious feel of his bare chest against my back, flesh to naked flesh. I felt his growing erection against my buttock and so I responded by squeezing my body more tightly against him.

'Hmm,' he sighed, and his breath tickled the back of my neck, making my skin come alive, reminding me of the self I had so lately rediscovered. I let my toes drift down to his foot. He inhaled quickly and jerked his foot away. I repeated the movement, aware that he was now fully awake.

'Hmm,' he said again. 'What time is it?' sleepily.

'Nine. Time to wake up.' I wriggled myself even more tightly into him and felt an answering twitch of hardness. Then slowly I turned around to face him and his eyes opened and we stared, expressionlessly, at each other. I broke the moment by placing a small kiss on the end of his nose and he smiled and closed his eyes once more, sighing deeply. I had always loved watching Dan sleep. I loved seeing him with his eyes closed. I loved the black curve that his eyelashes painted, and the smoothness of his skin inches from my face. It was when, to me, he looked at his most vulnerable and approachable. But as I watched him, his eyes remained closed, and his breathing assumed the same gentle rhythm of relaxation, so much so that I feared he had gone back to sleep. I kissed his nose again and put my arm out and stroked his naked shoulder, willing him to wake up, to pay me attention. 'Morning . . .' I don't know if he could sense the edge of insistence in my voice.

'Hmm,' he repeated, shivering. 'Your hands are cold. You're very awake.'

I traced my fingers over his arm, lightly, letting them slip over his skin until I felt the goosebumps ripple beneath my fingertips. His hand tightened over my hip, clasping it proprietorially, and pushed it away, slipping over my thigh and into my own warmth.

I pushed my hip towards him, invitingly. He opened his eyes and grinned at me and then he leaned over me. 'What a lovely way to wake up . . .'

I breathed in the familiar scent of my husband, secure and masculine, intensified by the night, infused into the warm cotton sheets, so that I was engulfed by the essence of Dan and I wanted to melt into him. 'Then what are you waiting for?' I whispered.

He raised himself and placed his body over mine, sliding between my legs. I squeezed my buttocks and raised my hips off the bed encouragingly and then saw his expression change; clouded confusion, closely followed by tired resignation and a long sigh. I could feel him soften against my thigh. 'Sorry,' he said. 'Just tired, I guess.'

'Don't worry,' I smiled, and said with forced enthusiasm, 'Never mind. There's always later.'

'Yeah,' he said, 'later,' and rolled off me. 'Sorry, babe.' He ruffled my hair and then lay back on his pillow and looked at his watch. 'Time to get up.'

'Yep.' I bit my lip, suddenly feeling that I could easily burst into tears. I slid out of bed and reached for my robe on the back of the door and pulled it around me, trying to generate some warmth. 'I'll make us some tea. Why don't you run a bath, and I'll bring it to you?'

'I'm so lucky to have you,' he called after me.

The cool wind had disappeared, leaving behind a beautiful calm day and I vowed to cast off my dismal mood and enjoy it.

'Let's eat outside,' Dan said. I was pleased that he seemed so relaxed. 'I'll lay the table, if you like. Unless there's anything else you'd like me to do?'

'Let's use the pretty cloth, the one we bought in the market at Carcassonne.' I had a momentary flashback: Dan and I, with Laura skipping between us, walking through narrow mediaeval streets. We stopped outside a shop that caught our attention with its wares spreading out onto the gloomy cobblestones: baskets brimming with the ubiquitous dried lavender; pale golden candles ridged into honeycomb shapes; and cheery yellow and blue Provençal linen in untidy but tempting piles. I saw Dan standing inside the shop, grinning at me as I piled crisply starched goodies into his arms. Laura was busy squirreling shell-shaped soaps into a print-lined basket, holding each one up to her nose before laying them down carefully. Dan bought the basket for Laura too. It was one of those memories that compose an important mental photograph, and when I looked at it, it reminded me not just of the place, but of an especially happy time, when everything seemed so settled and sorted, and I wished I could feel like that now.

'Then you'll want the blue glass plates.' Dan was already reaching up for them, taking them down from their home on the pine dresser.

'I've put some fizz in the fridge.' He seemed surprised and so I shrugged. 'I thought as it's such a beautiful day we'd make the most of it.'

'Is that necessary? Don't you think it's a bit OTT?'

'Surely you'd want to impress the lovely Ellie,' I joked.

'Why on earth would I want to impress her? What a daft thing to say.'

I'd been expecting him to laugh, to tease me in return. I put my hands up. 'Whoa, steady on . . . I was joking . . .' He nodded, but he still looked irritated and it seemed as though a cloud had threatened our perfect sky. Dan disappeared to I didn't know where, until about half an hour later I heard Pink Floyd filtering through the sitting room doorway, and as I peeled and chopped, with the sun streaming in through the windows, I couldn't resist singing along to the words I knew so well. Then I heard Dan 'Er humming . . .' in my ear and he startled me so much the carrot leaped out of my hand and onto the floor. He picked it up and placed it on to the chopping board in front of me.

'Someone sounds happy,' he said. I thought that was funny, bearing in mind the lyrics I was singing along to, 'Wish You Were Here', couldn't really be described as happy, could they?

'Sorry,' I said. Dan hated people singing along; he said it ruined the music.

'I love to hear you singing.'

'Liar. I know you hate it.'

'Not you. Only other people.'

'Ha ha, don't believe you, but thanks anyway. Listen, I'm sorry, sweetheart. You're right. Let's not have champagne . . .'

'If you want it, we'll have it,' he said.

'Maybe it might seem as if we're trying too hard.'

He put his arms around me and pulled me in tight, squeezing all the breath out of me. I felt him kiss the top of my head and I wanted to freeze the moment into a concentrated nugget of happiness. He took hold of one of my arms and spun me around as though he was dancing with me, almost knocking me off balance.

'Hey, steady,' I laughed. 'You'll have me on the floor.'

'Maybe I should do just that . . .'

He had that way of looking at me that could still make my stomach flip over, even after all this time, even after everything.

'Come on, we've got stuff to do . . . '

'Killjoy!'

'I've got to go and pick some chard and some beetroot . . . unless you want to . . . That's if you'd recognize them . . .'

'I think I'll stick to polishing glasses and napkin folding and fantasizing about my wife.'

'Yeah, right,' I giggled and even felt my cheeks go pink. But as I collected a basket it occurred to me how much more freely he flirted with me outside of the bedroom when there was less chance of a follow-through. But that was just cynical and I wasn't doing cynical today.

◇ ◇ ◇

Ellie was fashionably late. She arrived looking flushed at around one-thirty. I'd begun to think, hope even, that she might have forgotten. 'Sorry,' she said, breathlessly. 'Bloody Coco . . .'

I noticed that there was no dog, just a lead dangling limply from her right hand and a bottle of champagne clutched firmly in her left. I looked at Dan, wondering if he'd noticed the champagne and was sharing my own thoughts of 'out to impress'. But he was too busy watching her.

'I stupidly let her off the lead and she buggered off. There's a bank full of rabbit holes and I think she might have gone down one . . . Bloody dog! I've been calling for her for the last ten minutes. I didn't know what to do and I thought you'd be wondering where I was.' She looked all femininity and vulnerability. Standing, framed by the rose-covered arch, in her pale pink blouse and skinny white jeans tucked into cowboy boots, and all that thick glossy hair tumbling round her shoulders, she could have doubled for Shania Twain.

Dan just carried on looking at her while I said, 'Oh no! Poor you. I'll come and help.'

'That's so sweet . . . Would you mind if I just went back and had another yell? Sorry . . . I hope I'm not spoiling lunch.'

'No. Absolutely not. Nothing that won't keep. I'll give you a hand.'

Dan spoke for the first time. 'You'd better stay in charge of the oven, babe. I'll go with Ellie. I'll get a spade.'

'Oh Lord, I don't know . . . we'd never know which hole she's gone down. What a complete nightmare . . . Oh . . . this is for you . . .' she must have remembered she was still holding the bottle.

'How very kind. I'll put it in the fridge – let's hope we can celebrate Coco's safe return.'

'Yes,' she smiled, bravely. Poor thing, she looked like she could burst into tears at any moment. Her hand hovered over Dan's arm, like she was an invalid, or something. Clutching Ellie's cold champagne to my chest I watched them as they set off towards the footpath that linked our two properties and, as their voices faded into indistinct murmurs, I turned to go back into the house and felt as though the cold from the icy bottle had seeped right through me. The house, in contrast to the bright sunlight of the garden, seemed dark and gloomy, and I really needed a drink. I was tempted to open the champagne but then thought how bad it might look if something dreadful had happened to the bloody terrier, like I was celebrating. And I did mind about it, really I did. It would be an awful death, stuck in the dank darkness, buried alive, cold and starving slowly, wondering when your beloved was going to come and rescue you. Perhaps the air would run out so that the poor little thing would suffocate.

My eyes kept being drawn to the face of the kitchen clock as the minutes ticked by. The lamb was resting, the gravy made and the vegetables decanted into dishes and placed in the warming oven. I reached for the bottle of red wine sitting on the worktop next to the Aga. It was the bottle Dan had opened to go with the meat, and I had been allowed to steal a little for the gravy. I filled my glass and drank it far too quickly, and then re-filled it. Steady, I told myself. At this rate I'd have polished off the entire bottle before they got back. I poured myself a glass of water and drank it in two long draughts. Half an hour had passed since they'd set off. I played with the idea of perhaps going to search for them. I could insist that they come back to eat, like some sensible person always did in the best dramas. 'Come back,' I could hear myself say. 'You must eat. You'll need your strength . . .' I could transform myself into the caring, concerned nurturer that they would both appreciate and feel gratitude towards, instead of the staff relegated to the kitchen while the stuff of real life got lived somewhere else. I would take Ellie's arm, offer her a clean handkerchief and a strong shoulder. I'd lead her into the kitchen, pour her a drink and give her hand a squeeze. We would be like sisters sharing in her misfortune, while Dan fluttered about on the periphery, making him superfluous rather than me.

Forty-five minutes had passed by the time they returned. I was standing near the window and I saw them coming through the little gate that bordered our front garden. Ellie's head was downcast, and her feet seemed to drag. There was no dog. I went to the front door, opened it, and stepped back to let them in. I couldn't help thinking it was all rather ridiculous, acting as though there had been a significant crisis, almost like a death in the family, when all that had happened was that the bloody terrier had done what terriers do best and gone hunting. I felt wrong-footed, and unable to say what I wanted to say, so I said lamely, 'No luck?'

Ellie shook her head. 'God, I'm so sorry. Lunch and everything, keeping you waiting. Is everything ruined? And you were so kind to ask me.'

'We heard what we thought was a very faint whining noise. I dug there, but nothing . . .'

'How frustrating,' I said.

'Obviously she had to be there, near where we were. But we just couldn't find her. She must be stuck, stupid little dog.'

'I'm sure she'll come back. I wouldn't be surprised if she hasn't turned up by the time we've finished lunch. She'll follow your scent won't she?'

'Oh, yes, I suppose she might.'

'I think you need a drink – a glass of champagne. Dan? Why don't you open Ellie's bottle? I hope you're hungry, that you can manage something?'

'A little.' She smiled bravely. 'At least there aren't any major roads nearby, and my house is so close . . .'

'Yes,' I said. 'Thank God for that.'

'She'll turn up when she's hungry,' Dan said as he handed her a drink. They stood watching me get everything from the Aga. Dan was standing near to her as if he needed to be close in case she tumbled. He was wearing his most pathetic, doe-eyed expression of concern, as if he was almost sick with worry.

'Oh my God,' she said, when she saw the joint, and the roast potatoes and parsnips, 'a proper Sunday roast. How amazing . . . Now I feel even worse about Coco. I stupidly thought as it's so warm today we'd be having something cold . . . Oh God, I'm so sorry . . . look how hard you've worked . . .'

'I suppose cold would have been more appropriate on a day like today,' Dan said, disloyally.

God! He loved his meat and two veg, did Dan.

Ellie saw me frown at him. 'Heavens, no,' she said. 'Honestly, this is so nice. Such a change from all those fancy Mediterranean dishes everyone's into. Good to see there are still some corners of the earth that Ottolenghi hasn't penetrated yet.'

I bit my tongue to stop myself from asking 'Otto what?'

When we were all three of us seated in the sunshine with my unsuitable roast and all the trimmings piled high on our plates; when the salt and pepper, mint sauce and gravy had been passed, I said, 'I can't believe I haven't asked you what your book's about,' but Ellie didn't appear to hear me. She just carried on eating as though I hadn't said anything. So I asked again.

'Your novel, Ellie. What's it about?'

'Sorry?' she said.

'She obviously doesn't want to say,' Dan said.

I blushed. Honestly. I felt my cheeks go pink and I heard myself mutter 'sorry'.

I racked my brains for some other topic of conversation to cover the awkwardness. 'So . . . how long have you had Coco?'

Dan glared at me, and raised his eyebrows and mouthed 'well done'. I mean, for God's sake. It was only a bloody dog. I began to feel humiliated by them both, so I poured more wine into my glass and gave it one more try.

'How did you start out, writing, that is?'

'I used to be a journalist, on *Mode*.'

'Oh? I didn't realize you were in fashion. How glamorous.' The connection made sense. I had watched her daintily attacking the overcooked piece of leather that had started off life so promisingly as tender pink lamb, pushing her food around the plate and guessing that, judging by her skinny frame, she probably had the sort of food issues that came with the job. I could imagine her sitting, beautifully groomed, at one of those catwalk shows, poised in the front row with her spiral-bound notebook and leather-clad photographer.

'Must be very different, though – going from real people to invented characters.'

'When I was a journalist I had a knack of getting people to tell me things they wouldn't tell other people.' She was staring at me so directly that I felt uncomfortable. 'I still find uncovering other people's secrets is a really good skill to have, and it helps give me ideas.'

I shuddered, as though her teeny cowboy boots had just pirouetted over my grave. 'Sadly we don't have any secrets for you to uncover.' My mouth smiled, but my eyes didn't.

'Everyone has secrets, it's just that some are bigger, more interesting, than others.'

'Well I'm sure you must have loads of experience . . . secrets . . . to draw upon, from your own exciting life . . .' I was really trying to say: "Watch out, 'cos I know *your* secret".

'I can't imagine you'd get any inspiration round here. We're a fairly dull lot,' Dan said.

'You're *definitely* not dull,' she said, staring directly at him.

'Actually you're right,' Dan said, returning her look. 'Because I'm a little bit unpredictable . . .'

I swear her cheeks flushed. I felt confused by her, caught off balance and struggling to understand the reason for it. Dan seemed oblivious to what was going on. Like most men, Dan was surprisingly adept at only reading face value, especially when it came to attractive women. Funny really, when you thought it was supposedly his business to work women out. I'd love to be that simple and straightforward, but life's all about subtexts. And I was beginning to wonder whether Dan was her subtext. Had she targeted my husband for some reason? It's not a competition, I wanted to say. Dan's married. To me. But what made it hard was the fact that it was me who felt like the outsider because Dan was obviously being drawn in, lapping up her flattery and attention.

I gathered the dirty plates together and retreated to the kitchen. I could hear their voices through the open French windows. At one point Dan burst out laughing, a really loud, from-the-belly sort of laugh, and the thought struck me that I hadn't heard him laugh like that in a long time, at least not with me. And I admit I felt jealous. I'd forgotten how he laughed, how *we* used to laugh together. And I could also hear Ellie chatting away as if she'd known him forever. I almost felt guilty about returning to break up the party. Almost.

Apart from the company, it was a perfect afternoon. The sun was still warm on the terrace, washing it in a soft yellow afternoon light. Fat bumblebees buzzed in and out of the lavender like miniature fluffy helicopters, and I could see one of the hens debating whether or not to risk a scavenging foray towards the table. My life: simple and uncomplicated. Okay there were a few lumps and bumps; problems that, if I'm honest, I would rather not have. But we managed. Considering, it was all fairly sorted. There was the garden, which I loved. And I was almost embarrassed to admit that I also loved looking after the house. A home bird, that was me. Not like the swallows who set off on their three thousand-mile adventure twice a year, but I suppose like a little sparrow – a stay-at-home bird. Simple, straightforward, unsophisticated. I loved tending to things. Not remotely glamorous, but I loved it. I really did. I wouldn't want to swap with *her*. She was the one on her own, living her life – one could argue – vicariously, through the lives of other people.

I sat down and tried to retune in to their conversation. 'Did you ever fancy writing a novel?' Ellie was asking Dan as he refilled her glass. He neglected mine and replaced the bottle between them.

'Yeah. As a matter of fact I did.'

'Did you?' I said, reaching across him to get to the bottle and helping myself. 'You never told me.'

'Don't you have to write for work?' she asked.

'Not really. I'm an account man, not a copywriter. I'm better with clients and managing other people than being creative. But I still fancied the idea of being a proper writer.' Dan leaned back in his chair, rocking on the legs, elbows crooked and hands behind his head. I wanted to tell him to stop, to remind him how the chair got broken last time. But that would have made me sound even more boring.

'You should have a go. You'll never know until you try.'

'Yeah. Something for my retirement, maybe. I started one, once . . .'

'A novel?' I was so taken aback by this revelation that I wondered if he was actually making it up. I laughed and then noticed he was frowning. 'Are you serious?'

He ignored me and continued talking to Ellie. 'When I was at university. You know, the usual angry young man thing. Thought I was going to be the next Salinger.'

'What sort of things did you write about?'

'Sex and drugs and rock and roll,' I said. 'Those were his major interests.' I snorted, but they both ignored me.

Dan swung back towards the table and sighed, folding his arms in front of him. Then he leaned across and helped himself to a cigarette from Ellie's packet and glanced at me as he lit it. His look seemed to say '*Tough* if you've got a problem.' As he blew out a long stream of smoke, he answered slowly and deliberately. 'You know that game of chance you play when you're on the brink of a decision – how you don't know which fork to take, and all the emotional crap that gets in the way? I was writing about this really sorted guy who'd worked out the formula for getting it right.'

I was holding my breath, wondering where this was going.

Ellie said, 'Which was?'

'Never think about anybody else, put yourself first, always. Otherwise if you can't make yourself happy, how the hell are you going to make anyone else happy? I liked the idea of being free of any emotional baggage – no guilt, no responsibility, just freedom to live life as you want to.'

'Sounds a pretty selfish way of looking at life,' I said.

'Not really. I just wanted to work out how to make the right decision and not worry about hurting other people.' Dan said.

'Was it autobiographical?' Ellie asked.

'To the extent that I don't believe we can shake off our own subjectivity.'

'And you obviously succeeded.'

'Succeeded?' Dan asked.

'In getting your own formula right. I mean, just look around, it's all perfect.'

Dan looked down at his plate, and then glanced at me before looking directly at Ellie. 'Not exactly perfect . . .' Dan said.

'Dan!' I blurted. 'What do you mean?'

His eyes had hardened, but he formed his lips into a parody of a smile. He had drunk too much, I reasoned. It was easiest to blame the wine. And if I blamed the wine, I didn't have to blame us. He shrugged like a petulant child and took another draw of his cigarette, and then he stubbed it out on to the middle of a blue glass plate.

Ellie had the grace to look embarrassed. 'Listen, I'd better get going. Go and search for that bloody dog.' She stood up.

Dan stood up too, and so did I. 'It's nearly her supper time. I'd better go and waft my scent around so that she can follow it back to the barn. You've got my number?'

I nodded. 'And you've got mine. Inside your copy of *Rebecca*. Call us if there's any news.'

'Of course. And thank you both so much for lunch . . . and for everything . . . It really has been lovely.'

I was left in my customary place, up to my elbows in hot soapy water, quietly seething. Me and the washing up and a husband I barely seemed to know. Thank God she'd gone. I scrubbed at the roasting tin so hard I could almost see my face in it. I could still hear myself: 'More lamb? How's your glass, Ellie? Dan . . . you'll finish off these potatoes won't you? Oh, thanks, yes, it is good isn't it? I picked the rhubarb this morning . . . we're very lucky. Yes, I *know* it looks just like the rainbow chard I gave you with the lamb . . . Cream? No, really. It's fine. I'll manage. Coffee? Mint tea? You just sit there and chat, you two, while I go and do everything.' Not that they noticed whether I was there or not. No. They'd both succeeded in making me feel like a complete idiot. And most of all I felt deeply hurt by what

Dan had said about his life; and about what that said about *our* lives.

I sensed the tension in him as he made a show of reorganizing the dishwasher I'd already stacked.

'Shame about the dog,' I said, determined to break the silence, even if it meant edging a step closer to the inevitable confrontation.

'Yeah. She seemed really upset. She's had it since it was a puppy, four years . . .'

'I thought she didn't want to talk about it.'

'Well obviously, she talked about it when we were searching for it . . . her.'

'Ah. Of course. Silly me.'

'Are you okay?'

'Me? Fine. Why shouldn't I be?'

'I dunno. You just seemed . . . well . . . a bit aggressive, that's all.'

'Aggressive?' *I'd* been aggressive? That was rich. 'How?'

'The way you were talking to her, as if you were being deliberately confrontational.'

'No way!'

'Well . . . maybe I'm wrong. But that's just the way it appeared.'

'Like asking her what her book was about?'

'Well you did push it.'

'Seemed a reasonable question. And thanks, by the way, for making me feel *this* high.' I pinched my thumb and forefinger together, leaving a two-millimetre gap.

'What is *wrong* with you?' He slammed the door on the dishwasher, making the crockery rattle.

'Me? There's nothing *bloody* wrong with me. But it sounds as if there's quite a lot wrong with you.'

'Meaning?'

'All that stuff about your novel, and your *sorted* life. How do you suppose that made me feel?'

'It was a novel, for Christ's sake. Fiction! Anyway, it's not about how it's meant to make *you* feel. Sometimes it's not all about you. And that was a long time ago. It's so unimportant.'

'And I suppose *she* was interested . . . unlike *me*!'

'You're seriously overreacting . . .'

I pinched my lips together and concentrated on polishing a fork. 'Don't tell me you didn't notice how much she was flirting with you . . . and you with her, for that matter.'

'That's a ridiculous thing to say. She's just being friendly.'

'To you, maybe.'

'Well from what I saw she was perfectly friendly towards you. You were the one who was acting like the ice maiden.'

'You just can't see it, can you?'

'No. Whatever it is you think I should be able to see –'

'She's dangerous.'

'That's silly and childish. And nonsense.'

'Is it?' To be honest I don't think I'd framed the thought in my head until it was out of my mouth. Was she dangerous? Did I really think that? Wasn't she just a bit screwed up? Shouldn't I be more sympathetic and understanding? Wouldn't I be a bit weird if I'd been through what she'd been through? Wasn't I guilty of being insensitive and not making allowances, guilty of being over-protective of my marriage? I just didn't want her upsetting the status quo like this, just when I hoped we were nurturing the tender shoots of our relationship back to life. And here I was pushing him away, the very last thing I wanted to do. 'I'm sorry, Dan. Perhaps you're right. Maybe I'm just being stupid. But it would have been nice if I'd known about your novel.'

He walked over to the doorway. 'I'm going out.'

He seemed to be gone for an age, and Dan wasn't a great one for taking himself off for a walk. Not if it involved grass under his feet. And if he ever did venture out into the countryside 'Mr Kitman', as I called him, required a Gore-Tex jacket (nothing red or yellow – too many rambler connotations), army-surplus combats and a sturdy pair of hiking boots. He wouldn't have been seen dead in a Barbour or a tweed cap like the rest of the men in these parts; oh no, that would have been far too *county* for Dan. I think the other husbands viewed Dan's wardrobe with a modicum of suspicion, not quite *pukka*, I suppose, with that whiff of metropolitanism about him. I wouldn't go so far as to suggest they thought him effeminate, but I do remember Sally once told me that Patrick reckoned Dan had more outfits than Barbie's Ken. Frankly I was surprised that Patrick admitted he knew who Ken was, but there you go. No. Going for a walk in his jeans and blue suede loafers was definitely out of character. I suppose I could have called his mobile, but I didn't really know what I'd say to him. He'd probably just think I was checking up on him, and I didn't want him to think that.

Eventually I went upstairs for what I hoped would be a soothing bath. I lay in the tub, letting the water lap over me, occasionally twiddling the hot tap with my toes and letting my thoughts drift over Ellie's behaviour. If she *was* playing some kind of game it was probably because she was feeling vulnerable and lonely. This relationship, this psychotic man in her life, would be enough to make anyone behave strangely. Perhaps she saw in Dan all the lovely safe masculine qualities that I loved so much. He was so normal and straightforward she'd be bound to feel at ease with him. And here I was behaving like a jealous fishwife. If I'm honest, I also think the reason that I felt calmer had a bit to do with the fact that my alcohol level was dropping. Too much red wine, Dan had often pointed out, sometimes made me aggressive, and I wondered if perhaps I had gone a little over the top, maybe overreacted a teeny bit.

When I went downstairs I found him sitting in his usual place, remote control in one hand and the *Observer* in the other. He looked up from the paper and seemed to want to read my mood before speaking.

'You okay?' I asked.

'Fine. You?'

'Where did you go?'

'Oh just walking, clearing my head. You feeling better now?'

I nodded. 'Walking?'

'I went back down the track to see if I could find the dog. Then I bumped into Nick Gale's boy taking pot shots at the rabbits with his air rifle. I was worried he might have shot the damned dog. But he's a sensible lad so I can't believe he'd do anything like that.'

'God, I hope not.' I went over to the sofa and perched next to him. 'That would have been too awful. Imagine having to tell her . . . just horrid.' I shuddered, and then moved closer, so that my leg pressed against his, relishing the cosy feel of his body against mine.

'She'll come back, I'm sure of it. Probably just having fun exploring her new territory.'

'I hope so. It's a shame the way it messed up lunch, though. The lamb was like leather.'

'It was fine.' He folded the paper in half and laid it over the arm of the sofa and then placed his arm around my shoulder.

'I should have done something cold . . .'

'Well, perhaps. But I love roast lamb. You know I do.'

I put my hand on his knee and he placed his hand over mine and gave it a squeeze. 'I'm really sorry, Dan, about the way I reacted . . . if I behaved badly. I just felt so thrilled that I'd got a new friend, and then she seemed to go all weird on me. I was confused. I should have made more allowances for her, and now I feel really mean for the things I said. Silly, aren't I?'

'A bit.'

'She's quite complicated, though.'

'You are a one for over-analyzing, aren't you? Now, can we stop talking about her? Because I don't know about you, but to be honest I feel as if she's already occupied far too much of our day.'

'I agree.' God, wouldn't it be nice to be like a man, so simple and straightforward. Instead of, as Dan said, always looking for the worm in my perfect apples, like I do. I kissed his cheek and nuzzled my nose against his scratchy skin. 'You smell of nicotine.'

'Do I?'

'Yep.'

'Sorry. She led me astray.'

I punched his arm playfully. 'I'm the only person allowed to lead you astray!'

He grabbed my wrist and pulled me tighter to him, laughing softly. 'That's very dull of you.'

'Yep, dull and safe, that's me. But talking of leading you astray . . .' I stroked the tip of my tongue across his ear lobe and blew into his ear.

'Eeeeugh, that tickles,' he laughed.

'Why don't we have an early night?' I said, trying to make my voice sultry and suggestive.

'Do you know, that's just what I was thinking.' Dan grabbed hold of me and pulled me across his lap, and then he leaned forward and covered my face with his. His chin, as it closed against mine, felt scratchy and hard, but to me it was just the best feeling in the world as our lips met. I sighed, and all the tension of the day, and of the previous week, and Ellie and the bloody dog, and Dan and our bitter words melted from me.

Dan drew back and I opened my eyes to find he was gazing directly into them. 'I love you, Mrs Burton,' he said. 'Just remember that, when you start getting arsey about other women who can't resist throwing themselves at me. It's you I love . . .'

'I know. I'm just being stupid. And I love you, Dan.' I hugged him as tightly as I could, and then I stood up and took his hand. 'Come to bed with me.'

'I'll follow you up. I've just got to check my emails and then I'll be with you.'

'Don't be long,' I said.

He came up to bed about half an hour later and he made love to me more tenderly than he had in many weeks. I felt safe and reassured that everything was all right, and the last thing I remember is drifting towards sleep in his arms.

That Sunday lunch with them both was the first time I realized there was another side to her. She made some reference to uncovering secrets, and it was just the way she looked at me. It was really strange, like she was threatening me or something. I thought she was being really mean at that lunch. I'd just lost the dog and I was upset. Honestly, I thought she'd be suffocating down some rabbit hole. You hear about that all the time, don't you? So I thought it was a bit unnecessary to be so hostile. So, as she was being so tricky, I concentrated on Dan. He's such a sweetheart. I don't think she really appreciates him at all. Can you believe he'd never even told her he was interested in writing . . . that he'd started to write a book at university? I mean, what was she on? Still, other people's marriages are none of my business – but to be honest I do find them fascinating, don't

you? I reckon you can distil all the problems into either money or sex and I reckoned they'd got both.

I would have liked to carry my post-coital euphoria over into the following day, but sadly Mondays were never my favourite day and this one was stacking up to be a stinker. First I'd set off to muck out the hens and found one of my black Orpingtons missing. I had to do a head count of the remaining nine 'girls' twice over. I couldn't understand it because the gate to the pen was securely closed, and I remembered going out after my bath and counting them all on the perch in the dusk. They *always* put themselves to bed at sunset without fail. I suppose I must have just assumed that she was in there. Could she have nested down in the garden, maybe sneaked into one of the sheds and was now foraging around somewhere and would turn up later? But in my heart I realized that she'd probably served as Mr Fox's dinner, poor little girl. I was stupidly attached to my hens and loved the way they all had their individual characters. I'd had Nina – they were all named after divas – for over three years and she was spectacularly beautiful with her beetle-black, iridescent feathers. I felt miserably irresponsible for not taking more care of her.

Then I carried out my morning check-up of the vegetable garden and discovered my baby purple sprouting broccoli plants all bitten down to the soil. I couldn't believe it. Somehow all my carefully spread and pinned netting had come adrift and so the birds had managed to get in and feast on my lovingly nurtured seedlings. And I'd only checked them over yesterday morning. All those weeks spent propagating the seeds, pricking them out, growing them on in pots and then finally positioning them in the vegetable bed – all that effort gone for nothing overnight. Still, I wasn't giving up that easily. I'd buy some ready-grown seedlings from the garden centre and try once more. I guess it all added to the satisfaction in the end. Nothing rewarding ever came without effort, did it? And I was not going to let some fat bloody pigeon beat me. Sometimes gardening could be a depressing business.

Never mind, to cheer me up I had the dirty laundry to deal with, and then the kitchen to tidy; all before I hit the supermarket shelves. As usual when I gathered together my bag, purse, list, phone etcetera I couldn't find my keys. More and more these days I seemed to spend ridiculously large chunks of time trying to find lost 'stuff'. I was still searching when the postman's van pitched up. It wasn't Brummie Bob, our usual postie, but a woman I didn't recognize, which explained why she was an hour later than normal.

'Morning,' I called out. 'Bob on holiday again?'

'Gone to see his daughter in Australia.'

'Lucky chap,' I said. I knew that 'the daughter' had had a baby a couple of months back so Bob and his wife had been itching to go and meet their new grandson.

'Do you know the people down the road – in the barn conversion?'

'Ellie Black.'

'She got a dog?'

'A little Jack Russell. Why, have you seen it?'

'I nearly ran over it. It ran straight out in front of me just as I got to her place. There didn't seem to be anyone around. It's going to get itself killed, or cause a nasty accident.'

'I'll pop up there now and see what I can do.' That dog was managing to cause an awful lot of bother. I hurried along the lane and was outside her house in under five minutes. Her car wasn't there, but the dog was bouncing up and down at the front door as though it had got a spring in its backside. 'Coco!' I called softly. Considering she'd been out on the tiles she looked remarkably clean and tidy, apart from some rather muddy paws.

'Coco,' I repeated, bending down towards her. She shied away from me nervously, and then tentatively sniffed my outstretched hand. 'Good girl,' I said, gently. 'That's it, good girl.'

Now what? On the off chance I tried the front door handle and was surprised to find it unlocked.

'Hello!' I called out through the open doorway, though I don't know why I expected an answer when her car wasn't there. 'Hello . . .' I called out again, 'Ellie!'

'Come on, Coco. Good girl.' I grabbed her collar and hoiked her in through the door and shut it behind me. Now what was I going to do with her? I didn't fancy being responsible for muddy paws all over Jules Gale's new beige carpets, or Ellie's beautiful sofas. The kitchen. That's where she'd been shut in last time. Coco's claws scraped noisily over the waxed floorboards as I dragged her towards the door.

'Come on,' I coaxed. She was obviously wise to being locked up and tried to resist, but I pulled her in and closed the door. Then I checked for a water bowl and told Coco that she was a good girl once more, which was a big lie as she'd caused everyone so much trouble, especially me. Bloody little dog! More than anything else I would have liked to give her a giant kick up the backside, but that would have been cruel, and I certainly wasn't cruel.

The sitting room was open plan so Ellie's desk was just two paces from where I was standing with my hand on the kitchen door handle. The computer was switched on, flashing Ellie's life story at me. I took the two steps over to the desk and watched the display of Ellie form in front of me. I leant forward to get a closer look and my pendant swung down onto the keyboard, crashing into it. The computer started whirring and clicking and the slide show dissolved from the screen, revealing a page of double-spaced typing. I wasn't snooping; well I wasn't *meaning* to snoop. I couldn't help it, my eyes just tripped over the words and I couldn't help but read them. Halfway down the page, a phrase leaped out at me and I felt the hairs on the back of my neck stiffen.

'Thought I was going to be the next Salinger,' Tim says, bitterly. It's as if all the disappointment of his life, his marriage, everything, is condensed into that one statement and I look at him and I know that he wants me as much as I want him.

The words swam out of focus. Those were the words Dan used. Wasn't that what he'd said? About wanting to be the next Salinger? What the hell was I reading? I scanned the lines once more, just to make sure my eyes weren't deceiving me. No, there was no doubt. There it was, in black and white, on her screen. But what did she mean, the disappointment of his marriage? Him wanting her? This couldn't be right. She couldn't be writing about Dan, about *us*. Why? Why on earth would she do that? My eyes galloped over the rest of the page:

Later, when lunch is finally over, I leave. I feel sure he'll follow me so I dawdle along the footpath pretending to search for the 'lost' dog. But I am almost home by the time he catches up with me. We walk back to my house in silence, each of us savouring the thought of what's to come. And when he sees the dog, safely confined in my little kitchen, he says: 'What a pair of clever girls you are.'

My hand was trembling so much the mouse rattled beneath my fingers. The dog! Was she saying it wasn't really lost? That it was just a scam, to get time alone with Dan? I needed to read more, to be sure, to convince myself that what I was seeing was real. Could this be some kind of fluke? But no, this wasn't a coincidence. She was writing down what had happened. But was it true? Was she inventing this stuff, or was it real? I had to read more to find out just what the hell she was playing at.

I knew there was a chance she might come back and catch me, but so what if she did? Didn't I have every right to confront her? Wasn't there some law against this? Was she insane? I had no choice but to risk it. I tried to calm my shaking hand in order to slide the mouse pointer up a few pages and I read as fast as could.

I know everyone's eyes are upon me when I get out of the car. I can guess what they are thinking, especially the women. Who is she? Where's the husband? I know only too well how threatening a lone woman can be. I will be weighed up and judged, to see how predatory I seem, to see how trustworthy I might be; I could have worn something that said, 'yes, I'm safe', something nondescript, but the safe option was always the boring one. Instead I had opted for full-on glamour. I can sense the tension as I walk up the steps to the terrace, and I can read the questions in all those curious faces. I love that; in another life I should have been an actor. I think I'd have adored that feeling of walking onto the stage, holding the audience in the palm of my hand, just like playthings, just like my own toys. I loved the play-acting, the wearing of masks, inhabiting different roles, leaving your audience guessing who you really are.

As a child I'd learnt how to act for survival, but now I devoted my skills to the art of having fun. And here assembled, like presents beneath a Christmas tree, are all my new toys, my new playthings.

What I hadn't bargained for was that underneath the wrapping I'd find a surprise waiting for me. I thought I'd done my research fairly thoroughly; I thought I knew exactly what I was going to get. But I was wrong.

I was much too streetwise, too cynical to believe in love at first sight. But lust at first sight, that I can buy in to. He looks at me for a fraction of a second longer than he should, and I hold his eyes with mine. That's when I know that he knows, that we both know. When we're introduced I just nod and smile slowly. He takes my hand in his and as he lets it fall, his fingers slip slowly across my skin. A sensation like an electric shock pulsates through me and I pull my hand away and look at it. I look up again and he is watching me, and I know he felt it too. I get my pack of cigarettes out of my handbag and offer him one, which he takes. I try to light them both but he sees my hand is shaking, so he takes the lighter and lights first mine, then his, staring at me all the time. We exhale and the two streams of smoke merge into one. All of this takes just a couple of minutes, but I feel we've known each other for a very long time.

'Bella,' he says. 'Nice name.' The first time I hear his voice.

'Thanks.' I want to smell him. I have to stop myself from leaning forward. My eyes fix on his mouth and I am vaguely aware of someone handing me a glass of champagne. I feel myself acting normally on the outside while inside I am on fire. I have to be introduced to the others so I am forced to move away, but all the time we are talking to other people I know that he is as aware of me as I am of him. I am only half listening to the conversation I am involved in; I am unable to shut him out. There's an undercurrent of anticipation, like knowing a monsoon is on its way after months of drought. I know I shall have him. It is inevitable. And I know that he knows this, too.

I could feel the blood draining from my head and my knees giving way. I could easily vomit. I needed to sit down. I needed some air. I didn't want to stay in this room a second longer. I staggered to the front door and grabbed at the handle, then slammed it shut behind me, blinking in the harsh sunlight and choking on the clean air. I ran back down the lane to the sanctuary of my kitchen and made myself a strong cup of coffee to steady my nerves. I sat down in Dan's chair and hugged the warm china to my chest and there, sitting right in front of me in the middle of the kitchen table – where I knew they had certainly *not* been before – were my keys.

5

'How was your day?' Dan asked, as he helped himself to a cold beer from the fridge.

'Do you think you could pour a glass of wine for me?' I asked.

'Sure. That bad?'

'I've had better.' I stood in front of the Aga clutching the glass, tracing my fingers over the tears of condensation and then wiping the moisture on my jeans, distractedly. Dan opened a packet of nuts and poured them into a bowl and then offered them to me. I shook my head. I dreaded the conversation getting on to Ellie and the bloody dog, but I decided to get it over with.

'Good news,' I said, although from the flatness of my voice you'd never have guessed it. I told myself to try and sound brighter because I didn't want him to ask me what was wrong. All day long I'd wrestled with whether or not I should tell him what I'd read on her computer. I wanted to, I really did, but the trouble was I just had this nagging sense of uncertainty, a hangover from Sunday lunch. Maybe it was the way they'd laughed together, or the way he'd talked to me in front of her, as if he was hinting that his life hadn't really worked out; the fact that he'd gone out for such a long time that he really could have been with her. I was so close to spilling it all out but something stopped me. Even if it wasn't true, what would Dan think? He'd be hurt, insulted that I should doubt him, and it would undo all the good things that had happened between us. The only thing I could do, I reasoned, was to wait and watch and say nothing for the time being, and try and believe that she was just using Dan and me for her story; that she was making it up, that we were just her plot fodder.

'Good news?' he repeated.

'The postwoman nearly ran over Ellie's dog this morning. It was just running around in the road outside her house, apparently. It obviously found its way back . . .'

I paused, staring at Dan, alert to any sign of uneasiness. 'Thank God for that.'

I went on: 'So I went down there, and there she was, trying to get in the house. The last thing I could risk was the bloody dog going off again.' Again I studied his reaction, to see if he reddened, looked guilty in any way, but he seemed to be just listening, normally. I was *watching* him. Hard as I tried not to be, I was suspicious of him. I knew then just how potent her little drop of poison was. 'But anyway the door was unlocked . . .' I continued with my story but omitted the best bit. 'So I left her in the kitchen, filled her water bowl . . . didn't know what else I could do, really.'

'I knew she'd come back.'

'Did you?'

'Yep. When she was hungry. That's what they do.'

'I had no idea you knew so much about dogs.'

'I don't. But it's logical, isn't it?'

'As I said, I don't know.' I knew that there was an edge in my voice, that I was sounding chilly and distant. I just couldn't help it.

Dan let out a long sigh. 'What's wrong?'

'Nothing's wrong.' I took a mouthful of wine and couldn't bring myself to meet his eyes.

'Have you spoken to her?'

'I sent her a text . . . and she didn't text back.'

'Well you know how crap the signal is.'

'Not *everywhere*.' I couldn't tell him that I'd kept my phone sitting in the signal hotspots practically all day, just to see whether she replied or not.

'Whatever. I'm sure you'll hear from her shortly. And now we can forget about Ellie and her bloody dog for a while.'

'That would be nice,' I said, under my breath.

He gave me a sideways glance, and then shook his head at me, like a disapproving parent.

When the house phone started to ring I just looked at it and Dan looked at me.

'It's bound to be for you,' he said.

I crossed the kitchen and picked it up from its cradle on the wall. 'Hello?'

'It's Ellie. I just wanted to say thanks so much for finding Coco and putting her in the kitchen. That was such a wonderful surprise when I got back.'

'Good.'

'I would have been distraught if anything had happened to her.'

'Yes,' I said.

'And I wanted to say thank you for yesterday, for lunch. It was all so lovely and I'm only sorry that Coco and I messed it up.'

'Well thank heavens she's back now.' I realized I had to sound reasonably normal for Dan's sake. But it was a real struggle to keep my voice level.

'I feel awful at making such a fuss. Stupid little dog. I won't let her off the lead again in a hurry.'

'Won't you?' I said. 'Or maybe you'll leave her behind next time . . .' Careful, I told myself. 'So everything's all right . . . Did you manage to get lots of writing done?'

'Everything's absolutely fine and yes, I did get quite a lot done, thanks.'

'Good. Well, terriers are notorious, aren't they?' I couldn't believe how well I could keep up this charade.

'Listen, I was wondering if you and Dan are free next Saturday. I'm having some people to supper and it would be great if you could join us.'

'Hang on, I'll check with Dan.' I placed my hand over the receiver. 'She's asked us for supper next Saturday night.'

'Can we?'

I shrugged. 'So you'd like to go?' More than anything, I wanted him to say 'no', 'let's not,' 'let's say we're busy . . .'

'It's up to you. I suppose if we're not doing anything . . .'

'Saturday would be fine,' I said to her, feeling as though an invisible noose was slipping around my neck.

'Great. Around 8.15. See you then . . . if not before . . .'

'Absolutely.'

I replaced the receiver and turned to Dan. 'Dan?'

'Yeah.'

'Do you love me?'

'What kind of silly question is that?'

'Well do you?'

'Of course I do.'

'Because you know I really do love you, don't you?'

'Yes. I do know. Now, what's for supper? I'm starving.'

I got the feeling she'd been in my house. Sorry, correction, I knew she'd been in my house because she told me. But I got the feeling she'd been snooping in my house. I thought I'd ask them to supper so I could watch her . . . see if she looked guilty around me. Test her out. But I knew when I spoke to her on the phone she was guilty as hell.

I don't know how I was getting through each day, haunted by what I'd read. Ellie invaded all of my thoughts. I hated myself for it but she just wouldn't go away. Whenever the phone rang I jumped out of my skin, expecting it to be her, and when there was a knock at the door I dreaded finding her on the other side. When I drove past her house I kept my eyes firmly fixed on the road in front of me so that I wouldn't have to wave or stop to say hello. Even as I searched through my wardrobe for something to wear on Saturday night, I realized I was carrying this image of her in my head; all girly-girly pretty-pretty in her macaroon colours and skinny jeans which I couldn't seem to help comparing and contrasting against my own collection of assorted shades of vermin. It felt ridiculous. I felt ridiculous. I yo-yoed between denying to myself – no, really believing that Dan wouldn't, couldn't, be having an affair with her – to then piecing together all his behaviour and examining it forensically and thinking it might be true.

I decided to get away from the village, to put some space between myself and *her*, and I hadn't told Dan I was going to Birmingham. I felt sneaky and guilty, and wondered how he must be feeling if deception on such a small scale as mine could be so unsettling. But then I wasn't used to not telling him things. The Bullring was jam-packed with jostling people armed with offensive carrier bags. My temper was frayed, having been stuck in traffic for half an hour longer than necessary, and mostly because I just felt so bloody awful.

'Looking for something special?' the shop assistant asked.

God, I found it so annoying when they did that. 'No. Just looking, thanks.'

What was I supposed to say? 'Well . . . if you really want to know . . . just something that will make me seem half the size I am; something that in spite of what you see will transform me into a vision of loveliness; something that will make my husband fall in love with me all over again despite the fact that there is this drop-dead gorgeous predator who may, even at this very minute, be indulging in text sex with him. Oh, you haven't got anything in at the moment? There's a surprise . . .'

'Mum! Here you are!' My daughter arrived in a bomb-burst of hair, colour and noise. 'Where have you been? Is your phone switched off?' Her long blonde ringlets framed her head in a wild halo, which she tossed constantly this way and that around her head. I doubted that she would have been able to speak at all without the accompanying dramatic affectation.

'Hello, darling,' I gave her a hug, feeling her skinny little frame that seemed so fragile and vulnerable she might snap like a twig in my arms. Her bracelet-strewn arms jangled around my ears as she hugged me back. 'I've been looking for you everywhere.'

'I thought I said I'd be on the fourth floor.' Selfridges was familiar territory for us, and we each had our separate hunting grounds; Laura's being on the first floor where the likes of Top Shop and Juicy Couture were situated.

'Well I thought you'd be at Hobbs, or even Jaeger, but I didn't imagine I'd find you at Whistles. What's the occasion?'

'Oh God, don't you start. You're beginning to sound like the assistant.'

'Sorreeee.'

'No . . . no . . . take no notice of me. You know how much I love shopping.'

'Okay, then. Give me a clue.'

'Supper. Saturday night. Casual.'

'Casual. O-kay,' Laura repeated slowly. I knew exactly what she was thinking. Why would I have chosen to come to Birmingham to shop? Why, especially, when we were supposed to be, how I hated the expression, 'tightening our belts'? But I couldn't explain to Laura that I was shopping for confidence; that I was searching for something to help me face Ellie's bloody screensaver; something that might help me cover up my anger . . . and disguise my fear. I'd booked a haircut for the end of the week and I'd even flirted with the idea of perhaps squeezing in a visit to the nail bar before the end of today. I knew this wasn't really normal behaviour, but I wasn't really feeling normal.

I attempted to justify myself to my daughter. 'I haven't bought anything new for ages, and I feel dowdy. Middle aged and dull.'

'Who's giving it?'

'Oh just a new neighbour . . .' I tried to sound vague. I didn't want to make a big deal of it in front of Laura.

'Not the novelist that Dad mentioned?'

'Dad mentioned her? When?'

'When we had lunch yesterday –'

'He didn't tell me you had lunch.'

'Didn't he? Well it's hardly a secret,' she said, giving me a sideways look. 'We often do on Tuesdays – he says it's his way of making sure I eat something. I get to choose. It's cool.'

'I didn't realize.'

'It's not like he's been deliberately keeping it from you, he probably just forgot to say.' I could sense Laura getting defensive.

'Forgot?' What other things wasn't he telling me?

'It's hardly important.'

'No,' I said, keeping my voice light. 'It's not.' I didn't want to spoil our time together. It wasn't Laura's fault. Dan might not have told me, but *she* had. She wasn't the one deceiving me.

'So,' I said, cheerfully, 'What's the plan?'

'I'm taking you to Jigsaw.'

I pasted the veneer of a smile on my face as we walked out of the artificial world of the Bullring and into the daylight. We almost crashed into a balloon seller plying chirpy cartoon characters printed on shiny helium lollipops. There were lots of other mother and daughter couples just like us. The world was going about its normal business and I wondered how many people around us were also struggling to hold on to the fragile strings of their lives. The wind coming down Corporation Street was chilly and I pulled my cardigan tighter around me. Laura never seemed to notice the cold. She was wearing leggings, black ballet pumps, and a sort of diaphanous chiffon tutu that skimmed the tops of her slender thighs. A faded denim jacket that she'd probably picked up from some flea market somewhere finished off the ensemble. She was a great one for vintage finds, stretching her meagre allowance and still managing, always, to look fabulous and hip, or 'cooool' as she would say.

She hooked her arm through mine and guided me up the hill. I caught sight of our reflections in the window of Primark, Laura tall, reed slim and beautiful; and me, squat, frumpy and middle aged.

'I can't wait to meet her.'

'Who?' I pretended that I didn't know who she was talking about. The fact was that Ellie's name had never been out of my mind.

'The *writer*. Ellie. Isn't that her name? Eleanor Black? What's she like?'

'She's okay.'

'I can't believe we've actually got someone exciting in the village for once. *Nothing* ever happens in the village. I can imagine the place must be *buzzing*.'

'Yes, probably. Though she strikes me as being a bit odd, to be honest.'

'She might be able to help me, with contacts.'

'Oh I wouldn't have thought so.'

'Mum . . . God . . . hello! She's a writer, of course she might. She used to work on magazines. On *Mode*, apparently. She might be able to help, give me some advice.'

'Oh I doubt that,' I said, too quickly.

'How would you know?'

'I don't. But she's been out of it for a long time. She's a novelist now, not a journalist.'

'But even so, she must know that world. At least more than anyone else I know does. I might come back this weekend.'

It seemed that the buildings on either side of the street were pressing in towards me and the sky was a lead weight crushing me into the pavement.

'I don't think that's a good idea . . .' The words tumbled out before I could stop them.

'Sorry?' Laura stopped in the middle of the pavement, so I turned back to her.

'Well we don't know anything about her,' I said awkwardly, realizing how unconvincing I must sound.

'What else do we need to know? Like, she knows the world I want to get into. I mean, what *is* there to know? Don't you like her, or something?'

'I'm just not sure about her.'

'You don't have to like her, do you? You could just be excited for me.'

'Excited for *you*?'

'Oh Mum. Don't be silly.'

'Why am I silly?' I shrugged myself deeper into my cardigan and felt Laura's hand slip out from the crook of my arm.

'You don't want me to come back . . . you don't want me to meet her?' She folded her arms in front of her chest and set her chin defiantly. Laura was not easily dissuaded from doing what Laura wanted to do.

'It's not that I don't want you to come home. I didn't mean that. Of course I want you to come back. It's just Ellie. I'm not sure about her. Come on, let's shop.' I reached out for Laura's arm but she shrugged my hand away.

'Then tell me why.'

'Look, we're causing a traffic jam.' A woman with a buggy was struggling to get around us. I heard her mutter under her breath '. . . for God's sake . . .'

'Sorry,' I muttered. 'Come on, Laura.'

She stamped her foot on the pavement and sighed, heavily. 'Mum . . . honestly . . . just tell me what the problem is?'

'I don't know.'

'Then if you don't know, there isn't a problem.'

'Laura . . .'

'Is it something she's done? Something she's said to you?'

'Laura, just leave it, and accept what I'm saying . . . please . . . darling.'

'Look, Mum. I finish my degree next year. Do you have any idea how difficult it is to get into journalism? How hard it's going to be to find a job? Even getting some work experience is a nightmare. Obviously I've got to exploit every possible useful contact. At least Dad understands that. And frankly, so what if you don't get on with her? You don't have to, do you?' I wanted to slap her. She could be so damned stubborn. 'I can't understand why you're being so weird about her.'

I had to take a deep breath, to try and calm down. 'Do you want to come shopping with me, or not?'

Her mouth twisted defiantly. An expression I knew all too well. 'Actually I did say I'd meet George in the library. Look, you don't mind, do you? I mean you're probably better shopping on your own.'

'Laura . . . come on . . . don't be silly. We can have a nice day.'

'I really did promise George, and he said he'd help me with my project. And I have to take all the help I can get. You know what it's like . . . or maybe you don't . . . I'll come home at the weekend, see you then . . . Love you . . .' And with that she turned on her heel and melted into the shopping crowds.

Deep in my stomach the gnawing ache which had been there since I'd read Ellie's screen grew worse and it felt like my insides were being rung out. Why did Laura and I have to have this strained relationship? Why did she seem to get on so much better with her father than with me? He spoiled her. At nearly twenty-one she should be able to understand the fact that the world didn't entirely revolve around her. 'I should be excited for her . . .' for God's sake. No, Laura believed she was the centre of the universe. The price of being an only child. And Dan had fuelled it.

Things had never really been plain sailing. But then all normal families have ups and downs, don't they? We'd had the horrible mid-teens when she seemed to loathe not only me, but Dan as well. Life was always a constant battle about something. The usual stuff, I suppose. Some of it seems really minor, remembering back. Dyeing her hair, using too much black eyeliner so that she looked nineteen when she was only fifteen, trying to sneak out wearing what Dan would call a fanny pelmet, coming home an hour later than agreed, so that I'd driven into Worcester to comb the bars and nightclubs while Dan waited at home in case she turned up there. Of course it all turned out okay in the end, but not before I'd convinced myself that she'd been abducted, raped, murdered, run over . . . It was all about growing up, making her own decisions, becoming her own person and breaking away from me. Some of the rows had been worse than others. Take the row over getting her ears pierced. I'd had this rather old-fashioned idea that she should wait until she was sixteen, like I had to. But all her friends were getting them done. She was as white as a sheet when her friend Katie brought her home. They both looked guilty as sin and scared. Apparently Laura had fainted and Katie didn't know what to do. They'd had to sit in the piercings place drinking sweetened tea, getting her into a fit state to come home. 'Why on earth didn't you ring me?' I cried. 'I'd have come to get you, you twits. You should *never* have got the bus home.'

'I thought you'd be mad at me,' she said, pathetically.

'Not mad, darling. Worried.' Honestly.

I could have coped with just the ears, but I nearly dropped dead with shock when I realized she'd gone and got her tongue pierced as well. I was convinced she'd catch something life-threatening, some terrible disease like Hepatitis C, or B, or A or whatever it was. But thankfully everything was okay in the end. She got bored with it after a few weeks and the horrid stud was removed, and it was never mentioned again. Then there was the tattoo. I cried when I saw the tattoo, not in front of her, obviously. I just couldn't see the point of desecrating her perfect skin with a stain that would stay there forever. But once I got over the initial shock even I had to admit that it was quite tasteful, for a tattoo. A simple little butterfly just above her left ankle, so it could have been worse. And she was thrilled with it.

We hadn't had any terrible medical dramas to speak of. Just a broken arm when she fell off her pony the one and only time she went to pony club camp. No, no medical dramas other than the major one which neither she nor I would ever mention to *anybody* else, ever.

I'd had a panicked phone call from her: 'Mum, you've got to come to Birmingham. Please, straight away, and don't tell Dad.'

I'd jumped into my car and I was knocking on her door just an hour and a half later. She looked pale and puffy eyed, so I knew she'd been crying a lot. I thought perhaps it was something to do with her course, or maybe with Archie, her boyfriend. I was preparing myself for whichever support role I'd have to adopt, when she ushered me through to the kitchen and shut the door on the rest of the house. She put the kettle on and I knew she was struggling to tell me what the matter was.

'Darling . . . whatever it is, you can tell me.'

'Oh Mum,' she flew into my arms and her body started convulsing with sobs. 'Oh Mum, I don't know what to do.'

'Ssssh,' I'd whispered into her hair. 'It's all right. Whatever it is, it'll be all right.'

'No it won't,'

She broke away from me and started busying herself with making tea, but I could see her hands were shaking and fat tears were dripping onto the kitchen worktop. Poor Laura. I took her hand and guided her into one of the chairs by the kitchen table before taking over the tea-making. Sitting down opposite her, I hoped she'd calm down enough to tell me what was the matter.

'I'm pregnant,' she said.

'Oh my God!' I said. I couldn't help it. I know it probably wasn't the best reaction, but I honestly hadn't expected this news. I had thought of lots of other things it might be, and I suppose with hindsight this was probably a pretty obvious possibility, in the circumstances. 'I mean . . . oh darling. Goodness. Do you know how long . . . how many weeks?'

'Six. Just six. I've known, obviously, since four. I did a test as soon as I was a couple of days late. But I didn't know what to do. I haven't told Archie yet, not until I've decided.'

I suppose I couldn't be blamed for having such a mixture of feelings. Wouldn't anyone else be the same? For a moment you think your whole world has fallen apart. And then you realize that you're being selfish, self-centred and that actually it's not your world that's fallen apart at all, it's just all the thoughts and plans and assumptions that you'd made for your daughter's future that, actually, in the real sense are nothing to do with you. She was over eighteen, she was an adult. And it wasn't as if she was sleeping around; she had a steady boyfriend – Archie, whom she'd known since school. He was a nice boy. I liked him. Not that, again, it was really anything to do with me, but I didn't believe he was going to be *the one* for Laura. He just seemed a bit, well, hopeless really; hopeless in a very endearing sort of way. Whereas Laura had this wonderful sense of ambition, of an exciting future, and lots of drive and energy to get there, Archie seemed happy just to play lots of rugby, have a good time with his mates, maybe do a couple of ski seasons, bum around, and hope that at some time in his rose-tinted future he'd fall into a job.

It was all her fault, she said. She'd screwed up. She got really pissed one night. Didn't realize that the fact that she threw up an hour after taking her contraceptive pill might make it not work. While she was explaining all this, I was working out in my mind what we would do. I could take care of the baby and she could finish her studies, if that's what she wanted. In the space of a few moments I had completely rearranged my life in order to accommodate this new person. I was mentally sorting out the spare room, maybe putting Laura in there, putting the baby in Laura's room. God, I'd almost chosen the nursery paper. I kept reassuring her that if she wanted to keep it we'd work it out. But she was adamant. I suppose she also felt that it wasn't fair on Archie, either.

The next few days are a bit of a blur for me, and hopefully for Laura too. There was a pill to take orally, and then another to put inside her a day later. And then the cramps and bleeding started. I'd spent the first night in Birmingham, sleeping on her bedroom floor. I called Dan to say that Laura had a bad tummy, was feeling vulnerable, wanting her mummy. And then after the pessary was dealt with, I brought her home to look after her. It was dreadful seeing her go through it. My poor little girl, and poor little baby. I could never let Laura know how upset I was, deep down, about the abortion. It was her life, her decision, her baby. And she made me promise, made me *swear*, never to tell her father, and I know this is a dreadful thing to admit, and that in the grand scheme of things this was such a minor thing, but I was just so pleased that for once I could honestly feel that she was, however temporarily, more mine than his.

◇ ◇ ◇

I had coffee with Sally. We talked chiefly about our mutual friend. Sally told me that she's got this mother that gives her all sorts of problems. She's in a care home, suffering from some kind of personality disorder and dementia. 'That's pretty horrible for her to have to deal with,' I said. I didn't add that I thought the best thing would be for her to be given a one-way ticket to Zurich. I hope you don't think me callous, but I can't do old and sick. Sally wasn't sure which care home her mother was in, but thought it was somewhere on the outskirts of Malvern.

Sally said, 'Poor darling, she sees her once a week, but I know she finds it very difficult. It is very sweet of you to take such an interest. We all love her. She's an incredibly kind person, you know.'

And then I was so pleased to feel that I was fitting into the group, because Sally said, 'Has Amelia mentioned the village quiz to you? You really ought to be on the committee, with your expertise.'

6

My mother's room stank of TCP and Yardley's English Lavender soap. Small tables were placed haphazardly, covered in the flotsam from the wreckage of her previous life. A vase filled with garishly painted miniature porcelain tea roses, photographs of Laura, Dan and me placed in modern silver-plated frames; a box of CDs with an assortment of popular classics, Christmas carols, Catherine Jenkins and Aled Jones 'specials'. At some time in the distant past a set of fitted wardrobes had been constructed, but the doors no longer closed, defeated by my mother's excessive collection of garments. Flaccid limbs of blouses and jackets struggled through the gap, as though trying to escape their wooden coffin.

'Cassandra! You're not listening to me, are you?'

'Sorry.' I couldn't help flinching when she used my name in that tone so unique to her. She made it sound like a cracked whip. I was rubbing moisturizing cream into the scaly skin of her calves. 'The girls could do this for you,' I sighed.

'It's not the same. Not the same as when you do it. You're family. I'd rather it was you.'

'But I'm not here all the time.' I rocked back on to my heels and replaced the lid on the jar of emollient. It stuck to my hands, coating them in paraffin-scented, gelatinous goo.

'You look tired,' my mother said. She was always so brutally honest.

'Yes, I suppose I am.' There was no way I could really talk to her, to tell her why I felt so exhausted, so drained. I couldn't remember the last time we'd had a real conversation.

'You should wear more make up, get some colour in your cheeks, like I do. Daniel must think you look pale. Pale and interesting, they used to say. But there's interesting and there's ill. You're not ill, are you?'

'No, Mum, I'm not ill. Just tired.'

It was scary the way she could lock into my thoughts. 'You'd do well to hang on to that husband of yours. You don't want to be on your own, like me. It's lonely being on your own, especially when your family doesn't come to see you.' It was funny how she'd changed her tune. When Dan and I announced we were getting married she was horrified, appalled because he wasn't the right sort of chap at all. Not what she'd envisaged for me or, more importantly, for *her* as a son-in-law. Whatever I did in my life was a reflection on her, after all. Dan was a northerner, and he had silly socialist ideas. Perhaps as Dan had come to appreciate the comforts of capitalism, a true child of Thatcher – not that he'd ever admit it in a thousand years – my mother had come to accept – no, not accept, but *tolerate* him.

'I'm not well. My feet hurt. And I've got a pain in my head. My bowels are playing up again.' She was quiet for a moment and her chin dropped down towards her chest, and she started to cry. If I chose to look closely I knew I wouldn't find any tears. 'I'm always in pain. I wish I was dead.'

'That's an awful thing to say, Mum. What would we do without you? Don't cry. I know how brave you're being.'

'Why don't you come and see me? You never come. You just let me rot in here.'

I could only stomach a visit once a week, and even that left me feeling wretched. 'Well I'm here today . . .' It was like pacifying a small child, and I was now the parent figure. I had to be the mother to her which she had never been to me. I did miss the fact that I couldn't talk to her, or couldn't talk to the person I imagined a real mother would be. The person that I hoped I was to Laura.

'That Laura . . . she hasn't been to see me . . . not for months. And why hasn't she come? I am her grandmother . . .' She narrowed her eyes to sharpen the edge of her words. 'I bet she's been to see her other grandmother – though why she'd want to spend time in her company I can't imagine.'

I ignored the barb she'd thrown at Dan's mother. It wasn't surprising that Laura should choose to see her. She was loving and affectionate, normal. 'Laura's been busy. She's studying, and she's doing really well.'

'Is she? I expect she must take after me, then. I did really well at school. Do you think she takes after me?'

Again I ignored her. I spent most of my life praying that I didn't take after my mother, and one thing I was one hundred per cent certain of was the fact that Laura would *not* take after her.

'Well I expect she'll come and see me when she wants something. Everyone comes when they want something. She'll come when she needs money. Your hair's too long.'

'Dan likes it long.'

'It doesn't suit you. You're too old.'

'You're probably right.' Childish, I know, but I didn't want to give her the satisfaction of knowing that I'd already booked the appointment for tomorrow.

'Let me give you some money to get it cut.'

'No, really, it's okay.'

'But I want to give you some –'

'No! I don't need any money, Mum.' She used her money as emotional currency, blackmail currency. If she paid, she owned.

'I don't see why I can't look after my own daughter.'

'You're very kind and generous,' I said.

'It used to look so nice when it was shorter. You were more like me.'

'Yes.' A good reason to cancel that appointment.

'You *are* like me, you know.'

'Am I?'

'Matron said she thought you were pretty.'

'That was nice of Matron. I expect she was just being kind . . .' Saying what my mother wanted to hear, no doubt. They had Mum sorted, all right.

'No. She wouldn't have said it to be kind. But you don't look pretty today.'

'Well, anyway . . .' I always hated these conversations because I knew where they led. On cue she started to study my face intently, as if she was examining her own face in a mirror. This was another of our loving little routines. I shook my head and bent my neck forward, trying to make my hair hide my face, willing this game of 'mirror, mirror', to end. To my mother I knew I could only ever be a poor reflection.

'You should take more care of yourself. How is Dan?'

'He's fine. Working hard, as usual.'

'Hmm. Working hard. You know what men are like. If you made yourself more attractive he might work less hard –'

'Mum –'

'It's no good "mum-ing" me. I know what I'm talking about. I always kept myself smart for your father. I had my hair done once a week, had nice clothes, always something hot on the table for him when he came home. I was a very good wife to him, you know.'

'Yes, Mum.'

'He loved me, really loved me . . . How many years is it now?'

'Thirty-three.'

'Thirty-three . . . and he was . . . How old was he?'

'Forty-eight.'

'Forty-eight. Yes. I was trying to remember the other day, someone was asking me. I still miss him.'

I don't remember a specific moment when I first understood the truth about my mother; when I realized that she didn't love me, that she wasn't capable of love in the conventional sense. And in the same way I don't remember a specific time when I realized that what I felt for her wasn't love either, but fear. I could anticipate her mood swings like a barometer sensing the slightest shift in air pressure, and my own moods had to be adjusted like sails running before a constantly shifting wind. Sometimes there would be periods of calm, and I would enjoy the brief lull, soaking up the warmth of her attention. I made myself believe each time that this was how life would be. But the peace never lasted very long. She needed turbulence and tempest in order to feel alive. And my poor father had been just too weak to handle her. It was only after my father's death that I fully appreciated how much she had depended on him, not just for love and companionship, but for her sanity. He was the rock upon which she had anchored herself, and once the seismic shift happened and the rock shattered, she was left drifting helplessly. There was nothing I could do. Nothing anyone could do.

A carer breezed in with a tea tray with two cups of tea, already poured. Her arrival acted like a switch, flipping Mum's mood. 'Thank you, darling,' she smiled. 'You're so kind to me.'

'Anything for you, lovey.' The carer brushed her hand lightly over my mother's shoulder as she passed and avoided making eye contact with me. There was only one slice of cake on the tray, and the tea was both strong and milky. It might have been my imagination, but I felt it was their way of letting me know, getting their point across, that they thought I was a bad daughter, a cruel daughter, not visiting my poor mother often enough.

After the carer had closed the door behind her, my mother leant forward and lowered her voice. 'The girls here, they steal my money, you know.'

'No they don't. You mustn't say things like that.'

She raised her voice. 'Who are you to tell me I mustn't say things like that? It's true. Oh you don't know . . . What do you care? I'm telling you, they take my money.'

'When do they take your money?'

'When they go shopping for me.'

'You give them the money for shopping, so they're not taking it.'

'They keep the change.'

'Because you tell them to.'

'Why do you always try and twist everything? Why do you never believe me? They shouldn't keep the change, should they?'

'No, I suppose not. You should ask for it back.'

'I daren't. And I wouldn't have to if you went shopping for me, would I?'

I knew the scent of defeat. It smelt of TCP and cheap lavender. Everything was all my fault.

'I do, Mum. But you tell me I always get the wrong thing.'

'I don't.'

'You do! Last time you threw everything in the bin, said it was rubbish.'

'You're lying. I would never have done that. And anyway, the tights you bought for me were too small. I gave them away. The grapes upset my stomach, that's why I'm in pain now. I didn't like to say . . .'

'So maybe the girls get it right.' I could hear the little girl petulance in my voice that she always managed to bring out in me.

'They do. *They* listen to what I want.'

'That's good.'

'But they take my money. Maggie, the one who brought the tea. She's the worst.'

'I thought you liked her. You said she was your friend.'

'Huh, cupboard love. Why do you think she's so nice to me? Smarmy little bitch.' I flinched. That was her favourite insult, and one she often used on me.

'Do you want me to have a word?'

'And make my life a total misery? No I don't! If you had any sense . . . Oh, never mind.'

Silence fell between us and the clock ticked interminably. We were locked into this tortuous relationship where I would continue with my charade of caring for her, trying to be dutiful by looking after her physical requirements while defending myself against her mental demands, and she would continue with her pendulum swing between love and hate. Because I never knew which one I was going to get, she put me into a permanent state of alert. Dan said I was conditioned, like a Pavlovian reflex, into always looking for the worm; that I spent so much of my life on heightened alert; that I was overly watchful and obsessively protective; that I was easily threatened and distrustful. But I didn't think I was. Not always. Not all the time, anyway.

'Lovely to see you, Mum.' I stood up and walked over to the chair where she sat, her face animated by her anger. I brushed her cheek lightly with my lips. I would wipe them as soon as I was out of her sight.

'Oh go on then, go . . . You never stay long, do you?'

'I stay as long as I can, Mum. Same time next Thursday. Have a good week.'

My legs wobbled as I made my way back down the stairs. Sometimes I fantasized that if I could get away with it I'd put a pillow over her head and press down with all my strength until the life, all the hatred and bile, drained out of her. After all, she made me feel like I was already serving a life sentence.

'Mrs Burton . . . Cassandra . . . could I have a quick word?'

'What? Oh, yes, of course.' Matron had poked her head out of her office and was beckoning me to join her. I wondered what my latest crime would be. Mum had a habit of accusing me of dreadful things to the staff, so I found myself often having to give an account of myself. The worst so far had been stealing one of her life policies and pocketing the cash. I hadn't, but the facts weren't really the point. The point was that she could be at the centre of the storm, watching everyone running around – well, me, actually – trying to prove their innocence. So I braced myself for my latest misdemeanour.

'Is everything all right?' I asked, tentatively.

'Oh fine. No, nothing's wrong. In fact your mother's been on fine form. Did she mention the life story project?'

'Life story project?'

'Yes. Some of our residents are putting their life stories on tape. It's a local company going around all the care homes, offering the service. We think it's good for their memories and obviously nice for the families to have. Oh dear, I hope she wasn't saving it as a surprise.'

'I don't know, maybe. I shall look forward to hearing it, then.' It would indeed be interesting to hear how Mum re-wrote her history. Still, no harm in it that I could see.

'Is that what you wanted to talk to me about?'

'Er, no. Your mother tells me that you're a very keen gardener.'

'She did?'

'Yes. She said that you've started a business, and that you were very good at it.'

'Did she?' This was new. Praise from my mother?

'Oh yes, she's very proud of you.'

'I don't know about that,' I said.

'Well, the thing is, I've actually got a bit of a favour to ask.'

This wasn't at all what I'd been expecting. 'Fire away.'

'We need someone to take over the garden club. Just once a week for an hour or so now that we've got the new greenhouse designed to accommodate the wheelchairs. You know the kind of thing . . . seedlings . . . flowers, a few vegetables . . . I wondered if you'd be interested? I'm afraid it's voluntary but we'd meet all your expenses.

Quite a few of our residents are keen on the idea. They do miss their gardens. I'm sure I would ... and they get tired of bingo and war-time sing-alongs. It's easy to forget how active they might have been ... and all that knowledge they must have.'

'Well, I'm flattered to be asked. But I'm not sure I'd be very good at running a group.'

'You don't know 'til you try. How about giving it, say, a month's trial and then if it doesn't work out, no harm done, eh?'

'Well, maybe ...' I said, hesitantly. 'What day were you thinking of?'

'We could fit in with you, but Thursdays would be fine, or even Wednesday mornings if that was better?'

'Let me check my diary, though I'd imagine Wednesday morning might be best. Then I could see Mum afterwards instead of coming on Thursdays.'

'She might want to come to the club.'

'Mum? I don't think so. She never was very keen – didn't like getting her nails dirty.'

'She takes such a pride in her appearance, doesn't she? She always looks so elegant. She really might want to come along if you're there because she'll see more of you – in fact it was she who suggested you might like to do it. She's very proud of you, you know, constantly talking about how she misses you when she doesn't see you. All the staff are very fond of her . . .' She must have read something in my face because she added quickly, 'Although I do know she can be difficult – especially towards you.'

'Indeed she can,' I said. The not so subtle little guilt trip hadn't passed me by. I 'got' the 'she really doesn't see enough of you' message. I didn't know if I really wanted to take on the garden club, but Matron had successfully pushed all the right buttons on my guilt monitor. 'I'll give you a call when I've had chance to think it over.'

'Thank you. We would all be so grateful.'

I got into the car and wound the windows down so that I could drink in the unpolluted air. If I said no I would just be confirming what a difficult and selfish person I was; all the things my mother really thought about me. And if I said yes I knew that she was showing me that she still had the power to manipulate me into doing exactly what she wanted.

CHAPTER

7

I could hear Dan singing in the shower. There was a time when the sound would have made me feel happy, giving me the sense that all was well with the world; happy in the knowledge that I had a contented husband. But tonight I wanted to shut it out, because I didn't want him sounding so happy that we were going to Ellie's house. I closed the bedroom door but I could still hear him. I decided the safest thing would be to be out of the bedroom before he was out of the shower, for fear I said anything I might regret, or in case he read something dark in my mood. I focused on finishing off my face as quickly as possible so that I could be out of the way. But just a few minutes later he was in the bedroom, towel wrapped around his waist, damp hair sticking up around a scrubbed and shaved pink face. 'Hi babe,' he said, grinning at my reflection, and then he came over and planted a kiss on the back of my neck. Seeds of cold water dripped from his hair onto my skin and tickled, making me shudder.

'Your hair looks nice,' he said. I'd been to the hairdressers that morning and came out with it all bouffant, so that I looked like I should be smiling from the cover of a sixties knitting pattern.

'Do you like it? Thanks.' I'd pulled a brush through it a few times to flatten it and to get some of the lacquer out of it, and it looked all right, maybe just a little fuller than usual and so I was happy. Happy? Okay, satisfied then.

'Doesn't seem long since you last had it cut . . .'

I knew what he was really saying: that we were on an economy drive. I turned to face him. 'My mother paid for it.' It was a lie, but I didn't feel too guilty. I mean if we were going to judge each other on the potential scale of deceit, mine was a very small offence.

'I thought you hated her paying for anything.'

'I do, but sometimes it's easier just to go along with her. Appeasement, for a quiet life.' I turned from him, back to the face in the mirror that didn't really look like me. I hoped I looked a bit better than me, but I didn't want to look like I'd gone to too much effort because that would have flagged up some kind of insecurity, which I know would have been correct; but I didn't want her to know that. The mirror and the light in the bedroom was rubbish for putting on make-up, and my eyesight wasn't what it was, so I had to squint into one of those magnifying mirrors. I'd got to that age when looking in the mirror was never a particularly edifying experience, but I do remember a friend – maybe Amelia – saying once that in ten years' time you'd be glad to look like you do today. I guess it's some comfort to think that when I'm eighty I'd give anything to look like this.

I'd bought a pair of stretchy white jeans from Joseph at huge expense, and because they were long and my legs were short, I had to wear high heels. I didn't have any high enough so I'd had to buy a new pair of shoes too. I probably spent far more than I would have done if Laura had been with me; partly because Laura would have scolded me over our economy drive, and partly because the small act of rebellion distracted me, albeit temporarily, from the misery I was suffering.

I'd dressed my bottom half and wrapped my dressing gown over the top, so I could postpone the 'I haven't seen that before . . .' conversation. I didn't want to finish dressing while Dan was in the room because I hadn't taken off the labels and I knew he'd be bound to spot them. So I just faffed about with cotton buds, blusher brushes and lip liners and then pretended to linger over choosing earrings from my jewellery box, while Dan got dressed in the background. I watched him surreptitiously from the mirror and found myself wondering how he would be viewed through another woman's eyes. The towel was on the floor and so I could see his firm, white buttocks. He had a good body; compact and strong, and just enough hair on his chest not to be gorilla-like. Everything that I took for granted would be fresh and new, unchartered territory to someone else . . . I wondered if the touch of a new hand on his body would generate the kind of electricity that we used to have. Once, Dan only had to look at me in a certain way, a sort of sideways glance with a slow blink of his eyelids and a twitch at the corner of his mouth to make me feel weak. Did *she* feel like that?

Unaware of my scrutiny, I watched him open up his shirt drawer and pull out the blue and white stripes; I watched him purse his lips as he considered the decision, and then put it back. Next he pulled out the plain blue Thomas Pink shirt and repeated the process. Finally he settled on the blue and white Boden gingham which Laura had given him for his last birthday. He unfolded it and laid it on the bed, and then pulled on a pair of plain white cotton boxers. Socks next, pink and orange squares, very daring and also a present from Laura, and finally navy blue chinos. He was totally unconscious of my watching him and I had to bite my tongue when he sat on the bed and removed the socks he'd only just put on. So, he would be barefoot in loafers. How carefully he was putting together his look. Finally he put a comb through his hair and splashed on his aftershave, Chanel Égoïste. 'See you downstairs,' he said.

I nodded, got up from my dressing table and picked up the damp towel from where he'd left it in the middle of the floor and threw it into the dirty laundry basket. How well I could continue to perform my role.

I took my new Jigsaw silk embroidered tunic out of the wardrobe and slipped it over my head. I faced the mirror and agreed a temporary armistice with the image looking back at me.

When I went downstairs I found Dan sitting on the sofa watching television with Laura, his arm around her shoulders, and she was cuddled up to him. She had a habit of stuffing the knuckle of her thumb into her mouth so that it looked like she was sucking on it, but she wasn't. He turned his head in my direction, looked me up and down, and smiled.

'I haven't seen that before, have I?'

'What, this?'

'I don't remember it.'

'Did you get that in Birmingham?' Laura smiled at me, all sweetness and innocence.

'Birmingham?'

'Yeah, on Wednesday.'

'You went to Birmingham on Wednesday? You never said.'

'Well we all have our little secrets don't we?' I smiled.

Dan shrugged. 'Seems you do,' he said, and sighed one of his loaded heavy sighs that said so much more than words ever could. 'You ready? We ought to go. Walk or drive?'

'Let's drive up and walk back. One of us can collect the car tomorrow.'

Laura tore her attention away from *The X Factor*. 'Then you could take me round and introduce me. Pleeese.'

'We'll see.' Dan ruffled her hair and I shouted 'bye' over my shoulder.

◇ ◇ ◇

Bar forbidding Laura to go anywhere near Ellie, I hadn't come up with an idea to keep them apart. So for the moment I felt I had no choice but to run with it and deal with the fallout later. She was obviously still feeling sore at me, trying to land me in it with Dan. But there was no point in tackling her head on, because I knew I'd only end up pushing her further away which would make things worse.

'So you went to Birmingham?' Dan said as I buckled up my seatbelt.

'Yes. Has this seat moved?' I asked. I seemed to be leaning much further back than normal. I fiddled with the buttons down the left side of the seat. I never knew how anything worked in Dan's smart company Audi. Unlike my old heap, Dan's car was immaculate inside and out, with lots of unfathomable digital displays, gleaming chrome, polished walnut and squeaky-soft black leather; all stinking of newness and executive indulgence. It ordered you around, too, with lots of little audio cluckings like an officious old hen.

'Wouldn't have thought so. Anyway, why didn't you say?'

'Because I didn't want you to feel obliged to meet me, knowing how busy you are, and I wanted to catch up with Laura. Obviously I didn't know she was planning on coming back this weekend.'

'So you bought new clothes . . . and shoes . . . Did your mother buy you those as well?'

'Yes,' I said. 'An early birthday present.' I stared at the road ahead, not trusting myself to look at him. I heard him sigh heavily.

'Anyway, you never told me about *your* lunches with Laura . . .'

'What do you mean?'

'Laura said you often meet. You never mentioned it.'

'I'm sure I did.'

'You didn't.'

'Oh God, we're not going to have a row about this, are we?'

'No. Of course not.' More than anything I wanted to walk into Ellie's house with Dan at my side and on my side. 'Let's just forget it . . . talk about it later . . . try and have a nice evening, shall we?'

'That's what I always want. But you're . . .'

'What?'

'I don't know, Cass. Just odd at the moment.'

'Dan . . . don't . . .' We'd arrived. I opened the door and then slammed the beautifully crafted bit of *Vorsprung durch Technik* just hard enough to make Dan wince. There was nothing I could do for now. It was like I'd been cowering nervously in the wings and someone had just shoved me onto the stage. I squared my shoulders and took some deep breaths to try and feel calmer. Ellie had placed a row of clear glass tea lights along the top of the low brick wall which lined the edge of the path and pinned a string of illuminated stars around the top of the front door. Flanking the front door on either side were two huge terracotta pots, each stuffed with a six-foot-tall standard bay tree, their lollipop tops covered in a galaxy of teeny twinkly lights.

'Oh doesn't it all look pretty,' I said. My voice sounded reedy, stretched tight with tension.

I was glad that I hadn't brought her a bunch of my beautiful roses. Some of them were just at the perfect point for picking, fully open but not quite overblown. I could have chosen the most beautiful bouquet for her which would have looked wonderful on her desk, beside her computer. But instead I had opted for a jar of my famously hot lime pickle which I had dolled up with a lime green and white gingham lid cover. I pushed through the door and Dan followed close behind. Coco seemed especially pleased to see me. I tried to surreptitiously shake her off my new white Joseph jeans.

'Bugger off,' I hissed under my breath. Dan looked at me and frowned, unsure if he'd heard correctly, and I smiled as I bent forward and patted her. 'Good girl, Coco.'

The sitting room was empty but as we walked towards the kitchen I could see figures framed beyond the doorway to the terrace. I followed Dan through into the garden. Ellie saw Dan first and I watched her face break into a big smile of welcome, and I watched its radiance diminish as she turned to me, but I could have just imagined that. She curled her arm around his waist and left it there a moment longer than I thought necessary. She was wearing a pair of faded jeans with designer rips below her front pockets and across her knees, together with a sloppy white cotton jumper and those same Converse trainers. I swept my eyes around the other women guests and noticed that everyone was dressed in jeans and cosy jumpers and assorted flat shoes that didn't – unlike my three-inch heels – sink into the soft turf. Over to one side where Nick Gale and Patrick Priestley were head to head, I could see the smoke rise from a barbecue. As a table was also fully laid it was clear what form supper would take and I wondered if I'd be desperate enough to beg Ellie for something warm to wear later on.

'Now, let me get your drinks sorted. I've asked William to do the honours. I find the art of delegation is essential when one is entertaining single-handedly. Wait 'til you see what I've got planned for you, Dan. William!'

'Yes, my darling.' William detached himself from Sally and hurried over, obediently. 'Hello, Cass . . . Dan . . . Champagne?' My, my, I thought to myself, how quickly she'd found a niche for herself with our friends. William scurried off to get our drinks, leaving the three of us alone together.

'I see you've been shopping for pots,' I said. There were six of them arranged around her terrace, not quite placed as I would have placed them, and not quite filled with what I would have chosen. It was as close to a slap in the face as she could have given me without leaving a visible mark.

'Yes, thanks to your advice. Amelia knew of this place near Cheltenham and so we had a lovely day out together. Amelia's got such a good eye, hasn't she? She advised me on what to put in them.'

I thanked William as he handed me a glass of champagne. 'Dan thought you'd be far too busy so I couldn't have imposed on you.'

'Did you, Dan? That was very thoughtful of you,' I said. 'Amelia's done a much better job than I would have done, I'm sure.' I wondered, briefly, why Dan would have told her I was far too busy to help, bearing in mind he seemed so keen for us to be friends.

'Now, will you excuse me for a sec? I need to pass some canapés around.'

'I'll give you a hand,' Dan said.

'Would you? Thanks. They're in the kitchen. Follow me.' I stood for a moment, feeling alone and isolated, and yet here I was amongst my closest friends. Everyone was chatting, laughing, relaxing, having a happy time together without a care in the world, and then there was me. It was all so subtle, almost subliminal. Were it not for the shiny Apple computer that I could picture sitting on her pristine desk, just yards away from where I stood, I could almost have believed that I'd dreamt it all. I gulped at the champagne and listened to the lively voices of my friends: '. . . we had such a lovely day . . .' 'Ellie showed me what she's done upstairs . . . I just love the colour . . .' '. . . yes, a little wine bar in Montpellier . . .' '. . . she's made William promise to take me to this play . . .' '. . . I'm so pleased she's come to the village . . .' And then Dan's voice, 'Cass! You look miles away . . . are you okay?'

He was standing in front of me, brandishing a large plate covered in canapés: smoked salmon moussey things decorated with quails' eggs and salmon caviar; asparagus with *prosciutto*, although we were well past the asparagus season; *foie gras* on little circles of toasted *brioche* and topped with a dollop of chilli jelly. I looked at him and shook my head, 'No thanks.'

'You must. It'll soak up the alcohol,' he ordered.

I took one nearest to me and plopped it into my mouth. The chilli jelly fizzled onto the roof of my mouth, and was obviously a perfect balance for the silky rich pâté. Even though it was my first food of the day it felt like damp cardboard on my tongue. I struggled to chew on it and muttered a 'thank you' in Dan's direction. He moved off towards Nick Gale and so I made my way to Sally, Amelia and Jules. The dusk was closing in and I was just beginning to feel the chill nipping through my thin top. I couldn't stop myself from shivering. 'Cass!' Sally sidestepped to allow me into the group. 'Darling, how are you? Look at you, you look lovely. New top? And your hair, very glamorous.'

I shrugged and grinned. 'I see you lot all got the dress code right!'

'You put us all to shame . . .'

'Thanks. But if I'd known we were going to be outside I might have ditched the heels and worn something appropriate,' I laughed.

'Didn't Ellie say?'

'No. But she obviously told you.'

'And me,' Amelia added.

'Me too,' Jules said.

'Well she must have forgotten about *me*. Now there's a surprise . . .'

'Of course she wouldn't have forgotten about you. Probably that signal on your mobile.'

'God, don't you start, Amelia. You sound like Dan. I do check my messages – halfway up the stairs there's a hotspot and down by the chicken shed. There wasn't a message from her. Anyway the pots look lovely. Did you go to Foresters? I hope they gave you a good deal.'

'Do you know, I told Ellie that she'd be much better off going with you, but she was so thoughtful, not wanting to impose on you. Are you okay now?'

'I'm fine. I don't know why everyone seems to think there's something wrong with me.'

Amelia looked embarrassed. 'You mustn't think we've been gossiping about you, just concerned.'

'Well that's really sweet of you, but I really don't know why.'

'Well, there's your mother . . .' Sally said.

'And your business,' Amelia said.

'And Dan being so stressed,' Jules added.

'I honestly don't know what you're on about,' I said. 'Jules, did Dan say something?'

Jules raised her index finger to her mouth and glanced over in the direction of the men. She nodded and said *sotto voce*, 'I think he talked to Nick. Sorry. I shouldn't have said anything.'

I shook my head. 'Not at all. But Dan's usually so closed.'

'Let's not talk about it now. I'd hate them to hear us gossiping about them.'

'I honestly think they believe they're all we *ever* talk about,' Sally said.

Ellie joined us. 'What are you girls discussing so conspiratorially?'

'Just our men,' I said. 'And what about you, Ellie, how's your love life?' The champagne was fuelling my courage perfectly.

'Cass!' Amelia shot me one of her disapproving looks.

'What?'

'You can't just come right out with questions like that.'

'Can't I?'

'Of course you can,' Ellie said, giving me one of her best smiles. 'My love life's dead. Stone dead. Just the way I like it when I'm writing. I need to put all my passion into my book.'

'Is it a bit like being a method actor, you know, becoming the character, inhabiting them, letting them take you over until you turn into them?'

'Yes, I suppose . . . When I'm spending hours and hours inside someone else's head then I'm bound to become inhabited by them.'

'But isn't that the wrong way round? I'm confused, because as you've invented the characters, you're not inside someone else's head, are you? You're inside your own head, inhabiting yourself, in actual fact.'

'You're assuming that my characters are me?'

'How can they be anyone else? Or perhaps you're using other people to base your characters on, other *real* people.'

She raised her glass to her lips and stared unblinkingly at me for a moment longer than should have felt comfortable. I returned her gaze just as steadily and in that brief moment I felt that it was the first time she was revealing to me who and what she really was, and perhaps acknowledging that she knew who and what I was. Just as I waited for her answer, William appeared with the bottle, pushing it between us, brandishing it at Ellie's glass, and then at mine. 'Can't be doing with empty glasses – especially not our hostess's.' I held my glass out until he'd filled it to the brim, and then I drained a third of it, straight down.

'How's Patrick getting on with the food? I think it's probably time to eat. Dan,' she called over her shoulder. 'Can you come and give me a hand with the plates in the kitchen . . .'

I tried to move, but my heels were stuck in the soft turf. I pulled my right leg free but in doing so I overbalanced and my right heel got caught once more so that I was trapped with my feet pointing at awkward angles to each other. 'Oh God, Sally,' I grabbed at her arm and then my champagne spilled over Jules Gale's sleeve as she moved past me. 'God, Jules . . . sorry.' Sally grabbed me under the elbow but my legs buckled and I ended up landing on the grass with a thud. 'Oh God . . . how stupid . . .' I huffed as I tried to struggle back to my feet. Sally took one side and William the other. 'Come on, old girl, let's get you upright.'

'Thanks, William . . . Sally. Those bloody stupid heels.' I shoved my feet out of them, picked them up and stood barefoot with three inches of white Joseph trouser leg bottom getting muddy and damp in the dew. There was a big green and brown patch over my bottom and I saw Dan standing in the doorway, holding a pile of plates, watching me with an expression which I can only describe as utter scorn on his face. Amelia put her head close to mine. 'Cass, I think you'd better slow down – that was maybe a little over the top back there . . . with Ellie.'

'What?'

'Darling, you were a little strident, I thought. Probably the champagne talking.'

'Sorry. God, I wasn't, was I? That's what comes of not eating all day. Sorry, Sally, I wouldn't want to upset the lovely Ellie.' Sally gave me what you might call an old fashioned look and, not for the first time, I marvelled at how successfully Ellie seemed to be fitting into our lives.

I don't know how I got through the rest of supper. I remember shivering more and more as the night drew in. I neither asked for a jumper, nor did she offer one. I remember letting everyone else talk, disengaging but giving the appearance of listening. I think I did okay. Every so often I would dig my fingernails into my palms, to transfer the pain, to remind myself that it was real, that what I had seen on her computer was real. Looking around this jolly little gathering, with my friends smiling and chatting, relaxed and happy on a Saturday night I wanted to know: why me? Why had she chosen to fuck up *our* lives? Why not William? He was very rich, and charming. And why not Patrick? Patrick might well have been game. Not that I was wishing problems onto my girlfriends. I just wanted to understand why she had chosen us. Maybe we were the ones who were putting out the 'we're in trouble' vibes; maybe Dan had 'available' subliminally stamped over him. I wondered what would happen if I stood up and said: 'I've got an announcement to make: Oh, by the way, everyone. This lovely girl you're all falling over yourselves to welcome into our little community, well guess what . . .' Or perhaps I could suggest that she read us the opening chapters of her new novel. It was all just totally surreal. Our lives were becoming a novel, and how could I possibly tell where real life ended and fiction began?

At last it was time to say our goodbyes and thank yous. I couldn't bring myself to kiss her, but I had to stand aside and watch while she gave Dan a big, warm hug. Then we walked through her sitting room, my eyes inevitably drawn to her shiny Apple computer sitting in the middle of her desk. Then Dan hovered by the front door, mumbling about leaving the car until the next day. 'You can bring Laura to meet me,' Ellie said. 'Come for drinks before lunch if you like. I'll see you on Monday, Cass.'

'Monday?'

'The meeting for the village hall quiz. Amelia asked me to be on the committee, so I'll see you at Amelia's. In fact, why don't you call for me at ten and I'll drive you.'

'Perfect!' I cried out in a sing-song, happy voice.

We walked back down the lane. My stupid heels clip-clipped on the tarmac as I walked a couple of paces behind Dan. The moon made long skinny shadows in front of us and the world had taken on a monochrome hue. Over the hedge I could hear the heavy breathing from some of Nick Gale's prize beef cattle. An owl hooted and another one answered. A few yards ahead of us a dead badger lay against the verge, an oily black slick oozing from its innards onto the tarmac.

'Oh, poor thing,' I said. 'They are so stupid.'

'It was probably killed in a trap and thrown onto the road to make it look like an accident.'

'Really?'

'Yep. That's what farmers do these days.'

I was quiet for a few more paces pondering the lengths people would go to in order to cover up their tracks, and then I couldn't help myself: 'You're going to take Laura to meet her tomorrow, then?'

'Why?'

'Nothing.'

'You don't have a problem with that, do you?'

'Why would I?'

'God knows. I don't know what's up with you at the moment, Cass. Every time I looked across the table at you, you looked so bloody miserable . . . it was embarrassing.'

'I was cold – frozen, actually.'

'You could have asked her for a jersey.'

'She could have offered . . .'

'Do you have any idea how childish you're sounding?'

'Dan, fuck off!'

'Steady on. That's a bit unnecessary, isn't it?'

'Is it? Why don't you just stop getting at me for once? I really would rather, you know, if you can't say anything nice then just keep quiet. Shut up.'

'I don't know what's got into you.'

'Nothing's got into me. I'm fine. I just would like to have a conversation with you that somehow doesn't involve us biting each other's heads off.'

'I'm not biting your head off. I'm merely trying to talk to you.'

'God, you can sound patronizing sometimes. I'm *merely* trying to talk to you,' I mocked.

'You're just so strung out it's impossible to reason with you at the moment.'

I clamped my lips together. We'd both had far too much to drink and I didn't really want to have a screaming row in the middle of the road. For all I knew our voices would be drifting back up to the barn and all the other guests and our lovely hostess would be able to hear Mr and Mrs Daniel Burton ripping each other to shreds.

He carried on more softly, 'I'm just concerned, that's all.'

I took a deep breath. 'Thanks' I said as I exhaled. 'Now can we leave it?'

'If you want. But I've also been thinking about Laura's twenty-first.'

'I wonder why you'd be thinking about that.'

'You know why. Don't you think it's time –'

'When I'm ready. That's what you promised . . .'

'But you never are ready, are you?'

She'd made it pretty obvious during the evening that she was upset with me. I honestly thought that asking her to do my garden would be taking advantage of her, because there would have been that awkward thing about whether I should pay her or not, you know . . . me insisting . . . her refusing . . . So I just thought it would be more considerate towards her if I did my own thing, with Amelia.

I'd just said goodbye to the rest of the party – you know how it is when someone is the first to go? Everyone feels they've got to make a move too, so they all left pretty promptly. A few minutes later I was back in the garden, clearing off the table, collecting up dead bottles, when I heard their voices drifting through the night air. It's amazing how sound carries at night. I could hear them so distinctly they could almost have been just the other side of the hedge. She was shrieking at Dan like a fishwife. I couldn't believe it. You know, one minute she's sitting there meek as anything and then the next I could hear her yelling at him to fuck off.

Sally telephoned me on Sunday morning and she said how she'd thought Cass seemed really edgy and defensive. I recall she was drinking heavily, so heavily that she fell over at one point. Poor Dan, I really felt for him. I mean I felt sorry for her too, but for him it was all just so humiliating, really. I suppose if you pushed me I'd have to say she was showing some worrying signs, even then.

8

My head hit the pillow and the next time I opened my eyes the bedside clock told me it was 5.25. My thoughts span around my head like laundry on a turbo cycle but unlike stains, the mess in my head would not come out with a dose of Vanish. I lay awake and listened to Dan breathing steadily beside me and envied him. It was all right for him. Eventually I couldn't stand listening to him enjoying his contented sleep anymore and slipped on my dressing gown and headed down to the kitchen.

After I'd made myself a comforting cup of tea I pulled Laura's clean washing out of the tumble drier and got the ironing board out. The flat she lived in had a perfectly adequate washing machine, but she still brought her stuff home because she believed that it pleased me to mother her. She told me that, as I moaned at her because she couldn't be arsed to separate her coloureds from her whites, I would probably be happier doing it myself. I know that makes me into a mug but I think it meant that she came home more often, and unlike my husband and daughter, I'd never really taken on board that it didn't pay to be good at the domestic stuff.

I organized her clothes into a tidy pile and then set to work on her creases. It was fiddly work; a lot of her things were miniscule and some were downright immoral. But, as Dan had reminded me, she was nearly twenty-one, and if she wanted to wear knickers that consisted of two pieces of string and a piece of fabric the size of a postage stamp then I suppose that was up to her. I found ironing quite therapeutic – an outlet for my pent-up aggression, maybe. I thumped that iron down so hard sometimes that the legs of the board groaned in pain. I'd had to do my own and my mother's from around the age of ten or eleven; I didn't get pocket money unless I earned it from chores. And as I got better and faster at my jobs, Mum always found new ones to add on. She used to tell me that it was all good training for making me into a decent wife for someone. By the age of fifteen she even had me cooking the weekend roasts. Perhaps that's why I was soft on Laura, really, not wanting to repeat all that negative conditioning. Laura didn't get pocket money either – no, Laura got a monthly allowance, paid into her very own bank account so that she could spend it on whatever she chose. Except for clothes, because clothes were something that I liked to shop for with her, it was something we could do together, and it suited Laura, because if I paid she didn't have to use her allowance. Laura didn't have to do chores because she was always so busy studying for her exams; I never had time to study because I was always busy doing chores. I admit it could be argued that I was also partly responsible for spoiling her. It almost killed me to admit it, but our relationship had never been an easy one, and since she'd gone to university I was finding it more and more difficult to reach her – apart from that one time when she had really needed me. You would think that a shared secret would have created a bond between us, but instead it seemed as though she was somehow angry with me and I didn't understand why.

Laura had been what the health professionals called a 'challenging' baby. She looked like an angel, but at the time I sometimes wondered if I'd given birth to the child in *The Omen* – correction, had her excised from my stomach. I hadn't even managed to have a normal birth, which was why Dan was the first to hold her. I was too fuzzy, he told me afterwards, and he was worried I might drop her. I wasn't too fuzzy to notice that he wouldn't give her up. But from the moment he, at last, handed her to me it seemed like she just screamed and screamed and screamed. Her tiny little head would turn from delicate pink to livid beetroot as she filled her lungs and howled the place down. No matter how much I shushed and rocked and walked and crooned, Laura screamed. Even breastfeeding was a failure. For Laura, my milk seemed to be the concentrated essence of Brussels sprouts. I would present my nipple, ever optimistic for the first few days, and her whole body would tense, her head would strain away from me, and she would howl some more. My breasts became the battleground of so-called 'breast-feeding counsellors' drafted in to help fight the war taking place at number 12 Park Hill Road. I became used to having them manhandled by strange women; squeezed this way and that as they were pushed towards Laura's dainty, rosebud mouth, while a firm hand was clamped behind her head, forcing it towards me. It was amazing how much resistance was contained in that tiny little body. Laura was having none of it. I couldn't understand why, if she was hungry, she couldn't accept what God had specially prepared. During pregnancy I had imagined how much we would bond, my baby and I, during the nursing process. We would spend magical hours together, just the two of us, locked in our own little private world, forming a tie that would last forever.

'She's not thriving. She needs to eat,' the health visitor said. 'There's no shame in it. It happens to lots of people. It's nothing to do with you. You mustn't feel you've failed. And look on the bright side – you won't be a slave to her feeds for the next six months or so.'

When Dan picked her up she would stop crying. She would let out a big sigh almost straight away, and then her little body would soften as the tension melted out of her rigid muscles. Even before her first smile, her face seemed to be arranging itself into a pre-smile canvas of contentment, practising for when the beam would break out. And Dan would smile down at her, and they would look so beautiful together. I would busy myself with the steriliser and the bottles and the measures of powdered milk and then Dan would say:

'I'll feed her if you like.'

My ineptitude formed a drawbridge that everyone could cross in order to tell me what I should be doing; from how I should hold her to how long I should let her sleep, how I should push her around, how often I should feed her. Everything I did carried someone's caveat of 'perhaps you should do it like this . . .' I could just never get it right, it seemed. Then I began to fantasize about how it would be if I just went away and left them all to it. I began to wonder if perhaps Dan would make a better fist of it if I was out of the way. He seemed to know far better than I did what to do with her. She loved him. And I knew she didn't love me. I wondered if Laura really did hate me and whether she would be happier, if everyone would be happier, if I was out of the picture. And what frightened me most of all, what just seemed the *most* unnatural thing of all, was that sometimes, although I'd never admit it to anyone, I found myself feeling that I hated Laura too.

Sally turned up just after Dan and Laura had left to go and have their little pre-lunch drinkies with Ellie. I would have thought that, knowing Sally, she would have been busy preparing her own Sunday lunch, but I was delighted to see her. 'Glass of wine?'

'No thanks. Bit early for me.'

I looked at the clock: 12.15. 'I suppose you're right, and I did have quite a lot last night and woke up bloody early this morning. Still, at least I got all Laura's ironing done.'

'You ought to make her do it herself.'

'Yes, I know. But it makes me feel good to do these little things. Makes me feel needed – and I know you understand what that's like.'

Sally looked confused.

'You and Patrick, remember, that conversation we had at Amelia's?'

'Oh, vaguely.'

'Dan and Laura have gone to see Ellie, for drinks.'

'Yes, Ellie said they were going when I spoke to her this morning.'

Cosy, I thought. But then why wouldn't Sally call her to say thank you for the night before. I suppose if I was a normal guest I'd be doing the same. That was part of the entertaining 'deal' wasn't it, that all the girls could talk, have a post-mortem the next day about the kind of stuff that we women find so fascinating? It occurred to me, suddenly, that I might be the prime topic of conversation.

'I'd love a cup of coffee.'

'Coming right up.'

'You look tired, Cass.'

'Early starts and late nights. I'm getting too old . . .'

'Do you think you might be doing too much, taking on too much with all your gardening and everything?'

'My little jobs? They don't amount to very much. I haven't got anything big on, just a couple of border redesigns and an hour or two of maintenance here and there. It's good for me – gets me out of the house.'

'You just seemed a bit stressed, and I wanted to check you were okay.'

The kettle was boiling. I heaped a couple of spoonfuls of coffee into the cafetière and added the hot water. As I fiddled about getting cups and milk it gave me time to formulate how I was going to respond. All sorts of things were going through my mind; for instance, I just wanted to snap her head off and say, 'For fuck's sake, why is everyone so damned worried about me? It's *her* you should be worried about . . .' but that wouldn't have been the clever thing to do.

'That's really thoughtful, but honestly I'm fine. I mean, what makes you think I'm not?' I handed her a cup of coffee and perched myself against the Aga rail while I waited for her to answer.

'Well, nothing really, honestly. It's just that last night, well I didn't think you seemed yourself. You were very quiet during dinner.

I was worried about you. Is everything okay – with you and Dan, I mean?'

I laughed gently into my cup. 'That's funny, isn't it, because you were the one at Amelia's the other day saying that we were okay – welded together at the hip, I think you said.'

'I do think that. I really do . . . just so long as everything's okay.'

'You're incredibly sweet to be concerned. But really there's nothing . . .'

'You're okay with Ellie, aren't you? I just felt there was perhaps a bit of tension between you.'

'Honestly, Sally, there's nothing wrong between me and Dan, and nothing wrong between me and Ellie . . . I mean look at her . . . Laura's up there right now getting help with contacts.' I decided to change tack. 'How do you find her?'

'I think she's lovely. A real breath of fresh air . . . just what the village needs. And she couldn't be kinder, could she? I think she's really brave coming here, not knowing anyone, all by herself.'

'Has she mentioned to you anything about a husband . . . or boyfriend?' I wanted to find out if I was the only person she'd confided in about the madman she'd run away from. I wasn't planning to break her confidence, although to be honest, under the circumstances, it seemed more than a little crazy to care about respecting her privacy.

'No. She just said it was complicated, so naturally I didn't want to pry.'

'Like Amelia felt I did last night.'

'Well you did seem a little intense, but perhaps it was the champagne talking.'

'I wasn't drunk, Sally.'

'No . . . no . . . I didn't mean to say –'

'When I fell over, I really did get my heels stuck in the bloody lawn. And I probably seemed a bit tense because I was feeling the cold.'

'Sorry, I really didn't mean to . . . um, how's your mother?'

'The same. Charming and warm as ever.'

'Oh Cass, poor you. I think you're an angel the way you keep on going to see her.'

'I don't really have a choice.'

'No, I don't suppose you do.' Sally stood up and put her empty coffee cup on the sink. 'Thanks for the coffee. So you're okay, then? Everything's all right?'

'Yes,' I said, probably a little over-emphatically. 'I'm *fine*.'

'Good. So I'll see you tomorrow, at Amelia's.'

'Yep, I'll be there.'

I watched as she climbed into her car. And I had the strangest feeling. It was really uncomfortable; no, worse than uncomfortable. It was a feeling that bordered on alarm. Once again I sensed that the whole conversation had been heavy with subtexts, that Sally had most definitely come on a mission. I wondered then if Ellie had heard the row between Dan and me last night, and if she had, had she told Sally? Were they all now gossiping about us, picking over every nuance of our behaviour towards each other and towards other people? It was a nasty, creepy feeling of something dark and insidious gathering around me, and because it had no face or name I didn't know how I was going to fight it.

◇ ◇ ◇

'Mum, she's so lovely,' Laura gushed. 'She said she'd love to read some of my stories and then suggest where I should submit stuff to. She also said she'd try and get me some work experience, maybe even an internship on *Mode* . . .'

'That's good,' I said, keeping my face turned towards my bubbling saucepans.

'Yeah, she's really cool. She said I could go up there any time and hang out with her. God, how lucky am I to meet someone like that . . . on our doorstep? Is that all my washing? Oh thanks, Mum, that's really nice of you . . . I wouldn't have bothered to iron half of it as it just gets creased in my bag.'

'Well pack it carefully, and then it won't.'

'Okay. How long before lunch? I've just got to go and check Facebook.'

'Ten minutes, so don't be too long.'

Dan came and stood behind me. He put his hand on my shoulder and squeezed it gently. 'You okay?' he said.

'Yeah, fine.' I continued stirring the gravy, ignoring his hand. He let it slip and I heard him sigh.

'It's great what she's doing for her, isn't it? She said she remembered what it was like when she was Laura's age. How difficult it was to get a foot in the door.'

'But she doesn't know if Laura's any good. Wouldn't she want to know that, before pushing her forward?'

'I dunno, but she can see how keen she is. You should have heard Laura giving her the third degree about how she got into journalism . . . it was nice seeing her so fired up. Funny, 'cos I was never really sure about her doing media studies. If you could see the number of CVs that come into the agency . . . It's sad but true that the only way you get on is through knowing someone these days.'

'Isn't there anyone else we know – someone at work that might have contacts as well? I mean, I thought Laura was set on going travelling this summer, not working.'

'Well it may not happen this summer, and it may only be for a week or two, but she won't want to pass up an opportunity like this. She can travel anytime.'

'She should be having a break, having some fun with her friends while she's got the opportunity, before she has to knuckle down in the real world.'

'Yeah, well she's luckily being a bit more sensible than that. Funny, I thought you'd be pleased that she's being so sensible.'

'Well of course I am. How could I not be?'

'I don't know, Cass, I really don't know.'

Ellie might as well have been with us during lunch as all I heard was 'Ellie this . . .' and 'Ellie that . . .' After I'd cleared everything away I pleaded a headache and went upstairs for a lie down. I could hear Dan and Laura chatting together downstairs. Laura must have plugged her iPod into the sound system because I got drifts of music I didn't recognize. I could hear them both laughing, the sound of my husband and daughter being happy, enjoying a perfect family Sunday together. Knowing that they were happy should have made me happy, but it just made me feel alone. I must have dropped off to sleep eventually, because when I woke up the bedside clock said it was just before six, and when I went downstairs Dan told me that Laura had gone back to Birmingham already. He said she told him to say bye to me, that she hadn't wanted to wake me.

My first meeting with Laura. What can I say? Bright, beautiful, bubbly. A bit shy at first, which was rather charming. She made a big fuss of Coco while Dan helped me mix the drinks. He said he hadn't tried a Bloody Mary with freshly grated horseradish before, and that he thought it was one of the best he'd tasted. He also complimented me again on last night's supper. I asked him if Cass was all right. He looked a bit surprised; I don't know, it's hard to explain but there was this funny look that came into his eye – sad, almost like a wounded animal – and his shoulders just sort of sagged. I got the feeling he wanted to say something, but was afraid to. I didn't tell him that I'd heard the row between them, that I knew things weren't great, because I didn't want to say anything in front of Laura. So we took our drinks outside and I told her about my life on Mode, how I'd

143

got into journalism, my time in Rome. I sensed that Dan was much more relaxed than he had been the night before, like he was more himself, somehow. I thought Laura was very like him: same sense of humour, funny little mannerisms. Obviously I wanted to help her as much as I could, so I told her she could come round any time and I looked forward to really getting to know her. Of course I had no way of knowing that Cass would be really upset. I mean, why would anyone have been upset by someone helping their child? Honestly, the thought would never have crossed my mind in a million years.

It seemed another potentially 'perfect' Monday had arrived. Was it really only a week ago since I'd read all that bile? So much seemed to have happened, so much that seemed to change the way I viewed my little world and my own little family and my lovely, loyal friends. As I reached Ellie's I was sorely tempted to drive on past. I could say afterwards: 'God, Ellie, I'm so sorry. I can't believe I did that . . . I'm just so vague sometimes . . .'

She was all smiles when she opened the door, 'Come in, come in . . . It was so lovely to see you both on Saturday.' I hated the fact that she could look so normal and happy, as if she didn't have a care in the world, when she had just waltzed into my life, from nowhere, and was busy messing up everything that I cared about.

'And I loved meeting Laura. She's such a sweet girl,' she said. 'You must be so proud of her.'

'Yes,' I said. 'We are.' I hated hearing her say Laura's name. I couldn't look at her, so instead I stroked Coco, but she wouldn't shut up about Laura. I'd called Laura last night but her phone went straight to voice mail, and I'd texted her this morning to say 'please call me' but she hadn't. My fingers stopped their stroking motion on Coco's coat and I started pulling at the loose skin around the line of her collar, squeezing it between my fingers and twisting it around and around. Coco winced and snatched her head away from me, and then slunk off towards the kitchen, but Ellie didn't notice. 'I'm sure I'll be able to help set her up with some work experience, maybe even an internship. I still have lots of contacts.'

I didn't respond, but rubbed at an imaginary patch of dirt on the sleeve of my jacket. I knew I couldn't risk speaking in case I actually snarled. A vivid image flashed into my imagination of me throwing myself at her, clawing at her hair and scratching her eyes out, wrestling her to the floor and then smashing the light out of that lovely mask. I put my hand up to my mouth and cleared my throat and took a couple of deep breaths.

The intensity of my anger and my desire for violence had really shaken me, and for an instant I was afraid that this was how it felt to be unhinged, to suffer a moment of temporary insanity. Is this what they meant by diminished responsibility? As I struggled to calm myself, waiting for Ellie to lock up the dog and collect her handbag, or whatever it was she was bustling around doing, I felt a tiny nagging doubt drift like the wisp of a cloud over the rim of my mind. Was this what it felt like to be 'on the edge'? Was it really possible that my mind was playing tricks with me? But then I saw the computer, the shiny white case with the big silver apple emblazoned on its lid and I remembered the crunching noise that my pendant had made when it smashed against the hard plastic keyboard. I remembered the way the image of Ellie had dissolved to reveal the black and white virtual typescript and the words that had leapt from the screen and into my heart. 'I know that he wants me as much as I want him . . .' and I knew that I hadn't dreamt it. This sick bitch was at best using our story because she didn't have the imagination to make up her own; and at worst she was, right now, having an affair with my husband. That was the cold, hard reality.

'I'll drive you,' she said.

'No need.' I'd left the driver's door open and parked sideways on the drive so that in order for her to get out we'd have had to have moved mine. I was not going to be entrapped in her space. It was too intimate. It was bad enough having her in my van, but at least I could feel I was in control. I had the air conditioning fan on full blast so that I didn't feel I had to share her breath. Her proximity made me shiver with revulsion.

To say that I was gutted by the fact that Amelia had invited her onto the village hall quiz committee was a bit like saying you'd be mildly irritated if you'd accidentally shredded your £10 million prize-winning lottery ticket. She'd slotted herself into the community as perfectly as the final piece of a jigsaw puzzle. She was the exact fit: all that was needed to complete a perfect picture. What rearguard action could I have possibly taken to prevent it? Taken Amelia on one side and said . . . what? Oh, by the way, Amelia, I read on her computer that she's having an affair with my husband? And after Sally's little chat with me yesterday I suspected that if I said anything negative about Ellie, bearing in mind they thought she was so perfect, they wouldn't believe me. And it might also fuel their anxiety about me to know that I'd been snooping in Ellie's house.

I let Ellie lead the way into the house. She was obviously now familiar with the layout of Amelia's ground floor. She didn't need me to guide her through from the hallway, down the long, creaky-floored main passage where stern-faced gentlemen stared down disapprovingly from their gilded frames, then on past the open door of the morning room, turn right at the end by the drawing room and then take the side passage into the kitchen. I remembered it took me a long time to stop getting lost in the ancestral warren.

From the sound of female voices we obviously weren't the first to arrive. There were now – including Ellie – eight of us on the committee. Amelia, obviously; me; *her*; Jules who was great at drafting in Nick's agricultural vehicles when required for shifting stuff; Sally who was a whizz at blagging raffle prizes; Janice Davies from Rose Cottage who looked after the key to the village hall and who was the font of all local knowledge; Kate Holland, the young army wife here because her husband was on a two-year posting, and who had an 'in' with the younger mums at the local prep school; and Helen Clifford who had, in a previous life, been a professional caterer and was brilliant at all things to do with organizing 'do's'.

We were all sitting around Amelia's kitchen table. A tray of cups and saucers had been placed on one end with two cafetières full of coffee and a pot of lemon verbena tea, together with a plate of home-baked chocolate chip shortbreads. I helped myself to a cup of coffee and took a biscuit without hesitation, knowing just how good Amelia's cook was, but I was inwardly amused at Ellie's fastidiousness as she shook her head when Amelia offered.

'They look lovely, but I won't.'

'Firstly,' Amelia said, beaming benevolently at all of us, 'I'd like to welcome Ellie onto the committee and thank her for agreeing to help us out.'

A murmur of 'hear-hear' went round the table, and I just stretched my lips into the approximation of a smile and stared down into my coffee cup. I had taken my dog-eared shorthand notebook out of my handbag and had started to make a few notes. Ellie's notebook was leather, Moroccan-style, with gold tooling and tiny turquoise beads around the edges. Before I even saw the pen I could have guessed it would be of the smart fountain variety. I used a bog-standard clear plastic biro which I bought in a pack of 10 for £2.99 from the supermarket. Amelia was chairing the meeting, as usual, which was fine by everyone, as she made a very good organizer. We ran through everyone's progress so far and I wondered if I was imagining it at first, but I kept sensing Ellie's eyes upon me. Every time I glanced up I caught her lowering them, as if she'd been caught out. I felt like doing something outrageous, like sticking a finger up my nose, or dunking my biscuit into my coffee, to see whether it might come out in her book. I fancied we could play one of those children's games, where you have to copy each other.

Would I read about my funny little idiosyncrasies, my bad posture as I slumped over the table, my weird frizzy brown hair, my pale face, my too-thin nose, my flat chest and pear-shaped behind, would it all come out in the novel? Or was I too far ahead of myself, bearing in mind I had only read about Dan so far? But I was in danger of missing out vital instructions from our leader so I commanded my mind to stop wandering and to focus on what Amelia was saying.

'Okay, so can we please have volunteers for setting up on the day? We've got ten trestle tables here, but I reckon we could do with another half dozen or so from Newbridge Village Hall. And they've already told us we can borrow them so we might just as well round it up to ten. Jules, is Nick still okay to pick them up?'

'Does he have a choice?' Jules laughed.

'Great. And Cass, are you okay with the flowers.'

I nodded. 'Absolutely. As long as I can raid your garden if mine's a bit thin, Amelia?'

'Absolutely. I can give you a hand too . . .'

'Oh I can give you a hand, Cass. I adore flower arranging. I'd love to help out with that.'

'Great, Ellie. So I'll put you and Cass down as being I.C. flowers.'

I didn't comment, but stared down at my pad and concentrated on doodling a chain of linked sixes.

'I've got an idea,' Ellie said with a big fat, smug grin on her face. 'Why don't we, Amelia, when we go up to London, pop into Covent Garden market and see what we can come up with? We could get some flowers quite cheaply and,' she said, still grinning in my direction, 'it would save you a lot of trouble, Cass, if you're struggling to find stuff.'

'I . . . um . . .'

Amelia seemed embarrassed. 'Well, yes. That's a good idea, but I wouldn't want to tread on Cass's toes. You've always done the flowers in the past . . . and they've always looked *lovely* . . .'

'Oh God. I didn't mean . . . I hope I haven't come barging in like a bull in the proverbial . . . Sorry, Cass. I wouldn't want you to think I was trying to take over, elbow you out of your job. I just thought –'

'No. No. Not at all,' I managed to stutter. 'That's fine. Of course I wouldn't mind a bit. I think it's an excellent idea. Go for it.'

'Great.' Ellie beamed.

There was an awkward silence as Amelia tapped her pen nervously against the paper of her notebook. 'Um, right, where were we? Questions. Dan did such a good job last year. Do you think he would . . .?'

'Yes, he said he would.'

'Does Dan write them?' Ellie sounded impressed.

'No, he doesn't.' She carried on looking at me, obviously thinking I was going to elaborate on my husband's intellectual skills, or lack of them. But I didn't. I think the silence embarrassed Amelia so much that she felt she had to answer on my behalf.

'Actually I think he just gets them from the internet. We just try and slot in a few locally relevant ones: rivers, pubs, famous people from here . . . the usual.'

I continued to colour in the centre of the sixes in my manic doodling. I had pressed so hard on one that I had made a hole in the paper. I blotted my finger on the cheap, shiny black biro ink and then examined the mini mark of Cain on the tip of my finger. I wanted to stamp it in the middle of her forehead to show the world what she was – a bloody witch. I started to inscribe zigzag marks on my pad, forming an unending line of 'w's, and then I drew a horizontal line right through the middle of them.

Amelia said, 'Maybe you could put in a few literary ones for us, Ellie?'

'Well, as I said, I wouldn't want to tread on any toes, but I'd love to give Dan a hand, if he wanted.'

I sighed loudly, almost beyond the point of caring whether anyone noticed just how pissed off I was. I looked across at Amelia and saw a frown cross her face as our eyes met. She was probably thinking that I was being childish, sulking and behaving badly in front of our new friend Ellie who was, after all, only trying to help. I envied Amelia. She, to my knowledge, had never had a bad word to say about anybody. Her privileged background insulated her from the sort of insecurities which were responsible for most character flaws. She knew she was adored by William, and although it admittedly came at a price, she did live in a gorgeous house surrounded by beautiful things, *and* she had produced to order not only the heir and the spare, but a beautiful daughter to finish. Rather than spoiling her, this privileged life had engendered in Amelia an innate kindness and a truly benevolent nature. She was simply incapable of seeing the bad in people, which was one of the reasons we all loved her so much and the main reason why I was now finding her so irritating.

It was like being in the presence of a human moral compass, and in the past I wouldn't have minded her gently bringing me up short when I had been overly judgemental, or pointing out that I might have been insensitive to other points of view. I wouldn't have minded in the past because she was my friend and I trusted her. But she was going to London with Ellie. She had made friends with Ellie. And she was obviously annoyed with me.

All of them were acting like bees around a honey pot, and I was standing on the outside wondering why it was that I was the only one who could see through her. Just wait until you get to know her, was my only consoling thought. All that pretty, pretty front and perfect smile. It was as though I was separated from the unravelling scene by a plate glass window, one of those unbreakable, extra-strength, keep-everything-out, bulletproof jobs. I could see what was going on, like an audience watching the actors on a stage, but I couldn't participate. There was nothing I could do to alter or affect the action. It was like being back at school with the new girl who arrives and takes over, stealing your friends, and your boyfriend; suddenly she's like the most popular girl in the whole damned school, and you're the only one who knows that she's actually a malicious, manipulative bully. And there's nothing you can do about it because no one will believe you. They'd just think you were jealous or stupid. Only this wasn't school, and it wasn't my boyfriend she was stealing, it was my husband.

I don't know what else was discussed during the meeting. My mind had long since set off on a lonely hike. I was aware of Amelia closing her notebook, thanking us all for coming. People were standing up, collecting cups and saucers and returning them to the tray. Ellie was kissing Amelia, thanking her, saying how excited she was about next week. She'd call Amelia later to talk about it. I saw Ellie talk to Kate Holland, the young army wife. She was scribbling down her telephone number.

'Let's meet up,' she was saying. 'Come for supper. If your husband's away we should do something together. Maybe we could go to the movies?'

Kate was beaming at her. 'I'd love to. Call me and I'll do my best to get a sitter.'

Sally was suggesting coffee on Thursday. 'Why don't you both come?' she said to Ellie and me.

'Can I let you know?' I said quickly, before waiting for Ellie's answer.

'I really ought to get on with some scribbling. But maybe one evening?'

'Sure. I'll call you.'

'That was fun,' Ellie said, as I engaged the gear and let off the handbrake, concentrating hard on not ploughing up the gravel. 'Such a great bunch of girls. You've all made me feel so welcome. I can't tell you how refreshing it is after London. I feel happier than I've felt in ages.'

'So it's good for your writer's block, then. And your depression?'

'Depression? No, not me.' She laughed, as if the very idea was outrageous. 'You must be getting me confused with someone else, Cass.'

'But you told me . . . that day after we had lunch at Amelia's, sitting in your garden. Remember? You said you'd been suffering . . .'

'I've never suffered anything like that. Far too well-balanced,' she said, grinning at me and revealing her perfect, white teeth. But the smile didn't reach her eyes, I noticed. 'No, the thing about London, as I was saying . . . everyone's so full on, trying to prove how busy they are, that their lives actually mean something. It's all so bloody competitive. And the amount of grooming that goes on, like you wouldn't believe.' She prattled on but I was barely listening. I was revisiting our conversation and I remembered what she'd said. I knew I hadn't dreamt or imagined it. I remembered the look in her eyes, the tears, the touching . . . Why would she now deny it? I dragged my attention back to the present. She was *still* talking inconsequentially about London:

'Eyebrows have to be threaded, almost daily manicures, perfect hair all the time, and the obsession with being thin and having the right designer handbag that costs the price of a family car. Of course, for me it's fantastic fodder from a research point of view, but it's all a bit shallow. I love the fact that people are so much more chilled in the country.'

My white knuckles, clenched hard over the steering wheel, showed just how chilled I felt. I took a deep breath. I didn't want her to know that she'd thrown me off balance yet again. 'But what about your boyfriend, the fact that you had to run away, so that he couldn't find you? Aren't you nervous about going to London?'

'What boyfriend?'

'You told me about a boyfriend, a violent boyfriend. You said that's why you came here, to get away from him. You showed me the marks on your neck where he'd tried to strangle you.'

'Honestly, Cass, I don't know what you're talking about. You must be confusing me with someone else.'

I was so stunned that I couldn't speak. But she carried on, 'I'm really pleased that Amelia's coming with me to London. She mentioned she'd been longing to see the Romantics exhibition and I'd been given tickets, so I thought it would be really fun to take her.' She paused, and then flashed her eyelashes over those big, guileless eyes.

'I would have asked you . . . only Dan said that you weren't really into that sort of thing . . .'

'What sort of thing?' I asked, keeping my voice as level as I could.

'I think I was asking him if he'd ever taken you to Rome. He said he had, but that you wouldn't ever go back. I just assumed that you weren't that into galleries and museums.'

'Oh?' Too right I hadn't liked it. But not for cultural reasons. Was that the best he could come up with? An extension of the 'my wife doesn't understand me' line? A progression to 'my wife doesn't "get" culture . . . she's far too stupid . . .'

We'd arrived at her house. I kept the engine running while she thanked me for the lift. Something in me snapped. 'Ellie, I *know* you said you had depression, and I know you told me about a violent boyfriend. If you're saying that's not true, then one of us is going bonkers.'

'Don't worry, my memory's like a sieve these days, too. It happens to us all.' She was about to close the car door and then she leaned in again. 'I almost forgot. Can you let me have Laura's mobile number? I said I might pop up to Birmingham and meet her for lunch. Maybe you and I could go together,' she beamed.

'Sorry. It's in my phone. I don't have it with me . . . forgot to charge it . . . silly me.'

'Okay,' she said, brightly. 'You can let me have it later.'

As the car door slammed, my mobile started to ring. I don't think she heard it but, frankly, I was past the point of caring. I was too busy worrying about the possibility that I really was going mad.

Okay, that was it. I mean, really *it*. Enough was enough. I was *not* going mad. If anyone was mad here, it wasn't me. This woman was a complete and utter fruitcake. A total nutter. Weird just didn't come close. I *know* she told me about the boyfriend, and I *know* she told me about her depression. Without question, absolutely and most definitely. I didn't imagine her showing me the marks on her neck, or what she said about the involvement of the police. I didn't imagine the tears in her eyes when she had said how good it was to talk to someone who understood. I know what she had said.

I spent the whole afternoon attacking jobs around the house like some kind of demented lunatic in the hope that I could stop myself from obsessing about that bloody woman. But to be honest I found I could still obsess about her while scrubbing, polishing and vacuuming. She just refused to get out of my head. When I'd tamed the house into domestic submission, I decided I'd make an assault on the garden.

My shed was my special place, a place where I usually found peace: a little sanctuary where I had bags of soil and sand and grit for company; the stacks of old biscuit tins filled with seed packets, plant ties and labels; the old melamine-topped table and high stool where I would sit to prick out my seedlings. Hanging from the walls were my various tools and weapons: rakes, forks, spades, hoes and sharp-bladed shears. I had boxes of rose feed, clematis feed, tomato fertilizer, Growmore and Miracle Gro; mildew and rust sprays and organic slug pellets, all carefully organized and stowed in a way that usually gave me a warm glow of satisfaction. There was normally a sense of stillness in there, and lovely earthy smells, and the dust caking the windows filtered the sunlight like a soft-focus lens. But today there was something very wrong. Flies buzzed all over the windows obscuring the sunlight, more flies lay dead on the floor, crunching beneath my feet, while others buzzed angrily around my head. And there was the foul smell of something rotting; the sort of sickly-sweet stench of decomposition telling me something had died in there. I hunted around, fastidiously shifting stuff, wary of what I was going to uncover. And then I lifted an old, empty plastic sack and found underneath the carcass of Nina – my lovely black Orpington – with her milk-glazed eye, beak in rictus gape, feathers dull and dirty and her ribcage exposed, poor thing. I couldn't understand how she could have got there. Had she somehow got herself locked into the shed and I hadn't heard her? Had she gone broody and decided to nest away from the rest of her little flock? But there was no sign of a nest, no obvious place where she would have settled down and quietly got on with her business. And she was feisty enough to make herself heard if she was hungry. Could I have just let her die in my shed? Surely I couldn't have neglected her like that? And it struck me as strange that she'd been tucked underneath the sack, as though someone had covered her over. I opened up the sack and shovelled the shrunken little body into it and then tied the top and carried it to the wheelie bin. A thought struck me as I was closing the lid. No. She couldn't be that crazy, surely. Could she?

It was time to talk to Dan. Whatever the outcome, he needed to know what she was doing; he needed to see that she was unhinged, and most of all we needed to unite in order to protect ourselves from her because she might even be dangerous. I mean, one read about stalkers and things like that, but not in rural villages like ours. On the face of it, I could see why people would be inclined not to believe me because it did stretch the boundaries of credibility. Who *would* believe it? The trouble was, I realized, that it was only my word against hers, and I may well not be believed. And then what? Would everyone think it was me who was the crazy one?

I was still out in the garden when Dan got home, and in the middle of mucking out the hens. I was pushing the full wheelbarrow along the track towards the compost heap, and so I answered his wave with a shouted 'hi' and then he disappeared into the house. About five minutes later, when I'd moved on to the veggie patch and was busy collecting salad for supper, Dan reappeared dressed in a pair of running shorts and a baggy old T-shirt. 'Going for a jog?' I asked, rather unnecessarily.

'Yeah, I thought . . . as it's a nice evening. Need to get rid of some of the stress of the day, you know how it is.' He started doing his stretching while I was bent double over the lettuce. The stress of his day? Just wait until he heard about the stress of *my* day.

'Won't be long . . .' He swung the gate open and broke into an athletic bounce and had soon turned onto the lane and out of my sight.

I picked off the roots from the lettuce, chucked them on the compost heap and then put the basket back in the shed. I left the door open to get rid of the flies and the disgusting smell, and decided I would sweep the floor tomorrow when the light was better and the air fresher. Then I went into the house, scrubbed my hands and poured myself a large glass of wine and contemplated what I would say to Dan. He seemed to have been gone for a long time. In fact it was nearly dark when he walked into the kitchen. I was well into my second glass of wine and was almost finished putting together a vegetable lasagne from the Weight Watchers cookery book and spreading on the low fat fromage frais, which, I don't care what the book said, tasted nothing like a proper cheese sauce.

'Hi, babe,' he said. I thought he looked remarkably fresh for someone who'd just been punishing their body for well over an hour.

'Hi.'

'Hi. Did you know you've left the door to the shed open?'

'Yep. It's to get rid of the smell, and the flies. I found Nina.'

'Nina?'

'The hen . . . you know . . .'

'Oh yeah, Nina. Dead?'

'Very dead. Poor thing. And I can't understand how she could have got there. It's just really, really strange.'

I was surprised when he closed the gap between us and then pulled me towards him.

'Aw, your poor little hen. Come here,' he said.

He wrapped his arms around me, pulling me into him. His face was damp against my neck, and he smelt musky and masculine and in spite of my aversion to sweat-covered skin, I relaxed into him, instinctively grateful for his attention. Then my nose wrinkled, 'You smell of alcohol.'

'I just saw Ellie . . . I stopped by for a drink.'

'Oh?'

'Yeah. She was walking Coco in the lane when I went past. She said she wanted to talk to me about the quiz – that it had been suggested she give me a hand with the questions.'

'Did she?' He must have felt my body tense, because his arm slipped from my shoulders, but he let his palm hover against the small of my back.

'She told me you'd had a good meeting this morning. And she said she was going to help you with the flowers. Isn't that great?'

I moved away from him towards the bottle and topped up my glass, then took a sip. Dan gave me that sort of slow, lingering glance that I read as disapproving.

'Terrific.'

He bent over to untie his shoelaces and so his voice was slightly muffled, but he was still on the same topic. 'Must be nice for you all to have someone like her helping out.'

'Oh yeah. Definitely. A very useful contribution.' I slipped the dish inside the oven, closed the door, put the plates into the warming oven and generally tried to appear preoccupied.

'Well that's good.'

I finished clearing off the surfaces and started to wipe my hands down the front of my apron. 'Yeah. Nice. Really nice.' Our eyes met. This was not at all how I wanted the conversation to go. I took a deep breath.

'Dan, I need to talk to you, about her . . . about Ellie.'

'Oh please, not again . . .'

'No, it's important. Really important.'

He seemed nervous, shifty even. 'I need a shower.'

'But . . .'

And he was gone. I had that nagging sense of losing something very precious, and I was carrying out that same forensic revisiting of where I had been when I'd lost it, and punishing myself for being so careless. Only it wasn't that I had lost it, it was that someone else was stealing it. It was burglary. Ellie was burgling all that was good in my life, and I was just standing by and letting her get away with it. I busied myself with washing, drying and sorting the lettuce. I was almost grateful for the peace which had settled around the empty kitchen. I had time to try and scrape together my shattered nerves; I just needed to be able to turn my feelings over, spread them out in the palms of my hands and hold them up to the light. I needed to scrutinize them from all angles and examine what they were exactly, and maybe having done that I could then work out just what it was that I was supposed to do.

I measured the oil and lemon juice into a jam jar and then I heard Dan's phone bleep with a new message alert. His jacket was hanging over the back of the chair and he must have left his phone in the pocket. I carried on mixing the dressing, but the echo of the bleep stayed with me. Tomorrow was Tuesday; wasn't that the day that Laura said they sometimes met for lunch? Maybe that was Laura, now. I wondered what they talked about over lunch. I could guess what they'd talk about this week. It would be all about Ellie, and Laura's excitement and Dan's gratitude. Oh yes, I could guess what they'd say. 'Why was Mum being so peculiar?' Laura would ask, and Dan would say: 'I've been worried about Mum . . .' What would he tell her? Is that why he'd kept their lunches secret from me, so that they could discuss me? Oh stop it . . . stop it . . . I told myself, and took another sip of wine.

I wanted to check his phone. I really, really wanted to check it. And why shouldn't I read a text from my daughter to my husband? Wasn't Dan the honesty advocate? Taking Laura out to lunch without telling me wasn't part of an honesty policy. So it didn't matter if I knew about it, did it? I grabbed the phone before I could change my mind and quickly opened up the new message. But it wasn't from Laura.

Can meet you at Wagamama's at 1. Ellie xx

I could hear Dan moving around upstairs and I knew he'd be back down any second. I quickly marked the message 'unread', and then slipped it back into his pocket. I refilled my glass and drank half of it straight back. I could feel my cheeks turning pink. I threw the salad leaves into the wooden bowl and slammed the two silly hand-shaped servers down on the top. I had to keep my cool. I was so close to having an explosive confrontation with him, but I wasn't ready, not yet.

'Okay?' I said, as I poured him a glass of wine. 'Your phone beeped.'

'Oh?' He walked over to his jacket and took the phone out. I watched him, noticing his frown as he read the text. Then he put the phone back in his pocket.

'Anything important?' I asked.

'No.' He picked up his glass and took a long drink from it, then he started sorting through the pile of post, his head turned away from me. All the time I was saying over and over in my head, 'Just keep cool . . . play it . . .' I was like some kind of robotic Stepford wife, with my heart replaced by batteries. I dished up the lasagne, carefully placing it on one side of the plate so that he'd have room for the salad. I set it down in front of him, and then helped myself. Then we were both seated at the table. I had no appetite, but I made a good show of pushing my food around the plate. The fromage frais had congealed into a crusty, unappetizing excrescence.

'Mmm, this looks good,' Dan said.

'Are you meeting Laura tomorrow?' I dived straight in. I had to know whether my husband was a liar or not.

He stalled for time, finishing his mouthful, staring down at his plate and shovelling more fuel on to his fork. 'Why?'

'Because it's Tuesday and you often meet her on Tuesdays, don't you?'

'Sometimes.'

He looked at me and I tried to read his eyes. The trouble was, I was such a bad liar that I could hardly meet them with my own. I felt as if they were broadcasting the fact that I'd just sneaked a look at his mobile; that I'd snooped on him. My eyes travelled to the chair where his jacket hung, and then back to Dan. I sensed my face redden. A flicker of something unreadable passed across Dan's eyes and then he yawned, but it was the sort of yawn which didn't seem natural, the sort of yawn which was designed to demonstrate just how relaxed he was, just how insignificant what he was about to tell me was.

'I'm not sure if I'll have time to meet her tomorrow. I've got a big pitch to prepare for. I might even have to work late.'

'Work late? So you might stay in Birmingham overnight?'

'Yeah, maybe.'

He sighed and pushed his plate towards the middle of the table. I hated it when he did that. Then he leaned forward and propped his elbows onto the table, his hands clasping the sides of his temples in an attitude which I knew represented total exasperation.

'Cass, you know how important new business is. Surely you're not going to give me a hard time because I've got to put in a few extra hours?'

I wanted to scream. Instead, I refilled my wine glass, emptying the bottle. I took a sip before answering, and then met Dan's eyes directly and said, 'I need to talk to you about Ellie.'

A muscle on his left cheek seemed to give an almost imperceptible tick. 'Oh for fuck's sake, Cass.'

'No, listen, Dan. I think she's dangerous. She's trying to do something to me and she's using you and Laura. I think she's trying to make out that there's something wrong with me, mentally . . .' He was staring at me, his face appearing gaunt and strained. His lips were parted, so that I could hear his breath hiss sharply over his teeth.

'What are you saying?'

'I know this is going to sound bizarre, but there are things she's told me about herself, important things . . . and now she's denying she ever said them. Making out that I've imagined it.'

'Like what?'

'Like the fact that she said she suffered from depression . . . the fact that she's run away from a violent boyfriend . . . When I reminded her she said she didn't know what I was talking about. I *promise* you, Dan, I'm not making it up. And the little things, like not asking me to the cinema, telling the girls that she was worried about me . . . you've got to admit something's not right.'

I paused and waited, willing him to be reasonable, to respond to me properly, as a loving and caring husband should, longing for him to respect what I was saying and to believe *me* and not her. He seemed to be having a real struggle with his answer, like he was opening and closing his mouth several times before any words came out.

'Well, if you really want to know, she told me she's worried about *you*.'

'Is that what you talked about – me?'

'The thing is, your behaviour on Saturday night – you made it pretty clear that you weren't having a good time. And she probably heard us yelling at each other on the way home. And maybe you've said things to her, told her things?'

'Like what?'

'Oh I don't know – your state of mind, maybe?'

'Oh she's very clever.' I shook my head as I remembered once more our first cosy little chat in her garden. What a fool I'd been. 'So you are happy to listen to her, but not to me.'

'It's not a question of not listening to you. Of course I'll listen to you. I love you, Cass. You're my wife.'

'But . . .?'

'No "buts". But the problem is that someone looking in from the outside, listening to all these accusations of yours, might think you're being a little paranoid, because it doesn't exactly sound rational.' He was speaking calmly, as though he was the adult talking to a recalcitrant child. I wanted to shake him, to rock some sense into him, to make him see, but it just seemed pointless. 'So what I'm trying to say, Cass, is that if you don't want to appear irrational, then the best thing is to stop accusing her of all this stuff. It just . . . it just . . . oh sweetie, this is so difficult. It might make you sound as though you're losing it, and God help us we don't want that again, do we?'

'It's not me who's being irrational, Dan.' I stood up and started pacing the kitchen. I just felt that I was getting nowhere and I didn't know how to get through to him. I could feel my frustration and anger growing inside me. 'Did you talk to her about Rome as well?'

The mention of Rome had an almost electric effect on him. He suddenly looked wary.

'What about Rome?'

'She's taking Amelia to see the Romantics exhibition at the Tate. She said she hadn't asked me because you'd said it wouldn't be my sort of thing, because I hadn't enjoyed Rome.'

'I don't remember saying that.'

'How convenient.'

He leaned back in his chair and closed his eyes, for a moment, to illustrate his exasperation. 'Is that partly why you think she's got it in for you, because she's taking Amelia to London? That's ridiculous . . . and I think you've probably had too much to drink.'

That was typical Dan – attack, in his world, was always the best form of defence. But he'd pushed me over the edge. I could feel a surge of blood in my head, a wave of hurt and anger. My words tumbled from my mouth in a flood of accusation.

'Blame it on the drink, then.' I felt the room begin to spin and I wondered if I was slurring my words. 'But whatever it was that you said to her about Rome – we both know the real reason I didn't enjoy it, don't we?'

'Oh for God's sake. I thought we'd got over all that. Can't you just drop it? This is so ridiculous. You can't still be obsessing about something that happened *fucking years ago*!' I flinched as his voice rose. 'Don't you think it's time you sorted yourself out? Don't you think you ought to start dealing with these crazy obsessions of yours before you drive us both insane?'

'This is just what you do . . . making out it's my fault in order to cover up your fucking lies.'

'If anyone's the liar here, Cassandra, we know it isn't me, don't we?'

'What are you saying?'

'You know damned well what I'm saying.' Dan just sat there, shaking his head slowly from side to side.

He stood up. 'I'm going to watch the news . . .'

'Fine.' There was nothing I could do. The words kept going over and over in my head . . . 'nothing I could do . . . nothing I could do . . .' and I felt like something had died inside me.

Coco was barking her head off at someone outside, so I stuck my head out of the window to see why she was making such a fuss. Dan was standing there, dressed in running kit, rubbing his fingers through his hair, looking as though he wasn't sure what to do. 'Hi,' I said, and he smiled and said 'hi' back. 'Are you coming or going?' I asked. 'Because,' I said, 'if you're coming back why don't you join me for a restorative gin?' He said it sounded too good to miss, so he came in. We talked about Laura first of all. I said what a lovely girl she was and how happy I was to give her all the help I could. I told him that she'd already emailed me some of her stuff and that I was impressed with it. It was actually quite good. Raw around the edges and predictably self-conscious, but I thought there was some promise there. He seemed genuinely pleased to hear that, but then he would, wouldn't he? Then we talked about the quiz and he said he was delighted that I had offered to help him. I did say that I was worried that I didn't want to tread on Cass's toes, with the flowers, that she'd seemed a bit sensitive about it.

It was after I said that that I sensed there was something bothering him; I felt there was something he wanted to tell me, so I asked him outright if everything was okay. He didn't hesitate, honestly. He'd obviously just been waiting . . . I mean really wanting . . . to talk to me. First of all he apologized for Cass's behaviour on Saturday night. I said no need, don't know what you're talking about, although obviously I did; but I added I noticed she seemed a bit tense. I wasn't sure whether or not to tell him that I'd heard the row, but I decided I should. I said I thought she'd sounded quite angry and was there anything I could do. That I hoped there was nothing I had done which could have upset her. He told me that he was worried about her, that things were a bit tricky, and when he said he didn't know what to do he looked like a little lost boy. He said things were stressful at work and that he felt he needed to give Cass more of his time. He was so sweet, saying how much he cared about her. I said how lucky she was to have him and I hoped he didn't mind me telling him, but that she'd told me she felt she might be suffering from depression. I said I hoped that she wasn't feeling suicidal – that I gathered she'd felt like that in the past. 'Did she tell you that?' He seemed really surprised by that.

'She seemed to want to talk and so I listened,' I told him. He said he was really grateful to me for that and I said I would do anything I could to help, and then I gave him a hug. It just seemed the natural, friendly thing to do. He looked like he needed it so it was just the obvious thing, really. And then . . . Well, to be honest, I think we were both a bit embarrassed, so we started talking about Laura again.

I said I was planning on going to Birmingham the next day and maybe I'd call her up, take her out for lunch. He said he'd organize it, that it was the least he could do, considering I was being so helpful to Laura . . . so we agreed that I'd text him to confirm. It was all very innocent.

11

I fought with sleep all night, aware that Dan's side of the bed was empty. Exhausted but fully awake, I lay listening to the early morning silence, while the darkness melted into daylight. I couldn't stop myself from going over everything that had happened and coming to the same conclusion. It wasn't fair. Dan's accusations weren't fair. I was acting rationally. Anyone would feel the same as me if this was happening to them. I wondered where he had slept; the spare bed wasn't made up, so perhaps he'd taken himself into Laura's room. I listened for the sounds of him getting up. After a while I heard the hiss and gurgle of the pipes as he ran the shower. Then I heard his footsteps on the landing outside the bedroom. I held my breath as the latch lifted and he pushed the door open. The room was semi-dark but I could hear him crossing to his wardrobe in the gloom. Metal hooks of coat hangers slid against the steel rail as he sifted through his clothes, choosing a suit. A drawer slid open, then closed. Then another. I could picture him selecting socks, pants and shirt. All the time I pretended I was asleep, not moving, squeezing my eyes shut and trying to keep my breathing steady. I heard him whisper 'Cass . . .' but I ignored him, still pretending to be asleep. I think I sensed him standing over me, maybe looking down at me. I wondered if he would reach out and touch me, but he didn't. I heard his hand upon the doorknob once more, the quiet click of the latch shutting, the sound of his footsteps on the landing fading. After about ten minutes or so I heard the thud of the front door, and then the growl of his car engine.

I got up, dressed quickly and made myself a cup of coffee. I dropped the latch on the front door. I needed privacy and secrecy for what I was about to do. I went into Dan's study. A watery sun struggled through the ancient glass in the east-facing window. The wall occupied by the open fireplace was bare stone, with an oak lintel scorched and stained from two hundred odd years of wood smoke. There was no grate in the hearth, just a heap of ashes which, even though they hadn't been added to over the summer months, still gave off a lovely toasted-wood scent which made me nostalgic for autumn evenings and the onset of all things warm and cosy. Dan had squirreled away a lot of his personal treasures in his private space, treasures which illuminated the many different facets of his character and periods of his life. Centred above the fireplace was an award he had received for a lawnmower advertisement, which I remember had been shot in New Zealand. Beside that was a framed *Campaign* magazine article from when he had first joined the London agency, talking of Dan as the smart new kid on the block. He had a selection of cartoons and caricatures dotted around the walls, collected either because they amused him, or were connected to him in some way. His desk was a dark oak refectory table, covered in piles of papers and fat, shiny pink envelope files, in between which were dotted about little knick-knacky things: a pristine grey brick, a Rubik's cube, a Campbell's soup tin containing a selection of pens and pencils, including his special chinagraph markers. He had an ostrich egg placed on a little stand which some clever wag in creative had decorated with a picture of Dan and labelled 'I came first' as a tribute for one of his many awards. Dan loved eggs. He argued that as packaging went, you couldn't improve on them, aesthetically. There was a matching rather naff china pig and sheep which his old secretary had presented him with when we made the move to the country, and an assortment of stress balls which had been placed in his Christmas stocking over the years by Laura and me. He stored his

ELIZABETH FORBES

paper clips in a funny little clay bowl which Laura had made in
primary school. It was glossy and brown with red and blue swirls
under the glaze. I barely noticed these things anymore. Their
familiarity made them both unremarkable and stale on my eye. I just
simply picked them up, wafted a duster over the surface and plonked
them down again. But as I fondled them now, moving them around
in my hands, remembering the significance of each and every piece,
I felt keenly both my separation from, and their connection to, my
husband. It was strange to think these lifeless, inanimate objects
might have a more enduring relationship with him than that which
he had with me.

I didn't really know what it was, specifically, that I was searching
for. Anything, perhaps, that would prove to me that I was not being
obsessive and irrational. I needed what they call in counsellor-speak
'validation'. Diaries? Hardly. Not Dan's style at all. Phone bills, hotel
bills? They'd barely had time to inscribe their affair into any kind of
hard paper evidence. I just wasn't sure that I knew Dan any more. I
needed to find out whether the man I was married to was the man I
thought I was married to, if that made sense. Even though I felt Dan's
behaviour provided a full justification for what I was doing, my
stomach felt sore, as if it had been punched from the inside out, and
my limbs felt heavy, as though they were trying to swim through mud
and all my energy had been silted up by the flow of misery inside me.

I tried to pull open the top drawer of the filing cabinet but it
didn't budge. It was locked. I snagged my nail under the handle
thanks to the unexpected resistance. Surely people only locked
things when they had something to hide? I felt even more coldly
determined to find out Dan's secrets. I turned my attention to the
drawer which slotted beneath the table. My hands shook but I
steadied them. He was meticulously neat, and I was careful to replace
the little piles of business cards, the Pritt Stick, calculator, Sellotape
dispenser and so forth exactly as I had found them, but I couldn't see

any keys. I slid the drawer closed and looked around the room. There was nothing obvious on the desk, no little boxes or containers likely to contain a tiny key. Damn it. I still had the small cupboard to search, where he kept his stationery and computer bits and pieces. But, again, everything was neatly piled and placed with no obvious 'key' receptacle. I returned to the desk and sat down in Dan's chair. Then I picked up the Campbell's soup tin full of pens and tipped it upside down onto the desk.

There, in front of me, wasn't just the filing cabinet key, but another, more interesting-looking, intricately fashioned, antique key which I didn't recognize. I felt an adrenalin rush of euphoria, and the sick feeling in my stomach intensified. At last! I had been afraid that maybe Dan took the key with him. I picked it up and examined it closely, as if by doing so it would tell me where it belonged. But whatever it was, it couldn't be here in the study. The only things on the floor were a couple of piles of magazines and the log basket, and I'd searched the solitary cupboard. No, whatever it was had to be somewhere else in the house. Still, at least I could make a start on the filing cabinet. I unlocked it and slid open the top drawer and quickly scanned the little tag labels on the top of each divider. They were the usual mundane, domestic-type categories: electricity, water rates, tax, bank. Towards the back of the drawer I found one marked telephone, but when I opened it I realized it was only for the house land line. I searched at the back of the file hoping that I'd find his mobile account, but there was nothing. And then I remembered it was paid for by the company. I wasn't going to find any mobile evidence because all the bills would go to his office. I replaced the file in its sleeve and slammed the drawer shut and swore aloud.

Then I opened the bottom drawer and found myself staring at a space devoid of files, but filled by a large wooden casket. I just stared at it. I had never seen it before. The surface of the casket was silky smooth and cold to my touch. In the centre of the lid was a tiny inset brass square, engraved with Dan's initials, D.E.B. I tried to lift it, but I couldn't get my fingers under it. I slid the whole box towards the front of the drawer so that I could get some leverage from the back, and then managed to manhandle it up from the drawer. It was very heavy and awkward but I soon had it sitting on the floor in front of me. I picked up the key from Dan's desk and then got back onto my knees, praying that it would fit the lock. It slotted in easily and I heard a gratifying click as the mechanism turned. I paused, feeling queasy and lightheaded with a mixture of guilt, curiosity and fear of what I was about to discover. But the fact that it existed, the fact that Dan had possessions which were locked and barred against me made me certain that I had a right to know. Obviously we were living a lie. Obviously I didn't know my husband at all. Obviously the man I thought I knew inside out was a stranger to me, a deceiver and a liar.

But even through my fervent conviction that I had to know, a little voice warned me that I still had a choice before I crossed the Rubicon. I could turn the key back and replace the box in the cabinet, and let Dan keep whatever secrets he wished to keep from me hidden away. I could allow him his privacy and protect myself at the same time. There are some occasions when you are on one of life's precipices and you know that once you have stepped off it there is no going back; life will never be the same again. The little voice of rationality was still there, warning me that this was one of those occasions, and that I should step backwards. But it was too late. Like an assassin who has centred his target in the crosshairs, I was already squeezing the trigger. My hands were already on the rim of the lid, and I started to lift it.

The first thing I saw was a bundle of letters tied with a blue silk ribbon. I recognized my own hand on the envelopes, although it was a hand both neater and smaller than my current untidy scrawl. They were letters I had written to Dan during our courtship. They were post-marked south-west London and addressed to Dan at LSE; letters that he had kept from me to him, lovingly wrapped and stored in his little treasure chest. Seeing them there was almost as powerful an admonishment for what I was doing as Dan himself walking in on me and catching me in the act. How could I do this? But I was long past the point of no return. I picked them up and put them to my nose and breathed in – what? – memories? The paper felt smooth and cold in my hand, and the silky ribbon slipped through my fingers as I carefully untied the bow, releasing the pile so that the envelopes fluttered freely onto the floor in front of me. I opened the nearest one and started to read, and as I did so I was transported back to a small bedroom late at night, propped up against the pillows and crafting the words in my best handwriting.

'My darling Dan, It's now exactly one hour and twenty two minutes since we said goodnight, and I wanted to tell you how much I am missing you and wishing you were here with me right now, in my little bed. So when I finish writing this, I shall turn off the light and imagine you are here and think of all the naughty things I could do to you. I can barely breathe for thinking about what will happen when I see you at the weekend. It seems like forever, although I know it's only three more nights. And by the time you read this I shall hopefully be seeing you tomorrow!!!! I am going to be a very good girl and not ring you, so that you can get on with your revision, but I just wanted to tell you that I love you with all my heart and more . . .
C xxxxxxxxxxx

I laughed bitterly. *I am going to be a very good girl . . .* even then it was obvious where the balance of power lay in our relationship. I was always the one wanting more than he was prepared to offer, always the one having to be careful not to swamp him with the huge amount of love I had to give, and which I now knew Dan saw as neediness. It was over thirty years ago, but the memory of how I was feeling then was as vivid as if it had been last night. I was happy and in love.

I plucked another letter from the pile at random.

'Darling Dan,

I am writing this letter to you to tell you that I understand completely. The last thing in the world I would want is for you to worry about me. I shall be fine. Like you said, it must be hard being at university and making all those new friends and being tied to a girlfriend. I really do understand and I just want you to be happy. It would be nice to keep in touch and to know how you are. It's been a wonderful eight months and maybe it would have been better if we'd met up later on. But then we can't choose what life throws at us, can we? I just hope that you do really well with your course. I know you will, because you are very clever, unlike me, ha ha. Maybe we'll bump into each other in the pub and if we do I'd hate it if you felt you couldn't still say 'hi'. It would be good to know how you are. Anyway, see you around, as they say. C xx

P.S. I hope you won't mind if I pop and see your mum some time. She was so kind to me over Dad . . .

I remembered struggling to write those brave lines, saying how I would be all right when in reality I was devastated, completely falling apart. Dan had said he needed space, that it was all too much, we were getting too serious and he wanted a break. I suppose I had leant on him quite a bit after Dad . . . Nothing helped like being able to talk to Dan about how I was feeling. I couldn't talk to Mum because she was far too caught up in her own grief to have room for mine and she was . . . well, she was who she was, and so I just felt incredibly lucky having someone special of my own. And Dan understood because he'd lost his own father when he was fourteen to heart disease. All very different to the way I'd lost my dad, but I guess the grief, the loss, the hole left in our lives was the same. Dan seemed so sorted about everything and it was good for me to see that he'd survived it and seemed to be okay. The distraction of a love interest was brilliant for me. We used to have two-hour-long phone conversations late at night which, at the time, neither of us wanted to end. We'd go through those silly games of 'You put the phone down first . . . no . . . you . . . Okay, on the count of three . . .' and then 'Are you still there . . . ?' It was me who was *always* still there.

But the break, for me, wasn't great timing. He had told me that my neediness had made him feel claustrophobic and trapped. He said we were too young to be so serious. He said that it would be good for me to see other people, that we both needed space to grow up a bit. He wanted to be able to play football on Saturdays and go out drinking afterwards with the boys. He wanted to go on the uni ski trip with his mates and not feel guilty about going without me.

A couple of weeks later I had gone to see his mum and she had told me, a bit awkwardly, that she thought part of the reason we'd split up was because my grief had brought back bad memories for Dan, which made me feel even worse. But then I heard through a friend that he'd started going out with some girl on his course straight after the split, and when I asked her name I realized I'd met her. She'd been in the pub a couple of times and I remembered noticing the way Dan smiled at her and touched her arm when he talked to her. It didn't last long, though. She dumped him after a few months for a medical student. He was miserable and drunk late one night and so he called me. And I was just so damned grateful.

But I wasn't doing this to revisit our love affair, was I? I knew what was in those letters and didn't need to waste time on some self-indulgent reminiscence of all our good, and bad, times. I carefully retied the bundle and delved once more into the box. There was a collection of photographs of Laura, and some of the important childhood paraphernalia that we all like to keep, such as the Father's Day cards she had made for him. I almost tossed them aside carelessly, because these were not the things I wanted to find. I didn't want to find things that showed me what a sweet person Dan was. A good father, a kind man. A softie who kept silly little mementoes from his little girl's childhood. This was not the sort of thing I wanted to know about him – oh no, not at all. And then I found a postcard, standing on its edge, so tight up against the side of the box that I could easily have overlooked it. I slid it out. It had a picture of the Trevi fountain on the front. I was euphoric. This was more like it. Yes, this was definitely more like it. I nearly laughed out loud. Rome. How wonderfully appropriate. Rome.

I turned it over and started to read, struggling to keep my trembling hand still.

THEY SAY ACTIONS SPEAK LOUDER THAN WORDS. AND YOU WERE THERE WHEN IT MATTERED.
ARRIVEDERCI AND REMEMBER LA FIAMMA DELL'AMORE CONTINUA A BRUCIARE.
XXXXX

No signature, just kisses. And what the hell did that mean? Something of love continuing to something. There was no date on it. All I could say for sure was that it was from Rome and that it was from a woman.

I stared at it as if by looking at it for long enough some truth would reveal itself. But I wasn't looking for truths, I was looking for lies.

I think if I'm honest with myself, I'd known for years, but it had been easier to pretend. At least when I say 'I knew', I mean I suspected. I had suspected so strongly that I had confronted Dan about it. I knew instinctively. I don't know how, but I did. His client seemed particularly demanding. I couldn't understand why it was that Dan had to keep flying over there, spending a week at a time. And when he came home there was something about him, something almost indefinably different. It wasn't that he wasn't loving towards me. I'd say, if anything, when he first got back from his trips he'd be more so. And I got presents that seemed far more generous than usual. A gold bracelet one time; another time a set of dolphin earrings; a designer handbag. Lovely presents. But after the initial burst of romance upon his return, I sensed his withdrawal from me. He would disappear into his study after supper, saying he'd got papers to write, reports to read. And long after I'd gone to bed, I'd hear music playing down below. I remember thinking at the time that he was behaving a bit like a love-sick teenager. Eventually I had confronted him, sort of jokingly at first. I remember saying something like, 'God, Dan, you're going over there so often anyone might think you've got another woman . . .' and I remember to this day the look on his face when I said that. It was a look of sheer, blind panic. And I knew. Right then, just like that, I knew. Everything suddenly made sense. The presents, the guilt-fuelled attention towards me, followed by the pining for *her*. I'd backed off, of course. I mean I had a baby, a tiny baby. Laura must have been all of a year old. And I had to be careful. I had to be really careful what I said, and to know what the consequences might be. I had to be sure that if I did confront him, seriously confront him, and he told me that yes, he did have another woman, that I knew what I'd do if he said he was leaving me, going to live with her. And I didn't want that. I really couldn't have coped with that, after everything else. In the end I decided that I should just wait and hope that it would blow itself out. Instead of talking to

Dan I talked to the professionals, and they gave me drugs that numbed my feelings so that I wouldn't have to suffer the pain. I can't say I forgot about it. You don't ever forget about those sorts of things. The memories cruise like hungry sharks just below the surface of your subconscious, ever watchful for the next feeding opportunity. And right now they were back. Oh yes, they were back. I could feel them inside me, snapping away at these latest morsels.

I turned the card over and over in my hand and traced my finger across the handwriting. It was addressed to the Bristol office, so it was sent a long time ago, certainly more than fifteen years ago. It could be, what, eighteen – even twenty – years old, this postcard. And he'd hung on to it in his box of treasures. Calm, I told myself. Keep calm. It was a long time ago, a long time ago . . . I repeated the mantra to myself. 'A *long* time ago.' Not now. This wasn't happening now. Whatever had happened was in the past. We had had a lifetime together since then. I kept on taking deep breaths, trying to steady my racing heart. The box yawned wide open in front of me. I hadn't done with it. Oh no, I hadn't finished with it yet. My masochistic urge to hurt myself was not yet assuaged. I needed to feel myself bleed as surely as if I was wielding a blade against my skin. It made me feel real; it made me feel that I wasn't going crazy.

I started to empty out the entire box. Then I found a book of matches with the name of a hotel, the Majestic, Roma. What had he said when I'd confronted him? I'd been stupid. I'd been neurotic, possessive, jealous . . . suffering from depression. I needed help . . . oh yes, I remembered all right. He had used my own Achilles heel of insecurity to fuel my neurosis – to make me believe that I was imagining things, that my mind was playing tricks on me – and he'd succeeded in convincing me. And now, here in my hand was the evidence. And weirdly, the only thing that popped into my mind was how stupid of him. How very stupid of Dan to keep these little mementoes so that one day I could find out, have it all confirmed.

Maybe he wouldn't suspect that I'd go snooping into his personal secrets, but he might have thought that one day, if he happened to drop dead, someone – Laura or me – might have discovered these things.

I folded my arms over my abdomen and crouched forward on my knees, trying to ease the soreness in my stomach as a wave of profound sadness washed over me. Oh Dan. Why?

I don't know long I'd been sitting there, numbly thinking about things, mulling everything over in my mind, trying to piece together the fragments in order to make some sense of it. When the phone rang it made me jump. Caller display told me it was Dan. I let it ring until it went onto the message service. His voice mail told me he'd got a breakfast meeting at 8 a.m. and so he'd decided to stay in the company apartment. I felt a huge sense of relief that I'd got a respite from having to face him. I had another day to recover my senses, if that was possible. But I also wondered, could it be a coincidence that he'd chosen to stay away on the day he was having lunch with Ellie?

At dusk I set off down the lane wearing a pair of ancient trainers and some baggy tracksuit bottoms so that if anyone noticed me they might assume that I had taken up some new keep-fit regime. I didn't need to run, exactly. I was more of a power-walk kind of girl, and within a few minutes I was level with Ellie's. I accelerated as I passed, finding it hard to keep my head down so that I wouldn't be spotted, while at the same time trying to make sure that it was actually Ellie's head that I could see through the window. But, no, it was definitely the back of her head, seated at her desk, presumably tapping away at her keyboard, spewing poison. I could also see the dog, perched on the window sill, barking its stupid little head off at me. I ran even faster down the road and then I heard the front door open and Ellie call out 'Cass? Is that you?' I know it was stupid, but I couldn't think what else to do, so I leapt into the hedge and curled into a low ball amidst the vegetation, hoping that the cow parsley would hide me. I could feel the sharp sting of nettles against my bottom. 'Shit!' I said, under my breath. And 'Ouch!'

I waited for the sound of her footsteps but none came, and after a few more seconds I heard what sounded like the front door closing. The dog was still letting out muffled, intermittent yaps as if to say, 'She's still there . . . I know she's still there . . .'

I waited for the yaps to subside and then stood up and brushed myself down. The bloody barking started up again. I had a choice. I could either set out across the fields and do a huge circuit along the footpath to get back home, which would probably take about twenty minutes, or I could simply head back along the road and hope she didn't see me. Because if she did see me, I could guess what she'd say: 'I'm really worried about Cass, she was lurking outside my house last night . . .' It was beginning to get dark, and I didn't have a torch and, to be honest, I always found pitch-black open spaces a bit spooky at night. I waited for a few moments until the barking stopped, and then I set off, trying hard to sprint on the tips of my toes, but as I neared her house, the barking started up again. I bent low against the hedgerow on the opposite side of the road and continued running, but I tripped the sensor on the security light and so there I was, lit up like a rabbit in a headlight. I couldn't stop myself from glancing towards Ellie's front window, and there she stood, looking out at me, with this big silly grin on her face, waving.

That went well, I told myself, as I slammed my own front door shut behind me.

I was halfway through a bottle of chardonnay when the telephone rang. The sound made me jump so much that I spilt cold wine over my hand. Lately I seemed to jump out of my skin at the slightest thing, like I was primed, on heightened alert for attack. I hadn't had anything solid, bar a couple of cheese-flavoured rice cakes, all day. It was Dan's mother, and I was worried she might notice the faint slur in my voice.

'Cass, love. It's me.'

'Hello, Pat,' I said. 'How are you?'

'Mustn't complain.' Pat never complained about anything, she always seemed to be inexplicably contented with her lot. Widowed for years, her son living two hundred miles away, but at least she had Dan's sister, Maggie, close by. Maggie and Dan weren't close. She thought that Dan had got above himself, putting on airs and graces and turning his back on his working-class roots. If Dan was a champagne kind of socialist, Maggie was more of a bitter shandy sort of girl. I know that she resented the fact that Dan and I didn't see enough of Pat. But, then, we did live so far away. Sometimes Pat would come and stay for a few days, but I guessed she never felt really comfortable. Perhaps she didn't want to feel she was interfering, or getting in the way. She was thoughtful like that. A proper sort of mum.

'Dan's not here, Pat. He's staying overnight in Birmingham . . .'

'Not to worry. How are you, lovey?'

'I'm fine. Absolutely fine. We're all fine, thanks.'

'Well, you know, I was just checking you're not getting too lonely with Laura away, and Dan working so hard. I know how you feel these things, Cassandra.'

'No, no . . .' But something caught in my throat and I felt the prick of tears. For a second or two I didn't want to speak in case she guessed. A caring voice on the other end of the phone was the last thing I needed. I mean, it was lovely, but I couldn't cope with sympathy if I was to hold myself together. Not from Dan's mother, because she would tell Dan.

'You could do with a holiday, you two. Some time together wouldn't do either of you any harm.'

'Hmm, maybe. We had our five days back in April, which was lovely. But it's difficult getting away, what with the agency and everything.'

'Well he shouldn't lose sight of what's important – you and Laura. The Lakes are lovely at this time of year . . .'

I smiled into the phone. 'Yes. I believe they are.' And of course they were very close to Pat. 'We must come and see you, Pat. I'll talk to Dan and we'll try and get something sorted. It's been a while, hasn't it?'

'Well that would be nice. Sometime, dear. I'd love to see you both – and Laura, of course. But it's you I'm worried about.'

'I'm *fine*, Pat. Absolutely fine. And it's kind of you to ring.'

'Give my love to that son of mine, and tell him to take care of you.'

'I shall. Thank you.'

I replaced the receiver. It was sweet of Pat to call, but all I could think was that Dan had spoken to her about me. Was he laying foundations? And what would she report back to him? That I sounded depressed and drunk?

The last thing I did before climbing into bed was to check my mobile. I had a missed call and a text from Laura. She of all people knew if she really wanted to talk to me she should call the landline. I opened up the text:

'Thought u wd like 2 no had a gr8 lunch with Dad and Ellie 2day. Xx

◇ ◇ ◇

I got back from Birmingham around six-ish. I had to go and collect Coco from Sally's because she'd been looking after her for me. I stayed for a quick glass of wine and I told Sally that I'd met Dan and Laura for lunch because I was trying to help Laura with her work experience, internship

. . . whatever you'd like to call it. I said to Sally that as things were a bit delicate with Cass at the moment that Dan had said it might be best not to mention it to her. Sally agreed that she wouldn't mention it. I said it's no big deal but after that row I heard, and the way she was on Saturday night, I wouldn't want to upset her even more. I mean, with the way her mind was at the moment, she might read more into it than was there to read, if you know what I mean. So after that I went home. I settled down for a writing session and lost track of time.

I suppose it was about 9 . . . 9.30-ish – almost dark. Yes, that's right, it was almost dark because I'd put the lights on. Coco started to bark like a lunatic. At first I ignored it, thinking it must be a hedgehog – we get a lot of those – or even a fox. But she wouldn't quieten down, so eventually I got up to look out of the window, to see if there was anyone out there. Well, can you imagine my surprise when I thought I caught sight of a figure disappearing into the hedge? It was very disturbing, but I couldn't be sure it wasn't the shadows playing tricks, so I tried to settle back to work. Coco started barking again. I got up once more. It had got dark enough for the movement outside to trip the security lights, and imagine my surprise when I saw Cassandra there, all lit up and suspicious-looking. I opened the front door and shouted 'Hello . . . Cass . . . are you okay?' but she was running away, back down the lane towards her house, pretending she couldn't hear me. I thought it was very odd. I mean, even if she was just going for a run, then it was a bit late . . . a bit dark . . . to be doing it. And thinking about it, I reckon it was her that I'd seen leaping into the hedge. I think she was spying on me, you know. I do. I can't think what else she would have been doing there. And of course, with hindsight, it's obvious, isn't it, what she was doing?

I had yet another night of interrupted sleep, with my thoughts buzzing around my mind like flies trapped in a lampshade. Everything seemed to be going wrong: Dan, Laura, my friends; there just didn't seem to be any corner of my life where it felt okay. The only reason I dragged myself out of bed was because I'd made a commitment, and I couldn't cope with the fallout if I didn't turn up, so I had no choice but to pull myself together. Perhaps some might argue that the distraction of giving a garden session to a group of care home residents was just the tonic I needed.

I approached the greenhouse with a fair degree of trepidation but when I saw about half a dozen of the residents already assembled in a little group, ready for me, I knew I'd done the right thing. Imagine if I hadn't turned up. Matron and the staff would have every reason to believe all the dreadful things my mother said about me.

'Good morning,' I said, breezily, 'I'm Cassandra, Deborah's daughter. And I've come to help out with this morning's gardening session.'

'Whose daughter?' said one of the two ladies I didn't recognize, nudging the other.

'I don't know,' she said. 'But she's somebody's daughter.'

'Deborah's,' I repeated.

'Who's Deborah?' the second one asked.

'Her mother,' the first one said.

'Right then, perhaps if we could go round and I could learn who everyone is . . .'

I introduced myself to the two ladies I hadn't met and repeated my hellos to the others that I had, and then suggested we make a start. Fuelled by the warmth of the morning, sunshine, and penned in by wheelchairs and walking frames, I surprised myself by how much I was looking forward to our session. And so far, there was no sign of my mother.

'I used to grow all my own veg.' Jim, the old boy who always wanted you to make time for a little chat, was the first to speak. He had such a quiet voice that I had to lean close to him. He had that fusty old man scent – dry, slightly sour and tinged with essence of whiskers.

'Did you, Jim? And what did you grow?'

'Oh you know . . . the usual. Beans, onions o' course, and my wife, Betty, she loved her beetroot, she did.'

'That's right,' said Edith. 'Beetroot. Pickled in vinegar. Nothing like it. Mind, you had to be careful not to get it on your clothes. Bugger to get out it was.'

I giggled. 'Didn't have Vanish in those days, Edith.'

'No. Didn't 'ave no Vanish. 'Course I remember when we didn't have no washing machines, neither.'

'Kept you fit, though, dint'it?' Jim said. 'That's why people are obese. No exercise. They wanna get outside, get some fresh air in their lungs, 'stead of sitting in front of a computer all day.'

'Shut up! I don't want to hear any more from you.' Vera had been sitting slumped sideways in her wheelchair, not saying a word, and for all I knew didn't have a clue what was going on around her.

'That's not very nice, Vera,' I said.

'Fuck off!' she said.

'You can fuck off, you silly old cow,' Edith snapped back.

'Um . . . okay. I thought we'd sow some lettuce and carrots today. And I've brought along some tomato plants.'

'I hate tomatoes,' Vera said, grumpily. 'Don't agree with my stomach. It's the acid.'

'That's a shame,' I said. 'Perhaps you might like the carrots.'

'Humph,' she grunted, and let a great stream of dribble drop down onto her sleeve.

'Do you know how old I am?' another old lady, Babs I think she was called, asked me.

'No, I don't,' I replied, and almost said, 'Do you?' but stopped myself. 'How old are you?'

'I'm nine.'

'No she's not,' said Jim. 'She's ninety. You're nine-*tee*, Babs, not nine.'

'Yes, that's right, nine.' She shouted. 'I don't live here, you know. I'm waiting for my mother. Do you think you could telephone her and ask her to come and get me?'

This was really testing me. 'I'll call her in a minute, Babs. Shall we do some gardening first?'

'She'll be worried about me. She won't know where I am. I've got to catch a bus.'

'No you don't. Your mother's dead,' Jim said, unsympathetically.

'No she's not, because *she* said . . .' pointing at me, 'she'd telephone her, so how can she be dead?'

'I'm sorry, Babs,' I thought it best to come clean. 'I'm afraid she is dead.'

'Well when did she die?'

'Quite a long time ago,' was my educated guess.

'Oh.' Babs seemed to take this bad news stoically and propped her chin into her hand with her elbow supported by the arm of the chair. There was a solitary whisker on her chin which I swear was two inches long. 'Then who's going to collect me from school?'

'She's a bloody fool,' Vera assured me.

'I'm sure she isn't,' I said. I was way out of my depth. This was about refereeing, not gardening. I was almost pleased to see my mother approaching.

'Here she comes, the Queen of Sheba,' Vera said.

'Hello, Mum,' I said, trying to sound cheerful.

'Well, you never know what the day's going to bring, do you? Hello, darling,' she said, all smiles and warmth. 'She's my daughter, you know. This is Cassandra.'

Jim and Betty, who seemed to be the most lucid of the group, nodded politely and said, in unison, 'Yes, we know.'

'Are you my mother?' Babs said. Everyone ignored her.

'She's got a gardening business. She's very clever.'

'No, Mum, I'm not . . . really I'm not . . .'

'I need the toilet,' Babs said.

'She's just attention seeking, take no notice,' Betty said.

Babs pushed herself out of the wheelchair and started hitching up her skirt.

'Babs, no. Wait. I'll get a carer. Hold on.'

'I can't wait . . .'

'Oh God . . .' I rushed to the French windows and yelled, 'Help!'

Then I turned back to my little group. A large puddle had appeared at Babs's feet. The others were regarding it indifferently. Thank God a carer appeared. 'Oh dear, Babs. Never mind. Let's get you cleaned up, shall we?' She guided Babs gently back into the wheelchair and sped her off. I hoped that she might be back to mop up the puddle which was putting a bit of a dampener on my gardening class.

I decided the best thing was to pretend it wasn't there. The smell was evil, though.

'Does anyone have anything they'd like to plant over the coming weeks?' The ammonia fumes were making my eyes water.

'Pansies,' Jim said. 'Winter-flowering pansies. They'll cheer us up when it gets cold and miserable.'

'I never really liked pansies much,' my mother said. 'There's something a bit common about them. I suppose it depends on the colour. You know, I particularly dislike yellow pansies.'

'Let's have lots of yellow ones, then,' Vera said.

'Ignore her, Cassandra. She's just a difficult old woman. That's what you are, Vera, a difficult old woman . . .'

'I'm sure she isn't, Mum. I guess she's just a bit . . .' What could I say? A bit demented?

'Fuck off,' Vera said.

'We could have a mixture,' I said, attempting diplomacy. 'That would be no problem. And how about some Savoy cabbage and maybe some cauliflower?'

'Are you sure, Cassandra? I mean they can get them so cheaply at the supermarket. Is it worth the effort, I wonder?'

'I just thought, as it's a gardening club, it would be satisfying to grow a few things. Anyway, I'm going to transfer the tomato plants into big pots. Anyone want to help?'

'Jim, you'll help Cassandra, won't you? And Betty, dear, I'm sure you'd like to get your hands dirty.' My mother had only been with us for under five minutes, but was already acting like royalty, dishing out orders to her subjects. I envied Vera her style of revolt.

'Now Cassandra, you must remember they're a bit . . .' she dropped her voice and mouthed in a loud stage whisper '. . . doolally.'

'Who's doolally?' Vera said.

'You are,' my mother said.

'Mum!' I said.

'What?' my mother said.

'Nothing,' I said.

◇ ◇ ◇

When it was time to leave I climbed into my car and, despite having enjoyed the last hour more than I thought I would, I was left with the uncomfortable suspicion that there might be a degree of madness within all of us. Was it something to be afraid of, or was it really a portal of escape from the bleak prison of our minds, like where those poor old souls were waiting for nothing more than a swift and peaceful death? Was life so empty for them that their minds rescued them, placing them into a more bearable reality? And could that really be happening to me? How do we classify madness? What did it mean to be sane? I certainly didn't feel sane right now, with everything going on in my head. And did that mean it was impossible for me to tell whether or not my reality was 'real', or distorted?

I needed someone to tell me whether or not I was thinking like a crazy person. I really needed a friend, someone I could confide in, someone I could trust and someone who might understand, so I called Sally on my way home.

'Listen, what are you up to? Can I come and steal a cup of coffee?'

'What, now?'

'If you're free.'

'Sure.'

'I'll be with you in five minutes.'

Once the two Labradors had quietened down and we'd said our hellos, Sally filled our cups with fragrant fresh coffee. She shunted the old newspapers and junk mail to one side and then we both sat down at the kitchen table. It was a new kitchen table, along with the rest of the kitchen; smart, hand-built units painted the colour of creamy unsalted butter, and topped with glittery black granite. The new kitchen had been part of Patrick's penance.

I tried to stifle a yawn, but failed. 'God, sorry. This coffee's just what I need.'

'You look tired.'

'Thanks,' I laughed, drily. 'That's what you said last time you saw me.' Most of the time I loved Sally's directness.

'Well then you *still* look tired. What's the point of telling you you look fantastic when you look completely washed out?'

'To tell you the truth, I haven't been sleeping that well. And I've had quite a testing morning. Can you believe I've been roped in to supervise a gardening class at my mother's care home? It's pretty bloody depressing. You know, they're lovely old things, but there's nothing dignified about old age. They're either incontinent or doolally, as my mother put it. Which is rich, coming from her. I suppose the only blessing is that once they lose their minds they're not really aware of what's going on around them. At least I hope they aren't, for their sake.'

'How are things?'

'With my mother? Same as usual. I made a quick getaway after I'd finished the garden session. I should have spent more time with her, but I just didn't feel I'd got the emotional energy left.'

All this was just a preamble to the real conversation I wanted to have, but I was nervous about getting to the point. 'How are the tickets going for the quiz?'

'We've sold fifteen tables of eight. So we've already got more people than last year. But I think we're right to do away with the tea and coffee sales. We only had about three takers.'

'I remember. Everyone wanted to get more wine when they'd run out of the stuff they brought with them. I mean, who wants a bloody cup of tea with their meal?'

'Well obviously not many, as we found out last year. Probably a lot better for us than alcohol, though.'

'Do you think?' No doubt she was not-so-subtly reminding me of my supposed drunkenness at Ellie's supper. 'I think I'll stick to red wine. It's full of antioxidants, apparently – just like tea. Or is it just that disgusting green tea I'm thinking of? Talking of which, are you still taking your daily vitamin cocktail?'

'You bet. It's the only way I can justify sustaining my incredibly unhealthy lifestyle. Patrick tells me he can hear me approaching long before he hears my footsteps. I rattle, like a percussion instrument.'

'Don't be silly, you don't.'

'Of course I don't, sweet pea, I'm teasing you.'

'Sorry. Need to work on my sense of humour these days. Well, whatever it is you're on, it's obviously working. *You* look terrific.' Patrick's affair had galvanized Sally into losing a stone, having her hair coloured and restyled and spending a fortune on new clothes.

'And what about Laura and Dan, are they okay?'

I put the cup to my lips and noticed my hand was trembling. I took a sip and it scalded my tongue, and then set the cup back carefully on the saucer.

'Fine.' I gave her a thin smile which contradicted my words.

'Really?'

'Okay, then. Not fine. Not fine at all, in fact.'

'What's up?'

'Oh, I don't know . . . everything . . . It all seems such a mess.' Sally said nothing, just waited for me to go on. 'Can I ask you something?'

'Sure.'

'You know when you discovered Patrick was . . . you know . . .'

'Playing around?'

'How did you find out?'

'I saw his mobile phone bill. I was emptying the bins, sorting stuff to recycle, and I saw his bill was much more expensive than usual, so I had a look. Before that he'd been behaving a bit strangely, so I suppose I was already suspicious.'

'How do you mean, strangely?'

'Finding fault over little things – like I couldn't do right for doing wrong. It's hard to explain, but you just kind of sense these things, call it intuition. There was nothing big I could put my finger on, but he was just different. I can't really say how, but he just was.'

'Did you snoop on him?'

'Of course I did,' she sighed. 'Especially after I'd seen the phone bill. There were dozens of text messages, a few hour-long conversations – honestly I don't know how he found the time to get any work done. Oh, and he never let his phone out of his sight, and suddenly he decides to put a password on it. So then I searched for his credit card bills, only surprise, surprise, he'd stopped putting them in the file with the others. It's the things they do to cover their tracks, not the tracks themselves. You don't think that Dan's up to something, do you? Surely not, anyone can see that he loves you, Cass. You're so good together, you two.'

'Are we? Honestly, Sally, I don't know anymore. I don't know *anything* anymore.'

'Is this something to do with Ellie?'

I nodded. 'Yep. But it's not just her. There's other stuff, too.'

'Oh God. Do you want to tell me?'

'I'm afraid that if I do, you'll think I'm crazy.'

'Of course I won't.'

'Promise?'

'Promise.'

I still felt in two minds about saying anything, like I was being disloyal to Dan, and would sound neurotic about Ellie, but I *had* to talk to someone before I really did go off my head.

'Ellie's been doing some really weird stuff. God, this is really difficult . . .'

'What do you mean, "weird stuff"?'

'Do you remember that lunch a few weeks back, when we went to Amelia's? Well afterwards I went back to her place and we had a couple of glasses of wine. She told me that she'd suffered from depression, that she'd been feeling suicidal, that she'd been running away from this violent boyfriend . . .'

Sally's eyes had widened. 'Seriously?'

'Yes. Seriously. It was all really heavy stuff. So I was sympathetic – how could I be anything else? I ended up telling her that I'd suffered too – all of which was *fine*. But when I mentioned it to her the other day she denied everything, like I'd made it all up.'

'But why would she do that?'

'I don't know. It's like she's trying to make it look as if I'm crazy, or something.'

'Well why would that make you look crazy?'

'Because she's saying that I must have *imagined* it. And obviously I wouldn't have imagined something like that. She also told you and Amelia that she was worried about me. I think she even told Dan that she was worried about me.'

'But we *have* all been worried about you.'

'You weren't worried about me before *she* arrived here, were you?'

'No. But you've been acting a bit strangely since then.'

'How?'

'Oh God, maybe a bit defensive and withdrawn?'

'Maybe I've got good reason to be. She had lunch with Dan and Laura yesterday, in Birmingham. And Dan didn't tell me.'

'Perhaps he didn't want to upset you. And might there be a reasonable explanation for them having lunch together? Especially if Laura was with them? That doesn't sound like a romantic tryst, does it?'

'So you think I'm being silly . . .'

'Well she has told me that she wanted to help Laura out. So maybe it's just that Dan's trying not to upset you at the moment. If he thinks you're being a bit . . . um . . . over-sensitive, perhaps he thought you'd be really upset, read something into it that wasn't there. Don't you think that's possible? Don't you trust him, Cass?'

'Did you trust Patrick?'

'Yes. I did. But Patrick's not Dan.'

'Well I'm afraid I don't truly trust Dan.'

'Oh Cass . . .'

'Surely I'm just being realistic. You of all people should understand that. Nobody knows what they're capable of until temptation steps in their path, do they? And besides, there's other stuff that I've found out about Dan.'

'Such as?'

'It's stuff from a long time ago. I don't have any proof that anything happened. Just suspicions and probabilities. Like you said, intuition.' I had reached the point where I should tell her about Ellie's book, but something stopped me. So far she hadn't exactly been sympathetic towards my fears.

'Maybe you're right, maybe I'm being stupid,' I said. 'Neurotic, perhaps.'

She smiled, wryly. 'Maybe a bit. I honestly wouldn't worry about it, Cass. I'm sure it's all innocent. And trust me, she really does like you a lot. She's truly very fond of you. She's far too nice to do anything with Dan. I'm sure that the lunch was all about helping Laura. And I can't explain that stuff about her violent boyfriend. Maybe you did dream it . . .'

I had to hide the feeling of sickness that I felt. 'Yeah, maybe that's it.' I finished my coffee and stood up. 'Thanks, Sally. You've been a great help, listening to me. I feel much better already.'

She patted my arm affectionately. 'Good. Anytime. I'm always here for you, remember that.'

13

As I drove away from Sally's I felt deflated and despondent. It was so obvious what she really thought, just like everyone else. The Ellie they saw was not the same person I saw. I was the outsider, standing on the opposite side of the thick glass window, shouting my head off to warn them, but they couldn't hear me, or if they did, they refused to listen.

When I got home I checked Call Minder, but there was nothing, not a single message from anyone at all. I'd tried phoning Laura first thing this morning, but it had gone straight to her voicemail, so I'd left a message asking her to call me. But she seemed not to want to speak to me and, if I'm honest, I really didn't want to hear how much fun lunch with Ellie had been.

I felt oppressed by the interior gloom of the house. Usually I didn't notice the silence, or if I did it was a peaceful feeling that I found soothing. Now it just seemed to signify the extent of my loneliness, my isolation from the rest of the world and the shadows taking over my life. The low ceilings were suffocating, stifling my ability to breathe freely. It was beginning to feel like a prison; no longer the house I loved, where I felt safe.

I was also dreading seeing Dan tonight. Could I face him across the table? Chat to him as if everything in the world was okay, as if we had no problems? Could I pretend so convincingly? It just seemed that everything about us was based on deceit and lies. I couldn't trust him anymore. I didn't know him anymore. I almost wished that

Laura hadn't sent me that text telling me about lunch so that I'd be able to test out whether Dan *would* lie or not. If I was to take a bet on it, I'd say 'yes', most definitely, because that's what he was, a liar. Otherwise he'd have told me the other night, when Ellie's text came through. The problem was that the boundaries between right and wrong were blurred. It was all so confusing. The fact was that I'd snooped on Dan. What was it they said, snoopers never learn anything good? But you wouldn't snoop if you hadn't been given reason to distrust, would you? If I hadn't snooped the other night I wouldn't have known about that text. But it could have been innocent, well innocent-ish. Perhaps Dan just wanted to avoid having a scene with me about the lunch arrangement. And if lunch was supposed to be a secret, then Laura wouldn't have told me about it. It was all so fuzzy, because it wasn't really Dan who'd given me reason to distrust him – it was her, Ellie. Okay, no, it wasn't just Ellie, it was also Rome. I just couldn't think straight. That postcard and the matches. I'd Googled that phrase from the postcard on my phone, and what was it? 'The flame of love keeps burning.' Well what the fuck was all that about? That's hardly innocent. But did I need to be upset about it now when it was all so long ago? God, my head was really hurting.

I went straight up to our bedroom. I drew the curtains against the fading daylight and pulled off my jeans, before sliding between the sheets, and my thoughts drifted back down the years to Rome.

Rome. A place I never wanted to return to, ever. At least Dan had been right about that. I thought I was over it. I'd packed it away into a little suitcase and put it up in the loft, out of the way, where I wouldn't have to think about it for years, and then maybe, sometime in the future, we'd have a clear-out of boxes and suitcases and I'd open it up and say 'Oh goodness me, here's Rome.'

I was supposed to go with him. I had my ticket and everything. I was terribly excited because, for one reason or another, we hadn't really been away since Laura was born. This would be our first trip together since our honeymoon. Dan had a client to visit, and so it meant that the agency would pay for the hotel and Dan's flight. Dan's mother had offered to come and stay and look after Laura, so everything was all sorted. And then, the day before we were due to go, Dan came back from work and said everything had changed. There was a crisis in Rome and he needed to work all the time he was there. He said if I went I'd have to amuse myself. He said it would be okay because we'd be able to have dinner in the evenings, although he couldn't guarantee how early he'd be finished. He just said, 'Sorry, Cass. I know you're going to be disappointed, but I promise I'll make it up to you . . .' And so what could I say? I hardly relished the thought of being a solo tourist. I suppose I could have done all those museum-ey things by myself, but the point was that he and I were supposed to have a romantic time together. So I was angry. I was angry, hurt and disappointed. I went into a mega sulk and told him to go by his bloody self . . . and then I didn't speak to him before he left. He called a couple of times while he was away, but I couldn't bear to speak to him. In the end I began to feel guilty about my behaviour; I began to think: poor Dan, having to give up his holiday too. I felt terrible about how difficult I'd been, and how silly. I decided that any time together in Rome would be better than no time together like this. I called Dan's mum and asked her if she'd mind coming after all. There was still a couple of nights left before Dan was due to return, so I figured it would be worth it, to surprise him. I got to the hotel around six o'clock. Dan had obviously taken the room key with him, so the porter helped me with my suitcase and used the master key to let me in. I hung my things in the wardrobe and then decided to take a quick shower. I'd closed the bathroom door because there was a draught from the bedroom. I'd just stepped out of the shower when I heard voices. I heard, quite clearly, both a male and a female voice. She was laughing – giggling in a sort of flirty way. For an awful moment I wondered if the porter had put me in the wrong bedroom and that I was naked but for a meagre towel in some strangers' bathroom. But when I looked at the mirror shelf I recognized Dan's things – his toothbrush and toothpaste, his razor. So I knew that I couldn't be wrong. Anyway, as I strained to listen I could make out Dan's voice quite clearly. But the tone of the voices had changed. They were speaking quietly, more urgently. I heard the word 'suitcase' mentioned, and 'clothes'. I'd left my jeans on the bed, and my boots on the floor. And then I heard Dan whisper 'Fucking hell . . .' My hand was hovering over the door handle. My heart was pounding and I don't think I'd ever felt so frightened. Looking back it seems amazing how quickly your brain can assimilate these things, work out what's happening. I guessed straight away. Then, as my hand closed on the bathroom door handle, I heard the click of the door to the passage, and I heard Dan call out my name. He tried to smile, to appear pleased, but he couldn't quite manage it. Instead he looked like he'd seen a ghost. The loving surprise reunion I'd envisaged consisted of me confronting him about what I'd heard. Of course he denied I'd heard anything. He said it was the television. He said he'd switched it on when he came into the bedroom. I said what I'd heard was definitely an English voice, and why wasn't the television on now, but he wouldn't have it. Once he'd got over the initial shock, he lied quite smoothly. There was no evidence of anyone else using the room. Obviously I searched. The housekeeping department were very thorough – boringly diligent, in fact. The sheets were changed daily so there was no chance of finding a stray hair, pubic or otherwise. The bins were emptied and the complimentary toiletries replaced. I couldn't even work out if she'd availed herself of the body lotion or the shower cap. She must have left her things in her own room. So I was left with no proof. No concrete evidence, merely circumstantial. Even the matches I'd found after all this time were only circumstantial. Maybe he'd saved them because *I* was there with him. The problem was I couldn't force myself into believing that, much as I wanted to. Especially now that I'd seen the postcard.

I must have dozed eventually, because I wasn't aware of anything else until Dan opened the bedroom door and switched on the light. 'Here you are . . .' he said.

I blinked awake and turned towards him, squinting against the glare. 'Oh, hello,' I muttered foggily.

'The house was in darkness but your car was here. I couldn't find you. I was worried . . .'

'Migraine,' I sighed and managed to give him a small smile. His face was scrumpled into a frown of concern, and I noticed he had a new, crescent-shaped scratch on the side of his nose.

'Poor you. You haven't had one of those for such a long time. I'll get you some pills . . . Have you taken anything?'

I shook my head.

'And a nice cup of tea. It's chilly in here. Would you like a hot water bottle?'

'No, no, there's no need for that, really.'

'Rubbish. I'll get one for you.' He reached across and squeezed my shoulder, and then bent forward and planted a kiss on top of my head. After he'd gone I listened to the vague sounds coming from downstairs; the hiss of water from the kitchen tap, the clunk of the kettle on the Aga hotplate, all the sounds of comforting domesticity. And Dan, full of concern, looking after me, being a loving and caring husband. 'Please,' I prayed silently, 'make this Dan the real Dan.' And not just his guilty conscience.

A few minutes later he was back with a hot mug of tea, a glass of water, a choice of paracetamol and ibuprofen, and the cashmere-covered hot water bottle which I reserved for guests. I took two of each, handed the water back to him, and then lay back on the pillows. Dan passed me the mug of tea.

'Thank you,' I said.

'Darling, I'm really sorry about the other night. I didn't mean to upset you. I should be more understanding, especially at the moment when you're obviously not feeling yourself. And I'm sorry I didn't get back last night. It was all arranged last minute, and the meeting was so bloody early this morning. Were you okay?'

'Yep, I was fine. Your mother rang.'

He nodded. It was impossible to know if that nod meant 'I know', or just plain 'fine'.

'Are you hungry?'

I shook my head. 'Not really. I haven't done anything . . . for supper, that is . . . I was feeling so horrid . . .'

'Don't worry. But I'd be happy to get something for you. I've lit the fire and it'll soon warm up if you feel like getting up.'

'Thanks.'

'That's all right, babe,' he said. He sat down on the bed, placed his hand on my head and started stroking it tenderly. I put the tea down on the bedside table and closed my eyes, savouring the feel of his warm palm skimming over my scalp. 'Poor darling,' he murmured. He started to massage his hands into my hair and it felt so good I could feel my whole body relaxing against him. His fingers worked with a gentle pressure on my head and down where all the tension had made knots where my neck met my scalp.

'That's really good,' I said.

He was being so kind that I wanted to put off the moment when I'd ask him about lunch with Ellie, because I knew as soon as I did Dan would withdraw from me. I grabbed hold of his arm, scrunching my fingers into the cotton of his shirt sleeve. I wanted things to be normal, I wanted things to be all right. I wanted it all to be some awful dream from which I was now waking up into warm reality. A wave of affection swept over me. My Dan. My husband. My lovely Dan. I loved Dan. But it wasn't a dream. I couldn't hold it together any longer. I let out a huge sob.

'Hey,' he said. His fingers stopped circling over my head and he leant forward so that he could look at me. 'What is it? What's all this? Come on baby, don't cry. This isn't going to make that head any better.'

He put his arms right around me, lifting me and pulling me towards him, and then somehow he was lying on the bed beside me. I buried my face against his chest. I sobbed so hard that my breath came in gulps and all the time he kept on stroking me soothingly, murmuring, 'There, there . . . come on . . . poor Cass . . .'

And then it was spent. The storm had passed. 'Okay?' He released me so that he could look at me once more. I was aware of my face being wet, puffy and revolting. I took the handkerchief he offered me and blew my nose noisily.

'Sorry . . . God . . . sorry . . . poor you . . . not what you were expecting to come home to.'

'Well no, but hardly poor me – more poor you. Listen, I'm sorry for not being more understanding. I should be more supportive, especially when you're feeling so vulnerable. But there is stuff we've got to sort out . . . stuff we really can't put off forever . . .'

'I know. But I've just been feeling so tired. I can't remember when I last got a good night's sleep and things . . . well . . . I just need to feel a bit stronger, and get things into perspective.'

I *wanted* him to be able to say that yes, I did have everything in perspective, because he *wasn't* having an affair with Ellie, that he *hadn't* had an affair with some woman in Rome – and that the postcard was easily explainable . . . and the locked box . . . was that easily explainable too?

'What things, babe? Do you mean Ellie?'

'Her. And other stuff. Anyway, Laura texted me, said you had lunch with her.' I slumped back against the pillows. Dan sat up from his lying position, and handed me the cup of tea.

'Yep. I took her out with Laura. She was in Birmingham so I had to, I couldn't not – not with all she's doing. It was a bit of a thank you.'

'Was it fun?' I asked. Dan stood up and untied his tie and threw it towards the armchair. Then he undid his cufflinks and put them on the chest of drawers.

'It was okay, yeah, fine.' He undid the first two buttons of his shirt and then unzipped his trousers and slipped them off, lining up the seams before folding them carefully over the chair arm while I watched. 'I'm just going for a quick shower.'

I nodded, and then I realized that I was slurping noisily on my tea. How attractive.

When he came back into the bedroom he was wearing just a towel around his waist. His hair was damp, and clung to the back of his neck.

'Feeling any better?' He sat down on the edge of the bed and took my hand in his and gave it a squeeze. I could smell soap and shampoo.

'A bit,' I put on a brave smile.

'That's good.'

He stood up and started moving about the room, pulling out clean boxers, a T-shirt, jeans from the wardrobe and socks from the drawer. He threw them onto the bed and then unwrapped the towel from his waist so that he was standing naked in front of me. He rubbed the towel around his penis and then down between his legs.

'You're watching me,' he said.

'Sorry,' I said, automatically.

'I'm finding it hard to read your expression . . .'

'I was miles away . . .'

'Ah, I just thought you were checking me out.'

'I like watching you. You've got a good body.'

'Thank you. So have you.'

'Oh Dan,' I laughed. 'You're such an unconvincing liar . . .' and then I realized what I'd said and so I bit my tongue.

'Am I?'

'I . . . er . . . I don't know . . .' I could feel tears pricking behind my eyes again. I smiled at him and squeezed my nails into my palm. 'Yes,' I confirmed. 'An unconvincing liar . . .' Listen to me . . . a convincing liar lying to another convincing liar. 'Dan,' I said, 'We are all right, you and me, aren't we?'

'I hope so, babe. I really hope so.'

'I just feel everything's getting on top of me right now.'

'I know, sweetheart. Believe me, I can tell. Do you think it might be an idea to get some pills from the doctor? They might help you sleep, and then you might see things a bit more clearly. Like you said, get things in perspective.'

'Maybe,' I said

'I know what you'd like. Don't move.' He put his hand up to emphasize his command and then disappeared out of the bedroom for a few moments before reappearing clutching a small blue bottle: Juniper warming oil from Neal's Yard. 'A massage. Hmm? How would you feel about that?'

'Are you sure?' Dan hadn't offered me a massage for *years*.

'You'll have to take your top off – get rid of that blouse thing – and turn onto your tummy. Make yourself comfortable and available, Mrs Burton!'

He poured the oil into his palms and warmed it before spreading it over my shoulders and down my back, and then finally slid his hands inside my pants, and over the curves of my buttocks. Then he worked his way up to my shoulders once more. He stroked in slow circular motions, soothing and caressing, like he was talking to me through his hands. I felt all the tension drifting away from me. My body felt heavier as it began to relax, sinking deeper into the mattress. I don't know at what point Dan sensed the change in me, but I became aware of a change in the way he was stroking me, moving his attention away from my muscles and onto other parts of my body. Suddenly he tugged on my pants and slipped them over my bottom, down my legs and then pulled them off my feet. My body tensed as I wondered what he would do next. He started working on my buttocks once more, his fingers squeezing and kneading, and then they began to probe between my cheeks. I wasn't sure that I really wanted him to slide his fingers into those places but, as his stroking grew more insistent and rhythmical, it became impossible to ignore the delicious feelings of sensuousness which were flooding through me. I kept my eyes closed all the time, partly because I almost wanted to pretend that I was someone else, because I felt self-conscious and not fully able to let myself go with him, and by inhabiting the darkness behind my eyelids, I could leave 'me' behind. But as his hands delved deeper, the ripples of pleasure spread out, lapping like waves against the edges of my mental resistance. My breathing became shallower and faster and I rolled onto my back, twisting my head back into the pillows.

Just when I felt I knew exactly what would happen next, he put his hand against my hip and pushed it firmly, rolling me back onto my tummy once again. I felt his leg straddle mine, slotting it between my legs, nudging my legs open. Next he had his hands underneath my pelvis, hoiking me upwards onto my knees. He paused for a moment and I sensed he was looking at me. 'Oh God . . .' he murmured and I knew now what he wanted. I felt the hot tip of him gently exploring against me, sliding it up and down, almost teasingly, and then he thrust into me so hard that I cried out and almost collapsed back onto the bed. But he kept a firm hold on my hips, pulling me back towards him, keeping his body upright so that he could drive deeper and harder. Each time he slammed into me I yelped. He was so deep that I could feel my insides bruising but the pain felt good and, besides, I couldn't have stopped him. It had been a long time since we'd fucked like this. He had driven me up the bed so that my head was level with the headboard. I lifted myself up slightly, placing my hands on the top of the wooden panel. Then I felt Dan's hand slip over my shoulder so that he could brace my body harder against his. His fist formed a claw which began to dig into my collar bone. His fingers got nearer to the flesh of my throat and then he started to squeeze the soft tissue, making me choke for breath. I levered my hands against the headboard to give me strength to jerk my head so that his hand released slightly, and then I coughed his name, 'Dan . . . Dan . . . Dan . . . you're strangling me . . .'

Almost as soon as the words were out he exploded, as if the thought of strangling me had pushed him over the edge . . . 'Oh fuck . . . !' he cried, 'Fuck, Cass, oh God . . . !' and then he collapsed down onto my rump. He was too heavy and my knees were trembling, and so I leaned sideways, tipping us both onto the bed. He slipped out of me and murmured 'Oh shit . . . !'

Afterwards we lay like spoons, with Dan cradling me in his arms, and dropping light kisses on the top of my head. 'That was amazing . . . you're amazing.'

I sighed, 'Am I?' Every time a negative thought stalked me I tried to shoo it away. It didn't matter that Dan's aggression had smothered my own pleasure. It didn't matter that I'd felt like a sex object, rather than a loved wife. As we lay there, just holding each other, I told myself that this was what it felt like to be loved. I wasn't going to think about the postcard, or Rome, or Ellie. I felt safe now. It was me that my husband had just made love to, me that was here, wrapped safely in his arms. Maybe I could save our marriage by locking away all my bad feelings and just get on with the business of our life. That woman was not going to come between us. I wouldn't let her. All I needed to feel secure was for Dan to be loving and attentive, and that's what he was being, tonight. I didn't want to leave him or, more to the point, him to leave me. Life without him would be miserable.

I'd be so lonely. And the thought of what it would do to Laura was just unimaginable. For all I knew she'd choose to live with Dan and then I'd be completely on my own – no husband, no family, maybe no friends. What was preferable, this lovely space with Dan, right now, or being torn apart by things which might exist only in my imagination? Not really a tricky question.

After a while Dan rolled away from me. I opened my eyes drowsily. He threw the sheet back and got out of bed.

'You're going?'

'I've got a few things to do downstairs. I might get a sandwich. Why don't you come down and join me? You should eat something. How about I make you my special egg mayonnaise?'

'Sounds irresistible.'

I joined him about fifteen minutes later, after I'd had a quick shower and wrapped myself into my dressing gown. He was busy at the sink, peeling boiled eggs. He glanced round, 'Hi.'

'Hi. Glass of wine?' I went to the fridge and opened it, checking in the door for the white wine left over from last night. 'Funny,' I said. 'I could have sworn there was some wine left in here. Maybe you finished it?'

'Cass . . .' Dan put the egg down and turned around to face me. 'There's two empty bottles by the back door.'

'Two?'

'Yep. Two.'

'But I didn't drink two bottles last night . . .'

'Well I don't know how else they could have got there.'

'From the night before?'

'No, because I put that one in the recycle bin before I left for work on Tuesday.'

'I know I didn't finish the bottle. I remember putting it in the fridge last night, honestly. And I certainly didn't work my way through a second one.'

Dan shrugged. 'Whatever . . .' he obviously didn't believe me. 'Might explain why you'd got a headache.'

'I promise you I didn't.'

'I spoke to Mum today.'

'And? Oh, I know what you're going to say . . .'

'That she thought you'd been drinking?'

'Well I had. I told you. And I hadn't eaten anything all day. I was upset . . . after what happened the night before.'

'Listen, babe.' He came over to me and wrapped his arms around me, and then kissed the top of my head. 'I think you should go to the doctor's, have a chat. Tell him you're feeling low. If you felt a bit less vulnerable you might cut down on the old drinking, eh? There's no shame in it, sweetheart, not when you decide to tackle it. Hey?'

'But I don't understand. Honestly, Dan.' Was it possible that I didn't remember? That I'd had some sort of blackout?

'Don't worry, babe. Everything's okay, it's all right. We just don't want you getting ill again, do we?'

'I'm not. At least, I don't think I am.' I sat down at the table and watched him while he buttered the bread, whisked mayonnaise, salt and pepper into the smashed egg. 'Tell me about lunch.' I tried to sound as normal as possible, because I knew I wouldn't get anywhere by attacking him or accusing him.

'Ellie's promising Laura all sorts of opportunities, which I'm pleased about. She's suggesting she organizes some kind of internship for her. But . . . I don't know . . .' his voice trailed off and he remained silent.

'What?' I asked after I realized he wasn't going to continue.

'Oh, nothing.'

'Go on.'

'There's just something. Oh, I don't know. Take no notice of me.'

'No. What? Tell me.'

'Oh, it's just, I don't know what I mean, really. It's just the way

Ellie seems so terribly keen on being involved . . . I'm not sure I'm really comfortable about it . . .'

'I think there's something frightening about her.' I said quietly, trying to keep my voice steady.

'Cass . . .'

'What?'

'I just meant she shouldn't be using her valuable time. I mean, she's a busy woman and I just feel really grateful to her for helping. If anything, she's *over*-helpful. Not frightening. I don't think she's frightening. That's silly talk. It's just that I feel a bit concerned about how we repay her for all this. Obviously that's why I bought her lunch yesterday, to say thank you, but it's getting a bit embarrassing.'

'Oh.' I snapped my mouth shut, wishing I hadn't said anything.

'All this negative thinking, it's not doing you any good, Cass. Come on, let's take this next door and see how that fire's getting on.'

We sat curled up on the sofa together until it was time for *Newsnight* and then I told Dan I'd see him upstairs. I think I had fallen asleep because I remember thinking it was odd when I felt him shake me, saying: 'Here, drink this. Hot chocolate. It'll help you sleep.'

Dan was wrong about lots of things but right about the fact that I had to do something about my deepening depression. I was in danger of retreating far too much into myself and of isolating myself from everyone I cared about.

My introspection seemed to have infected the world around me, quarantining me from outside contact. Laura still hadn't called me and I was tired of leaving messages which were sounding more and more frustrated. I could have kept on trying, but I didn't want to have to listen to her excitement about bloody Ellie. I'd heard nothing from Amelia, and I didn't want to call her either, because no doubt she would tell me how much she was looking forward to her trip to London with Ellie.

I knew Dan would be pleased that I managed to get an emergency appointment with the doctor but I couldn't help but think from my own point of view that what I was doing was an admission of defeat. Depression was a form of mental illness, wasn't it? – so I must be mentally ill. What did that mean? Unstable? Irrational? Mad? I certainly wasn't mad. I'm not sure I was even irrational, but I did feel unstable; or, more correctly, I would say destabilized. I waited in the waiting room for my consultation in the consulting room, running through what I would say about why I was here. I decided it was probably best to keep it all to the bare minimum; I wasn't about to go in there and say, 'Actually I've got this weird neighbour who's playing silly little games, including planting empty wine bottles in my kitchen to make it seem like I've got a serious drink problem . . .'

'So,' he said. 'What can I do for you?'

'I think I'm suffering from depression . . . My husband is worried about me.'

'And what about you, what do you think?'

'I think I'm feeling pretty low.'

'And people, apart from your husband . . . Do you think others around you have noticed a difference?'

'God, yes. Everyone keeps on telling me how they're worried about me. If I had a fiver for every time I'd heard that recently.'

'How's your sleeping?'

'Bad. I toss and turn and then wake up early with all these thoughts just pummelling my brain. I'm so tired, to be honest. Although I did sleep really well last night for the first time in ages.'

'So you said you're feeling low. Does that mean you find yourself preoccupied with negative thoughts?'

I nodded. 'Definitely. Oh yes. Like I've got this inexplicable sense of guilt and feeling of anxiety in my stomach that won't shift. But I don't think the *whole* world's against me, and it's not that *everyone* dislikes me . . . just my friends, really.' There was a box of tissues on the desk, so I took one and blew my nose. Then the doctor opened a drawer and pulled out a questionnaire. 'Would you mind filling this in for me?'

It had questions like: do you feel hopeless? Do you feel useless to everyone? Do you ever think people would be better off without you? Do you have suicidal thoughts – some of the time? All the time? Never? It didn't have any questions about psychopathic neighbours, but I worked my way down the list anyway, and handed it back to him. He read through my answers and then looked at me. I had the awful feeling that his face was a mirror and the reflection coming back at me was cracked and distorted so that the 'me' seen through his eyes wasn't someone I recognized.

'From your score on this I would say that you are *mildly* depressed, Mrs Burton, and of course depression does distort your thinking, causing negative thoughts and so forth.'

'Ah . . . really . . .' I thought, 'that explained everything.' If only . . .

'I can give you antidepressants to increase your serotonin levels, which should make you feel more able to deal with things. But if you have problems that are making you feel like this, it won't make them go away – you'll still have the problems.'

'But I'll be better able to fight them, because I'll feel stronger?'

'Hopefully, yes.'

'Then that sounds a very positive way forward, doctor.'

He printed off a prescription and signed his signature with what seemed like a simple tick.

'It might be an idea to talk to someone, as well.'

I was speaking to him, wasn't I? 'Like . . .?'

'Like a counsellor. It could be arranged if you felt like it.' He looked at me steadily, and spoke gently. 'Have you been having any thoughts of harming yourself?' I had a sudden flash that I was watching characters on some trashy soap opera, that this conversation wasn't really one which could involve me. I felt oddly detached from a surreal-seeming situation. But then didn't that describe my life perfectly these days?

'No. Absolutely not,' I said firmly, as if the question was absurd. 'I just know that it would be good to get some proper sleep and then maybe I'd feel better able to deal with things.' I paused and he remained silent, just nodding in that professional, understanding manner. My eyes shifted away from his to the beige vertical blinds which were discreetly blocking off the view from the window, but which seemed to make the small room airless and claustrophobic. He continued with the silent treatment, still nodding. I wasn't going to fill the space, so I folded my arms in front of my chest and double crossed my legs, making myself smaller in the chair.

'I'd like you to come back in two weeks and we can see how you're feeling then. And if you change your mind in the meantime – about some form of counselling – just call my secretary and we'll go from there.'

I returned to the waiting room and had to wait for my Cipramil prescription to be dispensed. I sat there, hoping that I wouldn't see anyone I knew. I hated those waiting room chats, although they could be quite funny. I mean, the way you say 'hello, how are you?' when obviously you're not okay because you wouldn't be at the doctor's, would you? But when I saw Jules Gale come in I could feel my cheeks go pink as I said overly cheerfully 'Hi Jules . . . good to see you . . . How are you?'

She sat down on the chair next to me. 'Smear . . .' she mouthed, silently 'with the nurse. So boring.'

'Oh yeah, poor you.'

'How about you Cass? Are you okay?'

'Thrush,' I said. I honestly couldn't think of anything else to say. 'Such a bore . . .'

'Ouch. Natural yoghurt is good.'

'Is it? Well I'll give it a try . . . Just picking up some . . . you know . . . cream.'

'Mrs Burton . . . Cassandra Burton . . .'

'Here,' I said. I stood up and went over to the hatch to collect my prescription, delving in my purse for the money to cover the fee. And then the stupid woman behind the counter said in a very loud voice, 'Do you need this Cipramil on repeat, Mrs Burton?'

I looked straight at Jules. It was a reflex action and she was just smiling at me and nodding, like she knew *everything*.

◇ ◇ ◇

Dan was really pleased that I'd taken his advice at last. His only negative comment had been to question the GP saying I was *mildly* depressed. 'I'd say you were *severely* depressed,' he said, 'but maybe you didn't tell him everything. Anyway, let's hope you'll soon be feeling better, eh Cass?'

I couldn't fault him for the degree of concern he showed, tiptoeing around me, treating me almost as if I was an invalid. 'How's your head? . . . How are you feeling? . . . Are you okay? . . . Cass, are you really okay?'

'I'm fine,' I kept repeating. I almost found it easier to stay out of his way and away from his questions; and so went to bed soon after supper and attempted to read, but the words on the page refused to register, unable to make themselves heard above the story in my own head. Dan brought me hot chocolate. He sat down on the bed and took my hand, and looked at me with a face full of concern. 'I'm worried about you, Cass. What can I do?'

'But I'm fine. You don't need to do anything.' I mean, what could I say? I couldn't say any of the things I wanted to say, so it was easiest to say nothing. I don't really know what I was waiting for, what I thought would change in our situation. I suppose I hoped that the drugs would work and that I'd feel stronger. But whether that would mean that Dan and I would sort things out I just couldn't really say. The way I now saw it, I had a battle with myself on two separate fronts. Both of them had Dan in the middle, but one assault came from the past, and one from the here and now. The one I could square up to in the here and now was the one which no one gave any credence to. I was living up to my name – poor Cassandra, whose warnings no one would listen to – while the other assault from the past meant admitting that I'd been spying on Dan. So I wouldn't really be mounting my own defence – or more correctly, attack – from the moral high ground, would I?

It wouldn't exactly be the cleverest thing to say, for example,

'How dare you keep these mementoes locked away in your special box, these special things that mean so much to you, so that one day I'll come sneaking along and break open all your secrets?' Hmm, not a very good position from which to win whatever it was that would constitute a win. Maybe that was the place to start from: what did I want to achieve in the end? What did I want from all this? Easy, actually. I wanted Dan to be the loving and loyal husband that I'd *mostly* believed him to be. I wanted him to be satisfied with me, so that I didn't have to feel that I didn't somehow live up to his ideal; that I wasn't clever enough, or thin enough, or young enough, or amusing enough to be *enough* for him. And I wanted Ellie out of our lives. And I wanted *my* daughter to appreciate me and love me as much as she seemed to love her father. Was that such a lot to ask for?

Over the next couple of weeks I could sense that my depression was beginning to wear Dan down. The more I withdrew into myself, the harder he tried to reach out to me, but I just didn't seem able to lower my defences. I suppose I must have felt that it was okay because in a small way it was a means of punishing him. I know that sounds irrational, because it was hardly an effective punishment when he'd got no idea what it was all about. And to give poor Dan his due he kept on trying. 'I don't know what to do to help you,' he said. 'You know I'd do anything, Cass. You know I love you, don't you? But I just don't know what to do . . . Perhaps we could go away, would that make you feel better?'

'We can't afford it, can we? And you're always far too busy.'

'But if it would make you feel better, get you smiling again, it would be worth it.'

'Really, Dan? Do you mean that?'

'Well of course I do.'

'Your mother would like to see us. Maybe a night in the Lake District.'

'I was thinking of somewhere a little more romantic than that.'

'Rome, perhaps?'

'Oh Cass. Don't . . . please don't push me away.'

'I'm not . . .'

But I was. I just couldn't seem to help myself.

I called the day after lunch to say thanks, but his phone went straight to voicemail, so I left a message saying how much I'd enjoyed it, how much I'd loved chatting to Laura. What a terrific daughter he had – talented, beautiful. I heard from Sally that Cass had been to see her, and that she had seemed a bit – how did she put it? – manic, I think. Sally didn't give me the details and I didn't know whether or not Cass knew that I was meeting Dan and Laura for lunch, so I couldn't guess the reason for her behaviour, but then I'd also seen her acting so oddly outside my house that night, hadn't I? Oh, and by the way, tell me if I'm going too fast for you, too much detail. I just find it easiest if I tell you everything. Okay?

So, Jules Gale popped in for coffee the next day and naturally Cass came up in conversation and Jules said that she'd just seen her at the surgery. 'Cipramil,' she said, 'I could have sworn that was an antidepressant. I'm sure that's what the receptionist said. Perhaps she was getting confused with Canesten.'

'Poor Cass,' I said. 'I told you she was going down, didn't I? I told Sally and Amelia that I was worried. That day, when we first properly met, she hinted about feeling suicidal. I was so worried about her but I think she was just in denial. It's what we all do. But it's nothing to be ashamed of, nothing to be frightened of. I mean, I'm sure we're all just a hair's breadth away from snapping sometimes. And the good thing is that she's doing something about it. Poor Dan, he must be terribly worried

about her – and Laura doesn't need this to fret about. I wonder if Dan's told her.'

I called Dan's mobile later that evening, but again it went straight to voicemail. He was obviously up to his neck looking after her. I called Laura then to say hi and how much I'd enjoyed lunch. And I also said I thought I'd soon have some good news for her. I said that I was sorry to hear that her mum wasn't well. But she didn't seem to know anything about it. She said she hadn't spoken to her mum for a week or so. 'Oh,' I just said. That's all. I didn't go into detail – it wasn't my place to tell Laura, was it?

But they weren't close, were they, Laura and Cass? I mean they couldn't be close if Laura didn't even want to speak to her, could they? I was speaking more to Laura than Cass was. So she wasn't a good mother, was she? I was surprised that Dan didn't call me back, especially after I'd called another couple of times. I just wanted him to know that I was there for him . . . if he needed me . . . if Cass needed me . . . Did I think he was ignoring me? No . . . no . . . definitely not. But I was surprised not to hear from him – especially as I'd told him I was going off to London and that I might have some good news for Laura.

I think I must have been only mildly depressed because I could still get out of bed in the mornings and go through the motions of doing what I had to do. I wasn't one of those catatonic types, not engaging with anything. Not washing, letting their personal hygiene go to pot, withdrawing completely from everyone. No, I wasn't that bad. The doc had told me that it would take about fourteen days for the pills to kick in, so I tried my best to keep myself occupied, doing small things, little constructive things to keep me busy. Thank God the garden club had been cancelled because the weather had been so bloody awful. Even though it was held in a greenhouse, the residents still had to walk across the garden to get to it, and so it was deemed "too risky" for their "frail constitutions". That didn't help my mood, to be honest. Long dreary, sodden days meaning I couldn't get out into the garden. I decided to get on with some therapeutic chutney making which always made me feel good, turning some home-grown produce into delicious treats for the winter months. I'd got two wheelbarrow loads of Bramleys waiting for me, so I planned a cosy little afternoon for myself. I joined the afternoon play on Radio Four, pulled out the chopping board and looked for my favourite, sharpest Sabatier knife but it seemed to be missing, along with all sorts of other things. I was beginning to wonder if we'd got a family of borrowers living with us. I found a substitute and started peeling and chopping the apples and onions. I added sultanas, raisins, ginger, mixed spices, salt, muscovado sugar and lots of malt vinegar. The scent of the pickling liquor filled my nose, making my mouth water. All I had to do now was let it bubble away, uncovered, and watch it turn into a lovely, gooey, caramel-coloured relish.

Fiddling about in my kitchen soothed me, like a sort of mental massage, calming my nerves and chaotic thoughts. But even the thought of a massage came with other emotional baggage. I rubbed my hand over the top of my apron-covered abdomen and realized I'd drifted away from the voices on the radio. It was a play about a woman who'd suffered a stillbirth and was haunted by dreams of her unborn child. I remembered when I was newly pregnant with Laura. At first I had felt like I was carrying an alien inside me. I was terrified by the thought of not knowing who this child was going to be, of what she would turn into, of how I would cope with the responsibility. Sometimes I got so frightened that I explored the idea – only in my mind, of course – of getting rid of 'it'. I'd never voiced any of my fears to Dan. But pregnancy causes all sorts of peculiar emotions. They say your hormones are all over the place, like having bloody awful, endless, premenstrual tension. And it hadn't helped that I'd felt so sick all the time. I lost a stone in weight in the first three months. Some people blossomed into picture-book images of beautiful, rosy-cheeked Madonna types, the archetype of perfect maternity. Not me. I looked like a zombie from vomiting all day long. Sometimes I even imagined that this thing growing inside me was actually trying to kill me. I didn't dare share my dread with anyone else for fear of what they might have thought of me. I mean, it's not the sort of thing you hear pregnant women say, is it? 'God, I hate being pregnant so much I think I want an abortion . . .' I knew I wasn't really *normal*. Maybe, like my mother, I wasn't cut out for motherhood after all.

I kept my nightmares to myself and struggled through the eight months of torture, hoping that things would be all right when the baby arrived. But of course they weren't – all right, that is.

The phone made me jump, as always, probably because I never expected it to bring good news. I glanced at caller display but the number was withheld. I knew the voice on the other end straight away, though.

'Cassandra, hello. It's me, Ellie.'

'Hello.'

'I'm in London with Amelia and I've done something really stupid. I'm wondering if you could do me a huge favour . . . I know it's a bore and you're probably terribly busy . . .'

I was tempted to say, 'Well actually, yes I am. Frightfully busy making frightfully important apple chutney.' But I didn't. 'No. Ask away . . .'

'I've arranged to meet this man and I've got to cancel, and I stupidly left his number sitting on my desk. I wonder if you'd be a complete angel . . .'

I could barely answer. How many times had I fantasized about somehow gaining access to her house? I felt a surge of sheer, unadulterated euphoria at the thought that here she was, actually *asking* me, *inviting* me to go inside her house.

'How do I get in?'

'If you look at the edge of the terrace, where the grass starts, there's a line of bricks and somewhere near the middle one of them is loose and you can lift it up. You'll find a little box underneath, with a key inside. The telephone number is just sitting on my desk, on the back of an envelope, I think. Call me from my landline when you've found it. You're such an angel, Cass. Thanks so much.'

'Not at all. I'll go now.'

I pulled the preserving pan off the cooker and took off my apron. Then I collected my glasses and my car keys before locking the front door behind me. I must have been lifting up bricks in her garden within five minutes of her telephone call. I located the small box, together with the key and then plunged it into the lock and the door clicked open. My heart was thumping in my chest. I needed to calm myself down before I called her. But first I had to find that bloody number. I walked over to her desk. The computer wasn't there, so my euphoria drained away almost as quickly as it had come. All my fantasies about discovery were thwarted. No bloody computer, no bloody novel. The envelope was propped up against the base of a wooden carving. The name Stephen Myers was printed in capitals above a telephone number. I picked up Ellie's phone, dialled her mobile and quickly read her the number.

'Thank you so much, Cass. I can't tell you how grateful I am.'

'No, no, not at all,' I said.

'Speak soon.' And she was gone, leaving me in peace, in her house.

Her desk was neat and uncluttered. I sat down in her chair and placed my hands on the smooth polished wood. I closed my eyes for a moment and pictured Ellie sitting there, with her long legs stretched out in front of her. Then I opened my eyes and let them roam over the surface, looking for any clues about who this woman really was. I stroked the space where the computer would have been, remembering the day when I'd read all that awful stuff about Dan and her. And then I saw it. Sitting on one side of the desk, a wicker tray holding a stack of paper. Could I dare to hope that this was the manuscript? Was she so stupid as to invite me into her home with this lying around? I pulled the basket towards me. This was it, I was sure of it. She'd printed off a hard copy and left it sitting on the side of her desk. And then she'd invited me in. She wanted me to read it. This was by invitation.

I read the title page:

GASLIGHT
by Eleanor Black

Nothing could have prepared me for what I was about to read.

The last page. I started with the very last page she had written.

> 'How? How can you get away when she watches you all
> the time?'
>
> 'A little something to help her sleep, that's all. Leave
> the key for me . . .'
>
> I turn away from him and walk towards the city
> without looking back.

I flicked back towards the start of the section, ignoring the sick,
leaden feeling in my stomach. I had to know. I found the start of the
chapter.

CHAPTER TEN

> I've made sure that I've chosen the seat directly
> opposite Sophie because I can't seem to get enough of
> looking at her. Tim is examining the menu.
>
> 'What would you like to drink, Bella? You're not
> driving, are you? Let's order a bottle of something.'
>
> 'Sounds lovely,' I said. 'I feel like I've got a lot to
> celebrate.'
>
> 'Like?'
>
> 'Oh, meeting you, coming to the village, new friends,

NEAREST THING TO CRAZY

a new life. You . . . Sophie . . .' the wine arrived. 'Let's drink to our future together.'

We clink our glasses and drink. 'Now, young lady,' he says. 'I don't mean to be a dull old dad, but don't forget you've got to work on that essay of yours this afternoon.'

'Boring . . .' Sophie says. 'It's got to be handed in tomorrow,' she explains to me. 'It's pretty much finished. I've just got to have a final read through. Don't fret, Dad, it's all cool.'

'That's fine. But you've got to get a decent mark. It's important,' he says to me, 'for her degree. Otherwise,' he warns, 'you'll be heading for a Desmond. A Desmond in Media Studies . . . kiss of death. Do you have any idea how many CVs cross my desk? Well the Desmonds never reach it. They go straight in the bin.'

'A Desmond?' I ask.

'Tutu . . .' Sophie fills in for me. 'Dad thinks he's so uber cool. You want me to get a Damian – don't you, Dad?'

'A first?'

'Well done,' Tim mouths to me and smiles. It gives me the warmest feeling, sitting with these two very special people. The man I love and Sophie. Soon we shall be one perfect unit, I remind myself, and my life will be complete.

'Yep. But I won't. I'm not that sad. I have a life too. And if I'm going to be any kind of social commentator . . .'

I watch with amusement as Tim raises his eyebrows, '. . . then I need to get out there, see what's going on in the world. Don't I, Bella?'

'Sure,' I nod. 'In my day we didn't do university. We served apprenticeships instead. Mine was more of a shopping and dry cleaning apprenticeship.'

Sophie appears confused but is too embarrassed to ask what I'm talking about. I guess she thinks she should know what a shopping and dry cleaning apprenticeship is. Bless.

'Making myself indispensable to my editor. Passing her a tissue if she sneezed, monitoring her nails for chipped polish – all the vital things that a leading glossy editor needs.'

'Really? And you didn't mind?'

'Of course I minded. She drove me round the bend with her petty demands. But I was ambitious and knew that if I played my cards right I'd be able to move up the food chain. We followed the laws of the jungle, like in any competitive business. If you want to be successful you've got to be ruthless. Do you think you could be ruthless, Sophie darling?'

'Sure I could,' she nods vigorously. I sense that she liked being called 'darling'. 'Definitely. Yes, I could.'

'Steady, love. I hear what Bella's saying, but we are in the twenty-first century, not the 1980s. I think we can all be a little bit more touchy-feely, can't we?' He looks at me. I wonder if he's realized what he's just said but – as my gaze rests on him for a moment or two longer than convention allows – if he didn't before, he certainly does now. He shoots me a knowing glance and I smile back before turning my focus back to Sophie.

'Sure,' I say. 'Touchy-feely is good. But if you can temper it with a bit of hot-blooded ruthlessness – a bit of passion, if you prefer – then that, in my book, will take you all the way.'

Sophie is nodding, as if the secrets of the Holy Grail

have just been revealed to her. Her father is wriggling
in his seat. Perhaps he's thinking about some other sort
of grail. She's so sweet. Sweeter, actually, than I
expected, considering. I suppose I'd imagined she'd be
more sophisticated, more worldly and ambitious, more
like I was at that age. She's pretty, very pretty. Good
wide forehead, greeny-blue eyes and thick tawny lashes
that match her hair. She's coloured her hair but it's been
done badly. The paler stripes of blonde have an orangey
hue that tell me the story of some cheap little backwater
salon. I'd have to sort that out. I'm pleased to see that
she's got good teeth. I would have expected that. Her
clothes are okay-ish. They show me she has some sense
of style, although again she obviously shopped at all the
wrong places. I see it all the time – young girls who've
grown up following the example of some god-awful
frump of a mother, instilling in them their own
dictionary of non-style. It's damned hard to change a
lifetime of dodgy indoctrination. I'll have my work cut
out. But it will be very satisfying, for both of us.

The little voice of reason in my head was fading to an almost
inaudible whisper; 'it's fiction . . . it's a novel . . .' it told me. 'It's made
up . . . remember it's her imagination . . .' I slammed the cast-off page
back down on to the desk and read on.

'Would you like me to try and arrange some work
experience for you?'
'Would I? Oh my God. Dad . . . I can't believe
. . . that would be amazing. Do you really think you could?'
'Sure. Maybe in your Christmas holidays?'
'I've got four weeks then.'

'Okay. Give me your dates and I'll see what I can do. I plan to be in London myself for some of the time. There's always lots of parties and networking to do in the publishing world. We could have some fun together . . .'

'Where would I stay?'

'My flat.'

Tim sounded surprised. 'You've still got a flat in London?'

'Oh yes. I'd never give up my little flat. It's lovely. In Notting Hill. You'd love it. You could come up, too, Tim, come and visit us, check Sophie's okay. Wouldn't that be fun?'

'What shall I tell Mum?' Sophie said.

'We'll think of something.' Tim winked at me.

But she might be making this up . . . you might not know what Laura really said . . . remember it's a novel . . . the voice repeated as if by rote.

After lunch we say goodbye to Sophie. She says she has to work on her essay, and I make a show of the fact that I need to do some shopping. Tim says he's heading back to the office, and so we go our separate ways.

Fifteen minutes later I see him by the canal, where we'd arranged to meet. He is leaning against the curved brickwork fifty metres short of the tunnel entrance, not looking in my direction, but staring into the oily depths of the murky brown water. His collar is hitched up against the chill wind, his hands stuffed deep into the pockets of his coat. My red shoes make loud clicking sounds against the flinty pavement. Still he keeps his eyes fixed on the water, not looking at me. I walk on, not varying my pace when I draw level with him. He glances up as I pass him and our eyes meet briefly. He looks dreamy and removed, as though he's been in some other world, and is now surprised to see me. The only sign of recognition is a tiny half smile that lifts one side of his mouth. I carry on walking but the change in the rhythm of my heels signals to him that I have slowed my pace. I hear his footsteps behind me. I turn my head slightly to one side so that I can see his shadow gaining on me. The wind whips at the thin fabric of my skirt, brushing cold draughts over my thighs. I keep walking towards the tunnel, and when I reach it I stop and wait, keeping my head down. Tim's shadow grows larger and envelops me in the darkness. I hear him suck in his breath, but still he doesn't speak; he just gazes at me as if he's in a trance. I lean my shoulders back against the cold bricks and thrust my hips forward, longing for him to touch me. Still he stands in front of me, his feet planted squarely, hands in his pockets, fixing his eyes on mine. I can't read his expression. Could it be anger? Or, more likely, lust? Although he hasn't touched me, my skin feels alive, tingling all over my body. I feel my nipples grazing against the fabric of my bra and I want him to touch them, to release them, to roll them between his fingers, to clamp his lips over them and suck them. I need to touch myself. I stare at him as I put my hand up to my blouse and undo the button which strains against my cleavage. I slip my hand inside and rub my hand over my left breast, brushing it against my nipple, and then – still not letting my eyes leave his – I let my other hand drift downwards, and I slip my finger inside my knickers and touch the wet heat between my legs, and then I moan.

'Oh my God.' He steps forward, he reaches behind me and clamps my buttocks into his hands and squeezes hard. I can feel the solid length of his cock push against me. My finger is slick with wetness and so I rub it over his lips. His tongue laps at it, tasting me delicately at first, then takes it deep into his mouth and lets it slide out again. He nibbles lightly on my fingertip, all the time staring at me, then suddenly he clamps his teeth down harder, painfully, and I gasp and try and slap his face but he twists away so I miss, catching my nail on his nose . . .

Dan had a scratch on his nose. When he came home and saw me upstairs. I noticed. A crescent-shaped mark. Her fingernail had put it there. So it was true. It was all true. I *had* to read on, even though her words were destroying me . . . and my life with Dan.

Then he lifts me up and I wrap my legs around his hips, crossing them behind his arse, and he rocks me up and down over his erection. The warm wool of his trousers rubs right against the nub of my clit and I am so aroused that I come straight away. My legs judder and convulse against him. 'Come on, baby,' I breathe into his ear, 'Fuck me.'

'No.'

'What?'

'You'll have to wait . . . not here . . .'

'Bastard!' I hiss and bite his neck.

'Bitch!' he hisses back and threads his fingers into my hair, pulling on it and laughing quietly. 'Patience . . .'

I drop my legs back onto the floor. They threaten to give way. I hitch my skirt back down and straighten up.

I give him a burning look.

'I plan to do this properly. I want time to fuck you in every way I've imagined. A lot of time . . .'

'How? How can you get away when she watches you all the time?'

'A little something to help her sleep, that's all. Leave the key for me . . .'

I turn away from him and walk back towards the city without looking back.

This was insane. She was manipulating me, fucking with my mind. I wanted to be sick. I wanted to shower. I wanted to scrub myself all over. I wanted to rip this fucking manuscript to shreds. I wanted to burn down her house, rip *her* to shreds. My anger felt volcanic, seismic, nuclear. I was like a woman possessed. No, no 'like' about it, I *was* a woman possessed. I slapped the last few pages back onto the stack, and then turned the whole thing over again, so that I could see 'Chapter One' on the top sheet. I didn't care that the room was growing dark, I didn't care that people might notice my car outside *her* house. I didn't care about anything, except reading this fucking book.

GASLIGHT

by Eleanor Black

CHAPTER ONE

You never know what the day's going to bring. That was one of my mother's little homespun aphorisms. You couldn't argue with that. Nor could you argue with her. There was a certain logic to it; good or bad, she'd be right. That day I got home from school and she told me about Dad. The only thing I could think of to say was, 'Well, you never know what the day's going to bring . . .'

She looked at me but I knew she wasn't seeing me. Her eyes were all misted up.

'Your father's dead and that's all you can say?'

She got up from the kitchen table, pushing her chair back so violently that it fell right over backwards, hitting the floor, wood splintering against stone. I watched her pull her hand back like it was in slow motion. At around 45 degrees it stopped, and then it accelerated towards me through the unresisting air. She hit me so hard that I crashed into the kitchen cupboard. The doorknob smashed against my knee but I couldn't feel any pain in my leg. I was too busy tasting metal in my mouth, the metallic taste of blood where she'd smashed my cheek into my teeth. I must have looked a bit of a sight because she started to scream; she screamed and screamed and screamed until my ears hurt and I wondered if she'd ever shut up. 'Little bitch . . .' she yelled between her screams, 'little bitch . . .' I could see foam forming at the corner of her mouth. Not me, I thought, but you . . . rabid bitch . . .

'Your mother found him. It was a terrible shock for her,' the policewoman who was paid to be nice told me. 'And a terrible shock for you, too. Your mother . . . she's upset . . . she didn't mean . . . your cheek . . . it must be sore . . .' A kind hand reached out to stroke the blossoming bruise. I flinched, knowing that it would hurt if she touched me. You wouldn't get away with that these days, probably be deemed 'inappropriate', touching someone. She'd be CRB checked, though, wouldn't she? So maybe she'd be allowed to touch. Whatever. And maybe Mum wouldn't be allowed to touch. It was all my fault. Obviously. I knew it would be all my fault from the minute she told me he was dead.

Where was I? Oh yes, like I was saying, you never know what the day's going to bring, do you?

I always planned that when I was a mother I'd do it differently. I'd bake cakes that filled the kitchen with delicious smells as a welcome home from school. My child would be gathered up against a white starched apron and would plant kisses on to my flour-flecked cheeks, and I would ruffle my child's hair with pastry-encrusted nails. There'd be a dog snoring in its bed in one corner of the room. I'd have old china jugs stuffed full of roses and I'd pick up the fallen petals and rub them between my finger and thumb, knowing that they didn't feel half so soft as my child's skin, and I'd live in a beautiful house in that fantastical land that people called 'the country' where it was either always sunny, golden and green, or snow covered and robin infested, like a Christmas card. Except life never seems to work out the way you plan it.

My eyes flew over the pages, scanning the lines, reading the words so quickly that I barely had a chance to turn them into sense. I was trying to take in too much at once. I thought I must be imagining what I was reading, as if I was reinterpreting the words. But I wasn't. Some of the details were wrong, but there were enough correct ones for me to know that Ellie was writing about *my* life. The sentences swam in and out of focus, forming and re-forming their poisonous meaning as I read on. And it got worse, much worse.

'No . . .' I said aloud to the empty room. 'It's not possible. It simply isn't possible.' There was no way. There were laws in place, anonymity laws. No, I told myself. You're being hysterical. Slow down, go back to the beginning, take a deep breath and reread it, slowly. You've got it wrong.

> You never know what the day's going to bring. I picked up the letter, along with the rest of the post, and took it inside. I put it on the dresser in the kitchen, made myself a cup of coffee, lit a cigarette, even made a couple of phone calls, before I returned to the pile. I'd given up all hope. The way I viewed it, my baby had been stolen and I was never going to see her again. But as I unfolded the letter and scanned the neatly scripted words, I realized that everything had changed, that my life would never be the same again. I had found her or, rather, she had found me.

There was no mistake. I hadn't got it wrong. I felt the room spinning. I slumped forward, trying to get my head between my knees, but I slipped onto the floor, and then I must have passed out for a while; I don't know how long for, maybe just a few moments. When I came to I was overcome by tremors that shook my body. My teeth were chattering and I had cramps in my stomach. I crouched into a ball hoping that the convulsions would soon cease. I couldn't think of anything. It was just me and a sisal carpet against my nose, prickly and cold, and smelling vaguely of dog. 'No, no, no, no . . .' I heard a voice over and over again and then I realized it was my voice. My worst nightmare, the most unimaginably terrifying thing that could ever happen to me was there, above me, on a desk, typed clearly on a sheet of A4, as plain as you please.

The memory of the day I was told I could never have children of my own was still so vivid that I could reach out and touch it, smell it, climb right inside it and relive every excruciating moment. It was a hot day, a hot July day. Big, dust-filmed sash windows let in too much of the sun's heat, making the dreary mahogany-lined room stiflingly hot. There was a faint whiff of sour sweat coming, I guessed, from the consultant's shiny pin-striped suit. His steel-coloured hair was scraped back from a balding pate. He had some of those funny white pustules around his eyes, and half-moon glasses which rested on a bony escarpment halfway down his nose. He leaned over a leather-edged blotting pad, twirling a stiletto-shaped letter opener between his fingers. From the moment he started clearing his throat I knew I was in trouble. As I held my breath, waiting for him to speak, I remember the sound of the traffic providing a constant hum in the background, a hum overlaid with the thrumming syncopation of a taxi's diesel engine; the screech of a bus's brakes; the shrill roar of a jet overhead – sounds all mingling together to form the symphony of Harley Street. And inside the room, like a solo instrumentalist, a fly slapping against the window, while the consultant beat time, tapping the stiletto letter opener on the leather-edged blotting pad.

Being told I couldn't have children hit me at such a deep, fundamental level, I suppose, because it's what we're here for, our entire purpose in life. It's why we want to find a mate, why we have a sex drive, why we have a survival instinct, because it's all about the preservation and regeneration of ourselves. So it felt like a large slice of me had died. That there'd be nothing left of me. That I wasn't really *for* anything.

Dan said it was silly to feel that way. He said he loved me no matter what and that he could live without children; he said he'd married me for me, not because of someone he'd never met. Looking back, it's extraordinary how loving Dan was, and how understanding. When my periods started to dry up, about a year after our marriage, I put it down to things like stress. There'd been so many changes in my life. Maybe my diet wasn't as good as it should have been, not that I was ever too thin, or anything like that, the obvious things that you could assume were a rational cause. But when, after nine months, I'd been period free, I decided I'd go and see the doc, just to find out what was going on. At first he'd been reassuring and then, as he questioned me more and more, asking for my symptoms, suggesting that perhaps I might have others, I began to suspect what he was getting at. I had been feeling a bit weird – hot flushes, night sweats, odd aches and pains. He said he wanted to do some tests, take some blood, and refer me to a gynaecologist. Still I hadn't allowed myself to get too alarmed, thinking there would be some simple explanation, a remedy, like a course of antibiotics or a prescription to de-stress my life.

There was no way I'd been prepared for the diagnosis. Premature Onset Menopause was the official label. Apparently it affects about one woman in a thousand under the age of thirty, and I was one of those women. My ovaries had shrivelled and died, and so I could no longer produce eggs. No eggs, no baby. I tried not to mind. Maybe if I'd had some proper career that I could concentrate on, the reality might have been easier to bear. But I didn't. I'd always had unimportant little fill-in jobs. I'd worked in shops, waitressed in restaurants, been a receptionist in a smart hairdressing salon in Mayfair; I'd done all sorts of meaningless jobs that barely managed to pay my rent and food bills. The sort of life I'd been prepared for culminated – if viewed in terms of a successful career path – in marriage, and children. I'd got the husband, so now I needed the baby to give me the kind of purpose in life that I had been bred for. I had it all worked out in my mind; Dan would be the breadwinner and I would be the homemaker. Mum had seen to the fact that I wasn't fit for anything else. I'd been far too busy taking care of her to find time to study. Daughters didn't study, daughters carried out domestic duties. I was expected to marry, knock around earning a bit for a year or two, before getting on with the proper business of producing babies.

We had to start exploring all the other options, otherwise I knew I would have gone mad.

But how did she know? Was this all some horrible coincidence, some lucky guessing on her part? Or was there any way at all that she could have circumvented all the safeguards, all the anonymity laws, to track Laura down? It simply wasn't possible. There were only three people in the world who knew about Laura's conception, and they were Dan, me and my mother. Not Laura. Laura didn't know. I hadn't told Laura. I hadn't told Laura because I was afraid that she'd reject me for not telling her the truth so much earlier; that she'd reject me for lying to her for all of her life; that she'd reject me because I wasn't her genetic mother. And that was why Dan was, deep down, angry with me, because I hadn't been honest, and why I was angry with Dan because he had nothing to lose. That was why I believed Dan considered Laura to be *his* daughter, and not mine. We were all living a lie and it was my fault.

So how did *she* know?

I'd been in her house for over two hours. I needed to get home and plan what I should do next. Reluctantly I put the manuscript back. I took a last look around, checked that everything was as I had found it and finally replaced the key in its little box at the edge of the terrace. I somehow drove home, and although my body was back in my own kitchen, my mind was still reading over Ellie's poisoned prose. I dragged my thoughts back to the mundane domesticity of the scene I had left; was it really only two hours since I'd been listening to that radio play and thinking about sterilizing jam jars? None of that seemed remotely relevant or important anymore. I replaced the preserving pan on the simmering plate of the Aga, going through the mechanical motion of finishing off the chutney, scraping a wooden spoon across the base of the pan to see whether or not it left a clear trail of silver in the bottom. As I scraped, the liquid started to bubble into large blisters of heat which then exploded like tiny geysers, spraying my hand with molten sugar, but they didn't seem to hurt. Maybe my pain receptors were so overloaded that they'd broken down.

In my muddled head I tried to piece together the evidence, like the shattered fragments of a beloved object, broken beyond repair. I'd had an egg donor. I now knew her name: Ellie. We had 'egg shared'. Her husband had a low sperm count, so her eggs had to be fertilized *in vitro*. So in return for reduced fees, she had offered her surplus eggs to some other poor woman who was struggling to conceive. A wonderful gesture; a gesture for which I had felt nothing but gratitude ever since my pregnancy had been confirmed. But, according to her manuscript, her attempts at conception all failed. She was left childless, but with the knowledge that somewhere in the world, a child of hers *did* exist, and she might never meet her.

As I'd read on, I had learned more and more about my daughter and her biological mother. Ellie had, apparently, written to the clinic some years ago, when the anonymity rules changed. She'd told them that she realized she had no right to contact her genetic child, but she knew that at the age of eighteen, the child would have a right to contact her. She hoped that by letting the clinic know that she had no objection to being contacted, they could pass on her details, if ever they were requested. As simple as that. All she had to do was wait.

The manuscript informed me that 'Sophie' had written to the Human Fertilisation and Embryology Authority after her eighteenth birthday, asking if there was any information about her genetic mother and whether she had any siblings. She said that as an only child she had always been saddened by the thought she had no brothers and sisters. So she was curious to find out. Somehow the HFEA had put the two of them in touch and Ellie had found out where we lived so that she could come into our lives and fuck everything up. What was it she'd written?

> 'I felt like my life had been stolen along with my child.
> I needed to know this man who had created a child with
> me. And when I met him I knew how much I wanted
> him.
>   And so I made up my mind I'd take the whole thing
> back.'

So she was here to get both Laura and Dan, to steal them from *me*. But how did Laura find out, if there were only three people in the world that knew? And was Ellie really having an affair with Dan? Were they meeting up after dark, after I'd gone to bed, Dan having plied me with some ridiculous sleeping cocktail?

Oh my God! The hot chocolate. No . . . it wasn't possible . . . he wouldn't . . . not Dan . . . No, the whole thing was just too daft, too crazy, too *insane*. But I didn't know Dan any more. I didn't know what Dan was capable of. I didn't know he kept a locked box which contained his secret treasures, did I? My Dan wasn't my Dan at all.

I'd thought it was strange that night – the fact that he'd woken me up to give me something to help me sleep, when I was *already* asleep. And then the other nights, when he was being so attentive. This was crazy. This was mad. I tried to picture Dan in the kitchen, mixing hot chocolate powder with milk while, at the same time, grinding up sleeping pills in the pestle and mortar to knock me out so that he could creep out and go have fun with Ellie. It was daft.

Okay, you read it in novels, maybe even in murder trials, but not in middle England with boring middle-aged couples. Even so, I visited the medicine cabinet just to see, just to put my mind at rest. We kept all the pharmaceutical stuff in an old pine wall cupboard in the bathroom upstairs. It was one of those cupboards I kept meaning to sort out, with plasters that had lost their stickiness; leftover antibiotics that would never be any good to anyone, but which had been saved, just in case; Benylin bottles with sticky outsides; and half-finished packets of Lemsip. As I sifted through the contents there were several incomprehensible names stamped on white cardboard packaging, remnants of long-forgotten ailments. But sleeping tablets? I couldn't remember when either of us had taken them. Although there was lots of stuff in the cupboard which was unrecognizable, there was nothing that looked remotely sinister.

Dan wouldn't . . . I knew he wouldn't. I closed the cupboard doors and refolded the towels on the rail, picked up the bathroom bin to empty it, and then I thought . . . 'What if she gave them to him? What if she'd got sleeping pills and passed them to him?'

There was one more thing I needed to find out.

16

'Well you never know what the day's going to bring, do you? What a surprise,' my mother said.

'What have you said to Laura?'

'Well hello, mother dear, and how are you today?' My mother was sitting in her usual place, the armchair in front of the window, dressed like she was going to a Tory Ladies' Lunch.

'I need to know. What have you told Laura?' The smell of TCP seemed more pungent than usual.

'About what, dear?'

'About me. About her. You know what I mean.' I went over to her chair. I put my hands on either side of the wings and loomed over her menacingly. I had often fantasized about killing her, but she could have no idea just how close I now was to making that fantasy a reality. 'Tell me, mother. Just bloody tell me.'

'Stop it!' she shouted. 'Stop that at once. Go and sit down this minute.'

'No!' I continued to hold the chair. 'I'm not afraid of you. There's nothing you can do to me anymore.'

'Well it was obvious that you were never going to do it. She needed to know. I did the right thing.'

'When did you tell her?' I could almost feel the flesh of her throat between my fingers. I wanted so badly to squeeze that flesh, to squeeze all the breath out of her. But I let my hands slip from the chair. How was it possible that I had come from her womb? The idea repulsed me. I straightened up and took a step back so that I could see into her eyes more clearly. 'When?'

'When she came to see me after her eighteenth birthday. Hadn't you always said you'd tell her then? And you didn't. It wasn't right that you didn't. She had a right to know.'

'You had no right. No right at all. You're an evil old witch and my father knew that. That's why he couldn't stand to live with you anymore. He chose death, rather than carry on living with a monster like you.'

'That's not true. It was an accident.'

'An accident? What do you think he was doing with a rope around his neck swinging from the garage roof? An accident? Come off it, mother. You can't go on rewriting history because you can't face the truth.'

'Like you're doing,' she said. 'What's the difference? And your father loved me.'

'Then why did he choose the ultimate way to leave you?'

'Because I neglected him, because of *you*. Because I had to look after *you.*'

'No. Not my fault. You just made his life unbearable, like you've tried to do with mine, but it hasn't worked, has it? Because I've had Dan and Laura. But you couldn't bear that, so you wanted to take that away from me. You just couldn't bear it that I should be happy.'

'I don't know what you're talking about. Cassandra, you're really sounding quite unhinged . . .' But her voice sounded weak and shrill, like a frightened little girl. A little girl who deep down wanted to be mothered. Who, a great deal of my life, had expected me to be the one to do it.

'And tell me something else, this life story of yours, this person who's been coming to see you to take down your life story –'

'What about it?'

'Is it a woman, a red-haired woman?'

'Why?'

'And you've told her all about everything . . . about me . . . and Dad . . . about Laura?'

'It's none of your business. You've no right to know. It's my story.'

All the pieces were coming together. That explained why Ellie knew so much about me, even my childhood and my mother's funny expressions. My *mother*. 'Congratulations. You can't have the faintest idea just how successful you've been this time. Well done, Mother. Mother! If only you knew the meaning of the word!'

'Cassandra . . . !'

I'd held back from telling her how I felt, maybe from telling myself how I felt, for so long that I wasn't about to stop now. 'If only you could love like a mother should. Mothers are supposed to protect and nurture their children, not punish and destroy. Ironic isn't it, when you think about it, how you are a so-called natural mother, and I'm not. Just goes to show what an ambiguous word mother really is. I don't suppose you can understand what I'm talking about, can you? But it wasn't enough for you to be a rotten mother to me, you also wanted to make sure that I couldn't be a complete mother to Laura.'

All the colour had drained from her face. Her mouth opened and closed soundlessly and then she choked the words out: 'Cassandra . . . I think you should leave . . . get out of here . . .'

'Don't worry. I'm leaving. Goodbye, Mother!' I took one last look at her, hoping that I would never set eyes on her again.

I ran down the stairs and then paused outside Matron's office. 'I don't know when or if I'll be in again. So I'm sorry but I'm going to have to pass up the garden class.'

She opened her mouth to reply but I didn't hang around long enough to hear what she wanted to say. Okay, so Ellie hadn't got all the details right in her revolting book, but she had enough to let me know that she was writing about my life and my mother.

On the way home my mobile rang. I saw that it was Laura. I pulled to the roadside. How was I supposed to react to her now that

I knew she was aware of the circumstances of her conception? But, I reminded myself, she'd known for nearly three years and I'd only found *that* out a few moments ago. What I didn't know was whether she knew about *who* Ellie really was.

'Laura, darling,' I said.

'Mum! Mum, guess what? I'm just so excited. I couldn't wait to tell you. Ellie's just phoned me. She's sorted out some work experience, on *Mode* magazine. Two weeks in December. And, can you believe it, she says I can stay in her flat while I do it? God, how lucky am I? Mum? Mum . . . are you still there?' She didn't know about Ellie. Thank God. She wouldn't be talking about her like that if she knew.

'When in December?' The net was closing in. I wondered where we would all be by then. Would Laura have found out who Ellie really was? Would Dan and Ellie be forming part of that perfect unit?

'The first two weeks. I can't believe how kind she's being to me. Isn't that great?'

I didn't reply.

'I can go and shadow the fashion editor, providing I don't get in anyone's way, try and be helpful. God, I'll have to think about what to wear.'

'Yes, I suppose you will.'

'Mum . . . you don't sound that excited.'

'Laura . . .'

'Yes?'

'You know I love you, don't you? That I love you very, very much.'

''Course I do. But how lucky am I? I've called Dad and he was over the moon for me. He can't wait to thank Ellie. So if you see her, will you say just how excited I am? Oh, I know it's only work experience, and it's only a couple of weeks, but Mum . . . *Mode* . . . God, I can't believe it. I'm going out with some mates to celebrate.

But I'll be home at the weekend. It's the quiz, and Ellie said she hoped she'd see me there. Save a place for me somewhere, won't you Mum? Love you . . .'

And she was gone.

◇ ◇ ◇

When Dan got home I had to try and disguise the fact that I felt so weak and shaky. I wanted to run away from myself, to turn off all the lights and lock and bar the door of my head to keep myself out. If I could just go away somewhere, find some dark hole to crawl into and curl up into a tight little ball I might feel better, or safer. I just didn't know what to do with myself. Eventually I pleaded illness. I think I muttered something like '. . . must have eaten something'. But I wasn't so ill that I couldn't keep refilling my wine glass. I'd have to slow down, otherwise I might end up doing or saying something I'd regret.

When Nick Gale telephoned to ask Dan to help him shift some furniture, ready for the quiz on Saturday, it was hard to reconcile the fact that normal life was still carrying on out there, that people were just getting on with the minutiae of daily life.

Dan sounded relaxed and jokey, just like normal Dan. If only I could have screamed at him, 'We're not normal. Nothing's normal anymore. Don't you see what's happening . . . what *she's* doing?'

Over supper he said, 'You haven't touched your food. Stomach still bad?'

'Yeah. But I've taken some paracetamol,' I lied, and then, with wine-fuelled bravado, I said, 'I've been feeling so tired these last few days. I don't know what's the matter with me. It's almost as if I've been drugged . . .' I met his eyes, held his gaze.

His eyes didn't flicker. 'You look a bit peaky. Really pale.'

'Do I?' Peaky – that was almost funny.

'Did Laura tell you her good news?'

'Yes, she did. Dan, we need to talk. There's something I need to tell you.'

He pushed his plate away. 'Is it about Ellie again?'

'Yes.'

He held his hands up. 'I don't want to hear it.'

'You need to listen to me. This is important, Dan. Very important. You know she's in London with Amelia? Well, she called me today, asking me to go round to her house, to get a telephone number for her. So I did. And her manuscript was sitting on her desk. It's about us. It's about Laura. It's about you and her. Everything is there . . . even my father . . .'

I was finding it increasingly difficult to read Dan, but I think I saw, just fleetingly, an expression of sheer terror on his face. 'I don't understand.'

'She wrote about your lunch the other day, Dan. She wrote about what happened afterwards.'

'Nothing happened afterwards. What do you mean?'

'According to her manuscript you met up with her and nearly fucked her under a bridge.'

'What? That's ridiculous. She said that I . . . ? Oh come off it.'

'Is it true?'

'Are you serious? Of course it's not bloody true. Come on, Cass. As if . . . under a bridge? I mean *anywhere*, for that matter. This is potty. Laughable. But maybe that's just the way she writes her novel. Perhaps I should be flattered. Anyway, how do you know it's supposed to be me? Does it say "Dan Burton"?'

'No. You're called Tim.'

'So it's not me, then. It's some bloke called Tim.'

'Did you talk about Laura's essay and degree classification over lunch?'

'I can't remember, maybe. Why?'

'Because it's all there, in her story. And do you know what else is there?'

'Nope. No idea. Obviously . . .'

'Stuff she's learned from my mother. She's been interviewing her at the care home, pretending to be one of those companies that record your memory. I mean, can you believe it? Actually going in there, pretending to be someone else, getting all the information from Mum. It's just bloody unbelievable. But you know what? Do you know what's worse . . . even worse than you having an affair with her? Drugging me at night so that you can go and meet her or whatever it is you're supposed to do . . .'

'Oh come on, she didn't put that, did she?'

'Yes, she did. She put that. I know it's hard to believe, but it gets worse. By God it gets worse. My mother told Laura about the donor egg.'

'Oh Cass!'

'When she was eighteen. I should have guessed. You know what she's like, what she can be like. Probably annoyed with me over something, thought she'd get her own back. Well she really, really has this time.'

'But what's this got to do with Ellie?'

'According to her bloody manuscript, she is Laura's biological mother. It was her egg. You and Ellie made a baby together and she's so bloody unhinged that she thinks the three of you are going to become one lovely perfect little family unit, while for me . . . well God only knows what she's got in store for me. The loony bin, or worse!'

Dan was shaking his head. He pushed out his chair and stood up. 'I'm lost. Sorry Cass, but I can't take this in. Let me get this straight. Your mother told Laura, and somehow . . . somehow . . . coincidentally Ellie lands up here . . .'

'No, not coincidentally. According to the book, Laura wrote to

Ellie through the donor register – God, I don't really understand the details myself. But anyway . . . Ellie got the letter and Laura said she didn't want to meet her, but Ellie decided to track her down, move in on us all so that she could steal you both. Don't you see? This explains everything.'

'It's all bonkers. And if Laura knows, then why hasn't Laura said something? She's said nothing to me or to you. And yet you say she's known since she was eighteen. Sorry, but it just doesn't add up. Are you sure, Cass? Are you sure you haven't just had some really weird and wacky dream? Something caused by those new drugs of yours? I mean, they do say they can do funny things to you, don't they? Are you sure you're not imagining all of this?'

'I'll take you round there. Right now. I know where the key is. I'll show you the manuscript and you can read it for yourself. She's not back from London 'til tomorrow.' I stood up. 'Come on . . . are you coming? Let's go.'

'No. Absolutely not. Of course not. That would be breaking and entry . . .'

'Not with a key.'

'Well we wouldn't be supposed to be there, would we? We'd be burgling her, effectively.'

'Not if we don't take anything. And anyway, forget all that. Surely the point is that she's doing some pretty dreadful stuff to us . . . especially to me. And you're worried about the fact that we might get caught in her house? Well frankly, I don't give a toss whether she knows or not. She *deserves* to bloody well know.'

'Okay okay, calm down, Cass. Please. Let's think about this. So you're saying that Ellie is really Laura's mother, the egg donor.'

'God, Dan, I know this is difficult, but how many more times . . .'

'I think you've flipped.'

'Yes, I know you think that. That's what she wants everyone to think. That's all anyone keeps telling me, that they're "worried about me". I bet she's been feeding you stuff – do you know, I wouldn't be at all surprised if she's been making things up about me. And do you know what else I think? I think she comes into our house and moves things. I think she's had our keys copied and comes in when we're not here. When things go missing I reckon it's her. I think she murdered the hen and left her body in the shed to rot. Don't you think it was weird the way I found her, underneath a sheet of old plastic? Like the hen could have covered herself over before she died – I don't think so, do you?

'She wanted me to read that manuscript, you know. She did. That's why she left it there, sitting on her desk so that I'd see it. That's why she asked me to go round there and get that telephone number for her. Dan, you've got to see. She's fucking mental.'

'Cass –'

'Don't, Dan. For God's sake don't say you don't believe me. On my life . . . Laura's life . . . your life . . . I swear to you that what I am telling you is the truth. And you can see for yourself.'

'Look. I'm not going round there and that's that. But I'll talk to her.'

'Talk to her?'

'Yes. Tomorrow. I'll talk to her when she's back from London. And find out what the hell has been going on.'

'She'll deny it. She'll say it's me that's mad.'

'Well we'll see what she says. Now it seems to me the most important consideration at the moment is Laura, and if it's true what your mother says, that she learned the truth when she was eighteen – nearly three years ago – then we need to get that sorted out, don't we?'

'Oh my God, this is all just too awful. I can't believe what's happening to us.'

'You should have told her, Cass. You should have told her before, when she was younger. Like everyone advised.'

'Everyone! What do they know? The books, the

recommendations. We're not everyone. I wanted her to love me as her own mother. It's all right for you, but for me. God, Dan, I'm not even related to her.'

'You carried her in your womb. Without you she wouldn't be here, would she? It wouldn't have mattered to her. The fact is that she was wanted, really wanted. And she knows how much you love her, what a good mother you've been.'

'Does she? Do you think that?'

'Of course I do. Why wouldn't I?'

'You know damned well why.'

'All that was a very long time ago. I don't see it's going to be helpful to revisit all that stuff, do you? I think what's important is what's going on now. And that's what we've got to deal with. You'll have to talk to her, Cass. It's you that needs to do it, not me. She's coming home tomorrow night. You'll have to do it then. The sooner the better, so that we can get this whole bloody mess sorted out. Trust your mother . . . crazy old woman.'

He reached out and took hold of my hand. 'It'll be okay, Cass. I'm sure it'll be okay. Laura adores you, and the fact that she didn't say anything must mean that she didn't want it brought out in the open. She probably didn't want to upset *you*.'

'It just seems like my whole life is spinning out of control. You, Laura, my mother, my friends. And all since that woman has been in our lives. I hate her, Dan, I really, really hate her for what she's doing to us.'

'Ssssh. I'm sure there's a rational explanation.'

'Rational? Do you know she even wrote about that time when she came here for lunch, when the dog was lost, do you remember? And she wrote that the dog wasn't lost at all, that she'd used it as a ruse to get you alone. And that when you went for that walk later on, you went to see her.'

He was shaking his head slowly, wearing an expression of total incredulity. He was either a bloody good actor or else he really was telling the truth about Ellie. I had no way of knowing which.

'Dan, do you promise me that nothing was going on? That she really is making all of this up?'

'I don't know what else I can say. To be honest, I think you've got to take the whole novel thing with a huge pinch of salt. It hardly sounds like a credible plot to me. If what you say is true, then she's obviously some kind of fantasist – perhaps that's why she writes stories. Who knows? But I'll talk to her tomorrow. So . . .' he stood up and gestured me to come to him. 'A big day for all of us, hey? You, me and, most importantly, Laura. Forget all the other crap.'

'But how can I forget it? *Apparently* she's Laura's biological mother. God, I should have known it would end in tears, messing about with nature. Maybe I just wasn't meant to have children and now I'll lose Laura to her rightful mother.'

'I've never heard such rubbish. You can't just shove a lifetime away like that. You've got to have confidence in yourself, Cass. Laura loves you. Trust me.'

He held me and I felt my body relax into him. I still adored the smell of him, the security of the solid arms of the man I loved. Still loved. God help me, I still loved him. I reached out and put my arms around his waist and squeezed him towards me, as if I was trying to weld our bodies together. I sighed and felt some of the tension of this disgustingly horrible day melt away. I closed my eyes and breathed deeply and, for once, the fist in my stomach started to unclench. If only we could just stay like this, shut out the world and remain here, like this, just Dan and me. That's all I wanted. I wanted our lives back. I wanted normality.

'That's better,' he sighed into my hair. 'I love you, Cass. Please don't go somewhere else . . . in your mind . . . You know what I mean.'

I nodded. 'I don't want to . . . really I don't . . .'

'I know, I know.' He dropped his arms and took a step backwards away from me. 'I think I'll go and catch a bit of *Newsnight*,' he said. 'If you don't mind. Why don't you come with me? Take our minds off all this crap.'

I gestured to the washing up. 'I'll just clear up a bit. Maybe come in in a minute.'

As I stacked, washed, rinsed and dried I thought about Laura's antagonism towards me. It had kicked off around the time she went away to university, after her eighteenth, from memory. I'd put it down to the fact that she was trying to be grown up and independent, that this was all part of the growing up process, needing to separate herself from me, in order to become an independent woman. Now it seemed obvious that it was because she'd found out about me and my grand deception; that our lives had been one big lie. But how could she have borne knowing the truth, without saying anything? My heart bled for her; she must have been devastated. Poor darling Laura. That would explain why she wanted to punish me, why she always seemed so angry with me. I think Dan was wrong. I didn't think Laura loved me. I thought Laura hated me.

About twenty minutes later I poked my head around the door. Dan was holding his mobile, staring at the screen. He looked up at me and I swear he looked guilty.

Later, when he came to bed, I was almost asleep. He snuggled up against me and pulled me close. It felt so good to be near him, and I pretended that I was cocooned in a safe place. When he started to caress me, I responded to him with an urgency fuelled by the fear of what I might lose; and when he made sweet, gentle love to me, I allowed myself to imagine that this was my real world.

I woke up wanting to believe in the loving Dan of the night before. I kept running over what he'd said to me.

'My darling . . . you're so special . . .' he had whispered in my ear before he drifted off to sleep. His arms had remained around me as we slept spooned together, anchoring me to the bed – and to my sanity, it seemed. If he let go, if he cast me off, I'd spin away from him, beyond his reach, beyond the reach of rational thought. Was I losing my grip on reality? I didn't know any more which part of my life was the truth. This? Here with Dan, or between the poisoned pages of that witch's book? I wanted peace so badly even if it meant I had to kid myself that everything was fine. When it wasn't fine. At all.

As soon as Dan left for the office, my devils returned. The tenderness, the lovemaking, was all of that a cynical ploy to distract me from pursuing the truth? Oh God, I had bought a ticket for the rollercoaster and there was no way the seller was going to let me off until I'd completed the ride. I was a prisoner, held fast in the car; I couldn't escape the highs or the lows, I just had to wait for the next crest or dip of my emotions. And the next dip was coming up fast. I was obsessed with how to get through the next ordeal. I was like a puppet whose strings were held firmly in Ellie's hands. Like that balloon seller in Birmingham. All she had to do was let go of my string and I'd crash to the ground or float away into nothingness.

Somehow I managed to work my way around the supermarket even though I was in a somnambulant daze. Thinking about what to feed my family seemed just so mundane, so normal, that it didn't sit comfortably within the current landscape of my life. As if anyone would care about food, and whether I cooked lasagne or cottage pie. Or would they prefer steak? Baked potato or sweet potato? God almighty, it just seemed ludicrous.

At the checkout, the smiling woman – Barbara – at the till, said, 'Got anything nice planned for the weekend?' 'No, not really,' I'd said. 'You?' She did tell me but I wasn't listening. In fact, when I got back in the van to come home, I could barely remember that I'd been shopping at all.

I was halfway through unpacking all the stuff when Amelia's BMW appeared in the drive, her fiftieth birthday present from William. As the car drew up beside me she choked off some operatic diva mid-aria. She opened the door and climbed out. The door slammed shut with the sort of expensive click that Dan would appreciate.

'Ah, that explains why I couldn't get hold of you,' she said, by way of hello. 'You were out. And you hadn't got your mobile switched on.'

'No. Sorry,' I smiled. 'I didn't realize you were back.'

'Only just. I thought I'd come straight over, because I've got something for you . . . Here, let me give you a hand,' She kissed my cheek and swept up two handfuls of shopping bags and together we headed into the house. 'God, don't you just hate it all, shopping? So boring. Don't you ever get yours online? You know Waitrose will deliver from Malvern.'

'Dan's forbidden me to go near Waitrose as I'm always tempted to overspend, and I can't be doing with online. Or it can't be doing with me. Never can get it to work properly. Have you ever thought,' I said as I filled the kettle and stuck it on the Aga, 'just how much time one can waste trying to save time?'

'Suppose . . . Oh crikey, nearly forgot. It's in the car. Wait a sec . . .'

'I'll make coffee.'

'Love one.'

She reappeared, seconds later, with a basket filled with enormous white hydrangeas. 'For you. I thought they'd look lovely on your kitchen table.'

'They're beautiful. Thank you.'

She centred them on the table, having pushed away a pile of post and yesterday's newspaper. 'Covent Garden market. Have you been there? It's the most amazing place. Honestly, Cass, I was like a dog with six tails – so many flowers. It's huge. Terrifying. Anyway Ellie and I got everything sorted out. Phew, lovely, coffee, thanks. I'm *exhausted*.' She sank down into a chair and propped her elbows on the table while I started, somewhat distractedly, putting away the shopping.

'Have you lost weight? And, darling, you do look tired. I didn't think you seemed quite yourself the other day, at the meeting. There's nothing the matter, is there?'

'I'm all right, I suppose.'

'Hmm,' she continued. 'Ellie and I were talking about it. She was worried that she might have upset you, over the flower business. But I said you wouldn't have been remotely upset, probably just pleased to be relieved of it. You weren't upset, were you?'

I shrugged, stared down into my coffee cup. It was all just too draining. 'That all seems rather trivial now, to be honest.' I hadn't decided how honest I was going to be with Amelia, how far I was prepared to go, how much I could trust her to be my friend. 'Did you have a good time in London?'

'Wonderful. You'd have loved it. Only a couple of days, but you know what it's like . . .'

Actually I didn't. 'Hmm,' I said.

'We devoted yesterday morning to jobs, like sorting out the flowers. Thank God we took William's car, otherwise we'd never have fitted everything into mine or Ellie's. And the day before that we did the exhibition which was *wonderful*. If only there weren't so many people. You feel you're on a sort of conveyor belt and you stand back to get a really good feel of some fabulous painting, and then a load of people come and stand in front of you,' she laughed. 'One forgets how many people there are in London, and most of them seem to be foreign. And then at night we went to this fabulous fish place that Ellie knew and had a good old gossip. She's such fun. And her mother joined us.'

'Her mother?'

'Yes. She's incredibly young-looking. Lucky Ellie, having those genes. And isn't it exciting about Laura, and the work experience?'

'Yes.'

'Cass?'

'Hmm?'

'What's wrong? I can tell there's something . . . You don't have to tell me if you don't want to, but if there's anything I can help with . . . It's not something between you and Ellie, is it? She's very fond of you, you know. She kept on telling me how great she thought you were. The house, your garden, what a lovely girl Laura is, how well you've brought her up –'

The cup slipped out of my hand and crashed to the floor. I wished that I could crash to the floor with it. I grabbed some kitchen roll and started mopping up the spilled coffee, picking up the cup which had broken neatly in two.

'Careful. You'll cut yourself. Here, let me.' She took the pieces of china from my hand, placed them together to make a perfect fit. 'My china restorer could make a brilliant job of this, if you wanted. She's not expensive. Only charge you a fiver –'

'Oh for God's sake, Amelia. Just bloody leave it!' Her mouth dropped open in shock. I watched her soft blue eyes grow wide, clouded with confusion. 'Cass . . . I'm so sorry . . .'

I snatched the jagged pieces of china out of her hands and tossed them into the bin. 'It's broken and that's all there is to it.'

When I turned back to her, I noticed she was sucking her finger. When she took it out of her mouth a bead of blood formed.

'Oh God, I'm sorry . . . I'm so sorry, Amelia. That was so clumsy of me. See what I've gone and done. I've cut you. Oh God. How *stupid* of me.'

'It's nothing. Nothing. Honestly. Just, if you've got a plaster . . . You know what fingers are like. It'll stop in a minute.'

I gave her a piece of kitchen roll and she squeezed it onto the wound. 'Hang on, I'll go and get one.'

I felt dreadful. Truly dreadful. Poor Amelia. It wasn't her fault at all. She didn't know anything about what was going on. She was merely being her normal, uncomplicated, lovely self. And I was about to lose her as a friend, because I couldn't hold any compartment of my life together anymore. Did I really want this? No daughter, no husband, no friends? Then what? The only thing left would be the void, the void which I'd escaped in the past. But I didn't know this time. I really didn't know. It just felt like I was already in it, sucked into a giant vacuum of nothingness. No thoughts, no pain, no hurt.

My legs felt leaden as I descended the stairs. Amelia was leaning up against the Aga, still holding the sheet of kitchen roll which was now more red than white. I unwrapped the plaster and she held up her finger. I laid the sticky end around the top and rested the dressing side against the place where I had wounded her. But I could tell from her face that I hadn't just wounded her physically. I could tell that she didn't know what to say to me. She was offended, hurt and confused. I looked at the beautiful hydrangeas that she had placed on my table. And then I reached out and took her hand. 'I'm so sorry, Amelia. It's just that Ellie told me her mother was dead, that she'd electrocuted herself in the bath. So you see I'm feeling a little confused.'

'How very odd. That can't be right, you must have misunderstood.

I mean you must have got that completely wrong, because I promise you she's very much alive and kicking and in the rudest health. How strange, and what a dreadful thought.' She shuddered. 'Oh no, doesn't bear thinking about. That's really strange. Oh well,' she glanced at her watch. 'I'm sorry, Cassandra,' – she never called me Cassandra – 'but I promised I'd meet Ellie. I'm going to be late. Sorry. I'd love to stay and chat, really. Another time?'

'Of course. Another time.'

We kissed and said goodbye. Another part of my life I had successfully fucked up.

So, yes. That fateful day. God, I can still remember walking through the front door and just standing there, unable to believe what I was seeing. I mean, you never ever forget something like that. Amelia had dropped me off so I was quite alone. I didn't want to go further into the house at first, because I was afraid that whoever had done this might still be there. I wished I'd got Coco with me, but she was still at Sally's, otherwise she'd have let me know straight away if there was a stranger in the house, wouldn't she? But, honestly, you just wouldn't believe the scene in front of me. Talk about devastation. It was . . . well I don't know . . . words just seem inadequate. How do you describe that? It was just . . . horrible. I remember thinking who would do something like that? What kind of sick person would do this to another person?

I can't remember what time it was when I spoke to Dan. It might have been while the police were there, I'm really not sure. He called me, actually, not the other way round. I'd been meaning to, but I'd had other things to think about. So at first I was pleased to get his call, but then he started saying all this weird stuff about the book I was writing, and things I was supposedly saying to Cass. Honestly, as I said to him, he wasn't making any sense at all. I made him repeat what he'd said about the book because I wasn't sure I'd heard him correctly. And when he told me I was like, 'You can't be serious . . .' I said – and I shouldn't have been making light of the situation, it probably wasn't remotely appropriate – but I said, 'God, I wish I'd got that kind of imagination . . .' I think he said he'd call me later, talk to me later. I wasn't sure, but I really had enough to deal with without that kind of rubbish, don't you think?

18

The floodlights tripped as Dan's car came into the drive. Laura had originally planned to come back tomorrow afternoon, in time for the quiz, but Dan had said he would persuade her to come back tonight so that we'd have a chance to talk. It was going to be *the* single most important conversation of my life and I was feeling terrified.

I couldn't see them from the kitchen, because the windows occupied the wall to the rear of the house, but I saw the pool of light spread across the hall carpet, so I peeked through the glazed front door panel. From the protection of the shadows I watched them get out of the car. Dan walked around to the boot to lift out Laura's bag. She still used the rucksack that we'd bought her for her gap year. I'd suggested that she might like a suitcase instead, but she was adamant that a rucksack was much easier to cart around. Usually one of the first things she would do was empty half of it onto the utility room floor. Normally I would then go in, separate it out into two loads of colours and whites, and then I'd programme the machine and start the cycle. Before I went to bed I'd pull out the load, pop it into the drier, and put in the next load to wash, ready to do the same tomorrow morning. These were the normal, mumsy little things that I loved doing for her, even though I knew she was perfectly capable of doing it for herself. I'd felt for a long time like I was on borrowed time. Borrowed time. Time at school, gap year travelling, university life, getting a job – all things that would increase the distance between us, all flying-the-nest type things designed to get me used to the day when she would move all her stuff out for good. The day I dreaded, when Laura's room would become a spare room, when Laura would morph from resident to guest. Now it seemed more likely she'd turn from resident to stranger.

As they walked across the driveway, Dan put his free arm around Laura's shoulder and ruffled her hair playfully. How sweet they were together, father and daughter. Close. Look at how close.

Deep down I was afraid I'd already lost them both. I had done all I could to make them see how good I was. I'd taken trouble over preparing the supper. I'd washed my hair and carefully blow-dried it. I'd put make-up on and changed into tidy clothes. I wanted them to approve of me, to believe that I was special, to make them realize that they would miss me, that I was important to them.

Laura gave me a lovely hug and then immediately said, 'Sorry, Mum. Dying for a pee, back in a sec,' leaving Dan and me alone in the kitchen.

Dan put Laura's bag down and set his briefcase and laptop next to it.

'Have you said anything to her?' I asked, keeping my voice low. He shook his head. 'Something else has happened.' He just stood there with a really cool, sort of anxious expression on his face. I noticed he didn't remove his coat, and he was still holding the car keys, not placing them on the hook, as he usually did.

'What?'

'With Ellie,' he said.

'What about her?' I said, warily.

'Her house was trashed while she was away. The whole place vandalized . . . You hadn't heard?'

'No. Nobody's told me . . .' I stood rooted to the spot while my mind spun. 'Oh my God.'

'I called her, like I said I would. She was right in the middle of dealing with the police and everything. But she sounded in a dreadful state. Anyway I said I'd go round when I got home, to check she's okay.'

'No! You can't. No, Dan. I don't know what's behind all this, but knowing her there's some sort of trap, something devious going on. Don't fall for it.'

He stood there wearing that same cold expression, just shaking his head. 'Cass, I don't know what's going on in that head of yours. I told her that you'd been round there, as she'd requested, to get that telephone number – just to say that the house was obviously okay when you left it – and you know what?'

I shook my head. I could almost guess what was coming.

'She said she didn't call you. That there was no key left outside. That whoever broke in had come through the back door, smashing the glass, maybe getting the key off the hook nearby. She said she hadn't asked you to go into her house, Cassandra.'

Cassandra. I was being called Cassandra rather a lot, these days.

'Jesus Christ!' I sat down slowly. I wasn't sure I was capable of taking in what he was saying, what it meant.

'She's setting me up.'

'Is she?'

'Of course! You can't believe I did that . . .'

Laura was standing in the kitchen doorway. 'Did what?'

I just put my hands up in the air in a gesture of surrender. But Laura didn't notice.

'God, what about Ellie? Poor thing. Who would do something like that? Dad said she sounded really shaken. Hey, Mum. Do you think I should offer to go and stay with her, keep her company, help her clear up?'

I couldn't answer. I just shrugged and turned towards the Aga to fiddle with a pan that didn't require any attention. Next thing I knew Laura was speaking on her mobile.

'Oh hi, Ellie, it's me Laura . . . Listen, I was thinking, wondering if you'd like some company tonight . . . I could come and stay over if you wanted . . . You would? . . . No, it wouldn't be a problem at all . . . I think Dad's coming over now, so I'll come with him.'

'Is that all right, Mum?'

'I need to talk to you, Laura. About something really important.'

'Fine, Mum. We'll talk tomorrow, promise. But right now I think I should be with Ellie.'

I was just so tired, so exhausted by everything that I no longer had the will to argue. 'Fine,' was all I could manage.

While Laura fiddled about in her rucksack, getting out her washbag, clean pants, whatever, Dan just stood there watching me watching her.

'Will you be long?' I said to him.

'I really don't know,' he said, and then they were gone. So that was that. Alone again, me and the clock, tick-tick-tick.

Forty-five minutes. More than half a bottle of white wine, and forty-five long, drawn-out, excruciatingly painful minutes. Dan finally came home, shrugged off his coat, walked through the kitchen without speaking, just a nod of his head. A few moments later he was back, standing in the doorway, a glass of whisky in one hand, a cigarette in the other.

'You're smoking,' I said.

'Yep. Cass, we need to talk.'

'Do we?'

'I can't believe it, Cass. It's just disgusting. Unbelievable. "Bitch" scrawled on the mirror over the fireplace. Her clothes thrown all over the floor and . . . God . . . it's bloody horrible . . . whoever did it has even urinated on her underwear. She's in a hell of a state.'

'So the police have been?'

'Yeah, of course. They've been to take a statement and to check for fingerprints.'

Mine would be all over her desk. What else had I touched? I

hadn't been upstairs . . . Had I touched any of her personal things? I couldn't think. Apart from what I'd seen in the book I was hazy about what I'd done. I remembered waking up on the carpet, not knowing where I was or how long I'd been there.

'Cass . . . listen to me . . .' his voice was gentle, soothing. 'I think it might help if you saw someone, talked to someone. I think it might help us all, hmm? Will you? Will you do it for me, and for Laura?'

'You can't believe I did that. You really can't.'

'No, I can't. But then I can't think who else could have done it.'

'She did it herself. That's what she did. To make it look like I'd done it. She called me to make me go around there. To set me up. Why can't you see? The book, everything she's done . . . there's a huge pattern here. She thinks if she drives me insane she'll get you. I'll be nicely out of the way. A lot safer than murder, and Laura's a lot less likely to miss a mother who's crazy than one who's dead, or suicidal, don't you think?'

'I don't know what to think,' was all he said.

'You think I'm going insane . . .' I could feel the tears welling. A drop spilled out of my left eye and I quickly swept it away with my sleeve. 'Just why are you so defensive about her? Why is it that you won't hear anything bad about her?'

'Because it's all in your mind, Cassandra.'

'And what if it isn't in my mind, Dan? What if it's real?'

'But sweetheart, it isn't. You've got to stop this. It's all in your imagination.'

'Like Rome was in my imagination?'

'Yes, like Rome was in your imagination.'

But there was something about his face – a slight shadow, a darkening, just a flicker of something. He left the room, as though he needed to take time out, but he was soon back with a replenished glass.

'It doesn't really matter,' I said. 'What you did, what you're doing.

None of it really matters. The trouble is, Dan, it's just all too easy for you, isn't it?'

'Meaning?'

'It's all too easy to blame me, to dredge up my anxieties, my insecurities. It's all so convenient when anything gets in your way – when I get in your way – to accuse me of instability. You know how threatened that makes me feel, you know how to push my buttons and sometimes . . . well sometimes . . . I wonder if you're using it as a weapon in order just to defend yourself, and your behaviour . . . like some bloody great dirty bomb.'

'Well you would think that, wouldn't you?'

'I don't know. Maybe I would think that because it's true. But it seems to me that I'm never allowed to have thoughts that might be true.'

'Like before? Like all those years ago, when you ended up in the fucking Abbey?'

'Yeah. When I ended up in the loony bin, the *fucking* Abbey. My *nervous* fucking breakdown. I'm the one that's insane, so it always has to be me that's in the wrong. What the hell can I do? I just feel so powerless, Dan. I can't fight against you, can I? I couldn't fight against you then.'

'Fight against me? Do you know what it was like for me – for Laura and me, for us?'

'Yes, I do, Dan. Because you've told me, many times. You've said how you had to take care of Laura, how you had to get your mother to take care of her. You've told me what it was like to find me . . . to go with me in the ambulance, to wait while they pumped my stomach . . . to have to go through all the thought processes, the questions, the embarrassment of having to face up to the fact that we were dysfunctional . . . maybe even face up to your responsibility, your part in what had happened to push me over the edge. But you'd never really admit that you'd done anything . . . you'd never really be honest, would you? About how you were trying to push me out of Laura's life. How you were intent on getting her to bond with you so much more than me. About how, even then, you played on my insecurities in order to make you feel justified, and to make me look bad. I know you had an affair with some woman in Rome.'

'No, Cass . . . you are so wrong –'

'And you blame me, make me take the blame for falling over the edge . . .' My voice rose, until I was screaming at him: 'YOU FUCKING PUSHED ME, DANIEL BURTON . . . YOU FUCKING PUSHED ME . . .!'

'I've stayed with you. I stayed with you through all of that. Don't you think other men might have left you . . . might have had enough?'

'Well maybe you should ask yourself why you haven't left me. Maybe my inadequacies make you feel better, I don't know. Maybe you use my insecurities to cover up your own. It's all too fucking complicated for me. All I know, Dan, is that I've always had to feel grateful to you, grateful to you for staying with me, grateful to you for bearing to be with me – me . . . this fruitcake . . . this utter nutcase. This *person* – God am I really a person? – this *person* that you can manipulate and control with the smallest click of your fingers. Well now you've got an accomplice, and it's all so perfect, isn't it? You can both manipulate me as much as you like, it seems, and there isn't a damned thing I can do about it.'

'You're crazy!' he said. He picked up the car keys and grabbed his coat.

'What about her book, then? What about her fucking book?'

'There is no book, Cass. It doesn't exist.' He slammed the front door behind him. I was left standing alone in the kitchen. I was panting. I heard the car engine start and then drive away.

I picked up his laptop and took it into his study and set it on his desk. I wasn't really very good at computers, but I knew the basics. I knew how to do the internet, use Google; and I also knew how to activate 'in private browsing'. As I watched the screen come alive, and waited for all the files and gizmos to open up, I wondered why I hadn't thought of doing this before.

The first thing I did was to type Eleanor Black into the search window. I waited while the list of entries came up, something in the region of seven million, five hundred thousand entries. But I was only interested in page one and any that linked up with Amazon. There were Eleanor Blacks on Facebook, LinkedIn, and all sorts of other Eleanor Blacks, but I couldn't see any that appeared to have a chain of books attached to them. I flicked onto page two of the search result. None there either. Strange. I tried again, this time with 'Ellie Black', but same thing – lots of connections to black clothes but none to books. I didn't remember her mentioning that this was her first novel. But then did I remember her mentioning that it wasn't? I remembered, all too clearly, her saying how she liked to get into the middle of the action, sort of live her books. She was certainly doing that. But had she really not had anything published? Or was it the first time she was writing under her own name? Maybe there was some small shred of truth in all the lies she had spun to me. I remembered on her manuscript it had definitely said Eleanor Black below the title . . . what was it? *Gaslight*. Why gaslight? I know we lived in a country backwater, but we'd had electricity for quite a few years now. Idly, I tapped the word 'gaslight' into the search window. The first result was a movie title from 1944. And underneath that, good old Wikipedia's 'Gaslighting'. Just one click and it all became clear. At last, I began to understand the game she was playing.

'**Gaslighting** is a form of <u>psychological abuse</u> in which false information is presented with the intent of making a victim doubt his or her own <u>memory</u> and <u>perception</u>. It may simply be the <u>denial</u> by an abuser that previous abusive incidents

ever occurred, or it could be the staging of bizarre events by
the abuser with the intention of <u>disorienting</u> the victim.' [1]

There was no doubt. No reason to doubt myself anymore. I had been
right all the time and there was the evidence. She was deliberately
setting me up to make it look like I'd trashed her house. She wanted
everyone to think I was insane and she was succeeding.

I had no idea where Dan spent the night. I only knew that I was
awake long before the alarm went off at 7.30 a.m. and that his side of
the bed was untouched. I went for a shower and dressed quickly.
Then I phoned her.

'Hello . . .'

'It's me, Cassandra.'

'Yes.'

'I know what you're trying to do. I know about gaslighting. You
asked me to go round to your house, to get that telephone number for
you to set me up, didn't you?'

'I don't know what you're talking about. But what I do know is
that you rang me from my house and called me a fucking bitch, said
something about a book I've supposedly been writing. Cassandra . . .
I feel really sorry for you, honestly. But you're sick and it's time you
stopped doing things to upset me. You can't get away with it, you
know, you're going to be in real trouble. And now this latest . . . it's
all too much and I want you to stop it.'

'What latest?'

'As if you need to ask. My tyres, of course. Each one, slashed. I'm
sorry Cass, I don't want to involve the police because I know you're

---

[1] Wikipedia <u>http://en.wikipedia.org/wiki/Gaslighting</u> (accessed 26.4.2012)

ill, but they're going to find out it's you. I mean, you must realize, your fingerprints will be all over my house.'

'You fucking bitch!' I shrieked down the phone. Dan was standing in the doorway. I hadn't heard him come in. He looked rough; his face white, his jaw iron-grey.

I put the phone down. 'That's what was written on her mirror,' he said. *'You fucking bitch.'*

An image came unbidden, a cornered fox, a pack of baying hounds, lips snarling and jowls slavering, baring razor-sharp teeth, circling and watching in an ecstasy of anticipation, sensing with a primeval certainly that the moment was upon us. I could almost feel the remnants of my resistance seeping like lifeblood into the floor beneath me.

'How could you, Cass? Whatever possessed you? This has got to stop. I don't think you realize just how much trouble you're going to be in if you carry on this campaign of . . . of . . . God, I don't even know what to call it.' He ran his fingers through his hair in a gesture of exasperation that I knew all too well. 'What the hell did you think you were doing?'

'I didn't do it. Listen, I haven't been anywhere near her house. I've been here all night. If only you'd been here with me you'd have known that. Where were you?'

'I slept in the car for most of the night and then I went round to see Ellie, to see if she was okay. And that's when I saw what you'd done to her car.'

'Dan! I didn't do it.'

'Then why did I find a knife by her car? A knife just like one of ours.'

'It can't be ours. I'll prove it. I'll get it.' And then I remembered . . . the missing knife. I started to tremble and I could feel my lungs constricting, struggling for air. I had to think. I spoke quickly, desperately. 'One went missing. I couldn't find it when I was making

270

the chutney. It had gone, Dan. She must have taken it.'

'Oh Cass. You're sick. This isn't normal behaviour, this is madness. All of it. I just don't know what to do, how to handle you.'

'No, Dan. It's not true. I'm not sick. You have to believe me. I know what she's doing.'

'No more, Cass. He just stared at me, shaking his head slowly. 'I've got to get ready for the village hall. I've got stuff I need to do. I don't want to leave you alone. I'm worried about what you might do next. Will you be okay? Can I trust you not to do anything silly?'

'I haven't done anything,' I said. 'I just wish you would believe me.' Silent tears were dripping onto my cheeks, sliding down to my mouth. I could taste the salt.

'If only I could, Cass.' And then I was alone once more.

Because I simply didn't know what else to do, I put on my boots and my jacket and went outside into the garden. I almost felt calm, or was it just numb? Perhaps it was a belief that things couldn't possibly get any worse and so my emotions had just shut down. I didn't seem able to feel anything at all, apart from a sense of grim defeat. Even the thoughts of confronting Laura seemed to have dulled from sheer blind panic to a sense of unavoidable destiny. I had lost her. I hadn't realized it, but I'd lost her nearly three years ago. Everything since then had been a lie between us. She had kept her secret from me since the time my mother had told her; and I had kept a secret from her since the day she was born. I suppose you could say there was a kind of natural justice at play. Not only would she know I was a liar, but she would now believe that I was some kind of insane stalker. Funny, as my mother would have said, you never know what the day will bring.

It was a beautiful day. The sort of perfect day that makes it hard to believe that bad things can happen. Like 9/11. I remember people remarking that all of that murderous devastation unfolded on a perfect day, against that cloudless, infinite blue backdrop pierced by two identical towers polished silver by the sun's brilliance.

It was the kind of day that would normally have promised the scent of wood smoke from crackling logs. There, in the old lean-to, was our store neatly stacked and graded by Dan, with big fat logs at the bottom and little ones at the top. Their many shades of gold and amber harmonized with the dead and dying leaves that crunched and squelched beneath my boots. It was perfect early October weather, clear and sunny. The air had that slightly musty bonfire-ish taint, that damp, mildewy, hibernating essence of autumn, the season of poetic melancholy, of essential death and decomposition before a new cycle of life. A skein of Canada geese flew high overhead, honking their bossy commentary to one another. Oh, to be that free. And what was I to them? A tiny little speck of insignificance, whose imprint, whose legacy upon the earth would be no more than that of the withering oak leaf in my hand.

It had been a very long time since I'd had any suicidal thoughts. But now, engulfed by this torture – no nightmare, but reality – I felt the first, treacherous little demon come raking around the edge of my mind. Is it worth it? it said. Wouldn't it be so much better . . . ? I shook my head firmly and put my hands over my ears and said aloud, 'No . . . no . . . please . . . not again . . .' I couldn't let it happen again. I was better now, over it. I was *me*. Cassandra. I knew me. I had to hold on to that belief – that I really did know me. Normal. And sane. Most of all, sane. If I took the so-called easy way out – though there was nothing easy, to my mind, about taking your own life – I'd just confirm that I really was some crazy woman, crazy enough to leave her family without answers, without understanding. How could I do to my family what my own father had done to me? No, I still had love and compassion inside of me, even if I'd forfeited Laura's. I was not that old Cassandra. Without a shadow of a doubt, I truly believed that.

I was done with all that. I had blocked it out, as though it had all happened to another person, somebody I barely knew; like an anecdote I'd once heard related about an acquaintance. They say that suicide's a heritable trait, apparently. If that was supposed to mean like father, like daughter, it wasn't going to be me. Not this me. I was sane. Ellie was trying to drive me mad – maybe she even wanted to drive me to suicide – but I was *sane*. I was never going back to the mental hospital. *Never*. I had such *fond* memories of the place. I remember that from the outside it looked like a smart country hotel, a cruel kind of facade, perhaps, to assuage the consciences of those abandoning their loved ones. You left me behind, Dan. You abandoned me. You *made* me say goodbye to Laura. My arms ached from the moment I left her until the moment I was allowed home again. I so wanted you to bring her to see me. I thought maybe just once, for an hour, maybe one Sunday afternoon I'd look up and see you both there. But you'd decided on the tough love regime. But I wasn't there against my will, you said. I was told that by you, by the nurses, and by the professionals.

The pills were the highlight of the day because they provided some degree of numbness, dulling the edge of the pain in the same way that a hard rock can scrape the edge off a sharp blade.

People think that there is such a thing as a nervous breakdown. But I know there isn't, not as such. It's not so much a breakdown as a gradual erosion of all the little bits and pieces of yourself; little bits and pieces of your soul that shrivel through want of nourishment. You, Dan, didn't need me. Laura . . . none of you needed me anymore. And part of the problem was that I'd never really been convinced that you had ever needed me.

Therapy taught me that I shouldn't be so emotionally dependent upon you, Dan; that I had unreasonable expectations that you could make my insecurities better, by yourself. The way I heard it, I wasn't being fair on you, with my unreasonable expectations. So when I came back, all better, I'd swept up all my anger and stashed it deep inside the dustbin of my emotions. But do you know what? I never got around to emptying it, until now. And that lump of anger was still there, raw as ever. And I was not going to let you, Ellie or *anyone* take my daughter away from me.

I had to speak to Laura. I knew I needed to be strong and to shut out the doubts. I had to keep believing in myself even if no one else did. I went back into the house, changed out of my boots and picked up the keys to the van. I drove straight to the village hall, where I assumed Laura would be. I would ask her to come with me and we would go home and talk there, uninterrupted.

There were lots of cars I recognized in the tiny car park, as well as Nick Gale's trailer attached to his pick-up truck. It seemed slightly surreal in the circumstances to think back to last year when I was here with everyone else, with all my friends, bustling around with my flowers. But now I was no longer needed. It was as if I was being rubbed out of the picture, growing paler, formless and abstract; a series of watery, indistinct brushstrokes.

I paused in the doorway of the hall – invisible, it seemed, as I watched them all carrying out their particular duties. No one appeared to notice me, but maybe they were just ignoring me. I was becoming accustomed to this position of outsider, always looking on, observing, rather than participating in what should have been my life.

I couldn't see Laura. And I couldn't see Amelia or Sally, or her, either. I could see some of the other village women and Dan helping Nick Gale position the chairs around the trestle tables. Dan had his back turned to me. He said something to Nick, who nodded. And then he walked over to the door at the far end, the door which was normally shut because it was a fire exit but today it was propped open

– presumably to allow the workforce to go out for a fag. I could see that the tablecloths were on the tables and the flowers were set out. Small bunches of bluey-mauve hydrangeas in lime-green glasses. Simple and pretty. Hardly creative, I thought, bitchily.

I suddenly felt nervous about stepping inside to search for Laura. Perhaps Dan might humiliate me in front of Ellie and everyone; maybe accuse me once more of slashing her tyres. I could feel myself growing hot, clammy and light-headed. Cold water. I needed cold water. I reversed back to the entrance lobby and pushed open the door to the ladies' loo. The air was chilly, and smelt of industrial-strength disinfectant, Jeyes Fluid and cheap soap. I turned on the tap and splashed my face, then cupped my hands and gulped down a few mouthfuls of icy water. I turned off the tap and took a paper towel from the shelf and started mopping my face dry. In the quiet, I could hear the drift of voices coming through the top window, which was propped open.

As I tuned into the registers, I could make out Dan, and then Amelia and Sally. In between I could also make out Ellie, and then I was sure I heard my name. Every sinew in my body tightened and I held my breath, straining to hear. I craned towards the window like an FM aerial searching for the optimum reception.

'Poor Cass.' Now it was Sally's voice. 'I've been worried about her for a while, actually. She just hasn't seemed herself. At first I wondered if she was perhaps drinking too heavily . . . although maybe I shouldn't say that. And I remember you saying, Ellie, right when you first met her, that she'd confided in you.'

'That's right, she did. I was flattered, really, that she was being so open. But in a way I thought it was strange the way she disclosed so much to a relative stranger. And funny you should say about the drinking, because she suggested we have wine that afternoon instead of tea. Of course I didn't mind, it seemed just fun at the time. Do you remember, Dan? Didn't you have to come and collect the car that evening because she wasn't fit to drive back?'

'Yes, I remember. Maybe she felt safe, then, with you. Her drinking has been creeping up.' He didn't mention the two bottles the other night, and I was grateful for that. He went on, 'She's so fragile. Always has been. I blame it all on myself. It's my fault. I shouldn't have let this happen.'

'You mustn't blame yourself.' Ellie's voice. 'I think you've been incredibly supportive. It can't be easy living with someone who's so volatile. It must be really hard on you . . . and on Laura as well. It's funny, isn't it, how things seem to be all slotting into place, the strange things that have been going on? I think she was upset about our going shopping for those bay trees, Amelia, remember? It was like they just died, overnight. Like they'd been poisoned – I think I could smell bleach or something around the pots. I didn't like to say anything, obviously. But, you know, I think she must have poisoned them.'

'Oh, Jesus!' Dan exclaimed.

She was brilliant. I had to hand it to her. She had it all planned in labyrinthine intricacy. A chess grand master, every move foreseen, and every challenge pre-empted. I couldn't believe what I was hearing, but I was mesmerized by her cleverness.

Now it was Dan's turn to twist the knife in deeper. 'I've been trying to get her to talk to me, but I don't seem to be able to get through to her. She won't let me help her.'

'Because she's paranoid, Dan. Paranoid and irrational. How can you get through to someone when they're suffering from a mental illness? She needs treatment. She needs to be in a safe place.' Ellie's voice was soothing, clucking like a mother hen. 'Dan. It's not your fault. It's terribly hard on you and Laura. We must think about Laura. She can stay with me for as long as she likes if you think that might be . . . Oh dear, I don't know if this is the right thing to say. I mean I can't believe I'm saying this . . . if you think she would be safer away from Cass.'

Then Amelia's voice: 'Oh God. I'm so sorry, Dan. But when I called in to see her yesterday she just seemed so peculiar. She dropped a cup on the floor and when I suggested she get it mended she lost her temper and ripped it from my hands. She actually cut me. See, I've still got the plaster.'

'Amelia, I'm so sorry. I don't know what to say.'

'I know. It seems incredible that we're all standing here talking about our friend being a threat to anyone, but I suppose one has to think about what's best. I mean, we'd never forgive ourselves if anything happened to Laura, would we? And she must be kept away from you, Ellie. It's okay, Dan. Don't worry. You must try not to worry. She just needs help. Poor Cass . . . Oh dear, it's all so jolly difficult. I wonder if Patrick might be able to do anything – perhaps you could talk to him about getting some kind of restraining or protection order, to keep her away from Ellie.' I could feel myself sinking down. Patrick, Sally's husband, was a solicitor. Was I going to be confronted, now, by police, solicitors, charges? Was I really *not* dreaming all this?

'Do you really think that's necessary? I mean, not for my sake. I wouldn't want to make life any more difficult for you, Dan, than it already is, but if you think it would be safer for Laura. Goodness, I don't really know what to think.' I couldn't believe how sincerely concerned Ellie could sound.

'I think you've been incredibly thoughtful throughout. Too thoughtful.' I could picture Dan putting his hand on her arm; I could see him smiling at her, so gratefully. If only he bloody well knew. If only they all bloody well knew. 'And hard as it sounds, perhaps we do need to think about people's safety now . . . Cass's safety.' I'd heard enough. It was clear that Laura wasn't at the village hall, and I thought she must be at Ellie's house. If they were talking about solicitors and restraining orders, I might not have much more time in which to speak to her.

And there was another thing I needed to do. I had to get hold of the manuscript. It was the only proof I had that could back up my story. If other people could read what she'd written and see the awful filth on those pages, then they'd understand. They'd realize it wasn't me going mad, but her. Just the title page would be proof enough, surely. I just hoped they were so deeply locked into the conversation about how they could deal with the Cassandra problem that they wouldn't notice me leaving the front of the building. The car park wasn't full. There were lots of gaps between the cars. Nick Gale's pick-up truck was beside Dan's Audi. Amelia's BMW was beside Sally's Merc, and then there were half a dozen or so others between me and my van. I walked over to it without looking behind me. Although the full impact had yet to hit me, deep down I knew that my life here, in this community, was over. There was really nothing left for me at all. Dan? Would I want this Dan, who could truly believe all these lies about me? And he certainly wouldn't want to have the 'me' he now thought I was. And what about Laura?

I arrived at Ellie's. I walked slowly to the front of the house and tried the door handle, getting a sense of *déjà vu* as it swung open. I stepped inside. I heard the dog yap a couple of times from the other side of the kitchen door. Then I heard a voice, Laura's voice, call out.

'Hello?'

'Hi,' I said. 'It's me.'

'Mum!' She sounded really surprised. She was sprawled out on the leather sofa, but she sat up. I sat down opposite her, on the other sofa. Although the wood burner was blazing away energetically, to me the room felt chilled. 'All seems pretty tidy. Was there a lot to clear up?'

'Upstairs was the worst, but we attacked most of it last night.

Poor Ellie . . . it was just awful . . .'

'Hmm,' I shivered.

A half-drunk mug of coffee stood on the floor beside Laura. And then beside that was a stack of white paper. I could feel a vague wateriness in my stomach.

'What are you reading?' I tried to keep my voice even and my face neutral.

'Ellie's novel. God, it's so exciting. I'm completely hooked on it. I'm only halfway through, but it's gripping.'

'She said you could read it?'

She nodded. 'I said how much fun I thought it would be to read a novel *before* it's been published.'

'So . . . what do you think of it?'

'It's really good. Quite dark. There's some pretty nasty people in the story.'

'And do you recognize any of them?'

'Recognize any of them? No. Why would I? Oh, you think maybe she's basing her characters on people like us? Can I see any of our funny little foibles, you mean?'

'I suppose . . .'

She laughed. 'No, not really. Although the slimeball who molested her might have certain similarities with Sally's husband, if I think about it.'

I didn't remember anyone molesting her. I picked up a sheet from the pile on the floor and quickly scanned the lines. This was different. This was not the same style of writing. For a start it was written in the third person, and there was a character called Doug coming out of a privy, hitching up the buckle on his breeches. His breeches?

'Laura, what's this about?'

'It's about a woman who was a child evacuee in the Second World War. How she went to stay with this family here, in

Worcestershire, and the husband abused her. So when she's older she goes back to wreak her revenge on him. At least I think that's the gist of it. It's not finished. Her research is brilliant. That's why she came here, obviously.'

'It's set in the 1940s?'

'Well, yeah. That's when it starts. And then ten years later, early fifties, when the woman returns to get her own back.'

Once again I felt that my brain simply wasn't big enough to deal with this. So the manuscript I had read wasn't Ellie's book because, apparently, she was writing a historical novel – the book that Laura was reading. *That* was Ellie's book. Just how many books was the crazy bitch writing? No wonder she hadn't wanted to tell me what her book was about.

I got up from the sofa and walked over to Ellie's desk. Laura's eyes followed me. I stood in front of it, looking down, remembering when I'd last been there, what I had read of *her* novel. There was nothing about the Second World War in it. Nothing about evacuees. There was nothing about any of that, because her novel was all about *us*.

I had no choice. I put my hand on the drawer handle and pulled it open.

'Mum! What are you doing? You can't open up Ellie's drawers . . .'

I ignored her. I looked in the drawer. It wasn't there. I opened up the next drawer, and the next . . . nothing.

Laura had come over to my side. She put her hand on my arm. 'Mum. You mustn't do that. That's prying.'

'I know. But there's something I have to find.'

'What?'

'A manuscript. A novel she was writing.'

'But I've got it. It's over there.'

'No.' I couldn't keep the note of desperation out of my voice. 'She wasn't writing that one, she was writing another one.'

'Mum! What are you talking about? That's her novel. I've just been reading it.'

I put my hands on her shoulders. 'Laura, no. You don't understand. There's *another* novel. I've seen it. I've read it. It's about . . . oh God . . . it's about *us*! It's about you, and me and Dad, and *her*. I'm telling you, I've read the bloody thing.'

Laura had gone as white as a sheet. She pushed my hands away. 'Mum, please, you're frightening me.' Her mouth was open and she was looking at me in complete shock and confusion. 'Mum, I don't understand. I don't know what you're talking about. How can you have read it? Did she show it to you? Did she tell you she was writing about us?'

'No. No. I can't explain at the moment. I can't tell you. But I promise you, Laura, on mine and your lives, that I am not making this up. There is something really crazy going on here. She's trying to convince everyone that I'm mad, that I've been doing all these crazy things, and I haven't. It's her. She's the one that's crazy, but nobody can see it.'

'Oh Mum!' Tears were dribbling down her cheeks. 'Mum, you're really scaring me. Dad said . . . Dad said last night . . .' now she was sobbing, struggling to get the words out. 'Dad said that he was worried about you, that he thought you might be losing it. Oh please, Mum, don't behave like this. I'm really frightened. It's scary. Stop it, Mum.'

'Laura, I'm sorry. I'm really sorry and I don't want to frighten you. Come here . . .' I reached out for her, grabbed her and pulled her to me and squeezed her tightly. 'I love you, Laura. I love you so much. You know I'd never do anything to hurt you. I wouldn't let anything or anybody hurt you.'

'But Mum . . . Ellie . . . what you said . . . none of it makes any sense. And I'm worried, so worried about you. Tell me, Mum, tell me the truth. You didn't do this to Ellie's house, did you? It wasn't you that broke in?'

'Well of course it wasn't me. But that's what she wants everyone to think.'

Laura was shaking her head. 'Then why were your glasses here, upstairs, in her bedroom?'

'I've never been in her bedroom. I have no idea. What do you mean?'

'Last night. When we were clearing up the mess in her room, I saw your glasses, or a pair that were identical to yours, sitting on her dressing table. I picked them up, said they looked like yours. And she said . . . she said . . . she didn't know where they'd come from. You said you were looking for them last night, you said to Dad had he seen them. Don't you remember?'

I shook my head. 'No, I don't remember that.'

'And why would they be here, upstairs in her bedroom?'

'Because she put them there! Just like she planned it so that my fingerprints would be here. She asked me to come to her house, while she was in London. She called me, said she needed a telephone number, and told me where the key was. Now she's denying that she ever did that. So you see my fingerprints will be here. That's why she did it, to set me up. And her novel was here on her desk, like she meant for me to read it.'

I sank down onto the chair arm and hugged my arms across my stomach. Laura knelt down beside me and took hold of my hand. She started to stroke the back of it, as if she was tending to an invalid, which I suppose she believed she was.

'Ellie wouldn't do such a thing, Mum. I know she wouldn't. You've really got her all wrong. You see, she's worried too, concerned. And I know she wants to help you. She knows how difficult it is for you . . . for *all* of us.'

'Do you really believe that I could do this, that I could slash her tyres?'

'I don't know, Mum. I just don't know. I guess if you're sick . . .'

I took hold of her hand and clutched it between both of mine. 'The only thing I really, really care about is that you don't believe her. It doesn't matter about the others. It doesn't really matter what happens to me, but I want you to believe in me. Look at me, Laura. Just look at me.'

She met my gaze with her lovely, straightforward, clear greeney-blue eyes. 'I am not mad. There is nothing wrong with my mind. I am not imagining things, and I am not lying to you.'

'But Mum, it wouldn't be the first time you'd lied to me, would it?' she said.

'Oh, Laura. I am so sorry. So very sorry.' I collapsed against her and my daughter held me as I sobbed, her lips against my ear: 'Ssssh, Mum . . . it's okay . . . ssssh . . .' And then, through my tears, I saw Dan and Ellie framed in the doorway. Dan walked towards me, bent down and took hold of my arm while Ellie prised Laura away from me. I stood up, supported by Dan. 'It's okay,' he said. 'It's okay, Cass, everything's going to be all right. Come on. Let's go home.'

She didn't want to go without Laura. And for Laura you can imagine it was really difficult. She was upset and scared. I mean, it can't be easy, can it, finding out your mother is mad? Realizing that your own mother could be responsible for all that stuff – trashing my house, the car tyres. Inventing the book I'd supposedly written. God, what was going on in that woman's mind? I have to admire her. Really, the skill and ingenuity – and imagination to carry it all off. I still don't know why she chose to have it in for me. Maybe she really did believe that Dan and I were having an affair. Paranoid. Really paranoid. So, anyway, there was Dan in the doorway, gripping Cass's arm. He was being so kind to her. 'Come on . . .' he was saying. 'Come on . . . it's okay, everything's going to be all right.' She was looking at me, staring at me. My God, that look in her eye still makes me

shiver. Like evil. Really evil. If she could have killed me with a look I wouldn't be sitting here now, talking to you. Oh no. I would have died right there on the spot. I had never believed it was possible to see so much hate so clearly in someone's eyes. But it was there. I know this might sound strange, but I found myself thinking I could use that, in one of my stories. That look. The mind goes to funny places, doesn't it? But you'd know that better than anyone.

I just said to Laura, 'Laura, do you think it might be best if you stayed here with me, while your father sorts everything out?'

Laura was crying. Cass was screaming, 'No . . . no . . . Laura . . . please . . . you mustn't stay with her. She's evil. It's not safe for you. Please . . .' Such nonsense. And so upsetting. We were all holding our breaths in those moments, I think. All wondering what Laura would do. Then she sat down on the sofa. 'Is it okay? If I stay here for a bit, is that okay with you, Ellie?'

'Of course it is, honey,' I said. And then I sat down beside her and put my arm around her. Then Cass let out this ungodly scream. It was so chilling. Like an animal, like something that you might hear in the dead of night. It makes your blood run cold, really it does. We sat there together, both of us silent, listening as Dan's car drove off. I saw that Laura was still crying. I didn't know what to say to her, it was really difficult. All I could think of was, 'I'm sorry, so sorry, it's just awful for you. To see your mother like that, to know that she's unstable, I just can't imagine how that must feel.' She looked at me and I think I saw her lips tighten, like the glimmer of a faint smile at the corner of her mouth, so I felt I must be saying the right thing. I think, as I said before, it was obvious to me that she wasn't that close to her mother – thinking back to those times when she didn't call her, how she met her father for lunch and hardly ever her mother. I could understand Laura feeling like that, because Cass hadn't really been very much of a mother to her, had she? I was tempted to say that she'd be better off without her, but I thought it was maybe too early to say what I really thought. 'She'll be in good hands,' I said. 'You mustn't worry. You can stay with me for as long as you like. In fact, Laura,' I said to her, 'you must treat this as your home. I want you to know that I will take care of you, whatever happens to your mother.' You see how considerate I was being to her? I mean, what more could she have asked for? If I'd been her, I would have thought that life didn't seem so bleak after all. I mean, really, what did she have to worry about? With me there, with her . . . for her? 'So stop crying, now, hey. After all, you don't want to be all puffy-eyed for the quiz tonight, do you?'

'Quiz? I don't really think . . .'

'Nonsense. It'll do you good,' I said. 'Just what you need to take your mind off everything.'

'I'm not sure,' she said. And then she told me about the book, about what Cass had told her. The book that Dan had mentioned to me. I just shrugged and said, 'Like I told your father, I don't know what she was talking about. You've seen my book, read it. You know what I've been writing about.'

'I know,' she said. And then she said something like she'd never really thought that her mother had that much of an imagination, and how sure she'd seemed about it, like she was really convinced it existed.

'I know . . . I know . . .' I told her. 'The unstable mind can play some really funny tricks, and it just goes to show, doesn't it? That we never really know people as well as we think we do . . .'

She just sat there nodding, and I felt I'd reassured her, put her mind at rest, you know. Well . . . at least I hoped I had.

I climbed into Dan's car. The leather seats were ice cold against my back, far colder than the air outside. I shivered, and the shivering wouldn't stop. It started in my arms, then progressed to my shoulders, my chin, up into my head. My upper torso was almost convulsing with shock waves. I crossed my arms in front of me and squeezed my body back into the seat. Within minutes we were home. 'I never got the chance to speak to Laura . . . to tell her . . .'

'It doesn't matter, Cass. Not now.' Dan was opening his car door. He put one leg out. 'Come on,' he said, 'let's go inside.'

I just sat there, feeling like I was unable to move, like someone had pumped lead into my limbs. 'But she has to know that I know she knows. She needs to know about Ellie.'

'Come on, Cass. Later. Let's just go in, please. There's things we need to do, things we need to discuss. Please . . .'

I unhooked my seatbelt and pushed the heavy car door open and then almost fell out. My knees felt like they were going to buckle, as if the puppet master, the person holding my strings, had finally let go. I put my hand on the car roof to steady myself and took a few deep breaths to ease the crushing sensation across my ribs. 'I don't feel right, Dan. I just feel so weak.'

He came around to my side of the car and put his arm out to steady me. 'It's okay. Come on. That's it.' His voice soothed me and I relaxed against him and allowed myself to be helped through the little gate and down the leaf-strewn path leading to our front door. It looked different, somehow. It felt different, this homecoming, like it had some kind of temporary feel about it. I didn't sense I was coming back to a safe haven. That feeling you get after an exhausting day away and all you want to do is fall in through your own front door, put the kettle on, settle down in peace. No, this was new. As if I was in some kind of transition place – not my safe home anymore – and the man at my side wasn't my safe Dan anymore. There was me, and then there was *them*, and Dan was one of them. Me, Cassandra – just me, by myself, alone. I knew I wouldn't have much say or control over what happened next.

'But what about Ellie, the stuff she wrote about being Laura's egg donor? How could I have made that up, Dan? Seriously, do you think I would? And why, why would I do that? None of it makes any sense. You must see that. At least try . . . please . . . Jesus, Dan, I'm begging . . .'

'Enough, Cass. I don't know . . . I can't explain it. You . . . I . . . we both need help here. Sweetheart, if I don't call a doctor, call in some medical help, don't you see, I'd be failing in my duty? You know,' he paused, reading the lack of understanding on my face, 'my duty to you, as your husband.'

'It doesn't make sense. I mean . . . my mother. She admitted telling Laura, Dan. And Ellie went to see her, I know she did.'

'Enough, Cassandra. You've got to stop this torture . . . I'm going to call the doctor. Why don't you go and lie down and I'll bring you a cup of tea?' His face softened. 'It'll be okay. I promise it'll all be okay.'

There are some things I remember so clearly, and then other things which have become really hazy. I guess the medication they filled me with saw to that. I remember Dan bringing me a cup of tea, and then

I don't know what time passed – it could have been an hour, or three, I couldn't say – but two of them came. One was the shrink, for sure, and the other person was some kind of social worker. They asked me lots of questions, I think. To be honest it's all a bit of a blur and there's so much that I don't want to think about. It was the usual sort of stuff, you know, did I hear voices, what happened with my previous psychiatric *episodes* as they coyly termed it, whether I'd had thoughts about harming myself.

I remember saying something along the lines of, 'I don't expect you to believe me, but I don't hear voices telling me to do terrible things. If I'm guilty of anything, then it's of trying to pretend that things were other than they really were between me and my daughter. And I'm guilty of being jealous of the fact that I'm not my daughter's biological mother, but that Dan is her father. I'm threatened by that. And I'm threatened by the fact that the person who wants to destroy me is closer to my daughter than I can ever be. I am sickened to the very core of me by all that. It causes me the deepest pain imaginable that she is doing all of this to me. But it is not me that's insane, it's *her* you should be examining, sectioning, or whatever it is you're no doubt planning to do to me. I am not making any of this up.' I decided I'd try and play my ace card. 'Tell me, does the term gaslighting mean anything to you?'

'No, I don't believe it does.'

'It's a film, from the 1940s, about how you can manipulate someone into making them seem insane. It's what she called her book. That's what she's been doing to me, and all of you, everyone, yes, even *you* are being taken in by her.'

'Really. Interesting . . .' he said. But it was obvious from the way he said it that he didn't find it at all interesting. He opened up his briefcase and rooted around inside for a few moments. Then he produced a small bottle of pills. He scribbled my name on the label together with the dosage. Then he opened the bottle and took out a pill. 'Take this, now, please.'

'What is it?'

'Olanzapine. An anti-psychotic.'

There it was. My label. He thought I was psychotic.

He handed me a glass of water and I dutifully swallowed the tiny pill.

When the ambulance arrived, appropriately the earlier sunshine of the day had been obliterated by thick grey clouds and a fine drizzle was misting the air around us. Kind people in uniforms guided me up the steps and strapped me into a chair. The tremors started again and I hugged myself, as tightly as I could. I heard Dan say he'd follow behind, in the car.

I just nodded, dumbly. I was just so exhausted. All the fight had gone. There was nothing left, no more spirit to draw upon. Just my own body declaring war on itself as my life limped towards the final battle.

CHAPTER

21

'Mum . . . Mum . . . it's me . . .'

I opened my eyes and tried to blink away the shutter between imagination and reality. 'Laura, is that really you?'

'Yes, it's me.' I heard her fingers scrape over the starched sheet like she was searching for something. And then I felt her take my hand lightly in hers and squeeze her fingers around mine. Then she bent down and placed a kiss on my forehead. Her hair fell forward and brushed against my face and I could smell Laura, my Laura. I felt tears stinging my eyes and I bit my lip, chewing on a piece of dry, fraying skin, trying to control myself.

'How are you feeling?' She asked softly.

I just nodded and closed my eyes for a moment, wondering if, when I opened them, I would find she was just a fantasy. But no, she was still there. 'Darling,' I sighed. I felt so sleepy from the drugs. All I could remember were the odd wakeful moments – food, drugs, disjointed voices, sometimes Dan – and then drifting in and out of dreamless sleep. My limbs were glued to the bed so I stayed motionless, literally dead-still, as if rigor mortis had overtaken my body while my mind remained locked inside the prison of my subconscious. It wasn't entirely unpleasant because I no longer had to worry or fight against anything. I could just remain here, passive and immobile, while other people did whatever was required to keep me sedated but breathing.

'Mum, I'm so sorry.'

'Laura? You've nothing to feel sorry for. Wait . . .' I struggled to sit up, but the effort seemed too much.

'I'll help you,' she said. I think she must have found the button, because soon I could feel my head and shoulders rising towards her. She plumped the pillows behind my head and then she poured a glass of water and handed it to me. I took a couple of sips, feeling more awake now.

I licked my lips and my voice sounded strained and out of practice. 'Laura. I never got a chance to talk to you, about everything. I'm so sorry. You know what I'm talking about, don't you?'

'About me. About us. About where I came from?'

'Yes. About me not being your biological mother. Laura, I know that Granny told you. I am so sorry that I didn't . . . couldn't . . . wasn't brave enough. I just didn't want you to see me as any different. You see it's because I love you so much – you do see that, don't you?'

'Of course, Mum. And you always were my mum, always will be. Don't forget you carried me, gave birth to me. And even if you hadn't, it doesn't matter. It's you I love. You're my mum. That's all there is to it.'

'Ellie. Did she tell you the truth?' I was clutching Laura's hand now. She looked down at my fingers. She was wincing because I was grasping her so tightly, so I relaxed my grip and her hand stayed in mine. 'Laura. It was Ellie. Ellie who donated the egg. She's your biological mother. It's her – that's why she's here, in the village. She came to claim you, or so she said in that stupid book of hers. She wanted you and your father – how did she put it? – to make a perfect family, or something.'

I could tell there were a million thoughts swirling around Laura's head all at the same time. She seemed both angry and confused, as though she was struggling to control herself. I could see her swallowing hard, taking a deep breath. She looked down at our two hands, joined together. 'Mum, listen. It's not Ellie. She isn't my mother. God, that sounds so weird, calling anyone else my mother. Biological mother, whatever . . . But it's not her.'

'But . . . how . . . I don't understand. It's there, in her book. That's why she came here – to get you.'

Laura was shaking her head. 'There's something you need to know, Mum. Granny did tell me when I was eighteen about how I was conceived, and I admit I was angry. Angry and very confused. After a while I decided I wanted to try and contact the donor – apart from anything else I wanted to see if I'd got any siblings. And also I just wanted to know where I came from, to know my history, my real history. I thought I'd love it if I'd got brothers and sisters somewhere in the world. So I contacted the place, the Human Fertilisation and Embryology Authority, and they said that even though the anonymity rules had been in place at the time of my birth, my donor, your donor . . . I can't call her my mother,' she grinned at me, 'can I? Anyway she'd written to them sometime and left her details on file, in case I – well she wouldn't have known about me, specifically, would she? – but in case her daughter, because I think she'd have been told a daughter resulted . . . but anyway, that's not what's important. The important thing is that I wrote to her. I got a letter back from her husband. It was a really sweet letter, but Mum, she'd died. She had breast cancer. She died six years ago. He sent me a picture of her, and I suppose I look a bit like her. Same hair colour, frizzy, wild. He – Adam – also sent me this little potted history of her family. I've got a half-sister and brother – teenagers – but he said it would be hard on the children to know about me in the circumstances. So he's asked me to hold off any thought of contacting them until they're older. I can understand that. I guess it's bad enough losing their mum without having the shock of learning about me. I'm the lucky one. I've got you – I've still got my mum. And that's why, in the end, I decided not to tell you. I didn't see the point in upsetting you . . .'

'So you've known all this time that that poor woman was dead.'

'Yes. Sad, isn't it? But I imagined that you hadn't told me about how I was conceived because you wanted me to believe I was yours. And I am yours, always will be. I love you, Mum.'

I sobbed. 'Sorry . . .' I said, choking back tears. 'I'm just so sorry. But then what about Ellie? Why? Why did she write that?'

'In her book – the book that she said doesn't exist?'

'Laura, I know I haven't been honest with you in the past, but I promise you I'm not mad.'

'No, Mum. I don't think you are.'

'You don't?'

'No.'

'You believe the book existed? That I wasn't making it up?'

'Yes. I do believe you, Mum.'

'But how? Why? What's happened?'

'Are you sure you're well enough for all this? I don't want to give you too much excitement all at once.'

'I'm getting better and better by the minute,' I managed to grin at her. 'Please, go on.'

Laura didn't want to go to the quiz that night. I could understand that, of course I could. I called Dan – I mean he was the quizmaster, after all, and the evening kind of depended on him. He was quite terse about it, considering everything I'd done to help. But then he was under a lot of pressure, one way and another. He just snapped, saying something like. 'Of course I'm not doing the effing quiz.' So I offered to do it for him. Then he was a bit nicer. He said that would be good. That he'd see Laura after he got back from the hospital. The NHS is amazing, I do think that, I honestly do. I mean you all work so hard and when you really, really need it – in an emergency – it all just works so efficiently, doesn't it? At

weekends, even – everything just seemed to happen so quickly. So anyway, I left Laura at around six and I said she could carry on reading the book if she wanted to. She said she'd got to the end, but then I told her there was more on the computer if she wanted to go to the file, and that if she really wanted to read it there were a few more chapters on there she could look at. She seemed grateful, and I thought it would do her good to have something to take her mind off everything that was going on. Poor thing. It was all just so upsetting.

Anyway, when I got back from the quiz, the house was in darkness, which I thought was odd. At first I thought perhaps Laura had gone to bed, but no, she wasn't there. I called Dan to see if he knew where she was, but he didn't answer. So I sent a text, just saying have you got Laura, is she safe? A few moments later I got a text back saying, thanks, she's with me. And that was that. I was so concerned that I went round there. Well it's only just up the road, after all. I could see the lights on. I knocked on the door. After a few moments Dan came to the door. He looked dreadful. Just drained, white, exhausted. Poor man. What a day he must have had.

'Dan,' I said, 'I'm so sorry. What can I do?'

'Nothing, nothing at all. You've been fantastic,' he said. I told him that I hadn't really done anything – well no more than any other good friend would have done – and that I'd call tomorrow to see how they were, how things were. I told him that the quiz had been a success, even though there'd obviously been a bit of a shadow cast over everything, you know, everyone trying not to mention Cass, but of course it was all anyone was thinking about. But I didn't tell Dan that – no, of course not.

Oh, and I also said that they weren't to worry about any of the damage, you know, the car tyres, the house, all of that, the trauma, I said it was all okay. And then I went home.

I suppose it was about an hour or so after Laura had left that Dan arrived. I had made an effort to stay upright. I'd even got out of bed and had a little walk around the ward, although my legs felt really wobbly. For the first time in I don't know how long I actually felt like I wanted to eat something. Honestly, I couldn't believe how my life could turn around like that, like everything suddenly seemed almost okay. So when Dan arrived he found me sitting up, hair brushed and smiling.

'You look a bit brighter,' he said.

'Laura came to see me. Has she spoken to you?'

'No. I missed her. She sent me a text saying she needed to talk, but I thought I'd see her later, after you.'

'Good. She's got a lot to tell you.'

He looked puzzled, curious.

'That book of Ellie's, the one she says she's writing . . .'

'God, Ellie and her bloody books. What now?' He raked his fingers through his hair and I realized just how exhausted he must be. I had mixed feelings about him being here, because I was pleased to see him, really pleased to see him, but I was just so disappointed in him, in us, that he never believed me. That he'd brought me to this. And if it hadn't been for Laura . . . well God knows what would have happened to me.

'You know I don't really understand about computers. But Laura was told by Ellie that she could read her novel on hers.'

'Okay. And . . .'

'Well the thing is, apparently Laura closed the file down by mistake. And when she went to reopen it, the mouse pointer showed up some information, about when the file was modified, or something like that, does that make sense?'

'Yeah, I suppose.'

'Well this book she's writing, the last time she modified the file was almost a year ago.'

He looked confused. He shook his head. 'I don't understand what the relevance is.'

Even in my drug-muddled head, I could see the relevance straight away when Laura told me. Was he going to continue to be deliberately obtuse?

'It means that she hasn't touched the book for nearly a year – she hasn't been writing it, it was already written a long time ago. It's all been a cover up. Oh, for God's sake Dan. Do I have to spell it out? It means that she's been busy writing another book, the one that I read.'

'I can see it means that she hasn't edited that file, but there could be other files, there could be an explanation.'

'Well, yes. I suppose there could. And you might choose to believe that, especially as you always seem so inclined to give Ellie the benefit of the doubt – even to the extent that you have had me put in here.'

'Cass, don't.'

'Let me finish, Dan. It's time I was heard properly. And believed, for once.'

He just stared at me and, as usual, it was impossible to guess what was going on in that mind of his.

'Laura saw another file. It was a file called Laura. So naturally she was curious, and opened it. And guess what . . .'

'Go on . . .'

'It had the book in it. *Gaslight*. The one I told you about. Laura read the first chapter, maybe a bit more. That was enough for her to know. So she went home. Picked up her USB stick, whatever that is, and downloaded it. So she's got a copy. She spent most of today reading it. It exists, Dan. We've got a copy. I wasn't making it up – none of this should have happened to me. And you didn't believe me. You chose to exploit my insecurities once again.' I hadn't realized just how angry I was. Maybe I'd been holding it back, maybe the drugs were doing their bit, numbing my emotions. But now it seemed like the real me was finally taking shape again. I wasn't the watery, indistinct shadow in the background. I was me – Cassandra – with a slow, simmering, but undeniable rage growing in my belly.

'Oh, and I almost forgot the most important news. She's not Laura's donor mother – but I know you never believed she was, did you? Laura wrote to the real donor when she was eighteen, thanks to my mother – so that part was true – and discovered that she'd died some years ago. She got a letter from her husband telling her all about it. That's so sad. But you know, Laura said she loved me. That she'd decided there was no point in telling us about it. Just to let things lie as they were, because she didn't want to change things between us. That I was the only mother she could ever have. So isn't that nice?'

I was on a roll. I went on, 'But I don't understand why. What was it about Ellie that made you want to protect her? Why did you believe *her* over *me*, Dan? That's what I find so hard to understand.'

Dan's face was going through some weird contortions. Like he was really struggling with something . . . maybe realizing just what a shit he had been to me. About how disloyal he was not to believe me. And you know what, suddenly I felt almost sorry for him. Because he was so weak – pathetic, even – like a wounded and confused little boy. But at the same time, for once I felt a surge of power, a power that made me feel I didn't have to mentally creep around the edges of Dan's sensitivities, his moods, his approval. For once I was free from guilt, free from all the lies. I hadn't realized just how much of a hold he had had over me. But suddenly it seemed clear that he'd been able to use my own deceit against me, as if it was a way to keep me down and submissive and in the place where he wanted me to be. It was as if a veil was slowly lifting from my eyes and I could at last see everything.

And as I watched his face, his fight with his emotions – his despair, even – he seemed to sink in the chair. His shoulders collapsed and this time both of his hands went up to his hair, tearing at the silvery threads. 'This is all just so difficult . . . so bloody difficult . . . I don't know, Cass, I just don't know what to say, what to do. You've always been so fragile, you know. I didn't want to see you going over the edge again, and now it seems that I've achieved the opposite of what I wanted. I just don't know what to do to make it up to you.'

'Perhaps you could start by being honest with me, perhaps now we could all start being honest with each other. Now that Laura and I have settled our truth, do you think it might be time for us to settle ours? Don't you think I deserve it after all of this? I want to know. I really want to know what the fuck happened in Rome.'

22

'Oh God, Cass. I don't know what to say . . . it just doesn't seem right, being in here. Talking in here. With other people around us.'

'So you've got something to tell me, then.' I felt as though a clamp had been fastened onto the valves of my heart, squeezing so hard that it started to thump in my chest in protest. I could almost hear the blood racing through my ears. I could feel myself on the verge of a panic attack, but I concentrated on breathing in out, in out, in out. I tried to keep my expression blank. I didn't want to show weakness in front of him. I wanted to stay like this, for as long as I could, in control for once. I just had to hold myself together.

'Perhaps you could take me home. Give me a minute, and I'll see you in the car park.'

'Are you sure? Will they let you?'

'Oh come on, Dan. It's not as if there's anything wrong with me, is there? I think once everyone knows the truth they'll be falling over themselves to apologize for having me here in the first place, don't you? I'll get my things and I'll meet you outside.'

'Okay. I'll be waiting.'

'Good.'

◇ ◇ ◇

'Would you like a glass of wine, Cass?'

'Yes, please. And by the way, I didn't drink two bottles that night.

I haven't been hitting the bottle, just in case you should get any ideas of that sort.'

'No.' He opened the fridge and took a bottle out. The bottle was open. He took a couple of glasses from the cupboard, filled both and handed one to me.

The phone rang. Dan looked at it warily, then picked it up. 'Oh, yes. Hello, this is Daniel Burton. Yes. That's right. No, she's fine. She's here with me now. Yes, she's quite settled . . . No, I don't see any need for that, but I'll call if there's a problem . . . Yes. I'll be with her . . . no I won't leave her alone, you have my word . . . Yes, tomorrow. Fine . . . by ten o'clock. Thanks.'

'The hospital,' he said, needlessly. 'They were worried. They want you back tomorrow. So we'll have to deal with that then, okay?'

'Fine. Do you mind if we go outside? I feel really claustrophobic in here. Like the house is a prison, though I can't imagine why I'd feel like that . . .'

'No.'

He followed me meekly as we stepped outside. It was almost six o'clock and it would soon be dark. The air felt fresh and clean in my nostrils. It was good to be away from the stuffy ward. And my head was beginning to clear. I wondered briefly if the alcohol would react with the drugs, but I was feeling dangerous, reckless, almost heady with a new-found sense of purpose, and confidence in myself. While Dan seemed to have reduced in stature, I felt taller, more substantial, that I had a right to occupy my own space, and a right to be me for once. It's strange how profound thoughts can flash through the mind so very quickly; in the space of time it took us to walk around to the terrace I had analysed the dynamics of our relationship. I hadn't realized just how apologetic I had been feeling all our married life; as if I was somehow lucky to still have Dan, lucky that he hadn't chosen to leave me, or take Laura away with him. I suppose above all, what helped was the realization that I had Laura's love, and that despite

Dan's attempts to make her seem more his than mine, it hadn't worked. I also found myself wondering whether whatever he told me, whatever he confessed to me, would make a difference to how I would feel about him in the future, whether I could feel any worse towards him than I did right now.

We each pulled out a chair on opposite sides of the table. I wrapped my pashmina around my shoulders and snuggled into its warmth, at the same time clutching the chilled glass between my hands. And I waited for Dan to tell his story.

◇ ◇ ◇

'It happened when Laura was about a year old.'

'What happened?' I said so quietly that I thought he might not have heard me.

'The affair.'

My breath caught and I wondered if he had heard *that*. 'Go on,' I said, feeling every muscle in my body tense. Be strong, I told myself. Be strong.

'She worked in Rome. It was stupid. God, how I regretted it. I can't tell you how much, Cass.'

'Rome. You were always having to go there, to see clients. And then that time in the hotel . . .'

'I know, you were right. You can't imagine what a shit I felt. It's no excuse, but you were so ill, so vulnerable. I didn't want to push you over the edge. I should never have done it. Like they say, a moment of weakness and a lifetime of regret.'

'Who was she?'

It was funny how shocked he was over that simple question. I mean, obviously I'd want to know who it was, surely that was the most natural question, the one he would have most expected.

'I thought you'd guessed . . . I'm sorry . . .'

'Guessed?'

'No . . . no . . .' he shook his head, took a large gulp of wine, reached into his pocket for a packet of cigarettes. For once he said, 'Do you mind?'

I shrugged. Then I took one myself. 'You've never smoked. You'll hate it.'

'Actually I do sometimes. I just chose not to tell you,' I said.

'Really?' He was shocked again, and that felt good. Like I was somehow getting my own back. But of course I wasn't. How could I?

'How would I have guessed?'

'Ellie. It was Ellie.'

It was like he'd punched me. I gasped and the world started to spin. I heard myself murmuring, 'No . . . no . . . no . . . no . . .' over and over. 'Dan . . . no . . . no . . .'

I was struggling for each breath, panting. The unlit cigarette fell out of my trembling fingers. Dan picked it up, lit it and handed it to me. I took a drag on it and the hit made me feel even dizzier. I coughed as the smoke hit my lungs. 'I don't understand. How . . . when . . . her being here. All this time? You knew her? That day? That first lunch? And all the time you *knew* her?' I was shrieking at him. 'That's why she was here? Because of you? And you knew? And all that time, what she was doing to me . . . you knew her? You brought her here? You had her here, in *our house*? Oh my God, Dan. Oh . . . my . . . God!'

He hung his head, and I knew he couldn't look at me. At least he had the grace to be ashamed of himself. Once again thoughts flew around my head like missiles striking targets, targets which then exploded into thousands of fragments of further thoughts struggling to make connections.

'Please,' I said. 'Would you tell me the whole story?'

'I met her in Rome. I was in the hotel one night and she approached me at the bar. It's the usual excuse – too much to drink, away from home. I was worried about you – depressed a bit, too, if I'm honest. We ended up in my room. It was like a bit of escape from everything for me, and I wanted to forget all about it the next morning, like it never happened. But I didn't reckon on what she was really like. If only I'd known. I wasn't in love with her, Cass. I was in love with you. God, this is so hard. It was just sex. I was stupid. But she wouldn't let go. It went on for about six months, I suppose, but when I said that I really never wanted to see her again, that she had to leave me alone, she told me she was pregnant.'

'With your baby?'

'Yes, Cass. With my baby. To be honest, I didn't believe her. I thought perhaps she was just saying she was pregnant to blackmail me into doing something stupid. She became hysterical, threatened to tell you, said she wanted to make a life with me, how we'd be perfect together. But that was never going to happen. I walked away. I didn't hear from her for three or four months, and then I got a phone call. She was in hospital in London and she wanted me to go, to be with her. You see, the baby had died inside her. I think she was about seven months gone, so she had to go through the birth. She wanted me with her and I just felt I should be there. It was all so sad. No matter how I felt about her, it was our baby.'

I think I let out a little yelp of pain.

'It was horrible. Just horrible. You can't imagine . . . But you know, what I still feel really guilty about is that I felt a sense of relief that I wouldn't have this terrible secret in the world that would threaten me . . . you . . . us, forever.'

How ironic, I thought. 'Go on,' I said. I wanted to feel numb, to convince myself that I was listening to a story being told by a stranger about people I didn't know. I was morbidly fascinated to know what happened next. I *had* to know.

'We kept in touch for a bit, or rather she did – I didn't contact her. Phone calls, the odd letter or postcard, and then she met someone and that was that. I felt free at last. I never wanted to hear from her again. Like I said, I'd always had this feeling that she was a bit crazy.'

'So when she turned up here?'

'I swear to you, Cass, I had no idea. I swear on Laura's life, I couldn't have been more shocked that day. I hadn't had any contact with her for fifteen years, maybe.'

'You hid it well,' I said, drily.

'Because I felt my life depended on it.'

'But she knew about me, about my depression.'

He nodded. 'I must have talked about it at the time. I was worried about you. She was sympathetic. It was good to have someone to talk to.'

'Did you tell her about Laura? About how she was conceived?'

Again he hung his head and was silent for a few moments before he answered. 'Yes,' he said so faintly it was just a hiss.

'I see.'

'When she was pregnant. I tried to make her see sense. To understand what it would do to you, knowing . . . well, I don't need to go into details, do I?'

'No. But it gave her a weapon, didn't it.'

'Oh yes. She had plenty of those.'

'So what happened, when she came here? After that first lunch at Sally's?'

'I went to see her. We got into a fight.'

'Did it get physical?'

'Yes.'

'Did you put those marks on her neck? The marks she showed me?'

'Oh God . . . yes . . . I suppose . . . you see, I told her to go. I told her that I'd do something to her if she didn't get out of our lives. I was desperate. But she just laughed at me, and said she'd got plans. And that if I got in her way then she'd tell you everything.'

'Why did you ask her to lunch?'

'She insisted. She was blackmailing me, Cass, through you and Laura.'

'How could you have been so bloody weak?'

'Because I thought I could deal with it. That she'd get bored and leave.'

'And were you having an affair with her – recently, I mean?'

'No, Cass. I wasn't. I absolutely swear I wasn't. God, I hate the woman. But I couldn't let that show, or she would have carried out her threats. And then she was getting so involved with Laura, and Laura was liking her so much. I was trying to work out what to do. And then it seemed like you were going crazy. Oh Cass, I know I behaved terribly. That it all went so bloody wrong. But she was just toying with me and I honestly thought she'd get bored and go away.'

'So – the lost dog?'

'A ruse, to get me on my own. And you have to believe me when I say that a lot of the time I wanted to get her on her own so that I could try and make her stop what she was doing.'

'And lunch in Birmingham?'

'She insisted.'

'And the book, did you believe me?'

'I don't know . . . yes . . . I suppose . . . I knew it was just the kind of thing she'd do. You don't know, Cass, but every time you talked to me about something she'd done, I went to see her to tell her to lay off. And every time you reacted to what she was doing, it was like she was winning – so I didn't want you to react, don't you see? And if you didn't react, if you just ignored it all, I thought she might just give up and go away. And then with the stuff going on with you, the drinking, trashing the house . . . God forgive me, but I began to get confused. I began to wonder if you really were going crazy, when probably the one who was really crazy in all of this was me.'

'And her,' I said, flatly. 'So what now, Dan?'

'Now you know everything she has no weapons. We can deal with her.'

'You could have told me all of this before, and she would have had to stop.'

'But then I might have lost you. And I didn't want that. I love you, Cass. I always did. I just wish you'd believed it.'

'People in love don't have affairs.'

He shrugged, the helpless little boy again. 'I can't explain or excuse it. It happened. And I have regretted it every day of my life.'

'Tell me something else, Dan. Why were you so set on me telling Laura the truth? Why did you punish me over the fact that I was keeping a secret when you were carrying all that?'

'Because I thought if you told Laura, then some of the threat from Ellie would be removed. A weapon taken away from her.'

'I see.'

We both fell into a silence, but the air felt heavy with unspoken thoughts. I was thinking about what she'd said, at that lunch, about how she had a gift for uncovering people's secrets, about how she liked the really big ones, and how she could use them. We were so busy using secrets to protect ourselves that we couldn't see just how much damage they could do, what weapons they could turn into. We were all guilty in some way – me, Dan, Laura – even my mother deceiving herself about my father's suicide. Maybe if we had been honest, all of us, then we'd have been safe. Maybe, maybe not. There was too much to think about, too many open wounds to know what would happen to us, whether we could weather this. To know whether or not I could forgive Dan. I think it wasn't so much the affair that made me hurt so deeply inside, not the physical betrayal, but the mental betrayal. That Dan could let me believe I was going insane in order to protect himself. Because no matter what he said, I couldn't understand how he could do that out of love for me. But maybe I'd need time to work that one out, and for now we needed to deal with Ellie.

'Do you see now why I needed to talk to you, to tell you all this, the real story? I know how plausible Cassandra can be. But you needed to know the facts of what really happened. You must be really glad, now, that you agreed to see me. It wasn't easy. I mean, if I hadn't been so tenacious, pestering your secretary, you could easily have missed all of this. I'm sure you realize now just why I was so insistent, why it was so important.'

'Oh yes, Miss Black . . . Ellie. I can see why you wanted to tell me your story. It's been a very interesting diversion.'

'A diversion? Surely it's more than that. Diversion implies that you don't quite believe what I'm telling you. And I can assure you that all of this – my story, as you term it – is the truth. I can't believe you – a professional with your credentials and qualifications – would be taken in by a psychotic woman. I know she's manipulative, but surely you, of all people, can see through her. I wouldn't insult your intelligence by suggesting you couldn't.'

'No, I'm sure you wouldn't. And you're right. I am more than able to see through the manipulations of psychotic women.'

'So you can imagine why I was so surprised – shocked, even – when I heard that you had released Cassandra from hospital so quickly. It just doesn't seem right, given that she is so obviously crazy. Sorry, that's not a very scientific expression is it? I think her husband is unreliable in his judgement. I think he's under some threat from her, or maybe he feels some misguided sense of obligation to her, I don't know. It's hard to say, isn't it? – what someone like that can do . . . can threaten. But I'm

NEAREST THING TO CRAZY

worried about them. Naturally I am, because I care. And I'm deeply worried about Laura, whether she's going to be safe. And that's without reiterating what she did to me. And I can't feel safe if she's in the community, can I? And if anything happened I'm sure you wouldn't want to be held professionally responsible. Obviously you'll now feel that you've got to reconsider your decision in the light of all this – your decision about letting her out, that is.'

'I want to thank you for all your time, for telling me all of this.'

'Well, thank you, Doctor. I was concerned that with patient confidentiality and all of that, you wouldn't be able to talk to me. But in all the circumstances, and I suppose given that Cass is a threat, then you're allowed to break that.'

'I haven't broken any patient confidentiality. I have merely listened to your story, so I've been able to piece a few things together.'

'So will you be . . . ? Forgive me . . . I can't think of a sensitive way to put this . . . locking her up? For all our safety. I don't need to remind you of what she did to me.'

'No, I won't be locking her up.'

'But why? Don't you fear that you might be being negligent – I mean, professionally negligent. That if anything goes wrong you might be at the wrong end of a law suit?'

'No. I have no fears in that direction.'

'You have to be joking.'

'I wouldn't jest about something this serious, believe me.'

'So all I've told you, all this time I've spent in here, telling you everything, has been a complete waste of both our times. Is that what you're saying, Doctor?'

'No. It hasn't been a waste of time at all. Miss Black . . . Ellie, you are a very convincing woman, and I admire your intelligence, I really do.'

'Thank you. But why do I feel there's a sting in the tail, Doctor?'

'Ah, yes. The sting. And perceptive, too. I've got another of your stories here. Mrs Burton passed it to me.'

'Mrs Burton?'

'Yes. Look, here's the title page, which you'll no doubt recognize . . . Gaslight by Eleanor Black. Your novel, I believe. I've read it, of course.'

'Let me see that – where did you get it? . . . I don't understand . . .'

'Mrs Burton's daughter found it – I believe you allowed her access to your computer and she happened to stumble across it. Which is quite a good thing, really, in the circumstances, because otherwise poor Mrs Burton might be in the unfortunate position of not being believed – which I think is what you intended.'

'I've never seen this before . . .'

'My dear Miss Black . . . Ellie . . . as the old saying goes, you can fool some of the people some of the time . . . but you can't fool me.'

'What do you mean? Are you saying that you are going to believe her over me? She must have somehow put this on my computer. I've never seen it before. She could easily have done that, uploaded it without my knowledge. She broke into my house, my laptop was there . . . she had every opportunity to have access to it. My God she's clever . . . really clever. You've got to believe me. Otherwise I'm terrified of what she's going to do next.'

'Ellie, it's time to stop. Not only have I read your novel, but I've also read some patient notes of yours. I had them sent to me from your doctor in London. It took a bit of tracking down, but we managed it in the end. Mr Burton knew where you'd given birth, so we followed the paper trail from there. You were diagnosed with Antisocial Personality Disorder, or Sociopathy . . . Psychopathy in common parlance, weren't you, my dear? After the loss of your baby. Tragic for you. It's all here, your description of Dan not letting you see your daughter – transcribed from a tape recording, I believe.'

'I never had a baby. I don't understand any of this. This is crazy, really insane. Can't you see, it's all a pack of lies. There aren't any medical notes, I'm not a psychopath. You've got to see, you have to believe me. Cass and Dan, they've concocted all this between them.'

'Ellie, it's time to stop all this if we're to have any chance of helping you.'

'But can't you see? – I don't need any help. It's not me that needs the help. How can you be so blind . . . so stupid?'

'If you continue to resist, to be in a state of denial, then there is nothing I can do to help. I'd like to refer you to someone.'

'But don't you see . . . it's not me, it's her. You've got it all wrong. Why won't you just listen to me? . . . You've got to believe me . . .'

What can we ever really know about anyone beyond the stories they choose to tell us? And how can we measure the truth within those stories unless we have lived those stories together. And even then, we each have our own lens through which we can distort, reinterpret, pretend. How truly honest are we with ourselves, let alone with anyone else? You see, thinking back on Dan's story I kind of believe him. But then there are things which make it hard to trust him completely. Because there are things that simply don't make sense in his story.

In his study there is a locked box in which Dan keeps his secrets hidden away. Within that box lies a small postcard and a book of matches. I ask myself why he would keep those amongst his treasures if he really didn't care about Ellie. Surely, I tell myself, he would have burned the postcard – maybe using those very same matches. Instead he chooses to keep them next to the precious mementoes of his daughter's life. And I don't understand why. But I can't ask him, because to do that I would have to admit that I had opened his locked box; and that I can never do; that is a secret I must keep forever. And will he, too, keep that postcard a secret from me? I don't know whether or not I can believe in Dan. In the end it all comes down to something indefinable, like a gut feeling, a desire, an act of faith; for what is belief but something we choose to accept without proof. And aren't we all just locked boxes, locked boxes stuffed full of secrets, and the only way we can ever really know each other is through the stories we choose to tell. But we'll never *really* know the truth . . . will we?

Acknowledgements

To Broo Doherty, my dear friend and brilliant agent for all her warmth, hard-work, encouragement and faith and to Tom Innes for so fortuitously introducing me to Broo in the first place; to all at Cutting Edge Press, especially to Martin and Paul for producing such a beautiful book, and for all their support, and for making it so much fun; to Sean Costello for his fine editing skills; to the extremely talented Alessandro Massarini for his picture of Marcela Angarita's hand; to Anira Rowanchild for her mentoring, enthusiasm and friendship; to Clare John and Dion Dhorne, my incisive writing buddies who were there at the birth; to Philippa, Neffy and Mary for reading the manuscript; to Chris Thomas for psychiatric advice – for the book, not me; to Janet Stones for counselling expertise; to Philip Briggs for police procedural advice, and to the Human Fertilisation and Embryology Authority for checking the facts.

Huge thanks and love to my family and friends for understanding when I was in the cave . . . especially my poor neglected husband Jamie . . . and for still being there when I came out.

The Inspiration behind
The Nearest Thing to Crazy

Crazy. A little word with so many meanings.
- I'm crazy about you
- You drive me crazy
- She's so funny, really crazy
- The crowd went crazy
- My parents will go crazy
- She's gone crazy
- She's crazy about her garden

The Nearest Thing to Crazy is a fairly ambiguous statement, because it's near, but not there. And whose crazy is it? Who is the arbiter who actually decides whether you're crazy or not? Because one person's crazy can be another person's normal. I find that scary. Is it like you have to go through some kind of laboratory-style observation devised by other people? And what if those other people are a little bit crazy themselves. And what's even scarier is they might have an agenda as to why they want people – other people – to think you're crazy.

In the old days, adulterous wives could be committed to mental asylums. Being a bit wayward, or independent-minded might condemn you to a life time in an institution. But that was in the olden days. Now we're over all that. It doesn't happen anymore. Or does it? I think it happens a lot. In fact I think it happens such a lot that we become immune to it, we begin not to notice it, or to take it as the 'normal' way of relating to each other. And this may be contentious, but I think it happens to women a lot more than it does to men, and I also think it happens 'woman on woman' as well as 'man on woman'.

If anyone tells you you're silly to think that; you must have got it wrong; you're over-reacting. You imagined it. That's a stupid thing to say. You're being neurotic. Your husband thumped you? Well, you probably wound him up and he is stressed at work. You're too stupid to apply for that job? The newspaper takes precedence over your conversation, your opinions are dismissed as you don't know what you're talking about? This is just the easy stuff. Take a look at the open forums on battered wives help web sites and over and over again women are told they are stupid and useless, powerless, and they eventually get brainwashed into believing it. And to reinforce that powerlessness, they get beaten, sometimes to death. Also, the important thing to understand, I think, is that mental abuse can be just as damaging as physical abuse, which is why the law is changing, right now, to reflect this.

During my research for The Nearest Thing to Crazy I came across a term called Gaslighting, derived from a movie 'Gaslight' made in the 1940s. It was all about a husband trying to distort his wife's perception of reality. If the gaslights flickered on and off, the husband told her she was imagining it. Her things went missing, only to turn up in the places where they belonged, so she felt she must have imagined they had gone missing. The distortion of her reality was quite literally making her think she was going crazy. So the term 'gaslighting' is now used as a shorthand when someone tries to convince you that you cannot trust your own reality. Has anyone ever said 'we never had that conversation?'; 'I never said that to you?'; 'I never agreed to that, you imagined it…' well, that's gaslighting.

On face value I suppose it can seem fairly innocuous, after all, we all have memory lapses, or selective deafness, and so overall one can tend not to notice it as anything other than slightly irritating. But if it's used continually over a long period, it's an insidious form of abuse, it destroys your self-confidence, it makes you fear for your sanity, and it can be so subtle that you hardly realize it's happening. And it makes you afraid to confide in people because you are scared they will only confirm your fears. 'Don't be so silly.' 'I'm sure that didn't really happen....' 'I'm sure it wasn't as bad as all that...'

It does seem to me that it is very hard to prove you are not crazy, when the seeds of doubt have been sown. If you are calm then you have disassociated, and if you are hysterical... well, enough said.

So I wanted to explore with The Nearest Thing to Crazy just how this could happen to a normal woman, in a supposedly safe, middle class environment, but also saddled with a history of something a lot of women have gone through: post-natal depression. How does the label of being a little bit unhinged affect your future? How far, and how effectively can it be used as a weapon against a fragile ego state. And how does it affect the power balance in relationships generally?

The fact that this kind of story is a recurring theme in women's literature makes me wonder really how much we have changed since the 'olden' days. Remember Jane Eyre and poor mad Bertha, the wife in the attic; and Jean Rhys's prequel, The Wide Sargasso Sea, contrasting the flamboyancy and colour of Bertha's Caribbean upbringing with her incarceration in the freezing wilds of Yorkshire. The magnificent Yellow Wallpaper by Charlotte Perkins Gilman – another mad woman in the attic. Wilkie Collins The Woman in White, locked away in a lunatic asylum. And then there is the perpetual favourite Rebecca where the methods used on the replacement Mrs de Winter are so subtle but nonetheless terrify' she reverts to a childlike state dominated by a Bluebear

319

husband. She is the invisible waif keeping to the shadows of Manderley while the dead Rebecca continues to assert her vibrancy and passion.

But not only did I want to distort my main character's reality, or gaslight her, I wanted to see if it was possible to do the same with the reader. In The Nearest Thing to Crazy, I see the reader being asked to believe in three different acts of fiction. Centrally and most importantly is Cassandra's story, who starts as a nameless narrator as an homage to Daphne du Maurier's Rebecca. Ellie, like Rebecca, breathes life and vibrancy into the plot, and I hope, through her stream of consciousness, talking to camera, story style is a device which helps to seduce the reader into believing her side of the story, at Cass's expense. Her informal style is meant to be intimate, gossipy, and therefore seductively believable.

Another layer is added through the fact that Ellie is a novelist, and she is writing a novel which neither Cassandra nor the reader knows is based on truth or fiction. Indeed, it is made clear that it is a novel, and so must be a work of fiction, but of all the narrative strands, it is the one which Cass can test against her own reality, because it contains certain truths. So far, then, there are three separate self-consciously aware fictions within the novel, framed within a fourth which is, of course, the overall novel told my me.

And I hope, by seducing my readers into believing any of these stories, and to suspend the knowledge that they are merely reading words on a page about people who have never existed, I can in a small way demonstrate the wonderful power of fiction, and the true magic of imagination. And at the same time, show how terrifyingly ----- it can be to distort someone's reality.

Elizabeth Forbes 18th April 2013

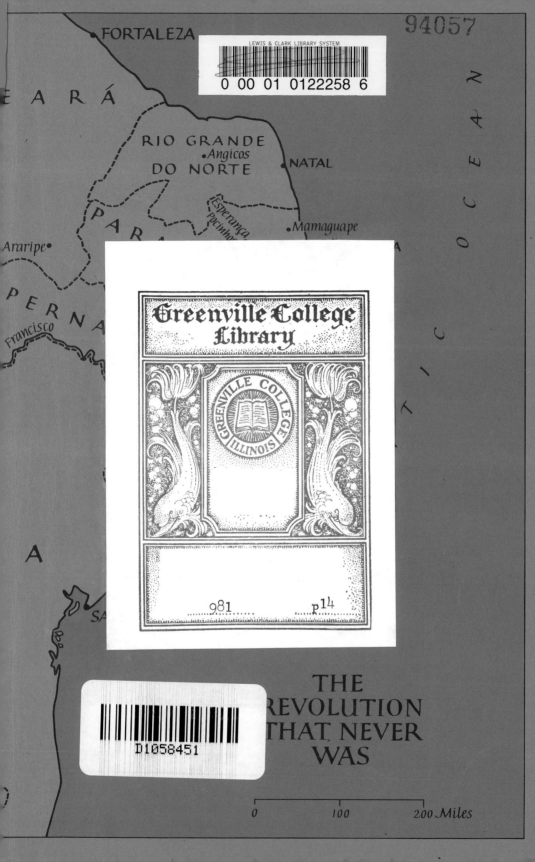

FORTALEZA

EARÁ

RIO GRANDE
•Angicos
DO NORTE
•NATAL

Araripe•

PARA

Esperança
Pocinhos
•Mamaguape

PERNA

Francisco

A

SA

THE
REVOLUTION
THAT NEVER
WAS

OCEAN

TIC

0   100   200 Miles

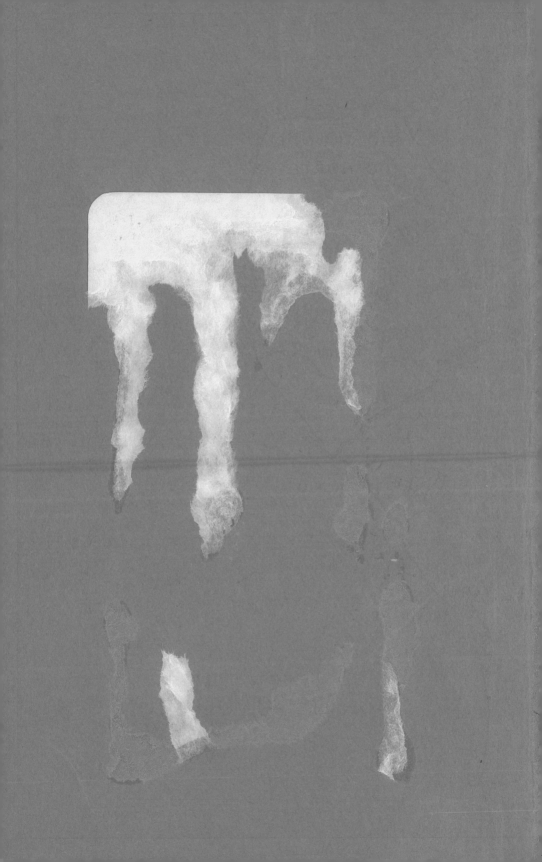

THE REVOLUTION
THAT NEVER WAS

THE THAT NEVER

Northeast Brazil 1955-1964

REVOLUTION
WAS

Joseph A. Page

GROSSMAN PUBLISHERS

NEW YORK · 1972

FIRST PUBLISHED IN 1972 BY GROSSMAN PUBLISHERS,
625 MADISON AVENUE, NEW YORK, N.Y. 10022
PUBLISHED SIMULTANEOUSLY IN CANADA BY FITZHENRY
AND WHITESIDE, LTD.
SBN 670-59706-6
LIBRARY OF CONGRESS CATALOGUE CARD NUMBER: 71-106293
PRINTED IN U.S.A.

PORTIONS OF CHAPTER FIFTEEN, "AFTERMATH," ARE RE-
PRINTED BY PERMISSION FROM THE AUTHOR'S "REPORT ON
NORTHEAST BRAZIL," PUBLISHED IN *The Atlantic*, JANUARY
1968, © THE ATLANTIC MONTHLY COMPANY.

"NOTES FROM A RECIFE JAIL" ORIGINALLY APPEARED IN
SOMEWHAT DIFFERENT FORM IN THE *University of Denver
Magazine* UNDER THE TITLE, "LETTER FROM A RECIFE JAIL."

to Roland Snyder

✿ ✿ Contents

✿ ✿ Introduction

IN THE EARLY 1960s the American public became aware that part of Brazil was on the verge of violent upheaval. Or so it seemed to the journalists and politicians who were sounding the alarm about the explosive situation in Brazil's vast, overpopulated Northeast. Visitors to the region reported that millions of peasants living in abysmal poverty were showing unmistakable signs of discontent, and that agitators—politicians, students, and the inevitable Communists—were busily fanning the flames. Americans disturbed by the success of the Cuban Revolution began to see Northeast Brazil as a battleground where the newly minted Alliance for Progress could be put to the test against the challenge of Castroism.

The Northeast did indeed turn into an arena, but the ensuing struggle was far more complex than most people at the time realized. For one thing, the Alliance for Progress found itself torn between its highly publicized humanitarian, reformist goals and the considerations of U.S. security that were the underlying *raison d'être* of the aid program. The latter prevailed very easily at the outset, as the American involvement sought first to preserve the basic structure of the status quo, and only incidentally to improve conditions in the region in ways that would not weaken the established order.

Northeast Brazil also provided the setting for a clash between advocates of immediate, violent revolution and those who called for the

radical redistribution of power through orderly, gradual, democratic change. Admirers of Fidel Castro were the leading exponents of the revolutionary approach, while Soviet-line Communists were among those who followed the peaceful, legal road to radical change. The revolutionaries suffered from erratic leadership, and failed to develop a broad base of support among the rural and urban masses. The radical reformers proved to be at the same time indecisive and overconfident. In the end, both groups found themselves overtaken by events in the rest of Brazil, and were totally unprepared, mentally as well as physically, when the moment of truth arrived.

Today the Northeast is a forgotten land, where millions of peasants still live in abysmal poverty. Since they show no outward manifestation of discontent, they no longer threaten U.S. security interests, and the American aid program that succeeded the now defunct Alliance for Progress has been reduced to suitably modest dimensions. An authoritarian military regime has suppressed the revolutionaries and the radical reformers, and all is quiet—deathly still, one might say.

Northeast Brazil merits rescue from history's dustbin. Its brief moment in the flicker of world attention provides an arresting case study of various approaches to the problems of underdevelopment in action and in conflict: nonradical reformism vs. revolution vs. legal radicalism; political vs. economic vs. military options; change vs. reaction. In addition, the struggle in the Northeast casts considerable light on the role of cultural and social factors and of individual personalities. For this reason, one must pay particular heed to the flavor of the ferment that convulsed the region.

I have attempted to be as scholarly as possible in writing this book. Yet there are some facts which I have seen fit to include but which cannot be footnoted for obvious reasons. I have checked out these facts in a conscientious manner, in repeated conversations with participants in the events I have described and with firsthand observers, taking full advantage of my six visits to the Northeast between 1963 and 1971, as well as trips to Paris, Cuernavaca, and elsewhere, and of my presence in Washington during the past three years. In my judgment, the story I am about to tell actually happened.

Several quirks of fate, including my brief sojourn in a Recife jail in 1964 (see the Appendix for details), have afforded me a unique access to individuals representing all factions in the struggle in Northeast Brazil. I hope I have done them justice.

It would be impossible for me to acknowledge the countless individuals who helped in the preparation of this book. The list would be too long, and would have to exclude those who spoke off the record or who might be unnecessarily embarrassed if identified. I can merely make known my heartfelt gratitude to all of them.

I cannot refrain from expressing particular appreciation to Emily Flint of the *Atlantic Monthly*, who gave me my first opportunity to write about Latin America; to the Institute for Policy Studies for its support of my 1967 odyssey to the Northeast; to my peerless publisher, Dick Grossman; and to my editor, Tom Stewart.

JOSEPH A. PAGE
Washington, D.C.
July 7, 1971

PROLOGUE

ONE ❦

❦ ❦ The Cast

AN HOUR BEFORE SUNRISE, Pedro Mota clambered aboard a bus parked on a side street several blocks from Recife's waterfront, joining assorted organizers, members, and hangers-on of Northeast Brazil's Peasant League movement.[1] Many of them had slept through the night on the dusty floor of a hall nearby, which served as Peasant League headquarters in the city. Now, barely awake, they headed north toward Mamanguape, some eight hours away.

The bus had seen better days. It was typical of the discards that turn up in the more remote reaches of the earth, to provide the creaking backbone for overburdened, underdeveloped transportation systems. Pedro Mota tried to sleep, but the seats were too close together and the roads too bumpy. Through an open window he watched groves of banana, coconut, and mango trees, dense patches of uncultivated brush, and the familiar sugarcane fields. Gently rolling hills softened the landscape, unlike anything he had seen in Chile, Bolivia, Peru, Ecuador, and Venezuela, countries he had toured in May, 1962, in an attempt to forge a link between the Peasant Leagues and other revolutionary movements in Latin America. It was closer, perhaps, to Cuba, which he had visited in the summer of 1961.[2]

Before long the bus crossed the state line into Paraíba. The eastern part of the state, which they were then traversing, was essen-

3

tially the private preserve of two families. It was also the region that produced the tastiest pineapples in all of Brazil. Several hours later, the group arrived at the little town of Mamanguape, the site of a rally to celebrate the founding of a rural labor union.

The prospect of addressing a large peasant audience exhilarated Pedro Mota. He knew what was wrong with Brazil and he never hesitated to say it. Put an end to the rotten system under which landlord exploits peasant, industrialist exploits worker, imperialist exploits everybody.

Pedro Mota had recently been expelled from the Brazilian Communist Party because, according to the Party, he had engaged in "adventurous and divisive activities incompatible with the sense of responsibility and discipline which ought to inspire true revolutionaries." [3] —activities such as speaking to peasants without the Party's permission and working with students who helped armed peasants invade and occupy sugar plantations.

Now he could hardly wait to speak. When his turn came, he stepped forward, clutched the microphone in his left hand, and gestured angrily to denounce the "North American imperialists" who were "sucking the life blood from Brazil." Beads of sweat trickled unevenly down the sides of his smooth, handsome face as he tossed his head back and forth and then shook it from side to side. The words poured out easily, without hesitation, reflecting his political apprenticeship as a student leader at law school.

The 600 or so peasants in his audience listened attentively. Summoned by bursts of fireworks, they had gathered in the early afternoon in front of the small wooden platform set up against a storefront facing the square. A makeshift cover of palms and branches provided shade for the notables who crowded the platform. Bits of colored cloth fluttered on lines stretched out across the open square.

A few listeners had come on horseback, remaining mounted as they viewed the proceedings from an adjacent plot of grass. One of them, a wizened Negro, crouched forward over the blanket-roll which served as a saddle and peered out from under his broadbrimmed hat. The peasants had patiently endured the rays of a burning sun for three hours while local politicians, labor leaders, and now a student attempted to stir them.

4

So far the crowd had reacted to but one speaker, a woman dressed in black. Elisabete Teixeira was the widow of João Pedro Teixeira, tenant farmer, stonecutter, and organizer of rural workers.[4] The landowners in eastern Paraíba had staunchly resisted all efforts to implant among their peasants the notion that the latter had any legal rights. Their repression had bred counterviolence on the part of the peasants, and this escalation reached its climax when a local politician-landowner hired a pair of rural policemen to ambush João Pedro. One afternoon as he was returning home to Elisabete and their eleven children, they gunned him down. Elisabete, a diminutive woman with piercing eyes and a firm voice, vowed to carry on his work and soon became the President of the local Peasant League. Three months later another bullet fired from ambush creased the forehead of Paulo Pedro, her thirteen-year-old son, hospitalizing him and scarring him permanently. At the same time Elisabete kept receiving threats on her own life. She claimed that the landowner responsible for all this violence was now offering a substantial reward to the person who would bring him her tongue. Her eldest child, eighteen-year-old Marluce, became so distraught at this that she swallowed a fatal dose of poison. Undaunted, Elisabete visited Havana, where she left one of her children in school. At the Mamanguape rally, she had urged the crowd to follow the example of the Cuban Revolution, and they had raised their arms to signify agreement and had answered her with excited cries.

Pedro Mota was eliciting no such response. Perhaps it was fortunate for him that the dissonant strains of a small brass band interrupted his speech. A procession approached from a side street. Priests, nuns, scrubbed children, and neatly dressed townspeople filed by the edge of the plaza. A group of men in their midst carried aloft polychrome statues of Saint Peter and Saint Paul. Few of the intruders could resist an anxious glance at the crowd in front of the platform.

The counterdemonstration distracted the peasants, who turned to watch impassively. When the last of the marchers disappeared around a corner, the attention of the audience returned to the platform. Pedro Mota was gone. The master of ceremonies, a soft-spoken, ebony-skinned Negro, introduced the afternoon's featured

5

speaker. A barrage of fireworks echoed the applause, and a riderless horse shied dangerously close to a small group of children.

Late arrivals on the bus from Recife had wondered why Francisco Julião was not aboard. Only when Mamanguape was an hour away did a pile of blankets stir, and the Honorary President of the Peasant Leagues sat up on the front seat where he had been dozing.

Throughout the long afternoon he had remained on the platform, his preoccupied gaze shifting from the crowd to the distant fields of sugarcane and then to the floor beneath him. His shirt was unbuttoned at the collar, which flopped over the top of a maroon, long-sleeved sweater. The bone structure above his eyes protruded and his forehead sloped back, lending a distinctive cast to his profile. The triangular shape of his head and the elevation of his cheek bones suggested a trace of Indian ancestry. Julião took hold of the hand microphone and began to speak—clearly, deliberately, emphatically.

"If Saint Peter and Saint Paul were alive today, they would not let themselves be carried around on anyone's shoulders. They would be right here, fighting on the side of the peasants. Jesus Christ, a rebel who fought against the Roman Emperor, who told the rich to humble themselves, he too would be here, with us." The effect on the peasants was electric. There were frequent bursts of applause.

"You must stand together, arm-in-arm with your brothers. Alone you are a drop of water. United you are a waterfall. In unity you can be a Peasant League, together like a closed fist. The League is the people marching, the landlord fleeing, his *capangas* [private police] disarmed. It is the birth of true justice, the dawn of true liberty. And the League's first task will be a land reform that will rip out the large estates by their roots."

The audience forgot the others on the platform. There was just Julião, all by himself, a slight, pale figure radiating a mystic presence. The peasants seemed to see only him and hear only his words, as he spoke in their own terms of their own anguish. He held them with a gentleness and a simple language that his listeners fully understood.

"It is the present system that is responsible for the hunger, disease, prostitution, and illiteracy that we see all around us. What we must do is create a new system which will provide schools, hospitals,

6

and jobs for everyone. It does not matter what we call this form of government. What is important is that it will benefit *every* Brazilian, and not just the landlords, industrialists, and American companies.

"In Brazil today there are 80 million people, but only 15 million voters. The Chamber of Deputies is composed of 250 landowners, 80 bankers, 50 industrialists, and only 20 or 25 men who fight for the peasant. How can you expect such people to pass a land reform law? I confess to you that I no longer believe in elections."

With the edge of the palm of his right hand he carved a deft pattern of gesticulations in the hot, heavy air, occasionally jabbing with a finger to punctuate a phrase.

"Therefore, let the poor people of Brazil unite in order to win back their own country. Let there be land without landlords, factories without industrialists, banks without bankers.

"There are those who say they want to bring about change, but insist that it be achieved without violence. But are we not living right now in the bosom of violence? One baby of every two born in Northeast Brazil does not survive his first year. Disease and hunger are everywhere. Is this not violence? The landowners torture and kill peasants and burn their huts. Does this not count as violence? I promise you that one way or another, we are going to have a revolution."

An ovation followed, and a throng of well-wishers surrounded Julião. His wife, Alexina, a hard-eyed blonde in blue jeans and leather boots—the chief courier between the Leagues and Fidel Castro—stood silently at his side. The peasants, with Julião's words ringing in their ears, returned to their homes in the countryside.

Recife is the capital of the state of Pernambuco, largest and most important city in Northeast Brazil, hotbed of radicalism, the Calcutta of the Western Hemisphere[5]—"the Brazilian Venice," as some imaginative boosters like to call it. Or as some local cynics pun, *Re-sífilis, Cidade Venérea*—"Re-syphilis, Venereal City."

As the 1960s dawned, a sense of excitement and anticipation pierced the city's tropical shroud. Political power seemed to be shifting, slowly but perceptibly, from a small circle of wealthy families to a broad-based populist movement. Liberals and progressives of every

7

hue, ranging from devout Roman Catholics to Communist Party members, were uniting in a massive effort. Their goal was to democratize the governance of the city and state, to utilize political power to bring social and economic justice to the masses of rural and urban poor, and thus to change the societal structures which they felt had condemned the Northeast to backwardness and extreme poverty.

Recife provided more than just a setting for the new movement. Truly deserving its reputation as the capital of underdevelopment in Latin America, the port city served as a constant reminder of the magnitude of the task at hand. It provided an environment that was enough to shock anyone with a spark of conscience into action.

For example, there was the housing problem. Estimates put the number of slum-dwellers in Recife at more than 60 per cent of the city's nearly one million inhabitants. Colonies of shanties, called *mucambos,* clustered in the mud along the riverbanks to be washed away by an occasional flood during the rainy season, yet always resurrecting themselves when the waters receded. A constant flow of peasants from the sugar zone and the interior transfused these fetid urban blotches. Typical was Coque, nestled among fingers of earth which beckoned the brown waters of the Capiberibe River. Tiny wooden huts roofed with tile or covered with boards housed a community which grew to exceed 20,000 people. Small boats and rafts were the most convenient way to get in and out of Coque, drifting past outhouses on stilts which slumped carelessly into the water. The road to the municipal airport passed by Coque, but a row of white-washed buildings spared visitors from the view.

The people who inhabited the *mucambos* by the rivers were the *dramatis personae* of what nutritionist Josué de Castro has called the "Crab Cycle." They fed upon crabs which fed upon human excrement in the river mud. "And with this meat, made out of mud, they [the people] build the flesh of their bodies and the flesh of their children's bodies. They are 100,000 individuals, 100,000 citizens made out of crabmeat. What their bodies throw off is returned to the mud, to be made into crabmeat again." [6]

Brasília Teimosa exemplifies how slum communities came into being. Fugitives from the great drought of 1958 began squatting on a land fill protruding into Recife's harbor and built to hold petroleum

8

tanks. Police would come in and tear down the shanties. The owners would return to rebuild them when the police left. Finally the authorities gave up, and a wretched slum spread like a sore. It was consummately appropriate that the settlement took the name of Brasília Teimosa, or "Stubborn Brasília," a tribute to the tenacity of its inhabitants.

In addition to the *mucambos* along the river and shore, even larger slum communities covered the hills on the outskirts of town. One of the big problems here was that in the rainy season the soil would loosen and cause slides which swept the shanties down the steep slopes. The quality of the dwelling places worsens (and the skin color of the inhabitants darkens) as one leaves the main road and climbs to the top of one of these hills. It is ironic that the poorest of the poor have the best view, as the lush green landscape spreads below and gives way to the red tile roofs and white skyscrapers of the city, and the azure sea beyond. (A similar phenomenon occurs in Rio, where the lower classes built their *favelas* on the spectacular hills which surround the city, while the rich and middle classes live along the shore. It is instructive to note that developers have begun to remove the *favelas* and herd their inhabitants to barren new communities many miles from the center of the city.)

Unemployment and underemployment affected most of those who dwelt in the *mucambos*. It was popular to refer to them as *marginais,* or marginal people. On the other hand, urban poverty helped to breed two distinctive types of work for which the city became well known.

Recife is one of the great centers of prostitution in the world. In July, 1961, a French monk who conducted extensive research on the subject in Brazil estimated that there were 30,000 prostitutes in Recife.[7] Of these he has calculated that 20 per cent worked full time, while the rest held regular jobs in bars or restaurants or even worked as maids in private homes. The lure of jobs which proved nonexistent drew many of them to the city.

The other type of "job" for which Recife had become famous was the practice of begging. Downtown Recife was infested with beggars, pawing and tugging prospective donors. Their bodies were often cruelly misshapen, as if by some mad practitioner of the plastic

9

arts. The forms could suggest all kinds of images to one whose sensibilities had not been dulled by frequent contact with such sights—to one who sought escape from these subhuman visions. Thus one could encounter Question Mark, with his curved spine, and Number Four, sitting on a bridge with one leg twisted over the other. There was the Frog, a woman whose trunk was folded against her thighs, keeping her close to the ground as she hopped from place to place. And the Snake, a man with no nose and twisted limbs slithering sideways along the sidewalk. Worst of all was the Lump, a blob with flippers, perched like Humpty-Dumpty on a wheelchair, one side of his head caved in, grunting at passersby. On Sunday mornings at a church near the center of town, several mendicants regularly took up their own collection, jerking and shaking in grotesque counterpoint to the strains of an organ.

This was the misery that spawned the new populist coalition, which in turn fed hope to the increasing numbers of "marginal" people who were becoming politically conscious. The emerging movement had its cause, the oppressive underdevelopment of Recife, the state of Pernambuco, and the whole of Northeast Brazil; it also had its leader, Miguel Arraes, man of the left, nationalist, and outspoken advocate of radical change by legal means. Arraes, cautious and skillful politician, had recently been elected Mayor of Recife. He was now about to seek election as governor of the state. The populists were on the move, and a genuine democratic revolution seemed within their grasp.

There were also some nonpolitical "legal revolutionaries" at work in Recife—such as Celso Furtado, an economist who was struggling to modernize the economy of Northeast Brazil. He had declared war upon underdevelopment in the region. His weapon was a unique government agency, the Superintendency for the Development of the Northeast.

SUDENE, as the Superintendency was commonly known, was a federal agency responsible directly to the President of Brazil. It was charged with the monumental task of planning, coordinating, and implementing the economic development of all of Northeast Brazil. As the agency's creator and first director, Furtado assumed responsi-

bility for devising solutions to Brazil's most pressing and persistent problem—the extreme poverty and backwardness of the immense, densely populated Northeast.

Celso Furtado seemed more than equal to the challenge. His qualifications for the job included scholarly achievement, intellectual versatility, and personal magnetism, plus the prime advantage of being a native of the region.

An economist of international repute, he had earned a doctorate from the Sorbonne in Paris in 1949, and had worked for a decade on problems of underdevelopment, first as a member of the United Nations Economic Commission for Latin America and then as a director of Brazil's National Development Bank.[8] His book, *The Economic Growth of Brazil,* has long been a standard text in several countries.

At the same time he bore the touch of the Renaissance Man. As a youth he had almost become a concert pianist. He had also sampled a literary career, working his way up from reporter to editor-in-chief of a popular magazine in Rio de Janeiro and contributing essays on subjects ranging from Mahatma Gandhi to American cowboy movies. He wrote a book of short stories entitled *From Naples to Paris: Tales of Expeditionary Life,* based on his experiences in World War II as a lieutenant with the Brazilian Army in Italy, which received favorable notices from the critics.

In addition to his intellectual attainments, Furtado possessed an abundance of charisma. He was remarkably adept at impressing people. Canadian journalist Gerald Clark, for example, once called him "one of the most inspiring and exciting men that I have ever met." [9] Young, handsome, cool, and competent, Furtado appealed to a younger generation, weary of the oft-repeated slogan, "Brazil is the country of the future," and impatient to take immediate steps toward progress and development. There was something almost hypnotic in his steely, grey eyes and the soft tones he used to convey the urgency of what he was trying to do for the Northeast.

Despite these formidable assets, Celso Furtado soon discovered that he had to develop and utilize a keen sense of politics in order to survive. SUDENE had the authority to disperse most of the money allocated to the Northeast by the federal government. Yet in exer-

cising this authority, Furtado had to walk a slack wire, swayed by the vagaries of national politics, the meteoric rise of Miguel Arraes, and the agitation of Julião and his Peasant Leagues in the countryside. At the same time the more boisterous of his enemies on the right kept insisting that he was an agent of the Communist Party, while a small group of highly intelligent industrialists and landowners in the Northeast set out from the very beginning to chip away quietly, steadily, and insidiously at the foundations of his fledgling agency.

SUDENE's command post in Recife was the Juscelino Kubitschek Building, the sort of soaring cement-and-glass edifice that had come to symbolize progress in Brazil. Its top floors had been originally designed as a hotel, but a lack of funds had delayed completion indefinitely. SUDENE, at the time looking for quarters, simply moved in and negotiated the lease later.

From his offices on the top floor, Furtado could look out over a tranquil expanse of the South Atlantic, or inland to the cane fields on the outskirts of the city. He had little time to enjoy the view.

Meanwhile, in Washington, John F. Kennedy had begun to hear of Northeast Brazil. He had staked out Latin America as an area of special concern from the very first days of his administration, and had launched the Alliance for Progress as "a vast cooperative effort, unparalleled in magnitude and nobility of purpose, to satisfy the basic needs of the [Latin] American people for homes, work and land, health and schools. . . ." [10] He quickly made the Northeast a top-priority target under the Alliance. As he stated on July 15, 1961, "no area is in greater or more urgent need of attention than Brazil's vast Northeast." [11]

President Kennedy's interest was a direct result of the enormous influence of *The New York Times*. On October 31, 1960, *Times'* readers were startled to discover that "the makings of a revolutionary situation are increasingly apparent across the vastness of the poverty-stricken and drought-plagued Brazilian Northeast." The warning was sounded in a front-page story by the *Times'* enterprising Latin American correspondent, Tad Szulc.

After a grim sketch of the horrors attributable to the region's eco-

nomic and social underdevelopment, Szulc described how extreme leftists were taking advantage of the situation to stir up trouble in the cities and countryside: "Cuba's Premier, Fidel Castro, and Mao Tse-tung, Communist China's party chairman, are being presented as heroes to be imitated by the Northeast's peasants, workers, and students." He then underscored the region's strategic value to the United States: "Recife is the support base for the southern string of tracking stations of the South Atlantic guided missile range of the United States Air Force." His main point flashed from a quote attributed to a "high municipal official" in Recife, who warned that "the Northeast will go Communist and have a situation ten times worse than in Cuba if something is not done." A second article entitled "Marxists are Organizing Peasants in Brazil" appeared on an inside page the next day and focused on Julião's Peasant Leagues.

The sensationalist tone of Szulc's reporting touched a nerve sensitized by the Cuban Revolution. Kennedy, in the final days of the presidential campaign when the articles were published, took careful note of them. Shortly after his inauguration, his newly designated Special Assistant, Arthur M. Schlesinger, Jr., made a fact-finding trip to Latin America and returned with more horror stories from the Northeast. During his brief stay in Recife, Schlesinger had visited the countryside with Celso Furtado, and had been shaken by the sight of "one bleak, stagnant village after another, dark mud huts, children with spindle legs and swollen bellies, practically no old people. . . . In one hut a baby, lying helplessly in his mother's arms, was dying of measles." [12]

At the same time an ABC-TV documentary film, *The Troubled Land,* lent an even greater impact to the reports President Kennedy was receiving. In one memorable scene, a landowner brandished a pistol at the camera and swore he would kill any of his peasants who tried to organize.

To translate anxiety into action, the President decided to set up in Recife a mission of the United States Agency for International Development to coordinate Alliance for Progress efforts throughout the region. The attitude that quickly crystallized in official Washington was that while American neglect and mistakes in the past might have helped to bring on the Cuban Revolution, Northeast Brazil was

the postman's second ring—indeed, a much more critical challenge, for at stake was the whole of Brazil and the rest of South America. In other words, a domino at the head of the line was beginning to totter.

For the next couple of years Northeast Brazil became a "must" stop on everybody's trip to South America. Politicians and government officials, academicians, journalists and writers, distinguished visitors from many countries, all followed one another in and out of Recife to have a firsthand look at the revolutionary stirrings. The list included: Peace Corps Director, Sargent Shriver; George McGovern, head of the Food for Peace Program; Edward M. Kennedy, an assistant District Attorney from Massachusetts with an interest in foreign affairs; Yuri Gagarin; Dr. Henry Kissinger; Adlai Stevenson; John Dos Passos; and a young freelance writer for the *Christian Science Monitor* named Ralph Nader.

Northeasterners could truly feel that the whole world was watching. Whether the world understood what it saw was another question.

TWO ✥
✥ ✥ The Setting

IF NORTHEAST BRAZIL WERE an independent country, it would be the third largest and second most populous nation in South America.[1] Only the rest of Brazil would hold more people. In 1955, the population of the region was nearly 20 million. It is now passing 30 million. Though the boundaries of the Northeast vary slightly depending upon which government agency or author one relies, only Argentina and the Brazilian remainder would contain more square miles than even the smallest configuration of the region.

The Northeast occupies the easternmost edge of the continent. To the west, the rain forests of the Amazon Valley stretch for hundreds of miles. Rio de Janeiro lies on a line 1,157 miles to the south and slightly to the west. Thus, from a geographical perspective the Northeast is not exactly in the main stream of South American (or even Brazilian) life, a fact which proponents of the "domino theory" tended to overlook.

The region contains four quite distinct parts: the sugar zone, the coastal cities, the backlands, and a transitional area known as the *agreste*. The sugar zone, a humid strip along the coast, never penetrates more than seventy miles inland. The soil is a dark clay, rich and moist, originally nourishing rain forests and now under cane cultivation. The coastal cities, swelling in recent years as a result of migrations from the countryside, include Recife, the "capital" of the

Northeast, Fortaleza, Natal, and João Pessoa. Approximately one-half of the region's population is concentrated in the sugar zone and coastal cities. The *agreste*, hilly and subtropical, yields food for the cities on the coast and for the towns of the interior. The backlands encompass three-quarters of the land surface of the Northeast and hold about 29 per cent of the inhabitants of the region. This is the arid *sertão*, covered with prickly, stunted trees and brush which the Indians called *caatinga*, the "white forest." Droughts occur here on an average of one per 7.3 years. At times reaching disastrous proportions, they have given the backlanders their nickname, *flagelados* (the scourged), driving many of them from their homes. Yet the population of the *sertão* remains surprisingly dense.

Estimates of per capita income in the Northeast range from $50 to $140 per year. The figures fail to convey the gross disparities in income distribution among sectors of the population. About 2.5 per cent of the people in the Northeast receive 40 per cent of the region's total income. Land ownership and distribution is similarly imbalanced. A 1963 survey in the state of Pernambuco revealed that 690,000 rural families were living on land suitable for the support of 110,000 families.[2]

Illiteracy is high. In rural areas it may exceed 80 per cent. Figures tell but part of the story. A Peace Corps volunteer told the author in 1969 that some of the peasants with whom he was working were unaware of the causal connection between sexual intercourse and reproduction.

Life expectancy is as low as thirty-five years for 80 per cent of the population. Infant mortality during the first year of life has been estimated at 60 per cent. In the countryside and in the city slums, those who suffer from only one species of intestinal parasite are a small and fortunate minority.[3]

A 1957 survey by the United Nations Food and Agricultural Organization (FAO) concluded that the average daily food consumption in the Northeast amounted to only 1,990 calories, considerably below the recommended minimum need of 2,500.[4] A 1967 sampling in the southern section of Pernambuco's sugar zone revealed peasants consuming only 1,299 calories daily.[5] What makes this remarkable is that according to the laws of medical science, a person doing

absolutely nothing for twenty-four hours is supposed to need from 1,440 to 1,512 calories to maintain basic metabolism.

Comparative figures compiled by a U.S. government task force in 1963 [6] demonstrated one result of this chronic underconsumption. The body weights and heights of Northeastern boys and girls between the ages of five and eighteen were 10 per cent below the standard weights and heights for American children in the same age group. Men and women above forty-five years of age in the Northeast showed a steady decline in body weight. The opposite is true in the United States.

But even worse can be said about hunger in Northeast Brazil. A team of nutritionists from the Federal University of Pernambuco has warned that the undernourishment of children in their first year can produce mental debility.[7] A study of infants in the sugar zone disclosed that only 4.4 per cent received milk from their mothers after they passed the age of six months. The most common reason was simply that the mother had no milk for breast-feeding. Other causes include illness on the part of the mother or the child, or a new pregnancy. Once deprived of their mother's milk, these infants assumed a diet that was seriously lacking in vitamins and proteins. Among the legacies of childhood malnutrition are fatigue, nervousness, a limited attention span, and inadequate muscular development. The professor who directed the study charged that lack of proper nourishment during these early years is producing a legion of mentally retarded human beings in the Northeast. In the words of a young university professor from Recife, "the poverty here paralyzes the mind as well as the body."

This, then, was the ceaseless and voiceless violence to which Julião, Arraes, and Furtado were reacting in the early 1960s. These were the depths of degradation from which the poor were attempting to crawl. It is important to keep in mind that if these conditions spawned ferment in the Northeast, they also placed certain limitations upon those seeking change. Starving, disease-ridden peasants do not make the best soldiers in the army of national liberation.

An understanding of conditions in the Northeast during this period requires some knowledge of how they developed. Let us pause briefly, therefore, to examine their historical background.[8]

17

The Portuguese first came to the Northeast in the early years of the sixteenth century. They established a few trading posts along the coast for commerce with the Indians. In 1534 the Portuguese crown gave to Duarte Coelho what was called the "captaincy" of Pernambuco—a land grant stretching some 250 miles along the coast and, in theory, as far inland as the line drawn by the Pope as part of the famous Treaty of Tordesillas (dividing the New World between Spain and Portugal). Under the terms of a captaincy, the grantee enjoyed virtually sovereign powers, which included the rights to found towns, distribute land, and collect taxes. In return, the crown could levy export taxes.

Coelho arrived in 1535. He set himself to the task of founding a colony, the purpose of which was to grow sugar cane. The Portuguese had learned to cultivate cane on the island of Madeira, and had found that the plant prospered in the Northeast's climate and soil. To aid in the production of sugar, Coelho imported technicians, most of whom were Jews, the so-called New Christians (in reality forced converts) who were beginning to feel the heat of the Inquisition in Spain and Portugal and sought refuge in the New World.

Though the Indians put up some resistance, Coelho was able to set up two towns and five plantations in the first fifteen years of the captaincy. Labor was a problem. Captured Indians proved totally unsuited to the rigorous demands of work on a sugar plantation. It soon became apparent that the only solution lay in the African slave market. In 1559, 120 blacks from the Congo were shipped to Pernambuco, the start of what was to become a booming slave trade between Brazil and Africa.

The Negroes filled the need perfectly. They came from an agricultural society in which slave labor was not unknown. They were strong and healthy, necessary qualities for survival on the plantations. Over the years some managed to escape to the interior. In 1630 they founded their own Republic of Palmares, which lasted until 1697.

The plantations began to multiply and prosper. Their success attracted attention from abroad. The French made several tentative moves in northern Brazil, but failed to secure a foothold. The Dutch were more persistent. In 1624 they captured the city of Bahia, to the

south of Pernambuco, and held it for almost a year. In 1630 they seized Olinda, one of the two towns originally founded by Duarte Coelho when he arrived, and the nearby port of Recife. The Dutch made no efforts to change the social and economic life of Pernambuco, and their occupation left no legacy when in 1654 a long struggle by native Portuguese, Indians, Negroes, and people of mixed blood culminated in their expulsion from the region. But while in the Northeast the Dutch had learned all about the technology of sugar production, and they soon created their own sugar industry in their remaining New World colonies. This marked the beginning of the decline of the Northeast's sugar industry, a slide from which the region has yet to recover.

Pernambuco and the other captaincies of the Northeast settled into a century and a half of relative stability. Though colonists pushing inward began to grow cotton and raise livestock, prosperity still depended upon the price of sugar. Competition from the West Indies caused economic difficulties which eased in the latter part of the eighteenth century when a series of revolts disrupted production in the Indies and war in Europe increased the demand for Brazilian sugar.

It was during this period that the plantation system developed into an institution that was to have profound effects upon life in the Northeast.[9] The plantations were virtually self-sufficient enterprises. The owners, called *senhores de engenho,* had absolute control over their properties. They maintained a paternalistic, highly personalized relationship with the slaves, salaried workers, tenants, and independent farmers (often relatives) on the plantation property. The *senhor de engenho* provided physical security for those who lived on his land. His influence often extended beyond the boundaries of the plantation. If the local authorities arrested one of his people, it was not unusual for him to lead an armed force into town to free the man from jail.

The slaves who worked in and around the plantation mansion often enjoyed the advantages of being treated in many ways like members of the owner's family. The owner's children were wet-nursed by black women, grew up with the young blacks, and were introduced to the mysteries of sex by precocious black girls. On the

19

other hand the tenants (mainly ex-slaves and mulattos) led particularly insecure lives. The *senhor de engenho* could expel them from their plots of land at any time for no reason, and often forced his sexual attentions upon their wives and daughters.

Roman Catholicism exercised a substantial influence over plantation life. Many owners built their own chapels and engaged priests to minister to the spiritual needs of the inhabitants. This included religious education, which served to reinforce the plantation system. The peasants were imbued with a sense of fatalism toward the travails of their earthly life, as well as with a strong respect for authority. Their Catholicism tended to be primitive, interspersed with superstition and the pagan beliefs which the blacks had brought to Brazil from Africa and had never really relinquished.

Inevitably, the political system that evolved from this neofeudal structure was designed to uphold it. Certain *senhores de engenho* in the sugar zone and large landowners throughout the rest of the Northeast assumed the role of political bosses in their immediate environs. They became known as *coroneis* (colonels). Their grip remained unchallenged in most places even up until the 1950s.[10]

The nineteenth century was marked by great political turbulence in Brazil. In 1807 the Portuguese royal family, fleeing from Napoleon, set up a government in exile in Brazil. Fifteen years later, after the court had returned to Lisbon, the Brazilians declared their independence from Portugal. They established a monarchy of their own under an Emperor, Dom Pedro, son of the Portuguese king. In 1889 the monarchy was overthrown and Brazil became a republic.

In the meantime, a long antislavery campaign finally achieved abolition in 1888. Though Northeasterners played prominent roles in the campaign, this milestone had little real effect on the blacks working on the region's sugar plantations. Most of them remained as dependent as ever on their masters. This era also saw the evolution of a new relationship between landowner and tenant, popularly known as the *cambão*. The word literally refers to the yoke which hitches pairs of oxen together. It came to describe a leasing arrangement whereby the tenant, instead of paying rent in cash or crops, had to work several days a week for the landowner without pay. A strict application of the *cambão* effectively bound tenants to the dictates of

20

the plantation owners. For the newly emancipated blacks, it was a not-too-subtle continuation of their previous state of servitude.

Yet significant change did come to the Northeast during this period. As the sugar industry continued to decline because of competition from Cuba, a new product, coffee, took over as Brazil's most important export, and the locus of economic power in the country permanently shifted from the Northeast to the coffee-growing regions of the south.

In addition, technological developments that occurred at the close of the nineteenth and start of the twentieth centuries brought about a profound transformation in the structure of the Northeast's sugar industry. New methods of production requiring extensive capital outlays led to the construction of large sugar mills, called *usinas,* throughout the sugar zone. Railroads connected the mills with the ports. The wealthiest plantation owners participated in this expansion, as did investors from outside the region. The *usinas* made it uneconomical to refine sugar on the plantations where teams of oxen provided power for the machinery, and as a result many of the *senhores de engenho* had to limit their operations to growing cane. They thus became mere suppliers. The mills began to buy out many of the plantations and to grow their own cane. The governments of the states, whose boundaries roughly corresponded to those of the old captaincies, supported this drastic change by making it easy for the mill owners (called *usineiros*) to borrow money. In the long run this resulted in the concentration of economic and political power in the Northeast. A relatively small number of family groups owning mills survived the ups and downs of the first half of the twentieth century.

The *usineiros* soon developed a tradition of not ploughing any of their profits back into their sugar operations. They preferred instead to indulge in conspicuous consumption—trips abroad, expensive apartments in the city, etc.—and to invest in other enterprises, some of which were not located in the Northeast. Displaying a remarkable lack of business initiative, they refused to modernize their mills.

By the 1950s and 1960s the Northeast's sugar industry was beginning to show the results of the *usineiros'* attitudes. Machinery was old and run-down. The growing and cutting of cane was barely

mechanized. Land that could have been used for other cash crops or subsistence crops was allowed to lie fallow. Only 34 per cent of the area under cane cultivation was fertilized, and 36 per cent of this land was on slopes which had inclines of 20 degrees or more and hence had to be worked by hand.[11] According to one popular story, a certain plantation owner kept cultivating the slopes of a steep hill near his house for the aesthetic delight of being able to look out the window from his bed and gaze upon a green curtain of cane.

Meanwhile, an emerging sugar industry in southern Brazil began to overtake the Northeastern producers. The southerners were soon growing and refining sugar at a lower cost than their competition in the Northeast. Between 1946 and 1961, when the overall demand for sugar was greatly expanding, the Northeast doubled its sugar production. Over the same period the southerners showed a tenfold increase. In the 1960s, the per acre yield in the south reached 24.3 tons of sugar, as compared with 16.2 tons in the Northeast. In a free market the Northeast's *usineiros* would have been out of business.

The Northeastern sugar producers therefore used every political resource at their disposal to force the federal government to help them. Whenever hard times came, they insisted that it was the government's duty to bail them out with bank loans and outright subsidies. In addition, they took advantage of the overpopulation of the sugar zone—their abundance of cheap labor—as the basis for an argument that amounted to crude blackmail: the government had to keep the sugar industry of the Northeast afloat to prevent all these people from starving to death.

And so the government kept the *usineiros* in business, enabling them to keep their workers in a state of semistarvation, and thus in readiness for the next crisis. It was a vicious cycle, and its preservation was the function of the Sugar and Alcohol Institute, a federal agency created during the Great Depression and, as one might expect, under the political control of the Northeastern sugar industry. The Institute buys sugar from the mills of the Northeast at artificially high prices, and then sells it at home and abroad. The United States, under its sugar quota, pays price supports for much of this sugar, and thus participates in the perpetuation of the system.[12]

The peasants who depended upon the sugar monoculture for their

existence found themselves trapped in an incredibly exploitative process. Their wages remained quite low and failed to keep pace with rising food prices. The price of food in the plantation stores was generally from 30 per cent to 50 per cent higher than in the towns, and the store owners cheated their customers as a matter of course. In slack periods the owners extended credit to the peasant. The mill would then pay the peasant's salary directly to the store owner, who would deduct what he claimed was owed and return the rest to the peasant. The latter, usually illiterate, had no way of checking on the store owner, who could withhold almost anything and get away with it. A not-uncommon variant was for the mill to pay its workers in paper chits redeemable for food at the mill or plantation store. The net result of this system of distribution was that the peasant ended up paying about one-third of his meagre salary for the privilege of spending the other two-thirds. Little wonder that he turned to the comforts of *cachaça*, a strong alcoholic drink made from sugarcane.

There were several categories of worker in the sugar zone. Mention has already been made of the tenant who paid his rent by working several days without pay—the *cambão* arrangement. Some sugar workers lived in the nearby towns. Still others were migrants from the interior who came to the sugar zone for the harvest season. But by far the most common type of worker was the *morador,* who was given the use of a small hut on the property of the mill or the plantation. There he lived with his wife and numerous children, crowded into a room or two, without light, water, or sanitation facilities. They sometimes had the use of a tiny plot around the hut where they could raise foodstuffs. The worker had no legal rights to this property and could be expelled at any time virtually at the whim of the landowner. This discouraged the peasant from making improvements. The long hours he had to spend in the cane fields likewise made it difficult for him in his struggle for survival. Occasionally he was permitted to clear off some unused land at the top of a hill where he might grow some food, but more often than not the next year the landowner would reclaim the land and put it under cane cultivation. Of course no payment was ever made for the worker's efforts in clearing the land.

⋎ Until the 1960s none of these workers enjoyed any effective legal protection, for before that time what few laws existed for his benefit were never enforced. Since most sugar workers were illiterate, they could not vote. Very few had any money to spend on anything except the bare necessities. They thus existed beyond the reach of the legal and political processes, and outside the money economy. In the mid-1960s the sugar industry of the Northeast employed some 450,000 peasants, while more than 2 million were dependent on the industry for their sustenance.

In the 1930s and early 1940s plantations distant from the nearest mill and not served by adequate roads were being shut down by their owners. Peasants living and working on these plantations remained as tenants. But at the close of World War II the price of sugar went up considerably. A number of *senhores de engenho* who had left their plantations now returned and wanted to begin growing cane again. First, however, they had to expel the peasants from their lots, where the latter had been raising subsistence crops. These tenants reacted like any peasant whose hunger for a plot of ground had been satisfied. Clinging to their plots, they resisted the landowners, and unrest spread throughout the sugar zone. It was in the midst of this unrest that the first Peasant League was born.

Meanwhile, in the vast interior of the Northeast, economic and social conditions evolved from a considerably different set of circumstances. The *agreste*, which marks the transition from the tropical sugar zone to the semiarid backlands, owed its settlement to the sugar industry. Large cattle-raising estates furnished animal power for the plantations and meat for the population concentrating along the coast. Cotton and foodstuffs were also cultivated. The *agreste* did not attract a large rural proletariat. Many peasants leased land under the *cambão* arrangement. Others were sharecroppers. In addition, a large number of small property-owners—a rural lower-middle class —came into being. Discontent arose among those paying the *cambão* when salaries in the region reached a level which made the value of several days' work per week over a period of several years exceed the value of the land which the peasants were leasing.

Originally explored by adventurers in search of precious metals, the *sertão* (arid interior) soon attracted a tough breed of permanent

settlers willing to fend off the Indians and endure the inhospitable climate. The governors of the captaincies extending into the *sertão* distributed to family and friends huge land grants which generally extended from riverbanks back into the interior. These estates became ranches for raising livestock. In addition, the soil adjacent to the rivers was found suitable for growing cotton. Here too the *cambão* evolved as a system of land tenure and employment, and eventually aroused the same sort of dissatisfaction which sprung up in the *agreste*.

The *sertão* has always been Brazil's number-one disaster area. In addition to the droughts, heavy rains often cause flash floods that severely damage settlements along the banks of the few rivers that traverse the interior.

Ever since the Great Drought of 1877–79, which killed an estimated half-million people in the state of Ceará, the federal government initiated a series of programs designed to go beyond mere emergency relief and defend the inhabitants of the *sertão* against the ravages of future droughts.[13] Federal commissions and agencies were formed, plans drawn up, and public works projects begun. Yet the droughts still came in their usual fashion and wreaked their usual havoc.

A principal reason for this failure to solve the problem of the droughts was the absence of a consistent and comprehensive program. The government was forever making false starts, and seemed unable to decide how much federal money should be allocated to the Northeast. The natural instinct of Brazilians to improvise was a difficult habit to break, and improvisation was no way of dealing with the recurring dry spells.

The plight of the Northeastern interior found its way into the depths of the Brazilian national consciousness through the medium of several literary masterpieces emanating from the region. Graciliano Ramos' *Barren Lives*, for example, etches a terse, unforgettable account of a grim cycle in the life of a herdsman and his family, who survive one drought only to face the ravages of another. *Rebellion in the Backlands*, by Euclides da Cunha, transmits a harshly unsympathetic picture of the federal government's repression of a peasant uprising in the *sertão*. As a result of these classics, Brazilians tend to

25

regard the Northeast with pangs of guilt tempered only by a sense of romanticism.

Inhabitants of the *sertão* originally included runaway and freed slaves as well as the usual gamut of mixtures to be found in the Northeast (Negro-Portuguese, Portuguese-Indian, Indian-Negro, and combinations of all three). Except for a few plateaus which escaped the droughts, the *sertão* seems hardly fit for human habitation. But the *sertanejo*, or backlander, survived and multiplied.

Among the distinctive characteristics of the *sertanejo* is the fact that he is an honest man. Ranch owners, accustomed to pay their employees one of every four calves born to the herd each year, can rest assured that no more than that percentage will be taken. Isolation from the rest of the country makes the *sertanejo* suspicious of outsiders, and marks his speech with quaint anachronisms. If he must travel to other parts of Brazil in search of work or is driven from his home to a coastal city because of a drought (the *sertão* seems constantly in the throes of migration), he never loses his attachment to this barren land and will return as soon as he can.

One of the most fascinating aspects of life in the interior is the periodic outburst of religious fanaticism, usually inspired by the appearance of some bearded and robed messianic figure. These backlands prophets play upon the *sertanejo*'s deep-rooted mysticism, a tendency bred by an interaction of frustration, isolation, and partly digested Roman Catholic doctrine. Thus, the struggle for existence that marks the daily life of the backlander is thought to be punishment for his sins, requiring penance and sacrifice. The tradition of the *promessa* or promise, whereby an individual pledges some act of sacrifice if God grants him a request, was derived from this belief.

These attitudes blended nicely with a popular belief known as Sebastianism,[14] which the earliest settlers of the interior brought with them from Portugal and implanted in the region. According to this tradition, Sebastian, a Portuguese king who vanished in Africa in 1578 while fighting the Moors, would some day return in triumph, bringing with him great earthly rewards for those who believed in him.

The first violent manifestation of Sebastianism in Brazil occurred at Serra do Rodeador in Pernambuco in 1819–20. A prophet gath-

ered together a group of followers to await King Sebastian, who was expected back at any moment to lead them on a crusade for the liberation of Jerusalem. The movement featured prayer, religious ceremony, and military drill in preparation for Sebastian's imminent appearance. Instead, Brazilian army troops arrived with orders to disperse the settlement. The faithful remained unperturbed, steadfast in the belief that their King would protect them, and that the attacking troops would lay down their arms and join the movement. They didn't.

Sebastianism reached its peak with the incident at Pedra Bonita, also in the interior of the state of Pernambuco. In 1836 a charismatic psychotic attracted a group of backlanders with his prophecies of the impending return of the King, who was going to create a paradise on earth for believers. The followers of this prophet immersed themselves in the usual occult religious practices, which took place around twin 100-foot pillars. On May 14, 1838, the prophet declared that King Sebastian could not break the enchantment which kept him from appearing, until the ground at the foot of the pillars was bathed with blood. His followers accepted the word and for three days indulged in a sacrificial orgy. Mothers dropped their children from the tops of the pillars. Adults jumped or were pushed. The final toll: thirty children, twelve men, eleven women, and fourteen dogs.

The most famous of these outbreaks of religious fanaticism in the *sertão* did not involve King Sebastian. Antônio Conselheiro was the very image of the backlands prophet, right out of central casting— long hair, flowing beard, tattered blue robe, hypnotic gaze. He had taken to the ascetic life after his wife ran off with a police officer and eventually acquired the reputation of being a holy man. People came to him for advice: hence the name, Anthony the Counselor. Soon he had gathered about him a considerable following to whose spiritual needs he ministered in a most stringent way. His basic teaching was that suffering is the most sublime virtue. His followers built a city, Canudos, in the interior of the state of Bahia, and attracted national attention when they refused to acknowledge the authority of the republican government that took over after the fall of the monarchy in 1889. Several army expeditions attempted to quell the rebellion, but Antônio's *sertanejos* used their innate guerrilla skills to inflict heavy

losses on the invaders. Finally, a large force overwhelmed the defenders and exterminated them to the last man, woman, and child.

About the same time, north of Canudos in that part of the *sertão* where the states of Pernambuco, Paraíba, and Ceará come together, a diminutive priest named Padre Cícero was beginning to gain fame as a miracle-worker.[15] Suspended by the Church and exiled to this remote corner of the interior, he offered a message of hope to peasants who lived in a region parched by terrible droughts. In the first decades of the twentieth century, his spiritual hold translated itself into political power, and the entire state of Ceará came under his control. Working out a *modus vivendi* with the Church, he institutionalized his rule in a welter of religious processions, public flagellations, and other daily rituals marked by considerable fervor and an occasional miracle. Already a popular saint at the time of his death in 1934, he is still widely venerated today throughout the interior of the Northeast. Legend has it that he will someday return.

A tradition of banditry stems from the same poverty and isolation that produced the apocalyptical mysticism of Antônio Conselheiro and Padre Cícero. Just as plantation owners were a law unto themselves in the sugar zone, so outlaw bands roamed the interior in defiance of feeble attempts by federal, state, and local authorities to establish law and order. These bandits affected a distinctive style of dress and often enjoyed Robin Hood-like reputations. The best known of the lot was the bespectacled Lampeão,[16] whose gang was not broken up until 1938. Government agents beheaded Lampeão, his mistress Maria Bonita, and the rest of his captured colleagues, and exhibited the heads throughout the backlands to prove to skeptical peasants that the legendary leader was indeed dead. For many years thereafter the government official responsible for the gang's demise received threats of death from Lampeão fans. The severed heads eventually found their way to the medical school of the University of Bahia. They were preserved in formaldehyde and became a tourist attraction, until Lampeão's surviving relatives convinced the government that this was unchristian, and the heads at last received a proper burial. Lampeão and Maria Bonita have become favorite subjects of Brazilian film-makers in recent years.

This was the setting from which the Peasant Leagues emerged.

The first members of the Leagues were tenants and salaried workers in the sugar zone. Their attitudes, motivations, and reactions reflected an environment that had changed very little over the centuries. The same could be said of the plantation owners and upper-class families who controlled the wealth of the Northeast. On every social level the Northeasterner tends to be introspective, embracing a pervasive regionalism which is celebrated and reinforced by tradition and strong cultural roots.

When the Leagues aroused worldwide interest in the early 1960s, foreign observers tended to ignore these factors. They were quick to assume that "revolution" in the Northeast could ignite upheaval in the rest of the country, to view the Leagues in Cold War terms, and to stress comparisons with the Cuban Revolution. But despite its sugar monoculture, the Northeast is not Cuba. And the relevant question at the time was not whether Francisco Julião was another Castro, but whether he could become another Padre Cícero or Antônio Conselheiro.

PART ONE

THREE 🗢

🗢 🗢 Francisco Julião
and the Peasant Leagues

AS DWIGHT D. EISENHOWER ENTERED the third year of his first term as President, U.S. relations with Latin America reflected the "don't-bother-me-now-I'm-busy" attitude which had crystallized in Washington during World War II and was to continue until the Cuban Revolution. State Department policy maintained an unwavering support of stability and the status quo. In an editorial expansively entitled "Our Hemisphere," setting the tone for its annual review of business and finance in Canada and Latin America, *The New York Times* expressed a guarded optimism for 1955, and concluded by reiterating the basic U.S. prescription for economic development in Latin America: the Latins should "help by creating a favorable climate for investments and trade." [1] The assumption was that progress required the fostering of stable conditions which would attract foreign (i.e. American) capital.

In January, 1955, Latin American stability resulted from a distinguished roster of dictators, which included Batista in Cuba, Pérez Jiménez in Venezuela, Perón in Argentina, Rojas Pinilla in Colombia, Somoza in Nicaragua, Stroessner in Paraguay, and Trujillo in the Dominican Republic. Chile, Peru, and Ecuador enjoyed respectably conservative governments. In 1954 the suicide of Brazil's Getúlio Vargas and the overthrow of Guatemala's Arbenz had eliminated two presidents who had been troubling the waters by pushing

33

for change. Indeed, on New Year's day the new government in Guatemala announced that the land Arbenz had expropriated from the United Fruit Company as part of an agrarian reform had been given back to its former owner.

The American public remained consummately uninterested in events and conditions below the Rio Grande, a fact of life recognized (and encouraged) by the sparse coverage given to Latin America by the nation's press. Only when outbursts of violence shattered the calm did heads turn south. In this regard, January, 1955, was an exceptional month.[2] The year had hardly begun when assassins machine-gunned to death the "strong man" President of Panama, José Antonio Remón. A week later, on January 10, the first reports of an invasion of Costa Rica from neighboring Nicaragua became public. From then until the end of the month, Americans read about the unsuccessful attack against Costa Rica's President, José Figueres, a prominent member of the so-called "democratic left" in Latin America. The affair assumed comic-opera overtones when the Nicaraguan dictator Somoza challenged the diminutive Figueres to a duel. Over this same period of time, there were stories of political unrest in Peru and Bolivia, "red" plots in Cuba and Guatemala, and the beginnings of Perón's attack on the Catholic Church in Argentina.

Accustomed to such goings-on south of the border, Americans could hardly take them seriously. More important things were happening in the Far East, where the Communist Chinese were putting pressure on Formosa and the offshore islands. At home, the Democrats had won control of both branches of Congress. Senator McCarthy, tarnished by the Army hearing, was beginning his quick fade into history. And a Senator from Texas, on becoming Majority Leader, tried to dampen rumors that he was a prospective presidential candidate by commenting: "I am conscious of my limitations. I think it's fair to say nobody but my mama ever thought I'd get as far as I am." [3]

Meanwhile, in Caxangá, an outlying section of the city of Recife, a group of peasants paid an unpublicized visit to a lawyer[4] and set in motion a chain of events which would have far wider repercussions

34

than the murder of a Panamanian president, or a ruckus in Costa Rica.

January in Northeast Brazil is midsummer, a time of searing, stifling heat. The peasants had driven their horse and wooden cart along the broad, badly maintained Avenida Caxangá, past Recife's only golf course to the edge of the city, the eastern bank of the Capiberibe River. The Sunday morning traffic had been light, only a fraction of the usual swirl of trucks, buses, and trolley cars. Still the peasants felt much more at ease when they turned down a dirt side road cutting through a dense blanket of vegetation which seemed to smother every trace of city noise. They came to a halt in front of a large, colonial-style house with faded yellow walls. An adjacent grove of banana and mango trees held back the morning sun.

[The spokesman for the peasants, a tall man named José de Prazeres, was carrying some papers rolled up and tied together with a piece of string.] While his companions waited on the porch of the house, he entered through an anteroom. He found himself in an office. A chandelier dangled from the ceiling. Pale-blue shutters rested against the sides of the windows. A desk littered with papers partially blocked the whitewashed fireplace opposite the door. Shelves burdened with musty law books covered much of the wall space.

To the left was a living room where two casually dressed men sat reading the Sunday papers. One of them, a big, pot-bellied mulatto with close-cropped, thinning hair, looked up as a clock chimed and noticed José, hat in hand, waiting respectfully in the doorway.

"What do you want?" he asked, instinctively putting his hand to his mouth, but not fast enough to conceal a missing front tooth.

✗ "I would like to speak with the Deputy," answered José.

The other man, whose head had been buried in the *Diário de Pernambuco*, folded the newspaper on his lap and looked up from a red rocking chair. "I am the Deputy," he said in a soft voice. "Come in, please."

(Francisco Julião, lawyer, state legislator, and part-time man of letters, beckoned to his visitor. José preferred to remain standing, and after exchanging the usual amenities with Julião, he told why he had come.

José de Prazeres was a tenant on a plantation called Galiléia in the township of Vitória de Santo Antão, some forty miles west of Recife on the outer edge of the sugar zone. The plantation, like many others, had ceased producing sugar in the late 1930s, and its owner, Oscar de Arruda Beltrão, had gone to live in Vitória. Before leaving, he had divided up most of the plantation among the peasant families who had worked for him. As tenants, they continued to grow sugar and other cash and subsistence crops on the property. Each month they paid their rent in cash or crops to the administrator of the plantation, José Francisco de Souza, an old peasant better known by his nickname, Zezé.

Living conditions at Galiléia had always been primitive, but no more so than elsewhere in the sugar zone. In the old days the peasants had worked for Beltrão, growing cane and producing sugar. Now they worked for themselves, but things had not much improved.

In contemplating their grim existence, Zezé, José de Prazeres, and some of the other tenants thought that the denizens of Galiléia might improve their lot if they united in some sort of mutual-benefit association. They could, through monthly contributions, establish a fund which might be used to hire a schoolteacher for the children, and to form a cooperative for obtaining credit for the purchase of seed and implements. In addition, the survivors of deceased members could draw upon the fund to defray burial expenses. In this way members could escape the humiliation, albeit posthumous, of being carted to the grave in a common coffin furnished by the municipal government for all charity burials in the township. Their goals were so modest that if they had been able to wait a decade or so, the peasants could have had a Peace Corps Volunteer assigned to help them.

And so Zezé, José, and the rest of the Galiléans, 140 families in all, formed what they solemnly called the Agricultural and Cattle-Breeding Society of the Planters of Pernambuco. Being very concerned with legal formalities, they went to a local judge, Dr. Rudolfo Aureliano, who drew up the legal documents which the law required of any beneficial association. They also paid a call on their landlord in Vitória.

Oscar Beltrão, whose family had owned Galiléia since 1887, at

first saw nothing wrong with the Society. Indeed, he could divine at least one positive advantage such a Society might offer, since Zezé suggested that one of its collateral purposes might be to create a special fund from which a member disabled by sickness or injury could draw to meet his rent payments. He was also quite pleased when his tenants asked him to become their Honorary President. (A "humble gesture," a Brazilian journalist later described it, "like that of a dog licking the hand that beats him." [5]) On January 1, 1955, speeches, fireworks, dancing, and other festivities formally launched the Society. In buoyant spirits, Beltrão announced to the tenants that they could use his timber to build a chapel as the Society's initial project.

It didn't take long for the honeymoon to end. Beltrão's son and heir, who lived in Recife, had been for some time planning to convert the plantation into a cattle ranch. Since this would require the expulsion of the tenants, he became alarmed that they had organized. Some of the neighboring plantation owners also expressed concern lest the idea spread. Together they convinced the Honorary President that he had been duped, that a Society of peasants was unheard of, subversive, probably Communistic, and certainly not to be tolerated. As a clincher, they added that the peasants were probably out to reduce their rent payments.

Beltrão immediately saw the error of his ways. After consulting his lawyer, he renounced his post as Honorary President and ordered the peasants to disband their Society. To his great surprise, they balked. He tried to have some of them ejected. They resisted. He fumed. Zezé, José de Prazeres, and others went to Recife. They appealed to the Governor of the state, General Cordeiro de Farias, an authoritarian conservative who lent credibility to the "gorila" epithet traditionally applied to Brazilian officers dabbling in politics. He chased them away, and later complained to his staff about their "seditious" attitude. They approached some lawyers, all of whom demanded substantial fees. They asked for help at the State Legislature. Someone told them to see a state deputy named Julião.

José de Prazeres paused and seemed to be holding his breath. Julião did not hesitate. "I'll defend you," he said. "I'm a deputy. The state pays me. You won't have to pay me anything."

His companion, a local lawyer and long-time friend named Jonas

de Souza, had been examining the documents while José spoke. "These papers will have to be notarized and filed, and the registration fee must be paid," he said turning to Julião.

"Yes, and the Society will have to elect officers as soon as possible. Can you hold elections this week?"

"Yes, Doctor," nodded José gratefully.

"Then we shall visit Galiléia next Sunday and see what needs to be done."

Julião was one of the very few Recife lawyers who would represent peasants in legal matters. Though he lived and worked in the city, he had never forgotten his childhood in the countryside.[6] His sentimental attachment to rural life was deep-rooted and constant, a quality not uncommon among intellectuals of the Northeast.

Francisco Juliano Arruda de Paula was born on February 16, 1915, in the municipality of Bom Jardim, some eighty miles northeast of Recife on the outer edge of Pernambuco's sugar zone. He was named for his paternal grandfather, Francisco de Paula Gomes dos Santos. His mother, a devout Catholic, customarily gave her children the names of saints, and February 16 was the Feast of St. Juliano. By the time he reached elementary school, the name had been shortened to Julião.

Both his grandfathers were *senhores de engenho*. Francisco de Paula was something of a romantic, a tall, gaunt man given to treating his slaves as part of the family. His sugar plantation, Bôa Esperanca (or Espera, as the peasants called it) was one of the most prosperous in the area. Julião has written that "in the heart of every plantation boy there lives a *senhor de engenho*." [7] To the young Julião, his namesake soon assumed heroic proportions.

Manoel Tertuliano Travassos de Arruda, his maternal grandfather, was a more traditional landowner. Short, stocky, imperious, he shouted commands in a booming voice. His conversational tone was only slightly less boisterous. It was not unusual to see him setting out on long hikes to survey his properties. His energies extended in other directions. Twice married, he sired twenty-seven sons and daughters by his legal wives, and an unrecorded number of illegitimate children. The white goatee which became one of his

38

trademarks gave him an air of respectability which helped him as a lawyer and local political leader. Manoel Tertuliano ruled his domain with a firm hand. It was said that he introduced the *cambão* to the region, a dubious distinction which his grandson would never forget.

Julião spent his youth on the plantation, along with his four brothers and three sisters. (One of his sisters died during childhood.) He was a typical plantation boy, wet-nursed by a black maid, toughened by work during the harvest season, riding and swimming with the sons of tenants and servants, wholeheartedly committed to the simple pursuits of country life.

When Julião was thirteen, his father sent him away to school. Riding on horseback to Limoeiro and thence by automobile to Recife, he enrolled in the Instituto Carneiro Leão, a private boarding school. Most of his classmates were the sons of large landowners. At first it was an unhappy experience. The combination of city life and scholastic discipline made him feel like a wild animal in a cage. But eventually he adapted and survived. Shy and introverted, he read a great deal (mostly novels) and daydreamt even more. It was during this period that he came into contact with Marxism, as developed in Engels' *Anti-Düring*.[8] The book greatly impressed him, and although still grasping for an ideology he began to think of himself as a "man of the left."

He completed the four-year course in 1933 and then, because of financial difficulties, taught for a year or two in an elementary school in Olinda, a suburb of Recife. After toying with the idea of becoming a surgeon, he entered law school in Recife.

In the late 1930s Brazil was ruled by Getúlio Vargas, a dictator who modeled his so-called New State after the Fascist regimes of Italy, Spain and Portugal. Political police were ubiquitous and kept a particularly watchful eye on the university students. Thus when a friend of Julião's wrote him a long letter defending Karl Marx and it somehow fell into the hands of the authorities, an order went out to arrest Julião. Police broke into the house where he was staying, seized him, and searched his room, even cutting open his mattress.[9] They took him prisoner for a day and a night. In the New State the experience was not unusual but it left an impression.

On December 16, 1939, Julião and 119 of his classmates received their degrees from the oldest law school in Brazil. Most were the sons of the rich and had jobs waiting for them in commerce or industry. A few settled down to practice law in Recife or the handful of other large cities in the state. Julião was in the latter group.

In 1943 he married a fifteen-year-old girl who had once been his pupil during his school-teaching days. The couple rented a modest house in the Caxangá district of Recife, on the edge of town near the highway leading to Bom Jardim. Julião maintained his close contacts with the plantation, which no longer produced sugar. Fresh fruits and vegetables from Espera were delivered regularly to his house. Alexina presented him with two daughters and then two sons: Anataílde (nicknamed Tata), Anatilde (Tidinha), Anatólio (Tulito) and Anacleto (Teto). Julião and Alexina were married within the Catholic Church and had all their children baptized—facts which suggest that the couple continued to respect the traditions of the Northeast.

Julião embarked upon a legal career in Recife and devoted part of his practice to the representation of peasants. This was a difficult undertaking. A governor of Pernambuco once remarked: "To my enemies, the law; to my friends, facilities." The aphorism nicely catches the yawning chasm in Brazil between the letter of the law and its actual application. The administration of Brazilian justice was customarily flexible, but it bent only one way—in the direction of wealth and power. Nonetheless, beginning in 1941 Julião defended peasants in the courts of Recife and in other towns in Pernambuco and the adjacent states. He soon gained a reputation among the rural workers, tenants, and small farmers, especially in the area around Bom Jardim.

At the same time he developed a taste for politics. The electoral process in Pernambuco operated on two levels. The powerful family groups and their rural allies (the "colonels") dominated the state and excluded outsiders from the exercise of any effective power. The only opportunities for ambitious newcomers lay on the outer fringes of the system, where small parties competed for minor offices. Julião plunged into the game with enthusiasm. In 1945 he joined the Republican Party, a center-conservative splinter group.[10] The leader of the Republican Party was an ex-President of Brazil, Artur Ber-

nardes, a conservative but also an economic nationalist who opposed foreign mining concessions and supported state development of petroleum resources. These nationalistic postures appealed to Julião, who aligned himself with the left wing of the party. He ran unsuccessfully for federal deputy in 1945 and for state deputy in 1948. In the latter election, the Republican Party nominated its own gubernatorial candidate, who promptly urged his supporters to vote for one of the other candidates. These machinations so disgusted Julião that he left the Republican Party to join the Brazilian Socialist Party (PSB), whose ideological orientation was much more akin to his own. The PSB, originally known as the Democratic Left, was composed of a small circle of intellectuals who talked a great deal, mostly to each other. They did not have any real popular base, a shortcoming amply demonstrated in every election. Julião at least injected a bit of freshness into the Pernambuco branch of the Party, and in 1954 he was elected a state deputy, the only PSB candidate to win a seat in the legislature that year.

In addition to lawyering and politicking, Julião pursued literary ambitions. He liked to write sonnets and also tried his hand at fiction. His first book, a collection of short stories entitled *Cachaça*, was published locally in 1951. The title story depicted the practice of landowners in certain areas of paying their workers in a cheap whiskey made from sugarcane. Julião's prose style caught the flavor of the countryside and won him plaudits among Recife's small intellectual elite. Gilberto Freyre, Brazil's renowned sociologist who makes his home in Recife, wrote a laudatory introduction which pointed to "pages of intense interest for all those who dedicate themselves, in Brazil, to the study of the man of the interior, of the common man, of the man of the people." Shortly thereafter, Julião completed his first novel, *Irmão Juàzeiro*, which focused on the conflict between a peasant and a landowner in the interior. The book was not published until 1961, when the author's fame assured an improvement over the limited circulation of *Cachaça* (which is now something of a collector's item).

It was abundantly clear from the outset that Julião and the Agricultural and Cattle-Breeding Society of the Planters of Pernambuco were destined for each other. It was a perfect match. As Julião took

41

up the defense of the Galiléans, his sentimental dreams and social conscience intersected. He must have known at the outset that a campaign to help the Society would have more promising implications than individual lawsuits involving peasants. But he could never have imagined the length and breadth of these implications.

One week after José de Prazeres's visit to the house in Caxangá, Julião made the trip to Galiléia. A large crowd of peasants greeted him with cheers and fireworks. They threw flowers at him. The scene would be repeated many times. His message to them would also be repeated many times: "I shall do everything I can so that these petals will never turn into stones." [11] A meeting took place in front of the house of old Zezé, who had been elected President of the Society.

Julião became their legal adviser. (Later he would be promoted to Beltrão's old post, Honorary President.) He first saw to it that the Society was properly organized and registered under the laws of the state, and he undertook to defend the tenants Beltrão was attempting to evict. He also made good use of his seat in the state legislature, from which he spoke out in support of the Galiléans. This was not the first time he had taken a public position on rural matters. At the close of World War II when the Vargas dictatorship fell and constitutional democracy was restored in Brazil, he had issued a manifesto urging that something be done to alleviate the misery of the peasants of the Northeast.[12] But words, no matter how eloquent, were never going to bring about change in the Brazilian countryside. The situation required a build-up of pressure at the grass-roots level. The Galiléans, with their modest organization, had unwittingly devised a mechanism that could create such pressure and translate it into movement. A local newspaper dubbed the Society a "Peasant League," no doubt hoping to stir memories of and to suggest a connection with Peasant Leagues organized by the Brazilian Communist Party in 1945 and disbanded soon thereafter. The name stuck.

The rural power structure did not take kindly to any sort of peasant organizing. From the onset the landlords made every effort to nip the new movement in the bud. At times their tactics were rather naive and quaint. Julião has described the reaction of one of his own relatives, a wealthy landowner, when he heard that his tenants were

in the process of forming a League. He called them together and made them recite some prayers with him. Then he delivered the following homily:

"The land on which you live I inherited from my father. And you, what did you inherit? Nothing. Therefore I am not to blame for being rich nor are you to blame for being poor. Everything has been ordained by God. He knows what He is doing. If He gives land to me and not to you, to reject this is to rebel against God. Such a rebellion is a mortal sin. Let all men accept God's will so that they will not incur His wrath nor lose their souls. You have to accept poverty on earth in order to gain eternal life in heaven. The poor live in God's grace. The rich don't. In this way you are more fortunate than I, since you are closer to heaven. Hear what I tell you and take my advice. Let him who has joined the League leave it." [13]

The peasants somehow did not sympathize with the plight of their rich landlord and would not abandon their League. Two weeks later, the landlord had them jailed, and Julião had to get them out on *habeas corpus.*

The reaction of Julião's relative was mild in comparison with how landowners customarily dealt with disobedient peasants. The story of Antônio Vicente and his sons has been cited as a more typical example of what peasants had to endure.

Antônio Vicente was an old man who had lived for many years as a tenant on a plantation called California.[14] He had worked hard to improve the small property which he leased, and was able to support his large family on it. One day the landowner told him he would either have to pay more rent or give up part of his land. When old Antônio refused both options, the landowner ordered him to tear down the second of two huts which he had built on the property. Antônio's crippled son, José, lived in it with his family. The threats which accompanied the order caused Antônio to comply, and he built another hut for José several miles away. Because he was partially paralyzed, José could not farm for himself but had to walk to his father's hut to obtain food. The trip required him to take a road which ran through the plantation. One day the landowner's son, Clélio, who lived on the plantation and administered it, decided to have some great sport and at the same time teach a lesson to any of

43

the other peasants who might contemplate balking at one of his father's commands. He and two of the plantation *capangas* (private armed police) went hunting, and they used José as game. Their prey could not move too well because of his disability, so it didn't take long for the trio to run him down and shoot him. The local authorities professed no interest in investigating the murder. Nor did they bestir themselves when another of Antônio's sons, Manoel, was tied to the back of a jeep and dragged around through the brush. (Actually it would have been difficult to investigate that case, since the driver of the jeep was the local police chief.) Manoel was so badly hurt that he went crazy and shortly afterward ripped open his own stomach with a knife. Antônio Vicente then joined the nearest Peasant League.

There were numerous other incidents, perhaps not quite so dramatic, but just as brutal. The prevalent attitude of the landowners was nicely encapsulated by Chico Romão, one of the most famous of the "colonels" of the backlands, when he said: "The Leagues are like an epidemic. . . . Our reaction is the bullet. Many bullets. The *sertão* is not a playground." [15]

What contributed to this "reign of terror" in the early years of the Peasant League movement was the attitude of the Governor of Pernambuco, General Cordeiro de Farias.[16] His enemies liked to point out how badly misnamed he was, since *cordeiro* in Portuguese means "lamb." He took an inflexible position in favor of law and order as it traditionally existed in the countryside. His state police supported the status quo to the hilt and did their best to crush any peasant resistance to the exercise of prerogatives by the landowners.

Despite the intensely repressive climate created and maintained by the landowners and police, Peasant Leagues somehow managed to multiply. There is a dearth of reliable data about this formative period of the movement. In all probability a number of factors contributed to the survival and growth of the Leagues.

First of all, an undercurrent of unrest did permeate the fringes of the sugar zone and make at least some peasants particularly receptive to the idea of organizing. The Galiléans were not the only tenant farmers who had been raising subsistence crops on rented lands and now felt threatened by owners intent upon putting their land back

44

into sugar production or converting their plantations into cattle ranches. These peasants, unlike the landless rural workers employed in the sugar mills, could at least feed themselves in a minimal sort of way, and thus were in a position to take a chance upon participating in the new movement.

In addition, a number of these peasants belonged to fundamentalist Protestant sects which did not have any institutionalized clergy and thus had to develop their own indigenous leadership.[17] Some of these lay leaders played prominent roles in the organizing of Leagues.

The abortive efforts of the Communist Party to set up its own Peasant Leagues immediately after World War II might have helped to raise the consciousness of some peasants and make them more receptive to the new movement. It is difficult to measure what impact, if any, the Communist organizing had upon the peasants of the Northeast. When the Peasant Leagues became established and widely known in the early 1960s, Communist writers predictably gave all the credit to the Party.[18] Indeed, according to a recently published article on the Leagues, José de Prazeres himself had participated in the postwar Communist Party efforts to gain a foothold in the countryside, and had much more than a mutual benefit society in mind when he helped to form the Agricultural and Cattle-Breeding Society of the Planters of Pernambuco.[19]

Another factor which might have boosted the new Leagues was the awakening of intellectuals and socially conscious elements of the middle class to the desperate situation in the Northeastern countryside and the pressing need for some kind of land reform. In August and September of 1955, left-wing intellectuals sponsored in Recife a "Congress for the Salvation of the Northeast" and the "First Congress of Peasants of Pernambuco," and peasants from the new Leagues participated.[20] These meetings served to give some measure of encouragement to the peasants and may have fortified their resistance to efforts by landowners to repress their fledgling organizations.

An ancient Northeastern custom helped to publicize the new Leagues throughout the region. Guitar-playing troubadors crisscrossed the region and entertained the peasantry with topical songs. This was the medium through which the bandit Lampeão and others

had attained folk-hero status. This was also the most effective way to reach illiterate peasants. The *violeiros* began to sing praises of the Leagues and the growing number of peasant heroes and martyrs born of the struggle. Performing in little towns, in front of plantation stores and on the large estates, they spread word of the movement throughout the *agreste* and even into the barren reaches of the *sertão*.[21]

During this formative era Julião did everything he could to help the Leagues. The reputation he had developed as a lawyer who represented peasants proved useful in attracting new members. As the activities of the Leagues and the reactions of the landowners stirred up an increasing amount of litigation, he soon had more legal work than he could handle by himself, and he sent Jonas de Sousa and other lawyer friends into the countryside to provide legal assistance to League members. His idea of setting up a League office, which he called a *delegacia* (headquarters) in many municipalities gave the peasants a psychological boost. They normally associated the term with police headquarters. Now they had a *delegacia* of their own, and it connoted a feeling of protection which helped to offset their dread of the police. Finally, one of his associates has written that Julião's house in Caxangá had all the atmosphere of a plantation manor, except that the peasants who came there were welcomed as guests.[22] This unaccustomed treatment in familiar surroundings made a highly favorable impression upon the peasants.

There were others, however, who were negatively impressed with Julião's efforts to protect and expand the new Leagues. The most notable manifestation of this attitude toward him was the "Captain Jesus affair," in late 1956.[23] Julião was meeting with the peasants of Galiléia one Saturday afternoon when a state police officer, Captain Jesus Jardim de Sá, cut the telephone wire from Vitória to Recife. He then arrested Julião, despite the fact that state deputies were supposed to enjoy immunity from legal prosecution. Taking his prisoner to Recife, he delivered the troublesome lawyer to an army colonel who served as an aide to Governor Cordeiro de Farias. The colonel was horrified at Captain Jesus's blunder, and immediately released Julião. The outraged deputy went straight to the state legislature, where he set up a howl of protest. The other depu-

ties, most of whom had no special affection for Julião, were nonetheless upset by this encroachment upon their immunity, and demanded an investigation. A week later Julião, along with two of his colleagues from the legislature, returned to Galiléia. This time they were surrounded by an army of *capangas* hired by one of the local landowners. Only quick thinking by the deputies (one of whom, it is interesting to note, was Miguel Arraes) averted bloodshed. The incident revealed how perilous it could be, even for state officials, to tamper with the style of life which had evolved over the centuries in Northeast Brazil.

The professed goal of the Peasant League movement was agrarian reform. Julião and those working with him constantly stressed the need to bring about a radical change in the entire system of landholding and agricultural production in the Northeast. But they seldom elaborated any detailed description of the new system they were advocating or specific methods of achieving this end.

Julião's first attempt at carrying out a specific agrarian reform project could hardly be considered radical. The controversy over the Galiléia plantation had persisted over the years. Finally Julião, with the support of Governor Cid Sampaio, procured the passage of a law expropriating the plantation. A Rio journalist, Antônio Callado, noted that the state was paying Oscar Beltrão a handsome price for his rock-strewn property—"a price which would not even have occurred to Shylock." [24] The expropriation foreshadowed what was to become a popular (at least in some quarters) formula for the solution of the agrarian problem in Latin America: "land reform = advantageous real estate transaction for landowner." Indeed, a number of landowners subsequently approached Julião with hints that he agitate for the expropriation of their properties.

Callado's criticism might have been premature, because Julião knew what he was doing. For Peasant League members the expropriation had political value. It was the first time that the peasants had *forced* the government to do something. It presaged greater things to come.

Julião made other attempts to instill a political consciousness in his peasant followers. On May Day, 1957, he brought about 600 peasants to Recife to participate in the traditional workers' demonstra-

47

tions. On May 13, 1958, he assembled some 3,000 peasants in the city to celebrate the anniversary of the abolition of slavery in Brazil.

The landowners and their political representatives responded by invoking the spectre of the International Communist Conspiracy. According to their way of thinking, any talk of land reform had to be part of a "red" plot. Julião had a ready answer. In his *Peasant's Primer,* he reported that a landlord once told his peasants that the Leagues were bringing communism to the Northeast. When the peasant asked what communism was, the landowner replied that communism took people's goods away from them, mistreated people's daughters, and destroyed people's religion. The peasant observed that as long as he could remember, landowners were depriving peasants of their property, raping their daughters, and persecuting anyone who belonged to a Protestant sect. "If what you talk about is 'communism,'" the peasant concluded, "then we already have it and the Leagues are against it." [25]

This engaging tale could not hide the fact that the Peasant Leagues were receiving very close attention from the Communist Party. From the very beginning the Party supported Julião. Recife's weekly Communist newspaper gave him a great deal of coverage, going to the extreme of publishing the times of his arrivals at the airport when he was returning home from a trip. [26] Clodomir Moraes, a lawyer and state deputy who often helped Julião, was a Party stalwart. When Party leader Luís Carlos Prestes made his political stopovers in Recife, Julião was often on the platform with him. In 1957 a delegation from the Pernambuco State Assembly was invited to visit Eastern Europe. Julião was among those who made the trip to Poland, Czechoslovakia, and the Soviet Union.

Americans conditioned by the Cold War subsequently jumped to all kinds of sinister conclusions about Julião's connection with the Communists. While a working relationship did exist during this period, it is essential to keep in mind its context. Recife was still very much a small town, at least for its intellectual community. Communists were by no means social outcasts, but rather were often respected members of this community. Everyone knew everyone else, and personal ties arising from family or friendship transcended ideology. Indeed, a U.S. official stationed in Recife during the late 1950s

developed a cordial personal relationship with Hiram Pereira, a Party leader, when both men discovered their mutual interest in the theater.

In the 1960 presidential campaign the Brazilian left (including the Communists) backed Marshal Henrique Lott, an army officer said to be a nationalist, against Jânio Quadros, Governor of the state of São Paulo. It was a poor choice, since Lott's drabness contrasted unfavorably with Jânio's color and charisma. Julião went along with the rest of the left, especially since Lott had backed up the peasants with a pithy pronouncement that "the Leagues have as much right to exist as the Military Clubs," and he did his best to rally his followers behind Lott. On September 27, 1960, the peasants paraded in Recife in support of Lott and listened to a speech by Communist leader Luís Carlos Prestes. Behind the speakers' platform were a series of gigantic sketches of Lott, Prestes, Arraes, Julião, and a bearded Cuban who had become the most recent hero of the Brazilian left. A month later when the votes were tabulated, Quadros had received 48 per cent and Lott only 28 per cent of the 11.7 million ballots cast.

A discovery that Julião himself made in 1960 profoundly affected his relationship with the Communist Party and the rest of the radical left. In March of that year he made his first trip to Havana. The circumstances of the trip were curious. The unpredictable Quadros had decided to visit Cuba as part of his campaign for the presidency, and invited Julião, among others, to accompany him. Julião could not resist the offer. He had developed a taste for traveling abroad and was on his way to becoming an inveterate political tourist. He accepted, and covered himself by announcing that he was going "to Cuba with Jânio, but to the voting booth with Lott."

The visit was supposed to last for eight days, but Jânio, true to form, abruptly cut it short after five days and took his entourage home with him. He never clarified why he left (or why he went, for that matter), but such was his political style. The trip was long enough, however, to whet Julião's appetite, and shortly afterward he returned for a long visit. From that point on, he was an ardent *fidelista*, proclaiming over and over again his solidarity with Castro and the Cuban Revolution.

Julião had been a Socialist for some time and had consistently worked toward the establishment of a Socialist system in Brazil as a long-range goal. His discovery in Havana was that a Latin American country had achieved this goal in the course of a relatively brief struggle. The dream had become a reality, and Julião saw no reason why it could not also happen in Brazil.

His rhetoric quickly changed its tone. In 1956 he had written: "I do not want to make any revolution in the sense of shedding the blood of my neighbor or of seizing power by force." [27] Now he began to hold up to the peasants of the Northeast the example of Cuba and China. By the end of 1961 he was declaring that Brazil needed radical structural change which could come about only as a result of pressure from the masses, and that because of the inevitable resistance of those now in power it was unlikely that this process would be peaceful. In a magazine interview he noted that "arms will not be lacking, as there is never a shortage of arms in a civil war in any country." [28] He constantly emphasized his opposition to applying foreign solutions to Brazilian problems in a mechanical way. But he left no doubt about his immediate goal. He began to call for "agrarian reform or revolution," and for land reform "by law or by the sledgehammer" (*na lei ou na marra*).

Seven months after Julião's first visit to Cuba, the United States discovered Julião, as Tad Szulc's *New York Times* articles raised him to the status of an international celebrity. Julião was unaware that such good fortune had befallen on him. At the time the articles were published he was touring the People's Republic of China.

FOUR ✵

✵ ✵ Miguel Arraes and the Urban Coalition

AS JULIÃO AND HIS PEASANTS WERE discovering each other in the countryside, a populist politician in the city of Recife was beginning to put together the elements of a constituency which was to develop quickly into a serious threat to the Pernambucan status quo.[1] In 1959 Miguel Arraes was elected Mayor of Recife representing a loose coalition of liberals, Socialists, Communists, progressive Catholics, workers, students, and intellectuals. This was not the first time that a leftist leader had taken the helm of Recife's municipal government. What made Arraes's victory worthy of special note, however, was the fact that his political future clearly encompassed the possibility of bigger things to come. Many of his supporters insisted that his political skills and popular image would propel him into higher office and enable him to achieve revolutionary goals within the existing framework of constitutional democracy.

Unlike Julião, Arraes did not seem, at least at first blush, to have been born to the role he was about to assume. His personality, both public and private, showed unmistakable traces of the *matuto,* or backwoodsman—qualities incongruous in an urban political leader. He was a consummately suspicious man, and this quality colored his every move as he made his way through the political underbrush. A heavy set chain-smoker who projected an avuncular appearance, he was able to capitalize upon his outspoken bluntness and reputation

for honesty—features which proved to be invaluable during his spectacular climb to political prominence. He was above all a complex man who knew his way around the "old politics," yet rode the crest of a new wave which many thought would sweep the country.⌉

Miguel Arraes de Alencar came from the southwest corner of the state of Ceará, Padre Cícero country. Araripe, the small town where he was born in 1916, lies at the foot of a range of hills close to the point at which Ceará converges with Pernambuco and Piaui, the most backward of the Northeastern states. It is an arid and nowhere land. He was the only son in a family which included six younger sisters. His parents were middle-class and of modest means but saw to the education of their children. Miguel went to law school in Recife. Five of the girls became school teachers, while one went on to win a university degree in philosophy. After graduation Miguel stayed in Recife to work for the Sugar and Alcohol Institute. In 1945 he married a local girl whose sister was the wife of industrialist-politican Cid Sampaio. Shortly thereafter, Miguel himself took the plunge into Pernambuco politics.

In order to understand the meteoric rise of Miguel Arraes, one must first know something about the Pernambucan political scene, which in turn requires some grasp of the national political scene. Politics in Brazil between 1930 and 1964 reflected the indelible influence of one man, Getúlio Vargas.[2] Most of what transpired during this period, even after he vanished from center stage, is understandable only in terms of a continuing struggle between his followers and his enemies.

Getúlio Vargas assumed the presidency of Brazil in 1930 as a result of a military coup. Seven years later he staged another coup to create what he proclaimed a "New State," which turned out to be a mild version of the regimes already established in Portugal, Italy, and Germany. Yet Vargas was an unlikely dictator, a short, chubby father-figure known to all simply as Getúlio. He was a master at political manipulation and government by improvisation. But he did make one institutional change by centralizing a great deal of power within the federal government.

In World War II Getúlio opposed the Fascist dictators and sent Brazilian troops to Italy to fight on the side of the allies. By the end

of the war, the contradiction between Brazil's authoritarian government and the democracies on whose side Brazilian soldiers had fought lent substantial support to Getúlio's enemies. On October 29, 1945, the military deposed him.

The restoration of democracy in Brazil meant the return of party politics. And Getúlio had left his mark upon the political process. His traditional antagonists belonged to the Union of National Democracy (UDN), a conservative party with a predominantly urban upper-class base. To oppose the UDN, Vargas himself had founded not one, but two parties. The Social Democratic Party (PSD) represented his attempt to unify those elements of the rural power structure which had been willing to cooperate with (or be bought off by) him. After his fall the PSD inherited the machine he had created from the coterie of local politicians who had supported him and the intervenors he had appointed to take over states whose governors had opposed him. In addition, during the war he had designed the Brazilian Labor Party (PTB) to mobilize the working class into some sort of populist movement, taking advantage of his image as the "Father of the Poor," and attracting support which would otherwise go to the Communists.

In 1950 Getúlio pulled off a startling comeback by winning the presidential election on the PTB ticket. He did this by drawing considerable help from his old friends in the PSD, despite the fact that the PSD ran a candidate against him. But four years later, frustrated by his political enemies, he took his own life in dramatic fashion. In the 1955 election the PSD's Juscelino Kubitschek succeeded in getting enough PTB support to gain the presidency.

Although in theory the UDN and the PSD were conservative and the PTB progressive, none of these parties represented any clear ideology. Their machinations derived from back-room deals and the pull of personality. This was doubly true of what went on locally in the underdeveloped areas of the country. In the Northeast the political game was the preoccupation of wealthy family groups who wrapped themselves in the banners of the national parties without such regard for positions taken by the national leadership. Party discipline barely existed. If your local enemy belonged to the UDN, you joined the PSD. It was as simple as that. Thus in the 1950 presi-

dential elections Vargas found that he could not seduce the PSD chieftains in Pernambuco, so he managed to secure the backing of the UDN in the state—despite the fact that the UDN's motivating force was supposed to have been opposition to Vargas.

Family groups belonging to the PSD had been ruling Pernambuco for many years. Their success was due to an alliance with local bosses, the "colonels," who were able to deliver the vote in the interior. The literacy requirements of the federal Constitution were liberally interpreted when one of these "colonels" brought several truckloads of his peasants to the polls. The usual procedure was to give each peasant a slip of paper with his name written on it. The peasant would then copy his "signature" in front of an election official and vote as the "colonel" had directed.

Miguel Arraes enjoyed his first real taste of politics in 1948, when one of the PSD governors appointed him state Secretary of the Treasury. Though brother-in-law Cid Sampaio belonged to the UDN, Arraes assiduously avoided identification with that or any other party. This early cautiousness was to be of great future value, since it facilitated his efforts to build a new coalition of voters in Pernambuco. During his service with the PSD government, he made many useful contacts with the PSD bosses in the interior.

In 1954 the PSD gave its gubernatorial nomination to General Osvaldo Cordeiro de Farias, an army officer who had long been involved in politics and whose political ambitions seemed to grow with the years. He had evolved into a hard-line anti-Communist conservative with an unswerving hostility toward Vargas. Indeed, he had been one of the strategists behind the 1945 coup which had ousted Getúlio. The UDN chose as its standard-bearer João Cleofas, a colorless oligarch and perennial loser whom Getúlio had appointed his Minister of Agriculture in 1951 as a reward for the UDN's support in Pernambuco. Cleofas was a hopeless candidate and lost badly.

Cordeiro de Farias kept the state government of Pernambuco on course. He continued its conservative, rural orientation, catering to the interests of the PSD families and their "colonel" allies. Opposition mounted on several fronts. As the city of Recife continued to grow, its problems proliferated. The indifference of state govern-

ments to these problems was not new, and urban voters had always been unsympathetic to the incumbent governor. This traditional animosity intensified. Students and intellectuals, customarily leftist and thus hostile to the elitist character of the state government, increased their protests. Miguel Arraes, who was now a member of the state Assembly, played a prominent role in this growing movement of opposition. He led a number of legislative fights against the administration, and for his efforts received a "Deputy of the Year" award from a state association of journalists.

But what spelled real trouble for the PSD was the growing strength of the UDN opposition. A number of Recife-based industrialists with ideas which were relatively progressive for the time and the place were extremely unhappy with the economic policies of Cordeiro de Farias. They saw opportunities for expanding industrial development and expanding internal markets being thwarted by shortsighted measures intended for the immediate benefit of the landed oligarchs. In 1957 as a protest against an increase in taxes promulgated by the state government, these industrialists declared a lockout, closing down factories and businesses in Recife and some of the other cities. The lockout did not last long and was not meant as an all-out economic war on the state government. It was rather a purely political gambit designed to project onto the political scene the name of the leader of the UDN forces, Cid Feijó Sampaio.

Cid (prounced "Seed-jee" by Northeasterners) Sampaio seemed hardly the sort to lead a political breakthrough which would have startling implications for Pernambuco. At the time of the lockout he was fifty years old, an industrialist and an *usineiro* (sugar mill owner) belonging to one of the oldest families in the state. By any standard other than that of the day he would have been considered a sound, respectable conservative. But in Pernambuco in 1958, as he mounted his bid for the governorship, he drew heavy fire from the right. For Cid decided that he wanted to do something—not terribly much, but something—for the poor people of the state. It seemed to be a matter of good business sense. After all, people with no money could hardly be expected to buy anything.

The Communist Party openly supported Cid, and he openly acknowledged their help. Although Communist support for a non-

Communist candidate was nothing new, Cid's PSD opponents made a big thing of it. It became a prime issue, especially when Recife's Archbishop, before leaving on a trip to Europe, declared: "Candidates who adopt ideological principles and action contrary to the doctrines of the Church cannot be voted for. Not even one who, though from a traditional Catholic family, becomes a mere tool of the reds, and gets up on platforms at rallies staged by Communist leaders whose hands are stained with blood." [3]

The Vicar-General of the Archdiocese subsequently cited Pope Pius XII's condemnation of alliances with the Communist Party as justification for the Archbishop's position. But this matter was not all that clear-cut. People recalled how the hierarchy had for the same reasons bitterly opposed the mayoral candidacy of leftist Pelópidas Silveira, one of whose sisters, incidentally, was a nun. Yet after Pelópidas had won, the Archbishop did not refuse his appropriation of city funds for the construction of a seminary.

The emotional intensity generated by the campaign succeeded in completely obscuring the substantive issues separating the candidates. For the first time in Pernambuco modern mass-media techniques were used intensively, as Cid attacked the PSD machine and the PSD partisans shouted "Communist" at Cid. The PSD had good reason to worry. The federal government had recently revised voting lists. As a result, Pernambuco had lost 200,000 registered voters. Most of these were in fact phantom votes (often the names of the dead) used by the PSD bosses to assure victory for government candidates. In the end, Cid held his conservative base among the Recife industrialists and merchants, and his overwhelming majority in the city carried the day for him. He won by more than 100,000 votes.

The PSD losers naturally claimed that the Communists were about to take over Pernambuco lock, stock, and barrel. They even spread the story that Luís Carlos Prestes, the Party's leader, was buying a home in Recife to be close to the action. Cid ignored their howls as he blissfully set about dismantling the PSD machine in the interior and replacing it with his own UDN machine. Shortly afterward, maintaining his spirit of defiance, he visited China, and enjoyed an audience with Mao Tse-tung.

Miguel Arraes served as Cid's campaign manager and put to good use his PSD contacts in the interior. His preoccupation with the gubernatorial race caused him to neglect his own campaign for reelection to the state Assembly, and he lost his seat. But Cid appointed him back to his old job as Secretary of the Treasury.

He did not remain long in the new administration, since 1959 was election year in the cities. With the fresh taste of victory driving them on, the emerging populist elements in Recife saw a golden opportunity to capture City Hall. And they felt certain that Miguel Arraes was the candidate who could do it for them.

The new force represented a coalition of left and center-left groups which embraced Communists, Socialists, liberals, and progressive Catholics, workers, students, and intellectuals. They saw Arraes initially as a successor to Pelópidas Silveira, the rotund "big daddy of the left" who had been a recent and popular mayor. Cid and his conservative UDN friends didn't relish the prospects of Arraes' candidacy. Cid had higher political ambitions and saw his brother-in-law as a potential rival. The industrialists and merchants of the city looked with disfavor on the forces behind Arraes. But in the end they reluctantly backed him, since the alternative was a win for the PSD crowd.

Arraes won handily. Again there were yowls that the Communists were about to take over, though none of the complainants ever specified what they thought the Communists would do with a city (save govern it in the manner of the numerous "red" mayors in Italy and France). Though Cid had kept his distance from the Party after he became Governor, Arraes did not. He appointed Hiram Pereira, one of the Party leaders in Pernambuco, to the post of Secretary of Administration, and Aluísio Falcão, a Party member, as Director of the city's Division of Cultural Affairs.

The presence of avowed Communists within the municipal government culminated a spectacular comeback for the Party in the Northeast, and reflected its growing power and prestige on a national level. What made this quite remarkable was that a quarter of a century earlier the Party seemed to have committted, both in Pernambuco and elsewhere, a mistake of suicidal proportions.

On Sunday morning, November 24, 1935, as Pernambuco's gov-

ernor drifted across the Atlantic on his way to Lisbon aboard the German dirigible "Hindenburg," the Communist Party launched an armed rebellion in his state, as part of a coordinated effort to overthrow the government of Brazil.[4] If one discounts an aborted coup in El Salvador in 1932, this was the first and only time that a Communist Party bound to the Moscow line ever tried its hand at violent revolution in Latin America.

The Pernambuco "putsch" began in the early hours of the morning when armed civilians attacked police stations and jails in various working-class districts in Recife. By 10:30 a.m. the rebels had cut the city's telephone service and were distributing pamphlets published by something called the National Liberation Alliance, calling for "BREAD, LAND AND LIBERTY for the people."

At the same time mutinies were breaking out in several military installations. At the barracks of the Seventh Military Region in downtown Recife, a ruddy-faced sergeant, whose trim figure bore witness to his job as a physical education instructor, signaled his co-conspirators and shot two lieutenants in the stomach. One of them later died from his wound. For this act of violence, the Army would never forget the name of Gregório Lourenço Bezerra.

This uprising turned out to be a blunder, as few workers and soldiers joined the "revolution." By early afternoon government troops had driven the insurgents from downtown Recife. The rebels sent part of their force to the nearby suburb of Jaboatão, so notorious for its leftist sympathies that people referred to it as "little Moscow." The rest of the rebel contingent holed up in the tower of the Church of Largo da Paz, which commanded the southern approach to the city. They fortified the tower with heavy machine guns and waited. Government forces soon arrived and surrounded the church. A big shoot-out ensued, demolishing the tower and forcing the remnants of the rebel group to surrender. Those who had betaken themselves to Jaboatão suffered a similar fate. Officials put at 150 the total number of fatalities on both sides. There are those who believe that the insurgents lost many more than 150, both during and after the rebellion. By some miracle, Gregório Bezerra survived both the battle and his capture. He was given a lengthy prison sentence.

Other uprisings occurred simultaneously in Rio de Janeiro, Natal,

58

and at scattered points throughout the country. The Communists enjoyed their only success in Natal, the capital of the state of Rio Grande do Norte, where they managed to topple the state government and hold power for three days. By the end of November, the whole thing was over, and the status quo survived.

Until the early 1930s the Brazilian Communist Party had been a relatively small movement with not much of a popular base.[5] In these formative years it had devoted most of its time and energy to squabbling, first with the anarchists and then with the Trotskyists, over who was to lead the extreme left in Brazil. What enabled the Party to develop so rapidly that in a few short years it could deem itself ready to attempt a violent revolution was the leadership of Luís Carlos Prestes, one of the most remarkable figures in the history of Brazil.

Prestes was an army captain in charge of a fortress in southern Brazil when he joined an uprising which had broken out in São Paulo in 1924, one of a series of rebellions undertaken by young army officers. What made Prestes' move so spectacular was that he kept it up for almost three years, meandering all over the vast interior of the country, using guerrilla tactics, and trying unsuccessfully to incite the rural masses to revolt. The march of the Prestes column was an amazing feat, covering some 21,600 miles, and Prestes himself became a popular figure whose heroic dimensions have seldom been equaled in Brazil. He and his men came to epitomize the struggle of the poor against the rich. Within the army itself, admiration for Prestes's courage and strategy was boundless. Come what may, his mystique somehow remained intact. He was always to be known by his nickname, Cavalier of Hope.

Though exiled in Buenos Aires, Prestes began to involve himself in politics, taking advantage of his large following. When he declared in 1931 that he had joined the Communist Party he gave the Party a tremendous boost. He spent some time in Moscow and worked for the Comintern (Communist International). In 1934 the Brazilian government allowed him to return, and he put his prestige to work for the Party. The following year he became Honorary President of the National Liberation Alliance, a Communist-led coalition of leftist forces designed to mobilize political opposition to the

government of President Getúlio Vargas. The Alliance marked an attempt to seek power through legal, constitutional means, but by mid-1935, extremists within the Party felt certain that the time was ripe for violent revolution, and they succeeded in convincing Prestes. It was a monumental miscalculation.

Vargas seized the opportunity afforded by the ill-fated uprising to repress the left. Prestes, whom the insurrectionists had proclaimed as the new "President of Brazil," managed to keep ahead of the police until March 1936, when he was finally arrested. He and other Party leaders and militants received lengthy prison sentences. The Communist Party was outlawed.

Several weeks after the end of World War II, Getúlio Vargas ordered the release of Prestes and the rest of Brazil's political prisoners. With his regime tottering from the growing opposition of those who demanded a return of constitutional democracy, Getúlio needed all the help he could get. The Communists in turn supported the President—proof, if any was necessary, of Prestes' unswerving adherence to the Party line, since Vargas had turned Prestes's wife over to the German Gestapo, and the Nazis had murdered her. These maneuvers could not hold back the inevitable, and on October 29, 1945, the military deposed Vargas.

Yet Prestes and the Communists managed to maintain a great reservoir of public sentiment in their favor. In the elections which followed the fall of Vargas, Communist candidates did quite well. The Cavalier of Hope, taking advantage of Brazil's peculiar election rules, got himself elected to the Senate from the Federal District (the city of Rio de Janeiro), and to the Chamber of Deputies from the Federal District and four states, including Pernambuco. He chose to accept the Senate seat. The Communist candidate for President received 10 per cent of the national vote. Fourteen Communists were elected federal Deputies. Among them was Gregório Bezerra, whose role in the 1935 revolt did not prevent the people of Pernambuco from casting ballots for him. The trend continued in the state election of 1946. The Party won twelve of twenty-five seats on Recife's city council, and placed thirteen deputies in the Pernambuco legislature.

But the Communists were not long in their role as an opposition

political party. As the Cold War dawned, the new Brazilian federal government took an increasingly militant anti-Communist stance. In May, 1947, Brazil's Supreme Electoral Court declared the Party to be "anti-democratic" and hence illegal under the Constitution. In October Prestes and all the Communist deputies in Congress lost their seats. For the next seventeen years the Party functioned just beyond the fringes of the law, never putting up candidates of its own, but working with (and sometimes within) other political parties and institutions.

In Pernambuco the Communists cultivated the base of support and sympathy that had made them choose Recife as a key target in the 1935 coup. In 1955 they added to their popularity by helping to elect as mayor of Recife Pelópidas Silveira, a vigorous, progressive administrator.

Yet the 1935 experience had left its mark. For the Communists it was a reminder of the years in jail which had befallen them as a result of precipitous, ill-advised action. They were not about to repeat their mistake. For the army units stationed in the Northeast, the victory over the rebels was kept alive through a tradition of constant commemoration. This was especially true of the officers, who would not forget their comrades who had been killed. Nor would they lose sight of those who had participated in the revolt.

The Communist Party in Pernambuco geared its activities to the demands of the Party's leadership. The high command in Rio faithfully followed the line as set in Moscow. This centralized and tightly disciplined structure was virtually the reverse of the way in which the other political parties operated in Northeast Brazil.

In 1954 the Communists discreetly backed the UDN standard-bearer, João Cleofas. They were still supporting Getúlio Vargas nationally, and Cleofas was Getúlio's man. In addition, the Party realized the necessity of breaking the PSD stranglehold on Pernambuco.

In 1958 Cid Sampaio received full and open Communist support. In the height of the campaign, the Party brought in its number-one drawing card, Luís Carlos Prestes, and the Cavalier of Hope attracted big crowds in Recife and the suburbs. Prestes appeared on the same platform with Cid, and they were photographed together.

When one considers in retrospect how amazingly fast things moved in the short span of time between 1958 and 1964, the Communist strategy was unquestionably correct. The 1958 election not only broke the PSD hegemony but also proved to the progressive elements in Pernambuco that they could shake the status quo. But what no one could have foreseen was the sudden emergence of a politician who could galvanize this new political force and use it for radical ends.

The Communists were, of course, quick to recognize the potential of Miguel Arraes, and they used all their influence among intellectuals, students, and workers to promote him. Arraes in turn included Party members within his inner circle of advisers.

The new populist movement challenged more than just the entrenched economic and political interests in Recife and the state of Pernambuco. The cultural establishment, presided over by Gilberto Freyre, also found itself on the defensive.

Recife's most distinguished resident made an inviting target, for his star was already on the wane. In 1933, with the publication of his seminal work, *The Masters and the Slaves,* the silver-haired social historian earned the destinction of introducing Brazil to its own cultural past. He succeeded in instilling in many of his countrymen an appreciation of the strengths of their multi-racial heritage, up to that time the source of an inferiority complex for upper-class and educated Brazilians.

But by the late 1950s, time was beginning to bypass Gilberto Freyre. The younger intellectuals in Brazil were no longer regarding him as the last word in his field. Much of his later work was found to be a rehash of what he had said in *The Masters and the Slaves.* His idyllic picture of plantation life was questioned. And he was accused of stifling the development of sociology in the Northeast, mainly through his influence upon the federally-supported Joaquim Nabuco Institute of Social Research, his own personal creation and base of operations in Recife.

Freyre's political outlook made conflict with Arraes and his supporters inevitable. Born in 1900, he was descended from a family that traces its Brazilian roots back back to the seventeenth century. During the 1930s he strongly opposed the Vargas dictatorship and

spent several years in exile abroad. With the restoration of democracy after World War II, he was elected to the federal Chamber of Deputies, but subsequently lost in a bid for re-election. He has often called himself a "leftist," and once went so far as to claim that he was an "anarcho-syndicalist." But in Recife, a hotbed of leftism, people recognized him for the conservative that he was. His political ties linked him to the UDN party. On the international scene he has served as an unremitting apologist for the African colonial policies of Portugal, frequently writing and lecturing on the subject. The Portuguese in turn have awarded him an honorary degree from the prestigious University of Coimbra, and frequently invite him to visit Portugal and the African colonies.

It was ironic that although Freyre took a substantial portion of his formal education in the United States (B.A., Baylor, M.A., Columbia), his work did not receive wide recognition in this country until he had gone out of style in Brazil. The University of Recife established an Institute for the Sciences of Man, which managed to function outside the ambit of his influence. And SUDENE, through its Division of Human Resources, would soon use some of its funds to subsidize sociological research by young scholars who did not belong to Freyre's circle.

Thus, the assault on the status quo in Recife embittered Freyre, who in turn did not even try to conceal his distaste for the new populist movement. Meanwhile, Arraes' backers made no secret of their hopes to elect him Governor of Pernambuco, and then to promote him for the Vice Presidency, with the ultimate dream of making him President of the Republic.

FIVE

✇ ✇ Celso Furtado,
SUDENE, and USAID

IN THE WAKE OF THE DISASTROUS DROUGHT of 1958, Antônio Callado made a trip through Northeast Brazil and returned home to Rio de Janeiro with material for a sensational series of newspaper articles. He told of an industry he had found flourishing in a barren land where no industries were thought even to exist. The articles, which ran in September, 1959, exposed to the glare of national publicity the "industrialists of the drought," large landowners who were making tremendous profits out of federal drought relief.

Callado's principal disclosure concerned the construction of reservoirs, which he dubbed "the most fantastic and unjust of the world's lotteries." [1] The irrigation resulting from these public works projects made landowners in the *sertão* rich overnight. The decision where to put the reservoirs was a purely political matter, not dependent upon rational resource allocation but rather subject to the whims of local politician-landowners. The latter had gained control over the National Department of Works Against the Drought (DNOCS), the federal agency responsible for antidrought programs in the Northeast. They therefore had reservoirs built to suit their own self-interest. Once a landowner hit the jackpot and had his property irrigated, he could do what he pleased with his newly watered soil. A provision in the federal Constitution all but prohibited the government from expropriating private property for the benefit of the general

public. There was no way to force a landowner to adopt modern agricultural techniques and use his irrigated land in a way that would
provide work or food for his numerous tenants. So the owner pocketed
as much as he could, and the landless peasants living and working
on or near his property continued to eke out a marginal existence.

Callado also described why some large landowners actually resisted federal drought relief. Their property was adjacent to dry
river beds, where they were growing a type of palm tree that furnished wax for candles. The sale of this wax provided a lucrative
source of income. More moisture would be harmful to these palm
tress, and thus the landowners opposed any project that might create
a flow of water through these riverbeds. They refused even to consider the benefits that more water might bring to the peasants in the
immediate environs.

Reports of irregularities in federal programs designed to help the
Northeast were not new. From the very beginning of such efforts
incompetence had served as the handmaiden to corruption. Dams
and reservoirs were built in the wrong places, and funds for emergency drought relief found their way into the pockets of politicians
and their friends. By 1959 DNOCS acquired a very unsavory image,
especially after reports of graft during the 1958 drought relief efforts.

Callado, an urbane journalist with a large national readership,
helped catalyze public indignation. His articles were vivid and hard-
hitting. More important, they appeared at an opportune moment.
For Callado's good friend, Celso Furtado, was engaged at that very
moment in a struggle to persuade the Brazilian Congress to adopt a
completely new economic policy toward the Northeast. Indeed,
Callado had made his trip to the region at Furtado's behest.

President Juscelino Kubitschek had turned to Furtado for advice
in the aftermath of the 1958 drought in the Northeast.[2] Public pressure had been mounting as thousands of *flagelados* streamed out of
the interior in search of food and work, while stories circulated
about the misuse of federal funds for their relief.

Kubitschek was a chief executive who liked to do big things. He
was building the new capital city of Brasília in the wilderness. He
had grandiose ideas about economic development. During his term
of office, Brazil was growing at a dizzy pace, at least in the south.
But the Northeast remained stagnant. In 1955 the region contained

32 per cent of Brazil's population, but generated only 13 per cent of the nation's income.[3] And things had not much improved. So Juscelino decided to use the drought to do something big for the Northeast.

Furtado, then an economist with the National Bank for Economic Development in Rio, responded by preparing what came to be known as the *Furtado Report.* In it he stressed the disparity between the level of development in the south and in the Northeast. He charged that a number of economic policies followed by the federal government were responsible for maintaining, and even worsening, this disparity by favoring the growth of the south at the expense of the Northeast. As the value of the Northeast's exports abroad deteriorated while the cost of imports from the industrialized south of Brazil increased, capital drained out of the Northeast to the south. In other words, the Northeast had been contributing to the growth of the south! He then drew up a plan that proposed a radically different approach to the Northeast's problems. Up to that time the government's concern had generally been couched in defensive terms. Measures had been formulated to alleviate the effects of drought. Furtado wanted a positive program which would reach the causes of underdevelopment throughout the entire region. His *Report* suggested several ways to deal with these causes.

The proposed strategy involved: (1) a policy of industrialization for the region; (2) a colonization project which would transfer people out of the overpopulated Northeast; (3) a more rational use of land in the sugar zone; and (4) an irrigation policy which would encourage increased food production in the *sertão.* Responsibility for working out and executing this grand strategy would vest in a new federal agency with broad powers and ample funds at its disposal.

Furtado submitted his report to Kubitschek early in 1959, and the President embraced it eagerly. Legislation embodying some of its recommendations was quickly drafted. The keystone of the new strategy was to be a new federal agency, the Superintendency for the Development of the Northeast (SUDENE), which was to draw up a master developmental plan for the entire region.

SUDENE was to have sweeping authority and would be responsible directly to the President. It would receive as its budgetary allotment 2 per cent of Brazil's total fiscal revenues. The governors of

the Northeastern states would sit as members of SUDENE's Deliberative Council, involving local interests in policy-making functions.

After a strenuous political battle, the federal Chamber of Deputies approved this legislation in May. In December the Senate, aided by the impact of Callado's articles, followed suit. Shortly thereafter, to the surprise of no one, Kubitschek appointed Celso Furtado as the first Superintendent of SUDENE.

It was also no surprise that the master plan worked out in detail by SUDENE closely followed the lines of the *Furtado Report*. The next step was to secure congressional approval of the plan, an effort delayed by the presidential elections of 1960 and the succession of Kubitschek by the controversial Jânio Quadros.

Meanwhile, Celso Furtado was pressing forward to secure what he felt was an important source of support for SUDENE and its master plan. Tad Szulc had used the front page of *The New York Times* to sound the alarm over the emergence of "Castroism" in Northeast Brazil, and the Kennedy administration was growing apprehensive about unrest in the region. So Furtado flew to Washington with a request for $400 million in U.S. foreign aid.

On July 14, 1961, he met with President Kennedy and made his usual good impression. At the same time he felt encouraged by the President's interest in his proposals. Several New Frontiersmen opined that the master plan might be just the sort of imaginative program the United States should back as a countermeasure to the growing appeal of Fidel Castro in Latin America. As an upshot, Kennedy dispatched a study team to Recife.

This was by no means the first American discovery of Northeast Brazil. During World War II the region served as a staging area for the transport of men and materiel across the South Atlantic to Dakar on the west coast of Africa. The U.S. built a large air base near Natal, the capital of the state of Rio Grande do Norte, and installations in Recife and other points along the coast. On January 28, 1943, President Franklin D. Roosevelt and President Getúlio Vargas of Brazil conferred aboard a U.S. destroyer in Natal harbor.

Dollars spent by the American troops temporarily stimulated the economy of the Northeast. The Americans also set up a number of health posts and made a few attempts to expand food production in

the region. The U.S. also loaned some technical assistance in a search for natural resources, although most of these efforts centered on the Amazon basin. At the end of the war the troops were withdrawn, bequeathing to the natives the air base and many buildings. They also left behind one cross-cultural transplant, the tomato, which they had brought with them and introduced to the Brazilians.[4]

From 1950 to the Cuban Revolution, U.S. aid to Brazil took the form of technical assistance under the so-called Point Four Program and an occasional developmental loan. Northeast Brazil received a tiny share of this modest effort. One reason, suggested by Professor Stefan H. Robock, was that "many top Brazilian officials who were close to the United States Embassy and Point Four personnel sincerely believed that the Northeast was a lost cause and that aid should not be wasted on the region." [5] (In addition to the small amount of U.S. aid channeled into the Northeast, various United Nations agencies managed to provide some technical assistance, although the U.N. had meagre resources for economic development.)

Thus the United States had done little in the Northeast before economist Merwin L. Bohan arrived in Recife on October 23, 1961, to begin a comprehensive study of the developmental needs of the region. Working rapidly to comply with President Kennedy's mandate, Bohan and his team produced a lengthy document urging a substantial commitment of American aid. Their report suggested both a long-term and a short-term program. The latter was designed to "show prompt results as a clear expression of the concern of the governments of Brazil and of the United States, acting within the Alliance for Progress, for the economic and social welfare of the population of the region." [6] It included the drilling of water fountains and wells, the construction of Quonset huts in the sugar zone to serve as "Alliance for Progress Labor Centers" for health and educational services, literacy and vocational training, and the formation of mobile health units. The cost of such an impact program would have been $33 million.

The long-term program encompassed anti-drought measures, road construction, community water and health projects, and the creation of agricultural settlements that would drain part of the surplus population out of the Northeast and into the vast, empty inte-

rior of Brazil. The program would have extended over a period of five years and cost nearly $400 million (the exact amount that Furtado had originally sought from Washington).

When one considers the time pressures under which it was produced, the Bohan Report was a competent, commendable attempt to set the U.S. aid program in the Northeast off on the right foot. Bohan, an experienced foreign service officer in the State Department, was familiar with the Brazilian scene. He had been a member of the Joint Brazil-United States Economic Development Commission, founded in the early 1950s as part of an American effort to study ways of removing obstacles to development in Brazil. The team he headed fully appreciated SUDENE's role in the Northeast, and worked closely with Furtado and his young technicians. The recommendations of the Report followed closely the thrust of SUDENE's master plan. So far, so good.

But at this point, political factors began to rear their ugly implications. On a national level the unpredictable Jânio Quadros had outdone himself by resigning from the presidency on August 25, 1961, to the utter amazement of most of his countrymen. Vice President João Goulart of the PTB (Brazilians could split their vote between presidential and vice-presidential candidates) assumed the office only after outflanking an attempt by elements of the military to stage a preventive coup. Certain officers distrusted Goulart because he had been Getúlio Vargas' protégé, and more recently had cultivated strong support from the left. A last minute compromise enabled Jango, as he was popularly called, to become President after he agreed to the reduction of some of his constitutional powers. But concern in Washington mounted as the Goulart government began to display what seemed to be leftist tendencies. At the same time the forces behind Mayor Miguel Arraes were initiating their campaign to put him in the Governor's Palace, and Julião was talking more and more of revolution. These trends greatly increased the anxiety level in Washington.

It is crucial to keep in mind the domestic political situation in the United States. Kennedy had just been stung by the Bay of Pigs fiasco, and the Cuban Revolution had shifted to an openly Marxist-Leninist line. The Democrats were highly sensitive to accusations

that they had "lost" Cuba just as they had "lost" China fifteen years earlier. The liberal gloss of the Kennedy administration could not survive anything that smacked of another such "loss."

Hence, even before the Bohan mission arrived in Brazil, the U.S. Embassy in Rio de Janeiro was worriedly pondering whether Northeast Brazil posed a political threat to the rest of Brazil and the United States. The conclusion reached by the Embassy was that radical forces in the Northeast did in fact pose a serious challenge which had to be quickly and effectively countered.

To do so meant interfering in the domestic affairs of Northeast Brazil, a tactic from which the Embassy did not shrink. And the most convenient vehicle through which this policy of intervention could be effectuated was the Alliance for Progress.

The Embassy decided therefore to utilize the U.S. aid program in the Northeast for immediate, political purposes. This amounted to a rejection of the possibility of working effectively with SUDENE. Furtado's agency had committed itself to long-range economic development the success of which depended in large part upon the avoidance of damaging political entanglements. As Professor Riordan J. A. Roett III of Vanderbilt University has observed in his extensive study of the SUDENE-U.S. relationship: "Forced to choose between supporting SUDENE and long-range modernization, and immediate impact and the possible thwarting of the radical left, the United States chose the latter and alienated the developmental agency." [7]

While Bohan and his team were making their study, the Embassy was pondering how to manipulate U.S. aid to the Northeast so it would have the desired political impact. An American technician with experience in Brazilian educational matters had just visited the Northeast and returned to Rio with a plan for a school construction project in the state of Rio Grande do Norte. Ambassador Lincoln Gordon rejected his choice of location. The Embassy decided to go ahead with the project, but in Pernambuco rather than Rio Grande do Norte, on the principal ground that the "democratic forces" supposedly represented by Governor Cid Sampaio needed help from the U.S.[8] With an election coming up in 1962, the strategy was to attempt a crash construction program that would provide some tan-

gible evidence of progress, and thus benefit the candidate whom the Sampaio forces would nominate to oppose Arraes for governor.

This was, of course, not the only time that the Alliance for Progress was utilized to serve short-term political ends. In 1966 Senator Ernest Gruening, then Chairman of the Senate Subcommittee on Foreign Aid Expenditures, did a little-noticed case study on "United States Foreign Aid in Action," which documented how the U.S. used its aid program to attempt to influence the 1964 Chilean presidential election.[9]

The American decision to politicize their aid program in Northeast Brazil was to saddle Celso Furtado with an additional burden of staggering proportions. Although he was a highly skilled technician and kept insisting that "I have not trained myself to be a politician," he knew full well that his program for the Northeast would have a profound political impact on the region. Throughout his entire career with SUDENE he would demonstrate the ineluctable nexus between economic development and the political process. His cardinal rule was to remain aloof from the game of party politics. "One must avoid a connection with politics," he said in an interview in Recife in 1963, "for this is the only way of surviving here." His strategy: "I get along with all groups. That's how I keep my power." But as he struggled to wield what amounted to political power without getting caught in partisan politics, the Americans were planning to plunge their aid program into the depths of the political thicket.

Meanwhile, conservative elements in the Brazilian Congress were stubbornly blocking SUDENE's proposed master plan and the appropriations for it. A PTB Senator (and large landowner from Furtado's home state of Paraíba), all but accused Furtado of being a member of the Communist Party, and charged that the master plan was designed to foment civil war in the Northeast.[10] This was an old charge. According to Arthur Schlesinger, Jr., "during the fifties the American Embassy regarded him with mistrust as a Marxist, even possibly a Communist." [11] And there were fantastic stories occasionally appearing in the Brazilian press that the Federal Department of Public Security, Brazil's FBI, had a dossier listing him as a participant at the founding of the Communist Information Bureau (COMINFORM) in Yugoslavia in 1947, and as the head of a Communist

Party cell in Rio.[12] Nonetheless, Furtado was obliged to defend himself against these wild allegations.

Concurrently, Cid Sampaio was trying to undercut Furtado by urging that the President of SUDENE's Deliberative Council be given power equal to that of the Superintendent. This was a subtle move on the part of a representative of the more intelligent industrialists and landowners in the Northeast to cripple the agency at birth, as a prelude to taking complete control of what remained.

SUDENE's surprisingly numerous supporters rallied to the support of the new agency. On December 8, 1961, a mass meeting was held in Recife and a one-hour pro-SUDENE strike shut down much of the city. (Professor Albert I. Hirschman has observed that this was "the only [protest movement], to the writer's knowledge, ever to have been staged in support of an economic planning agency!")[13] The pressure proved effective, as the Brazilian Congress quickly gave Furtado what he wanted.

Having procured his first appropriations and the approval of his plan, Furtado turned to the question of foreign aid.[14] He strongly felt that the development of the Northeast was exclusively Brazil's responsibility. No nationalist could tolerate any other premise. The proper role of foreign aid, in Furtado's view, was to support Brazilian plans to projects which the donor-country decided were in its interest to support. These would remain Brazilian plans or projects and should in no way be considered as actions *jointly* undertaken. Thus, ideally Furtado would have preferred U.S. loans which SUDENE could utilize as it saw fit to carry out the master plan (assuming, of course, that the U.S. approved of the master plan). Since the Alliance for Progress under its enabling legislation could not grant such general loans, Furtado would have settled for loans to be applied to specific SUDENE projects.

The Bohan Report, submitted to Washington in February, 1962, followed the SUDENE master plan fairly closely, at least with regard to long-term projects, and hence was acceptable to Furtado. He assumed that the Report would form the basis for an American aid program the emphasis of which would be on these long-term projects. He further assumed that such an aid program would require a modest American presence in the Northeast. (Indeed, this seems to

72

have been an assumption of the Bohan Report itself.) What he did not realize was that U.S. officials were now regarding the region as a major security problem. He did not know that the Report would be virtually shelved because it failed to take sufficient account of these political considerations.

President João Goulart had in the meantime been invited to Washington, where, among other things, he was to sign an agreement for the establishment of an aid program in the Northeast. The agreement, drafted in Washington in accordance with standard Alliance for Progress procedures, was sent to Rio prior to Goulart's departure. Before Goulart left, Furtado read it and made certain objections which arose from his view of the role of foreign aid. He felt it implied that the American aid mission to be set up in Recife would have some control over the whole program of development in the Northeast, including projects to be financed by Brazil alone.[15] Such an arrangement, in his view, would lead to messy political attacks from nationalist elements in the region. At a meeting at the home of Foreign Minister Santiago Dantas in Petrópolis, Furtado urged that the U.S. mission function like a bank, approving or disapproving U.S. loans for projects. Goulart and the Foreign Minister agreed.

On April 13, 1962, as part of Goulart's agenda in Washington, the U.S. and Brazil signed what was called the Northeast Agreement, providing for the allocation of $131 million of American aid in the Northeast over a two-year period. The Agreement committed the U.S. to a five-year effort, which seemed to follow the recommendations of the Bohan Report in that it would include both short-term impact projects and long-range developmental programs. Responsibility for agreeing upon which of these projects and programs would receive American aid was vested in the USAID mission, and in SUDENE or "other agencies . . . as may be designated by the Government of . . . Brazil." The projects and programs were to be drawn from the Bohan Report and the SUDENE master plan, or might be undertakings "which may be mutually agreed to."

Professor Riordan Roett has analyzed at some length the Agreement and the negotiations leading up to it in order to identify the sources of the conflict which subsequently arose between SUDENE and USAID. He points to a basic disagreement in interpretation:

73

SUDENE believed that it would be the exclusive representative of the Brazilian government in all foreign-aid negotiations in the region, and would thus have the right to pass upon projects which USAID might want to enter into with other Brazilian agencies. The American position was that the Agreement permitted USAID to deal directly with other agencies so long as the Brazilian federal government approved. A second difference resulted from Furtado's assumption that the U.S. aid program would stay close to the guidelines of his master plan. But as Professor Roett has written: "For the United States, the Agreement meant that it could now begin to combat, firsthand, the Communist menace it had identified in the Northeast." [16] If engaging in such combat required giving foreign aid to individual state agencies, then USAID was prepared to do so, despite the fact that this would lead to the type of involvement in local politics which Furtado felt would be fatal to any program of regional economic development.

Why, then, did Furtado accept the Agreement without a protest? Part of the answer lies in the pressure that had begun to build under SUDENE, especially from right-wing sources, to stop planning and start producing. A fight over the Agreement would have exposed him to charges that he was being an ideological (or "Communist") obstructionist to foreign aid. It might also have put him in conflict with Goulart. Moreover, in the days which followed the signing of the Agreement there were assurances from Goulart and others to the effect that the Alliance for Progress would in no way compete with SUDENE, but rather would complement the job of the agency. In other words, SUDENE would still be in charge.

Furtado pushed ahead with his master plan, and USAID began to staff what was to become a sizable mission in Recife. And on June 6, 1962, USAID signed a $1 million accord with Governor Cid Sampaio of Pernambuco to undertake a school construction program.

The use of the Alliance for Progress to counter the burgeoning political movement of Miguel Arraes was by no means the only direct U.S. intervention in the internal affairs of the Northeast. The Central Intelligence Agency had its eye on the ferment in the countryside, and was secretly planning its own strategy to dampen the revolutionary ardor of Julião and others like him.

PART TWO

SIX ❧

❧ ❧ Julião on the Rise

ONE OF THE MORE COLORFUL Julião stories, which probably contains truth and myth in equal parts, begins at a secret meeting of twenty large landowners eager to retaliate against the leader of the Peasant Leagues.[1] One suggested that since Julião was a lawyer, he could be bought off. "He might refuse the offer," replied another. "Or worse yet, he might take the money and use it to buy machine guns. It would be better to shut him up permanently." They all thought a bit, and finally one announced, "Leave it to me. I'll fix him myself." His plan was to shoot the state deputy while the latter was making a speech at the Legislative Assembly. The would-be assassin loaded his revolver on the appointed day and drove toward the Assembly. But he soon began to have second thoughts, and suddenly a strange foreboding came over him and shattered his resolve. At that moment a voice within him clearly pronounced the words, "Don't kill him. Don't do it." The man had always believed in spiritualism and never disregarded such messages. He turned his car around and headed home at a speed unusual even in Recife. The next day, repentant, he confessed everything to his intended victim. Julião thanked him, and later drew up a list of names of those at the clandestine conference. He gave it to his lieutenants saying, "If anything happens to me, I want to meet these twenty in hell."

Opposition to Julião within his home state of Pernambuco was al-

77

ways frenetic, but it was never more imaginative than the assassination plot of the twenty landowners. Some opponents, like Governor Cid Sampaio, tried to undermine the Peasant Leagues with reforms. In a speech on July 6, 1961, Sampaio hailed his reform efforts and confidently predicted that "at the end of my term in office there will no longer be any agrarian reform problem in Pernambuco." [2] His optimism was woefully misplaced.

Cid was trying to quiet the turmoil in the countryside through a land reform administered by the Company for Resale and Colonization (CRC), a so-called "mixed" company, 80 per cent of whose funds came from the state government and the remainder from federal and private sources. The CRC bought up land to establish peasant cooperatives. (It had taken over the Galiléia plantation after the expropriation.) The program was a flop. The CRC had little money, and could only nibble at the outer edges of the agrarian problem. The agency planned to settle 5,000 families in colonies over five years. According to official figures, more than 200,000 peasant families were landless in Pernambuco. Moreover, reports circulated that the CRC was exhausting its modest resources by paying high prices for poor land, as plantation owners disposed of property they couldn't otherwise unload. According to one report, prices were set by a tripartite commission composed of representatives of the landowner, the state government, and the CRC,[3] an evaluation process plainly not designed to discourage hanky-panky.

Others opposed the Peasant Leagues by attacking Julião personally. Julião's enemies and critics, both at home and abroad, could not confine themselves to assessing the merits of his ideas and activities. Instead, they impugned his motives in every way possible, a tactic made difficult by Julião's romantic idealism and his failure to indulge in a weakness shared by many political luminaries in Latin America —he did not use his position to get rich.

A favorite charge, leveled first by his political opponents[4] and later by foreign observers,[5] was that Julião was a large landowner himself who should begin agrarian reform at home by dividing his property among the peasants who lived on it. On several occasions his enemies even dumped truckloads of peasants on his farm, and then accused him of calling the police to remove them. (His support-

ers deny this, and maintain that the farm provided at least temporary refuge for a number of peasants who had been driven from their homes by their landlords.) This line of attack does not seem to have been taken seriously except by a few foreign commentators. No stretch of the imagination could make Julião into a large landowner. Espera contained 692 acres. Julião's father, while he was still alive, had split the property equally among his seven children, so that Julião himself owned less than 100 acres.

This accusation—like others leveled against him—had obvious political overtones. It did not receive wide publicity until April 14, 1962, when an article in a national magazine purported to expose "The Other Face of Julião." [6] The charges made by the author seemed tailored for use by Julião's opponents in the elections for federal deputy in October. They also amounted to a diversionary tactic. His enemies would have been delighted to see him devote his time and energy to administering a peasant cooperative, just as those to whom revolution in Latin America is abhorrent were overjoyed to see Che Guevara in the field with a gun in hand.

Other accusations were hurled at him. It was said, for example, that he was a coward; that he fled from the platform at the first sight of hostile disruptions of rallies or political meetings; that he had once taken refuge in a church when police arrived to disperse a demonstration in downtown Recife; and that he hesitated to go into the nearby state of Alagoas to organize Peasant Leagues.[7] Now, Alagoas happens to be the Brazilian equivalent of Sicily or the state of Guerrero in Mexico, remote spots whose claim to fame rests on the predisposition of the inhabitants to indulge in violent acts. The life of anyone attempting to organize peasants in Alagoas would surely be uninsurable. Indeed, at one point Julião actually received a message which read: "If you come to Alagoas, you will end up indoctrinating corpses." [8] Julião never pretended to be a militant who would lead his peasants into violent confrontations. He did not enjoy good health and was frequently incapacitated by migraine headaches. Nor did he delight in affecting the masculine, "tough guy" image that certain other Brazilian political leaders tried to project. He did on occasion defend Alagoan peasants in court, but, in general, he seemed to think revolution by suicide was a contradiction in terms.

Julião's enemies also delighted in calling him a cuckold, a serious charge in Brazil, as in virtually every Latin country, where the unfaithfulness of a wife is viewed as a substantial derogation of her husband's masculinity. His marriage with Alexina had not been a happy one despite Alexina's wholehearted participation in Peasant League work. Julião had never refrained from exercising what was considered as a husband's prerogative in Brazil, and had engaged in several extramarital love affairs. Alexina, being of high spirits and modern outlook, had done likewise, and Julião seems to have eschewed the double standard prevalent in the Latin world. At least until 1963, both parties apparently agreed that each would be free to pursue outside amatory interests but maintain the façade of married life. There is no evidence that his enemies' whisper campaign based upon this unusual arrangement had any ill effect on Julião's work.

Julião was, of course, charged with being a Communist. Since the cold war still raged in all its fury, the accusation clearly connoted that he was part of the International Conspiracy emanating from Moscow. The landowners, who saw a "red" plot behind every threat to them, could never be dissuaded by evidence of the actual relationship between Julião and the Communist Party as it developed in the early 1960s. The peasants, thoroughly conditioned to cries of "Wolf!" by the landlords, did not seem to be moved by the charge.

In view of the persistency of the accusation, it is curious that an incident that occurred in early December, 1961, during Julião's visit to Goiânia, the capital of the state of Goiás in central Brazil, was completely ignored by his enemies in Pernambuco. Julião delivered at the university a rather inflammatory speech which provoked a hostile reaction from some sectors of the local populace. At a subsequent rally in the city, he had to confront some of this hostility in his audience. The highly respected newspaper, *O Estado de São Paulo*, described him as "contradictory and unsure of himself," and quoted him as saying: "What I want in truth is revolution, and to transplant the regime of Cuba, of Russia, to Brazil. I am a communist, and it doesn't matter that they brand me as such." [9] According to this account, the crowd booed and began to shout "Get Julião!," the speaker fled from the platform, and the meeting broke up in a pushing-and-shoving match among members of the audience.

Since Fidel Castro had declared himself to be a Marxist-Leninist three days before this incident, Julião's admission has been cited as an example of his slavish devotion to the Cuban Premier.[10] On the other hand, the newspaper account suggests that Julião may have lost his head in the pressure of the moment and blurted out his admission in an act of defiance. Julião now denies ever having made the statement. Given the reliability of the Brazilian press, he might possibly be telling the truth.

In any event, the incident passed completely unnoticed in Pernambuco. Julião's political opponents failed to make use of his declaration either at the time it was supposedly issued or later during the 1962 election campaign.

On the theory that the best defense is a good offense, Julião replied to the various accusations made against him by taking advantage of his access to the national and international press and making sensational charges against his critics. The most famous of these appeared in an interview he granted to the West German magazine *Stern*.[11] He described three incidents of brutality equaling anything in the existing catalogue of atrocity stories. One involved a peasant who stole food from a plantation owner. The owner had the thief stripped, smeared with honey, and tied down to the ground on stakes next to a huge colony of voracious red ants. In the second, a landlord punished one of his peasants by making him stand in a large vat filled with water up to the peasant's mouth. Once a day the peasant was fed a piece of dry bread. He had to drink the water in which he was standing and into which he was discharging his own excrement. After three days he fell to his knees and drowned. The third case involved a peasant who stole cane from a plantation. As punishment and as an example to like-minded peasants, his body was cut up into pieces and thrown to the dogs. What created a loud stir when the interview was reprinted was that Julião claimed that two of the landowners involved in these incidents were state deputies in the Pernambuco Legislative Assembly.

On the whole, these charges and countercharges had little, if any, impact upon Julião and his enemies. The accusations flew back and forth at a time when Julião's star and that of his Leagues seemed in full ascendancy on both national and international horizons.

Always a visionary, Julião planned to create a national peasant movement that would link his Peasant Leagues with peasant groups in other parts of the country, yet remain under his leadership. As part of this grand scheme he hoped to forge alliances with working-class and student organizations, and at the same time to construct a political coalition between the Brazilian Labor Party (PTB) and his own Brazilian Socialist Party (PSB).[12] With his peasant constituency, Julião probably felt he could dominate the PSB and deal with the PTB on an equal footing, thus effectuating a nationwide peasant-worker alliance.

These grandiose ambitions required Julião to deal with the PTB's João (Jango) Goulart and Luís Carlos Prestes of the Communist Party, both of whom had plans of their own for the future course of political development in Brazil. These plans excluded a role for free-lance rural revolutionaries, but did require the services of a subordinate who could front as the leader of a national peasant movement. Julião was the natural choice for the job, and both Jango and the Communists were courting him.

In 1960, Julião was invited to a peasant congress at Londrina in the state of Paraná in southern Brazil.[13] The Communist Party, with help from the then Vice President João Goulart, arranged the meeting. Julião brought with him Zezé of Galiléia, who was now something of a national celebrity, and a delegation from the Pernambuco Peasant Leagues. The lawyer-deputy from Recife was named Honorary President of the congress. Later, on his way home from his trip to China, he crossed paths with Goulart in Moscow. In a subsequent interview in Rio de Janeiro, Julião disclosed that they had met in a hotel, and claimed that Goulart had actually agreed to merge his PTB with the Brazilian Socialist Party.[14] Nothing ever came of this meeting, which suggests that Goulart might merely have been dangling bait in front of Julião.

Meanwhile, the Communists, though they had been backing Julião from the first days of the Peasant Leagues, had for some time entertained misgivings about him. Simone de Beauvoir reported that as early as 1960, during the Quadros-Lott presidential campaign, Luís Carlos Prestes had been expressing vigorous criticism of the Peasant Leagues in private.[15] Yet the Party had preserved its façade

of support for Julião, and in 1961 seemed in a fairly good position to co-opt him.

The Communists made their move early in the year. Julião met privately and secretly with Prestes in Rio de Janeiro.[16] They talked about the possibilities of forming some sort of nationwide peasant movement. The Communists had for some time controlled a peasant group known as the Union of Farmers and Agricultural Workers of Brazil (ULTAB), which they used for the purpose of organizing coffee and sugar workers in the state of São Paulo in southern Brazil. ULTAB was reformist in orientation, spending most of its time at collective bargaining and other efforts to improve working conditions. Prestes offered to merge ULTAB with the Peasant Leagues. Julião would become the leader of this new union, but naturally he would have to accept conditions, such as the Party's retention of ultimate control. The proposition failed to tempt Julião in the slightest, since he realized full well what these conditions would do to his position of leadership. He also knew that at that moment his Leagues were much more dynamic and had a much greater growth potential than ULTAB. He countered by urging Prestes to accept the development of autonomous peasant groups and leaders in various parts of the country, arguing that diversity could lend more strength to the movement than the concentration of all peasant organizations within a monolithic structure. Then a common program could be forged in a democratic fashion at a national conference. Prestes, a firm believer in the hierarchical necessities of revolutionary organization, was not pleased at Julião's proposal.

The conference that Julião had in mind took place later that year when President Goulart, in an effort to broaden his political base, called for the first National Peasant's Congress. Some 1,600 delegates representing rural movements from all over Brazil gathered, in mid-November, in Belo Horizonte to discuss agrarian problems. Brazilian leftists of every conceivable hue turned up, as well as a number of prominent national politicians taking their cue from Goulart and seeking a piece of an emerging rural constituency. While the Communists from ULTAB pushed a reformist line, Julião stole the show. Although only three months before, at the first Conference of Peasants and Rural Workers of Pernambuco, Julião

83

had signed a manifesto making relatively moderate demands for progressive change in the countryside,[17] he now unfurled the banner of "Radical Agrarian Reform." His slogan caught the temper of the moment and proved especially appealing to the students attending the conference. He carried a majority of the plenary session, and the Congress adopted a Declaration urging "a radical transformation of the present agrarian structure of the country, with the liquidation of the monopoly on landholding exercised by the large landowners, principally through the expropriation of these holdings by the federal government, substituting in place of monopolistic landholding peasant ownership . . . and state ownership." [18]

At this time the Brazilian Constitution stated unequivocally that the federal government could not expropriate land without paying the owner "prior indemnification, at a fair price and in cash." Brazilian law also prevented illiterates from voting, thus making it impossible for peasants to elect representatives who might enact an effective land reform law in Congress. Little wonder that Julião expressed his doubts that the Declaration of Belo Horizonte could ever be realized through legislation. The realities of the situation made it clear that the Declaration was a revolutionary document.

The Belo Conference was a turning point in Julião's career. While the meeting was still in progress, President Goulart made him a concrete offer which, though neither party has ever revealed the exact terms of the proposal, would have put Julião in a position to use and benefit from the resources of the federal government. However tempting that possibility might have been, Julião turned it down, fearing that by accepting he would compromise his independence and become a mere paid agent of the government. From that time on, Goulart did everything he could to undercut Julião. And at the same time, the conference opened an irreparable breach between Julião and the Communists, who were unhappy with the revolutionary tone of the proceedings and with Julião's continued refusal to accept the Party's line. Though it was not immediately apparent, Julião was now very much on his own.

The split with the Communists surfaced first. On February 6, 1962, just three months after the conference, a Recife newspaper published what purported to be a telegram from Clóvis Melo, a local

journalist whom the paper called the leader of the Communist Party in Pernambuco. The telegram stated: "The international trips of the socialist deputy to the Pernambuco Assembly amount to a business which brings personal gain to Julião and nothing more." [19] The article also quoted an unnamed Communist official who called Julião "an imposter and an opportunist." (Several days later in a letter to the editor, Melo denied that he was the leader of the Party in Pernambuco and that he had made the derogatory reference to Julião,[20] but most knowledgeable readers did not take the disavowal seriously.) On September 11, Julião gave an interview that left no doubt about his feelings toward the Party.[21] He accused the Communists and certain elements of the middle class (this was probably a reference to Goulart) of conspiring to set up a "Syndicalist Republic" by means of a *coup d'état*. What a "Syndicalist Republic" might be he never made clear, but he probably had in mind something like Perón's Argentina, with Goulart in the title role, the Communists supporting him, and dissidents like himself marked for elimination. In the same interview he said that the Communists no longer backed him because he refused to be the Party's stooge. The Communist newspaper in Recife, *A Hora,* published a pair of articles replying to Julião in a firm and barely fraternal tone.[22] One argued that the reactionaries could easily destroy the Peasant Leagues if the latter failed to form a united front with the urban workers (whose unions, the article neglected to add, were dominated by the Party). The other noted rather condescendingly that Julião's Leagues were merely a restructuring of the Peasant Leagues the Communist Party had founded just after World War II. From that point on, Julião's name never darkened the pages of the Party's newspaper.

Julião's break with the Communists resulted from a profound divergence in their attitudes toward the style and substance of what both sides saw as the coming revolution in Brazil. Julião, relying on the authentic traditions of the region, felt that the peasant's religious faith and innate mysticism could be well-springs of revolutionary consciousness. Brazil is essentially a rural nation, and Julião believed that the Brazilian revolution would resemble the Chinese, in that it would begin in the countryside. He often expressed admiration for Mao's Chinese Revolution. Yet he neither joined nor expressed

85

sympathy for the pro-Chinese elements which split off from the Brazilian Communist Party early in 1962 and formed their own "Communist Party of Brazil." The Moscow-line Communists, he would charge, were inflexibly tied to the dogma that revolution must emanate from the urban working class; they wanted to convert the peasants into orthodox Communists without regard for the cultural forces that for centuries had shaped life in the Northeastern countryside; they sought to compromise with the middle class in an attempt to manipulate the revolution from above, rather than to encourage an awakening peasantry to make their own revolution from below.[23]

The Communists, for their part, charged that Julião was overwhelmed by success and taken in by his own charisma, an egotist who thought he could personally orchestrate the Brazilian revolution. In addition, they were undoubtedly nervous about his use of revolutionary rhetoric. Violence at this time, the Party argued, would be counterproductive, since it would provoke right-wing elements to overthrow the government. Julião's views were dismissed in familiar terms: "leftist extremism, the childhood disease of communism."

The feud between Julião and the Brazilian Communist Party disturbed even Fidel Castro, who learned of it shortly before May Day, 1962. Julião was in Havana, and Fidel suggested that he come to the airport to welcome Prestes, who was arriving for the festivities. Never one to say no, Julião accompanied Fidel but was rudely snubbed by the Cavalier of Hope as the latter disembarked. Later at the hotel, Julião told Fidel about the feud. Castro resolved to visit Prestes in his room to try to patch up the rift. A half-hour later he returned to Julião and said with a disconsolate shrug: "The Cavalier is there, but all Hope is gone."

Meanwhile, Julião's dispute with Goulart was simmering. It finally boiled over in the summer of 1962, in the state of Paraíba, just north of Pernambuco.[24] The Peasant League movement had spread to Paraíba early in 1959 when João Pedro Teixeira, a peasant who had been to Pernambuco and had witnessed the growth of Julião's new movement, founded a League in Sapé. Sapé is located in the transitional area between the sugar zone and the *agreste*, where

many of the sugar workers lived in huts on plantations and had the use of a plot of land on which they grew cash and subsistence crops. They were obliged to sell their cash crops to the plantation owner, usually at poor prices, and to work for the owner three days per week at a salary less than the going rate. The peasant's right to his hut and plot of land was uncertain, and landlords were wont to move resident workers in and out of their huts to prevent them from claiming any special rights as a result of improvements made by the peasants in the property. Thus the region provided fertile ground for peasant organizing.

A principal activity of the new Paraiban League was to provide legal assistance for peasants who wanted indemnification for improvements or who wanted to pay annual rent instead of working three days a week for the landlord. The peasants made claims in court and thus could avoid eviction as long as these legal proceedings were pending. The owners, unaccustomed to any challenges from their workers, often resorted to violence, and bloody clashes occasionally erupted. On March 17, 1962, peasants on a plantation north of Sapé slashed to death two of their landlord's private gunmen and wounded the plantation administrator in a battle that left two peasants dead. The landowners vowed vengeance.

Shortly thereafter, two men dressed as cowboys ambushed João Pedro Teixeira and shot him to death. The killers were subsequently captured and turned out to be rural policemen. They implicated several landowners, including one prominent politician. The policemen were imprisoned, but those actually responsible were never prosecuted. Julião vigorously protested the murder and sent a well publicized letter to Goulart's Minister of War, urging him to confiscate the weapons Julião claimed the Paraiban landowners were stockpiling.[25] He also prominently displayed the widow, Elisabete, who succeeded João Pedro as President of the Sapé Peasant League. She accompanied him on several trips to Havana and to the south of Brazil. But she also began to alienate other peasant leaders in the state with her increasingly militant talk about revolution.

As the Peasant Leagues in Paraíba multiplied and expanded, Julião found it increasingly difficult to control them. A young Paraiban agronomist, Francisco de Assis Lemos de Souza, rose to a posi-

tion of leadership within the movement and was soon quarreling with his colleague from Recife. Assis Lemos, who enjoyed good relations with the Communist Party, maintained a more pragmatic and less revolutionary approach than Julião. He wanted to concentrate on improving the peasants' living conditions. In early 1962 he attracted the attention of President Goulart, who was looking for an opportunity to undercut Julião. He instructed his Minister of Agriculture to provide funds for the establishment of medical posts in rural areas where the Paraiban Peasant Leagues were active. This was a tangible benefit for the peasants and greatly enhanced Assis Lemos' prestige. He soon became President of the Federation of Peasant Leagues of Paraíba. In July, 1962, Goulart visited Paraíba and was hailed by a procession of 16,000 peasants.

When Assis Lemos ran for state deputy in 1962, Elisabete also entered the race. There was talk that Julião had put her up to it in an attempt to draw votes from Lemos. If so, the plan misfired, for Elisabete lost badly. After that Julião had very little to say about the course of the Peasant League movement in Paraíba.

Julião, though he did not know it yet, was in trouble. By alienating both Goulart and the Communists, he had isolated himself on the left flank of Northeastern politics, and the consequences—especially of his split with the Communists—were profound. The Peasant League movement in the Northeast required leadership and coordination, especially if it was to maintain a revolutionary tack. Yet Julião knew full well that a regional revolution could never succeed, and therefore he had to seek allies in other parts of the country. He needed financing, which could come only from southern Brazil and from abroad. He also had to keep up his international contacts.

But Julião was only one person. It thus became necessary for him to delegate responsibility and to rely upon subordinates. When he broke with the Communists, he could no longer make use of their smoothly functioning apparatus, and he had to expand his own organization. The Belo Congress helped him to accomplish this, for it enabled him to attract a number of individuals, mostly students, who had become thoroughly disenchanted with what they saw as the conservatism of the Communist Party. These new supporters were eager for action. Their enthusiasm created other problems—

whether they could function under Julião's direction, and whether they would remain under his control.

Communist opposition meant much more than the mere absence of Party support. The Peasant Leagues, because they were loosely structured and scattered throughout the sugar zone, offered an irresistible target for infiltration. The Communists began to move in and to attempt to wean control of the Leagues away from pro-Julião elements. This competition served only to confuse the peasants and detract from the struggle for land reform. Factionalism, the congenital disease of the left, had made its inevitable appearance, and would soon spread with great intensity.

Celso Furtado, in an interview in 1963, perceptively posed another difficulty that Julião faced as he adopted an openly revolutionary stance. He noted that the Communist Party since 1935 had occupied the extreme left of the Brazilian political spectrum and had achieved a monopoly on the use of revolutionary rhetoric. But the Party never really *did* anything revolutionary. As the Communists began to be dislodged from their comfortable spot on the extreme left by Julião and other left-revolutionaries inspired by Cuba, the latter found that they could not emulate the inaction of the Communist Party. They began to feel the pressure of having to *do* something, or else forfeit to someone else the right to advocate revolution with any degree of credibility. Thus the stability which the Communists had created on the left could no longer continue. Furtado's conclusion was that "when you pass from words to action, you have to pay a very high price, especially if conditions for revolution do not exist."

The year 1962 began with Julião having outflanked the Communist Party and finding himself on the far left end of the political spectrum in Northeast Brazil. He did in fact begin to feel pressure to translate words into action. The moment had arrived for the Peasant Leagues to produce some visible forward movement toward the revolution—not necessarily an armed uprising, but at least the successful stirring of a revolutionary consciousness among the peasants and the forging of some sort of revolutionary infrastructure. In short, it was time for something to happen.

SEVEN 🌿

🌿 🌿 Julião Descending

FRANCISCO JULIÃO'S RHETORICAL SKILLS DID NOT include a feel for coming up with the felicitous epigram. But in the course of his career in the Northeast he did issue one memorable maxim. During an interview in 1963 with Antônio Callado, he observed, somewhat ruefully: "To agitate is a beautiful thing. To organize is what is difficult."[1]

By mid-1962 Julião could look back with nostalgia upon the early years of his peasant movement. This was a romantic and relatively uncomplicated period, already beginning to assume the aura of living legend. With some help from Julião the Leagues had reproduced themselves in a manner more spontaneous than contrived. Perhaps Julião was not "a social agitator like Christ and Moses," the historical epitaph he appropriated for himself in a 1962 speech,[2] but during the formative years he did play a rather simple role in his efforts to stir the peasants of the Northeast. But now things were changing. Julião and others were talking about the immediate necessity for radical reform which under existing circumstances could not be achieved by peaceful means. There were dark hints of the inevitability of violence. Since conditions had not reached a point where the peasants would rise in a spontaneous revolt against their oppressors, it seemed logical that those who were urging what amounted to revolution would have to provide a plan of action, a disciplined organi-

zation, and a cadre of leaders who could execute the program. Agitation alone would no longer suffice.

It would be no easy job. For one thing, nobody really knew how many Peasant Leagues were already in existence, and how many peasants belonged. Claims ranged from Julião's solemn estimate that League membership had passed the 100,000 mark[3] to the statement of a Catholic priest working with rural workers in Pernambuco to the effect that as of January 1962 he would be very surprised if twenty Leagues still existed in that state.[4]

There is some evidence indicating that Julião actually believed that the Leagues were as far flung and as numerically strong as he kept insisting. His writings assume the existence of a mass peasant movement throughout the entire Northeast. Such idyllic self-delusion reflected the triumph of theory and ideology over the harsh dictates of reality. It would prove a serious weakness in the crucial period ahead, when the need for action would expose the impotence of the spoken and written word.

Whether planned violence became a part of the League program of action in 1962 is debatable. But in the early days it was clear that the Leagues did not espouse violence. Although Recife newspapers blamed several armed clashes in the countryside on the Leagues, these charges were never substantiated. Landowners occasionally claimed that League members set cane fields on fire, but Julião adamantly denied the accusation. He argued that the peasants could burn down the entire sugar zone if they really wanted to, but it made no sense for them to destroy resources which, in the event of an effective land reform, would eventually belong to them.

Nor do the Leagues seem to have adopted a policy of instigating squatters' invasions of plantations or sugar mills during this early period, although one can find a random newspaper reference to such clashes, usually after peasants were evicted from their homes. Occasionally these evictions resulted from a desire on the part of the landowner to discourage Peasant League membership. (In one extreme instance, a landowner's private police were reported to have branded a peasant's forehead with the initials of the landowner in front of the peasant's wife and children because the peasant had joined a League.[5]) For the Leagues to respond with demonstrations or inva-

sions was more a matter of self-defense and even organizational necessity than of official policy.

By 1962, however, the Leagues had very definitely taken to the offensive. The *Chicago Daily News* reported one incident in which peasants picketing a sugar mill near Vitória de Santo Antão circulated a petition which read:

> Our men have the hunger of the damned. We need some decent food.
>
> The 1,500 peasants who demonstrate for agrarian reform on the fallow lands of Constâncio Maranhão demand: sixty-six pounds of flour, beans, sugar, meat.
>
> If this petition of the people is not granted, these same people with their troubled spirit will have to apply the "hammer," because our aim is: the land should be for him who works it.[6]

At least the Leagues had chosen an appropriate target. Constâncio Maranhão was the pistol-waving landowner in the ABC–TV documentary *The Troubled Land.*

The Leagues also developed fervent support for Fidel Castro in 1962. Despite Julião's insistence that Cuba was merely a symbol and Castro merely another hero in his wonderfully eclectic revolutionary pantheon (along with Moses, Jesus, Saint Francis of Assisi, Mao Tse-tung, Ben Bella, Thomas Jefferson, Abraham Lincoln, and others), his words often carried thinly veiled implications that Cuba was to be more than just an inspiration. He once told a Rio journalist: "We are all Cubans. The Cuban Revolution is ours. Not just symbolically but concretely. Whoever dares to touch Cuba today . . . will be directly provoking the Brazilian people into an immediate and limitless struggle." [7]

And so stories began to circulate that Peasant League people were recruiting volunteers from Northeast Brazil to go to Cuba and help defend that beleaguered isle from American aggression; that peasants and students from the Northeast were receiving guerrilla training during their visits to Cuba; that mysterious shipments of arms and money were coming into the Northeast from abroad. One Re-

cife politician went so far as to charge that Julião had a cache of Czech guns hidden in the backyard of his house in Recife.[8]

Reactions to all this varied widely. General Artur Costa e Silva, the army officer in command of troops in the Northeast (and later to become President of Brazil), was not in the least disturbed by talk of armed uprisings. He put it bluntly: "Julião is a bluffer." [9]

The Communists looked upon the turmoil that the Leagues were causing as a mere extension of Julião's program of agitation. They would not dignify what was happening by viewing it as part of any revolutionary plan. A Party journal asked: "And now? What could they offer as a form of struggle to the peasants? Land reform was the order of the day. But what sort of land reform? That was of no interest. The thing that counted was only to agitate." [10]

The respected Rio newspaper, *Jornal do Brasil,* aimed shafts of ridicule at the Peasant League rebels. An editorial declared: "Mr. Julião, a conspirator and an agitator, speaks of beards and arms. He forgets that this is not Cuba. Armed bearded men in a democratic and civilized Brazil (in this country there were never any Batistas) are not revolutionaries—they are police cases. Or worse, they are caricatures. Caricatures which do not merit fear. They provoke laughter. . . ." [11]

At the same time some observers were advancing the theory that Julião was actually a *moderating* influence on explosive elements in the Northeast. Those who shared this view looked upon his inflammatory language as merely a device to hasten reform. They argued that this kind of talk enabled his oppressed followers to let off steam, and at the same time pressure for meaningful changes in the agrarian structure. The fact that he never spelled out any program involving the use of violence fortified this rather benevolent interpretation of his movement.

Finally, it should be noted that during this period a special commission from the federal legislature was conducting an investigation of the Peasant Leagues. It failed to turn up any significant evidence of subversion, and at one point issued the observation that the Leagues were in fact seeking structural change in the countryside.[12]

What were the Leagues really doing? Many of the rumors about their activities had little basis in fact. For example, Julião himself ad-

mitted in an interview with the *Times'* Tad Szulc that he had never made any real plans to send volunteers to fight in Cuba, but that agitation against U.S. aggression was just a method to politicize the peasants.[13] The frequent trips to Cuba do not seem to have produced a single legitimate peasant guerrilla. As one of Julião's lieutenants afterwards observed: "There was nothing to learn in Cuba about fighting in the Northeast. For the peasants who went, it was like a picnic, a weekend. The whole thing was a tremendous waste." [14] Finally, despite all the talk about guns, no one ever uncovered any significant stockpiles of weapons that could be used to mount a serious threat against the government.

Yet it would be inaccurate to dismiss the Peasant League movement as generating words without action. For there was in fact an attempt by people connected with the Leagues to stage a genuine insurgency in 1962. Although Brazilian security officials produced documentary evidence purporting to incriminate Julião,[15] he has continued to disclaim any connection with the "Dianópolis caper." What actually happened was that Julião lost control of certain militants within the Peasant League movement, and they went off on their own to plan and prepare for an armed insurrection in the Brazilian interior. The idea was to set up several training camps to serve as bases for small fighting groups composed mostly of students. These cadres would also attempt to enlist both the active and passive support of local peasants. Julião objected vigorously, but in vain.

The "Dianópolis caper" represented a drastic departure from the strategy Julião had devised for the Leagues, which derived their strength from conditions in the sugar zone in Pernambuco and Paraíba, and which had grown and prospered in response to specific social and economic pressures. Now an attempt would be made to achieve the instant radicalization of peasants in different areas far removed from these pressures. It is true that from a purely military point of view the remote and sparsely populated interior offered certain advantages over the relatively compact sugar zone. But these advantages never came close to outweighing the plan's obstacles. Parallels with the Che Guevara operation in Bolivia are obvious. The "Dianópolis caper" was a forerunner of that ill-fated venture.

The idea sprung from the fertile imagination of Clodomir dos

Santos Moraes, Julião's chief lieutenant. Clodomir was a lawyer from the state of Bahia, on the southern fringe of the Northeast. He had come to work in Recife and had served for a while in the state legislature. He had become friendly with Julião, and was one of the few state deputies who would accompany the Peasant League leader on investigatory trips to the countryside. He was also a card-carrying Communist. When the mood struck, Clodomir could be a delightful raconteur, embellishing his stories with a deft torrent of detail. A cigarette often dangled jauntily from the corner of his mouth. Yet there was a certain unmistakable toughness about him, which his quick wit tended to exaggerate. Some considered him ugly, but he projected a magnetism that attracted followers. His wife, a beautiful Czech, was said to speak nine languages.

Clodomir was the man with connections in Havana. It was he who brought Julião and Fidel together. By 1961 he had committed himself wholeheartedly to Julião's cause. In December he was censured on the front page of the Communist Party newspaper in Recife.[16] In June, 1962, he was expelled from the Party for "adventurism." [17]

Thus Clodomir shifted from the left wing of the Communist Party to the left wing of the Peasant League movement. Within the latter he found an important ally, Alexina. Julião's wife was an activist within the movement, and in this as in other matters she remained unwilling to subordinate herself to her husband's interests. Both Clodomir and Alexina were convinced that the revolution was within reach. Julião disagreed, but was swept along. In this he demonstrated one of his most serious weaknesses, an inability to say "no" and make it stick. Looking back on this crucial period, Julião observed in a 1969 interview that Clodomir "couldn't tell where reality ended and fantasy began. So he began to live in a fantasy world. It is very dangerous to work with a man like this." [18]

Given the clandestine character of the "caper," the dearth of confirmable detail is not surprising. Both the claims made by the Brazilian government and the denials made by Peasant League sources seem to reflect considerable exaggeration. Indeed, one American professor not at all sympathetic to the Leagues has expressed doubt whether the "caper" ever took place.[19] An examina-

95

tion of published sources,[20] weighed against random references made by Peasant League people still reluctant to discuss the incident, suggests the occurrence of the following events:

In November, 1961, a small group of Northeasterners journeyed to the state of Goiás and purchased several farms in and near the municipality of Dianópolis, some 600 miles north and slightly east of Brasília, the capital of Brazil. Goiás is one of several enormous, underpopulated states in the Brazilian interior, its northern tip extending beyond the latitude of Recife, its bottom reaching almost as far south as Rio de Janeiro. To the east of the upper part of the state lies the vast *sertão* of Northeast Brazil. When Brazilians talk about opening up the interior of their huge subcontinent of a country, they invariably cite the potential of Goiás in hopeful terms. The founding of Brasília in the southern part of the state and the beginning of the construction of a highway from Brasília to the mouth of the Amazon were intended to spur the development of this remote, tropical region in the central highlands. Indeed, land speculation by foreigners (mostly American) attested to the ultimate validity of this vision of the future.

Obviously immigrants settling in and around Brasília and the new highway would require food. This seemed eminently sensible when the Northeasterners arriving in Dianópolis announced plans to raise livestock and cultivate grain on the farms they were purchasing. It also made sense, as they said, that their efforts were being financed by a group of investors, Northeasterners who had formed something called (no doubt with tongue very much in cheek) the Capitalist Company of the Northeast, with a view toward taking advantage of the opportunities that Goiás offered.

As the months went by, the representatives of the Capitalist Company of the Northeast began to display an unusual social consciousness. They paid their own farm workers well and provided them with medical and dental services. They also encouraged both their own workers and workers in the vicinity to organize. By June, 1962, there was talk of the formation of Peasant Leagues in the Dianópolis area.

Clodomir Moraes was in charge of the Dianópolis group. Using the Capitalist Company as a cover, he had assembled a small nucleus

composed mostly of students. The Dianópolis operation was one of several similar projects initiated in 1962. Other camps were set up in the states of Bahia and Maranhão, in areas on the fringes of the Northeast. The young guerrillas-to-be collected small arms and trained on long marches throughout the countryside. They also tried, without much success, to enlist local peasants. The weapons assembled were not, as some have charged, shipped in from abroad, but were either purchased or stolen from the army. At this time it was easy to get hold of guns in Brazil.

The Dianópolis group had internal problems. The students did not adjust well to the rigors of guerrilla life. According to Clodomir: "The expenses of the training camps soared as a result of the insistence of these young people on complementing the sparse guerrilla diet with a steady supply of cookies, jellies, and canned food. In addition, they maintained that they were entitled to weekly visits to the prostitutes of the neighboring villages . . ." [21]

The security of the "caper" was not at all tight. In São Paulo students talked freely about the camp and some even visited Dianópolis on a lark as part-time guerrillas.

The Brazilian authorities, of course, were fully aware of what was going on, and kept the various camps under close surveillance. According to Julião,[22] in the fall of 1962 Pelópidas Silveira, then Vice Governor of Pernambuco, informed him that security officials linked him with this guerrilla activity. Julião insisted that he had nothing to do with it, but immediately sent word to the students in the field to close up shop and return to Recife to help in the 1962 state election campaign, which was just getting underway. Clodomir claims that "peasants and workers" expelled the students from the camps.[23] In either event, in late November the army raided the Dianópolis farm.

What actually happened during and after the raids is difficult to ascertain from the conflicting and often patently exaggerated stories emanating from the area. One paper reported that Clodomir was caught on the spot, and then a few days later reported him turning up in southern Brazil. The most imaginative item was a suggestion that the guerrillas had chosen Goiás because its flat terrain and network of rivers were especially suited for the landing of aircraft.[24]

Since the Governor of Goiás was a reformer of suspected leftist tendencies, his enemies were eager to associate him with any sort of illegal and/or subversive activity. Thus reports from the scene stated that among those who were arrested was an official of the state government. (Later the Governor was cleared of any participation in the "caper.") The authorities did make some arrests and did find some weapons. The Peasant League newspaper, *A Liga,* announced that the weapons had been planted by government officials, and were in fact the property of Point Four, the U.S. technical assistance program that predated the Alliance for Progress.[25]

The worst was to come. On December 13, state police in Rio de Janeiro arrested Clodomir, a girl named Célia (Clodomir's wife had apparently returned to Czechoslovakia), and an unidentified young man in a station wagon on the outskirts of the city. The vehicle contained some weapons. It belonged to Julião. According to one version of the story, the Communists had fingered Clodomir to the police. Julião dismissed the whole affair as a frame. He added, apparently with a straight face, that the guns found in the car were Point Four weapons, clearly demonstrating Clodomir's innocence. The militantly conservative Governor of the state of Guanabara, which is coextensive with the city of Rio, was delighted to have Clodomir in the hands of his police, who within a month would receive nationwide publicity for their attempt at achieving a final solution to the beggar problem in Rio by dumping a group of helpless mendicants into the bay. The ex-deputy from Pernambuco disappeared from view into the maw of a Guanabara dungeon.

As if the loss of Clodomir were not sufficiently serious, on November 27, 1962, a commercial Brazilian airliner crashed near Lima, Peru, on a flight from Rio to Lima. Discovered in the wreckage was a pouch belonging to one of the unfortunate passengers, a Cuban official who had been attending an international conference in Rio. The pouch contained documents that referred to the clandestine activity of Clodomir and the others in the Brazilian interior, and established a connection between the Cubans and the would-be guerrillas.

This embarrassing disclosure resulted in the suspension of the modest financial support the Peasant Leagues had been receiving from Cuba as of late 1961. Castro had been reluctant, even then, to

contribute to the Leagues because he had doubts about their revolutionary potential. Now he was certain. The loss of Clodomir further damaged the solvency of the movement, since he had taken charge of fund-raising both at home and abroad. This left Julião with two sources of international funding, a committee in Paris that collected money from labor unions in Western Europe and student groups in Czechoslovakia that were raising money to be sent to the Northeast.[26] His principal domestic source was a big landowner from Rio, who also happened to be a practicing Marxist.[27] Thus the "caper" succeeded in worsening the already shaky financial condition of the Leagues.

What happened in Dianópolis vindicated Julião's insistence that insurgency operations were inappropriate at this time, but vindication was of little comfort to him. Because of the ambiguous nature of his connection with the "caper," the Peasant League leader suffered a damaging loss of prestige, catching abuse from all points of the political compass. The militant revolutionaries considered the affair to be a demonstration of incompetence. The conservative elements on the left disavowed what they saw as dangerous "adventurism." Julião was caught in the middle, and there wasn't much he could do about it.

On a local level, meanwhile, the shift to more militant action by the Peasant Leagues in Pernambuco was proving no more effective in bringing Brazil closer to the brink of revolution. (The major problem which the Leagues faced, competition from the Catholic Church, the Communist Party, and other groups seeking to establish a power base in the countryside, will be discussed at length in Chapter 11.) Julião also had to deal with the difficulty of furnishing effective leadership on the local level. One of his most trustworthy lieutenants was a law student named Joel Câmara.[28] Unlike Clodomir, Joel did not entertain grandiose illusions of implanting an insurgency in the interior of Brazil, but instead he shared Julião's vision of nurturing an indigenous revolutionary movement among the peasants of the sugar zone. Yet in January, 1963, Joel, like Clodomir, was in jail.

The radicalization process has been known to dehumanize even those individuals whose first steps along the road to revolution were

motivated by the loftiest of humanistic impulses. The dynamics of frustration and repression, as they interact with the overwhelming sense of urgency which drives these individuals, can put a man's spirit to an agonizing test. Yet there are others who somehow succeed in preserving their humanity and the purity of their ideals in the face of pressure which invites the corrosions of anger and bitterness. Joel Câmara was such a person. His ideological convictions were straightforward and simple. "I am a Socialist, a Christian, and a revolutionary," he once remarked during an interview. "A Socialist because I believe wealth should be divided among all the people. A Christian because the example of Christ as a revolutionary leader is more relevant and easier to grasp than that of Marx. Christianity is spiritual. I am spiritual. Brazil is steeped in spirituality. Materialism can never take root here. The socialism of the Bible, not that of Marx, Lenin, and Trotsky, is what will eventually prevail in Brazil. Finally, I am a revolutionary because this is the only way to take power."

At first blush Joel did not look very much like a revolutionary. He was a scrawny, pale, polite youth with yellowish buck teeth. He came from a lower-middle-class family. His father was an actor. A teacher at the university remembered him as "a nice boy, always smiling and laughing even while he talked about machine guns." (Joel did, in fact, have a fascination for machine guns.) But he did not always smile and laugh. There were times when he would become excited about something which concerned him deeply, and a hard gleam would flash from his eyes. It was this gleam that signaled that he would not hesitate to put his body on the line when he deemed it necessary.

Joel first received public attention in 1961 when he and a fellow law student won an essay contest with their study of conditions in Recife's House of Detention. Their paper exposed the disease, brutality, homosexuality, and lunacy rampant in the fortress-like jail adjacent to one of the city's worst riverbank slums. The authorities failed to appreciate what the students had done, and labeled them subversive.

Later that year Joel made the trip to Belo Horizonte to attend the National Peasant's Congress. It was an exhilarating experience. He

met and befriended a group of young Trotskyists whose sincerity greatly impressed him. At the instigation of the Communists, they had been excluded from participation. Joel protested and helped them at least gain permission to pass out their leaflets at the meeting. For this the Communists directed at him what would be the first of many verbal assaults.

Joel's big discovery at the Congress was the existence of a revolutionary group from his own home state. He introduced himself to Julião, joined the Peasant League movement, and quickly assumed a position of responsibility.

Though Joel was city born and bred, he chose to do his work in the field and became an on-scene legal advisor to peasants who belonged to the Leagues. He soon learned that the living law, as it operated in the countryside, was considerably different from what he had been studying at school.

"You ask about the law," he said in a 1963 interview. "I will tell you about the law. On one plantation the landowner had the habit of drinking too much rum and then running naked through the peasant huts. The peasants complained to the police, who shrugged their shoulders and laughed. Finally one peasant caught hold of the naked landowner on one of his nocturnal visits and threatened to carve away his manhood with a knife. The landowner kept his pants on after that.

"I tried to use legal methods, but it was useless. The case of José Firmino is an example. His landlord wanted to evict him from his farm in Bom Jardim, and José called upon me for legal assistance. We secured witnesses and prepared a writ. But when we came into court, the landlord's private gunmen frightened away the witnesses. The judge saw everything, but all he could say was 'Take it easy, take it easy.' He was afraid to protest.

"The next day I was told that the gunmen were setting up an ambush for me in town. But I thought up a new idea. I got hold of a large cherry bomb, for it was almost the Feast of São João (Saint John), and I went into town with several peasants. A small boy told us where the gunmen were hiding. I approached alone, and when I heard their pistols click, I jumped into a hole at the side of the road. They began to shoot, but I kept very still. Then they came out after

me. I lit the cherry bomb and threw it at them. There was a big explosion, and when I looked up, the gunmen were running away. I could write you a whole book," he concluded with a twinkle in his eye, "if you could send me a machine gun."

The Bom Jardim incidents, which occurred in July of 1962, resulted in more publicity for Joel. In order to defend José Firmino from the gunmen who were trying to evict him from his home, Joel decided that the time had come for a paramilitary operation, based on defensive guerrilla tactics. He stationed peasants armed with their primitive hunting rifles at the approaches to José Firmino's hut, and devised a signal system, based on the explosion of fireworks, to warn of the enemy's approach. (One bang = approach of landowner's men; two = peasant wounded; three = approach of police or army.) He even gave the plan a name, "Operation Espada," after the plantation upon which these actions took place. His chief partner in "Operation Espada" was one Dequinho, who happened also to be Julião's brother and the manager of the family farm, Espera, which was not far away.

It was all great fun while it lasted, which wasn't very long. The newspapers back in Recife published scare stories about guerrilla warfare breaking out in Bom Jardim, and quoted a local police official as declaring that "Joel's activity is part of a well organized subversive plot to implant anarchy throughout the interior." [29] Shortly thereafter the police arrested Joel, Dequinho, and some peasants, and turned them over to the army. Unfortunately Joel, because of his literary bent or perhaps with an eye toward history, had put "Operation Espada" in writing, even to the point of drawing a detailed map of José Firmino's hut and its surroundings. The army general in command immediately called a press conference, exhibited the captured documents, and announced that the whole thing was straight out of Mao Tse-tung's handbook for guerrilla warfare. "They kept asking me and asking me about this, and I kept insisting that I made the whole plan up and did not copy it out of any handbook," Joel reminisced in 1969, "but they wouldn't believe me. So I finally told them that I got the idea for 'Operation Espada' from an article in the Brazilian military magazine, *Revista Militar*, and that seemed to satisfy them." The newspapers gave it sensational cov-

erage, even reproducing the map, and heralded the start of revolutionary activity in Pernambuco. But they quickly dropped the story when the army failed to press charges and released its prisoners. Recalling the incident during our recent interview, Joel became animated and declared with a grin: "Joe, I did what I did with five peasants armed with five old rifles, guns from the days of Buffalo Bill. Imagine, just imagine what I could have done with one machine gun!"

The Communists of course vehemently denounced what Joel was doing, and tried to ridicule him. They took to calling him "General Joel," and spread stories that he was crazy. Yet the peasants were fond of him and would kill a chicken and prepare a special meal in honor of his visits. The police took due note of this, and kept telling the peasants that the only reason he came into the countryside was because he liked to eat chicken.

The fact that Joel survived his constant forays into the countryside must be attributed at least in part to his great good fortune (and perhaps also to the Smith & Wesson revolver he carried). There were a number of close calls. One example was the incident in Sarinhaém, a municipality on the coast of Pernambuco, south of Recife.

"A landowner had destroyed the hut of a peasant widow, so the local League organized a protest in the nearby town. The peasants marched carrying the remains of the widow's personal property. I was at the head of the line, and an American reporter was with me. The town politicians and the priest organized a counterdemonstration, a procession of children. As we approached the church, the children began their march while the priest rang the church bells and shouted over the loudspeaker attached to the tower: 'Deliver us, Saint George, from these devils; let us pray, brothers, that Saint George defends us.' We tried to talk with the priest, but two gunmen came out of the church. We retreated, and the reporter and I took refuge in the police station. When we tried to leave, the gunmen shot at us, and a policeman shot back. The procession of children was in the cross fire, and a five-year-old girl was killed."

Joel's activity was for the most part confined to the northern part of the sugar zone. He clearly was not engaged in any planned insurrection, but was utilizing violence as a defense against real and imagined aggressions by the landowners. (There is also evidence which

indicates that some of this violence might have been part of the intramural squabbling between the different groups trying to organize peasants.[30]) Though he had very little, if any, outside help in the form of money and supplies, he welcomed all the rumors about the existence of armed, organized peasant bands, because "it kept the landowners and the police in a great state of confusion." His best weapon was secrecy: "One minute of surprise is worth a plane with an atomic bomb."

But Joel's career lasted only through 1962. In January, 1963, in the municipality of També, where his friends the Trotskyists were organizing peasant unions, some peasants from the local League had invaded three sugar plantations. The police dispersed them, made several arrests, and reportedly seized a number of rifles and Molotov cocktails. Under vigorous interrogation the arrested peasants blamed Joel for organizing the invasions, and on January 14 he was picked up by the police in També. A comedy of errors ensued, as the police released him by mistake and put him on a bus to Recife. Discovering the gaff, they wired the state police in Recife to rearrest him and send him back, but it proved unnecessary, for Joel himself, upon arriving in Recife, took the next bus back to També, and was apprehended upon arrival. He spent some time in the També jail, where he fell in love with a local girl who had come by with a group of friends to have a look at the "notorious guerrilla leader" who was gracing their local jail. Shortly thereafter he was shipped to Recife and imprisoned as a subversive under the so-called Law of National Security. He thus gained the opportunity to experience, firsthand and for some time, the conditions in Recife's House of Detention.

Julião once said of Joel that "his only defects are purity, idealism, and courage." [31] There were others within the Peasant Leagues who exhibited a wider range of shortcomings. Take, for example, Padre Alípio de Freitas, billed as "the people's priest," a bald, ruddy-faced bundle of energy who passed through the movement like a zany whirling dervish, lending a dash of color, dispensing confusion even-handedly, and ending up, like Clodomir and Joel, behind bars.

Padre Alípio's background was obscure, so much so that one cynic suggested that he had infiltrated the Peasant League movement as a spy for the Church. Others doubted that he was a priest at

all. "He didn't talk like a priest," a League functionary once commented. "If he was one, he wasn't very serious about it." The Padre was originally a native of Bragança in Portugal. According to one rumor, he had been expelled from Angola, one of the Portuguese colonies in Africa, for stirring up the blacks against their colonial rulers. Julião claimed in a 1962 newspaper interview that he was "a theologian, multilingual, a professor of international law, and a captain in NATO." [32] Another report pictured him as a chaplain for the U.N. peace-keeping force in the Congo. Leftist causes greatly attracted him. He attended a World Congress for Disarmament and Peace in Moscow in 1962, as well as a Congress of Leaders of the Christian Left in Brazil. In the 1962 interview Julião described him as "an authentic Christian." Seven years later, in a more reflective mood, Julião mused that Padre Alípio "was in fact an anarchist. He followed Bakunin more than Christ." Julião added that despite his leftist leanings, the Padre was not much of a Marxist.

Padre Alípio spent some time working with peasants in Maranhão, a large, sparsely populated state in northern Brazil. A number of young people were attracted to him, and it became fashionable for students to invite him to their meetings, where he would violently denounce the "oligarchs." He went south for a while in 1962, and because of his "scandalous" behavior the arch-conservative Cardinal of Rio de Janeiro issued an order barring him from the exercise of his priestly functions. This didn't slow him down a bit. On June 26 he sent the Cardinal a letter declaring that the order was unnecessary, since he found it impossible to perform the duties of a priest under the Cardinal's "pastoral orientation." [33] The letter went on to attack the Cardinal's advisors, an "elite" group which functioned as "instruments of imperialist domination."

Despite the Cardinal's order, Padre Alípio kept his cassock on, and turned up in the Northeast, where he campaigned with Julião in Pernambuco and Paraíba during the 1962 elections. His role remained unclear. Julião named him to the Peasant League's National Directory, a group which seemed to exist only on paper, and even disclosed to the press that the Padre was his confessor. The presence of a priest on the platform with him undoubtedly helped offset attempts to convince voters that Julião was an anti-Christ, or the devil

incarnate. The problem was that the Padre would not just stand there, but he would deliver speeches, and he simply could not control his urges to use provocative, anti-military language. Army officials arrested him in Recife after a vituperative outburst, in which he urged peasants to turn in their hoes for rifles, and released him a few weeks later. After a similarly worded speech at the law school in João Pessoa in Paraíba, troops armed with submachine guns apprehended him as he left the building. By mid-November he was loose again, and he returned to Rio, where he displayed no loss of enthusiasm in a television interview. He disclosed that while imprisoned he had engaged in two hunger strikes, one of which protested the U.S. blockade of Cuba; that there was no truth to the story that he was about to go to a socialist country because he did not deserve such a reward, and anyhow "there is a revolution to be made here"; and that because 70 per cent of the Brazilian congressmen were big landowners, agrarian reform could be achieved only "by the hammer." [34]

Julião was not very happy about Padre Alípio's trip to Rio. He had suggested that the priest go back to Maranhão and take charge of the "northern region" of the Peasant Leagues. But the "northern region" was probably as nonexistent as the National Directory, and the Padre had no intention of returning to the boondocks. He much preferred the delights of Rio, where he did some writing for *A Liga*, the Peasant League newspaper, and at the same time had a torrid love affair with a pretty blonde medical student. He soon drifted away from Julião's movement and became active in a radical Catholic group called Popular Action. Within a short time he was back in jail. On May 28, 1963, a Recife newspaper reported that the army was holding him incommunicado, and that he had requested a clean cassock and a Bible. Except for an article in *A Liga* lamenting the death of Pope John which he managed to smuggle out that June,[35] he was not heard from again.

Julião's decision to utilize the dubious talents of Padre Alípio reflected a lack of judgment which was to plague him consistently. At times this shortcoming was actually a side effect of another of his weaknesses. Maria Ceales, for example, was a young law student whose oratorical skills were greatly enhanced by the captivating

qualities of her physical appearance. Julião found her green eyes irresistible, and for a while she fronted as his "secretary." She accompanied him on the trip to the peasant congress in Londrina in 1960. Though she came from a family of large landowners in the state of Ceará, her views were definitely progressive. She relished delivering revolutionary speeches to the peasants, and quickly earned the nickname of "La Pasionaria of the Northeast." It was her idea to "infiltrate" SUDENE and try to use the resources of the developmental agency to help the Peasant Leagues. Julião had his doubts about this, since he did not want to antagonize Celso Furtado, but once again could not say no. She got a job with the agency and utilized it to coordinate Peasant League activity throughout the Northeast. However, she was not very discreet about what she was doing, and soon enemies of SUDENE were pointing to her as an example of "Communist" activity within Furtado's organization.[36] Maria Ceales proved to be too much of an extrovert and a bit of an authoritarian in her approach. She also liked to take credit for things with which she had no connection. She soon clashed bitterly with some of the other Peasant League organizers and Julião finally had to ease her out of the movement.

These reverses, among others that the Peasant League movement suffered during late 1962 and early 1963, were only superficially offset by Julião's election as a federal deputy. His triumph in the October, 1962, balloting was an upset from which great satisfaction could be derived, since both the Pernambuco establishment and the Communist Party opposed his candidacy. The office carried with it immunity from arrest, new prestige, travel benefits, and an opportunity to strengthen connections in the south. But there were serious disadvantages as well. It meant that Julião would be further removed from his power base in the Northeastern sugar zone, and would be devoting even less time to the development of a revolutionary consciousness among the peasants, a handicap made even more severe by his lack of a cadre of effective subordinates. It also exposed his perpetration of a manifest contradiction, since he was going about condemning Brazil's version of the democratic process and at the same time playing the electoral game.

Why did he run for federal office? Some of those close to him felt

it was a big mistake. His enemies saw it as proof that he was no more than an opportunist. Julião himself has offered an answer which is far from satisfactory. In a 1969 interview he explained that he ran for federal deputy in order to gain a platform from which he might denounce the elections. Yet he might have done the same thing either by openly refraining from indulging in the political game, or by renouncing his mandate after the election.

Julião's decision to run seems to have been a logical extension of his other efforts to broaden the Peasant League movement. It reflects the dilemma in which he found himself in 1962: he saw the futility of attempting a regional revolution, which could have been easily crushed by the federal government even without U.S. military aid, so he sought to develop some kind of national peasant-worker alliance which would conform to more traditional models of socialist revolution. He thought that his election to the Chamber of Deputies in Brasília would facilitate this process. But things in Brazil were moving too rapidly. People were no longer asking whether there would be a revolution, but when it would occur and what direction it would take. The peasants in the Northeast, however, were simply not ready to participate. Lacking a reliable team of organizers, Julião soon discovered that not only was he unable to keep his movement politically abreast of the pace of national developments, but he was also ill-prepared to meet the challenge of other groups trying to organize peasants in his own home state.

If Julião's candidacy was a contradiction between what he said and what he did, the newly elected federal deputy quickly rediscovered his consistency in January, 1963, when he denounced the national plebiscite which would determine whether President Goulart should assume the full powers of his office. When Goulart took over following the sudden resignation of Jânio Quadros, he had to agree to a limitation of the powers of the presidency in order to assuage those elements of the military and the right wing who were bitterly opposed to him. The compromise which was reached nonviolently in typically Brazilian fashion called for a national plebiscite on the restoration of the full constitutional powers of the presidency. Julião called the vote a "farce," and advised his followers to abstain.[37] He explained that the plebiscite would be of no use to the peasants, since

it would not bring them any closer to a radical agrarian reform. His position succeeded only in isolating him from the rest of the left, which gave full support to Goulart and helped him win back the authority he had yielded in order to reach the presidency. Within the context of national politics in Brazil, Julião never really recovered from the consequences of this puzzling display of independence. The Communist Party took the opportunity to blame him for the fiasco in Dianópolis.[38] The Brazilian Socialist Party came close to expelling him. A Socialist leader said of him: "He is not a scoundrel: he is a mystic, a reverse Savonarola, insanely eager to jump into the fire." [39]

Meanwhile, back in the Northeast, Julião's revolution was being swept out from under him. Others were replacing him as the most important revolutionary figure in the region. The most important of these rose to statewide prominence just as the Leagues were falling into disarray. The year 1962 witnessed the dawn of a "new politics" in Pernambuco. And the man of the hour was Miguel Arraes.

EIGHT 🌿

🌿 🌿 The Rise
of Miguel Arraes

ALTHOUGH THE PEASANT LEAGUE MOVEMENT WAS beginning to show
signs of disintegration in 1962, unrest in the countryside and in the
cities of the Northeast intensified, and the international press continued to place Julião in the vanguard of what many were calling the
"Brazilian pre-revolution." By 1962, however, the Mayor of Recife
had clearly replaced the Peasant League leader as the most important spokesman for Northeastern radicalism.

Not that Miguel Arraes ever proclaimed himself to be a revolutionary, in the usual sense of the word. He consistently believed in
working within the system to effectuate radical change—and many
people agreed with him that he could do so within the framework of
Brazil's Constitution and without violence. His populist coalition
was on the march.

The urban problems confronting Mayor Arraes were of staggering proportions. A survey taken during his administration revealed that 27 per cent of Recife's streets were paved, 6.6 per cent
were served by public transportation, 48 per cent were reached by
the water system, 36.8 per cent were serviced by municipal garbage
collectors, 45.4 per cent had lighting, 12 per cent were accessible to
telephone lines, and 20.1 per cent were connected to the city's sew-
age system.[1] Incredibly, in a city whose population was fast approaching one million, there were only 6,500 telephones in operation.

In his 1959 campaign, Arraes had called for low-cost housing, an expanded water supply, better transportation, and more schools. But the financial resources available to a Brazilian mayor are minimal. In 1956, for example, municipalities had received only 9 per cent of all government tax revenues in Brazil.[2] Thus, Arraes could do no more than dent the armor of wretchedness that encased the city. He did initiate public works projects in some of the shanty neighborhoods, and achieved a reputation as a good administrator.

His most significant and controversial program was the one designed to make radical reforms possible—the Popular Culture Movement (MCP), an effort to promote educational and cultural activity at a grass-roots level. The MCP's principal project was adult literacy training. Those who conducted the program used a *cartilha*, or primer,[3] specially designed for Recife illiterates. Arraes's opponents claimed that the *cartilha* was subversive, and in the context of conditions in Recife and throughout the Northeast, it certainly was. Lesson one taught that "the vote belongs to the people." In Lesson 24 the pupil learned that "a good politician always stays at the side of the people." Other dangerous notions propagated by the *cartilha:* "Hunger, sickness, unemployment, and illiteracy are some of the social evils of the Northeast"; "A worker in a trade union is a strong man"; "Democracy is a government of the people, by the people, and for the people." The theory behind this approach was that Recife's adult illiterates could best be motivated by the hope that literacy would lead to enfranchisement, which would in turn enable the newly qualified voter to do something about his own poverty. What he was most likely to do, of course, was to vote for Miguel Arraes and others like him.

Thus the MCP's critics charged that the program was a blatant attempt to radicalize the city's poor and to consolidate and expand Arraes's electoral base. The fact that a number of known Communists moved into the MCP caused the chorus of protest to intensify. MCP supporters replied that the function of popular education and culture was to sensitize individuals to themselves and their surroundings; if such a process led to dissatisfaction and an urge to change things, this was the fault of conditions in Recife and the Northeast. But in fact, certain MCP activities had direct political overtones. A

festival of guitar-playing minstrels, who were brought into Recife from the interior to perform to the theme "The Land Belongs to Him Who Works It," proved highly successful. (On the other hand, a photo exhibit on Albania thoroughly mystified those peasants and workers who went to see it.)

There is no question that the literacy program would, however indirectly, help proponents of radical change. And it seemed to have a much better chance of working than the efforts many leftist-nationalists were then directing toward amending the federal Constitution to give the vote to all adults regardless of literacy. The conservative makeup of the federal Chamber of Deputies and Senate gave such an amendment no chance at all of passing. But if enough illiterates could be taught to read and write and qualified for the vote, the composition of those legislative bodies might change sufficiently to enable the Constitution to be amended.

As the MCP struggled to reduce illiteracy and thus presumably increase Arraes's electoral strength, the Mayor of Recife set out to capture the governorship of Pernambuco. His ambition put him on a collision course with the incumbent brother-in-law Cid Sampaio.

The inevitable split between Arraes and Sampaio came into the open during the 1960 presidential campaign, in which the Mayor backed Marshal Henrique Lott, while the Governor supported Jânio Quadros. The colorful Jânio caught the voters' fancy with an exciting campaign and won handily. He carried not only the state of Pernambuco, but also the city of Recife—an indication that the left was far from in complete control of the city's politics. Yet Cid gained little political capital from Jânio's victory. The new President began to make noises like a leftist-nationalist. When he professed an interest in the problems of the Northeast, it was Mayor Arraes, and not Governor Sampaio, whom he summoned to Brasília for consultation. And when he abruptly resigned, his successor, João Goulart, was clearly more sympathetic to the political views of Miguel Arraes. Meanwhile the death in 1961 of Arraes's wife, Cid's sister-in-law, dissolved the personal relationship that had bound the two men.

Cid Sampaio nourished the hope that he could win the nomination for national office in the 1965 elections. Thus it was essential for him to pick his successor, as proof of his political muscle in the

112

Northeast. Arraes had now moved so far to the left that the conservative elements that comprised Sampaio's base of support were horrified at the thought of Arraes moving into the Governor's Palace. Cid, therefore, had to stop Arraes at any cost.

The political jockeying that characterized every state election in Pernambuco was much more frenzied than usual in 1962. Arraes from the very beginning was the man to beat. He obtained the nomination of President Goulart's PTB (Brazilian Labor Party), which was strong nationally but weak in Pernambuco. The PTB leadership had put forward another candidate, but the left-leaning rank and file wanted Arraes, and the PTB bosses could not resist its pressure.

The PSD (Social Democratic Party) was unhappy at being out of power since 1958, especially since Governor Sampaio of the UDN (National Democratic Union) had been making appointments which cut down the power of the PSD bosses in the interior. But the party could not agree on an electoral strategy. An alliance with the hated UDN was out of the question. A PSD landowner-politician, Paulo Guerra, had already accepted the vice-gubernatorial nomination on Arraes's ticket—an indication of the latter's willingness to play the political game to the hilt—but the leaders of the PSD could not bring themselves to make a deal with Arraes when he firmly refused to denounce communism publicly and pledge not to appoint Communists to positions within his administration. So after much deliberation and hesitation, the PSD nominated its own candidate for governor, a man with little popular appeal and no chance to win.

Cid Sampaio was in a more difficult position. That perennial loser, João Cleofas, badly wanted the nomination of the UDN. Cid, whom the law prevented from running for reelection, desperately sought a more dynamic candidate for his party. His efforts were in vain, as the old war-horse got the UDN nod. Cid could do nothing but throw all his influence behind Cleofas and hope for the best. At the same time, taking advantage of a peculiarity in Brazilian law, Pernambuco's Governor ran for federal deputy in the nearby state of Alagoas in an attempt, as he sanguinely phrased it, to bring about the "union of the Northeast." [4]

Most of the family groups that dominated the economy of Pernambuco backed Cleofas, who was a large landowner himself and

had good connections within the existing power structure. Cleofas was part of what was referred to as the "system," just as Governor Sampaio had been part of the system. For Cid, despite his progressive attitudes, never really went beyond what one astute observer has called "diversionary developmentalism," or programs which would not upset the system. But Arraes was something else. He posed a real threat to the status quo.

Yet curiously enough, there were a few members of the system who found Arraes acceptable. He had carefully nurtured certain contacts he had developed during his tour as Secretary of the Treasury in the cabinet of a PSD governor. The biggest dividend he reaped from this was the support of a powerful PSD family group that owned most of the western part of the state.

It is doubtful that Arraes's broad popular appeal could have prevailed over his opposition, which could bring into play seemingly limitless funds. Fortunately for Arraes, he found himself the beneficiary of financial support from one of the richest men in Brazil.

The chief contributor to the Arraes campaign was José Emírio de Moraes, a middle-aged entrepreneur who had amassed a huge fortune through aggressive investments both in the Northeast and São Paulo. His Northeastern holdings included sugar mills, farmlands, the only cement factory in Pernambuco, brick and tile factories, and limestone quarries. When in the region, he lived in a palatial modern mansion along the beach.

José Emírio was a typical *nouveau riche*. He did not belong to the system in the Northeast, and as often happens to hard-driving, ambitious outsiders, he longed for the prestige that would flow from social recognition from the established families. Such recognition, however, was withheld. Further, he was once on the verge of becoming the Brazilian Ambassador to West Germany—an honor which he saw as the crowning achievement of his career—but his nomination was blocked by the PSD-UDN coalition that controlled the federal Senate and by the Brazilian Foreign Office. Finally, he was outspokenly nationalistic and anti-American, often criticizing what he considered to be unfair competition from U.S. business interests in Brazil. These factors combined to motivate him both to bankroll Arraes and to put himself up as a candidate for the federal

Senate from Pernambuco. Arraes in return promised to lend political support to José Emírio's campaign. For the stocky, greying industrialist, this would be sweet revenge upon the upper-class Northeasterners, the Senate, and last but not least, the "North American trusts."

Arraes's enemies delighted in referring to José Emírio as an "out-of-stater," though he was a native Pernambucan. The conservative newspapers often called him "the billionaire from São Paulo." [5] But if Arraes had outside backing, so did Cleofas. The gubernatorial campaign had aroused a great deal of national interest. Right-wing elements in the center-south of Brazil realized full well the dangers posed by Arraes and his movement, especially with its potential for spreading beyond the Northeast, and so they tried to nip it in the bud. Their weapon was an organization called the Brazilian Institute for Democratic Action, or IBAD. A principal function of IBAD was to channel funds into a target city or state in order to influence the outcome of local elections. Early in the campaign IBAD set up shop in Recife. Cid Sampaio, who was guiding the Cleofas campaign, assigned one of his brothers-in-law to act as liaison between IBAD and anti-Arraes, pro-Cleofas forces. Their activity was no secret, and gave Arraes a good issue. He used it to the hilt, loudly complaining about IBAD's presence.[6] There was even talk that money from U.S. firms doing business in Brazil found its way into the fund that the IBAD office in Recife had at its disposal.

A principal thrust of the "stop Arraes" strategy was to play upon the fears of "atheistic communism" harbored by many middle and lower class Catholics. As the election drew near, a group known as the Adult Catholic Action Movement ran daily front-page advertisements in one of the local papers railing against the "red menace." Other less subtle approaches were used. Pictures were distributed showing Arraes on his knees in prayer with rosary beads from which dangled, instead of a cross, a hammer and sickle. On August 29 a column in a Recife newspaper told the following story: "After a rally in També, candidate Miguel Arraes was invited by the local mayor to have lunch in the latter's residence. The invitation was accepted. At the exact moment when Mr. Arraes passed through the gates of the mayor's residence, there fell to the ground with a shat-

tering crash a framed picture of the Sacred Heart of Jesus. On the following day the residents of També began to pick up the pieces of glass and fragments of the picture frame in order to exorcise the evil spirit." [7] The columnist then printed a poem which referred to Arraes as the "Anti-Christ."

Finally, to top off the religious aspect of the campaign, Father Patrick Peyton of the international Family Rosary Crusade turned up in Recife to hold a rally just before the voting. Of course there was no official connection between this rally and the political excitement gripping the city, but it would be naive to suspect that the scheduling of the rally so close to election day was a mere coincidence.

The Archbishop who had campaigned against Cid Sampaio in the 1958 election had since been transferred out of Recife, and his successor decided to remain formally neutral in 1962. Arraes probably benefited from this, as well as from the support he received from many liberal and left-wing Catholics who were outspoken in their contempt for the argument that a win by Arraes would result in the forcible imposition of "atheistic communism" upon the citizens of Pernambuco. Arraes's sister, Violeta, was very active within the progressive wing of the Catholic Church, and her contacts proved useful. To counter the religious propaganda his enemies were spreading in the interior, Arraes began to travel around in the company of three priests, whose appearances on the platform with him at rallies effectively diminished the effect of talk that he was the candidate of the forces of evil.

The net result of the injection of religious factors into the campaign was summed up by an American observer who commented: "The people got the message that communism is evil, but were not at all convinced that Arraes was a Communist." Arraes at first refused to comment on the charge, constantly repeated by the local papers, that he was the "candidate of subversion." Finally he declared: "Everybody knows that I am not a Communist and that I haven't made any deals with the Communists, just as I have made no deals with the other forces which support me." [8] The Communists, sensitive to the political atmosphere, helped by not bringing Luís Carlos Prestes to Recife to campaign for Arraes.

The public denial which Arraes issued served only to intensify the attacks on his Communist ties. Supporters of Cleofas built a replica of the Berlin Wall in downtown Recife. Gilberto Freyre denounced Arraes for his acceptance of Communist backing. Things reached a grand climax when just before the election a full-page newspaper ad [9] reproduced a cartoon showing Arraes constructing his own "Berlin Wall," Fidel Castro holding the blueprint, Nikita Khrushchev pushing a wheelbarrow full of planes and guns and marked "commercial accords," José Emírio de Moraes wearing a jaunty bow tie and stirring a vat marked "$ cement $," and Luís Carlos Prestes piling bricks. At the bottom of the page was the caption "The Price of Liberty is Eternal Vigilance."

Perhaps the "stop Arraes" forces might have been able to win if they had been able to find a half-way decent candidate. But João Cleofas was hopeless. In the middle of the campaign a newspaper published a photo of him sitting on the veranda of his plantation, wearing riding boots, and looking for all the world like an old slave-owner. He had nothing positive to say, and worse than that, from a political point of view, he was popularly identified as the candidate supported by the United States. (It was no secret that the Americans too were nervous about Arraes. A Recife newspaper quoted a Northeastern Governor as saying that on his recent trip to Washington during an interview in the White House President Kennedy asked whether Arraes was going to win.[10])

Meanwhile, the Mayor of Recife was taking advantage of the publication of a popular song entitled "The Deeds of Miguel Arraes," which made him out to be a legendary folk-hero. The wandering minstrels of the Northeast picked it up and sang it throughout the interior. Somewhat later in the campaign, Cleofas' people began to call Arraes "Joe Nobody," a derogatory expression in Brazilian slang. The sobriquet backfired, for it was a perfect slogan, far better than any his own supporters had been able to devise. Miguel Arraes, the taciturn man from the back country, was indeed a "Joe Nobody," a face in the crowd, the candidate representing all the "Joe Nobody's" who had never been allowed to participate in the political life of the state.

The controversy over Arraes's candidacy overshadowed every-

thing else. No one seemed to notice Julião's campaign for federal deputy, except that some members of the state's Electoral Commission for a while contemplated taking action against him for using "subversive" slogans such as "Agrarian Reform or Revolution," and "Agrarian Reform By Law or By the Sledgehammer." And in a quiet ceremony in Recife during the last week of the campaign, General Artur Costa e Silva turned over command of the Fourth Brazilian Army to a dour, diminutive General named Humberto Castelo Branco.

As the campaign came to a stormy close, Recife's conservative newspapers were confidently predicting a victory for Cleofas. The stodgy UDN candidate went even further. On September 30, seven days before the election, he gravely announced: "Certain of defeat, the Communists plan to sacrifice lives—a bloody plan which will be ready for execution long before election day." [11]

Neither prediction came to pass. When all the votes were counted, Arraes was declared the winner. His 40,000 vote margin in the city of Recife was more than enough to offset Cleofas's strength in the interior. Arraes's total margin was a slim 13,000. José Emírio de Moraes won his Senate seat, and Francisco Julião was barely elected to the federal Chamber of Deputies. In Alagoas the voters decided that they didn't need a Pernambucan to represent them in Brasília, and they handed Cid Sampaio a resounding defeat. All in all, it was a great triumph for the left.

Cleofas journeyed to Rio de Janeiro, where he informed the press that "communism has taken power in Pernambuco." [12] Disgruntled right-wingers were wondering in private why the UDN and PSD bosses in the interior had not "arranged things" so that Cleofas would have obtained enough of a majority in the countryside to offset the Recife vote. IBAD closed down its Recife office, but Cid Sampaio's brother-in-law kept the anti-Arraes forces organizationally intact.

On inauguration day, January 31, 1963, Miguel Arraes gave the best speech of his career, rising to the occasion with an inspired delivery worthy of the elegant phrases written for him by his cousin, a professor of Brazilian literature.

"They tried to make me out to be an agitator, a bomb-thrower, a

man who was going to shatter the foundations of law and order in Pernambuco," he declared to a standing-room-only crowd in the Legislative Assembly.[13] "Then afterward they said I was really a 'nice guy,' and would change my political philosophy. Well, let no one deceive himself: they couldn't turn me into an agitator or a bomb-thrower, and they're not going to turn me into a 'nice guy,' selling out to the privileged groups I have always fought and can now more effectively fight as Governor of the State."

An unhappy Cid Sampaio tried hard to mask his fatigue and listen attentively. The outgoing chief executive had remained in his office in the Governor's Palace with two assistants until 4:30 that morning. They had been making a final, frantic check of the files, to see to it that nothing politically embarrassing was left behind for the new Governor to exploit.

"At this very moment," Arraes continued, "there are millions of Brazilians who think as I do, who share my outlook, who are capable of holding office, men who represent the Brazilian Revolution. These Brazilians constitute a brotherhood of nonconformity: they will not conform with poverty, with hunger, with backwardness, with illiteracy. It is the fraternity of those who detest the glorification of misery, and therefore fight against the false cult of tradition embraced by nostalgic intellectuals interested in maintaining the status quo above all else. For them, tradition means the people in the slave quarters and them in the mansions [a subtle slap at Gilberto Freyre]. No one treasures the traditions of our past more than our people themselves: but they treasure the authentic and legitimate traditions of Pernambuco and the Northeast: the traditions of work, of resistance to the invader, of struggle for freedom; the heritage of whites, blacks, and Indians, masters and slaves, soldiers, merchants and priests, the true heritage of the people of the Northeast and the people of Pernambuco. . . .

"I believe I possess everything a man needs for his work," the new Governor concluded, "and something else—a quality that has best been described by one of our poets:

I have only two hands
And a feel for mankind."

NINE ❧

❧ ❧ Enter the Americans

SUNDAY AFTERNOONS AT THE GUARARAPES AIRPORT on the outskirts of Recife are curiously festive occasions. Large numbers of people stroll along the concourse and climb up to the roof-deck to watch planes take off and land. As is customary in Latin America, crowds of friends and relatives gather to welcome or bid goodbye to travelers, but once a week one does not need any special reason to visit the airport. Families enjoy outings, couples hold hands, teenagers exchange gossip. For some during the early 1960s it was a chance to stop by the newsstand and peruse the most extensive collection of leftist and ultraleftist literature to be found anywhere in Northeast Brazil.

On July 30, 1961, the Sunday throng was larger than usual and in a state of excitement. President Kennedy's brother was coming.

Edward M. Kennedy, then twenty-nine years old and an Assistant District Attorney in Massachusetts, was in the process of preparing himself for bigger and better things to come. A key facet of this preparation involved crisscrossing the globe on fact-finding tours. He arrived in Recife in the course of an extended journey through Latin America, and would spend forty-two hours examining the problems of the Northeast. His entourage included a law school roommate (John V. Tunney, later to become a Congressman and then a Senator from California), a professor of Latin American history, a Texas businessman, and a journalist.

The group spent Sunday evening with Governor Cid Sampaio and the next day journeyed to the plantation Galiléia for a firsthand look at the original Peasant League. Old Zezé gathered some fifty peasants in front of his house to hear the youthful visitor. (Julião was out of town at the time.) Kennedy, in his shirt sleeves, conveyed his brother's greetings and then delivered a five-minute speech which was translated by no less eminent an interpreter than Celso Furtado.[1] The conversations which followed demonstrated the level of mutual understanding that characterized the confrontation. Kennedy posed to the peasants such questions as, "What do you want your children to be when they grow up?" (Apparently nobody gave the obvious answer, "Alive.") The audience responded with such requests as, "Doctor, what we would like is that you ask your brother to withdraw the police from here. There are no disorders, and the police are not necessary."

Finally, someone mentioned that the nearby town needed a generator to meet a severe shortage of electricity.[2] The young Assistant District Attorney made a note of this, and when he returned home he pulled some of the many strings available to him in Washington, and a generator was sent to Recife. Cid was reluctant to furnish any aid to a Peasant League stronghold and delayed shipping it to Galiléia. It was not until Arraes became Governor that the machine was delivered. Much publicity attended the "inauguration" of the new generator. The only problem was that the local folk did not have the money to install it properly and to purchase gasoline for it. So when the "inauguration" was over, the generator was stored in a shack. Eventually it was put to use. Professor Neale Pearson has reported that in June, 1965, Zezé and other peasants took him to see the generator, which was supplying electricity for a school.[3] They claimed that the machine had been given to them by President Kennedy.

Other forms of "people-to-people" foreign aid proved more successful. During one stretch in 1963, a crew of American technicians employed by Bell Laboratories to do work on the U.S. missile tracking station on Ascension Island was delayed for some time in Recife, a relay point for men and materiel in transit to the station. Some of the men "went native" and moved in with prostitutes in the red-light district along the beach. One night at a party in the large apart-

ment house in a fashionable seaside district where many of the city's better whores and kept women resided, the ladies complained about the electrical system in the building. It seemed that the supply of electricity in the apartments was inadequate, and some of the girls owned hi-fi phonographs which caused short circuits at inconvenient moments. The American technicians, well into their cups, boasted that if they had a mind to do it, they could fix the wiring throughout the whole building in a couple of days. The Brazilians scoffed at this claim and a friendly argument ensued, until the Americans declared they would carry out their boast. The next day they visited the Pan American hangar at the Guararapes Airport. Pan Am managed the Ascension Island installation and stored in the hangar equipment which would be later shipped to the base. The Brazilian employees in charge of the hangar were not noted for their vigilance, and the loss of materiel in transit was common. The technicians quietly pilfered wiring and other necessary items from the storeroom and went to work on the apartment building. Within the promised time period they not only completed the rewiring but as a bonus to their lady-friends they even installed dimmer switches—no doubt of considerable occupational use. On another occasion the irrepressible technicians borrowed equipment from the hangar to build a rudimentary road inland from a beach, much to the delight of the fishermen-relatives of the ladies, who were having a difficult time getting their fish to market. As one of the technicians later commented: "We were the type of skilled people who could give real foreign aid, not like those kids in the Peace Corps." [4]

These incidents suggest that foreign aid can be a delicate matter, dependent for success in large measure upon a rapport and mutuality of purpose between donor and donee. Without these factors, aid efforts can produce results which run counter to the stated goals of assistance programs.

Citizens of Recife had long been accustomed to the sight of foreigners, both resident and transient. Ships from many nations anchor in Recife's harbor, and their passengers and crew take rest and recreation ashore. According to Gilberto Freyre, an American missionary visited Recife as early as 1838.[5] Many others have followed, both Protestant and Catholic. American Southern Baptists and Pres-

byterians administer schools in the city. U.S. Air Force officers and enlisted men are stationed in Recife to man a small weather station and facilitate the flow of supplies to the U.S. missile-tracking stations on the Brazilian island of Fernando de Noronha and Britain's Ascension Island in the South Atlantic. Several countries maintain consulates in Recife, and the U.S. had for some time based a modest technical-assistance mission in the city.

But the massive influx of Alliance for Progress funds and personnel was something far different—an attempt to affect in a significant way the economic, social, and political processes of the region in a manner consistent with the aims and needs of U.S. foreign policy. In 1962 the American presence in Northeast Brazil began to proliferate by leaps and bounds because of the installation of a large U.S. Agency for International Development (USAID) mission in Recife. And in a short time the Americans were in serious conflict with a substantial number of Brazilians.

The USAID mission in Recife came into being as a result of the so-called Northeast agreement signed by the United States and Brazil on April 13, 1962. Under the terms of the Agreement, USAID was to supervise the application of $131 million in Alliance for Progress funds to be allocated over a two-year period. To carry out this mandate, the Americans decided to set up a mission staffed by technicians who, working with SUDENE, would plan and administer aid projects in accordance with the guidelines of the Agreement.

Bruno B. Luzzatto was named to head the mission in April, 1962.[6] Born and educated in Italy, a production manager for Italian aluminum plants for the twelve years prior to World War II, Luzzatto had become a naturalized U.S. citizen and in the immediate postwar period had worked on the Marshall Plan in Rome and Paris. In the decade prior to his appointment to the mission he had been with the World Bank in Rio de Janeiro. Thus his background included experience in economic development problems and a firsthand exposure to life in Brazil. He had to begin his new job pretty much from scratch, since the only American aid presence in Recife up to that time consisted of a handful of technicians working under the old "Point Four" program.

Luzzatto did not last long. He had some very definite ideas about how to staff and run the mission, and an unfortunate brusqueness which easily antagonized people. In his view, the key to success or failure of the USAID effort lay in obtaining the confidence and full cooperation of the Brazilian technicians in SUDENE. To accomplish this he wanted a small, "low-profile" mission staffed by Americans with a solid grasp of the Portuguese language and a feel for the Brazilian way of doing things. His ideas were quite close to Furtado's: USAID should operate like a bank, funding projects which the mission approved as being consistent with the goals of the Alliance for Progress.

The U.S. Embassy in Rio de Janeiro, however, decided on a large mission. Luzzatto did not get along well with the Consul General in Recife, nor with Ambassador Lincoln Gordon. He did not fit into the image of the young, aggressive executive types who were coming down from the States to fill USAID posts in Brazil. He also had problems in his relations with the local press, which had been on the receiving end of an incredible amount of publicity about what the Alliance for Progress was going to do for Brazil, and kept badgering the new mission director for specific information.

In mid-July of 1962, Ambassador Gordon suddenly removed Luzzatto from the Recife mission and sent him back to Washington. To fill the opening, Gordon turned to John C. Dieffenderfer, an Assistant Director for Planning and Programs in the USAID mission in Rio de Janeiro.

It must have been obvious even then that the Recife job was a hot seat. The developmental problems of the Northeast were overwhelming, the political climate intense, and the pressure to produce results kept building in what seemed to be a geometric progression. In addition, the inflation that was wracking Brazil's economy made it imperative to move quickly and decisively with aid projects, lest the allocated funds (which for the most part were in local currency) lose much of their value. In spite of all this, Lincoln Gordon sent into the fray a man with little background in Latin American affairs and without a working knowledge of the Portuguese language.

John Dieffenderfer had studied economics at Amherst, Roman and comparative law at Oxford, and American law at Yale. He prac-

ticed law in Cleveland and then spent five years with a management-consulting firm in Chicago. Somewhere along the line he developed a deep interest in Latin America, and he coincidentally communicated this to one of his associates. The latter, as it happened, had once worked for Lincoln Gordon, and when Gordon was named Ambassador to Brazil, the associate recommended Dieffenderfer to him. One day in August, 1961, Gordon contacted Dieffenderfer and invited him to join the USAID mission in Rio de Janeiro. Much impressed by Lincoln Gordon and in enthusiastic agreement with the Latin American policies then being spelled out by President Kennedy, Dieffenderfer accepted, and on February 8, 1962, he arrived in Rio. Until the Ambassador dropped the Recife mission in his lap, his only contact with the Northeast had derived from a careful reading of the Bohan Report.

Dieffenderfer was originally designated as the temporary Director of the mission. But since this was a crucial, formative stage, and some rather far-reaching decisions had to be made, his temporary status was removed on November 1, 1962.

The new Director accepted the challenge wholeheartedly. He tried, perhaps too hard. By nature achievement-oriented and self-demanding, he felt himself driven by a combination of other factors as well: his own idealism; the relatively short amount of time left both in his two-year tour and the two-year period during which, under the Northeast Agreement, $131 million in U.S. aid was to be allocated; and the attention the mission was attracting in the United States. There were constant visits from American journalists and political figures, and weekly progress reports had to be sent to USAID in Washington. It was no secret that President Kennedy was watching the Northeast. The superimposition of health and serious domestic problems during his tour in Recife did not help Dieffenderfer. As things developed, he became prototypically "uptight."

Though the Northeast was declared to be a top-priority target area under the Alliance for Progress and the publicity attending the Northeast Agreement was sufficient to arouse the greatest of expectations, the success of American aid to the region obviously depended upon the sort of Americans who were to administer the program in Recife. The decision to set up a large USAID mission in

125

Recife made the Northeast unique, since it was the only *region* in the world which was deemed to merit its own USAID mission. (Every other country which was receiving American aid had a single mission in the capital, except for Pakistan, which had two missions for obvious geographical reasons.) The problem was that there was no ready pool of able and dedicated U.S. technicians sufficiently familiar with the language and culture to operate effectively in the Northeast. The need to assemble a large staff in Recife within a short period of time led to the recruitment of people such as the five technicians who came to the Northeast directly from Haiti as a result of "Papa Doc" Duvalier's decision to expel the USAID mission from Port-au-Prince. Their knowledge of Creole French was not much help when they arrived in Recife. The competition for qualified personnel was intense, since there were many other USAID projects that required staffing in the center and south of Brazil. The net result was that while some of the technicians attracted to the Northeast were enthusiastic about the unique problems they would be dealing with, too many others were career foreign-service types who were merely putting in their time.

Sociologist Gilberto Freyre once commented that "the Alliance for Progress came in a difficult time to begin work, and some of the leaders sent here do not have a knowledge of Brazilian conditions to act in the right psychological way." [7] Observers complained specifically that John Dieffenderfer and others in the mission lacked a feeling for the Brazilians, a serious charge in view of the importance of personal relationships within the closed Northeastern society.

Language proved a substantial barrier, since few Northeasterners speak English. The fact that much personal contact with Brazilian officials required the use of an interpreter slowed things down, increased the risk of misunderstanding and did not sit well with some ultra-nationalistic Brazilians. The USAID people took crash courses in Portuguese, but this inevitably served to consume time which might better have been spent on developmental projects.

Considerations of health, education, and housing made technicians with families hesitant to come to Recife, which was rated as a hardship post. The influx of Americans necessitated the organization of a school for dependent children and resulted in the foundation of an

American colony of homes in the fashionable Boa Viagem section along the beach. Americans working for the U.S. government could ship automobiles to Recife, and the presence of large cars on the narrow streets of the city added an obviously incongruous touch. The custom of selling these cars locally at a fantastic profit—a fringe benefit for Americans stationed in Latin America—might have delighted the few rich Brazilians who could afford to buy them, but did not reflect well upon the aid program as a whole.

Sharp criticism of the quality of the USAID operation came to light in 1963 when the Recife mission earned the distinction of becoming the first U.S. government agency to be Naderized. What made this deliciously, if accidentally, appropriate was the fact that mission chief John Dieffenderfer was the only person in Recife who drove around in a Corvair.[8]

Ralph Nader was on the second stop of a trip through South America and had originally planned to devote only a couple of days to Recife. But he became fascinated with the ferment and remained for more than a month, concentrating his attention on the USAID mission. He wrote a series of three articles which appeared in the *Christian Science Monitor* that September and concluded that the mission was in sad shape.

Nader scored the low morale and frustration of USAID personnel, and cited complaints by lower echelon technicians that they were not encouraged to offer criticism or suggest changes in policy. He also pointed to a general lack of "enthusiastic commitment" on the part of USAID people:

> Time seems to weigh heavy on their hands and if not working on crossword puzzles or engaged in friendly banter, they are likely to saunter over to the collection of pocketbooks and select a title for an afternoon's reading. A visitor wonders what connection such stories as "The Case of the Screaming Woman," "A Very Private Island," "The Road to Laramie," or "The Sin of Susan Slade" have to do with improving living standards in the Brazilian northeast. Perhaps of more concern is the type of leadership which tolerates such diversions.[9]

The large USAID mission required considerable administrative support, one reason for the increase in U.S. consular personnel in Recife. Before the U.S. "discovered" Northeast Brazil, the Consulate was a small post manned by a Consul and a couple of Vice-Consuls. The size of the Consulate began to increase gradually in late 1961, and over the next few years the rank of the top U.S. diplomatic official in Recife was upgraded from Consul to Consul General to Minister

Consular officials were, of course, involved in activities which went far beyond administering to the needs of the USAID mission. The economic and commercial section of the Consulate kept data on the health·of the region's economy and made economic and financial information available to any Americans wanting to invest or do business in the Northeast. (During these years of unrest, American businessmen displayed little enthusiasm for putting money into the region.) The political section kept a close watch on the region's political pulse. Much of this work involved merely reading and clipping newspapers and collecting available documents. It also required maintaining as wide a range of local contacts as possible. The political officers maintained a complete dossier on all the region's political figures.

The political section of the Consulate also provided cover for the performance of intelligence work by Central Intelligence Agency (CIA) agents disguised as consular officers. Virtually every U.S. Embassy and major Consulate has its "spooks," as these agents are commonly known. In 1960 and 1961, the CIA man in the Recife Consulate was one of the two or three Vice-Consuls assigned to the post, and enjoyed the reputation of being extremely well informed about local goings-on. "He really got around," one observer noted with admiration. His replacements were not so highly regarded. In early 1962 there were two CIA men in the Consulate, and two years later the number had increased to three, an indication of the attention the Central Intelligence Agency was paying to Northeast Brazil.

The senior CIA official in the Consulate coordinated both the gathering of intelligence and the execution of covert operational activities, making good use of Brazilian nationals willing to cooperate.

The extent to which the CIA participated in attempts to defeat Miguel Arraes at the polls remains unknown, but it is difficult to believe that Agency operatives sat on their hands during the 1962 campaign.

The CIA did enjoy one remarkable success in the Northeast. In late 1962, a personable, good-looking young man arrived in Recife with his wife to begin work promoting the formation of agricultural cooperatives in the countryside. He ostensibly represented the Cooperative League of the United States of America (CLUSA), a private organization devoted to the cooperative movement. His appearance at this moment of mounting unrest in the Northeast was no coincidence. He was in fact an undercover agent of the CIA.

After completion of his Agency training, he had taken a crash course in cooperativism. The CLUSA official who arranged his dispatch to Brazil was H. Jerry Voorhis, one-time California Congressman (whom Richard Nixon unseated in 1946), and at that time the President and executive Director of the Cooperative League.[10] These funds were channeled into CLUSA by private foundations known to be CIA conduits. In 1967 *The New York Times* reported that between 1963 and 1965 CLUSA received $526,500 from these conduit foundations.[11]

The CIA-CLUSA man proved to be uncommonly gifted. His circle of close acquaintances included key personages in the American community, left-wing intellectuals in Recife, and rural labor leaders. A graduate student who was unaware of his affiliation and who used him as a source for a monograph on the rural labor movement of Pernambuco noted rather ingenuously that his "reputation as the most expert of the observers of Northeastern politics is well deserved." One American in Recife who did suspect what he was doing, in assessing his intelligence-gathering skills, concluded, "the CIA really got its money's worth from him."

His work in the countryside went beyond the collection of information and the organization of cooperatives. He also dispensed CIA funds in an attempt to affect the struggle for control of the rural labor movement (an activity that will be described in Chapter 11).

As early as 1960 the group of American aid technicians in Recife included a so-called Public Safety Advisor, whose function was to

help local law enforcement agencies. The expanded USAID mission continued to administer a public safety program. The interest displayed by American officials in the capabilities of Brazilian police forces had obvious political and security implications. The U.S. Army Area Handbook for Brazil, prepared by the Special Operations Research Office of American University (which also conducted the ill-famed "Project Camelot" in Chile) and published in July 1964, presents a detailed survey of the military state police of Pernambuco and concludes: "The problem of equipment and facilities for the Pernambuco forces, together with those for all state police of the country, is continuously under study by police experts of the United States in cooperation with the Brazilian Government." [12]

The United States Information Agency (USIA) functions abroad under the title of the United States Information Service (USIS), so that no one will confuse its acronym with that of the Central Intelligence Agency. In Recife one of the principal tasks undertaken by USIS was the promotion of the Alliance for Progress. A saturation publicity campaign ensued. As one USIS official noted: "We sold the Alliance like it was a Jacqueline Susann novel." [13]

At one time USIS displayed an interest in the way the wandering minstrels of the Northeast were publicizing the feats of Julião and his Peasant Leagues. Tad Szulc of *The New York Times* reported that "when a United States propaganda official was recently apprised of the activities of the Brazilian *viola*-players, he suggested that a well-known United States labor-union folk singer be sent to the Northeast to counter Julião's propaganda—in English." [14] This proposed project was never executed.

American corporations had very little visible presence in the Northeast during this period. The most important were two textile firms which shipped cotton from the interior to mills on the coast. The First National City Bank and several other companies had modest operations in Recife and elsewhere. Firestone and Union Carbide participated in the construction of a synthetic-rubber plant near Recife. An American company owned the Brazilian electric power company, but under the written terms of its enfranchisement it was in the process of being taken over by the state of Pernambuco in a relatively uncontroversial manner. U.S. corporations with fac-

tories in the center-south of Brazil maintained distributorships in the region. Thus the leftists did not have any really good physical targets upon which they might vent their anger at U.S. imperialism. In the analysis of Marxist theoretician Andre Gunder Frank, the economy of the Northeast was a satellite of the economic interests of the center-south, which in turn was a satellite of the economic power of the United States.[15]

The foregoing sketch of the quantity and quality of the American presence in Northeast Brazil during the early 1960s sets the scene for an account of the outbreak of conflicts which severely strained U.S.-Brazilian relations in the region. Within a relatively short period of time the USAID mission had become embroiled in various controversies which totally frustrated any hope of reaching any of the lofty goals of the American aid program.

TEN

🌿 🌿 The Americans and the Nationalists

"OUR DUTY HERE IS TO BLOW UP the Alliance for Progress." The proponent of this violent proposition was by no stretch of the imagination an extreme leftist. A slender, handsome young man, he had once spent several years at an American university, and was now working on a literacy program sponsored by the state government. The views that he expressed in an interview in June, 1963, reflected a radicalization experienced by a number of moderate nationalists and progressive Catholics who had been attracted to the banner of Miguel Arraes.

"We need money, but all the U.S. wants is propaganda, with all those Alliance for Progress signs they are putting up everywhere. How much does the Alliance help Brazil shape its own destiny, and how much does it keep Brazil from being independent?"

The graceful movements of the hands, the earnest facial expression and a measured tone of voice lent a priestly air to his discourse. It was easy to overlook certain logical inconsistencies which occasionally surfaced through the emotional rhetoric.

"What has to be done is to remove 90 per cent of the U.S. personnel here. And Dieffenderfer should be back planting potatoes. The State Department has made a big mess. They always do the wrong thing, and the Russians do the right thing."

His approach to literacy: "We have to show the peasant that he

should be a subject, not an object, and that he can make choices, and that he should never let anyone take away from him his capacity to make choices. We must call his attention to the hard facts of life, and enable him to see the Alliance for Progress for what it is."

The conflicts which developed between USAID and SUDENE shortly after the buildup of the American mission began contributed significantly to the atmosphere of hostility which soon clouded U.S.-Brazilian relations in the Northeast. As noted earlier, language problems and a cultural barrier made it difficult for most of the U.S. technicians to deal with any Brazilians. There were other factors which caused specific tensions between USAID personnel and their counterparts in SUDENE.

The Brazilians who joined Celso Furtado's team were young and enthusiastic, long on idealism but short on experience in the technical aspects of economic planning and development. They believed in Furtado's plan and the assumptions behind it. Some of them were arrogant and perhaps overly aggressive. The USAID technicians were older men. They tended to treat their SUDENE counterparts in a paternalistic way. They also tended to want things done the "American way." The Brazilians resisted.

USAID officials felt they could work with Furtado, whose intelligence and goodwill they respected. But in November, 1962, President Goulart made him federal Minister of Planning in addition to Superintendent of SUDENE. For the next few months, a crucial period in the USAID-SUDENE relationship, Furtado had to spend a great deal of time in Brasília and Rio de Janeiro, and the relationship went from bad to worse. Ralph Nader's article in the *Christian Science Monitor* described this deterioration and noted "a tendency for most AID personnel to stereotype SUDENE as being noncooperative. This attitude is quickly transferred to new AID arrivals. One such technician, on his second day in Recife, said to a United States consular officer: 'SUDENE people are impossible to work with.' He had not even been over to SUDENE's offices." [1]

The USAID people brought with them inflexible political attitudes which could not readily adapt to the turbulent Northeastern scene. They were horrified at the slightest hint of communism, and were quick to draw ominous conclusions about the omnipresence

133

and omnipotence of the Party. Their anxieties were heightened by the hard line that the CIA agents in the Recife Consulate were taking toward what they saw as a serious Communist threat to the Northeast. Periodic stories in the Brazilian press about the alleged Communist affiliations of Celso Furtado and some of his lieutenants made matters worse,[2] as did reports that the CIA considered one of Furtado's chief deputies a Party member and had information that SUDENE technicians had attended Communist congresses in Cuba and the Soviet Union. Since this was a convenient explanation for what they felt was obstruction on SUDENE's part, the USAID people came to believe very soon that SUDENE was under Communist influence.

Leftist-nationalist Brazilians saw nothing wrong in working with the Communist Party to achieve mutually desired goals. They considered red-baiting to be divisive and irrelevant. SUDENE, because of its reformist nature, attracted many leftist-nationalists and even some Communists. Furtado himself knew that his agency contained a small number of Communists, but saw no harm in this so long as they did their work. The cold-war anti-Communism of the Americans proved irreconcilable with the political tolerance of the radical reformers within both SUDENE and the emerging populist movement of Arraes.

The case of Naílton Santos is uniformly cited by USAID officials as an embodiment of their problems with SUDENE. Naílton was a twenty-seven-year-old Negro with a law degree from the University of Salvador in the state of Bahia. He was originally the head of the SUDENE department in charge of training technicians, and later became chief of the agency's human resources division. According to the USAID people, he was a Communist (with pro-Chinese leanings), anti-American, and especially anti-Caucasian-American, and above all else, he was absolutely impossible to work with. An article in a Brazilian magazine had named Naílton as one of the Communist sympathizers within SUDENE,[3] perhaps because of his personal friendship with an ex-Party leader from Pernambuco who had once been a Communist agent in South America and a personal friend of Stalin.

The facts suggest that these descriptions of Naílton were a bit

overdrawn. A heavy-set bachelor with a resonant voice and an engaging sense of humor, Naílton could not have been much of a racist, since one of his closest friends in Recife was a white USAID technician. The two were drinking companions who frequented the city's night spots together. Indeed, the USAID technician was a lumbering, good-natured fellow whose chief responsibility seemed to have been to provide for his mission a means of communication with Naílton.

An American who had the opportunity to watch Naílton at work felt that he greatly enjoyed baiting USAID officials and taking them for a ride. He cited one incident when Naílton engaged in a heated argument with a couple of top USAID people and began to wave his tie at them. The tie was decorated with a painted Chinese dragon, a souvenir from the trip to China he made while a student leader in Bahia. A more objective U.S. observer concluded that Naílton's problem was that he had a low opinion of most of the USAID staff and did not suffer fools gladly.

Even more serious than the linguistic, cultural, and personality differences between the Americans and the Brazilians was a deep and basic misunderstanding which went to the heart of the USAID-SUDENE relationship. Although Celso Furtado had drawn up his own detailed scheme for the economic development of the Northeast, U.S. policy-makers still found it necessary to dispatch to Recife in late 1961 the study-team which in a short time produced the Bohan Report. As pointed out in Chapter 5, the Bohan Report concurred with SUDENE's Master Plan in certain respects, especially with regard to long-term programs, but also suggested a number of impact projects which ran counter to Furtado's emphasis on the crucial need for structural economic change in the region. Some nationalistic Brazilians resented the very existence of the Bohan Report. They felt that the Northeast was a Brazilian problem which had to be solved by Brazilians, and furthermore the fact that a Brazilian strategy for development had already been conceived made it presumptuous for foreigners to intrude with proposals which were inconsistent with this strategy.

Furtado himself had originally hoped that USAID's function could be limited to the financial underwriting of SUDENE pro-

grams which appealed to the Americans. This apparently had been an underlying assumption of the Bohan Report, of which Furtado generally approved. It was soon made clear, however, that the U.S. would go beyond the mere disbursement of funds, and that American and Brazilian technicians would work together in teams on specific projects. Some Brazilians interpreted this to mean that each SUDENE project in which USAID would participate would have Brazilian and American co-directors, an arrangement which was of course politically indigestible. The fact that some of the joint projects would involve the spending of Brazilian as well as American money strengthened Brazilian objections to any trace of U.S. control over such projects. In addition, the Brazilian understanding originally accepted the creation of a small USAID mission in Recife. The rapid accumulation of a staff, which by June 30, 1963, included 133 American technicians, took the Brazilians by surprise and caused considerable resentment.

The USAID mission had to operate within the guidelines set down by the U.S. Congress in the foreign aid legislation which governed the Alliance for Progress. Some of these restrictions, such as the need for strict accounting procedures, irritated the Brazilians, who often saw this as bothersome red tape at best, and at worst as unwarranted interference in domestic affairs. The latter charge was leveled when USAID insisted that it had the right to withdraw funding from a program at any time if the program proved inconsistent with U.S. policy. This was one of the major obstacles to the signing of one agreement involving an education project. Dieffenderfer took the position that USAID could terminate its participation if it determined that what was going on in the schools being built with American money would not be acceptable to the U.S. Congress.[4] SUDENE viewed such a restriction as an attempt by the Americans to exercise control over Brazilian education. A proposal to put together an aerial map of a large portion of the Northeastern interior, undoubtedly a prerequisite to road-building and water and mineral resource surveys, met with disapproval by SUDENE for purely nationalistic reasons. The project was to be done with technical assistance from the U.S. Air Force, and USAID deferred to pressures from above in imposing the condition that the U.S. receive one

print of the map. SUDENE refused, to the dismay of USAID officials who displayed their insensitivity to Brazilian nationalism by failing to comprehend why this offended the Brazilians.

These differences between USAID and SUDENE were soon overshadowed by a decision on the part of U.S. policy-makers which destroyed any vestige of hope that the two agencies could work together in a productive way. USAID began to put the Alliance for Progress to immediate political use by negotiating directly with certain state governors the Embassy wanted to support. This, of course, meant bypassing SUDENE.

The implications of this decision are obvious. SUDENE from its birth had been engaged in a delicate balancing act which required it to stay out of the toils of local politics in order to accomplish developmental results which would have far-reaching political implications. In addition, the fledgling agency had to jockey with existing federal agencies to establish and maintain its supervision and control of a wide range of activities relating to economic development in the Northeast. To maintain the local support he needed, Furtado had to take great care in exercising the considerable powers at his disposal, since decisions regarding where to locate what projects would obviously affect local politics by making incumbent officials look good. Thus it is easy to understand why SUDENE interpreted the Northeast Agreement as giving it the exclusive right to represent the Brazilian government in foreign aid negotiations. The situation was complex enough without adding the impact of politically oriented decisions by a foreign government regarding foreign aid.

It cannot be argued that "noncooperation" by SUDENE forced USAID to seek ways to circumvent Furtado's agency, since the first instance of a direct agreement with a state occurred as the Recife mission was just beginning to function. The school program into which USAID entered with Governor Cid Sampaio on June 6, 1962, has already been described in Chapter 9. It was funded apart from the $131 million U.S. commitment, and amounted to a desperate and unsuccessful attempt on the part of USAID to help defeat Miguel Arraes. The failure of this dabble in local politics did not discourage the Americans. For as U.S. officials determined that the national government of President João Goulart was veering to the left,

the Alliance for Progress became a major instrument of a policy to lend support to state governors who were friendly to the U.S.[5]

The American strategy for the Northeast was phrased in a felicitous way by a USAID official in Rio, whose memo on the subject has been quoted by Professor Riordan Roett: ". . . it seems to me that each of the nine governors must be made to feel as sharply as possible that he is in competition to demonstrate to the United States that he is ready quicker and with better assurance of making good use of our money than any other eight governors."[6] Implicit in this strategy was that the Americans would decide what constituted "good use," and would utilize political criteria in making these decisions. Thus the "competition" among the governors of the Northeast would relate to their political activities, which the Americans hoped would respond to the "carrot" of aid dollars.

The prime candidate for these dollars in the Northeast turned out to be the Governor of the state of Rio Grande do Norte. Aluísio Alves, though a member of the conservative UDN party, enjoyed the reputation of being a progressive politician with a bright future. To John Dos Passos, he represented "one of the young men with a passion for social service who represent a new breed of Brazilian politician."[7] In certain ways he resembled Cid Sampaio. American officials quickly tagged him as a man the U.S. could do business with, and in July, 1962, he visited Washington and met with President Kennedy. Shortly after his return he signed a manifesto with USAID officials from Rio committing the latter to contribute to the economic and social development of Rio Grande do Norte.[8] That they would also be contributing to the building up of a political opponent of President Goulart did not pass unnoticed. The agreement was reached without consultation with SUDENE, though the Brazilian agency would still have to participate in its implementation, because the funds were to be drawn from the $131 million under the terms of the Northeast Agreement, which made SUDENE a necessary party. Governor Alves wanted to begin with a school construction project, and journeyed to Recife with some specific plans.

As might be imagined, SUDENE was not very happy about USAID's new tactic. The SUDENE division which had jurisdiction over education was just in the process of getting organized. The

original Furtado plan did not include primary education as a target. SUDENE instead committed itself to the training of college-level experts in various technical skills. This reflected a conscious decision by Furtado regarding resource allocation. He felt that the long-range developmental needs of the Northeast could best be served by focusing on the university. It was only after USAID signed the education agreement with Governor Cid Sampaio that SUDENE began to show an interest in going beyond the original Furtado plan.

Further, SUDENE's Human Resources Division, with which Governor Alves had to deal, was headed by Naílton Santos, who did not take kindly to what USAID and Alves had done. There were others of the same persuasion within the Division. An additional factor which made SUDENE people even more reluctant to cooperate was the obvious point that the agreement with Alves was politically motivated, and they were not eager to involve themselves in any move against President Goulart, in whose cabinet Furtado was serving and upon whose continued support SUDENE depended.

By the end of November the Rio Grande do Norte school-construction project had still not been finalized, and Governor Alves was angry. He flew to Brasília and demanded action from Goulart, who apparently acceded to this pressure. Alves then sent a telegram to SUDENE declaring that the President was behind the project, and a few days later SUDENE signed the agreement.

It might be appropriate to digress for a moment and note the outcome of the Rio Grande do Norte school-construction project. Governor Alves and his staff did not hesitate to make political use of their American aid in their decisions on where to locate new schools. The state Secretary of Education eventually resigned, charging, among other things, political interference and the transfer of funds in violation of the agreement with USAID and SUDENE. The USAID mission became involved in a hassle over the auditing of the program. By April, 1965, only forty-five new classrooms were completed out of the 1,000 which had been planned. And as for the political future of Aluísio Alves, the government deprived him of his civil rights in 1969 on charges of corruption while in office.

The election of Miguel Arraes added a further complication to the USAID-SUDENE relationship. The fact that most of the

Americans in Recife had rooted for Cleofas was no big secret. The CIA agents in the Consulate had confidently predicted an easy win for the UDN landowner, in part because their imperfect grasp of Portuguese forced them to rely heavily on information from the relatively few Northeasterners (mostly upper class) who could speak English. The policy which the Consulate followed reflected this judgment and colored the attitudes of many USAID officials. When Arraes won, the American colony readily accepted the claim by Pernambuco conservatives that the Communists were about to take over the state.

Shortly after the election the Hispanic American Report noted that "American Ambassador Lincoln Gordon and U.S. Agency for International Development (AID) representatives were watching Arrais [sic], hoping that in 1963 he would become more moderate." [9] If genuine, this hope easily qualified as the by-product of pure arrogance. The Americans had made an effort (albeit feeble) to defeat Arraes. Now he was supposed to become "moderate" and work with them. One wonders whether an American governor, approached by a foreign (or even federal) agency that he believed worked actively for his defeat, would have been any more cooperative than Arraes proved himself to be.

During the campaign Arraes hinted at what would be his position regarding the Alliance for Progress. He said on several occasions, when asked his views on foreign aid: "I will not negotiate with foreign powers. I am not the President of the Republic." [10]

His inaugural address gave further indications of what was to come. In a philosophical nod to the left he spoke of the need to "liquidate exploitation by foreign capital." He had this to say specifically about the Americans: "Today we are one of the most internationally known areas of backwardness, misery, and hunger, a kind of cancer which the whole world knows and fears its spread. The cancer of the Northeast preoccupies the Americans, who imagine that our sickness can be politically contagious and contaminate our neighbors, and therefore, I don't know whether they do this ingenuously, they give us powdered milk, as if our hunger was different from theirs, as if it was not, as is the entire world's hunger, constantly being reborn. That is black humor and it isn't funny, nor does it re-

solve, nor can it resolve, the plight of a single Northeastern family, let alone the plight of the Northeast." [11] Several weeks later in an interview with a *Newsweek* reporter he said of the Alliance for Progress: "You are only giving us chocolates and candy, while what we need is jobs. You talk of us as if we were an international menace, and what we are is a poor region full of suffering and human problems. What we want is very little—your understanding. But you behave like those soldiers in *The Teahouse of the August Moon*—you insist on making us into something we cannot be." [12]

A *Newsweek* article in February, 1964, depicted Arraes as a hardline anti-American: "Virtually the only things American which Arraes does not denounce are the Marlboro and Winston cigarettes which he chain-smokes. 'Americans are for burning,' he shrugs." [13] An agency of the state government fortified this image by staging an exhibition of pen-and-ink sketches, many of which attacked the U.S., on a river barge tied up near the main post office. One of the sketches depicted a half-starved Brazilian stretched out on the ground with Uncle Sam standing over him. With one hand Uncle Sam was drawing blood from the Brazilian's veins with a syringe, with the other he was releasing aid dollars from an eye-dropper.

Considerable evidence, however, supports the argument that Arraes did not take orders from the Communist Party and was not unbendingly hostile to the U.S. A high American official who observed him at close hand has described him as "a cunning, pragmatic, hard-to-outfox politician who was using the Communist Party more than they were using him." [14] The state government always supplied police protection for buildings occupied by U.S. officials whenever political demonstrations were being held and there was the slightest threat of a move against the American presence. (Such threats never at any time materialized.) Pernambuco officials were very cooperative in processing USAID personnel en masse through the state driver's test. There was never any hint of a policy on the part of the state of Pernambuco to harass Americans. And Arraes himself enjoyed cordial relations with several U.S. officials.

A number of on-scene American observers have expressed the opinion that Miguel Arraes was enough of a pragmatist to realize the

benefits he might reap from U.S. aid given in such a way that it would not compromise his political position on the left. Those holding this view, point to the common goals of the Alliance for Progress and the Brazilian nationalist-leftists, and conclude that something could have been worked out between the Americans and the Governor of Pernambuco. Yet U.S. officials made no really serious overtures to Arraes.

During the crucial months in 1962 and early 1963, the U.S. Consul General in Recife was D. Eugene Delgado-Arias, a charming, intelligent, cultured, "old-school" diplomat who much resembled a Spanish count. He could not bring himself to deal with Arraes and his supporters on any level. Like many upper-class Northeasterners, he regarded Arraes as the devil incarnate. He did not even attend the Governor's inauguration.

Shortly after Arraes took office, Dieffenderfer called upon him and informed the Governor that USAID was prepared to work with him on the agreements which had been signed by his predecessor[15] (in a vain attempt to keep Arraes out of the Governor's Palace). They included the education accord, which has already been discussed, as well as agreements on health, housing, colonization, and water supply. Arraes was cold and aloof toward the American mission Director, and exuded distrust from every pore. He put Dieffenderfer off, and on February 12, 1963, established a study team to reexamine all the accords. The six-man group was headed by the newly appointed state Secretary of Education, a Catholic leftist. Rumors about the Communist leanings of the group began to circulate around the USAID mission.

The final report of the study-team[16] reached Miguel Arraes on May 1. A few days later he released the document to one of the local papers, which published it in full on the very morning that Ambassador Lincoln Gordon was in Recife to address SUDENE's Deliberative Council. The report found that the Pernambuco accords were in violation of both the Brazilian Constitution and the Northeast Agreement, and recommended that the Governor abrogate them. Arraes followed the recommendation, with the result that for all intents and purposes the Alliance for Progress was for the moment dead in the most populous and important state in the Northeast.

American reaction to the report ranged from Ambassador Gordon's curt statement that "I am not a lawyer; therefore I cannot discuss the legal aspects of the Alliance for Progress," [17] to the private comments of USAID officials that the report was "sophomoric" and "a phony."

The argument based upon the unconstitutionality of the accords rested upon the premise that an individual Brazilian state could not enter into agreements with foreign powers, since the Brazilian Constitution reserved that function to the federal government. With respect to the education accord, this contention was weakened by the fact that one of the signatories was the federal Ministry of Education and Culture. The insistence that the Northeast Agreement required SUDENE's participation in every accord which involved the Alliance for Progress was derived from a Brazilian interpretation of the wording of the Agreement. USAID interpreted the same wording differently, and amazingly enough these conflicting views were never resolved.

The report also attacked various aspects of the Alliance for Progress, and the ways in which restrictions on the disbursements of American aid gave USAID the power to intervene in Brazilian affairs in a way which the authors of the report found unacceptable. USAID's unilateral decision to hold up funds under the Pernambuco education accord because of the late filing of a report was cited as a specific example of unwarranted foreign interference, since it meant that USAID could secure the immediate paralysis of a program— which might conceivably cause Brazilian schools to be shut down.

As if all this were not enough to exacerbate Brazilian-American relations in the Northeast, on the very same day that the report was made public, another Recife newspaper published a translation of a *Newsweek* article in which John Dieffenderfer accused SUDENE of impeding the Alliance for Progress: "I cannot spend a cent of American money without SUDENE approval. They determine how resources will be utilized and whether our participation is desired. We are relegated to a negative role. Our only power of decision is to say no." [18] More pointedly, he observed that SUDENE was precariously organized with such inexperienced youths that it could not utilize the resources at its disposal. He added that within

SUDENE there were certain persons who "are not particularly interested in seeing the success of the efforts of the United States." On the following day Furtado's chief deputy replied that "if we had the experience of the North Americans, we would not be in a state of underdevelopment." [19]

Dieffenderfer's remarks were certainly inconsistent with USAID's pursuit of the Rio Grande do Norte agreement (which was far from "negative"). He later claimed that his statements to the *Newsweek* reporter were off the record.[20] From the beginning of his tour-of-duty in Recife he had been under pressure from a continuous stream of American journalists and politicians, all looking for some visible evidence of progress to report. The extent to which SUDENE was to blame for the absence of such evidence is questionable, but one can readily picture a seasoned reporter getting an inexperienced and thoroughly harried government official to let his hair down and tell all.

Though the USAID mission was the principal focus of strains in U.S.-Brazilian relations, other aspects of the American presence in the Northeast caused problems. For example, the increase in the size of the U.S. Consulate in the Northeast attracted criticism from people in the Arraes movement. In August, 1963, Arraes himself complained about the presence of fifteen vice-consuls in Recife.[21] His figures were incorrect—at its high point the Consulate contained ten consular officials, a nurse and a clerk—but the thrust of his charge clearly implied that all these U.S. officials were there to meddle in local affairs.

In fairness to the Americans, it should be noted that Arraes never complained about the activities of the French Consul, a jovial, porcine ex-Resistance fighter who was wont to pop up in important local political circles and openly supported Arraes. However, the U.S. presence was backed up by considerably more muscle than the French could ever bring to bear, and this made nationalistic Northeasterners both nervous and indignant.

There did seem to be an exchange of intelligence information between U.S. and Brazilian security officials. Julião's charges that the Paraiban and Pernambucan police sold to the "FBI" copies of files on local peasant leaders[22] may not have been entirely off the mark.

The U.S. Consulate in Recife maintained a complete dossier on all the region's political figures, and these files included photos which might well have been procured from the local police. In the light of the use to which similar data was put during the U.S. intervention in the Dominican Republic several years later, the uneasiness which some Brazilians felt about the American presence is totally understandable.

The human element certainly played a part in the deterioration of U.S.-Brazilian relations in the Northeast during the early 1960s. It is possible that American officials and technicians fluent in Portuguese, familiar with conditions and customs in the Northeast, and sympathetic to the aspirations of the nationalist-left might have dulled some of the hostility Northeasterners were directing toward the United States. But the decision to use the Alliance for Progress as a means to interfere in local politics, the intense pressures from Washington to produce quick results, and the deep-rooted unwillingness of American policy-makers to tolerate radical structural change in the Northeast combined to produce serious restraints upon what any U.S. official might accomplish. The failings of the particular individuals bound by these restraints merely served to make matters much worse.

PART THREE

ELEVEN

🌿 🌿 Chaos
in the Countryside

THE MAIN HIGHWAY HEADING SOUTH FROM RECIFE RUNS parallel to
the shoreline along one side of the Guararapes Airport through what
in mid-1963 optimistic Northeasterners were calling an "industrial
park." Very little industry had located there, but plans had been
drawn and hopes raised. In anticipation of the coming industrial development the state government had even begun a housing project
on the hills just beyond the airport. A slightly faded sign advertises
the contribution of Alliance for Progress funds.

A highway checkpoint marks the outer edge of Recife's suburbs
and a change in topography. Occasional patches of green shrubbery
interrupt a long, desert-like stretch of sand. Then the sugarcane
fields made their inevitable appearance, a thick green rug
smothering the hills. At one spot where the road cuts between two
steep, stalk-covered slopes, the ghost of a Negro worker from a
nearby plantation is said to appear at night and frighten unwary mo-
torists. The highway emerges from the cane fields, passes a huge
synthetic rubber factory, and nods gently in the direction of the
town of Cabo.

A stream of visitors made the trip from Recife to Cabo in 1962
and 1963. For the Catholic Church, which had tolerated poverty
and injustice in the countryside for centuries, had reacted swiftly to
Julião's call for revolution, and had moved to blunt the appeal of the

new Peasant Leagues. The Church's response to Julião was Padre Antônio Melo, a youthful parish priest in Cabo.[1]

Padre Melo, one of fifteen children, was a native Northeasterner from the unobtrusive mini-state of Sergipe in the southern part of the region. He had been assigned to Cabo in 1961 at a time when Governor Cid Sampaio was making preparations for one of his pet projects, the construction of a plant which would utilize alcohol, a by-product of the Northeast's sugar industry, in the fabrication of synthetic rubber. Alliance for Progress funds, as well as investments from several American companies, helped make possible this venture, which was supposed to create a new industry and new jobs for the region, and new markets for the sugar mill owners. (These hopes remain unrealized up to the present day.) The factory would be built on the site of a sugar mill. The state government had promised to take care of the peasants who would be displaced, but Padre Melo's bishop had the foresight to realize that such promises were not made to be kept, and so he assigned his young priest to watch out for the interests of the peasants.

It was a smart move that got the Church in on the ground floor of a serious social problem, for the state government predictably reneged on its promise and began to force peasants to leave their homes upon receipt of a very small token payment. Padre Melo protested, but got nowhere. Then he tried something more dramatic: he went to the peasants' homes, encouraged them to resist expulsion, and announced that he would physically block the police the next time they tried to evict a peasant. His tactic worked. The state government gave in, declaring in writing that the peasants could stay until other suitable homes had been arranged for them. Padre Melo, because of all the publicity generated by the incident, became a national hero. He continued to work among the peasants, and was soon competing with Julião.

A visit to Cabo in mid-1963 revealed Padre Melo in fine fettle, a bit bewildering even to one forewarned of his eccentricities. His parish office adjoined the church and also served as a reception hall and dining room. In one corner of the long, sparsely furnished room was a hammock, into which the twenty-nine-year-old priest deposited himself without the slightest self-consciousness. He began to

sway back and forth in a vigorous rhythm, his graceful hands gesturing, his face responsive to the emotional pitch of his voice.

"The agrarian structure is old. There has been no change since colonial days. The old system is the cause of our poverty. The problem is to change the structure. If Congress does not pass an agrarian reform law, there will be a social convulsion in which all groups will participate." The hammock creaked softly as the words poured out in a forceful yet unhurried flow. The only visible signs of excitement were the flashing in his left eye (his right eye was clouded), a rise in the pitch of his voice, and a tendency to poke at the legs of his listeners.

"Land not producing should be confiscated by the government and distributed to the peasants." When asked about compensation to the landowners, he almost lurched out of the hammock. "Pay? Why? For what? It is contrary to the social doctrine of the Church to let a landlord keep nonproducing land while peasants nearby are hungry." In an aside, he noted that Prince Rainier owned a big, nonproducing tract of land in central Brazil. Julião he characterized as "the alarm clock who awakened us to the problem, but for political purposes and not for finding a solution." He swung both feet up on the hammock and was now lying on his side. "*The New York Times* has been here to see me, and they have taken movies of me for American television."

The interview came back to a more serious note. "President Kennedy is a true Christian, yes," he said, sitting up suddenly and resuming his metronomic swing. "But the Wall Street capitalists control Congress and want to keep Latin America enslaved. They want to continue taking their profits out of Brazil."

Padre Melo concluded with a declaration: "I am against both capitalism and communism. I am in favor of a socialist form of government, like that of Israel, Yugoslavia, or Sweden."

At this point he called out to the next room and a group of peasants entered. They picked up pieces of paper from a desk in the corner and crowded together. On Padre Melo's signal, they broke into song, nasally but with no lack of determination. *"Camponês avancai na batalha . . ."* ("Advance, peasant, into battle . . .") Padre Melo beamed approvingly. "It is the Peasant's Hymn," he an-

nounced as they finished the rendition. "Words and music by Aureliano Vicente Silva, a peasant himself." He nodded in the direction of a bushy-haired man whose unshaven face broke into a shy grin. "He is a Protestant," another peasant interjected solemnly, "but he plays the organ in church for Padre Melo."

The Brazilian communications media, always quick to create and exploit new "stars," made the mercurial Padre Melo a symbol of the radicalized rural priest. The Padre did not shrink from the spotlight. In 1961 he disclosed that he was "just a lighter of bonfires." [2] Testifying in Brasília before a federal commission investigating the Peasant Leagues in 1962, he insisted that those responsible for violence in the countryside were not the peasants, but the "reactionaries." [3] After the gubernatorial election in Pernambuco he vigorously denied that Miguel Arraes, whom he had supported, was a Communist.[4] Though he professed public concern over reports of the use of force by the Peasant Leagues, his relations with Julião were cordial. After his successful defense of the peasants against the state government, the Peasant League leader paid him a congratulatory visit which was well publicized in the press.[5]

In certain quarters Padre Melo's postures evoked an unsympathetic reaction. In February, 1963, one of Brazil's more vitriolic right-wingers included the young priest's name in a list of prominent Roman Catholics whom he charged with being "crypto-Communists." [6] Locally an angry landowner threatened to riddle his cassock with bullets. Another landowner told an American official that the biggest threat of subversion in the rural areas came not from the Communist Party, which at least was visible, but from "red priests," such as Padre Melo, who were subverting the system from within, advocating the "plague" of land reform.

The truth of the matter, however, serves as a commentary on the hopelessly retrograde mentality of the landowners. For Padre Melo did not belong to the leftist element within the Church which saw radical change as the only answer to Brazil's problems, and worked with leaders like Miguel Arraes and with known Communists—in fact with anyone seeking to restructure Brazilian society. Padre Melo was the most vocal representative of a group of young priests who sought to divert the rural labor movement from the radical

goals set by Julião and others. The influence exerted by these priests was, at least in the short run, profoundly counterrevolutionary, a fact duly noted by intelligence officials in Washington. Padre Melo made Marxist noises,[7] although more often than not he sounded more like Harpo and Chico than Karl, but by late 1963 he was openly accepting money from the ultraconservative Brazilian Institute for Democratic Action (IBAD), denouncing Miguel Arraes and proclaiming his support for the presidential ambitions of a right-wing politician[8] described by the *New Republic* as the candidate of "milk, motherhood, and the American flag." [9]

The interest of the Catholic Church in the plight of the Northeastern peasants reflected the pioneering efforts of a bishop in the state of Rio Grande do Norte.[10] During the 1950s he put together an organization known as the Rural Assistance Service, which provided health and educational programs in the countryside and began to organize rural workers into unions, or syndicates. The Service declared itself free of political ties, but was explicitly anti-Communist and did not seek radical changes in the social and economic structures of the countryside. The syndicates attempted to help rural workers enforce their legal rights and to bring about a mild sort of land reform. Conditions in the countryside of Rio Grande do Norte were not quite so grim as those in Pernambuco, a factor which contributed to the popularity and success of the bishop's programs (though the landowners did resist what he was trying to do).

Meanwhile in Pernambuco the Church watched the activities of Julião and his Leagues with alarm. The traditionalist clerics were content to maintain the Church's identification with the landowners and to denounce the spread of "communism" in the countryside. But progressive elements, especially among the younger padres influenced by the encyclicals of Pope John XXIII, realized that a more positive approach would be necessary. Some of them had visited Rio Grande do Norte and viewed with admiration the work of the Rural Assistance Service. So on July 25, 1961, twenty-five Pernambucan priests met to discuss the growing political unrest in the countryside. They decided that the most effective way to confront the problem would be to organize rural unions.

At this time the legal status of rural workers was not very clear.

In 1943 the minimum wage laws were extended to cover farm laborers, but they were never enforced, at least in the Northeast.[11] Other labor laws affecting all workers were theoretically interpreted to apply to rural workers, yet in practice they too were ignored. In 1944 legislation was enacted which sanctioned the formation of rural unions. Upon recognition by the federal Ministry of Labor these syndicates supposedly had the same legal status as urban unions. But the political situation in the countryside was so unbalanced that it was both useless and dangerous to encourage the formation of such peasant organizations. Indeed, when the Pernambucan priests held their meeting, only five recognized rural unions existed throughout the whole of Brazil.

Nonetheless, the young padres felt certain that a rural labor movement organized within the framework that the law in theory provided could effectively counter the forces Julião had unleashed in the countryside. And so they went to work.

Padre Melo became a combination front man, mouthpiece, and dispenser of charisma among the peasants. But the mastermind behind the operation was a rotund, energetic mulatto, Padre Paulo Crespo. The two men worked well in tandem (at least during this early period), Padre Melo cavorting in the glare of publicity, Padre Crespo putting together an organization behind the scenes.

The keystone of their movement was SORPE, the Rural Orientation Service of Pernambuco, a Church-sponsored organ modeled after the Rural Assistance Service of Rio Grande do Norte and designed to find peasant leaders and train them in Christian trade unionism.[12] These peasant leaders would be used to organize rural labor unions which would follow SORPE's guidance. The new unions would seek the harmonious solution of differences between peasants and landowners, and sugar workers and mill owners, as a preferable alternative to class conflict. They would also encourage the formation of cooperatives as a means of improving the peasant's lot, and provide legal and other services.

Padre Crespo emphasized the distinction between the new unions SORPE was creating and Julião's Peasant Leagues: "The Peasant Leagues, by themselves, . . . are not the best instrument for the solution of the peasant's problem. By their very constitution they more

closely resemble a beneficent society, without positive goals. It is more a paternalistic organization than a society in which the peasants themselves struggle for their own development. . . . In the midst of all these contradictions, there arose the rural unionism movement, as a force of pressure, for the perfection of our democracy. It is the final hope for the peasant. . . ." [13]

It should be noted that in spite of these lofty sentiments, the SORPE approach to rural unionism developed a paternalism of its own. Young lawyers who came into the movement quickly assumed positions of leadership, and Padres Crespo and Melo never displayed any inclination to defer to the peasant leaders they were training and relinquish their overall control of the forces they set in motion.

Nor did they realize that they were receiving support from the U.S. Central Intelligence Agency. The young CIA agent working as a Cooperative League (CLUSA) technician had moved quickly and quietly to develop close contacts with SORPE and Padre Crespo. Before long he was channeling CIA funds into the movement to help pay salaries and expenses for SORPE and attract people who might not otherwise have contributed their efforts to rural unionization. He also worked very effectively with SORPE people to urge the new rural unions to found cooperatives that could furnish a wide range of agricultural services. These cooperatives eventually did produce material, bread-and-butter benefits for their members. But more important to U.S. security interests was the fact that their organization and administration diverted peasant leaders away from the political struggles of the Pernambucan countryside, where they might have become involved in efforts to bring about radical change in the status quo. Though discontent was utilized in convincing peasants to form cooperatives, the cooperative movement never hid its acceptance of existing political and economic structures. As the CLUSA-CIA man himself once noted: "In convincing the peasant that the misery of his condition is unnecessary, one must be careful not to push him to the extreme of revolt against the authorities and vested interests who have held him in his present state." All in all, the CIA strategy to support SORPE and to found agricultural cooperatives was a well conceived, well executed move to help defuse the revolutionary potential of the rural labor movement in Pernambuco.

The federal government was not at all pleased with what the Padres were doing, especially when SORPE people began to seek recognition from the Ministry of Labor for the rural unions they were organizing. Under Brazilian law there could be but one recognized union of rural workers in each municipality. Thus official recognition of a SORPE-affiliated union meant that the priests had a monopoly over legally sanctioned union activities within an entire municipality.

In May, 1962, the first Congress of Rural Workers of the North and Northeast met in the state of Bahia. Representatives of Church-controlled unions dominated the meeting, which the Communists later charged had been sponsored and financed by the big landowners.[14] The federal Minister of Labor took the occasion to recognize twenty-three new rural unions, five of which were located in Pernambuco. In June a group of Pernambuco syndicates banded together to form a statewide Federation of Rural Syndicates; in October it achieved recognition from the Ministry of Labor.[15] The Federation was under the firm control of Padre Crespo and his SORPE associates.

While the priests were organizing unions in the Northeast, the Brazilian Congress was debating land reform. The issue had suddenly become highly popular on the national level—remarkable in view of the fact that a few years before "agrarian reform" was considered a "subversive" topic, not to be discussed in polite company. Politicians from President Goulart on down were now loudly rendering lip service to the need for a solution to Brazil's rural problems. Everyone had a different solution, of course, and the federal constitution still forbade the expropriation of private land without full and immediate compensation, thus making it impossible for the government to break up the large estates in the interior.

But then on March 2, 1963, a strange thing occurred. The Brazilian Congress passed a comprehensive Rural Workers Law. The law spelled out all the various rights and benefits granted to farm laborers and formalized the rights and responsibilities of the rural labor unions. It was the first piece of federal legislation to deal exclusively with rural workers. And it created hardly a ripple.[16] Perhaps the lack of excitement was due to the fact that it repeated things which

had already been legislated (such as the application of minimum wage laws to rural workers). In addition, the law still did not cover all the various kinds of rural workers to be found in the countryside. Perhaps also people assumed that the new law would suffer the same sort of nonenforcement enjoyed by other similar laws.

Yet the new law turned out to be highly significant. In Pernambuco Governor Miguel Arraes, upon assuming office, brought about some startling changes. He ordered the state police to remain neutral in disputes between peasants and landowners. The latter, deprived of their traditional allies, complained loudly. On April 10, 1963, an association of landowners took a full-page ad in a Recife newspaper, listing in an open letter to the Governor incidences of violence allegedly committed by the peasants in recent weeks.[17] The next day in the same newspaper Arraes issued a full-page reply, listing all the acts of violence which had allegedly been committed by landowners against peasants over the same period of time.[18] Official recognition of the peasants' side of the law-and-order issue was a novelty in Pernambuco. The peasants, upon discovering that one source of intimidation against them had been removed, were encouraged to organize and demand their legal rights with even more vigor.

In addition, Arraes decided that the minimum wage laws in the sugar zone should be enforced, and used all his influence to compel the mill and plantation owners to observe, rather than wink at, their legal obligations. This also abetted the growth of the rural unions, which now could pressure the owners and secure actual monetary benefits for their members.

As the rural unions began to assume a new importance in the sugar zone, it became increasingly obvious that the priests had stolen a considerable march on everyone else, since they had been organizing syndicates for some time. Leftist politicians and political groups had always been cognizant of the potential power of a rural constituency, especially if the federal Constitution could be amended to give illiterates the vote. President Goulart's Brazilian Labor Party (PTB) had used the unions to establish a base of support among the urban workers. Now Goulart realized that the key to control of the rural workers lay in the union structures which were taking shape in the countryside.

Brazilian labor law vests decisive power in the federal government. The Ministry of Labor supervises the collection and distribution of the so-called "union tax," which is paid by employees and employers. The Ministry also has exclusive powers over the recognition of individual unions and statewide federations of unions. The Regional Labor Delegate, who represents the Minister of Labor in each state, can "intervene" in a local union by removing its leadership. President Goulart did not hesitate to utilize these powers in an attempt to secure control of the emerging rural labor movement in Pernambuco.

But Miguel Arraes had his own designs on the rural workers. It was no secret that he was seriously considering a bid for a vice-presidential, or even a presidential, nomination in the 1965 national elections. He would have to present himself as the candidate of the Northeast—which would require backing from the rural workers of the region and their unions. Though Goulart could not legally succeed himself as President, he still pursued political power, and his ultimate ambitions were a source of speculation. In any event, he looked upon Arraes as a rival. And both he and Arraes opposed the Church-sponsored unions.

The Communist Party, from its traditionally secure urban base, decided to follow a double-pronged policy of infiltrating the existing Peasant Leagues and at the same time forming rural unions which would be under the Party's control. The infiltration program did not seem to work, but proved unnecessary as the Leagues foundered in a sea of confusion. On the other hand, the Party did enjoy some success in competing with the priests in a race to organize unions. Arraes gave support to the Communists, and they in turn backed him in his maneuvering *vis à vis* Goulart.

The rural labor movement in Pernambuco spelled eventual doom for the Peasant Leagues, in the absence of the outbreak of revolution in the countryside. The unions had legal status, and were in a far superior position to secure monetary, medical, and educational benefits for members, as well as a share of political power. Early in the game Julião took the position that his Leagues and the unions could exist side by side. "The Leagues are the mother of the unions," he was fond of reiterating. He urged League members to join unions and

vice versa. But he continued to spend considerable time away from the Northeast on trips abroad and to southern Brazil, and he never did develop a strong local organization. As a result first the priests began to outflank him with their unions, and then Arraes and the Communists drained away some of his support. Though Julião supported Arraes's candidacy, the Governor did not hide his contempt for the Peasant League leader. In a conversation with a reporter from *Newsweek* Arraes said of Julião: "I have my own methods, he has his; it's up to the people to judge who is right." [19] In a later interview he dismissed Julião as "just another politician." [20]

So Julião tried to keep his Leagues intact while at the same time competing with the priests and the Communists for control of the rural unions. What added spice to the struggle was the appearance of a group of young Trotskyists and a group of Communists who had split from the Party and were following the Chinese line. These splinter elements also entered the competition, never able to penetrate beyond the fringes but nonetheless contributing to the mass confusion which characterized the Pernambucan countryside in 1963 and early 1964. The jockeying was often Byzantine: Arraes vs. Goulart on the upper level; priests vs. Communists vs. Julião vs. Trotskyists vs. Maoists on the local level, with various alliances forming and dissolving in rapid succession.[21] And in the midst of the din, technicians from SUDENE were attempting their own pilot land reform project in Pernambuco.

Organizing activities in the sugar zone had been suspended during the 1962 gubernatorial campaign, as virtually all the various rural leaders (including Padres Melo and Crespo) supported the candidacy of Miguel Arraes. But in January, 1963, several weeks before Arraes took office, a bloody clash erupted on a large sugar mill in the southern part of the state, a grim reminder that the big landowners were not about to roll over and play dead.

The incident resulted from a demonstration staged by a group of about eighty peasants in front of the office of the mill. The peasants worked on plantations belonging to the mill, and were demanding the bonus wage which the law obliged the owner to pay them at the end of the year. The owner happened to be a federal deputy, a member of Goulart's Brazilian Labor Party. The demonstrators in-

cluded women and children, and were displaying clubs and knives in a rather aggressive manner. According to one report, several of the peasants carried revolvers. The Peasant Leagues were apparently behind the demonstration.

The politician-landowner, accompanied by his hired gunmen, came out of the office to talk with the peasants. Discussion soon escalated into confrontation, which finally erupted into violence. Five peasants were killed and several more wounded. At least one of the gunmen was also hurt. The state police took their usual stance, maintaining the right of the landowners to protect themselves with hired gunmen. The best that Julião could do was to fall back on a shop-worn liberal response, and call for an investigation.

Shortly after the incident, there appeared in the southern part of Pernambuco's sugar zone a dynamic, charismatic organizer who began to put together a rural union. Gregório Bezerra's hair was now white, but the former Army sergeant and federal deputy was as physically fit as ever. His presence was not related to the recent shooting, but it did signal the beginning of the Communist Party's campaign to gain a foothold among the rural workers.

The area in which Gregório was working was the most wretched part of the sugar zone, dominated by large mills which exploited a landless rural proletariat. There were but few sharecroppers and small tenant farmers bound in a feudal relationship to plantation owners. The Peasant Leagues had enjoyed scant success here in the south, and because of this Julião was actually accused of protecting the interests of the big landowners. The truth of the matter was that as a general rule only those peasants who had the use of some land of their own dared to join the Leagues. Those who worked for the large mills usually did not have any land to fall back on for subsistence, and hence were more vulnerable to retribution from the mill owners. Clearly the Peasant Leagues could not offer these workers protection and benefits that would make it worth their while to join. But the unions, especially after the law of March 2, 1963, were something else. They were legally recognized as representing the interests of rural workers and were better able to stand up to the pressures of the landowners.

Gregório concentrated his efforts in the largest town in the area,

Palmares. Governor Arraes made available certain facilities which abetted these efforts, and other Party members joined Gregório in the field. One of them came from as far away as the territory of Acre, a remote corner of Brazil bordering on Peru and Bolivia. But the President of the newly formed union was not a Party member. He was a former member of the Peasant Leagues, who had once visited Cuba with Julião.

The Party's organizational activities paid off, as the federal Minister of Labor not only recognized the Palmares union, but included within it twenty-two other municipalities! The creation of this giant union made it impossible for the priests to wrest control of it away from the Party, but it also gave the Communists only one potential vote in the statewide federation of rural unions, of little use in any attempt to take control of the federation away from the priests. As a result, the Palmares union never bothered to join the federation.

In comparison to the violent rhetoric of the Peasant Leagues, the positions taken by the Palmares union seemed rather conservative, as the Communists agitated for tangible benefits on behalf of the sugar workers. The union did, however, constantly emphasize the theme of class conflict between landowners and peasants. During the next year the union sponsored numerous strikes and demonstrations. For some peasants these were like festivals, an opportunity to parade around the plantations and into town, but without any real grasp of what was happening. Others were beginning to develop political consciousness—especially after being organized by the Communists into small cell groups on each plantation.

Of more immediate importance to all the workers in the area was the fact that the mill owners, under pressure from Arraes, were paying the legal minimum wage. As *Newsweek* put it: "The new money hit Pernambuco's half-starved economy like a desert cloud burst." [22] The peasants suddenly found themselves with money in their pockets and rushed to exercise their new privileges as consumers. Palmares and the nearby towns reflected the new prosperity as shopkeepers and merchants profited from the purchasing power of the sugar workers.

In addition to their success in Palmares, the Communists also helped to administer a hard blow to the Church-controlled move-

161

ment in the town of Jaboatão on the outskirts of Recife. This was the home base of Padre Crespo, and he had organized the local rural union. Jaboatão was close to Recife and at the same time extended into the sugar zone. It contained several industrial plants, as well as a couple of sugar mills. The town had always provided a large pool of workers who could be easily transported to Recife for labor demonstrations. It also enjoyed the reputation of being a hotbed of Communist supporters—so much so that people commonly referred to the town as "little Moscow." Thus it was not surprising when an effort was made to pry the township's rural union away from Padre Crespo.

A peasant leader who had once been part of Crespo's organization began to agitate against the Padre's union. He was assisted by the Arraes government and by Communist and Peasant League agitators who sparked demonstrations against Padre Crespo. The Regional Labor Delegate, representing President Goulart, finally "intervened" in the union, removing its pro-Crespo leadership in August, 1963, and scheduled new elections for November. A period of great confusion ensued, with charges and countercharges, demonstrations and counterdemonstrations. Even Padre Melo leapt into the fray, defending his colleague on radio and television. In his inimitable style, he went so far as to denounce Arraes as "a man dominated by hate, who does nothing else but hate." [23] On the eve of the election, Padre Crespo realized that his slate of candidates couldn't possibly win, and he withdrew, relinquishing control of the union to a group of leaders who had close ties with Arraes and the Communists. In February, 1964, the Regional Labor Delegate struck again, intervening in Padre Melo's Cabo union and installing new leaders who belonged to the Peasant Leagues.

Left to their own devices, the Leagues did not do well in the competition with the priests. In Bom Jardim, Julião's home town, and even in Vitória de Santo Antão, the municipality where the Peasant League movement began, Church-connected groups controlled the rural unions. Vitória did remain a hotbed of Peasant League activity. João Alfredo, a young law student, and a schoolteacher named Maria Celeste coordinated agitation which consisted mainly of invasions of plantations. In late 1963, João Alfredo broke with Julião, ap-

parently over tactics, and a bitter feud ensued.

Meanwhile, Joel Câmara languished in Recife's House of Detention, writing his memoirs and attending law school classes in the company of several prison guards. The competition for control of the rural unions had completely soured him. "It was ridiculous," he reminisced in 1967. "The countryside is enormous. There was room for everybody. There were plenty of peasants to be made politically conscious. The enemy was the big landowner. Instead, the groups were fighting among themselves. Why waste time with these petty feuds?" Joel was released in December, 1963. His disillusionment was so great that he washed his hands of the entire business and did not return to the Peasant League movement.

The young Trotskyists whom Joel had befriended at the 1961 National Peasant's Congress in Belo Horizonte suffered a somewhat different fate. These students from southern Brazil, members of what they called the "Leninist Vanguard," found irresistible the opportunity afforded by the ferment convulsing the Pernambucan sugar zone. Eager to participate in what seemed to them a genuine revolutionary experience, they left their books to carry the banner of Leon Trotsky's Fourth Internationale into the Northeast. Brazilian journalist Antônio Callado found them to be closer to anarchism than Trotskyism: "They seemed to me more like followers of Norman Mailer, let us say, than old Leon." [24]

The Trotskyist mini-group chose for its theater of operations També, a municipality in the northernmost part of Pernambuco's sugar zone. They began to work among the peasants and to mount an attempt to seize control of the rural union, which was controlled by followers of Padres Crespo and Melo. Until his arrest in January, 1963, Joel Câmara worked in coordination with them. Though he was skeptical of their approach ("They came from the south, wore ties, and had no understanding of what was going on in the sugar zone"), he admired their fervor. Some time later, their efforts bore fruit and they took over the union. But in August their leader, a twenty-three-year-old student using the pseudonym "Jeremias," was killed in an ambush by a landowner's gunmen. This provoked the remainder of the group into convoking a "Peasant's Congress" in També on September 7, 1963. A manifesto announcing the Con-

gress called for a "United Front of Workers, Peasants, and Soldiers," and set forth a program which proposed a peasant's militia, "popular tribunals" to try and punish landowners, and the occupation of the properties of the big landowners. On the day of the "Congress," the state police arrested the three students who had signed the manifesto, and they were imprisoned under the Law of National Security. In October, the Regional Labor Delegate intervened in the. També union, ousting the leadership and putting an end to the Trotskyist adventure in Northeast Brazil.

Even more bizarre was the brief but eventful career of Júlio Santana, peasant leader. Júlio was a forty-year-old fisherman-farmer from the town of Cabo. He became involved with Julião in the Peasant League movement and soon rose to a position of leadership as a result of his native intelligence, oratorical skills, and aggressive personality. Júlio, however, liked to drink, and his bouts with the bottle brought out a violent streak that greatly disturbed his brethren in the Leagues. One day during a drinking spree he badly frightened the wife of a League official. The latter, aided by three friends, went after Júlio with a knife and cut him up badly. He was taken to a hospital and left for dead.

Several months later at a League meeting Julião was shaking hands with some peasants when a man with a big, black moustache walked up to him and said, "Julião, don't you recognize me?" It was Júlio, patched up with some rudimentary plastic surgery. "He was like a corpse, back from the grave," Julião recently reminisced.[25] Júlio insisted that he no longer drank, and asked to be taken back into the Peasant League movement. Julião consulted with some of the other League officials, and they agreed to give Júlio another chance.

It turned out to be a big mistake. Júlio went to work in the municipality of Sirinhaém in southern Pernambuco. In early 1963 the Peasant Leagues had organized the rural union in Sirinhaém, apparently with the support of one of the local sugar mill owners. Júlio became an official in the union, and soon began to feel that his leadership qualities were not being fully appreciated. According to Julião: "This was a time when the mill owners were being compelled to pay the legal minimum wage. The peasants in Sirinhaém had no

union experience. They were very impressionable and gave Júlio credit for what was happening. They began to look upon him as a savior. This went to Júlio's head. He thought he was making the revolution by himself. He began to drink again, to wear dark glasses, to carry a pistol, and even to have his own private gunmen." [26] Antônio Callado called Júlio Santana "a mixture of political leader and bandit," and "a first-rate anarchist." [27]

In any event, on July 7 Júlio assembled his large peasant following and forcibly took over the rural union. This marked the start of a frenzied struggle, as the Peasant League forces and Júlio captured and recaptured the union from each other. The local mill owner was quite frightened of Júlio and helped the Peasant Leaguers. Júlio had his own outside backing. Julião maintains that the Trotskyists were using Júlio to exert a divisive influence in the countryside. Another Peasant League leader insists that Miguel Arraes was using Júlio to combat Julião's influence. At one point Júlio appeared in Sirinhaém in an official jeep of the Regional Labor Delegate, Goulart's representative in Pernambuco. If Arraes had been behind Júlio, the Governor's support did not last long. On October 11 the state police arrested Júlio and imprisoned him in Recife's House of Detention under the Law of National Security. It was ironic that on that same day an advertisement appeared in a Recife newspaper announcing the creation of a "Central Syndicate of Rural Workers of Pernambuco." [28] It called for an alliance among workers, peasants, and soldiers, and denounced Julião. Júlio was listed as Vice President of the new group and João Alfredo, another ex-Peasant League leader, was listed on the Advisory Board. Only the Trotskyists protested Júlio's imprisonment.

Then came an appropriate footnote. A law student with a flare for the dramatic (who might also have been working with the Trotskyists) tracked down the police lieutenant who had arrested Júlio, captured him by surprise, took his machine gun, and paraded him and his driver through the streets of the town. The lieutenant managed to escape, and the police finally captured the student, who quickly joined Júlio, the Trotskyists, and Joel Câmara as the only political prisoners in Pernambuco.

In the face of growing opposition, Padre Crespo, Padre Melo, and

their associates in SORPE managed to rebuff efforts to pry the Federation of Rural Syndicates from their control. On November 18, 1963, the Federation called a strike against Pernambuco's sugar industry as a result of the failure of negotiations among the sugar workers, mill owners, and plantation owners. The Peasant Leagues and the Communists cooperated, and about 90 per cent of the state's sugar workers walked off their jobs. After three days the strike was settled, as the mill owners agreed to increase the minimum wage by 80 per cent, pay the year-end bonus required by law, and pay for the time lost during the strike.

Though the leaders of the Federation gained a good bit of prestige from the strike, their troubles were far from over. The Regional Labor Delegate announced that he was going to create two other "federations" of rural workers in Pernambuco, one to represent the workers in the *agreste* and the other to include the workers of the *sertão*. There was a certain surface logic to this decision, since the workers in each of the three distinct regions of Pernambuco did have different interests and problems. However, this was not the real reason behind the Delegate's proposal. The priests controlled the one existing Federation because of their power over virtually all the unions in the *agreste* and *sertão*. If these unions were placed into separate federations, the hold which the priests exercised over the remaining federation, which would encompass only the sugar zone, would be quite precarious and subject to change. And of course the sugar zone federation would be the largest and most powerful in the state.

In addition, there was disagreement within the priests' Federation over the question of relations with the Communists. The president of the Federation was a bona fide left-wing Catholic who favored collaboration with the Communists to achieve specific goals. Padre Crespo clung to a rigidly anti-Communist position and successfully fought every attempt to allow the Communists any influence within the Federation.

Another complication was the formation of a National Confederation of Agricultural Workers in December. This Confederation, known as CONTAG, would represent the various state federations on a national level. President Goulart saw it as an important vehicle

for the political manipulation of the emerging rural constituency and was determined to maintain control over it. One way he planned to do this was by creating "paper" unions and federations of unions, especially in the more remote areas of the country. However, the first President of CONTAG turned out to be the leader of the Communist-controlled Union of Farmers and Agricultural Workers of Brazil (ULTAB), a man whom the Party had put forward as a competitor with Julião in the early period when the Communists were trying to derogate Julião's position as a national spokesman for the interests of the peasants.

The intensely political nature of the convulsions in the sugar zone explained, at least in part, a curious omission in Celso Furtado's Master Plan for SUDENE. The agrarian problem surely rated the highest priority within any developmental scheme for the region, yet Furtado's proposals seemed to hardly touch upon the problem. The reason was the essentially political nature of the agrarian problem, putting it beyond the scope of SUDENE's capabilities. Furtado did have plans to create colonies of transplanted Northeasterners along a riverbank on the western edge of the Northeast, but colonization was an excessively expensive solution and would hardly make a dent in the overpopulation of the sugar zone.

The one interesting project which did materialize in the Pernambuço sugar zone came about not as a result of any planning by SUDENE, but through the initiative of a young, progressive sugar mill owner who made some of his lands in the municipality of Cabo available for a pilot land reform.[29] A number of peasants, under SUDENE supervision, were to rent the land and grow sugarcane which they would then sell to the mill owner. The project would be run on a cooperative basis. The Bank of Brazil was to supply credits for the purchase of equipment, and the USAID mission offered Food for Peace to tide the peasants over through the first months. Despite opposition from reactionary mill and plantation owners and hostile criticism from the Communists, the cooperative of Tiriri formally opened on July 30, 1963. Some observers called it the last chance for capitalism in the sugar zone.

The activities of the groups competing in the countryside reflected various philosophical and ideological approaches toward

land reform. Indeed, these approaches received a thorough airing in Recife in May, 1963, when the Joaquim Nabuco Institute of Social Research sponsored a symposium on "The Agrarian Problem in the Pernambuco Sugar Zone." [30] Julião, Padre Melo, João Alfredo, a peasant leader from the state Federation of Rural Syndicates, a representative of the plantation owners, and assorted professors, journalists, bureaucrats, and politicians exchanged views in a remarkably free and open debate. The commanding officer of the Fourth Brazilian Army, General Humberto Castelo Branco, presided over one of the sessions, and Governor Miguel Arraes delivered the closing address.

Under the layers of rhetoric, three basic positions emerged. On one end of the spectrum, a number of mill and plantation owners were convinced that there was nothing to reform. They viewed as immutable the highly paternalistic relationship between landowner and peasant, a product of the Brazilian mentality and national character. To this group, any change in the status quo was anathema.

At the other extreme were those who held that the root cause of misery in the sugar zone was the existing pattern of land distribution and tenure. This has been defined by the Inter-American Committee for Agricultural Development as a problem "of the relations between those who can grant the rights to land and those seeking lands to cultivate." [31] To alter this relationship required radical changes in the political, economic, and social structures of the region.

A middle position sought tangible benefits for the peasants under the existing system. This was essentially a reformist approach which offered the considerable appeal of immediate rewards yet left the region's power structure intact.

There is little to be said for the stand-pat position, which sought to prolong the genocidal conditions in the Northeastern interior. The radical vision suffered from several drawbacks. There was a limit to the nature and amount of radical change which could be accomplished within a regional context. The necessity of operating on a national, or even international, level required a dependence upon outside forces. Also the radicals were particularly vulnerable to competition from groups offering immediate tangible rewards to the peasants. The problem with the middle position was that it de-

pended in part upon the cooperation of an existing power structure which had traditionally evidenced a calloused attitude toward the peasants. In addition, the programs carried out by the reformers brought benefits to a limited number of the total peasantry. Both radicals and reformers were proposing solutions which would realistically require massive cash outlays, but neither group had the faintest notion of how to obtain such financial backing.

The overpopulation of the sugar zone loomed as the ultimate obstacle, and no one really came to grips with it. As the rural syndicates pressed for the legal minimum wage and the year-end bonus, the mill and plantation owners began to cut costs, and in some cases even to modernize. This meant reducing their work force. At the same time, the lure of better wages was keeping in the Northeast peasants who might otherwise have migrated out of the region. Unemployment and underemployment, already at unacceptably high levels, increased, and the crisis atmosphere continued into 1964.

At the same time, the influence of the Peasant Leagues had greatly diminished, and the Church- and CIA-supported rural unions were feeling severe pressure and were beginning to lose ground. More radical elements tied to Arraes, Goulart, and the Communist Party were increasing their penetration of the countryside, and it was becoming more and more obvious that something had to give.

TWELVE 🙢

🙢 🙢 The Revolution
in Forty Hours

ONE REASON THE STAKES WERE SO HIGH IN the competition for control of the rural labor movement was the wisp of a chance that the Brazilian Constitution could be amended to extend the vote to illiterates. Brazil's population was primarily rural. If the rural workers could be organized and persuaded to vote in a bloc, they could exercise a decisive influence at the polls. This no doubt in part explained Governor Miguel Arraes's preoccupation with the rural syndicates. But Arraes, consistently displaying an acute sense of the politically feasible, fully realized the obstacles which made a constitutional amendment hardly worth holding one's breath for. So he pursued an alternative course of action.

As Mayor of Recife he had supported the literacy efforts of the Popular Culture Movement (MCP), a city agency which worked to teach adult slum-dwellers how to read and write. The controversy over the "subversive" nature of the primer the MCP was using has already been noted. If the MCP primer caused conservative hackles to rise, the statewide program which Arraes instituted shortly after becoming Governor made the guardians of the status quo positively livid. The primer was soon rendered obsolete by a literacy method which taught people to read newspapers and write letters after forty hours of instruction.[1] This was to be "the Revolution in Forty Hours," as proponents of the new method promised.

The man behind the method was Paulo Freire, a slightly balding, slightly barrel-chested professor who radiated ebullience and innocence in equal parts.[2] Born in 1921 in Recife into a middle-class family, he suffered a firsthand exposure to the rigors of poverty during the Great Depression after the death of his father, a state policeman. The experience left a lasting mark upon his social conscience. He obtained a law degree but found legal practice unappealing, so he turned to the study of sociology and education. A devout, practicing Catholic, he took the social doctrines of the Church seriously and decided to do something about a national problem which had verbally occupied politicians for decades. He launched a direct attack upon Brazil's staggering illiteracy rate.

In 1961 Arraes's MCP was in high gear. Freire, then a Professor at the University of Recife, worked in the MCP's literacy program, but at the same time he was fashioning a unique literacy method of his own. In 1962 he was made Director of the University's Cultural Extension Service (SEC), one of the functions of which was to provide for adult education. This let him put his theories into action.

Although the SEC conducted a number of small experiments with the Paulo Freire Method, the most important and best publicized test of the Method became, surprisingly enough, a part of the Alliance for Progress. The USAID Mission in Recife had resolved to attempt some short-range impact projects in adult education, a fertile and almost untouched field of endeavor. At the same time, the education agreement which USAID had signed with Governor Aluísio Alves of the state of Rio Grande do Norte was in the process of execution. USAID decided to run a pilot project in early 1963 with the Paulo Freire Method in the municipality of Angicos in the interior of Rio Grande do Norte.[3] Since this was Governor Alves' home town, he was naturally quite enthused about the idea.

Though the actual class time expended in the Angicos project was a bit more than forty hours, in all other respects the Freire Method lived up to its billing. USAID financed the training of seventy teachers, who then used the Method to teach 299 illiterates how to read and write. President Goulart came up from Brasília to attend the final hour of some of the classes.

One of the these final sessions took place in the Angicos jail,

where a group of prisoners were being made literate. One of them was serving a life term for having committed a murder when he was twelve years old. He had become a singing minstrel of some repute, learning of current events and town gossip from passersby who stopped at the window of his cell, and then entertaining his fellow-inmates with verses which conveyed the news of the day. During the last class, with President Goulart in attendance, the minstrel raised his hand. The teacher refused to recognize him, but he kept waving. Finally Goulart interjected, "Let him speak." The minstrel stood up and spoke with the rhythm and inflection characteristic of the Northeastern backlander. He said that for many years he had sung his poems, but today for the first time he was going to write one. He picked up a piece of chalk and wrote on the blackboard a poem paying tribute to Goulart. As he traced out the words he recited the verses in a voice which matched the trembling of his hands, and when he had finished he repeated the whole thing. Then he turned to Goulart.

"Mr. President," he began, reciting a little speech from memory, "for twenty-seven years I have been trying to get a pardon. I have petitioned your predecessor and your predecessor's predecessor, and none of them answered. I have petitioned you and you never answered. But I am not going to petition again. Now I can write my poetry and send it out of the jail. I am no longer a prisoner. This young man," pointing to the teacher, "has taught me to write, and in so doing he has set me free."

It would have been a nice touch if Goulart had been so moved by this speech that he issued an immediate pardon. But he didn't. The minstrel remained in jail, where he began to publish his own newspaper.

Another sentimental incident stemming from the Angicos project did not even have a bittersweet ending. One of the local madames went to the young man in charge of the literacy project and accused him of discriminating against the town's prostitutes. "Everyone else is learning," she argued. So he decided to organize a special class for prostitutes. The only available classroom space turned out to be the visitor's room in the jail. Eight or nine girls came to the class, which was held early in the evening. There were no problems until the next visitor's night at the jail, which unfortunately fell on the same

night that the class was in session. When the wives of the prisoners saw the girls, they leapt to an obvious, if erroneous, conclusion, and made a vigorous complaint to the authorities. As a result the class had to be canceled. One of the girls, who was eighteen years old, had a letter written to Governor Alves: "I have been a prostitute since the age of twelve when I discovered the only one part of my body worth anything. For a moment, while I was attending the class, I almost believed that I had found a way to be free. But now it is finished, and I am sorry." The class was never resumed.

Despite the effectiveness of the Paulo Freire Method in pilot projects at Angicos and elsewhere in the Northeast, despite the growing interest educators from the center-south of Brazil and even from abroad were showing in the program, USAID discontinued its support in January, 1964.

The Method taught only simple, phonetic words, mostly nouns, and Freire had not been able to develop more than rudimentary plans for continuing adult education beyond the literacy stage. The inadequacy of follow-up procedures and materials helps account for the USAID decision.

Another factor entered into the American choice: the Method had become highly controversial. Its critics echoed the familiar chorus that it was "subversive." According to his most vocal enemies, the devoutly Catholic Freire was out to "Bolshevize" Brazil.

The critics were certainly correct about the Paulo Freire Method being "subversive." The acquisition of civil rights by large numbers of newly literate peasants could substantially "subvert" the existing distribution of political power in Brazil. Moreover the essence of the Method was to confront the individual illiterate with the reality of his disenfranchisement, make him grasp the relationship between his impoverishment and his status as a noncitizen, and channel his reaction to this realization into a force which would motivate him to become literate and do something to help himself.

There were various steps to this process. First, a group of students visited the area where classes were to be held and interviewed a number of inhabitants. This was the "romantic" phase, as the students collected answers which described local conditions with a certain archaic purity of expression. From the responses which their

questions elicited, the interviewers then compiled a list of twelve commonly used words which reflected the immediate environment and at the same time contained as many combinations as possible of recurring consonants and vowels.

Classes ranged in size from small groups of eight to gatherings of twenty-five or thirty. The teacher, usually a university student, assumed the role of discussion moderator. During each of the first eight sessions, the class viewed photographic slides which projected sketches of familiar objects or scenes. The moderator, using the Socratic method of questioning, attempted to prod the students into an awareness of themselves and the world in which they lived. The goal was for the students to achieve *conscientização,* or consciousness-raising, whereby the individual becomes critically aware of his existential situation. Motivation burst from the illiterate's realization of the gap between his own level of education, which put him on the same level as Brazil's most primitive Indians, and the level of knowledge reflected in the culture of modern technology, which he saw all around him. Once it dawned upon him that this gap was the cause of his own backwardness, there would be no holding him back.

The actual literacy teaching began in the ninth session, when the class would learn to pick out from a slide of a chart of various two-letter syllables the sound groupings which composed a word corresponding to a common object, whose likeness was also projected on the screen. While doing this they would also learn the five vowels. From this point on students would pick out their own words, usually with great enthusiasm, and the other eleven key words would be introduced to them in the same way. Soon they would be able to write not only the twelve key words but many other words which they could build from the consonants and vowels of the key words. The moderator would hold a contest to see who could go home and write the longest word. (In one class a woman won by bringing back "penicillin.") By the end of the forty hours the class could read and write five hundred words.

Those who were unhappy with the Paulo Freire Method contended that it was designed more to incite the untutored masses into a rebellious frame of mind than to make them literate. As one USAID official observed: "It wasn't really a literacy program but

rather a means of politicizing people. The goal of the Method was to arouse the politically apathetic and get them into an uproar." One of Freire's aides who subsequently became bitterly disillusioned with the turn of events in the Northeast now calls the Method a "revolution factory." An alternative, related charge was that many of those teaching in literacy projects in Pernambuco, after Governor Arraes decided to use the Method on a large scale in his state, were Communists and extreme leftists who were manipulating the Method to indoctrinate their students in Marxist ideology.

There was much truth to the allegation that Paulo Freire's Method would agitate illiterates and cause them to be highly dissatisfied with their position in society. However, as his supporters responded, this was society's fault, not the Method's. If the rural and urban poor, upon arriving at a sense of what man has done and can do, conclude that they can better their lot and that society through its political processes has no right to hold them back, so be it.

The degree to which certain groups were using the Method for political purposes is questionable. The essence of the Method was to make the student think critically, and thereby humanize him. As one of Freire's assistants declared: "The Communist Party does not present options. The Method teaches the peasant to make choices. The Communists dictate answers. The Method tells the peasant that he should remain a subject, rather than an object, and that he should not let anyone take the right of choice from him." [4]

A Communist moderator might, of course, use the classes for pure political indoctrination, and his students might never get any exposure to the Method. In addition, class discussion, especially during the first eight sessions, did touch upon political subjects, and a skillful moderator might abuse his role by attempting to influence the students' thinking about politics. In these respects the Method was subject to the possibility of improper use.

When Miguel Arraes decided to launch a literacy campaign throughout Pernambuco with the Paulo Freire Method, he expanded Recife's Popular Culture Movement (MCP) so that it could operate as a state agency, and gave it jurisdiction over the state's adult education program. Freire's Cultural Extension Service (SEC) at the University of Recife was supposed to work with the MCP

and train people (mostly university students) to be moderators under the Method. There is no evidence of Communist influence within the SEC. Freire ran his own show, and his second-in-command was a Catholic priest. A couple of individuals within the SEC who taught the Method to MCP moderators were considered Communists, but nothing indicates that they did not do their jobs properly.

The leading Communist within the MCP was Abelardo da Hora, a Recife artist who was in charge of the MCP's Popular Art Center. But he had nothing to do with the literacy movement. A number of university students within the MCP were members of a Communist youth group. Many of them secured assignments to teach the Freire Method in the Palmares area, where the Communists controlled the rural labor union. It is more than likely that they coordinated their work with the Party's program of action for the southern sugar zone of Pernambuco.

The Paulo Freire Method was not the only literacy program underway in Brazil at this time. The Catholic Church's Rural Assistance Service in Rio Grande do Norte had been conducting an active literacy campaign which made extensive use of radio broadcasts to reach the peasants. President Jânio Quadros had been so impressed with this campaign that he provided partial financing for a national program, called the Basic Education Movement (MEB), which utilized the techniques of the Rural Assistance Service's campaign and was under the direction of the National Conference of Brazilian Bishops.[5] João Goulart continued the program. By late 1963 MEB teachers were beginning to use a primer which eventually created almost as much controversy as the Paulo Freire Method. Its title was *To Live Is To Struggle,* and it taught sentences such as "Is it just for the people to live in hunger?" and "There is need for complete change in Brazil." [6]

The Freire Method, however, had caught the imagination of educators all over Brazil, and with the financial backing of the federal government it began to spread like the most contagious of ideas whose time had come. Training courses for moderators were set up in almost every state capital. The national plan for 1964 was to put about 2 million illiterates through the program (so adding them to the voting rolls). The "Revolution in Forty Hours" seemed within reach.

176

THIRTEEN ✻

✻ ✻ Countdown
to Catastrophe

ON AN EVENING IN JULY, 1963, a jeep made its way hesitatingly through a maze of cobblestoned streets and alleys in Goiana, a dreary town in northeastern Pernambuco.[1] The mud-spattered vehicle had navigated the rain-filled ruts and potholes of the highway from Recife, and was now trying to locate a small plaza on the edge of town. After much meandering through the empty streets, the driver finally made the proper series of turns and came to a halt at the rear of a political rally which was already in progress.

"He has just arrived," the speaker shouted, interrupting himself in the middle of a sentence when he saw the occupants of the jeep making their way through the crowd. "A great Latin American leader has just arrived." People began to applaud as Francisco Julião made his way to a platform perched on the back of a venerable truck. A string of light bulbs overhead illuminated the local politicians assembled on the platform. Julião climbed the shaky ladder propped against the rear of the truck, exchanged embraces with the men on the platform, and struck a pose of dignified interest as the speaker resumed his remarks.

He looked out upon a sea of brown faces, staring in blank concentration at the spectacle before them. The assembled townspeople, many of them recent arrivals from the countryside, were very attentive but hardly enthusiastic. It took the outbursts of obvious plants in

177

the crowd to ignite applause. Almost everyone in the audience wore dirty, shabby, torn clothes. Up front, a peasant whose shining eyes reflected either intoxication or a sadly deteriorated mental state planted his bare feet in mud which oozed between his toes. Both big toes veered off at an absurd angle from his instep. A vacuous grin wreathed his face. Behind him stood another peasant, a pipe dangling loosely from his mouth, a battered hat shading his eyes, and a tin pan pressed between his folded arms and chest. A group of young children amused themselves by mimicking the gestures of the speakers.

The light bulbs lured all manner of insect life, which descended *en masse* from the nearby fields. The politicians, most of whom were candidates for the local town council, demonstrated a complete indifference to the intruders. Only when an enormous, brightly colored bug perched on the shoulder of a candidate for mayor was there a defensive reaction, as the man standing behind him rendered a swift execution with his palm. The candidate acknowledged this service with a slight turn and bow, unmindful of the long, yellow stain on his white jacket.

When it was Julião's turn to speak, the master of ceremonies, a clean-cut youth with dark-rimmed glasses, introduced him as "the man who can save Brazil," and the audience dutifully applauded. Shifting his weight from one foot to the other, the Federal Deputy began with an explanation for his presence.

"On the first of May 3,000 peasants from Goiana walked all the way to Recife to attend a rally. At that time I promised I would return the visit, and that is why I am here." He then launched into a familiar denunciation of conditions in Brazil and declared his lack of faith in the electoral process. No one seemed to notice when he made a smooth transition to an electoral pitch.

"Let us defeat the reactionaries and elect an honest government. Let us put into office men like the candidates here tonight, men who will support Governor Arraes. Miguel Arraes is doing his best to improve conditions in Pernambuco. He has opened the doors of the Governor's Palace to the peasants. They can now sit in chairs where before only the wealthy were allowed to sit."

Julião's words received a tepid response from the crowd. He

178

sounded just like all the rest of the political pitchmen, a far cry from the social agitator whose disdain for elections had once evoked in many minds a vision of revolution in the rural Northeast.

The return trip to Recife seemed endless. Julião had a sore throat and said very little. A companion in the back seat of the jeep hacked away at stalks of sugarcane and distributed chunks to his fellow passengers, who chewed vigorously to extract the sweet juices and then spat out the roughage.

Approaching the outer limits of Recife, they turned off the highway and sloshed through pools of water which made the road almost impassable. Suddenly a mass of moving objects filled the narrow roadway ahead. The jeep lurched to a halt and tilted to one side as a wheel settled in a deep rut. A herd of humpbacked Zebu cattle, their long, droopy ears swaying back and forth, quickly surrounded the vehicle. A horseman rode in their midst, goading them on with a shrill, unearthly wail. The driver of the jeep remained faithful to his habit of switching off the lights every time he stopped. Everyone sat there quietly, unmindful of the possibility that a horn might penetrate the canvas covering of the jeep. Julião, in deep meditation, gazed off into the darkness.

The Peasant League movement no longer presented any semblance of a coherent revolutionary threat to the power structure in Pernambuco's sugar zone. *A fortiori* it had little national importance. The Leagues could still mount protests and even invasions of plantations, but these were more in the nature of annoyances to the authorities and pretty much confined to the area of Vitória de Santo Antão. At times these invasions annoyed even Julião, since it seems likely that he did not authorize many (if any) of them, and they were the cause of a bitter rift with the student, João Alfredo.

Concurrently his efforts to transfer the peasant movement into the cities were bearing no fruit. In 1962 he had written in a Mexican magazine that the Cuban Revolution "has demonstrated that revolution can be made from the countryside to the cities. . . . In Brazil revolution also can be made from countryside to city. . . ."[2] Though the Leagues failed to ignite an upheaval that could spread to the cities, Julião organizationally followed his 1962 dictum by trying

179

to set up "Urban Leagues" in Recife and other cities. One of his key lieutenants took charge of these new Leagues, which never amounted to much. Similarly planned "Women's Leagues," "Fishermen's Leagues," and "Students' Leagues" suffered the same fate. Organizing in the cities meant direct competition with the Communists, who had long been active among the urban workers. If Julião had serious problems in administering his rural movement, he surely did not have the resources to develop "Urban Leagues."

Nonetheless, these practical considerations did not deter Julião and his followers from "thinking big." A more uncharitable way to put it is that their dreams had no bounds. In October, 1963, they decided to amalgamate these barely existent groups into a "Political Organization of the Peasant Leagues of Brazil," in order to create a united front in the revolutionary struggle.[3] This new political organ was avowedly Marxist-Leninist, although it was never made clear exactly how it differed ideologically from the Communist Party and the splinter Maoist and Trotskyist groups.

This was also the period when Julião's marriage to Alexina reached the breaking point. Their liberal sexual arrangement had survived many strains, but by late 1963 Julião was openly living with a handsome brunette named Regina de Castro. Indeed, in mid-January, 1964, a Rio newspaper reported (erroneously) that he had remarried and was honeymooning in Rio.[4]

Regina, a lawyer and the wife of a SUDENE lawyer, had been working with Julião from the time of the National Peasant's Congress in 1961. Having fallen in love with him, she remained within the movement, putting to good use an apartment which she had near Ipanema Beach in Rio. It became a Peasant League headquarters in the center-south, where Julião, Padre Alípio, and others stayed during visits to Rio. Eventually pressures began to build. Regina obtained a legal separation from her husband and retained custody of her two children. During one of Alexina's trips to Cuba in the latter part of 1963, Regina moved in with Julião on a more or less permanent basis and soon became pregnant.

Julião's political activity in July and August, 1963, focused on local elections for mayor and city (or town) councilmen being held throughout Pernambuco. In Recife itself, the leftist movement

which had brought Miguel Arraes to the governorship sought to install in City Hall an engineer, Pelópidas Silveira, a member of the left wing of the Brazilian Socialist Party who had been a popular mayor of Recife, Vice-Governor of Pernambuco during the Cid Sampaio administration, and Miguel Arraes's Secretary of Transportation. Pelópidas, a rotund "big daddy of the left" with close ties to the Communist Party, enjoyed broad support and even attracted a campaign appearance from Communist war-horse Luís Carlos Prestes. The opposition nominated Leal Sampaio, Cid's brother. Pelópidas won, but by a margin of fewer than 9,000 votes,[5] suggesting that despite their growing optimism the radical left did not have much of an emerging majority, even in Recife. The leftists, however, made no secret of their plans to back Miguel Arraes for Vice President in 1965 (hopefully on a ticket headed by the popular ex-President, Juscelino Kubitschek), and to promote Pelópidas to the Governor's Palace in 1966. Their dreams too appeared to have no bounds.

This scenario threatened to isolate Julião even further because of his outspoken criticism of Kubitschek. "Juscelino was the leader who betrayed Brazil the most," he once declared. "He was most insensitive to the problems of the man in the fields. He impoverished them violently during his five years in office. He killed them. Brasília was built over the corpses of hundreds of thousands of peasants."[6]

Arraes had no such problems because of his caution and consummate political skills. He enjoyed a solid identification with the left yet had never overcommitted himself, rhetorically or otherwise, to any position that would prevent his from working with more moderate elements in the national spectrum.

He was cautious, partly because he was constantly under the close surveillance by important representatives of Brazil's military establishment. The Fourth Army had its headquarters in Recife and bore responsibility for the security of the Northeast. Though cynics were wont to question its actual fighting capabilities in terms of materiel ("bellicose junk," some called it) and personnel (drafted peasants), it was the only army in town. Arraes controlled the state police, but had no state militia.

The Brazilian armed forces had for many years built a tradition of

keeping out of civilian affairs, except to "defend the Constitution." Thus when efforts were made to keep Kubitschek from assuming the presidency after his election in 1955 and to keep Goulart from succeeding to the nation's top office after Quadros resigned, it was the Army (or at least powerful elements therein) that intervened to maintain constitutional processes. Once law and order had been restored, the troops returned to their barracks. The military establishment, however, made its own decisions about when the Constitution needed defending, so the political left had to consider how the Army would react to overt attempts to bring about radical change in Brazil.

Two of the most influential figures within the high command served as commanding officers of the Fourth Army during the early 1960s. General Artur Costa e Silva and General Humberto Castelo Branco had firsthand opportunities to observe the birth of the rural labor movement in the Northeast and the rise of the populist forces behind Miguel Arraes. Neither General had much sympathy with the left, and in August, 1963, Goulart replaced Castelo Branco with Justino Alves Bastos, a General he believed to be loyal to him. Indeed, Goulart's final instructions to Alves Bastos were: "Keep an eye on Arraes; he's very dangerous." [7] But if Goulart thought that the General was going to look out for the President's political interests, he was to prove very sadly mistaken.

On a national level there were certain high Army officers who had the reputation of leaning toward the left. Radical politicians made every effort to cultivate them. At the same time the most promising revolutionary element within the Armed Forces was thought to be the sergeants.[8] Certain radical elements worked at politicizing these noncommissioned officers in the hope that they would not take up arms in the event of a right-wing military coup attempt, and that they might even become a political pressure group capable of offsetting their more conservative superiors. Part of this program involved pushing a proposal to change the constitution to remove the provision that barred servicemen from voting. On several occasions protests by groups of sergeants lapsed into insubordination. A revolt of noncommissioned officers in the Air Force, Navy, and Marines broke out in Brasília on September 12, 1963, but was quickly crushed. The officer corps was quite upset and now had

an issue, the discipline of their troops, which caused them to take an even dimmer view of the radical left. The influence of the few officers who sympathized with the left was weakened, and certain officers began to think the Constitution might soon need defending.

Since Arraes had no military muscle at his disposal, his only road to power lay in the democratic process and strict adherence to the Constitution, to which he constantly reiterated a firm commitment. According to journalist Antônio Callado, Pernambuco was the "most democratic state of the union." [9] How much this would help the Governor in his bid for national office was another question. Many political figures in the center-south looked upon him as too provincial or too cautious for their tastes.

Meanwhile, President Goulart was proving increasingly incapable of coping with the inflation that was ravaging Brazil's economy and with the buffeting pressures for and against reform.[10] He refused to adopt stringent economic measures, since an orthodox anti-inflationary policy would hit hard at the pocketbooks of his working-class supporters, and insuperable political obstacles kept him from bringing about basic structural reforms. His constant talk of reform served only to arouse the dissatisfied and alienate the conservatives. Right-wing groups were now actively plotting his downfall, army officers were discussing their "constitutional duties," rural and urban workers being mobilized by the left saw their expectations frustrated, and groups on both ends of the political spectrum talked of acquiring arms.

On October 4, 1963, Goulart requested Congress to grant him power to govern under a state of siege for thirty days. Sensing that the President might be groping toward an authoritarian solution after the model of his mentor and idol, Getúlio Vargas, both the right and the left vigorously objected. On the 7th Arraes scheduled a speech to denounce the state-of-siege request. Before he delivered it, word reached Recife that Goulart had withdrawn the request. Since he already had an audience on hand, Arraes went ahead with the speech anyway. An hour later troops and tanks of the Fourth Army appeared in the downtown area and surrounded the Governor's Palace.[11] General Alves Bastos announced that these were merely "maneuvers." Later it was revealed that one of the first things Gou-

lart had planned to do under the state of siege was to remove from office both Governor Arraes and the militantly conservative governor of the state of Guanabara in the south. Apparently the President lost his nerve.

Meanwhile in the countryside the competition for control of the rural unions continued apace. In November the Federation of Rural Syndicates conducted its successful strike, which involved most of the workers in the sugar zone. But as has already been pointed out, the Federation and the Catholic priests behind it were under constant pressure from the radical left. As 1964 began, strikes and land invasions were still disturbing the tranquility of the cane fields. In mid-January, ten peasants were reported killed and nineteen wounded in a clash at a sugar mill in Paraíba between the state police and a large group of demonstrators supposedly belonging to the Peasant Leagues.[12] A sergeant used a machine gun during the battle, which also claimed the lives of several policemen. The authorities blamed Julião, who had visited the area several days before the outbreak of violence.

Throughout January and February peasants belonging to Julião's Leagues occupied a certain plantation in Vitória de Santo Antão. The owner had abandoned it in April, 1963, but now wanted it back. The peasants who had taken up residence on it refused to leave. Governor Arraes even made a personal appeal, promising food, shelter, and jobs to those who would move. A number of the occupiers took him up on this and were transported to the state fair grounds. Finally on March 3 a federal agency in charge of land reform expropriated the plantation.

In mid-March Clodomir Moraes emerged from a Guanabara dungeon and returned to Pernambuco. He resumed his work with the Peasant Leagues and went to Vitória de Santo Antão. On March 25 he explained in a Recife newspaper interview that the Leagues were opposed to land invasions. He accused the landowners of provoking invasions so that some state or federal agency would then expropriate the land at an inflated price. What the Leagues wanted, insisted Clodomir, was "confiscation, pure and simple." [13]

The increasing turmoil in late 1963 and early 1964 made it extremely difficult for SUDENE to carry out its mandate. Some of the

problems encountered by the development agency could be traced to Celso Furtado's frequent absences from the Northeast. Indeed, throughout this whole period he lived on a temporary basis in a small apartment near the beach in Recife, and continued to maintain his permanent residence in Rio de Janeiro.

Furtado had not been able to turn down Goulart's request that he take the sticky job of national Minister of Planning. During the final quarter of 1962, he labored heroically to draft a Three-Year Plan for the Brazilian economy.[14] The task took him away from Recife during a crucial, formative period, when SUDENE was just beginning to move and to have to cope with the expanding USAID mission. In the first few months of 1963, efforts to put the Plan into action consumed valuable time.

When Furtado was away from the Northeast his chief deputy became Acting Superintendent, yet lacked the power to make important decisions. Furtado could nullify anything the Acting Superintendent did during his absence. Often decisions that should have been made in the urgency of the moment had to be deferred.

The work on the Three-Year Plan did not result in any political gain for either Furtado or SUDENE. It caused the Director to be identified with the Goulart administration at a time when the latter was becoming shakier and shakier. The Plan's provisions for reform, especially in the countryside, worsened Furtado's standing with conservatives who had previously suspected him of being a subversive character of sorts. The tough stabilization measures envisioned by the Plan met with fierce opposition from organized labor. The Plan's acknowledgment of Brazil's need for more foreign investment drew criticism from the radical left. The Kennedy administration, suspicious of the leftward trend of the Goulart government, refused to provide sorely needed long-term financial support. In the end Goulart lacked the stomach and the political muscle to execute the Plan and dropped the whole thing by mid-1963, so that Furtado's effort to save the Brazilian economy was never given a chance.

When he returned to the Northeast on a more or less full-time basis, Furtado found relations between his agency and USAID at a low ebb. In addition, because of his absence some of his subordinates had built up little empires within the now formidable SUDENE bu-

reaucracy. This made it difficult to take action against the varied problems of development in a flexible and effective way.

The relationship between Furtado and Arraes during this period was enigmatic. Furtado himself did not become identified with the Arraes movement, yet he must have realized that the structural reforms he sought to achieve with SUDENE required the type of political support that a leftist-nationalist political force could best furnish. Arraes on his part joined with the rest of the left in denouncing Furtado's Three-Year Plan, but in line with his innate political caution, the Governor maintained a proper attitude toward SUDENE's Director in all other respects. Arraes did not seem to have any profound ideas of his own about the economic needs of the Northeast. His pet plan, the promotion of small "cottage" industries throughout the state, never got beyond the talking stage, and could scarcely compete with Furtado's prescriptions for the development of the entire region. A SUDENE official has characterized theirs as a "love-hate" relationship, with Furtado disturbed by what he considered Arraes's occasional lapses into demagoguery, and Arraes at times disenchanted by Furtado's cool intellectualism.

In late 1963 and early 1964, Furtado found himself under increasing pressure from leftist elements within SUDENE. The agency's employees were organized in a union and succeeded in going out on strike and shutting SUDENE down on several occasions. It seemed as if the labor unrest that was becoming quite common in Recife and the countryside had spread to the government agency itself.

More serious were the efforts to hinder SUDENE's application of a tax incentive program designed to attract private capital to the Northeast. A key part of Furtado's Master Plan for the Northeast sought to industrialize the region in an attempt to utilize the manpower which was a by-product of overpopulation and unemployment. If jobs could be created, then employees with newly acquired purchasing power would demand goods and services which would in turn create additional jobs. Under the law a corporation could invest in the Northeast a certain percentage of its tax liability to the federal government. In other words the company could take money marked for taxes and put it to work in the Northeast instead of paying it to the government. This was a plan similar to that used to attract in-

dustry from northern to southern Italy. But SUDENE would retain the authority to approve or disapprove of specific investment projects before this tax exemption would work.

There were valid reasons to move cautiously with such a program. Some opposition to it resulted from ideological revulsion at any capitalistic solutions. The Communist Party newspaper in Recife was especially critical of the idea of attracting outside capital to the region.[15] Some leftist-nationalists did not like a proposal to extend the tax incentives to permit non-Brazilian companies doing business in the center-south to invest their Brazilian taxes in the Northeast (and thus expand their penetration into the Brazilian economy). In late February, 1964, a labor organization dominated by the Communists transported armed peasants by truck to Recife and had them surround the SUDENE building in a bid to prevent a meeting which was going to discuss whether to allow foreign companies to take advantage of the tax incentives. The peasants carried signs denouncing "imperialism" and demanding "basic reforms." According to one of the local newspapers, the police stayed away and let the demonstration run its course.[16]

The conservative elements in Pernambuco sought to resist the mounting tide of strikes convulsing the state. In early February they resorted to the lockout,[17] a weapon which seven years before had successfully promoted the ambitions of Cid Sampaio. Now, as political positions polarized, landowners, industrialists, and merchants closed ranks to meet the threat from the left. Arraes called their effort "Operation Terror," and denounced it in a telegram to President Goulart on February 28.[18] If Arraes really expected Goulart to help, he was sadly underestimating the President's antipathy toward him. On March 3 the employers of Recife locked their doors. Arraes, left to his own devices by Goulart, somehow managed to settle the labor dispute which had given rise to the controversy, and the lockout lasted for only one day. The incident served to boost the Governor's already considerable popularity.

In the meantime, the "Revolution in Forty Hours" sputtered in the background. Paulo Freire's Method still had not yet left the starting-gate. The crash programs which were supposed to make thousands of peasants literate had not begun. The Method required

time to make the peasants conscious of their needs, but events in Pernambuco and the rest of Brazil were moving too quickly. Leaders within the state Secretariat of Education, the MCP, and Freire's SEC could not agree on what to do. Freire himself was politically naive and could not cope with what was happening around him. (At one point one of his associates informed the U.S. Consulate that he had actually joined the Communist Party for "opportunistic reasons," but this accusation has never been corroborated.) Furthermore, technical problems were slowing down the administration of the program. Resources and trained personnel were proving to be critically scarce. Freire, who had visions of using his Method all over the rest of Latin America and even in Africa, could not make it really work in Brazil.

More and more the ferment in the Northeast reflected the turmoil that had the rest of the country in an uproar. President Goulart seemed to be veering to the left in an attempt to break through the political impasse that prevented him from remedying economic and social problems that were rapidly reaching crisis dimensions.

In the center-south, conservatives were taking militant measures in their opposition to the President and the politicians who supported him. Organizations of Catholic women disrupted leftist political meetings.[19] On several occasions Miguel Arraes was their target. In February at a televised interview in São Paulo he had to use a rear entrance to avoid a group waiting to attack him. Later, during a speech in Juíz de Fora, he required the protection of a large contingent of state police, who were stoned by the hostile crowd.

In a desperate gambit, Goulart decided to appeal directly to the people. He staged a mammoth televised rally in Rio de Janeiro on March 13.[20] Appropriately enough, it was a Friday.

Much of the organizing for the rally was done by Communist-dominated labor unions. Prominently displayed in the audience were signs calling for the legalization of the Communist Party.

The nation's leading leftists appeared on the platform with Goulart. Lionel Brizola, the President's ultraleftist brother-in-law and a federal Deputy, delivered a violent address calling for the dissolution of Congress and the creation of a Constituent Assembly. Goulart, speaking with emotion which at times verged upon loss of control,

promulgated and signed with a great flourish two presidential decrees; one nationalizing privately owned oil refineries (all of which were owned by Brazilians), the other expropriating land located within six miles of federal highways, railroads, dams, and irrigation projects, and deemed to be "underutilized." He also promised future measures to deal with agrarian and tax reform, and the extension of the vote to illiterates and servicemen.

The March 13 rally caused a great sensation. In Recife a leftist newspaper ran a banner headline proclaiming the "Death Blow to the Large Estates." [21] It was much ado about very little, since Brazil's agrarian problem went far, far beyond the lands adjoining federal railroads, highways, and dams. Nonetheless, the left became positively manic about the "bold" step Goulart had taken. The right began to plan seriously for a *coup d'état*.

Ultraconservatives had been talking among themselves about a coup ever since Goulart took office. For them, he was the reincarnation of Getúlio Vargas. Certain high military officers had been thinking about the need to "defend the Constitution," and were now considering specific plans for action. The March 13 rally enabled the right to mount a "scare" campaign of such proportions that a half-million people demonstrated against Goulart on the streets of São Paulo on March 19. Conservative Catholic groups organized the march, which had an unmistakable anti-Communist tone. More significant was the fact that the demonstrators were mostly middle class, an indication that the bourgeoisie was now thoroughly frightened by what the President was doing. Further demonstrations were planned.

At the same time the plotters were receiving strong encouragement from Washington. The new administration was taking a more "pragmatic" approach toward Latin America. In March, 1964, Thomas C. Mann, President Johnson's Assistant Secretary of State for Inter-American Affairs, announced that the U.S. would no longer automatically oppose the overthrow of Latin democracies.[22] Charles Bartlett, a political columnist reputed to have excellent contacts in Washington, confided to his readers that this change of policy was meant to urge the Brazilian military to move against Goulart.[23] A U.S. Army officer attached to the Embassy in Rio had

extremely close relations with the Brazilian high command. Ambassador Lincoln Gordon, according to Professor Thomas Skidmore's excellent history, *Politics in Brazil,* knew all about the burgeoning conspiracy.[24] Indeed, the Ambassador canceled a trip he was scheduled to make to the Northeast at the end of March so that he could remain in Rio during this crucial moment.[25] The Embassy assured the plotters that the U.S. was behind them. This meant that the regime which replaced Goulart could count on substantial American aid. According to a respected São Paulo newspaper, the Embassy even offered arms if necessary.[26]

The conspiracy was not, as some Brazilians later charged, hatched in Washington. The events of February and March, however, clearly indicated that whatever the conspiracy gave birth to would be wrapped in an American flag.

Miguel Arraes returned from Rio to Recife five days after the rally, to be greeted by headlines that he was about to launch a "Rush Toward Reforms." It did not matter, at least to the press, that the presidential decrees signed at the March 13 rally did not give the state governors any new powers. Euphoria was the order of the day. The left exuded confidence. A Peasant League leader has recalled: "In late March one of the Communists said to me, 'We are going to take power,' and I answered, 'With what?' But he wouldn't listen. He believed that historical determinism was about to drop Brazil in his lap."

The conservatives did not do much talking. They were too busy accumulating guns.[27] Cid Sampaio led the Pernambuco plotters and kept in touch with the conspirators in the center-south. One of his brothers-in-law took charge of radio communications. A leading landowner politician was purchasing Czech submachine guns from São Paulo. They were packed in an innocuous manner and shipped to Recife in commercial busses. Five or six men from Pernambuco's Federation of Industries, an organization of businessmen dominated by Cid Sampaio, were taking lessons in how to use the weapons on weekends at a plantation near Recife. Their instructor was an official in the state association of plantation owners. They kept the guns in their homes.

It is curious that as all this was happening the Governor was con-

sulting with his associates about the volatile political climate. Arraes, cautious as ever, was not very exuberant. His concern was that Goulart might make a play for power which would result in his ouster from the governorship. He was still clinging to his stake in the democratic process.

But on the evening of March 29, the die was cast. A group of sailors had staged a violent protest against their superiors in Rio on March 26. Goulart, who had allowed the military to put down the sergeants' revolt in Brasília on September 13, now took the side of the demonstrators. On this fateful evening he made a televised speech in which he virtually condoned the sailors' breach of military discipline. "It was a decision little short of political suicide," notes Professor Skidmore.[28] At dawn on March 30 a general in the key state of Minas Gerais ordered his troops to march on Rio. It hadn't been planned in that exact way, but the conspiracy had now become an insurgency.

For two days Goulart and his allies on the left attempted to rally their forces to defend the government. A Communist labor group called a general strike. Work went on as usual. Goulart sent troops to intercept the rebel column. They couldn't seem to find the enemy.

In Recife during March 30 and 31 one sensed confusion and even a sense of paralysis. Bits of news filtered up from the center-south, but no one seemed to know what was happening or what to do. A Communist-controlled labor organization published newspaper advertisements that proclaimed the unity of all workers in the face of reaction and denounced the "enemies of progress and national emancipation." [29]

On the evening of March 31 Miguel Arraes drafted a manifesto in the name of the governors of the Northeastern states, expressing their "serene confidence in the pacification [sic] of the Brazilian family," and their "determination to preserve their legitimate rights." [30] He also released the following declaration of his own: "The State is calm and our position is one of support for legality, democratic principles, the liberties of the people and the prerogatives of the President of the Republic." [31]

Mayor Pelópidas Silveira issued a statement that he remained "as always, in favor of liberty." [32]

PART FOUR

FOURTEEN ✺
✺ ✺ The Military Coup

CELSO FURTADO HAD BEEN ATTENDING a session of an Alliance for Progress advisory council in Washington and was not fully aware of what was happening in Brazil. He flew back to Recife on March 31, just in time for the crisis.[1] One of the first things he did on his return was to give to the press a statement expressing the need to reformulate the thrust of the Alliance, because the elite groups holding power in Latin America had no intention of relinquishing what he termed their "constellation of privileges."[2] The implications of this proposition were about to descend upon him in a totally unexpected way.

Even after a telephone call to Brasília and a nocturnal visit to the Governor's Palace, SUDENE's Director was unable to find out whether Goulart had been able to quell the insurgency. A few hours' sleep at his apartment refreshed him, and at 7 a.m. he drove back into town to see Arraes.

Except for the usual obstacles presented by the early morning traffic, the approaches to the city were still open. As Furtado passed the Praça da República, a spacious park setting the Governor's Palace off from the rest of downtown Recife, he could observe how lonely and exceedingly vulnerable that modest structure was—tucked away on a gently rounded extremity of the Santo Antão district of the city, and overlooking the Capiberibe River as it curls

around in a 180 degree arc, merges with the turgid waters of the Be-
beribe River and heads out toward the sea.

Miguel Arraes was pacing back and forth, puffing furiously on a
Marlboro and in an obviously agitated frame of mind when Furtado
arrived at his office. He gave the Director an up-to-the-minute
briefing on events as they were breaking. He was beginning to hear
rumors that the Fourth Army was occupying parts of Pernambuco.
An Army officer had just stopped by to ask him what his reaction
would be if troops surrounded the Palace. He had replied that there
was absolutely no cause for such a maneuver, since the state was
calm; that he had already communicated to General Justino Alves
Bastos his hope and intent to keep the Northeast from being dragged
into the conflict that seemed to be breaking out in the center-south;
that he had taken steps to prevent the occurrence of strikes in Recife; and that he had already ordered the state police to cooperate
fully with the Army. He had given the officer a draft copy of the
manifesto of the Northeastern governors, and had told him to take it
to General Alves Bastos. But Arraes was still apprehensive about
what the General was going to do. He asked Furtado to pay Alves
Bastos a visit and sound out his intentions.

Fourth Army headquarters was conveniently located in the
nearby district of Bôa Vista, just across the Capiberibe River.
Within a short time Furtado was ushered into the presence of the
General, Justino Alves Bastos. A diminutive, dark-complexioned
career officer, Bastos was known for his keen sense of opportunism
that more than compensated for his intellectual shortcomings. (Following the well established Brazilian custom of making fun of all
public figures, his detractors liked to pun on his name to convey the
expression "Justino's full of shit.") "Goulart should either resign or
change his cabinet," the General informed Furtado. "What he
ought to do is bring serious people like you into his government."
The telephone rang, and Furtado, thoroughly puzzled by the General's vague comments, was asked to leave. He headed back to the
Governor's Palace.

Shortly thereafter, a military delegation headed by the Admiral
who commanded the naval forces based in Recife visited Governor
Arraes and began to make certain demands on him. They wanted

him to call for Goulart's resignation, to fire his Secretary of Security (the state official in charge of law enforcement), and to promise not to use the police against the Army. It soon became evident that they were indirectly pressuring *him* to resign. When Furtado arrived back at the Palace and was told what was happening, he suddenly realized that General Justino Alves Bastos had been putting him on.

Only later did Furtado grasp the full extent of the put-on. From the earliest moments of the conspiracy Alves Bastos had thrown in with the anti-Goulart movement. Indeed, the President's man in the Northeast was the first of the commanding officers of Brazil's four military commands to express support for the conspirators. This had given considerable confidence to Cid Sampaio and his associates in Pernambuco. The leftists, too busy being overconfident to check carefully on the the position of the military, had remained totally unaware of the General's decision.

Late at night on March 31, the military did have one serious scare, when reports were received indicating that a ship bearing arms and munitions was about to tie up at the private dock of Senator José Emírio de Moraes, Arraes's chief financial supporter during the 1962 campaign. It turned out to be a false alarm. The ship carried a cargo of mercury.

During most of the morning of April 1, a military officer had been making regular radio broadcasts assuring listeners that Recife was calm and that the state government and the Fourth Army were cooperating to maintain normality. Just to make sure, the Army arrested the head of Pernambuco's state police. At the same time General Alves Bastos was in constant consultation with other officers and the politicians who were participating in the conspiracy. Army units were making their way to a few labor union headquarters where some resistance to the coup might be expected. The troops had the streets to themselves, because Arraes, in his eagerness to avoid conflict, had ordered the state police to remain in their barracks. This left only one real problem: how to find a pretext to remove the Governor, who stubbornly clung to the only thing he had left—the legality of his position.

Earlier that morning, two ardent Arraes supporters met on the

street in one of Recife's modest middle-class suburbs. One of them had been trying unsuccessfully to pick up on his short-wave radio set some news of the insurgency in the center-south. "I guess there will be trouble here," he said softly. "Julião will bring his peasants into town. Should we try to find some guns?"

"We should have thought of that a long time ago," his friend replied with a touch of bitterness in his voice. "As for Julião, he's in Brasília, and even if he were here, he would be no help. The peasants won't fight. There's nothing we can do but wait. Our only hope is that the Third Army will stand by Goulart." Based in the President's home state of Rio Grande do Sul, the Third Army had intervened at a crucial moment to assure Goulart's succession after Jânio Quadros's resignation in 1961. The southernmost state in the union, Rio Grande do Sul was a long, long way from Pernambuco.

Naílton Santos, the chief of SUDENE's Human Resources Division, entertained no such illusions about the Third Army. The first thing he did that morning was to go to his office in the SUDENE building and clean out his desk.[3] The sound of loud voices in the corridor interrupted him. He emerged from his office in time to confront red-faced City Councilman Wanderkolk Wanderley and a rather belligerent entourage. Wanderley was one of Recife's most militant right-wingers, bearing impeccable credentials in the form of a wound he sustained as a military officer fighting against the 1935 Communist uprising in Pernambuco. He had organized a vigilante group and was now demanding that SUDENE "surrender all its weapons." Naílton, the ranking SUDENE official present at the time, invited him to search as many offices as he liked. Wanderley and his men stormed through the entire building but found no guns. Eyes narrowing behind the thick lenses of his spectacles, spittle dripping from the side of his mouth, the city councilman angrily called Naílton a "Communist," and marched out of the building. Shortly thereafter Naílton left, and immediately went into hiding.

Gregório Bezerra, himself a veteran of the 1935 rebellion, might have felt the same nostalgic urge which impelled Wanderley into action. Or he might have been deemed expendable by his Communist Party superiors. Perhaps he was just plain foolhardy. In any event, on the morning of the 1st Gregório slipped a .32 pistol and six

bullets under his belt, hopped into a jeep, and drove out of Recife toward Palmares.

It was business as usual for the USAID mission in Recife on April 1. Some female personnel were sent home during the uncertain morning hours, but soon a military officer announced over the radio that the Fourth Army had joined the "revolution," and that troops were now surrounding the Governor's Palace. From one of the buildings occupied by the mission, soldiers could be seen setting up machine guns at the approaches to a bridge which led to the Palace. The Americans breathed a sigh of relief, since they had been concerned over the possibility of violence resulting from a split within the Army. Across the river at the Consulate there were no such worries. Cid Sampaio and his Pernambuco plotters had kept U.S. consular officials informed of their plans from the very beginning of the conspiracy.

Troops and tanks appeared in force on the streets of Recife during the early afternoon. At 2 p.m. a crowd of university students gathered on the steps of the Faculty of Engineering.[4] The President of the Pernambuco Student's Union made a speech urging calm and arguing that a demonstration would be useless. Hotter heads prevailed and a mob started out toward the downtown area. When they reached the Praça da Independência and tried to turn down the street which led directly to the Governor's Palace, they came face to face with a line of soldiers with rifles and bayonets at the ready position. The students began to chant "Ar-raes, Ar-raes," and to heckle the soldiers, who fired into the air. More shouting, more firing, but this time some of the troops fired into the crowd, which quickly dispersed. Two students lay dead in the gutter. It was almost a carbon copy of a confrontation between students and soldiers in 1945 during a big demonstration against the Vargas dictatorship. There one student had been killed. He became a martyr, and his name is still remembered. This time the whole affair was generally considered foolish. The two dead students have long been forgotten.

Meanwhile Miguel Arraes had lunch in the Palace with members of his family and staff. The military insurgents and their civilian colleagues still did not know quite what to do with him. Later in the afternoon a delegation of officers returned to the Palace, now com-

pletely surrounded by troops. One of them informed Arraes that he had been removed from office. "You are free to go anywhere," he added. The Governor consulted with his staff. The consensus was that it would be dangerous for him to leave, since the military now had responsibility for him, but once outside the Palace he might risk injury or even death. Arraes replied to the delegation: "I do not consent to be deposed. I have my mandate from the people, and only they can take it from me. I will remain here, with my family." Their bluff called, the officers shrugged their shoulders and left.

Some of Arraes's more zealous supporters now criticize him for not going into the interior of the state with a radio car and as many loyal state police as he could mobilize. Then, they argue, he might have initiated a resistance to the coup which might have gathered broad support throughout the Northeast. With the benefit of hindsight the conclusion is inescapable that such a move would have been suicidal. Arraes never pretended to be a revolutionary. He had always been in favor of legality, democracy, and the Constitution. He was certainly not any kind of military leader. In the end, he stood by his principles. His mistake was to believe that legal means could bring about truly radical change in Brazil. At least he had the intelligence not to compound that error by resorting to force in a situation where his enemies had him clearly outmuscled.

In the late afternoon, another military group entered the Palace. Some of the men were carrying submachine guns. This time no polite requests were made. Arraes was placed under arrest, and at 8 p.m. he was finally taken from the building.

Furtado, who had been present at the Palace all afternoon, knew the end had come when this last delegation marched up the stairs. He walked out unmolested and slipped into his car. An officer beckoned him to get out and told him that his orders were to take everyone in the Palace to Fourth Army headquarters. SUDENE's Director coolly informed him that that was exactly where he was going. The officer saluted and Furtado drove away.

Cid Sampaio and some of his fellow conspirators were wheeling and dealing with General Justino Alves Bastos when Furtado arrived. The General was polite but firm. "You didn't help us at all. The Governor has been causing us many problems." Furtado told

Alves Bastos that he would close down SUDENE and await developments. He left the headquarters without being further detained.

Meanwhile, at the Legislative Assembly, the state deputies were debating over what to do about Arraes, who had not formally resigned. A cordon of troops surrounded the building, and lent an air of urgency to the deliberations. An ingenious solution to the impasse was finally devised. At 11:30 p.m., while Miguel Arraes was being held prisoner at a military installation in the city, a majority of the state legislature, after formal debate, voted with a straight face (45 to 17, with one abstention) to remove him from the governorship because he was now no longer able to carry out the functions of that office. Vice-Governor Paulo Guerra, one of the biggest cattle-raisers in Pernambuco, then succeeded to the state's highest office. As a Brazilian reporter subsequently described it: "Paulo Guerra passed through the military sieve and, being recognized as a serious man, was able to take office." [5] Legality had triumphed.

Meanwhile, President João Goulart was enjoying a similar taste of the strange workings of the legal process in Brazil. On the morning of the 1st he flew from Rio de Janeiro to Brasília, where he found no significant support against the insurgency. That evening he flew to Pôrto Alegre, the capital of the state of Rio Grande do Sul. Shortly afterward the President of the Brazilian Senate announced that the presidency was vacant, and Ranieri Mazzilli, the head of the Chamber of Deputies and next in the constitutional line of succession, was sworn in as Acting President.

Twelve hours later, with Goulart still in Brazil, these solemn proceedings received the ultimate sanction. Lyndon Johnson sent to Mazzilli a message conveying "my warmest good wishes on your installation as President," [6] and expressing admiration for "the resolute will of the Brazilian community to resolve [its] difficulties within a framework of constitutional democracy." Goulart, unable to interest the Third Army in a civil war, fled to nearby Uruguay on April 4.

In the course of a single day, a movement which had begun in the late 1950s and had been threatening to alter the balance of political and economic power in the most important state of Northeast Brazil collapsed like a house of cards. Military force, backed up by the

careful preparation of a group of civilian conspirators, prevailed in a sudden and seemingly effortless coup. The masses who were supposed to be behind Arraes did not lift a finger to help him. After some initial confusion in Recife during the uncertain hours of the morning and early afternoon, there was virtually no resistance to the takeover.

This marked the start of a time of great travail for the left. The new rulers would have to justify their actions. Blame would have to be assigned to those groups and individuals who "provoked" the military coup, which now, by virtue of its success, had been transformed into a "revolution." The winds of retribution were about to sweep across Northeast Brazil.

FIFTEEN 🌿

🌿 🌿 Aftermath

GREGÓRIO BEZERRA ALMOST DIDN'T MAKE IT to Palmares.[1] The police had thrown up several roadblocks along the way, but somehow let the tough, red-faced sexagenarian pass. When he finally reached the town where he had enjoyed such remarkable success as a Communist rural-syndicate organizer, elements from the state police and the Fourth Army immediately arrested him.

Fortunately for Gregório, the state police assumed responsibility for his safety. The Army officials in Palmares wanted to kill him on the spot. The military had not forgotten that in 1935 Gregório, then an Army sergeant, had played a leading role in the Communist uprising in Recife and had killed a lieutenant. It was now time to even the score. Some soldiers brought the ex-federal deputy to a nearby sugar mill, and would have finished him off but for the protests of the police.

So Gregório was taken back to Recife. There his luck turned for the worse. He fell into the clutches of Lieutenant-Colonel Darcy Villocq Viana, whose vindictiveness put Gregório's rugged physique to a severe test. The Colonel and his men first worked him over with iron pipes. A doctor who tried to intervene received a punch on the jaw for his trouble. They then stripped the old man to his underwear trunks. Colonel Villocq Viana was a man possessed, an avenging fury with a feel for the macabre. He ordered his men to

tie a rope around Gregório's neck and parade him through the streets of Recife.

The grisly procession did manage to turn a few stomachs, as on-lookers had to turn their heads and a couple of women fainted. The soldiers kept hitting Gregório, taunting him with shouts of "Communist" and "traitor." The spectacle reached a climax when the Colonel commanded that they pass by his own house, perhaps on the theory that the family that flays together, stays together. His wife, watching this parody of a Passion Week procession, broke into tears and begged him to stop. Gregório, in a last, defiant gesture, summoned up the energy to shout: "Here's what Western Christian civilization is like!" Unmoved, the Colonel bid his men to continue.

It was hard to imagine anyone Gregório's age surviving such an ordeal. Indeed, a story began to circulate that he had dropped dead from a heart attack. A local newspaper called this a "Communist rumor," [2] too late to stop an American correspondent from including it in a dispatch to New York. *Time* magazine subsequently reported Gregório's death,[3] which turned out to be much exaggerated.

Colonel Villocq Viana delivered his charge to one of Recife's prisons, but the white-haired Communist was in such a messy condition that the commanding officer of the prison would not accept him. So they took Gregório to a hospital and finally gave him some medical treatment. He was returned to the prison, where he managed to rehabilitate himself by performing exercises, in concert with a Catholic priest who had also been arrested after the coup and now shared his cell. He remained there for five years and was finally flown to Mexico in September, 1969, as one of the political prisoners freed in exchange for the return of kidnaped U.S. Ambassador to Brazil Burke Elbrick.

Joel Câmara had been leading a quiet, bourgeois existence ever since his release from Recife's House of Detention in December, 1963. Apart from writing up an account of his experiences in the countryside, he had completely forsworn his former life as a revolutionary, had finished his law studies, and was now doing legal work for a commercial firm in the city of Recife. On April 2, a lieutenant, a sergeant, and four enlisted men, all armed with rifles except for the

lieutenant, who carried a submachine gun, drove in a jeep to the office where Joel was working. They closed off the entire street and then sent word for Joel to come out with his hands raised. Bystanders were taken aback when the scrawny, buck-toothed youth emerged. Flattered by this impressive display of attention, the onetime Peasant League legal advisor surrendered himself to the patrol and was taken to prison. He luckily escaped physical abuse, but did spend forty-five days in a tiny cubicle. His father, concerned that the police might search their house for evidence which might be used against him, burned the only manuscript of his memoirs.

In the first days after the "revolution," the Army and the police (now under the control of the new state government) rounded up as many Peasant League leaders as they could find.[4] Clodomir Moraes was apprehended in a town in the interior. Assis Lemos, arrested in Paraíba, was brought to Recife, beaten up and imprisoned. Police invaded the plantation Galiléia in Vitória de Santo Antão and arrested Maria Celeste, the schoolteacher who had been leading Peasant League land invasions. They discovered the shack which contained Ted Kennedy's generator, and used this modest token of American aid as "evidence" of a plot to supply power to a radio transmitter which would broadcast subversive messages to the countryside. (The peasants' explanation that the generator was a gift from "President Kennedy" cut no ice with the police.[5]) The new state Secretary of Public Security ordered all Peasant Leagues closed down and all League material seized. In Bom Jardim Julião's brother Dequinho hid for a while in the fields and was finally caught and imprisoned. The most notable figure to escape the crackdown was Maria Ceales, Julião's ex-"secretary." For some reason the police wanted very badly to catch her, and left no stone unturned in an unsuccessful search.

Julião himself had a special fate awaiting him.[6] As a matter of poetic justice, if nothing else, he managed to avoid the indignity of a quick arrest. His career in the Northeast came to an end in a fashion befitting his role as a central figure in a revolution that never was.

At the time of the coup, he and Regina were living together in Brasília. Alexina had journeyed to Havana at the beginning of March in order to attend the wedding of their eldest daughter, who

was marrying an Ecuadorian student revolutionary. In late March Julião was back in Recife for a few days. He would return to Brasília to spend the Easter holidays with Regina, who was now well along in her pregnancy. Early in the morning of March 26 a close friend drove him to the Guararapes Airport for what was to be his last flight to the capital as a federal deputy. The main topic of their conversation was the impending visit of a German journalist who had once written in *Stern* a sensational story about Northeastern landlords torturing their peasants.

Gleaming skyscrapers neatly arranged in the red clay of an endless barren plateau project a splendid isolation which has become a hallmark of Brasília. The great distances separating the new capital from the nation's population centers were supposed to relieve the pressures on government officials and allow them to make decisions in a relaxed (if slightly rarefied) atmosphere. During the entire coup Brasília remained unruffled. There was a surrealistic quality to Goulart's quick visit on April 1 and the subsequent swearing-in of the Acting President—events played out against an ultramodern backdrop before a modest audience swallowed up by fast, empty spaces.

Conscious of his immunity from arrest, one of the privileges of a federal deputy, Julião continued to attend meetings of the Chamber of Deputies. But on April 7, as he entered the Chamber for the afternoon session, a friend warned him that the new government was about to suspend a number of legislators from office. Julião stayed in the building, and even made one of his infrequent speeches on the floor of the Chamber. As he was about to leave, he noticed a contingent of policemen outside, waiting for him. One of his colleagues had an official car at the door and offered him a ride. He slipped into the vehicle, managing to avoid the attention of the police.

That evening Julião disguised himself in the ragged clothing of a *candango*, the term for poor Northeasterners who left the region in search of work. He said good-bye to Regina and set out for Belo Horizonte in a truck filled with genuine *candangos*. By leaving Brasília, he was giving up the opportunity to seek asylum in one of the foreign embassies there. Not yet abandoning all hope, he had decided on an ingenious plan to throw his pursuers off the trail and take refuge in a place where no one would think to look for him.

Two days later, the government declared his removal from office.

On the afternoon of April 8 he arrived in the capital of the state of Minas Gerais, the site of his great triumph at the National Peasant's Congress in 1961. Wandering about the streets, he happened upon a rally celebrating the victory of the "revolution," and mingled with the crowd. Then he rested for a while at a small pension, where he went by the name of "Mr. Antônio."

Next came the difficult part of his odyssey. He set out from Belo Horizonte back *toward* Brasília—first by taxi to the city of Sete Lagôas, and then on foot through the back country. In the interior of the state he made a prearranged stop at the hut of a peasant family, where he paused for a few days. Here he was met by a friend from Pernambuco, who brought him some tragic news. Shortly after his disappearance from Brasília, a reporter had broadcast over a Recife radio program the news that he had been killed. His father, eighty-six years old, heard this and dropped dead from the shock.

Julião escaped from his sorrow by immersing himself in his natural surroundings. This brought him back full circle to his childhood on the plantation. As he continued on his trek, he began to relive his peasant fantasies. He might have been playing out scenes from his novel, *Irmão Juázeiro*, or from some as-yet unwritten tale of life in the countryside.

By early May he reached the Federal District. Instead of returning to Brasília, he went directly to a plantation in one of Brasília's satellite municipalities. Regina had already arranged for his arrival there, and had rented it for him. He was still "Mr. Antônio," now a bricklayer, dressed in peasant clothes, a growth of stubble on his face. During the day he did construction work on a small house. In the evenings he took to reading the Bible to his peasant companions.

On June 2 he received the news that two days earlier Regina had given birth to a baby girl. He scarcely had time to celebrate. The next morning, with a dense fog shrouding the plantation, a police patrol broke into the thatched hut that he was sharing with some peasants. He protested that he was only Mr. Antônio, a simple peasant, but his teeth and feet gave him away. The former were too cared for, the latter too soft.[7]

It was a long walk back to Brasília. His captors booked him and

then turned him over to the press for interviews and photographs. After these preliminaries, he was taken to a military prison, where he was treated passably well during a three-week sojourn.

On June 24, the Feast of São João, Francisco Julião returned to Recife. This was the day when his family customarily gathered at the plantation, and one of his sisters prepared the traditional holiday fare. But on this São João, Julião was not going to make it to Bom Jardim. He was flown into town in an Air Force plane and handed over to the Fourth Army.

They took him immediately to a jail in the suburb of Olinda, where from his cell he could see the São João bonfires in the distance. That night he suffered a severe attack of migraine headaches, the ailment that had plagued him for many years. To have to endure this without medication was merely an opener. Early in the morning a squad of soldiers came to transfer him to a more appropriate spot. They led him down a long, dark corridor, hit him several times on the back with a billy-club, and tossed him onto the cement floor of a tiny, tomb-like cell. At first he thought he was being buried alive. The migraines passed, but he came down with a bad case of the grippe. Once the darling of the international press, Julião now found himself in a lonely struggle for survival. With his Peasant League movement now smashed into oblivion, the ex-deputy fully realized that the Army would not be at all upset if he perished during the course of his confinement.

Meanwhile, he was replaced in the federal Chamber of Deputies by his alternate, Luís Pereira da Silva, a house-painter who had received 126 votes in the 1962 election.

The first weeks of the "revolution" were difficult for the entire rural labor movement in Pernambuco. Some landowners saw the coup as a signal that the "good old days" had returned, and meted out *ad hoc* retribution to peasants who had participated in the activities of the rural unions or Peasant Leagues. These would-be feudal lords and their gunmen administered beatings and other, more subtle forms of humiliation and torture.

Dan Kurzman, a reporter from the *Washington Post*, visited the area shortly after the coup and sent back an account of the situa-

tion[8]—much to the annoyance of the Americans in Recife, who were insisting that the new "revolutionary" government was performing superbly and that things couldn't be better. Kurzman's story was one of the very few critical reports on the "revolution" to be published in the U.S. The Fourth Army finally put an end to these barbarities. The landowners had made their point, however, and proceeded to ignore most of the rural labor legislation which the Goulart government had passed and the Arraes administration had enforced.

Four days after the coup, the new Secretary of Public Security in Pernambuco posted guidelines for law enforcement officials who had to deal with the rural labor movement.[9] The gist of this pronouncement was that the rights of the peasants were to be respected, and that the legitimate rural syndicates were not to be destroyed. As a practical matter, *de facto* control of the rural labor movement passed to the only leader the Fourth Army trusted—Padre Melo.[10]

His feud with Miguel Arraes in late 1963 turned out to be the best thing that ever happened to the young priest from Cabo. By the time of the coup, he was a full-fledged, well publicized opponent of the Governor, so that when the Army was looking for someone to tell them what to do about the rural labor movement, Padre Melo was the obvious choice. He became for a while an unofficial dictator, directing the Army and the police to intervene in virtually all the rural syndicates and naming new directors to replace the leaders he had removed.

Meanwhile, Padre Crespo found himself in trouble. Thanks to a couple of timely resignations, the new regime did not intervene in the state Federation, but in the postcoup hysteria newspaper articles began to appear criticizing the Padre for his "collaboration" with the Communists.[11] Crespo, it turned out, had sent a telegram to João Goulart expressing his support for the tepid agrarian reform measures the President had decreed at the now infamous March 13 rally.

Eventually the storm blew over and Padre Crespo remained at his post in SORPE. One reason for his survival was the fact that the Americans were not about to let their favorite Padre be purged. Someone from the USAID mission contacted a lawyer who had connections with officers in the Fourth Army and strongly urged

that the priest be spared.[12] Six months later Padre Crespo partici-pated in an open agreement between SORPE and the Cooperative League (CLUSA) which enabled the CIA to pump funds directly through its CLUSA cover into the cooperative movement in North-east Brazil.

With the fall of the Arraes government, the old politicians repre-senting the traditional power structure in Pernambuco assumed that they would move into the vacuum and run the state as they had in the pre-Arraes era. When the anti-Goulart movement had begun, there was no reason for them to believe that the Armed Forces would not return to their barracks once the "crisis" had passed and order restored. But in the days following the coup, one could detect indications that this time things might be different.

On the national scene the military leaders who had executed the coup chose one of their own, Marshal Humberto Castelo Branco, to be President.[13] Their civilian colleagues applauded and the Con-gress, which had no alternative, meekly ratified this decision. Castelo Branco was to serve out Goulart's term (to 1965), and after that the civilian politicians took it for granted that the presidency would re-turn to civilian hands. They chose to downgrade statements by high military officials indicating that it was now up to the Armed Forces to clean out the Brazilian body politic and set the country irrevoca-bly along the road to modernization. The suggestion was unmistaka-ble that important elements within the military felt that civilians could no longer be trusted with the nation's fate, and that it was now up to the Armed Forces to develop Brazil's long recognized poten-tial for greatness.

In addition, two days before Castelo Branco's inauguration, the military issued what was euphemistically termed the "First Institu-tional Act," a fiat that gave broad powers to the new Chief Execu-tive. The most significant of these powers authorized him to suspend summarily the political rights of any Brazilian for ten years. This meant that anyone subjected to "cassation," as this process was called, could not hold any government office, or even vote. The first list contained some obvious names—Goulart, Arraes, Julião—as well as some big surprises. Ex-President Juscelino Kubitschek and ex-President Jânio Quadros were included. Neither man could be con-

sidered "subversive" by any stretch of the imagination. But they were political threats to the new military rulers—another hint that the generals might be out of their barracks for a while. There were also indications that charges of corruption might qualify a politician for "cassation," lending further credence to the military's determination to clean house. President Castelo Branco, under the terms of the Institutional Act, could continue to issue "cassations" until June 15. Scanning these lists of names as they appeared in the newspapers became a national pastime for the next two months.

In Pernambuco an immediate manifestation of the military's preeminence occurred when Cid Sampaio tried to reap some reward for his anti-Arraes efforts. Cid had been one of the earliest supporters of the conspiracy, at both state and national levels. He felt he was now in line for an important appointment, and cast a covetous eye on SUDENE. Control of the regional developmental agency would certainly enhance his status as one of the leading industrialists of the Northeast. But there was one major obstacle to his ambitions. One of the leading military conspirators had been General Cordeiro de Farias, the ex-Governor of Pernambuco whom Cid had attacked so vigorously during his own ascent to the governorship. Cordeiro de Farias was now a key behind-the-scenes figure and wielded great influence with the high command. He also had a long memory. He not only vetoed any appointment for Cid, but even threatened to have him prosecuted, or subjected to "cassation," for his acceptance of Communist Party support during the 1958 gubernatorial campaign. So Cid did not have much of an opportunity to savor the success of the "revolution," as he had all he could do to blunt the General's wrath.

Though the military promised to "wipe the slate clean," it did manage to make certain exceptions to the standards it followed in its purge. Multimillionaire José Emírio de Moraes, the man who provided most of the money behind Miguel Arraes, kept his seat in the Senate and remained untouched by Brazil's new rulers.

The Paulo Guerra administration took over the state government of Pernambuco with only a few minor hitches. Miguel Arraes proved to be no problem. He was quickly trundled off to the tiny island of Fernando de Noronha off the coast of Northeast Brazil in

the South Atlantic, where he was imprisoned in a military installation. An attempt was made to include Padre Melo in the new state government, but the suggested appointment was not approved by higher ecclesiastical authorities. The Governor named Marco Antônio Maciel as his Secretary of Labor. A local newspaper called Marco Antônio a "soldier of democracy." [14] It was only later that someone discovered that under state law Marco Antônio, fresh out of the University, was too young to be in the cabinet. The law required cabinet members to be at least twenty-five years of age. So Governor Guerra had to find another Secretary of Labor.

On April 2 Mayor Pelópidas Silveira was arrested and imprisoned. Following the precedent set by the state legislature, Recife's City Council voted 20 to 1 to oust Pelópidas. "I have nothing against him personally," one of the councilmen commented afterward, "but we can't have a Socialist-Communist running around loose." [15] The Vice Mayor was immediately sworn in to fill the office.

In the days and weeks that followed the Fourth Army and the police rounded up anyone who fell within their broad definition of "subversive." Reports giving instances of their tough-minded approach to the task spread quickly throughout the state.[16] For example, Regina de Castro's estranged husband, a lawyer with SUDENE, went to visit his two children shortly after the coup. Unfortunately for him, they were staying at Julião's house, which the police had under surveillance. He was placed under arrest when he tried to enter. One of his SUDENE colleagues, who happened to be of Chinese extraction, was detained by the Army and found to have in his possession a letter written in Cantonese. He was held for fifteen days, until his captors found someone trustworthy to translate the letter. It turned out to be filled with family news from an uncle in São Paulo. Another SUDENE technician, who was in Washington at the time of the coup, had visited the Soviet Embassy in search of some literature on agricultural development. As is their custom, the F.B.I. photographed and duly noted his visit. When he returned to Recife, the police called him in and asked him to explain his business at the Embassy—a chilling example of the F.B.I.'s close cooperation with its opposite numbers in Latin America.

The authorities searched the homes of a number of intellectuals, and discovered and confiscated subversive books such as Graham Greene's *Our Man in Havana,* and Bertrand Russell's *Why I Am Not a Christian.* The jails were soon bursting at the seams and there were ugly incidents of torture. The police swept leftist literature of all kinds from the newsstands and bookstores, without ever bothering to compensate the owners. Recife's Communist newspaper was of course immediately shut down, and several weeks after the coup the city's other leftist paper ceased to be published. The three conservative newspapers gave the government no cause to worry. General Alves Bastos praised them by noting that they "have behaved very well, not bringing upon themselves any restriction on account of their actions." [17]

The "Revolution in Forty Hours" suffered a rather emphatic termination. One of the first things the Army did was to invade the headquarters of Paulo Freire's Cultural Extension Service (SEC) at the University of Recife, and confiscate all the materials which were being used in the literacy program. Freire himself was in Brasília when the coup began.[18] He returned to Recife on a safe-conduct pass obtained by one of the priests who worked for him. Under virtual house arrest, he was finally dragged off to jail in mid-June.[19] A number of his colleagues were also imprisoned.

Freire's experience illustrated one of the tragic characteristics of the immediate postcoup period. There was very little coordination or control over the repressive activities of the various Army colonels and captains who enjoyed command functions and of the various "delegates" who performed civilian law enforcement functions under the state Secretary of Public Security. For more than twenty-four hours after soldiers took Freire from his home, his wife and friends were unable to find out whether he was safe and where he was. Fourth Army officials at first denied that he had been arrested. They finally discovered that some captain had taken it upon himself to throw SEC's Director into jail.

During this time Justino Alves Bastos was too busy traveling around in the state from town to town, receiving homage from the local political bosses, to control his henchmen. Governor Paulo Guerra displayed no interest in restraining the hounds.

Ironically, these Communist-hunters caught very few real Communists. The leadership of the Party in Pernambuco disappeared when the coup began. Their contingency plans proved quite effective during the crisis, with the result that Hiram Pereira, Aluísio Falcão, and the rest of the Party's top brass made perfect getaways. Pereira escaped in clerical garb. (The ever-charitable Padre Melo subsequently denounced the priest who had helped him.) The only ones caught were marginal types, such as the artist Abelardo da Hora, the Party's leading local intellectual Paulo Cavalcanti, and of course Gregório Bezerra.

Virtually the entire national leadership of the Party, including Luís Carlos Prestes, also managed to escape. The most important Party figure captured by the Army was Carlos Marighella, who was shot in the stomach in a Rio movie theater. Marighella survived to break with the Party and become the leader of Brazil's urban guerrillas. In 1969 the authorities did not make the mistake they made in 1964. The police shot him to death in a street ambush.

One sector which suffered heavily in the repression was the Catholic left.[20] Many were arrested. Several priests were forced to leave Pernambuco. The authorities virtually destroyed the Basic Education Movement (MEB), the Church's literacy and adult education program. The MEB primer, *To Live Is To Struggle*, was declared subversive and confiscated. (Professor Neale Pearson has written: "One Army Intelligence Officer in Fourth Army Headquarters, Recife, Pernambuco, told this writer in August, 1965, that the contents of [the primer] themselves justified the April, 1964, Revolution." [21])

Coincidental to the crackdown on the Catholic left was the arrival of Dom Hélder Câmara in Recife. The Archbishop of Olinda and Recife, Dom Carlos Coelho, had died on March 7, and one week later the progressive-minded Dom Hélder, a Northeasterner who had been serving as an auxiliary bishop in Rio de Janeiro, was named to the post. Brazil's ultraconservatives had already marked Dom Hélder as one of the nation's "Communist clergy" because of his constant advocacy of reform and his disagreements with the staunchly traditional Cardinal of Rio de Janeiro. The diminutive prelate could not have picked a worse time to come to Recife. He ar-

rived on April 10, and the very next day armed soldiers invaded his Palace.

The pretext for this incident was the presence in the Palace of Arraes's sister.[22] Violeta had worked with Dom Hélder in Rio and was an old friend. She had heard rumors that the Army was about to ship her off to join her brother on Fernando de Noronha, and had gone to ask help from Dom Hélder. A squad of Army reservists, dressed in sport shirts and carrying submachine guns, followed her into the Palace. Other troops surrounded the premises. Dom Hélder, who was lunching with the Bishop of Sergipe, telephoned General Alves Bastos to complain that this was hardly a way to greet a new prelate. The soldiers eventually left and Violeta was permitted to return to her home. There she remained under house arrest until May 29, when she and her French husband were released and flew to Paris.

The same day his Palace was invaded, Dom Hélder and the rest of the bishops of Northeast Brazil issued a statement which expressed the hope that "the innocent, unavoidably detained in the first moment of inevitable confusion, would be before too long restored to liberty; and that even the guilty will be free of vexation and treated with the respect every human creature deserves." [23]

This gentle plea of course went unanswered, and Dom Hélder settled into his new post amid rumors of his imminent arrest. One may speculate that if he had made a vigorous public protest against the excesses being committed by the military and the police, he would probably have been imprisoned, and that this might have provoked such a reaction that the repression might have been halted, or at least tempered. On the other hand, since he had just arrived in the Northeast, he was not in a very strong position to speak out on matters pertaining to the region. Dom Hélder decided to sit tight and try to work quietly behind the scenes. In this way he survived the repression, and soon became the only public figure in the Northeast who could protest against what the "revolution" was doing.

Mention has already been made of the surprises on the first list of "cassations" issued by the Castelo Branco regime. One of the inclusions which caused broad international repercussions was the name of Celso Furtado. SUDENE's Superintendent, the apolitical techni-

cian, found himself excluded from public service in Brazil for ten years. Even those Americans who applauded the coup had difficulty reconciling their belief in the "progressiveness" of the new regime with this apparently senseless sacrifice of one of Brazil's most gifted economists.

The axe had actually fallen several days before the publication of the first list, when the Fourth Army intervened in SUDENE and summarily removed Furtado from his post. A general was named to replace him. On April 6 Furtado cleaned off his desk and attended the inauguration of the new Superintendent. Then he went straight to the airport and flew to Rio. He remained there for a short time, after which he left Brazil in *de facto* exile.

Conservative elements in Recife had always regarded SUDENE as a hotbed of Communist penetration. On April 3 a journalist referred to the agency as a "well equipped Communist machine." [24] It is not surprising, therefore, that attempts were made to discredit Furtado's organization. The Deputy Superintendent was arrested and jailed, along with several other technicians. (Naílton Santos managed to hide out in several hotels before escaping south to Rio and then out of the country.) The Army began several separate investigations into "Communist infiltration" of SUDENE. The press printed all kinds of charges, but there was a noticeable lack of substantiation.

Indeed, in the immediate postcoup period, the new regime and its enthusiastic supporters let loose a barrage of accusations creating the impression that their "revolution" had narrowly averted a Communist take-over. There were allegations of an elaborate Communist plan for a coup to be executed on April 2 (the accusers later changed the date to May 1, surely a more suitable day), and of a "blacklist" containing the names of persons to be liquidated by the "reds" once they seized power. The newspapers constantly informed their readers of the discovery of material which documented these grave charges, but seldom disclosed what these documents actually said.

But then on April 7, the authorities in Pernambuco finally made public the proof they had promised—incontrovertible evidence of the planned "red revolution" which the courage, devotion, and diligence of the Brazilian Armed Forces had nipped in the bud. In a

storehouse belonging to the Resale and Colonization Company, a state land reform agency which had been under the control of the infamous Miguel Arraes, the Army, and the police discovered 10,000 coveralls. Yes, 10,000 coveralls. It did not matter that there were no guns nearby, nor were the coveralls dyed red. As Wanden-kolk Wanderley declared in an impassioned speech to Recife's Municipal Council on April 10, who could ask for clearer proof that Arraes and his Communist friends had planned to issue these uniforms to the peasant militia they were about to create in order to take power in Pernambuco.[25]

For sheer nonsense, the affair of the coveralls topped even the uproar over the apprehension in Rio of nine Chinese—members of a trade mission from mainland China—carrying American dollars. Red Chinese with money equaled subversion. It was as simple as that. The ordinary processes of logical thought were held in abeyance during this particular phase of the new Brazilian "revolution."

Americans living and working in Brazil, as private citizens or as U.S. officials, hailed the "revolution" with near unanimous enthusiasm and gave full backing to the new regime. Ambassador Lincoln Gordon was the head cheerleader.[26] On May 5 in a speech to the Brazilian National War College he solemnly declared that the action of the Brazilian Army "may well take its place alongside the initiation of the Marshall Plan, the ending of the Berlin blockade, the defeat of Communist aggression in Korea, and the solution of the Cuban-missile base crisis as one of the critical points of inflection in mid-twentieth-century world history." [27]

The offices of the United States Information Service (USIS), both in Rio and Recife, did their part to promote the new regime. They did not hesitate to distribute the most incredible "documents" issued by the government to justify the "revolution." [28]

The acme of U.S. support (apart from a tremendous increase in American aid to Brazil immediately after the coup) came from the American business community in São Paulo. Despite the favorable press the "revolution" was receiving in the United States, these gentlemen were upset at the few articles and editorials which took the new regime to task for excesses such as the "cassations" of Juscelino Kubitschek and Celso Furtado. So they organized "truth squads" to

travel to the U.S. and "set the record straight." [29] They even contemplated hiring a press agent to write laudatory pieces on Brazil which would then be placed in American newspapers and magazines.

The USAID mission in Recife found that the "revolution" solved the problem of how to deal with SUDENE. The Brazilian agency adopted a policy of full cooperation with the Americans. In effect what this meant was that American notions about what was best for Northeast Brazil would now go unchallenged.

In early June President Castelo Branco visited Recife and received a conquering hero's welcome. A ceremonial troop of mounted horsemen, organized by Paulo Guerra as one of his first official acts as Governor, led the parade through the downtown streets. Gilberto Freyre, whose enthusiasm for the "revolution" knew no bounds—he had recently written that Castelo Branco was "the Brazilian de Gaulle, but without the latter's arrogance." [30]— stood next to the President on a reviewing stand lined with brass and local dignitaries. During his forty-eight hour stay, Castelo Branco accepted the titles of "Citizen of Recife" and "Citizen of Pernambuco" and was awarded the Guararapes Medal of Merit. He spoke at a meeting to SUDENE officials, signed a road construction agreement with USAID and was guest of honor at a gala luncheon sponsored by the businessmen of the state.

The President's visit symbolized the dawning of a new era in the Northeast. Despite the hopes of some ultraconservatives, the "revolution" did not set the calendar back ten years. Though the military had wiped out the Peasant Leagues and the populist political forces led by Miguel Arraes, these movements had left a lasting mark on the regional and national consciousness. Castelo Branco, who was a Northeasterner by birth, reiterated his determination to promote the development of the region. Forward looking businessmen saw the "revolution" as their golden opportunity to solve the Northeast's problems by expanding and rationalizing private enterprise. In so doing they could count on the full cooperation of USAID. The Fourth Army, the repository of ultimate power, maintained law, order, and stability with a firm, if at times iron, hand. A surge of optimism buoyed backers of the "revolution" who now sought to create a "new Northeast."

If one were looking for a symbol of the totality of the demise of the forces for radical change, a sentimental choice might have been the arrest of Zezé of Galiléia in mid-June. The police detained for questioning and then imprisoned the old man who had once enjoyed worldwide celebrity status as the President of the first Peasant League.

Those who had taken an active part in the precoup movements for radical change and did not flee from the Northeast underwent a period of great anguish, which was often both physical and mental. The usual sequence involved anxiety, investigation, arrest, and imprisonment, for varying lengths of time. Most of those who suffered were totally unprepared for their ordeals.

The reactions of the losers ranged up and down the emotional scale. A number of them recriminated against the Communists, who had encouraged agitation without giving serious thought to the possibility of a military coup, and had then vanished, leaving others to pay the price of unpreparedness. Some criticized Arraes for not mobilizing armed resistance to the coup. Others criticized Furtado for not giving SUDENE a forthrightly political thrust. Still others rationalized, rather limply, that any violent clash in the Northeast would have provoked intervention, à la Santo Domingo, by the U.S. Marines. A pervasive sense of depression and deep disillusionment prevailed, so much so that upon their release from jail many of these former activists could not even bring themselves to read newspapers.

With the benefit of hindsight it is easy to understand why things ended as they did in 1964. The recent Cuban Revolution, though scarcely comparable to what was happening in the Northeast, frightened people into magnifying into ridiculous proportions the first human stirrings of a peasantry which had endured an animal-like existence for centuries. Events, especially as they unfolded in the developed center-south, outpaced the slow process of awakening which was an essential prerequisite to effective political mobilization in the Northeast.

Francisco Julião, more romantic than revolutionary, nicely filled his original role as catalyst and messianic symbol. But the rush of events tempted him to undertake tasks for which he was manifestly

ill-suited. He was, in the end, a complex man who lacked the toughness of body and spirit to execute his own idyllic visions.

Those who sought radical change through legal, constitutional means sorely underestimated the tenacity of the local power structure, which was not about to hand over its privileges. They also overestimated the extent and strength of their own popular following. Miguel Arraes and his supporters hoped to apply the rhetoric of democracy to the reality of the Northeast. They failed to realize the inherent limitations of democratic action, which tends to fade before tanks and troops.

Celso Furtado's attempt to develop the Northeast through the mechanism of rational planning and implementation by an independent federal agency exercising wide powers failed because of the fatal interdependence of economic and political development. As he noted later, in a somewhat rueful understatement: "The struggle for power between the populist leaders and the traditional ruling class is the crux of a political conflict which tends to thwart every attempt at coherent planning by those who from time to time govern the country." [31]

Finally, the course of events in the early 1960's provides an instructive case study of U.S. intervention in Latin America, and the political role of foreign aid. Despite the idealistic trappings of the Alliance for Progress and concern some U.S. officials voiced for the impoverished masses of Northeast Brazil, it was clear from the outset that security interests were always paramount. From this perspective, the work of USAID and the CIA must be deemed a great success. The forces of radicalism were soundly defeated, the status quo remained secure, and the Northeast did not become "another Cuba."

How these short-range triumphs will look thirty years from now is another matter entirely. While the Northeast has remained relatively tranquil in recent years, the political forces of the entire country are polarizing at extremes formed by an increasingly authoritarian and repressive military regime and an opposition that has no choice but to function as an urban guerrilla movement. The precoup turmoil may yet prove to have been Brazil's 1905.

EPILOGUE
Or, What Ever Happened to Northeast Brazil?

IN 1969 PRESIDENT RICHARD M. NIXON SENT Governor Nelson A. Rockefeller on a series of visits to Latin America. The purpose of the mission was "to consult with the leaders of the other American republics on [Nixon's] behalf, and to help [the Nixon] administration develop policies for the conduct of [U.S.] international relations throughout the Western Hemisphere."[1] Governor Rockefeller and his entourage did not stop in Recife, nor anywhere else in Northeast Brazil.

Antônio Callado wrote numerous newspaper articles about the pre-1964 ferment in the Northeast, but after the "revolution" he chose the format of the novel to convey his ultimate interpretation of the debacle. *Quarup,* published in 1967,[2] describes the radicalization of a Pernambucan priest whose dream of setting up an Indian community structure embodying the pure communism of the Bible and modeled after the Guarani Indian Republic established by the Jesuits in the eighteenth century gives way to an active involvement in contemporary efforts to mobilize the peasants of the Northeast. The supporting characters suggest figures from real life, except that they all display unswervingly heroic qualities and carry on their struggle even after enduring postcoup imprisonment and torture. In the novel's final scene the protagonist, by now an ex-priest, rides off toward the *sertão* to join up with an insurgency led by refugees from the Pernambuco movement.

Callado's *roman à clef* reflects escapism from a sense of disappoint-

221

ment over the failure of the Brazilian left to offer any serious resistance to the military coup. It used to be fashionable to rationalize such passivity by parroting the maxim that "the Brazilians are a nonviolent people." But recent events, including reports of the systematic genocide of Brazilian Indians, belie this sanguine gloss of the Brazilian national character. The truth of the matter, *Quarup* notwithstanding, is that the military elements that seized power on April 1, 1964, completely crushed the movement for radical change in the Northeast, and those who participated in the movement have either escaped into exile or remain in the region but without any stomach for reviving their precoup activities.

Julião, for example, somehow managed to survive his ordeal in the dungeon, where he was kept in solitary confinement, unwashed and unshaven, for two months. The military then transferred him to a more comfortable prison cell, and in October 1964, put him into a spacious room in the Firemen's Barracks on the outskirts of Recife. During this time he penned a lyrical account of his last days as a free man and smuggled it out to a publisher. *Até Quarta, Isabela* (*Until Wednesday, Isabela*) takes the form of a letter to his new daughter, a beautiful, blonde, blue-eyed child. It is by far the best thing he has ever written.

For a while he shared his accommodations with an illustrious roommate, Miguel Arraes, who had been brought back to Recife from Fernando de Noronha island. The two men had ample time to discuss their previous differences, and when Arraes was transferred, they parted the best of friends.

In the meantime Regina, who remained free, was making every effort to secure Julião's release. After the euphoria of the first weeks of the "revolution" had passed, the military government found itself in a position of having to find legal justification for holding its prisoners. The civilian authorities preferred one set of accusations against Julião, while the Armed Forces brought charges of their own, which were processed in a military court.[3] Regina, who had been trained as a lawyer, helped file a petition for a writ of habeas corpus with the Brazilian Supreme Court, which had jurisdiction over the civilian charges. The writ was granted, and Julião was released on September 27, 1965.

He immediately left Recife and flew to Rio, where he lived quietly and clandestinely for a month. Then, on October 27, as a result of the military's displeasure with the results of state elections which had just been held, the Castelo Branco regime decreed its Second Institutional Act, dissolving all political parties and making the military's rule more openly dictatorial.

As soon as he heard about Act II, Antônio Callado realized that the "hard-line" elements within the Armed Forces would crack down again on suspected subversives, so he contacted Julião and advised him to take refuge in an embassy. Julião's first reaction was to disguise himself, and he turned up at Callado's house with his hair slicked down and wearing a wildly colored shirt. "He looked more Julião than ever," Callado recently recalled, "like some mystic from the *sertão.*" [4]

Initial efforts to find an embassy that would accept him were fruitless. The Chilean Embassy, which had sheltered many fugitives in April, 1964, refused to allow him to enter, as did the Algerian Embassy. At first the only sympathetic foreigners were, curiously enough, the Indonesians and the Bolivians. Julião was not keen to end up in either country. Finally, the Mexicans agreed to take him. So Julião in his disguise and a very nervous Regina crouched on the floor of Callado's Volkswagen, and the journalist drove them to the safety of the Mexican Embassy.

The Brazilian authorities granted him the customary safe-conduct pass, and he flew to Mexico. Regina, along with Isabela and the two children from her first marriage, joined him there. They lived for a while in Mexico City and then took up residence in Cuernavaca. His escape proved fortunate, for the military tribunal subsequently convicted him *in absentia* and sentenced him to nineteen years in prison.

Hampered by occasional illnesses and without any reliable source of income, Julião still manages to retain his good spirits and has not stopped thinking and dreaming about his beloved Northeast. Meanwhile in the district of Caxangá on the edge of Recife, an old friend lives in his rambling house amid memories of the past, trying in vain to preserve it from the ravages of time and the elements.

After leaving the Firemen's Barracks in Recife, Miguel Arraes

found himself the object of a tug-of-war between elements of the Armed Forces. The Supreme Court ordered his release in mid-April of 1965, and President Castelo Branco decreed that the Court's decision be upheld. But "hard-line" army officers investigating his alleged Communist activities kept arresting him. This harassment continued until late May, when Arraes took asylum in the Algerian Embassy and was allowed to leave the country. He flew to Algiers, where he has been residing ever since. A Brazilian military court has sentenced him to twenty-three years of imprisonment.

Other figures in exile include Paulo Freire, Clodomir Moraes, and Maria Ceales. Pelópidas Silveira, Joel Câmara, João Alfredo, and Paulo Cavalcanti are among those who have served prison terms and are now living quiet, absolutely nonpolitical lives in Recife.

From the very moment they seized power, the military rulers of Brazil stressed their determination to install a "new order" in their country. Their mission was to modernize the nation, to bring about necessary reforms, to eliminate corruption from public life, and to destroy all traces of Communism. Or so they said. A widely distributed propaganda poster announced that "until 1964, Brazil was the country of the future; and then, the future arrived."

Since their control over the country was virtually absolute, there was nothing to prevent the generals from decreeing basic reforms. The opportunity was theirs, but they shrank from it.

In Pernambuco, they returned political power into the hands of the closely knit family groups that ran things before the rise of Miguel Arraes. All political activity of course remained under the watchful eye of the Fourth Army, but Pernambuco's elite gave the military no problems. Paulo Guerra finished out Arraes's term as Governor, to be succeeded by Nilo Coelho, whose family owns almost all of the western part of the state. The fact that both men supported Arraes in the 1962 elections did not disqualify them in the eyes of the military.

Within the charade which passed for politics, no one looked after the interests of the poor. An "urban renewal" in Recife underscored the results of this lack of representation. The Mayor forcibly removed over 300 families living in shanties by a river near the center of town, and relocated them in a little valley behind the airport.[5]

They found themselves out of sight, cut off from easy access to the city, and unable to eke out any kind of living.

The Army and the police have kept a tight lid on any political activity which might challenge the status quo. Only the university students have protested vocally, but their occasional rallies and marches have been violently repressed. The presence of informers and the technique of random arrests have successfully demoralized the students. Six bombs exploded in Recife between March and July of 1966, but under the circumstances lending some credence to the popular belief that they were set off by "hard-line" elements within the Army.

The only real voice of dissent in the Northeast belonged to Dom Hélder Câmara.[6] Recife's Archbishop quickly moved into the political vacuum created by the military, and offered a glimmer of hope to those elements of the middle and lower classes who had once looked to Miguel Arraes for leadership. The military could not muzzle Dom Hélder, and he spoke of the need to transform the feudal society which had reduced the region's peasants to a subhuman state. He urged the formation of a new mentality that would enable urban and rural workers alike to free themselves from the chains of poverty, disease, and ignorance. His constant emphasis was upon nonviolence, in the tradition of Mahatma Gandhi and Martin Luther King.

In 1966 Dom Hélder faced his first direct challenge from the military when the bishops of the Northeast issued a manifesto protesting the plight of the sugar workers. A number of Army officers considered the document "subversive" and tried to prevent its publication. But Dom Hélder managed to gain the support of President Castelo Branco. Several generals were shifted from the Northeast, and the document was released.

This confrontation and its outcome provoked the wrath of Pernambuco's conservative establishment, and right-wingers began a campaign to vilify him and to label him a "Communist." Gilberto Freyre mounted an especially vicious attack against the Archbishop, and managed to accuse him of being a "Brazilian Dr. Goebbels" and a "Brazilian Kerensky" in the course of a single newspaper article.[7]

In the years that followed Dom Hélder and his supporters issued

several more documents, including an eloquent tract entitled *Development Without Justice,* protesting urban working conditions in the Northeast,[8] and a recent sequel, *Northeast: The Forbidden Man.* But the difficulty that they were never able to overcome was that they were confronting political problems without any semblance of political power of their own.

Those who had the power had their own ideas about how to develop the Northeast. Pernambuco's progressive industrialists and businessmen enjoyed control of the state government, backing from the Fourth Army, and enthusiastic support from USAID. They embarked on an ambitious plan which sought to attract new industries to the Northeast, stimulate public investment in the region's infrastructure (transportation, health, education, hydroelectric projects, etc.), and increase agricultural production, especially in the sugar zone. They listened closely to their USAID advisors, and turned the Northeast into a test tube for development, American-style.

Not to be confused by the facts, the promoters of the new strategy almost immediately hailed its success in a noisy burst of ballyhoo. They announced the dawn of a "new Northeast." A series of articles published in a national magazine and purporting to be on-scene reports described the region's growth in the most glowing terms.[9] (No one seemed to notice or care that the articles were paraphrased directly from promotional literature.[10]) Things reached a crescendo in August, 1967, when President Castelo Branco's successor and his Cabinet spent an entire week in the Northeast issuing proclamations affirming the wondrous development of the region.

One cannot deny that Recife and other Northeastern cities have enjoyed a remarkable expansion of their industrial capabilities over the past six years. The new factories and the increase in the number of automobiles on the streets are the most visible signs of progress. Yet a glimpse beneath the veneer suggests that the din of publicity celebrating the "new Northeast" is woefully premature.[11]

The push toward industrialization derives its impetus from an imaginative tax incentive device. A company doing business in Brazil may invest or reinvest up to 50 per cent of its annual federal income tax instead of paying it to the government. The particular investment requires approval by SUDENE. Investors may also obtain

226

credit on very liberal terms from the Bank of Northeast Brazil and from some state developmental agencies. An aggressive promotional program has publicized these investment opportunities.

By the end of 1968 statistics released by SUDENE indicated that new industries either already operative or in the planning stage would provide 123,300 new jobs. SUDENE claims that every job directly created would in turn stimulate four more jobs.

There are several difficulties with the industrialization program. First of all, it is still on a scale far too small to make a meaningful dent. About 50 per cent of the available work force in the greater Recife area is unemployed or underemployed. The population is increasing at a dizzy clip. The truth of the matter is that the developers of the "new Northeast" have been running in order to stand still.

Despite the continuing magnitude of the problem, murmurs of discontent have been heard from industrialists in Rio and São Paulo, who would rather invest in the center-south and earn more with their money. At the same time other underdeveloped and undeveloped regions of Brazil have obtained similar tax incentives, which enable them to compete with the Northeast for capital.

In addition, the new industries in the Northeast are naturally utilizing modern machinery, which demands fewer, more highly skilled workers. The existing manpower pool in the region is for the most part untrained and illiterate, although efforts are being directed toward vocational education.

The capital which has been coming into the Northeast takes the form of either new industry or investment in existing industry for purposes of expansion and modernization. In the latter case Northeastern entrepreneurs have often been forced to pay a 10 per cent "bonus" (euphemism for bribe or "kickback") to the outside investor in order to obtain these funds. Several foreign companies (American, French, and Japanese) doing business in the center-south have also found it advantageous to set up factories in the Northeast under the new law.

The infusion of fresh capital has neither broken the grip of the family groups which control the region's economy nor stimulated any improvements of conditions within existing industries. The new

investors are interested primarily in the maintenance of a good business climate. They find it expedient to work within the structure and not "rock the boat" by competing with the concentration of economic power within the region.

At the same time, workers in the textile mills and other older industries have had to accept less than the minimum wage set by law. Though living costs keep increasing, the federal government has allowed wages to lag behind as one of its arsenal of anti-inflationary measures. Because of the manpower surplus in the region, workers find it unwise to strike. Trade unions continue to exist, but under the domination of management or under the leadership of men apprehensive of what the Army does to anyone it labels an "agitator."

Occasionally a glimmer of meaningful reform flickers, such as SUDENE's attempt in 1968 to include in its Fourth Master Plan a requirement that new industries adopt profit-sharing plans for their workers and develop ways to involve workers in the management of the enterprise. This was by no means a subversive plot. SUDENE was merely implementing changes which were specifically declared desirable by the new federal Constitution promulgated by the military government in 1964. But a howl of protest both in the Northeast and the center-south forced SUDENE to withdraw the proposal. "Could you imagine," a Recife journalist explained, "some Negro sitting on the administrative council of a company, asking to see the books, complaining about common practices like a family company paying domestic maids out of company funds. It would be impossible. The cultural level here is too low. The workers would be manipulated to make trouble. Also to have workers helping to administer their own factories is socialism."

Meanwhile, interest in investment opportunities in the Northeast has stimulated a demand for another type of entrepreneur, the local consultant, an indispensable on-scene contact who can guide the prospective investor through the legal and practical intricacies of setting up a business in the region. This sort of work can be quite rewarding. One Recife consultant is making in excess of the equivalent of $30,000 per year. As he recently noted in an interview: "There is much money to be made in the Northeast."

The Northeast continues to suffer an unfavorable balance of

trade. The prices the region receives for its exports are below the prices the region pays for imports. Critics of the current industrialization program maintain it has yet to reverse this net capital outflow, a basic cause of the Northeast's underdevelopment.

An interesting feature of the "new Northeast" concerns what has happened to SUDENE and USAID. The demise of Celso Furtado stripped SUDENE of its glamorous mystique. While Furtado was spending a year in exile in Chile, teaching for another year at Yale, and then settling down as a professor of economics at the Sorbonne in Paris, SUDENE ceased to function as an independent entity responsible directly to the President, but in a governmental reorganization became a part of the federal Ministry of the Interior. The shock caused by Furtado's dimissal, the subsequent psychological depression suffered by the agency and a cutback in funds as a result of the government's anti-inflationary policy came close to destroying SUDENE. That it has managed to survive at all must count as a bright spot of the post-1964 period.

After the "revolution," SUDENE-USAID relations improved tremendously. Brazil's military rulers made it clear that they would tolerate no obstruction of developmental policies approved in Washington and eagerly embraced by those now in charge of the Brazilian economy. SUDENE would cooperate, or else, so that to a degree the agency had to become a rubber stamp for USAID projects.

By 1966 the number of USAID operatives in the Northeast exceeded 150. Some of their work was consistent with the specifics and/or the philosophy of Furtado's original Master Plan and the Bohan Report. Thus USAID provided loans and technical assistance for several ambitious hydroelectric projects which greatly increased the region's power supply. American aid helped to create roads, wells, irrigation facilities, and health posts.

Other USAID efforts have been of questionable value. A widely heralded program to stimulate small rural industries which would be financed solely by local capital proved for the most part unworkable. An attempt to remake the educational system in the American mold failed both in the Northeast and elsewhere because of widespread, determined resistance from students and others. The training of policemen in riot control under USAID's so-called Public Safety Pro-

gram has evoked recognition and resentment as an American effort to strengthen the status quo against any sort of popular unrest. A number of Northeasterners have expressed serious doubts about the "ABC Crusade," a literacy program administered by American and Brazilian Presbyterians and supported by Food for Peace. The "Crusade" rejects Paulo Freire's philosophy of *conscientização*, or making the illiterate aware and thus critical of his position in the social system, and instead seeks to train him to accept things as they are and make the best of them.

As of June 30, 1968, USAID had expended $249,462,000 in loans and grants to the Northeast.[12] An additional $40 million had already been obligated to ongoing projects.

SUDENE's industrial-promotion program and the various USAID projects just described left virtually untouched the Northeast's major problem—the sugar industry. The machinery in the mills remained antiquated, the feudal mentality of most mill and plantation owners persisted, and the misery of the sugar workers and their families actually increased. In 1968 a nutrition study of a sample group of rural workers in the area around Palmares revealed that they work consuming fewer calories than in 1962.[13] A French newspaper reported that in one small town in the sugar zone in southern Pernambuco "under 'normal' conditions all the infants born between the months of June and December 1968 have died." [14] In 1967 several mills near Palmares went bankrupt, and reports of widespread starvation reached Recife.[15] One story described desperate peasants eating rats to stay alive. The owner of a large mill began to pay his workers in script redeemable at the company store. For a number of weeks the store was empty, and the government had to rush emergency food supplies into the area.

Mill and plantation owners continue to flaunt the law with impunity. At times they simply refuse to pay the legal minimum wage. Or they find ways to circumvent their statutory obligations. One common dodge derived from the fact that the legal wage is calculated on the basis of a seven-day week. To earn it, a field worker must perform six full days of work. His daily task is assigned as piecework (so many square meters hoed, so many bundles of cane cut, or so many meters ploughed). To avoid having to pay the legal

minimum, the owner has his foreman assign to the peasant a one-day work load that is impossible to do in a day. When the peasant cannot finish it, he loses his right to the full legal minimum wage for the week and receives only five days' pay for six days' work.

The payment of wages in script, though forbidden by law, continues to be a common practice. Recently, peasants at one of the largest sugar mills in Pernambuco have been trading their script to office employees of the mill in return for 20 per cent of the script's value in cash. The office employees then sell the script back to the mill for up to 40 per cent of its value.

A land-reform law passed by the federal government shortly after the coup has been ignored. One of the requirements of the law is that each peasant working in the sugar industry shall be given two hectares of land for his own use near his house. No attempt has ever been made to force the mill and plantation owners to comply.

The once vital rural labor movement of Pernambuco has been unable to secure effective enforcement of rights that peasants supposedly have, or to obtain any new legislation to benefit workers in the countryside, since Brazil's military rulers have prohibited organized labor from functioning as an independent political force.

In the Northeast, the Army installed new leaders in most of the rural unions shortly after the coup. Padre Crespo managed to hold on to his control over the Federation. Padre Melo remained with his union in Cabo, but took advantage of his good relations with the military to bolster his designs on the leadership of the movement. In 1965 the inevitable happened, and the two priests quarreled bitterly. A difference of opinion over strategy provoked the split, which reached its nadir when Melo unsuccessfully tried to have Crespo ousted from the Federation. The feud has simmered on, and persists even to the present. Padre Crespo has never relaxed his grip over SORPE and the Federation, a fact which in the opinion of some observers has contributed to the failure of the Pernambuco movement to develop indigenous leadership. In early 1971 he announced he was leaving the priesthood in order to marry, but that he would continue his work with SORPE and the Federation.

In December, 1964, the Cooperative League (CLUSA) signed a contract with SORPE whereby the Catholic organization continued

to receive CIA funding. A number of agricultural cooperatives were founded, and most of them are still functioning today. CLUSA withdrew its financial support in 1967, at about the same time its link with the CIA was publicly disclosed, and responsibility for assisting the rural cooperative movement in the Northeast shifted to USAID and the Peace Corps.

U.S. involvement with the rural labor movement in the Northeast developed in the postcoup period through the work of the American Institute for Free Labor Development (AIFLD), a private, nonprofit corporation created by the AFL-CIO primarily as a tool to fight Communist and Castroite influences in the Latin American labor movement.[16] USAID provides most of the funding for AIFLD, whose policies closely follow those of the U.S. Department of State, and whose board of trustees includes representatives of American corporations with a substantial stake in Latin America.

As early as June, 1963, AIFLD officials were trying to organize a program in Northeast Brazil. But events were unfolding too rapidly, and AIFLD was unable to muster its resources in time to have an impact on the precoup ferment in the countryside. (AIFLD was active elsewhere in Brazil. Indeed, one of its officials has proudly boasted of the organization's contribution to the overthrow of Goulart.[17])

Not long after the coup, an AIFLD team arrived in Recife to involve itself deeply in what was left of the rural labor movement in Pernambuco. AIFLD arranged training courses for labor leaders and constructed several Peasant Service Centers. Emphasis has been placed on the development of "free and democratic unions," a highly dubious concept in a military dictatorship that will not tolerate aggressive and independent activity by labor, but AIFLD has not been troubled by this contradiction. So the rural unions in Pernambuco do hold democratic elections to choose leaders who draw handsome salaries, take courses from AIFLD, and do very little.

The Brazilian government was fully aware of the worsening conditions in the sugar zone, and decided upon a new approach to the problem. Following the recommendations of a USAID study undertaken by the Hawaiian Agronomics International Company,[18] the military regime announced, with appropriate fanfare, the birth of

232

GERAN, or the Special Group for the Rationalization of the Northeastern Sugar Industry. GERAN's goals were to bring about both the modernization of the sugar zone and a genuine land reform. The idea was to stimulate the adoption of new machinery and methods which would enable mill owners to produce as much sugar as they were then producing, but on half as much land. The remaining land would then be available for crop diversification and distribution to the peasants.

The creation of a new federal agency to deal with the Northeast's most pressing problem indicated in no uncertain terms SUDENE's loss of power, prestige, and importance. SUDENE was represented in GERAN's deliberative council, but shared responsibility with the Sugar and Alcohol Institute, the Bank of Brazil, and several other government entities.

GERAN's guiding philosophy, that of trying to encourage the mill owners to help themselves and thus incidentally provide relief for the impoverished masses, was thoroughly consistent with Washington's notions of "trickle-down" development. It seems incredible that those who for many decades had preserved a system which brought poverty, disease, and ignorance to many thousands of peasants were now to be rewarded by becoming the direct beneficiaries of more government aid.

GERAN could not of course force the mill owners to modernize. It had no authority to compel them to do anything, but instead had to sell them the idea of taking advantage of the new program. And there was much talk around Recife that GERAN was going to concentrate on the modernization of the mills and forget about the plight of the workers who would be displaced. USAID expressed concern over this possibility, and developed plans to transport these peasants to relocation centers, where they would be given training and technical assistance. The idea alarmed some Brazilians, who saw the proposal as an attempt to set up "concentration camps." But it never got beyond the planning stage.

GERAN was announced in 1966. In early 1967 it was in its organizational phase. Officials were expressing the hope that it would begin to show results in five years. That August the agency suffered an administrative shake-up, which continued for two years. In May,

1969, the government appointed an Army colonel as chief administrator of GERAN. His claim to fame was that he had been in charge
of security in Recife during the repressive period immediately after
the coup. In June, 1969, GERAN was still in the organizational
stage. By early 1971, only one Pernambucan sugar mill had had its
modernization plans approved by GERAN, but no action had been
taken. At the same time a new agency, GERA (Executive Group
for Agrarian Reform) had been created. In June, 1971, the military
regime announced a brand-new plan for agrarian reform, which
would involve the expropriation of land in the sugar zone (with cash
payments to the owners), and the transplantation of Northeastern
peasants to colonies along the new Trans-Amazónica Highway.
And so it goes.

While GERAN has been making its feeble effort to "rationalize"
the Northeastern sugar industry, American consumers have been
helping the mill and plantation owners resist change. Under the
Sugar Act, the U.S. purchases quotas of sugar from a number of
sugar-producing nations, including Brazil, at a price higher than that
of the world market. Almost all the sugar imported to the U.S. from
Brazil under the act comes from the Northeast. A U.S. Government
Accounting Office report calculated that in 1967 Brazil received a
$44.4 million subsidy as a result of the Sugar Act.[19] This windfall
enables the Brazilian Sugar and Alcohol Institute to buy sugar from
the Northeast at an artificially high price, making it worthwhile for
the Northeastern producers to maintain antiquated methods of production, and giving them no incentive to alter their ways. It is a curious contradiction that while the USAID mission in Recife tries to
encourage the GERAN program, State Department officials in
Washington have made no effort to urge Congress to amend the
Sugar Act to create pressures on backward sugar producers, such as
those in Northeast Brazil, to reform.

As American efforts in the Northeast intensified in the years following the coup, the American presence expanded perceptibly. The
Peace Corps sent a swarm of Volunteers into the region. By mid-
1967, 204 Volunteers were working in various communities
throughout the Northeast. Even the number of American missionaries increased. One by-product of this influx was a wave of anti-

Americanism. In Paraíba students accosted Peace Corps Volunteers and Mormon missionaries with cries of "Go home!" A joint Michigan State-SUDENE study of marketing practices in the Northeast for a long time floundered because of Brazilian suspicions that the Americans were connected with U.S. companies planning to move into the region. A campaign in the Recife newspapers vilified a Peace Corps girl falsely accused of sterilizing peasant women.[20]

The close relationship between Washington and Brazil's military regime was an underlying cause of these hostile manifestations. Since the Army suppressed all antigovernment criticism in the Northeast, anti-Americanism provided an indirect way for Brazilians to vent their dissatisfaction with the domestic political situation. In addition many Brazilians felt that their government had become intolerably subservient to the United States, and were alarmed at what they saw as a policy of Americanization being forced upon them. The American intervention in the Dominican Republic and the intensification of the U.S. involvement in Vietnam served to heighten animosities. In 1968 the U.S. substantially reduced its official presence in Brazil, at least in part because of the rising tide of anti-Americanism.

Meanwhile, the repressive grip of the regime seemed to loosen a bit as Marshal Artur Costa e Silva was chosen by his fellow officers to succeed Castelo Branco as President. Costa e Silva took office in March, 1967, and announced his intention to "humanize the revolution." But his administration failed to make any real progress toward social justice or structural reform to complement the mild economic recovery achieved by the government's stabilization policy. As Costa e Silva began his second year in office, opposition to the regime seemed to be getting out of control. Students mounted violent demonstrations throughout the country. Isolated instances of leftist guerrilla activity took place. Progressive Catholics intensified their agitation for social reform. The old politicians (Kubitschek, Quadros, the exiled Goulart, and others) attempted to form a united-front opposition political party in defiance of laws making such organizing illegal. Right-wing paramilitary groups, with the tacit support of certain Army officers, reacted with a terrorist campaign against the left, and conservative Catholics petitioned the Vatican to

do something about the "Communist infiltration" of the Brazilian church.

Things reached the crisis point when a federal deputy denounced the military as "torturers" because of their suppression of a student meeting. The government demanded that Congress remove his immunity from prosecution. The Congress refused, and on December 13, Costa e Silva decreed the Fifth Institutional Act. Congress was dissolved and the Army imposed a rigid press censorship. The wave of arrests which followed was reminiscent of April, 1964.

The universities came under serious attack, as students and professors fell victim to new purges by the police and the military. This proved too much even for Lincoln Gordon, then President of Johns Hopkins University, and he joined other U.S. specialists in Latin American studies in sending a telegram of protest to Costa e Silva.[21]

In the Northeast Act V meant the suppression of Dom Hélder Câmara and his followers. An ultraconservative Catholic group called "The Society for the Defense of Tradition, Family, and Property" campaigned for the Archbishop's transfer from the Northeast. The government expelled two American priests who were working in Recife and whose parish newsletter reprinted foreign newspaper articles critical of the regime. (A third American priest returned to the U.S. just ahead of imminent expulsion.) Press censorship kept Dom Hélder's name and statements out of the newspapers, except for an occasional mention on the religion pages. Police spies began to attend Sunday masses to check for "subversive" sermons. Terrorists shot bullets at Dom Hélder's residence, palace, and Archdiocesan office, and painted slogans such as "Death to Dom Hélder, the Red Archbishop." On May 26, 1969, one of his priests was brutally murdered. This plus the shooting and crippling of a student leader cast a pall of fear over Northeasterners who had been in any way expressing criticism of the regime.

The process of polarization has continued apace. A young student from São Paulo who tried to organize peasants in the Pernambucan countryside was arrested and so badly tortured that he attempted suicide and broke his back in a leap from a window in police headquarters. A group of students from the south were captured by the police after a gunfight in Recife. The students were accused of plan-

ning to kidnap the U.S. Consul. One of them was an American girl.

Washington has expressed some unhappiness with this turn of events in Brazil. What was billed in 1964 as a great triumph for Western Civilization is now a source of embarrassment for those who view dimly the destruction of democratic institutions, the censorship of the press, and the torture of students, priests, and nuns. For U.S. policy-makers, the chickens have come home to roost.

In May, 1970, a serious drought, the worst since 1958, once again turned the Northeast into a national disaster area. Peasants streamed into the towns of the interior and sacked stores and private homes in search of food. They even stopped freight trains and carried off food supplies. The once proud SUDENE, created to defend the region against the effects of future droughts, hastily set up a program of "work fronts," so that peasants might earn enough on public-works projects to keep alive. Refugees from the backlands—the *flagelados* —began to arrive in the city of São Paulo. *Le Monde,* the distinguished Paris newspaper, reported that "for the fifth time in a month, Pernambuco police stopped a lorry loaded with men and women who were going to be 'sold' [as bonded workers] to the large property owners in the state of Minas Gerais for eighty *cruzeiros*— less than $18 a head." [22]

Plus ça change . . .

APPENDIX

❧ ❧ Notes

CHAPTER ONE

1. The author was present on the bus and at the rally on June 29, 1963.
2. *Congressional Record,* March 25, 1963, pp. 4866–69.
3. *A Hora* (Communist Party newspaper, Recife), October 6, 1962.
4. For the story of João Pedro Teixeira and his family, see Lêda Barreto, *Julião-Nordeste-Revolução* (Editôra Civilização Brasileira, Rio de Janeiro, 1963), p. 130; Antônio Callado, *Tempo de Arraes: Padres e Comunistas na Revolução Sem Violência* (José Alvaro Editor, Rio de Janeiro, 1965), pp. 65–70; *Land Tenure Conditions and Socio-Economic Development of the Agricultural Sector: Brazil* (Inter-American Committee for Agricultural Development, Pan American Union, Washington, D.C., 1966), pp. 312–13; *Jornal do Comércio* (Recife), April 10, 11, 1962; *A Hora,* April 7, 1962; *Ultima Hora* (Recife), July 1 and 13, 1962; *The New York Times,* April 10, 1962, p. 17; *id.,* April 11, 1962, p. 18.
5. For an interesting portrait of Recife, see the article by Ralph Nader in the *Christian Science Monitor,* September 30, 1963.
6. *Jornal do Comércio,* July 11, 1961.
7. Josué de Castro, *Documentário do Nordeste* (Editôra Brasiliense, São Paulo, 1959), pp. 25–28.
8. The source for biographical information on Furtado is Alessandro Porro, "Porque Éle É um Cassado," *Realidade,* August, 1967, p. 76.
9. Gerald Clark, *The Coming Explosion in Latin America* (McKay, New York, 1963), p. 248.

10. Address by President John F. Kennedy, March 13, 1961, *Public Papers of the Presidents of the United States, 1961* (U.S. Government Printing Office, Washington, D.C., 1962), pp. 170–81.
11. Quoted in *The New York Times,* July 15, 1961, p. 10.
12. Arthur M. Schlesinger, Jr., *A Thousand Days* (Houghton Mifflin, Cambridge, Mass. 1965), p. 171.

CHAPTER TWO

1. For background material on Northeast Brazil, see generally *The Brazilian Northeast* (pamphlet prepared by the Brazilian Embassy, Washington, D.C., August, 1961), pp. 1–3; René Dumont, *Lands Alive* (Monthly Review Press, New York, 1965), Chap. 3; Celso Furtado, *Diagnosis of the Brazilian Crisis* (University of California Press, Berkeley, 1965), Chap. 9; Stefan H. Robock, *Brazil's Developing Northeast: A Study of Regional Planning and Foreign Aid* (Brookings Institution, Washington, D.C., 1963), Chaps. 1–3; Charles Wagley, *An Introduction to Brazil* (Columbia University Press, New York, 1963), pp. 33–53.
2. See *Northeast Brazil: Nutrition Study, March–May, 1963* (Report by the Interdepartmental Committee on Nutrition for National Development, May, 1965). The Interdepartmental Committee is composed of representatives from the Departments of Defense, State, Agriculture, HEW, and Interior, the Agency for International Development, and the Food for Peace Program.
3. See Ruy João Marques, *Aspectos da Saúde Pública no Nordeste* (Imprensa Universitária, Recife, 1964).
4. *Nutrition Study, supra* note 2.
5. Alberto Tamer, *O Mesmo Nordeste* (Editôra Herder, São Paulo, 1968), pp. 114–15.
6. *Nutrition Study, supra* note 2.
7. See Tamer, *op. cit. supra* note 5, pp. 105–27.
8. The best single study of the socio-economic history of the Northeast is Manoel Correia Andrade, *A Terra e o Homem no Nordeste* (Editôra Brasiliense, São Paulo, 1963). See also Josué de Castro, *Death in the Northeast* (Random House, New York, 1966); Andre Gunder Frank, *Capitalism and Underdevelopment in Latin America* (Monthly Review Press, New York, 1967), Chap. 4; Celso Furtado, *The Economic Growth of Brazil* (University of California Press, Berkeley, 1965); Tamer, *op. cit. supra* note 5.

9. See, generally, Gilberto Freyre, *The Masters and the Slaves*, abridged ed., (Alfred A. Knopf, New York, 1964); José Lins do Rêgo, *Plantation Boy* (Alfred A. Knopf, New York, 1966).

10. See Marcos V. Vilaça and Roberto C. de Albuquerque, *Coronel, Coroneis* (Tempo Brasileiro, Rio de Janeiro, 1965).

11. Tamer, *op. cit. supra* note 5, p. 26.

12. See Jerome Levinson and Juan de Onís, *The Alliance That Lost Its Way* (Quadrangle, Chicago, 1970), pp. 244–45.

13. See Albert O. Hirschman, *Journeys Toward Progress* (Twentieth Century Fund, New York, 1963), Chap. 1.

14. See René Ribeiro, "Brazilian Messianic Movements," *Millennial Dreams in Action* (Thrupp ed., Mouton, The Hague, 1962); Waldemar Valente, *Misticismo e Região: Aspectos do Sebastianismo Nordestino* (Instituto Joaquim Nabuco, Recife, 1963).

15. See Ralph della Cava, *Miracle at Joaseiro* (Columbia University Press, New York, 1970).

16. See Wagley, *op. cit. supra* note 1, p. 49; Eduardo Barbosa, *Lampião: Rei do Cangaço* (Edições de Ouro, Rio de Janeiro, 1963).

CHAPTER THREE

1. *The New York Times*, January 5, 1955.

2. *E.g.*, the front page of *The New York Times* had stories from Latin America on January 3, 4, 6, 9, 10, 11, 12, 13, 14, 15, 19, 21, 22, 23, 26, 1955.

3. *Id.*, January 2, 1955.

4. My principal source for the story of the peasants' visit to Julião's house derives from interviews with Jonas de Sousa during my own visits to the house in July, 1967, and June, 1969. My version of the encounter is consistent with that of Antônio Callado, who first wrote about it in a series of articles in the Rio newspaper, *Correio da Manhã*, in September, 1959. The articles are reprinted in Antônio Callado, *Os Industriais da Sêca e os "Galileus" de Pernambuco* (Editôra Civilização Brasileira, Rio de Janeiro, 1960), pp. 33–43. A second, quite different version of the encounter, for which I have been able to find no substantiation, first appeared in an article entitled "Nordeste: As Sementes da Subversão," by Mauritônio Meira and Hélio Passos, in *O Cruzeiro*, November 11, 1961, pp. 8–9. This version was subsequently reproduced by Gerald Clark, *op. cit. supra* Chap. 1, note 9, pp. 203–04, and Josué de Castro, *op. cit. supra* Chap. 2, note 8, pp. 7–17. It is

rejected by Professor Neale J. Pearson in his dissertation, *Small Farmer and Rural Pressure Groups in Brazil* (University Microfilms, Ann Arbor, Mich., 1967), p. 103, fn. 3. A third version, which downgrades Julião's role and makes José de Prazeres the prime mover of the Peasant League movement, recently came to light in Clodomir Moraes, "Peasant Leagues in Brazil," *Agrarian Problems and Peasant Movements in Latin America* (Stavenhagen ed., Anchor Books, Garden City, N.Y., 1970), pp. 462–64, fn. 10. This account is colored by the fact that both its author and José de Prazeres quarreled with Julião and disputed his leadership of the Peasant Leagues.

5. Meira and Passos, *op. cit. supra* note 4, p. 9.
6. Julião has described his family and childhood at length in *Cambão: La Cara Oculta de Brasil* (Siglo XXI Editores, Mexico City, 1968).
7. *Id.*, p. 21.
8. Francisco Julião, *Até Quarta, Isabela!* (Editôra Civilização Brasileira, Rio de Janeiro, 1965), p. 50.
9. *Id.*, pp. 48–51.
10. Interview with Julião, Cuernavaca, September, 1969.
11. Julião, *op. cit. supra* note 6, p. 110.
12. Interview with Julião, Cuernavaca, Mexico, September, 1969.
13. Julião, *op. cit. supra* note 6, pp. 111–12.
14. Sources for the story of Antônio Vicente are Meira and Passos, *op. cit. supra* note 4, pp. 9, 12; Julião, *op. cit. supra* note 6, pp. 131–37. Julião refers to him as Antônio da Mate.
15. Vilaça & Albuquerque, *op. cit. supra* Chap. 2, note 10, p. 56.
16. See Francisco Julião, *Que São as Ligas Camponesas?*, (Editôra Civilização Brasileira, Rio de Janeiro, 1962), pp. 44–45.
17. Interview with Gilberto Freyre, Recife, June, 1963.
18. See, for example, *A Hora*, October 20 and 27, 1962; *Novos Rumos* (Communist Party newspaper published in Rio de Janeiro), November 23–29, 1962.
19. Moraes, *op. cit. supra* note 4, p. 453.
20. See Clodomir Moraes, *Queda de una Oligarquia* (Gráfica Editôra, Recife, 1959).
21. See Julião, *op. cit. supra* note 16, pp. 34–41.
22. Moraes, *op. cit. supra* note 4, p. 453.
23. See Gondin da Fonseca, *Assim Falou Julião* (Editôra Fulgor, São Paulo, 1963), pp. 49–53.
24. Callado, *op. cit. supra* note 4, p. 142.
25. Francisco Julião, *A Cartilha do Camponês* (Recife, 1960), p. 5.
26. See, for example, *A Hora*, September 30, 1961.

27. Quoted in Barreto, *op. cit. supra* Chap. 1, note 4, p. 131.
28. Quoted in Meira and Passos, *op. cit. supra* note 4, p. 13.

CHAPTER FOUR

1. The prime source of the career of Miguel Arraes is Adirson de Barros, *Ascensão e Queda de Miguel Arraes* (Editôra Equador, Rio de Janeiro, 1965).
2. On the career of Getúlio Vargas, see Thomas E. Skidmore, *Politics in Brazil: 1930–1964* (Oxford University Press, New York, 1967), pp. 3–136; John W. F. Dulles, *Vargas of Brazil: A Political Biography* (University of Texas Press, Austin, Texas, 1967). For an engaging portrait of Getúlio, see John Gunther, *Inside Latin America* (Harper & Bros., New York, 1941), Chap. 23.
3. Quoted in de Barros, *op. cit. supra* note 1, p. 34.
4. The Communist uprising in Recife is described in Glauco Carneiro, *História das Revoluções Brasileiras* (Edições O Cruzeiro, Rio de Janeiro, Volume 2, 1965). See also *Diário de Pernambuco,* November 27 and 28, 1935.
5. See Robert J. Alexander, *Communism in Latin America* (Rutgers University Press, New Brunswick, N.J., 1957), Chap. 7.

CHAPTER FIVE

1. Callado, *op. cit. supra* Chap. 3, note 4, p. 6.
2. For an extensive discussion of the drought problem and the foundation of SUDENE, see Albert O. Hirschman, *Journeys Toward Progress: Studies of Economic Policy-Making in Latin America* (Twentieth Century Fund, New York, 1963), Chap. 1.
3. Andre Gunder Frank, *Capitalism and Underdevelopment in Latin America* (Monthly Review Press, New York, 1969), p. 245.
4. *The New York Times,* July 31, 1969, p. 33.
5. Robock, *op. cit. supra* Chap. 2, note 1, p. 128.
6. *Northeast Brazil Survey Team Report* (February, 1962), p. 2.
7. Riordan J. A. Roett III, *Economic Assistance and Political Change: The Brazilian Northeast* (University Microfilms, Ann Arbor, Mich., 1968), p. 12, published as *Political Change and Economic Assistance in the Brazilian Northeast* by the Vanderbilt University Press.
8. Interview with USAID official, Washington, D.C., October, 1969; in-

terview with Dr. Lincoln Gordon, Baltimore, Md., March, 1971.

9. *United States Foreign Aid in Action: A Case Study* (Subcommittee on Foreign Aid Expenditures, Senate Committee on Government Operations, U.S. Government Printing Office, Washington, D.C., 1966).

10. *The New York Times,* November 12, 1961, p. 43.

11. Schlesinger, *op. cit. supra* Chap. 1, note 11, p. 172.

12. *O Estado de São Paulo,* May 7, 1963; Glauco Carneiro, "Nordeste: Sinal Vermelho," *O Cruzeiro,* June 30, 1963.

13. Hirschman, *op. cit. supra* note 2, p. 88.

14. The following description of Furtado's role in the negotiations for foreign aid is based upon an interview with Furtado in Paris, May, 1968.

15. *Ibid.*

16. Roett, *op. cit. supra* note 7, p. 274.

CHAPTER SIX

1. Mauritônio Meira, "As Soluções da Estupidez," *O Cruzeiro,* November 25, 1961, p. 57.

2. *Jornal do Comércio,* July 7, 1961.

3. Meira, *op. cit. supra* note 1, p. 54.

4. See, for example, *Diário de Pernambuco,* February 6, 1962.

5. See Anthony Leeds, "Brazil and the Myth of Francisco Julião," *Politics of Change in Latin America,* Maier and Weatherhead, eds. (Praeger, New York, 1964), p. 190; Roett, *op. cit. supra* Chap. 5, note 7, p. 282.

6. Glauco Carneiro, "A Outra Face de Julião," *O Cruzeiro,* April 14, 1962, p. 20.

7. *Diário de Pernambuco,* February 6, 1962.

8. *Ibid.*

9. *O Estado de São Paulo,* December 6, 1961, p. 5.

10. See Tad Szulc, *The Winds of Revolution: Latin America Today—and Tomorrow* (Praeger, New York, 1963), p. 20.

11. See *Jornal do Comércio,* June 14, 1962.

12. *The New York Times,* January 23, 1961, p. 5.

13. The Congress is described in *Revista Brasiliense,* January–February, 1961.

14. *The New York Times,* January 23, 1961, p. 5.

15. Simone de Beauvoir, *Force of Circumstances* (Putnam's, New York, 1964), p. 535.

16. Interview with Julião, Cuernavaca, Mexico, September, 1969.

17. See Benno Galjart, "Class and 'Following' in Rural Brazil," *América Latina,* July–September, 1964.
18. Quoted in Julião, *op. cit. supra* Chap. 3, note 16, p. 84.
19. *Diário de Pernambuco,* February 6, 1962.
20. *Id.,* February 9, 1962.
21. *Jornal do Comércio,* September 11, 1962.
22. *A Hora,* September 15 and 29, 1962.
23. See Eckstein, "A Report on Brazil's Northeast," *Swiss Review of World Affairs,* December, 1962, p. 16; Barreto, *op. cit. supra* Chap. 1, note 4, pp. 79–84.
24. See sources cited in Chap. 1, note 4.
25. See Julião, *op. cit. supra* Chap. 3, note 6, pp. 159–63.

CHAPTER SEVEN

1. Callado, *op. cit. supra* Chap. 1, note 4, p. 58.
2. *Jornal do Comércio,* April 27, 1962.
3. *The New York Times,* November 18, 1961, p. 9.
4. *Jornal do Comércio,* January 27, 1962.
5. See Gerrit Huizer, "Some Notes on Community Development and Rural Social Research," *América Latina,* July–September, 1965, p. 128.
6. Quoted in Belden Paulson, "Difficulties and Prospects for Community Development in Northeast Brazil," *Inter–American Economic Affairs* (Vol. 17, No. 4, Spring 1964), p. 37.
7. Quoted in Barreto, *op. cit. supra* Chap. 1, note 4, pp. 49–50.
8. *Diário de Pernambuco,* January 22, 1964.
9. Quoted in Meira and Passos, *op. cit. supra* Chap. 3, note 4, p. 13.
10. Quoted in Galjart, *op. cit. supra* Chap. 6, note 17.
11. Quoted in *Jornal do Comércio,* January 12, 1962.
12. *Id.,* April 17, 1962.
13. *The New York Times,* January 23, 1961, p. 5.
14. Interview in Recife, June, 1969.
15. See, for example, *Jornal do Comércio,* December 21, 1962.
16. *A Hora,* December 9, 1961.
17. *Id.,* June 23, 1962.
18. Interview in Cuernavaca, Mexico, September, 1969.
19. Pearson, *op. cit. supra* Chap. 3, note 4, p. 125, fn. 1.
20. *Jornal do Comércio,* December 4, 7, 15, 16, 19, 21, 1962; *Congressional Record,* March 25, 1963, pp. 4866–69; *Documentation of Communist*

THE REVOLUTION THAT NEVER WAS

Penetration in Latin America (Hearings before the Subcommittee to Investigate the Administration of the Internal Security Act and Other Internal Security Laws, of the Senate Committee on the Judiciary, Pt. 1, October 2, 1963), pp. 99–102; *Id.*, Pt. 3, pp. 389–92; *A Liga*, December 11, 1962, p. 6, reprinted in *Ligas Camponesas: Outubro 1962–Abril 1964* (F. Julião, ed., Cuaderno N. 27, Centro Intercultural de Documentación, Cuernavaca, Mexico, 1969), pp. 75–84. That the "caper" actually occurred has now been unquestionably confirmed in Moraes, *op. cit. supra* Chap. 3, note 4, pp. 484–89.

21. Moraes, *op. cit. supra* Chap. 3, note 4, p. 487.
22. Interview, Cuernavaca, Mexico, September, 1969.
23. Moraes, *op. cit. supra* Chap. 3, note 4, p. 489.
24. *Jornal do Comércio,* December 19, 1962.
25. *Ligas Camponesas, op. cit. supra* note 20, p. 76.
26. Interview, Cuernavaca, Mexico, September, 1969.
27. *Ibid.*
28. The material on Joel Câmara is based upon interviews with him in June and July, 1963, July, 1967, and June, 1969; see also F. Novaes Sodré, *Quem É Francisco Julião?* (Redenção Nacional, São Paulo, 1963), p. 32.
29. *Diário de Pernambuco,* October 2, 1962.
30. *Jornal do Comércio,* January 13, 1963.
31. *Id.,* May 9, 1963.
32. *Id.,* September 11, 1962.
33. Reprinted in Aloísio Guerra, *A Igreja Está Com o Povo?* (Editôra Civilização Brasileira, Rio de Janeiro, 1963), pp. 19–23.
34. Quoted in *Ligas Camponesas, op. cit. supra* note 20, pp. 44–45.
35. *Id.,* p. 273.
36. See Carneiro, *op. cit. supra* Chap. 5, note 12.
37. See *Hispanic American Report* (Vol. 16, January, 1963), p. 81.
38. *Jornal do Comércio,* January 6, 1963.
39. *Ibid.*

CHAPTER EIGHT

1. My sources for these figures were Monthly Reports prepared by the U.S. Consulate in Recife in 1963.
2. *U.S. Army Area Handbook for Brazil* (Dep't of the Army Pamphlet No. 550–620, July, 1964), p. 297.

3. *Livro de Leitura Para Adultos* (Gráfica Editôra do Recife, 1962).
4. *Diário de Pernambuco,* September 2, 1962.
5. See, for example, *id.,* October 6, 1962.
6. For Arraes' testimony before a federal commission investigating IBAD, see de Barros, *op. cit. supra* Chap. 4, note 1, pp. 171–74.
7. *Diário de Pernambuco,* August 29, 1962.
8. Quoted in de Barros, *op. cit. supra* Chap. 4, note 1, p. 82.
9. *Diário de Pernambuco,* October 7, 1962.
10. *Id.,* August 30, 1962.
11. Quoted in de Barros, *op. cit. supra* Chap. 4, note 1, p. 85.
12. *Jornal do Comércio,* February 15, 1963.
13. The address is reprinted in *Palavra de Arraes* (Editôra Civilização Brasileira, Rio de Janeiro, 1965), pp. 9–24.

CHAPTER NINE

1. For a full account of the proceedings, see *Diário de Pernambuco,* August 1, 1961.
2. My sources for the generator story are various U.S. officials and J. Warren Nystrom and Nathan A. Haverstock, *The Alliance for Progress* (D. Van Nostrand, Princeton, N.J., 1966), p. 82.
3. Pearson, *op. cit. supra* Chap. 3, note 4, p. 108, fn. 3.
4. Interview in Washington, D.C., March, 1969.
5. Gilberto Freyre, *Guia Práctica, Histórico e Sentimental da Cidade do Recife,* 4th ed., (Livraria José Olympio Editôra, Rio de Janeiro, 1968), p. 11.
6. My discussion of various USAID personnel in the Northeast is based upon extensive interviews with Americans and Brazilians who had first-hand knowledge of the operations of the USAID mission during this period.
7. Interview in Recife, June, 1963.
8. Interview with John Dieffenderfer, New York, December, 1969.
9. Ralph Nader, "Brazil Aid Effort Rapped," *Christian Science Monitor,* September 7, 1963, p. 12. The other articles appeared in the *Monitor* on September 5 and 9, 1963.
10. See T. Hogen, *The Introduction of the Peasant to the Cooperative Movement* (CLUSA, Chicago, 1966), p. 9.
11. Sheehan, "Co-op Group Got CIA Conduit Aid," *The New York Times,* May 16, 1967, p. 37.

THE REVOLUTION THAT NEVER WAS

12. *U.S. Army Area Handbook for Brazil*, cited *supra* Chap. 8, note 2, p. 627.
13. Interview in Washington, D.C., January, 1970.
14. Tad Szulc, *The Winds of Revolution: Latin America Today—and Tomorrow* (Praeger, New York, 1963), p. 34.
15. Frank, *op. cit. supra* Chap. 2, note 8, pts. 3–4.

CHAPTER TEN

1. Nader, *op. cit. supra* Chap. 9, note 9.
2. See Chap. 5, note 12, *supra*.
3. Caneiro, *op. cit. supra* Chap. 5, note 12.
4. Interview in New York, December, 1969.
5. See Levinson and de Onis, *op. cit. supra* Chap. 2, note 12, p. 88.
6. Roett, *op. cit. supra* Chap. 5, note 7, p. 322.
7. John dos Passos, *Brazil on the Move* (Doubleday, New York, 1963), p. 189.
8. The Rio Grande do Norte projects are described in detail in Roett, *op. cit. supra* Chap. 5, note 7, pp. 314–19, 330–43; see also *Report of the Special Study Mission to the Dominican Republic, Guyana, Brazil and Paraguay* (Committee on Foreign Affairs, House of Representatives, May 1, 1967), pp. 28–29.
9. *Hispanic American Report* (Vol. 15, December, 1962), p. 962.
10. Quoted in de Barros, *op. cit. supra* Chap. 4, note 1, pp. 138–39.
11. *Palavra de Arraes*, *op. cit. supra* Chap. 8, note 11, pp. 13–14.
12. *Newsweek*, March 11, 1963, p. 55.
13. *Id.*, February 24, 1964, p. 36.
14. Interview in Washington, D.C., March, 1970.
15. Interview with John Dieffenderfer, New York, December, 1969.
16. Published as *Aliança Para o Progresso: Inquérito* (Editôra Brasiliense, São Paulo, 1963).
17. *Ultima Hora*, May 4, 1963.
18. *Jornal do Comércio*, May 4, 1963.
19. *Ultima Hora*, May 5, 1963.
20. Interview with John Dieffenderfer, Recife, July, 1963.
21. *Jornal do Comércio*, August 20, 1963.
22. *Ultima Hora*, July 18, 1962; da Fonseca, *op. cit. supra* Chap. 3, note 23, p. 67.

CHAPTER ELEVEN

1. Padre Melo's rise to prominence is described in Mauritônio Meira, "Nordeste: A Revolução de Cristo," *O Cruzeiro,* December 2, 1961, p. 28.
2. *Jornal do Comércio,* November 12, 1961.
3. *Id.,* May 6, 1962.
4. *Hispanic American Report* (Vol. 15, December, 1962), p. 962.
5. Meira, *op. cit. supra* note 1.
6. *Jornal do Comércio,* February 16, 1963.
7. He is still making Marxist noises. See Antônio Melo, *The Coming Revolution in Brazil* (Exposition Press, New York, 1970).
8. See Callado, *op. cit. supra* Chap. 1, note 4, pp. 50–53.
9. *New Republic,* January 4, 1964, pp. 10–11.
10. On the work of Bishop Eugênio Sales, see Pearson, *op. cit. supra* Chap. 3, note 4, pp. 149–50.
11. Sources on Brazilian rural labor legislation include Robert E. Price, *Rural Unionization in Brazil* (Land Tenure Center, University of Wisconsin, Madison, Wis., No. 14, August, 1964); *Land Tenure Conditions, op. cit. supra* Chap. 1, note 4, pp. 297–332.
12. Information on SORPE was obtained from interviews with Padre Crespo and members of his staff in Recife in June and July, 1963.
13. Quoted in Price, *op. cit. supra* note 11, pp. 50–51.
14. *A Hora,* June 16, 1962.
15. See Cynthia N. Hewitt, "Brazil: The Peasant Movement of Pernambuco, 1961–1964," *Latin American Peasant Movements,* H. Landsberger, ed., (Cornell University Press, Ithaca, N.Y., 1969), p. 374. Hewitt's study, which is based primarily upon interviews with SORPE personnel and others who remained in the Northeast after the 1964 coup, is an important source for what must be viewed as one side of the story.
16. See Caio Prado, Jr., "Marcha da Questão Agrária no Brasil," *Revista Brasiliense,* January–February, 1964.
17. *Diário de Pernambuco,* April 10, 1963.
18. *Id.,* April 11, 1963.
19. Quoted in *Jornal do Comércio,* February 16, 1963.
20. Interview with the author, June, 1963.
21. The sources which I have relied upon include Hewitt, *op. cit. supra*

note 15; Mary E. Wilkie, *A Report on Rural Syndicates in Pernambuco* (Latin American Center for Research in the Social Sciences, Rio de Janeiro, April, 1964) (mimeographed copy on file with the author); Callado, *op. cit. supra* Chap. 1, note 4; Recife newspapers published during this period (*Diário de Pernambuco, Jornal do Comércio, Ultima Hora,* and *A Hora*); *Ligas Camponesas, op. cit. supra* Chap. 7, note 20; interviews with persons connected with the Peasant Leagues and SORPE.

22. *Newsweek,* February 24, 1964, p. 36.
23. Quoted in Price, *op. cit. supra* note 11, p. 53.
24. Callado, *op. cit. supra* Chap. 1, note 4, p. 98.
25. Interview in Cuernavaca, Mexico, September, 1969.
26. *Ibid.*
27. Callado, *op. cit. supra* Chap. 1, note 4, pp. 97, 98.
28. *Ultima Hora,* October 11, 1963.
29. See Callado, *op. cit. supra* Chap. 1, note 4, pp. 135–50.
30. For a transcript of the proceedings, see *O Problema Agrário na Zona Canavieira de Pernambuco* (Imprensa Universitária, Recife, 1965).
31. *Land Tenure Conditions, op. cit. supra* Chap. 1, note 4, pp. 329–30.

CHAPTER TWELVE

1. Sources on the Paulo Freire Method include Callado, *op. cit. supra* Chap. 1, note 4, pp. 123–33; Paulo Freire, *Educação Como Práctica da Liberdade* (Paz e Terra, Rio de Janeiro, 1967) (especially the introduction by Francisco C. Weffort); "The Paulo Freire Method," unpublished paper by Robert Myhr, a Fulbright scholar in Recife in 1963–64; interview with Jarbas Maciel, assistant to Paulo Freire, in Recife, June, 1963; Levinson and de Onís, *op. cit. supra* Chap. 2, note 12, pp. 284–92.
2. The source for biographical information on Paulo Freire is Márcio Moreira Alves, *O Cristo do Povo* (Editôra Sábia, Rio de Janeiro, 1968), pp. 200–03.
3. Details on the Angicos project were supplied by USAID official Philip Schwab in an interview in Washington, D.C., October, 1969.
4. Interview with Jarbas Maciel in Recife, June, 1963.
5. Pearson, *op. cit. supra* Chap. 3, note 4, pp. 150–51.
6. See *Viver É Lutar: 2° Livro de Leitura Para Adultos* (Movimento de Educação de Base, October, 1963), pp. 8, 32.

CHAPTER THIRTEEN

1. The author was present in the jeep and at the rally herein described.
2. Francisco Julião, "La Izquierda en el Brasil," *Política*, April 15, 1962.
3. See *Ligas Camponesas, op. cit. supra* Chap. 7, note 20, pp. 529–30, 538–48.
4. See *Diário de Pernambuco*, January 18, 1964.
5. *Jornal do Comércio*, August 20, 1963.
6. Quoted in de Fonseca, *op. cit. supra* Chap. 3, note 23, p. 65.
7. Quoted in de Barros, *op. cit. supra* Chap. 4, note 1, p. 97.
8. See Barreto, *op. cit. supra* Chap. 1, note 4, pp. 26–34.
9. Callado, *op. cit. supra* Chap. 1, note 4, p. 103.
10. See Skidmore, *op. cit. supra* Chap. 1, note 8, pp. 234–52.
11. *Id.*, pp. 275–76.
12. *Diário de Pernambuco*, January 16, 1964.
13. *Id.*, March 25, 1964.
14. See Skidmore, *op. cit. supra* Chap. 4, note 2, pp. 234–52.
15. *A Hora*, January 22, 1964.
16. *Diário de Pernambuco*, February 25, 1964.
17. See Skidmore, *op. cit. supra* Chap. 4, note 2, p. 276.
18. *Ultima Hora*, March 1, 1964.
19. See John W. F. Dulles, *Unrest in Brazil* (University of Texas Press, Austin, Texas, 1970), pp. 257–63.
20. For descriptions and discussions of the rally, see Skidmore, *op. cit. supra* Chap. 4, note 2, pp. 284–93; Dulles, *op. cit. supra* note 19, pp. 267–74.
21. *Ultima Hora*, March 13, 1964.
22. See Levinson and de Onís, *op. cit. supra* Chap. 2, note 12, p. 88.
23. *Boston Globe*, March 23, 1964, p. 12.
24. Skidmore, *op. cit. supra* Chap. 4, note 2, pp. 325–26.
25. Interview with USAID official.
26. See Skidmore, *op. cit. supra* Chap. 4, note 2, p. 326.
27. Interview with conservative who participated in the gathering of guns, Recife, July, 1967.
28. Skidmore, *op. cit. supra* Chap. 4, note 2, p. 300.
29. *Diário de Pernambuco*, March 31, 1964.
30. *Palavra de Arraes, op. cit. supra* Chap. 8, note 11, pp. 135–36.
31. *Jornal do Comércio*, April 1, 1964.
32. *Ibid.*

CHAPTER FOURTEEN

1. Details of what befell Celso Furtado on March 31 were obtained in an interview with Furtado in Paris in May, 1968. They are corroborated by a timetable of events published in the *Jornal do Comércio*, April 2, 1964.
2. *Jornal do Comércio*, April 1, 1964.
3. Interview with Naílton Santos, Cambridge, Mass., December, 1969.
4. Details on the confrontation between the students and the troops were obtained in an interview with Robert Myhr, Fulbright scholar, in Recife, June, 1964, and from the *Jornal do Comércio*, April 2, 1964.
5. Murilo Marroquim, "Ação do IV Exército Contra Arraes," *O Cruzeiro*, April 25, 1964.
6. Tad Szulc, "Washington Sends 'Warmest' Wishes to Brazil's Leader," *The New York Times*, April 3, 1964, p. 1.

CHAPTER FIFTEEN

1. Sources for the Gregório Bezerra story are Antônio Callado, "Les Ligues Paysannes," *Les Temps Modernes*, October, 1967, p. 751; Márcio Moreira Alves, *Torturas e Torturados* (Idade Nova, Rio de Janeiro, 1966), pp. 59–61; interview with cell-mate of Gregório, Recife, July, 1967.
2. *Diário de Pernambuco*, April 5, 1964.
3. *Time*, April 17, 1964, p. 49.
4. See Alves, *op. cit. supra* Chap. 3, note 1.
5. See Pearson, *op. cit. supra* Chap. 3, note 4, pp. 108–09, fn. 3.
6. The source for the story of Julião's capture is Julião, *op. cit. supra* Chap. 3, note 8.
7. See *Jornal do Comércio*, June 7, 1964; see also *O Cruzeiro*, June 27, 1964, p. 142.
8. *Washington Post*, May 12, 1964.
9. Copy on file with the author.
10. My source on the fate of SORPE and the Church syndicates after the coup is an interview with the CLUSA-CIA man in Recife, August, 1965.
11. See for example, *Jornal do Comércio*, June 14, 1964.
12. Interview with USAID official, Recife, July, 1967.

13. For a discussion of the events which followed the coup, see Skidmore, *op. cit. supra* Chap. 4, note 2, pp. 303–21.
14. *Jornal do Comércio*, April 9, 1964.
15. *Id.*, April 3, 1964.
16. Information on the postcoup inanities and atrocities was obtained in the course of extensive interviews in Recife in June, 1964, and July, 1967.
17. *Jornal do Comércio*, April 10, 1964.
18. See Alves, *op. cit. supra* Chap. 12, note 2, pp. 203–05.
19. The author interviewed Freire and had lunch with him at his home on the day before he was imprisoned.
20. See generally, Alves, *op. cit. supra* Chap. 12, note 2.
21. Pearson, *op. cit. supra* Chap. 3, note 4, p. 154, fn. 1.
22. Interview with Mme. Violeta Gervaiseau, Paris, May, 1968.
23. *Ultima Hora*, April 14, 1964.
24. *Diário de Pernambuco*, April 3, 1964.
25. *Id.*, April 11, 1964.
26. Dr. Gordon has stated that he was so disturbed by the postcoup abuses of the constitutional processes that he considered resigning his Ambassadorship but was talked out of it by his Political Officer. See Levinson and de Onís, *op. cit. supra* Chap. 2, note 12, pp. 90–91. His words and actions during the postcoup period were in no way consistent with this recent disclosure.
27. The exact quote was supplied by Dr. Gordon in a Letter to the Editor in *Commonweal*, August 7, 1970, p. 379.
28. In June, 1964, a USIS official in Rio furnished the author with a copy of a newspaper published by the Brazilian government and entitled *Brazil Woke up in Time*. Though it was little more than propaganda attempting to justify the coup, the USIS official presented it to the author as a "fact sheet." In Recife several weeks earlier a USIS official "briefed" the author with "facts" unswervingly supportive of the coup.
29. See *Christian Science Monitor*, August 14, 1964.
30. *Life* (International Ed.), May 31, 1964.
31. Celso Furtado, "Political Obstacles to Economic Growth in Brazil," *Obstacles to Change in Latin America*, C. Veliz, ed. (Oxford University Press, London, 1965), p. 160.

EPILOGUE

1. *The Rockefeller Report on the Americas* (Quadrangle, Chicago, 1969), p. 5.

2. For the English translation of the novel, see Antônio Callado, *Quarup* (Alfred A. Knopf, New York, 1970).

3. Interviews with Julião and his lawyer, Recife, August, 1965.

4. Interview in Rio de Janeiro, July, 1967.

5. Interview with Peace Corps Volunteers, Recife, July, 1967.

6. See the recently published biography, José de Broucker, *Dom Hélder: The Violence of a Peacemaker* (Orbis Books, Maryknoll, N.Y., 1970). See also Page, "The Little Priest Who Stands up to Brazil's Generals," *The New York Times Magazine*, May 23, 1971, p. 26.

7. *Jornal do Comércio*, August 21, 1966.

8. *Nordeste: Desinvolvimento Sem Justiça* (Ação Católica Operária, Recife, May 1, 1967), reprinted in H. Câmara, *The Church and Colonialism* (Dimension Books, Denville, N.J., 1969), p. 131.

9. *O Cruzeiro*, June 3, 1967, p. 51; *id.*, June 10, 1967, p. 47.

10. Copies on file with the author.

11. Information on current economic conditions in the Northeast was derived from interviews in Recife in July 1967, June 1969, and January 1971.

12. *United States Assistance to Northeast Brazil: Summary Report, 1962–June 30, 1968* (AID/Brazil, Northeast Area Office, Recife, August 31, 1968).

13. A. Tamer, *op. cit. supra* Chap. 2, note 5, p. 115.

14. *Le Monde Diplomatique*, May 4, 1971.

15. For a report of the author's visit to Palmares in July, 1967, see Page, "Northeast Brazil: Rich Become Rich and Poor Poorer," *Denver Post* (Perspective Magazine), August 6, 1967, p. 12.

16. See, generally, *Survey of the Alliance for Progress* (Committee on Foreign Relations, U.S. Senate, Doc. No. 91-17, April 29, 1969), pp. 573–658.

17. *Id.*, p. 586.

18. "Diversification and Modernization of Agriculture in the Sugar Cane Zone of Northeast Brazil," Hawaiian Agronomics International, Basic Agreement No. AID/csd-842, Task Order No. 1.

19. General Accounting Office, "Foreign Aid Provided Through the Operations of the United States Sugar Act and the International Coffee Agreement," (B-167416, October 23, 1969), p. 23.

20. *Jornal do Comércio*, May 6, 1967.

21. *The New York Times*, June 1, 1969, p. 24.

22. *Le Monde* (English Language ed.), May 20, 1970, p. 4.

❧ ❧ Notes from a Recife Jail*

I FIRST VISITED RECIFE IN THE SUMMER OF 1963. It was to have been a brief stop on a tour of the entire South American continent, but instead became the high point of the entire trip. I traveled with a friend, whose current pursuits and idiosyncrasies compel me to refer to him as Roland Snyder. We were eager to examine at firsthand the unrest that had for some time marked Northeast Brazil as a "trouble spot." Remaining for more than the three days normally allotted to Recife by visiting Americans, we managed to obtain a close and long look at what was happening in the region.

Although we were able to interview most of the important personalities in and around Recife, it was Francisco Julião who most fascinated us. By sheer good luck we managed to persuade him that we were objective observers, so he allowed us to travel with him on several occasions to watch him in action. After more than a month's stay, we became convinced that Julião's Leagues were weak, disorganized, and generally overrated as a revolutionary threat.†

My plans for a return to the Northeast in the summer of 1964 were unaffected by the coup of March 31, 1964. I was spending the academic

* This is a revised version of an article which appeared in the June 1966 issue of the University of Denver Magazine. When I wrote that article, I had absolutely no idea why my captors were so interested in my 1963 traveling companion and so convinced of his presence in Recife. It was not until July, 1967, that Antônio Lucena informed me, most apologetically, exactly why the police were looking for the two of us.
† Our conclusions were published in a "Report on Brazil," *The Atlantic*, March, 1964.

year at Harvard Law School in pursuit of a Master of Laws degree. My most notable discovery during this sojourn occurred when I experienced my first brush with academic prostitution. Several acquaintances of mine—an official at the Law School and a graduate student at the University—asked me to become part of a "research team" they were assembling as part of their bid for a lucrative U.S. Air Force contract for an in-depth study of Latin America. I was to be the "field man" in Northeast Brazil. My initial impression was that this would involve bona fide investigative reporting into political, social, and economic conditions, until my two friends informed me that the object of the exercise was to determine how various sectors of the local populace would react to an invasion and occupation by foreign troops, and that I should concentrate on gathering "hard stuff." The graduate student elaborated, with a faint smile: "We want documents —pamphlets, even private correspondence—if you have to beg, borrow or steal them." These instructions so thoroughly astonished me that I never did get around to asking the nationality of the hypothetical foreign troops. (The Harvard group was not awarded the contract. A similar, subsequent research effort, the Army's "Project Camelot" in Chile, turned into a great fiasco when it was publicly exposed, and badly damaged the prestige of American academic researchers throughout Latin America.)

Although the American press had reported the many arrests that had occurred right after the coup, I felt no forebodings as I planned my departure. Roland was unable to come, so I set out on the adventure alone.

I arrived in Recife on Sunday, June 1. The atmosphere seemed calm and unchanged. That evening I telephoned Antônio Lucena, an engineer in Recife's sanitation department and a childhood friend of Julião's. Lucena, a cheerful, nonpolitical fellow who had spent a year at the University of North Carolina, had acted as interpreter for Julião whenever the latter granted interviews to Americans. "He's out of town now," a voice answered. "When he comes back, tell him to call Joe Page at the Hotel Guararapes," I replied.

It took about forty-eight hours for me to reach the conclusion that Lucena had to be in jail. I soon learned that the "revolution" had struck Recife with particular force, and that virtually everyone connected with the Peasant Leagues had been arrested.

As I discovered some three years later, Lucena was indeed behind bars. He was languishing in a dungeon in the nearby city of Olinda. I had spoken on the telephone to his son, who had relayed the message during a visit to the dungeon two days later. Lucena had been insisting that he had been Julião's interpreter, and nothing more, and now he seized at an apparent

opportunity to prove his innocence. Unfortunately, he misunderstood my telephone message. He called the Army officer in charge of the dungeon and told him that he could now furnish witnesses to the nonpolitical nature of his association with Julião; that *two* American journalists who had interviewed Julião in 1963 were now back in Recife; and that they would testify in his behalf. And he gave the officer our names. In this ultraparanoid stage of the "revolution," the only thing which interested the officer was that two Americans who had once talked with Julião were now in Recife.

Meanwhile, unsuspectingly, I went about interviewing American officials in the Consulate and the USAID mission, and contacted those of my Brazilian friends who had not been arrested. As compared with 1963, my first week in the city was utterly uneventful. One evening I took my first look at Recife's famous waterfront *zona*. By day a busy commercial district, the *zona* at night becomes the base of operations for many of Recife's prostitutes. They mill about in the streets and dance halls and offer something for every taste. Yet the sight of an attractive, gaily dressed girl with stumps for arms and legs bouncing along in quest of customers proved too much for me, so I sought refuge in a shed near the Governor's Palace where a "strip tease" show was advertised. It turned out to be very bad vaudeville (except for one act in which the girl started out naked and dressed to music).

I had been in Recife for nine days when I received an urgent phone call to report to the American Consulate. Pete de Vos, a Vice-Consul, had some interesting news.

"Did you try to contact Antônio Lucena, Julião's interpreter?"

"Yes, last week. But how did you find out?"

"Well, this morning the police called. They found out about it and questioned Lucena. He's in jail, you know. They say that he told them you're a notorious Communist agitator in league with Julião."

I felt almost flattered. "Wonderful. What do I do now?"

"We told them you're not a Communist, but you'd better go down to headquarters and explain things to them."

"Not alone, I'm not going, no sir," I replied inelegantly.

"Okay. I'll go with you."

We drove across one of the rivers which flow through Recife and parked in front of a whitewashed stone building overlooking turgid waters. A crowd of people cluttered the inner hallway, which exuded dinginess. Pete, his Ivy-League appearance decidedly out of place, led me upstairs to an office, which was full of people. He looked at the mob with impatience.

"We'll never see the Delegado today," he muttered. "Let's get out of here."

When we emerged from the building, he turned to me with reassurance. "Tell you what. I'll telephone him tomorrow morning and arrange a meeting. You'll be all right. Nothing will happen right away."

I nodded with some hesitation and thanked him for his efforts. He drove off, and I walked back to the hotel. It was mid-afternoon. Angry swarms of cars and ancient taxis rendered the streets impassable until the tan-uniformed policeman standing beneath an umbrella on the corner changed the traffic lights with manual controls reminiscent of the hand throttles of an old trolley car.

Feeling the heat, I decided to take a nap. The heavy, tropical air forced me into a deep slumber. Then, a knock—I awoke to a hazy consciousness. The knock persisted. I rolled out of bed and staggered to the door. Two men stood in the corridor. One, the only hotel clerk who spoke any English, was in an acute state of discomfort. He gestured toward his companion, a short, brown-skinned, hatchet-faced man in a rumpled white suit.

"He is the police. He wants to search your room and take you for questioning."

"It must be a mistake," I answered, and then switching to Portuguese, "I am an American."

"Yes, he knows. He wants to arrest you."

"Okay, okay," I grumbled. "At least let me put my pants on." I shut the door and slipped into my trousers. Still not functioning, I was unable to think of a single intelligent thing to do.

I reopened the door. Hatchet-Face, unsmiling and in dead earnest, marched straight for my belongings, which he began to paw. The clerk glanced at me nervously. I held my breath as the policeman turned to the considerable quantity of written material I had piled on a dresser. A paperback translation of the Brazilian classic *Os Sertões* (*The Backlands*) was on top. Unfortunately the English version of the title was *Rebellion in the Backlands*. He thrust the book at the terrified clerk.

"Translate," he ordered, and the clerk duly blurted out the Portuguese equivalent of the English title.

" 'Rebellion,' eh!" His eyes flashed with the expression of one who has uncovered the anticipated, and he began to gather together all my printed materials.

"Please let me telephone the American Consulate," I requested glumly.

"No, you cannot. You must come with me." He picked up one of my notebooks, and a fateful thing happened. A scrap of paper fluttered to the

floor. He snatched it up and read it with obvious relish. On it were written the names "Joseph Page, Roland Snyder."

"Joseph Page, that is you. Who is Roland Snyder?"

"A friend. He came with me last year on my visit to Recife," I replied. "He was unable to come with me this year and is now in the United States."

Hatchet-Face shot his best skeptical gaze at me and stuffed the paper into his pocket. I began to regret having brought with me the notebook I had used on the 1963 trip.

We left the room and walked down the corridor. As we reachéd the elevator, the doors opened, and a young, spectacled fellow, obviously American, emerged. He was, in fact, a Papal Volunteer, one of a group of Catholic laymen performing social services for bishops throughout the world. He had been doing construction work for the Bishop of Natal in northern Brazil, and a mutual friend had recently told him to look me up when he next visited Recife.

He stared at me for a moment and then asked in English, "Are you Joe Page?"

"Why don't you come back later," I responded. "This is sort of a bad time."

Hatchet-Face could not suppress a look of triumph as he put down my books and papers, stepped forward and exclaimed, "Ahah! Roland Snyder!"

"But . . . but . . . my name is Bernie," protested the newcomer in fluent Portuguese.

"Can you prove it?"

Bernie fumbled for his wallet, which contained a social security card and an Ohio driver's license.

"Your passport," Hatchet-Face demanded.

"I left it in my hotel."

"Then you, too, are under arrest. Come with us."

Hatchet-Face led us across the river to police headquarters. The crowds were gone, and the badly lit building evoked an air of seediness. We were taken upstairs and detained in a small room cluttered with cartons of confiscated books and pamphlets.

Hours passed during which the only notable occurrence was an electrical failure. Candles were procured, and the flickering light cast ominous shadows on the wall. Bernie and I conversed in whispers and were periodically ordered to silence by our guard, who was not hesitant to display the pistol he wore at his side.

Then they took Bernie from the room. I could hear an animated conversation in a nearby office. He returned, thoroughly upset.

"They kept asking whether I was a Communist," he reported in low, hurried tones. "I said no, and they asked why I was in the company of a notorious Communist agitator. I told them I never saw you before in my life, but they don't believe me."

At that moment another guard appeared and beckoned me to accompany him. Uneasy, I followed him to a shabbily furnished office. Hatchet-Face was sitting behind a desk. The dim candlelight served to accentuate the wrinkles lining his face. He motioned for me to sit down.

"I would like to ask you some questions," he began softly.

"If I am to be interrogated, I would like an interpreter so that I can answer in English."

"That will not be necessary."

"Then I would like to telephone the American Consulate."

"No need for that either." He shuffled some papers on his desk and then looked me squarely in the eye.

"We know that you are here in Recife with Roland Snyder, and we want to know where he is."

I was completely taken aback. "I told you he isn't here. He's in the United States."

"No, you are mistaken. He is in Recife. We know because there are witnesses who have seen him with you."

I had difficulty believing what I had apparently heard. I managed a weak smile. "You must be joking."

"No, I am serious. You will have to tell us where he is."

For some reason, perhaps the frustration at the hours of waiting, perhaps indignation at the absurdity of the whole affair, I suddenly became quite angry. "This is ridiculous, absolutely ridiculous," I declared. "You're all crazy. I am a writer. I'm an American. I demand to telephone the Consulate."

This proved to be a serious miscalculation. Hatchet-Face jumped to his feet, eyes glinting dangerously. "Very well," he snarled, with a gesture to the guards standing in the doorway. "Take him to the dungeon."

A sense of panic seized me as the guards grabbed me by the arms and searched my raincoat. I uttered a feeble protest to no avail. They hustled me out of the room and down a flight of stairs. Events were proceeding too rapidly for comprehension. We crossed a courtyard, and I found myself in front of a large, iron-grated doorway. A hulking guard clad in a loose-fitting, blue shirt emerged. A brace of keys dangled from his belt. I examined him desperately.

"I'm an American. I'm an American." My voice sounded hollow and foreign.

He smiled, revealing a gap between his front teeth. "Down here, that means very little."

He ushered me into the central chamber. On both sides were cellblocks teeming with prisoners. My new captor summoned one of them, a young man wearing only pajama bottoms, and unlocked the gate to the cells on the right side. I stepped inside, and the gate snapped shut.

"Come with me," said the prisoner, and we made our way toward the interior of the cellblock.

The stench of sweat was overwhelming. "How many are in here?" I asked.

"Forty in this block."

"What sort of prisoners are they?"

He turned with a look of amusement. "Political." Then his eyes narrowed. "You're a spy, aren't you?"

My denial had no apparent effect, and the thought occurred that I might not survive a long stay in this new environment.

We reached the innermost cell, a tiny cubicle already occupied by four men. They were lying prone, two on top of and two below the pair of cots attached to opposite walls. My appearance did nothing to disturb their catatonic state.

"You may lie down over there," said the trustee, pointing to the barren far wall. I deposited my raincoat on the floor and looked about in dismay. One of my cellmates, a Negro in tattered, filthy underwear, sat up and offered me a banana from a paper bag next to his cot.

"Thank you, no. I'm very thirsty. Is there any water?"

The trustee called to the adjoining cell, and another prisoner appeared with a battered lube-oil tin filled with what passed for water. I gazed at this repulsive liquid, decided to expose myself to an apparently inevitable attack of dysentery, and gulped down the "amoeba cocktail."

Admonishing me to stay in my cell, the trustee took the tin and left. The Negro stretched back on his cot and recommenced staring at the ceiling. None of my other cellmates moved, but their eyes were open. I retreated to the far wall. In the oppressive heat I did not hesitate to strip to my underwear. With newspapers as my mattress I had to choose between putting my head next to a pair of bare feet or the hole which served as the cell's toilet. The lesser of the two evils prevailed, and I reclined on the hard floor. I soon discovered that the bright light in the cell, combined with the drops of rain now spattering through the bars of the open window above me

made it impossible to sleep. Each minute dragged on interminably. I speculated on the probable length of my stay.

A half-hour passed. My emotions ranged between panic and terror. Time was my enemy. How long could I lie still? Some noise in the central chamber attracted my attention. Several people had entered. There was boisterous shouting. A cell door was opened. A pause, then the unmistakable sound of blows. Cries of pain, interspersed with laughter. I now knew I could lie still for a very long time.

Two hours later a voice called out, "American. American." I quickly jumped up, dressed, and evacuated my cell. One of the guards who had taken me to the dungeon was standing in the central chamber. He regarded me with disdain. "Come."

We returned to the office. Hatchet-Face was sitting smugly behind his desk. Next to him was a rotund mulatto in shirt sleeves. He was the police interpreter, but in fact his English was so rudimentary that his sole utility was to convert difficult Portuguese into simple Portuguese.

"Sit down," began the interpreter with a reassuring voice. "We want to ask you some questions." I complied, and a group of guards positioned themselves around me.

"Now, first of all, what are you doing in Recife?"

"I am a writer."

Can you prove it?"

"You have my briefcase. It contains letters from American magazines saying they are interested in articles about Brazil."

Hatchet-Face produced the briefcase and thrust it in front of me. "Show us the letters."

With fear mixed with suspicion I fumbled through the manila folders, but the one marked "Freelance Correspondence" had been removed. "It was here," I stammered, "but it's . . . it's gone."

"Ahah!" proclaimed Hatchet-Face. "You see! You're not a writer!"

I hung my head in despair. The interpreter sensed my mood.

"Wait, don't be upset," he said with reassurance. "We're not after you. We don't care about you." Pause. I felt better. "The person we really want," he continued, "is—Roland Snyder."

The expression on my face must have been exceedingly pained. "Oh, no," I groaned. "I told you he's not here."

"But we know he is," declared Hatchet-Face, imperiously.

"He was here last year, is that not so?" asked the interpreter.

"Yes."

"And you stayed at the same hotel, the Guararapes?"

"Yes, yes."

"And people there knew you both?"

"Perhaps."

"Not perhaps. Yes. And they have seen you both together in the last week."

"They must be mistaken."

"No, you are mistaken to try to fool us," interjected Hatchet-Face. "He was to meet you there tonight. We have been tapping your telephone. We heard you arrange the appointment with him."

"No, no, no," I moaned, convinced that they were utterly mad. I buried my head in my hands.

"We have no more questions," the interpreter announced, and the inquisition suddenly ended. "You may join your countryman in the next room. I regret that you had to be put in the dungeon, but it was necessary to teach you a lesson."

"I'm sorry."

"That is a good sign," observed Hatchet-Face profoundly, "when an American says he is sorry."

It was after midnight, but Bernie was awake. He was still shaken from the ordeal to which he had been put. Some armed guards had taken him out in a jeep, and he was given the distinct impression that this was to be his last ride. Instead, he was brought to his hotel, where he produced his passport. Nonetheless, they refused to release him and brought him back to police headquarters. He was confined in the office where I now found him. For his late evening entertainment, one of the guards became rather drunk and kept waving a pistol under his nose.

We stretched out on the floor. I found it impossible to sleep although the room contained seven other soundly slumbering prisoners.

The new day signaled itself with the appearance of newspaper vendors and an enterprising lad with a large coffee dispenser strapped to his back. This is the final indignity, I thought. They won't even feed us. In truth, prisoners had to buy their meals, or, as was more commonly the case, their families brought food on their daily visits. The office was much more informal and relaxed than the dungeon. This was because our roommates had been detained merely for "investigation" (and had now been confined to the office for some sixty days), while the unfortunates below had been arrested in a more formal manner.

Our new companions impressed upon us the need for urgent communi-

cation with the American Consulate. "Otherwise, they will keep you here for weeks," a young bank clerk told us. He agreed to help us smuggle a message through his brother, who was to visit him at noon.

At 9:30 a.m., however, Pete de Vos and Celso, a jovial Brazilian employee of the Consulate, marched into the Delegado's nearby office. In a few moments, they came into our room. Bernie was to be released immediately, but because of some alleged red tape I would have to wait until five in the afternoon. "I think they are interested in your notes," Pete confided.

It was a long day, enlivened only by the stories my companions told about the horrors perpetrated upon the peasants by the military and the landlords after the April 1 "revolution." In the early afternoon Hatchet-Face dropped by to tell me that "everything is going to be all right." I managed a smile and wondered what I would do if I ever met him in a dark alley.

Promptly at five, Pete and Celso reappeared, and I was released. They would not tell me how they had learned of my arrest, but I had reason to suspect that somebody working in the headquarters was an informer for the Consulate.

No official apology was ever tendered. When the Consul General lodged an informal protest to the military authorities, the Delegado responded by refusing to release my notes. I remained in Recife for two more weeks and became somewhat of a celebrity among the American "establishment" and the local conservatives, who were greatly amused by my experience.

When I arrived in Rio de Janeiro from Recife, the Associated Press was informed of the incident but decided not to run the story. I could not help but wonder whether a similar decision would have been reached if I had been imprisoned by Cuban police.

My notes were finally relinquished and sent by diplomatic pouch from Recife to Rio. They were handed over to me in the American Embassy. My captors had stuffed them into the nearest available container, which happened to be a large manila envelope apparently confiscated from a local professor. A crowning touch of nonsense, it is my most treasured memento of the experience. On it are stamped the words "National Library of Peking, People's Republic of China."

✿ ✿ Index

THIS BOOK WAS SET by Fototronic-CRT in 11 point Janson. The display faces are Monotype Janson and Foundry Optima Semi-Bold with Linotype Dwiggins ornaments. The composition, printing and binding is by The Colonial Press Inc., Clinton, Massachusetts. The paper is Sebago Antique. The end-paper maps were drawn by Joan Emerson. This book was designed by Judith Lerner.